Love On A Whirlwind

Love On A Whirlwind

J. Jean Elliott

Copyright © 2007 by J. Jean Elliott.

Library of Congress Control Number: 2007903369
ISBN: Softcover   978-1-4257-5823-3

All rights reserved. No part of this book may be reproduced or transmitted in any form or by any means, electronic or mechanical, including photocopying, recording, or by any information storage and retrieval system, without permission in writing from the copyright owner.

This is a work of fiction. Names, characters, places and incidents either are the product of the author's imagination or are used fictitiously, and any resemblance to any actual persons, living or dead, events, or locales is entirely coincidental.

This book was printed in the United States of America.

To order additional copies of this book, contact:
Xlibris Corporation
1-888-795-4274
www.Xlibris.com
Orders@Xlibris.com

38660

TO MY FATHER, JAMES DANIEL ELLIOTT, SR., SEPTEMBER 28, 1921-JANUARY 5, 1978: YOU DID TRY TO HELP ME AT THE LAST MINUTE. IT'S JUST THAT YOU WERE ILL AND NEVER HAD ANYTHING TO GIVE ME BUT ALL OF THE CREATIVITY THAT HAS ENABLED ME TO DO EVERYTHING, INCLUDING WRITING THIS BOOK THAT I DEDICATE TO YOUR MEMORY.

J. JEAN ELLIOTT

Could love come in as little as three days . . . ?

Rachel had not seen Felix in years, not since he had dated her older sister Devon, who she had then dumped for another man, whom she had then dumped for another man. Felix has never quite gotten over her. Now, Rachel and Felix are meeting again, where she will be a bridesmaid in her older brother George's wedding and Felix, George's best friend, is standing in as his best man. Rachel wants to spend her short time there sightseeing, so George asks Felix, who has been staying at the hotel for more than a week, to show his baby sister around. Felix is not averse to that and neither is Rachel, always having thought of Felix as a handsome man. He shows her around for three days and they have an absolutely glorious time. But now that they are falling, what's going to happen when Devon shows up, newly divorced and ready to take up with Felix right where they left off ten years ago?

"You have a beautiful wife, man," the stranger said.
"I think so, too," Felix agreed.
As the man moved pass their table, Rachel tried to cover the fact that the intent way Felix sat watching her had completely unnerved her, in addition to the feel of his hand still claiming hers so possessively.
"Why didn't you correct that man's assumption that I'm your wife?" she asked in a low insistent tone.
"Because he was right about you. You turned out to be as beautiful as your sister. As a matter of fact, while we're on the subject of kissing, I wonder if you taste like her?!"
The equally intent way Felix's gaze dropped to her mouth unnerved her even further in the wave of sensation that it sent knifing down her spine, although Rachel tried to hide this behind a show of nonchalance.
"I guess you'll have to taste me, and see," she said audaciously.
Bent on doing just that, Felix leaned over toward her. . . .

Chapter One

The tires screeched against the pavement as the yellow taxi rolled to a stop. Rachel Hardison felt a faint excitement at knowing after all the time she had spent flying on the plane and riding in the cab that she had finally reached her destination. Indeed, the ride on the plane had been smooth, the ride from the airport in the cab an interesting one, but now Rachel was finally there, at the Amber Heights Hotel in downtown Anchorage. Taking a cue from the cab driver that stepped from the car to remove her luggage from the trunk, Rachel slid the black strap of her bag onto her shoulder, clutched her gray toiletry case in that same hand and opened her door with her right one.

Straightening up to her full five-feet-eight-inch height after closing the car door behind her, Rachel inhaled a breath of the fresh clear air. So this was Alaska, she thought to herself as she took in the well-manicured grounds of the hotel and noted the brisk sunny weather. She was going to do a lot of sightseeing, she knew, even though her stay there was only going to be six days. And with George having lived here for the last five years, he would know every nook and cranny of the Alaskan landscape to take her to.

Alerted to the fact that the cab driver had retrieved the rest of her luggage from the trunk by the sound of it closing then, Rachel watched as he tucked two of the cases under each arm and picked the last two up in his hands.

"Follow me, Miss," he said in his native tone as he began to move toward the door of the hotel, luggage in tow.

"I'm right behind you."

As she followed the cabby to the hotel entrance after having switched the handle of her toiletry case into her right hand, Rachel had to smile to herself. Looked like her brother George had done pretty well for himself, judging by the swankiness of the hotel he worked at as general manager. Oh, but that was only the outside. Once inside the hotel behind the cab driver after being seen in by a red uniformed doorman, Rachel had to change her mind. Swanky was hardly the word to describe the place. More like muy magnifique!

"That'll be $15.75," said the cabby as he set her four pieces of luggage on the brown-carpeted floor in front of the reservation desk.

Reaching into the black bag slung over her left shoulder with that same hand, Rachel extracted a twenty from her wallet and handed it to him.

"Here you are, and keep the change," she said.

"Thank you very much, Miss, and enjoy your stay," the cab driver nodded, smiling slightly. Then tucking the twenty into his back pocket, he turned to go back the way he had come.

A brown-haired receptionist that had been busy with two others behind the check-in counter while she'd been involved with paying the cab driver came over to claim her attention then.

"Welcome to the Amber Heights Hotel," the woman began in a medium-pitched professional voice. "How, may I help you, Miss—?"

"Hardison. Rachel Hardison. I'm here to see my brother, George Hardison. He's getting married here this coming Saturday."

"Why, yes, of course, Miss Hardison, I'm Diane Mortemburg," smiled the receptionist, proffering her hand across the swanky counter to shake her right, forcing Rachel to have to swing the toiletry case back into her left. "I too am part of the wedding party. Just a minute, I'll page him for you."

"Thank you," smiled Rachel as Diane let go of her hand, causing her to drop her own back to her side.

As Diane moved away to page George on the intercom, Rachel took another look around the lobby. The sofas, armchairs and loveseats were grouped in sets of three around French Provincial tables in sophisticated shades of blue, brown, rust, and autumn gold and chandeliers and glass table lamps provided just the right amount of lighting. Yes, George had done well in planning to marry the owner of this hotel. She must surely come from a loaded family, if the rich looking appearance of this lobby was anything to go by.

"He'll be right out, Miss Hardison," said Diane, returning her attention to Rachel then. "In the meantime, why don't I check you in?"

"Yeah, that's a great idea." Rachel turned a relieved smile on Diane as she looked her name up on her computer. "I've had a long flight, and could use a rest."

"Yes, I see that you have flown in all the way from Atlanta, Georgia, in the Lower 48," smiled the brunette, who wore a blue uniform bearing the hotel's insignia. "How's about we hurry up and get you a room?"

"Yes, why don't we do that?" Rachel agreed.

She handed her a registration form and a blue Bic pen. Waiting patiently as Rachel filled it out and then handed both form and pen back to her, she gestured a hovering bellboy to come and pick the four pieces of her luggage that matched the toiletry case she carried up off the deep brown carpeting while at the same time handing Rachel a room key with the number 1125 on it. Just as Rachel accepted it from her, George emerged from around the corner and saw her standing there.

The grin that slid onto his well-hewn attractive face wreathed his face in a couple age lines as he approached Rachel in several quick strides of his long black-clad legs. The blue jacket he wore with the black slacks, which like Diane's, bore the insignia of the hotel on the lapel failed to conceal the strength of his sturdy five-feet-ten-inch frame.

"Rachel!" George cried excitedly as he took her into his arms as well as her pocketbook and toiletries case would allow just as the bellboy picked up her four other pieces of luggage. "It's about time you all got here! I've been waiting all afternoon for the family to put in an appearance! What's taken you guys so long?"

"Well, if you let me go, George Hardison, maybe I'll be able to tell you!" Smilingly reciprocating the bear hug he'd initiated with her free arm, Rachel waited for him to loosen his hold on her shoulders before dropping her free hand to clasp his wrist. With an oval face possessing symmetrical features, and surrounded by a neat short black fro, George was good looking for a 'brother,' in fact, one might even think he looked like the son of a movie star. "First of all, the good news: Mom and Dad are coming to the wedding. Second of all, the bad news: they're driving in cross-country. You know Dad's been just waiting for an opportunity to try out the RV he bought last year? This trip is what he's trying it out on. They'll be here either Thursday or Friday. Third of all and the worst news of all: Devon, our sister, is sadly not going to be here. She's in the midst of finalizing her mess of a divorce from Richard this week, and so, with any luck, won't be able to fly out here until next week, when it'll be too late."

Although George tried not to be disappointed, Rachel saw the pain reflected in his deep brown eyes and felt for him. He was getting married to a wonderful girl in just five days and not only were his parents arriving at the last possible moment to witness it, but Devon wasn't coming at all.

"Oh, well—just as long as Mom and Dad are here to see me tie the knot," George said a trifle ungraciously, twisting his wrist free of Rachel's free hand. "But for crying out loud! Devon had agreed to be one of the bridesmaids, like you are. Now, it looks like I've paid for an extra bridesmaid's dress and pair of shoes for nothing!"

"No, not necessarily," Rachel said, briskly taking hold of his wrist again and grateful that he had saved her the trouble of having to come off the monies for the dress and shoes herself. "I'm quite sure my dress and shoes will fit. That's why I arrived early; just in case they don't, we have plenty of time to make changes. Plus, as long as you kept the receipt to Devon's dress and shoes, you can always get a refund on them later."

"Yeah, I guess you're right." George raised his free hand to knead the back of his neck in an agitated fashion. "And it's a shame that no one is back home to see Devon through her divorce, what with everyone heading over here."

"Now, that's the truth," Rachel agreed, smiling to coax him out of his momentary melancholy. "Anyway, enough about Devon. . . . Why don't you tell me all about this lady you're going to marry? Devon—to mention her one more time—tells me she owns this hotel."

The grin was back on George's well-hewn lips as he motioned the blue-clad bellboy and Rachel to the elevators down a papered hallway striped in the same colors of blue, brown, rust and autumn gold that dominated the lobby. "Yes, her name is Stacey Lumas, and yes, she does own this hotel. I can't wait for you to meet her, Rachel, she's the greatest."

"She must be to have agreed to have two practical strangers in her wedding—even though we are sisters of the groom," Rachel stated realistically as she watched George push the 'up' button to call one of four in the elevator banks they had reached then. "So, where is she?" Rachel asked.

"Stacey had to go into town to handle some business, I'm afraid," George said a trifle airily. "She'll be back at the hotel by five this evening. You can meet her then. I'm sure she's going to love you. Just like I'm sure you're going to love her."

"I'm sure I will," Rachel agreed again, considering the fact a no-brainer. "And you can wrack your brains trying to explain to her how we've managed to come out looking so much alike."

"Oh, yeah . . . !" George indulged a mild laugh as the 'up' elevator doors opened and they stepped inside along with the bellboy carrying her four other luggage pieces, one strapped over his shoulder, one tucked under an arm and the other two carried from his hands. That he and Rachel looked alike was an inside joke. At thirty-one, George with his suntan brown skin and mannish looks looked just like their father. Devon and Rachel with their darker skin and dusky looks looked exactly like their mother.

No one on any upper floors called for an elevator 'up' and as a result, theirs quickly ascended to the eleventh floor, where the doors opened almost immediately. Stepping from the elevator behind her and George, the bellboy carried Rachel's luggage the several feet down the corridor until George stopped at Suite 1125. Taking the blue-tagged key from Rachel's unresisting fingers, George pushed the key in the lock, turned it and pushed open the door. Stepping inside, he was followed by Rachel and then the bellboy, who moved past them to carry her four pieces of luggage past the blue-carpeted living room and into the bedroom of the two-room suite.

"My, what a pretty suite . . . !" Rachel exclaimed, her brown eyes shining as she moved through the living room and into the blue-themed bedroom, setting her black bag and gray toiletries case onto the king-sized bed as she approached it. At the same time, George gave the departing bellboy a five and thanked him for his services before dismissing him to return to his post on the first floor. "And it has a view, too, I see!" Rachel pulled back the frilly print linen drapes that matched the bedspread in the bedroom and saw a breathtaking view of Flattop Mountain in the nearby Chugach State Park. Or so that was the name the friendly cabby had given her of the dark, murky mountain range on the way to the hotel.

"So, what does it cost for a person to stay in a suite like this a night?" she thought to ask artfully amid turning away from the window.

"If you're worried that you won't be able to afford to stay here, I'm covering the cost of your stay," George said in his abrupt alto, having followed her through the living area and into the lavish bedroom.

"Oh, George . . . !" Rachel was so pleased that she was sure it emanated from her like a mist. "You're letting me stay here for free?"

"Can't a brother do something nice for his kid sister?" asked George, shaking off the hug Rachel was giving him with both arms now. "Besides, I can afford it and I know you're on a budget, trying to live off a kindergarten teacher's salary."

"Man, you've got that right," Rachel stated, appreciative of his understanding of her lack of decent funds. "I'd ditch that job in a minute, were it not for how much I love those kids. Oh, and thanks also for paying for my bridesmaid's dress and shoes, I'm sure they'll fit perfectly."

"I'm sure they will," George agreed.

Planting a grateful kiss on his near cheek, Rachel jumped in the floor suddenly, taking George completely by surprise. "Man, I can't believe I'm actually in Alaska!" she exclaimed excitedly. "I have heard so many good things about this state!"

"Yes, this place has a lot to offer in the wintertime—snow-capped mountains, glaciers—even though they do come with freezing zero temperatures," George said informatively. "And then, in the summer, like now here in June, it gets no hotter than the low-to-mid seventies, and we have days that never seem to end. Alaska, North America's last frontier. . . . And more wilderness than we know what to do with."

"Yes, I've already planned to go sightseeing." Rachel grinned enthusiastically as she spun around the large bedroom.

"Surely, you're not planning on going sightseeing alone?" George was the voice of concern as he handed Rachel her blue-tagged room key and then watched her pick up a couple pieces of luggage and lower them onto the bed. "What would you do were you to run into a bear? They're plenteous in this region."

"Oh, I don't know—freeze, scream, run, try and climb a tree?" she prodded mockingly.

"Hardly," George disagreed, all serious. "You try and run, and a bear will outrun you. Try climbing a tree, and a grizzly will climb right on up behind you. No, you would fall to the ground and play dead, while putting your hands behind your neck. That will insure that at the most, the bear will sniff you, see you as non-threatening, and move on."

"Oh, I see," she said, trying not to be impressed by all he knew on the subject as she unlocked the first piece of luggage, a gray tweed Pullman of the American Tourister label, as were all of her others. "So, I would be endangering my life were I to venture out on my own?"

"You most certainly would, Kid Sister," George assured in dissuading tones. "That's why I'm going to supply you with a tour guide who knows this wilderness we call Alaska, to take you where you want to go. I'm sure that out of the six men who are my groomsmen in the wedding, I'll be able to find one who is just right for you. Which reminds me—guess who's standing in as my best man!"

"Who . . . ?" Rachel dared, brown eyes wide in curiosity as she began taking folded pieces of clothing out of the large Pullman and lowering them to the frilly spread-covered king-sized bed.

"You will simply never guess!" George taunted in his abrupt alto. "Felix Latham!"

"Felix Latham! But then, of course he would be your best man, you've been best friends since your freshman year in college! I'm surprised you've managed to keep in touch after all these years!" Rachel prided herself on the control she regained over her shock at his mention of the long forgotten name. "How is he doing after all these years?"

"He's fine, and is an actor currently on hiatus from a soap opera taped in New York City. Name of *As The Star Shines,*" George said.

"Felix Latham is an actor?" Rachel asked in amazement, not even trying to hide her surprise. "How come I've never heard of that soap opera?"

"Because you've been too busy attending school and college, Kid Sister," George teased her playfully. "Not to mention being too busy in the three years since graduation from said college getting established as a teacher to hear about it."

"I guess so," Rachel agreed as she returned to her task of removing another clothing item from the gray tweed Pullman on the bed. "So, how long has this soap been on the air, anyway?"

"Over twenty years, as a matter of fact," George said. "Felix has been on it for the last six playing the role of Joe Murray. He's won three Daytime Emmys for that role, as a matter of fact."

"Felix Latham's won three Daytime Emmy Awards playing a role on a soap opera?" Rachel stared in surprise.

"Uhm-hmm. First one five years ago for Best Male Newcomer, second one three years ago for Supporting Actor, and third one last year for Best Male Pairing In A Couple."

"Really . . . !" Rachel shook her head in amazed wonder, never having known the man wanted to act, much less well enough to win an award for it. "Wow! Felix Latham, an Emmy Award-winning soap opera actor!" she mused with a smile. "And didn't he date our sister Devon for a while?"

"Uhm-hmm." George adopted a reminiscent look as she remained standing in the middle of the floor. "They went together for four months, three days and seventeen hours before Devon dumped him on his duff for another man, whom she subsequently dumped for another man. I'm afraid that Felix is still in love with her."

"Then, be glad she won't be here for the wedding, and so, won't be able to play with his emotions," Rachel said thoughtfully.

"Now, of that, I am glad," George laughed in agreement before getting back to the subject. "Anyway, the reason for me bringing up Felix is that he would make a fitting tour guide for you."

"What makes you say that," she began, "when he's not a native of Alaska, either?"

"The fact that he's been here for over a week, he's been here since last Sunday. And he's upset half of my female staff getting them to show him around while they've been off duty. He's seen a lot in that one week, too. Far more than I got to see in my first week here."

"I don't wonder!" Rachel continued to muse as she unlocked the second piece of luggage, another large gray tweed Pullman, on the bed and began removing more clothing items. She'd always thought of Felix as a lady-killer with his killer good looks with the exception of not being able to keep Devon wrapped around his finger. Small wonder he became an actor. "So, is Felix staying at the hotel, or is he someplace else?"

"He's here, in Suite 1202. Maybe you'd like to visit him later. He's going to get a kick out of seeing how you turned out after all these years."

"I'm sure he will," Rachel agreed as she remained bent to her task. It was going to blow Mr. Daytime Emmy award-winning actor Felix Latham's mind seeing how she had filled out since he had last seen her at fourteen. "Okay, I'll let your Felix be my tour guide, if he has no objections, but I still rather wished you would take me sightseeing." She turned a look of her former mockery on him, knowing how George hated it when she didn't take him seriously.

"Hmmm, much as I'd like to," George said from his stance in the middle of the floor, "need I remind you that I have a hotel to run? Not to mention that I'm in the process of getting a wedding set up for this Saturday—my own, as a matter of fact?"

"Yeah, I know, I know, you're a busy man," Rachel sighed. "So, go. Leave me be to finish me unpacking and take a quick nap before I meet your fiancée." She threw a dismissing hand up in the air as she adopted the Jamaican accent.

"Okay, okay, I'll see you later." George took the few steps away from her to move back into the living room, which he crossed toward the door, where he curled a brown hand on the brass knob. "Come visit me up in the penthouse after you've rested, and I'll introduce you around to everybody."

"You live in the penthouse?" Rachel was surprised, and asked in amazement.

"Yes," George nodded his head. "It's also shares as an office for Stacey and me."

"I see." Rachel wondered in what other capacity the suite served him and Stacey as she followed her brother back into the living room. "Well, you're certainly doing well for yourself, my brother, as is Felix, apparently," she smiled.

"I guess so," George agreed, smiling as well. "Anyway, come on up after you've rested, and I'll show you around the place."

"Okay."

He had just pulled on the doorknob to open the door when he turned back to say to her almost as an afterthought, "Anyway, it's so good seeing you, girl!" he grinned.

"And it's good seeing you, George!" Rachel turned a rivaling grin on him as he stepped out into the corridor and disappeared on the other side of the door.

Left alone in the spacious two-room suite, Rachel returned to the bedroom, where she picked up the clothing items that she had emptied onto the bed, placed them into a drawer in the French Provincial dresser across the room, and put the two empty American Tourister Pullman luggage in the closet. Then, picking up the last two pieces of luggage of the same label—a smaller Pullman and a large carry-on that hung from a sturdy gray shoulder strap—out of the center of the floor, Rachel placed them on the bed and started to empty them in the same manner.

There really hadn't been anything else for her to do but take off the long yellow sweater she'd been wearing over equally yellow shirt and slacks, kick her shoes off into the floor and then fall back against the firm king-sized bed and go to sleep. But the more she tried to sleep, the more awake she became. It seemed that the slight jet lag she'd been suffering from upon her arrival at the hotel had fled in the face of George and Felix's success. To think that not only was Felix an award-winning actor now, but George was occupying the penthouse suite at what might be termed one of the poshest hotels in downtown Anchorage. It had to be worth at least $200 million. In harmony with that, George was doing so well that he could actually cover the cost of Rachel's stay at said multi-million-dollar hotel for her entire six-night stay there. Yes, truly, George had done well for himself. He had literally started on the bottom rung on the ladder and then climbed the ladder all the way to the top.

And then there was his fiancée, Stacey Lumas, who had put him there. She had been his employer for the past five years. That gave them plenty of time to fall in love to the point of wanting to get married. And Rachel wished the best for both of them. Still for her brother to find his true love in Anchorage, Alaska all the way from Atlanta, Georgia in the Lower 48 seemed odd somehow, especially in light of all the honeys he had dated in his twenties before relocating to Alaska five years ago. There was Rachel's fear too that George's fiancée would be a white woman, as there weren't that many 'sisters' owning hotels of the caliber of this one. Well, Rachel was going to find out, of that she was sure.

Gazing at the silver-toned watch adorning her left wrist, she saw that the time was two fifty seven p.m. George had said that Stacey wouldn't be getting back until five o'clock. That gave Rachel two hours to kill with absolutely nothing to do to pass the time.

She tried to imagine what the yet unmet Stacey looked like. Was she at least as tall as George, who stood at five-ten in his sock feet? Or was she short, petite? Was she slender, with curves in all the right places like Rachel was proud to acknowledge about herself? Or was she fat and out of shape? After all, love didn't care what one looked like on the outside, but was measured by what one was on the inside. And if Stacey was a white woman, was she the dreaded long-haired blonde that every black man fantasized about going to bed with? And was she a pretty woman, at least as good-looking as Rachel, or was she a dog in the face? Certainly, Rachel hoped George had used discretion in his choice of a potential marriage mate.

Crawling off the bed then, Rachel walked over to the French Provincial dresser, sat down in the make-up chair, and gazed at her appearance. Her reflection in the mirror did not disappoint. She was an attractive woman, a beautiful woman, with long relaxed off-black hair that was temporarily pulled away from a perfectly shaped round face to form a ponytail down her back. Her deep brown long-lashed eyes were large and luminous beneath perfectly arched black brows; she had high cheekbones, a gently flaring nose, and medium lips that most men she met wanted to kiss twenty-four/seven, perfect Halle Berry teeth. Rachel was not being vain in acknowledging her good looks. George and she had simply had very handsome parents that they had taken their looks from. Devon was even more beautiful than her.

Rising from the chair she had been sitting in, Rachel let her chocolate gaze take in the rest of her appearance in the long-sleeved yellow shirt and yellow slacks she stood in. There was a provocative fullness beneath the yellow shirt that she had never thought was going to come when she was fourteen years old. But the following year, Rachel had developed a D-cup bust-line with the hips to match. And being five-eight in height, she had long dusky Beyoncé legs that were more than most guys could take at one sitting. Hence, she was suspicious about the motives of the guys she dated, because they were all only after one thing and she had no intention of answering their boody calls. Not when she was having too much fun in her life in being on her own.

Giving up on the idea of taking a nap, Rachel tidied herself up quickly by neatly tucking her shirt back into the cuff of her pants and squaring both materials. She was going to go look up Felix—Mr. Award-Winning soap opera actor—see if he remembered her, and with that thought in mind, she withdrew her black bag from a bottom dresser drawer and touched up her mascara, blush and berry lipstick. Sticking her sock feet back into the black shoes she had discarded into the carpeted floor earlier, she then slung the strap of her bag over her shoulder, picked her room key up off the bed, moved back into the living room, opened the self-locking door and stepped out into the hallway.

The rich look of the same stripe-papered walls in hues of blue, rust, brown and autumn gold that had dominated the first floor immediately claimed her attention as she moved purposely down the hall to the elevators halfway down the corridor, reminding her of the elegant sophistication of the hotel. Stepping into the first elevator going up, Rachel pushed the button for the twelfth floor, where she stepped out into a corridor that was an exact replica of hers and that of the first floor. Again stripe-papered walls in the same colors dominated, continuing the hotel's rich feeling. Moving around the floor, Rachel sought out Suite 1202, which was just around the corner, not too far from the elevator banks.

No sound came from the inside of the suite, but that did not deter her purpose as she raised her hand and rapped on the white door. When no answer proved forthcoming, Rachel raised her hand and rapped again. Still no one came from inside to answer her knock. So she reasoned that wherever Felix was, he was not in his suite. Oh, well, she would have plenty of time to see him later, Rachel thought smilingly as she turned back in the direction of the elevator banks. Stepping into the first one that opened, she pushed the 'up' button for the fifteenth floor.

Here, unlike on the eleventh and twelfth floors, the lobby to the penthouse suite was colored in varying colors of red and gold. Again she was reminded of how successful George was as she again raised her hand and rapped on the red door. He answered the door a second later and stood surprised to find her standing there, rather than a treasured employee of sorts.

"Rachel! What are you doing here so soon?" he asked, glancing at the gold watch on his wrist. "It's only a quarter after three. I thought you were taking a nap!"

"Yeah, well, I thought I was taking one too," Rachel said, "but a funny thing happened on the way to that happening."

"What?" George prodded when she didn't go on.

"It appears that my jet lag has lagged on by. I couldn't fall asleep, couldn't take a nap. So, I thought I'd get up and take you up on your offer to show me around. May I come in?"

"Oh, of course, sure, come in," George said almost as another afterthought, opening the door wider to allow her entrance. Once done, Rachel saw that the suite like hers and the lobby was outfitted in beautiful French Provincial furnishings, with the exception that all the sitting pieces were a deep red, as was the carpeting. And just like the lobby, lights were everywhere. And the place was huge, allowing him to set up two offices to one side of the spacious living room. The suite also came with two large bedrooms—each with its own bath possessing Jacuzzi tub, steam shower and phone, and there was a guest bathroom with a simple glass-enclosed tub/shower. The place was so fabulous that there was also a kitchenette and a terrace.

"So, how do you like it?" asked George in a tone indicating he knew he had bowled her over.

"Like it? I love it!" The corners of Rachel's mouth were curved into a grin as they returned to the living room of the penthouse suite. "My God, George, you are living large up in here!"

"Yeah, I'm comfortable," George agreed somewhat immodestly.

"Before coming here, I took your advice and went up to the twelfth floor to see if Felix was there, but no one answered his knock," Rachel said.

"Yeah, I'm afraid Felix is in the street, as I said earlier. He'll come dragging in here sooner or later this evening."

"Hmmm, probably will," she agreed.

"Which reminds me, I neglected to ask before, but how're you doing? I mean really? And how're the kids treating you at school, since I touched briefly on the subject a while ago?"

"Just fine, George, just fine," Rachel said of her third year working as a kindergarten teacher in one of Atlanta, Georgia's premiere schools. "The kids are great, as always, and I love every one of them. Of course, like you hinted earlier, the pay is ridiculous, but as long as I keep my eye simple and don't crave too many material things, I do alright and can stick to my budget. Now, this trip to Alaska, it set me back a pretty penny, but it was necessary. I wouldn't miss your wedding for nothing, especially when I'm standing in as one of your fiancée's bridesmaids. Now, me, I'm blowing my entire June check on this trip, but I also plan to get a lot out of it."

"You mean sightseeing, don't you?" The smile returned to George's lips as he picked up on her train of thought. "Well, I may be too busy to take you out on my own, but I can spare the time to show you around the hotel. Come on, let me go pick up my penthouse card."

"Okay, I'd like that," Rachel said.

Picking the card to the suite up off a French Provincial desk, George slid it into his pocket. Then claiming Rachel by an arm, he propelled her to the door and out into the lobby/foyer, where he quickly saw her into an elevator going down.

He showed her the two large meeting/banquet rooms and the game room down on the first floor as well as a lounge, where one could have a drink and unwind after a long day. He showed her a cafeteria on the first floor where the eating was casual, and the three restaurants: one Continental, one, French and one Mediterranean, where more fancy dining could be indulged on the second floor. He showed her a large fitting/dressing men's room on the third floor and an equally large fitting/dressing/powder room for women on the same floor across the hall. He showed her the large kitchen, laundry/cleaning service and housekeeping department on the ground floor as well as a large indoor swimming pool and the twenty-four-hour Nautilus unisex fitness gym not too far from it, also on the ground floor. And then he introduced her to everybody—the maids, the housekeeper and assistant housekeeper, the concierge, a valet, the bellboys, the chefs, a couple of the waiters, one of the fitness instructors, one of the bartenders, a couple of friends who were part of the wedding party, his assistant manager and the reservationists. Yet Rachel couldn't help noticing that while she had wound up right where she'd started at the front desk, she still had had no sight of the best man. Felix hadn't shown up yet.

"I'll bet Mr. Hardison's introduced you to so many people that you'll probably never get the names straight, huh, Miss Hardison?" smiled Diane Mortemburg from her position at the front desk. She got off at seven, and it was only just now pushing a quarter until five.

"Probably not," Rachel agreed with a laugh at the woman; who had to be at least two years her senior. "Oh, and please, call me Rachel. After all, like you told me when I was preparing to check in, you're in the wedding party, too."

"Why, thank you, Rachel, I'll be glad to call you that." The woman smiled, showing her pretty teeth.

"Yeah, my sister Devon was supposed to stand in as a bridesmaid, also. Unfortunately, she's in the throes of a nasty divorce, and so, won't be free to travel until next week," Rachel told her.

"Oh, how unfortunate," Diane sighed genuine sympathy.

"Anyway, since we're somewhat on the subject, what colors are the bridesmaids' dresses, and how do they look? Not too bad, I hope?"

"Quite the contrary, they're quite attractive," Diane said. "They're beige, and have short cap sleeves, beige net scarving from the boat neck to the waist, and a fit-and-flare skirt. And Stacey has paired them with beige heels to match."

"Did I hear my name called?" asked a woman Rachel assumed was Stacey, who entered the double doors of the hotel then, black strap of her handbag slung over one blue jacket-clad shoulder, carrying some important papers in one hand.

"Darling, it's about time you got here," George said in a tone of half relief, half annoyance as the woman approached him. "I've been waiting all afternoon for you to get back."

"What was so important that you couldn't wait for me to get back?" asked the softly spoken woman as she curved an arm around his waist and stood up on her tiptoes to give him a kiss of greeting.

"My affection for you, for one thing . . . ! You know I love you so much that I want you in my line of vision twenty-four/seven!" George teased her playfully. "Besides, I have someone here that I want you to meet."

As Rachel listened to George begin introductions, she couldn't help rethinking what had occurred to her up in her suite earlier. It was a 'sister's' loss, as George was marrying a white woman. Only she wasn't the long-leggy blue-eyed blonde Rachel had imagined but a short semi-attractive Alaska Native with an oval face, brown eyes, freckles across her nose and long brown hair flowing down her back, much like Rachel's own off-black relaxed straight hair. And she was stout, although thank God she was in good enough shape not to have a paunch, a spare tire around her middle.

". . . Like you to meet Stacey Lumas, my fiancée. And Stacy, meet my kid sister, Rachel Hardison."

"How do you do, Stacey? It's good to meet you." Rachel smiled at the shorter woman she guessed to be about five-four, at the same time proffering a yellow-sleeved arm forward to shake her free hand.

"And it's good to meet you, Rachel," Stacey, who like George, wore black slacks under her blue jacket, smiled, showing pretty little teeth, well aligned though they were. "George has told me so much about you, all good, thank goodness," she laughed. "And thanks for agreeing to be in our wedding."

"No, thank you, for asking me," said Rachel as she let go of her hand and dropped it back to her side.

"And where's the rest of your family? In their suites resting up from their trips . . . ?" Stacey asked.

"No, I'm afraid that my mother and father are driving cross-country in an RV that Dad acquired last year, and so, they won't be here until either Thursday or Friday. And I know that this leaves you with a spare bridesmaid's dress and shoes on your hands, but George's and my sister Devon unfortunately won't be able to make the wedding, at all. She would have flown in with me today, but she is putting the finishing touches on her second divorce this week, and so, won't be able to get here until next week, when you and George will be on your honeymoon." Almost word-for-word Rachel found herself mouthing the explanation she had given to Diane Mortemburg only a moment before.

"Gee, I'm sorry to hear that, which leaves me a bridesmaid short. I'll have to think about whom I can put in her place that wears a size twelve dress and eight-and-a-half size shoes." Stacey managed to hide her disappointment, speaking matter-of-factly. "Anyway, since we're on the subject, that reminds me—I have your dress and shoes up in my room on the tenth floor. Come on up with me, and you can try them on, see if they fit," Stacey finished with a smile.

"Okay," Rachel smiled equally, relieved that she and George weren't sharing the penthouse in sin before the marriage. Or so that remained to be seen once she'd taken her to the tenth floor to try on her dress.

"George, these are caterers' estimates for a hundred people. Why don't you go over them, while I take your sister up to my suite?" Stacey handed George the papers she carried under one arm and watched him proffer a cursory look over them.

"Yes, I'll take these up to the penthouse, and go over them there," George said. "Come on, we can share an elevator together."

"Okay." Stacey turned to speak to Diane as George slid a blue-sleeved arm around her waist, prompting her to do the same to him. "We're still on for dinner at seven thirty?"

"Seven thirty, it is," Diane agreed.

"Very well, come on, Rachel. Let's go try on that dress."

"Okay."

Somewhat embarrassed at their mild display of affection in public, Rachel turned to follow George and Stacey away from the reservation desk and to the elevators down the hall. Yet before Rachel could take three steps forward, Felix Latham came walking in through the double doors, bringing a brisk wave of cool air in with him. He was not alone, but had a woman on each arm, one white and one black, both with looks befitting an actor of his obvious caliber. Felix was not paying attention to either of them at the moment, but had his brown gaze directed on his best friend, who was in the process of moving away from the reservation desk with his fiancée.

"Hey, slow down, my man," Felix began in his attractive tenor, fitting George with a laugh. "Can't a man have a kind word for a brother?"

"Felix!" Dropping his arm from Stacey's waist while she kept hers possessively in place around his, George turned to face his best man, relief flooding his attractive mannish features. "Man, where have you been? I've been waiting all day for you to get back here!"

"Why? You knew I'd be with the ladies, man. What did you want me for?"

"Man, I wanted to see if you could recognize this blast from the past!" Curving a hand around Rachel's wrist, George pulled her over toward Felix until she stood directly in his line of vision. Felix returned her boldly amused gaze for a moment, the long-lashed brown eyes in his attractive rectangular face narrowing perplexedly until he had placed her at last.

"Rachel—?" he began in his attractive tenor, dropping his arms from his two lady friends. "Oh, my God, it is you!" he cried, taking her into his arms.

"Yes, it's me," Rachel said as she reciprocated the arms he had warmly lowered around her waist by curling hers around his shoulders with equal congeniality. "How are you, Felix?"

"World's better, now that I've seen you!" Relinquishing his hold on her shoulders, Felix curved his hands over her upper arms and held her at arms' length so that he could give her the once-over. "Little Rachel Hardison! George's kid sister!" he grinned, showing perfect teeth. "Only you're not so little anymore, are you!"

"I'm afraid not," Rachel grinned, already having anticipated his shock. The last time Felix had seen her at fourteen, she had been flat as a board and straight as a rod. He couldn't say that about her now in either capacity.

"Rachel Hardison! George's kid sister . . . !" Felix laughed. "How are you? And what are you up to these days?"

"I'm fine, Felix, and am a kindergarten teacher in Atlanta," Rachel answered, grin sobering into a smile as she slowly wriggled her arms from his fingers. "And what about you . . . ? George tells me you're an award-winning actor on a soap opera."

"Yes, I've won three Daytime Emmys for the role I play of Joe Murray on *As The Star Shines*," Felix continued to flash his pearlies in a grin. "I'm currently on a three-week hiatus, which is how I can afford to be out here for a couple attending George and Stacey's wedding."

"Yeah, I'm on summer vacation from teaching at the school. That's how I can be here for the wedding," Rachel said.

"So, what about the rest of your family . . . ?" Felix asked curiously, grin sobering as he became serious. "What about Devon? Is she coming to the wedding?"

Rachel wondered when he was going to get around to mentioning his former flame, as she couldn't help noticing that he had completely forgotten about his two lady friends.

"No, I'm afraid she's not going to be here. She's in the process of getting a divorce this week, and so, won't be free to fly out anywhere until next week when it'll be too late," Rachel replied regretfully.

"Aw, what a shame. . . ." For the first time since they'd been talking, Felix's face fell, and Rachel knew immediately that it was just as George said: After all these years, he was still in love with Devon. Wait until he found out that she had been married twice and to men who didn't resemble him in any way, shape, form or fashion.

"Rachel Hardison! George's little sister!" Felix grinned then, again taking her back into his arms. "Anyway, it's good to see you! We've got a lot of reminiscing to do!"

"That, we do," Rachel agreed, grin back on her own lips as she reciprocated his hug by again circling her arms over his broad shoulders.

"Well, at least I'm glad to hear you say that." George took control of the conversation, the papers Stacey had given him earlier rolled up in one hand.

"Why is that?" asked Felix with the return of his curiosity, dropping his hold on Rachel's shoulders but maintaining a hold on both her hands.

" . . . Because Rachel's got it in her mind to go sightseeing while she's here these next four days. Well, I can't show her around, because of having to run this hotel and trying to get my wedding together. So, I told her that I'd ask you to show her around since you know each other from way back. That is, if you have no objection to acting as her tour guide over the next few days?" George asked.

The sadness that had been in the chocolate brown eyes was quickly replaced with a look of interest and flirtation as again Felix grinned at her. Rachel's heart skipped a beat at the notion that he was trying to excite her into wanting to be with him, especially when he was so extremely good looking and sexy to begin with.

"You want to go sightseeing tomorrow?" Felix asked unnecessarily.

"I sure do," Rachel replied.

"Then, I will be happy to be your tour guide," Felix smiled, bowing his head. "Like I said, girl, we've got a lot to talk about."

"That, we do," Rachel smiled in agreement as she continued to behold the bold gaze he had turned on her. At thirty-one years of age and six-foot-one, and along with a well-built physique presently covered in a thick woolly brown sweater over black cords, he was gorgeous for a black man, possessing long-lashed dancing brown eyes beneath straight even black brows, a strong yet gently flaring nose and the most kissable slim-lipped mouth one could ever hope to see in a sexy rectangular face.

"Good, well, now that the two of you've got that all settled, come on with me, Rachel, and I'll show you your dress." Stacey's request brought her back to the present as she dropped her arm from George's waist and prepared to turn away from him.

"Okay, Stacey," Rachel said, and affording Felix and George one last cursory smile, Rachel moved away from them behind Stacey.

Chapter Two

"It's beautiful!" Rachel exclaimed of the beige satin cap-sleeved dress Stacey showed her from a disarray of women's clothing on the king-sized bed in her tenth floor two-room suite moments later. That, plus a lack of George's toiletries being anywhere in view in the large blue-themed bedroom told Rachel exactly what she had wanted to know: Stacey was occupying the suite alone.

"Yes, I was hoping you'd think so. I chose a pattern that all my bridesmaids could wear more than once," Stacey said in her soft-spoken way, unaware that she was under inspection from Rachel. "Here," she said upon handing it to her, "go try it on."

"Okay."

Taking the dress, which was covered in cellophane plastic from her, Rachel moved off to her bathroom to slip out of her shoes, shirt and pants and try it on. She chose not to undress in front of her because she had an ulterior motive in going into her bathroom and undressing there—to see if she could possibly be hoarding some of George's toiletries in this more private area of her suite. But there was nothing on her sink except her own feminine needs and she had drying pantyhose hanging from the shower. And no woman in her right mind would have her man find her bedroom or suite in such sloppy disarray. Sure, it was none of Rachel's business that George was marrying a slob—or whether Stacey and George were sleeping around, but Rachel felt a great relief that they were not living in sin before the wedding. And sufficiently satisfied, she removed the cellophane wrap from the back-zippered dress and slid it on, all the while bending over so that her ponytail would fall forward so that she could pull the long-length zipper all the way up to the back of her neck.

"It's beautiful!" she repeated as she stepped out of the bathroom and back into the bedroom of the suite, admiring the fashionably designed beige satin flare-hem dress, which had same color veil detailing across the shoulders down to the form-fitting waist.

"And thank God, it fits you perfectly!" Stacey marveled from her seat to one side of her junky bed.

"Yes, I've already thanked George for buying Devon and me the dresses and shoes, even though she won't be here to appreciate hers." Despite Rachel's somewhat disparaging remark, it didn't stop her from modeling the expensive dress in the floor for Stacey's observation.

"Yes, that is unfortunate that Devon won't be here to appreciate hers," Stacey agreed regrettably. "I can't tell you how much I was looking forward to meeting my other future sister-in-law."

"Oh, don't worry—you'll get to meet her. It's just going to be a little later than you had expected to," Rachel assured her.

"Yes, of course, you're quite right," Stacey agreed, belatedly looking on the bright side. "Oh, by the way, here are your shoes." Putting her mind back on the matter at hand and rifling through the disarray on the bed, she pulled out a box of beige heels and handed them to Rachel. "Here. See how they fit."

"Okay." Settling against the foot of the bed, Rachel peeled her yellow socks from her feet and stuck them into the equally expensive designer beige heels. They would have felt much better had she a pair of nylon footsies on her bare feet, but besides having a little trouble getting them into the heels initially, once done, they too were a perfect fit.

"Very comfortable . . . !" Rachel grinned as she rose to her feet and walked tentatively around the floor. "They're a perfect fit!"

"Thank God!" Stacey's equally grinned thanks were genuine. "Two less items for me to worry about . . . !"

"Hey, I know what you mean." Grin sobering, Rachel stepped out of the heels, put them back in the shoebox, and then put the lid back on the box. Then she sat down on the foot of the bed and slipped her feet back into her yellow socks.

Rising back to her sock feet and moving around to her side of the bed, Rachel gestured for Stacey to undo the long-length back zipper of the dress, pulling her long black ponytail out of her way as she did so. At the same time she frowned in thought, causing several lines to etch across her forehead.

"Stacey, do you mind if I ask you a personal question?"

"What?"

"How old are you?"

Stacey laughed lightly. "I'm twenty eight."

"And you've actually owned this fancy hotel for the last six years?"

Again she laughed lightly, bringing in line her perfect small teeth.

"Actually, I had a rich uncle who owned two posh hotels—one here in Alaska, the other in Hawaii. When he died six years ago, he left me this one in his will and my brother Rick the one in Hawaii. He had no children of his own to leave them to," Stacey explained. "And with his two remaining brothers—one of which is my father—as his closest relatives, well naturally, Raj wanted to leave them with them. But they didn't want them. Too much of a hassle, they said, not to mention they had been working in careers of their own for over thirty years. So, my Uncle Raj ended up leaving them to Rick and me."

"Oh, I see," Rachel nodded, as that explained why her father wasn't owner of the Amber Heights Hotel instead of her. "Is your brother flying out for your wedding?"

"Yes, he is. And my father and mother will be driving in from Ketchikan. My father is going to give me away. They're arriving Thursday, possibly like your dad and mom."

"I see. Well, they'll find an absolute gem in George as a son-in-law," Rachel smiled.

"Tell me something I don't know!" Stacey laughed in agreement, and Rachel shared her opinion as she moved off to the bathroom to change out of expensive dress.

Once back in her yellow shirt and slacks and with the cellophane-wrapped dress safely in her hand, Rachel approached Stacey at the bed, where she sat resting amongst the clutter.

"You're not going to believe this, but I don't even know where your and George's wedding is going to take place. Where are you getting married?" Rachel hoped she wouldn't think her a total ninny to have traveled five time zones without any idea as to where the nuptials were going to be.

If the question seemed a silly one to Stacy, she kept her opinion to herself behind a polite smile. "We're getting married in the first meeting/banquet room on the first floor of the hotel on Saturday, at four o'clock. And we're having the reception at the second meeting/banquet room also there on the first floor."

"Oh, I see. I can't believe I never got around to knowing that," Rachel said with a self-mocking laugh.

"Yea, it's going to be a small but elegant affair. I can't wait," Stacey smiled.

"I'm sure you can't," Rachel continued to laugh, although this time sincerely.

"Say, would you like to join us for dinner?" Stacey asked then, changing the subject. "Everybody's going to be there—George, Felix, Diane from the front desk, and George's friends, Martin Rolf and Flip Hart, also part of the wedding party."

Rachel was so relieved to have been invited to join her and George for dinner that she was sure it showed on her face. It hadn't occurred to her until just that moment that there had been no plans made for her to eat, whether in one of the fancy restaurants or up in her suite alone. Of course, George probably simply hadn't gotten around to asking her to join him and Stacey and Felix for dinner yet, nor had Felix. That is, if Felix weren't still walking around with his black and white fan duo on his arms.

"Why, yes, I would love to join you all for dinner," Rachel smiled at her, her eyes beaming.

"Good. We're eating at seven thirty in the Continental Room." Having had enough of relaxing amongst the clutter on her bed, Stacey moved lithely to her feet. Checking whether her room key was safely in the pocket of her black slacks, she said, "Why don't you take the dress and shoes up to your room and put them away? I've got to catch up with George and go over the bids for the caterers for the wedding."

"Yes, I'll do that." Rachel draped the dress over her shoulder, tucked the boxed shoes under one arm, and slung the straps of her black bag over her right shoulder.

"Come on, we can share an elevator," Stacey said and saw her out of the suite. Rachel smiled in agreement, having no choice other than to follow her.

As she stepped off the elevator on the eleventh floor moments later, she fixed the freckled features with one last smile. "Tell George that I'll catch up to him later," Rachel said, dress and shoes in tow.

"I'll, do that," Stacey too smiled in agreement just as the elevator doors closed in front of her.

Left alone in the hallway, Rachel went to her suite and put the dress and shoes in her bedroom closet with her empty suitcases. The lavish two-room suite came with TV in the living room and the bedroom, a VCR, cable and DVD player in both, a wall safe, a work-desk area, a stocked mini bar and refrigerator, three multi-line phones—including one in the bathroom, AM/FM clock radio, in-room ironing board and a hair dryer. And there was even the luxury of a white terry guest robe for wearing after showering or bathing, not to mention a large and tasty complimentary basket of fruit that came with each suite. But Rachel was not interested in any of these considerable amenities as she stood in the floor perplexed, to decide what to do next.

A glance at the silver-toned watch on her left wrist showed the time to be five-thirty. That left two hours for her to kill before dinner. Well, she wasn't going to spend the hours alone.

With the straps of her black bag slung over her yellow shoulder and her room key safely in the bottom of it, Rachel stepped from the self-locking door and then took the elevator up to the penthouse.

Both to her surprise and delight, Felix answered the door upon hearing her knock, indicating that either he'd been standing nearby or that George was too far away from the door to answer it, himself. Which was odd, Rachel thought because the workday was over. Oh, well, she guessed he was still going over the caterers' estimates with Stacey as she smiled up at Felix, whose gorgeous rectangular features would pull on any woman's senses. Small wonder the man was an actor.

"Hi, Felix, I thought you'd be here," Rachel said as she stood there waiting for him to see her inside.

"Well, if it isn't George's kid sister!" The smile on his attractive mouth was teasing as he saw her into the suite. Immediately she saw the reason for him answering the door in place of George. George sat at his desk poring over some important papers, although he acknowledged Rachel's presence with a nod of his black-haired head. Stacey stood beside his desk poring over the papers with him and acknowledged her with a mere nod of her own brown-haired head.

"Get in here, girl!" Felix closed the door behind her and stood staring as his brown eyes perused her figure in the yellow outfit from neck to ankle. "You know, your body is out of this world! Is that an astronaut outfit you're wearing, or what!" he teased, mouth curved into an outrageous grin.

"Oh, please!" Rachel said with a grin of her own, even though he did speak the truth! Nevertheless, she felt herself flushing with embarrassment as Felix curved a congenial brown-sleeved arm around her shoulders to lead her away from the door.

"So, come on in here, and tell me what's happening with you, girl," he said as he led her into the living area.

"There's not much happening with me. What's happening with you? Or do I know already? I ask that because I went to your suite on the twelfth floor a couple of hours ago, and you weren't there. No doubt you were out with your two groupies. Or should I call them fans?"

She turned a coquettish smile up at him as she settled amid the red cushions of the first sofa and lowered her bag to the coffee table. Felix settled on the sofa beside her, a tickled smile playing about his own mouth as he pondered how to answer the questions without incriminating himself.

"You know how it is, Rachel. *As The Star Shines* is a very popular soap opera, and it has a big following even way over here in Alaska. And because of the role I play on the soap, people not only recognize me, but follow me wherever I go." Felix removed his arm from round her shoulders, but stretched it out across the back of the sofa behind her head in a proprietorial action he knew she couldn't miss.

"I see," Rachel said; her smile only tolerant now. "So, where are your fans now?"

"Running for their lives, no doubt," Felix answered. "I told them that in real life, I'm just as much a cad as I am on the soap opera."

"I see," Rachel remarked, although as yet he had explained nothing. "So, how are you a cad on the soap? Sleep around a lot?"

"Sort of. . . . I'm presently sleeping with my boss, her daughter, and her stepdaughter, without any of them knowing of the others. The veteran actress on the show was my first love interest; now, I have three," Felix finished, smiling plaintively.

"Your character's sleeping with three women all at the same time?" Rachel managed an outraged laugh at his shameless nod. "Felix, you should be whipped!"

"Are you asking for the job?" The dancing brown eyes were entirely flirtatious, yet even then it was impossible to tell whether he was being serious or not.

"So, you're saying that you are a cad in real life?" she asked.

"Of course not. You know how gentlemanly I behaved when I dated your sister Devon all those years ago. I've no intention of behaving any less gentlemanly as I show you around Alaska over the next few days."

"Well, at least I'm glad to hear that!" Rachel said on a relieved note. "Or I might have to remind you of the short courtship you two had before she dumped you on your duff and told you good riddance!"

"Oh, how short was it? I seem to have forgotten," Felix said, perfect teeth showing in a smile of disinterest.

"Actually, it was four months, three days, and seventeen hours," she was swift to remind him.

"You kept count of how long your sister and I dated?"

"No, George did."

"George did what?" Having finished with their work for the day, George, accompanied by Stacey, approached the sitting area just in time to catch the tail end of their conversation.

"Kept count of how long Felix and Devon dated," Rachel repeated her statement for her brother's benefit.

"Oh, you mean the four months, three days, and seventeen hours?" George laughed as he did the same and repeated Rachel's earlier spoken statement before settling on the adjacent sofa and Stacey beside him. "And then, Devon dumped you on your duff, and I doubt if you've gotten over her to this day."

Rachel was of the same opinion, although she chose not to voice it as she gazed up at Felix's well-groomed features. The smile had left that sexy mouth of his as he sat beside her on the sofa, a series of emotions flitting across his equally sexy face.

"Yeah, she was definitely the one that got away," Felix acknowledged humbly after a moment. "I have long since gotten over her."

"Well, I should hope so!" George continued to laugh.

With the three of them becoming silent then, Rachel again took control of the conversation, at the same time turning on the sofa to fix Felix with a wicked grin.

"Hey," she prodded him softly, "you remember that time you, Devon and I were sitting on the chaise rocker on my family's front porch? I was fourteen to Devon's nineteen and your twenty one, and I was sitting between the two of you trying to get into your business. Anyway, you were reading some kind of magazine, and you raised it up behind my head to keep me from seeing you as you leaned over behind my back to give Devon a kiss. Except that I, knowing what was coming, moved the magazine out of the way just in time for your kiss to intercept my cheek!"

"Yeah, I remember that." Felix's smile was reminiscent. "You know, you were such a bratty kid at fourteen. I wonder what you're like at twenty-four."

"No longer a bratty kid at fourteen. . . ."

"No, you're definitely not fourteen," Felix agreed smoothly.

"Hey, man, that's my kid sister you're hitting on!" George warned caustically.

"Funny, I thought she was hitting on me!" Felix remarked with a jocularity that made them all laugh. Then the atmosphere in the large penthouse suite sobered as George took over the conversation.

"So, where do you plan to take my kid sister sightseeing tomorrow?" he asked Felix.

"Well, I thought I'd start her on a walking tour of the city, starting at the Alaska Public Lands Information Center and ending at the Anchorage Museum of History and Art."

"You might rather start at the Log Cabin Visitor Center," Stacey interjected, "where friendly volunteers answer questions and racks of brochures line the walls. Oh, and be sure to observe the marble statue in front of Old City Hall next door, which honors William Seward, the secretary of state who engineered the purchase of Alaska from Russia."

"Alaska was purchased from Russia? I didn't know that." Rachel shook her head in amazed ignorance, having failed to remember that from her high school history.

Felix laughed. "Yes, Russia sold Alaska to the United States in 1867 for $7.2 million, or about two cents an acre. Ironically, $7.2 million was the value of the shipment of crude oil moved by tanker after the Trans-Alaska pipeline was completed."

"Very good!" praised Stacey of Felix's knowledge of her native state. "You've been paying attention to your tour guides this past week!"

"He ought to have," George agreed, fixing his friend with another jeering look. "He's been going out with enough of them. A different employee every day . . . !"

Felix's regard of his friend's scathing demeanor was one of amused satisfaction. "So, can I help it if I'm popular?" he laughed.

"Popular, indeed!" derided George in the same jeering demeanor.

"Hey, look man, you've got yours, I've still got mine to get!" Briefly fixing his friend with an equally demeaning look, Felix diverted his attention onto Rachel in one that was again entirely flirtatious, as if she would serve the capacity of being his as any other woman. "Do you have proper walking shoes for all the walking we shall be doing the next couple days? Something like these?"

Raising one foot off the floor, Felix showed Rachel the white Nikes sneakers adorning one foot, bringing with it an inner edge of relief. Aside from the black pumps she was currently wearing which were fit for evening wear, she had packed for her trip some white Nikes sneakers for hiking. In fact, they almost looked like his.

"Yeah, Felix, I brought some Nikes sneakers that look almost like yours."

"And what about a windbreaker, or jacket . . . ? The mornings tend to be cool here."

"No, I didn't bring either a windbreaker, or a jacket. I brought sweaters, and a coat."

"No, a sweater is not heavy enough to fight the cool Alaska summer mornings, and a coat is too confining. Come, my dear, we have to go shopping." Reaching out and curling a hand over hers, Felix moved to his feet and pulled Rachel to hers after thoughtful consideration of her heavy coat and seeing that it would never do. "If we're not back in time for dinner, start without us." Throwing the statement over his shoulder to George, Felix just did give Rachel a chance to retrieve her black bag from the coffee table and slide its strap back onto her yellow-clad shoulder before he had pulled her from the penthouse.

Once back in the elevator, Felix maintained a hold on her hand, sending a warm pleasure shooting up her arm. He pushed the elevator for the twelfth floor with his free hand as the doors closed on the penthouse floor. Rachel determined not to feel anything at his touch, knowing as she did that it was simply the impersonal claiming of her hand to keep her at his side.

"So, where are we going?" Rachel asked as the elevator began to descend to the twelfth floor.

"Wal-Mart," Felix said in his attractive tenor. "To get you a parka and some disposable film for all the many photos you'll want to take."

"Oh, that's right!" Rachel covered her mouth with her free hand. "It never occurred to me that I might want to take pictures on this trip. I didn't even bring a camera, or film!"

"Yeah, funny how I knew that," Felix laughed absently.

"Indeed," Rachel agreed.

Once on the twelfth floor, Felix went to his suite, where he slid into a gray woolen jacket, and then they took the elevator down to the eleventh floor, where Rachel entered her own suite and slid into the yellow sweater that matched her ensemble and that she had worn before. Then filing back into the elevator, they descended uninterrupted to the lobby.

Diane Mortemburg was still on duty at the reception desk and eyed them curiously as they began to cross the lobby, especially when Felix was holding so possessively onto Rachel's hand.

"We're going to buy me a parka," Rachel explained unnecessarily, smiling as they passed by the reception desk. "Apparently, according to Felix, my sweater is not warm enough for the Alaska summer mornings."

"Felix is right." A smile accompanied the affirmation. "And you'll need one in the morning, because we're having a cool spell, and it promises to be thirty-eight degrees come daybreak."

"Oh, I see." Rachel neglected to inform Diane that she had a heavy winter coat in her belongings to handle that since Felix had said it would be too confining for what they were going to do.

"Anyway, don't be surprised if we don't make it back in time for dinner," Felix said by way of apology. "This lady and I have a lot to talk about."

"So, you say," Diane smiled as they crossed the lobby and stepped from the hotel.

Outside, the cooling temperature warned that Felix knew what he had been talking about. In the gray woolly jacket he had pulled on over his shirt Rachel doubted that he had felt the slight chill in the air, while she in the lightweight yellow sweater was downright cold.

Fortunately he led her to a tan Pontiac Grand Prix not too far from the hotel door and quickly saw her into the passenger door. Rachel sighed in relief as he just as quickly moved around the back of the car and slid in behind the wheel.

"I should have known that a man of your career and popularity would have seen ahead and rented a car, and I am grateful," Rachel said as he started the engine of the car and turned the heat to low temperature. "There's nothing like having your own transportation when you want to go somewhere. And had I to have stood waiting for a cab, I would have been chilled to the bones by the time it got here. Either that, or I would have had to go pulling out my heavy coat—you know, of which you're too embarrassed to be seen with me wearing."

"Nonsense, I would simply have offered you my jacket—you know, like a gentleman would?"

"Oh, yes, of course, I forget how gentlemanly you are." Rachel's smile met the brief one he turned on her as he backed out of the parking spot and turned out onto the street.

"So, how come a woman as beautiful as you is still single?" Felix asked after a moment.

The smile remained painted on Rachel's mouth as he turned them onto a connecting street leading them away from the hotel. "I guess I've been too busy working to meet someone. Not to mention the fact that most men my age are only interested in one-night-stands. And I don't want to find myself at twenty-nine getting divorced for the second time as my sister Devon is presently."

"Yeah, tell me about her," Felix pumped her with a smile. "How'd she find herself twice-divorced at as young an age as twenty-nine . . . ?"

"That's really very simple, Felix," Rachel began, "she found herself at twenty one involved in a relationship that resulted from a one-night-stand. They got married and stayed so for six months; it didn't work out. End of first marriage. Her second divorce taking place now is happening because she came home one evening three months ago and found her second husband of six years in their bed with two women. End of second marriage. And Felix, they were so different from you. They didn't treat her with respect at all."

"Oh, I see. By that, I take it they weren't gentlemanly at all, huh?"

"Not at all," Rachel agreed.

"The poor dear. . . . She would have been so much better off if she'd stayed with me."

"Yes, she would." Rachel fell briefly silent after voicing the three-word response. She didn't need another reminder that Felix was still in love with her older sister, Devon. Abruptly she changed the subject.

"So, how is it that a thirty-one-year-old man as good looking as you is not married?" Rachel asked.

"I guess it's a matter of me never being in the right place at the right time," Felix said in his seductive tenor, turning another brief smile on her. "But then, I knew when I went off to acting school that I would be too busy honing my craft to date. That, plus as yet, I haven't had to work with anyone who floats my boat, so to speak. So, I've simply contented myself with being single."

"Now, that's exactly what I've done!" Rachel laughed. "Contented myself with being single . . . !"

"You're a lot better off," Felix said, "choosing to let the fates fall where they may."

"I agree with you," Rachel replied. Falling silent, she averted her luminous brown gaze to the scenery they were passing as they turned left onto Old Seward Highway.

"So, how long have you been a kindergarten teacher?" Felix asked after a moment, sweeping her with yet another brief glance.

"Three years."

"Really . . . ?"

"Yes," Rachel smiled, "and I absolutely love it. Children at that age are so adorable; you can't help but love 'em. But then, you probably know that."

"Yes, I do."

"And you love your job. . . . Playing the Daytime Emmy award-winning role of Joe Murray. A man who's presently sleeping with his boss, her daughter, and her stepdaughter . . . !"

Felix laughed outright behind the wheel at the mockery underlining her teasing tone. "Something like that," he agreed.

With her gaze lingering on his sexy profile, Rachel again changed the subject. "So, how's Elvis these days?"

Felix's mouth remained curved in a smile of pleasure at her mention of the Elvis Presley music collection he had stolen from his father.

"He's doing great!" Felix turned a fifth look on her from behind the wheel, albeit an amazed one that time. "How'd you remember about that? That was years ago!"

Her berry-lipped smile remained mocking as she continued to gaze at him. "Who can forget that you were an Elvis freak, the way you used to come out to the house playing his old cassettes in your car, and singing them to my sister? Not that I mean to bring her up again," Rachel went on, aware that she was going back on her own word, "but even at the age of fourteen, I could have told you no matter how infatuated you were with Devon's beauty that your relationship with her would not last indefinitely, that she was going to dump you sooner or later—and do you know why?"

"Why?"

" . . . Because she did not like Elvis. My nineteen-year-old sister could not understand why a twenty-one-year-old man who was coming to see her was interested in the music of a man who had been dead for decades."

"Hey, I don't care how long he had been dead, he was the King," Felix remarked with a laugh that showed his lack of shame for his love for the classics. "He was the best musical artist that my father could have ever taken an interest in. That man could sing rock-and-roll, raunchy blues, lilting boogie, operatic pop, and country tearjerkers. And to hear my father tell it, during the last decade of his career, Elvis Presley's live show in Vegas was the hottest ticket in America. Not to mention that they are still impersonating him almost thirty years after his death."

"Hey, you don't have to tell me," Rachel laughed. "I know Elvis was the King. The man died before I was even born, yet still, I don't mind listening to some of his old music. He had some serious hits, such as *Hound Dog, Jailhouse Rock, and Don't Be Cruel,* just to name a few. And I've seen several of those old movies he made back in the 1960's on the Classic cable channel. I loved *Girl Happy, Fun In Acapulco, G.I. Blues,* and *It Happened At The World's Fair.* God, those are some good old movies. Elvis was one gorgeous white man! And do you realize that in every movie he did back then, he got into a fight?"

"Who are you telling . . . !" Felix turned an incredulous grin on her in his surprise of her absorption with the deceased singer/movie star that he had been a fan of for years. "I have presently in my collection in New York City *Double Trouble, Paradise Hawaiian Style,* and *Viva Las Vegas,* to name a few. And you're right—Elvis did get in a fight in each of those movies. I'm surprised you noticed that!"

"Hey, like I said—the man might be dead, but he was talented. Devon couldn't appreciate that. She's never liked anything he's ever done. That's why I used to feel so sorry for you when you used to come to the house singing to her that she had you *'all shook up.'* My sister was a *'hard-headed woman.'* She stepped all over your *'blue suede shoes.'"*

"Yea, you've got that right." Felix laughed at both her knowledge of and mention of the old Elvis Presley classic tunes. "She did not *'love me tender.'* Not during the four months, three days, and seventeen hours that you and George say we went together."

"No." Rachel's long off-black ponytail bobbed from side to side as she smilingly shook her head in the negative. "She didn't treat you right."

"Now, that's Luther!" Felix reminded her with a laugh.

"You could be right!" Rachel's laugh agreed with him as she thought of the old song by the equally world-famous black singer.

Arriving at Wal-Mart then, Felix parked the car up near the front of the lot, extinguished the engine, and then slid from the driver's side to see Rachel from the passenger door. Aware that the yellow sweater she wore wasn't warm enough to fight against the chill in the air, he quickly escorted her into the department store, black purse strapped to her shoulder, where they made a beeline for the ladies' section. There the typical apparel met the eye from every direction—blouses, sweaters, dresses, socks, skirts, shirts, pants, jeans, slips, sleepwear, underwear, and so on. But Felix wasn't interested in any of these and quickly led Rachel to the coat section, where a number of parkas of varying colors and sizes were lined up on a lower rack.

"What do you think of this?" Felix asked, pulling a thick woolly parka of mud brown off the rack and showing it to her.

"Not bad," Rachel smiled, fingering the ribbed material, "except that it's too big."

At her mention of the word big, Felix's brown gaze lowered over the curves of her figure in a too assessing look that left Rachel practically blushing in the floor.

"What size are you?" he asked, eyes sliding back to her flaming face. "Aren't you about a twelve?"

The brown of Rachel's gaze settled on the sexy rectangular face in a deeply demeaning look. "You been with so many women that you can look at one and tell what size she is?" she demanded.

Felix did not back down from the intent look she had turned on him. "Are you a twelve?" he repeated, amusement flickering unabashedly in his dancing gaze.

"No, I'm a ten!" Rachel informed him primly.

The brown of his eyes dropped back to the provocative fullness of her breasts behind the yellow sweater pulled on over her equally yellow shirt and he sighed.

"Well, then, I guess this will never do!" Averting his incredulous gaze away from her, Felix placed the size twelve mud brown parka back onto the rack and began rifling through the rest of them for a size ten.

Beside him, Rachel continued to look at him in a statement of affront. "I feel like I've been felt up!" she said, her eyes lowering over his well-built physique in the gray woolen jacket, thick woolly brown sweater and black corduroy pants he wore in a similar appraisal.

His eyes settled on her in an equal expression of offense as he observed her own boldly assessing look. "Now, I feel like I've been felt up!" he said in his attractive tenor.

Rachel deliberately ignored the teasing gleam that had crept back into his dancing brown eyes as she accepted the mud brown ribbed woolly parka he was then handing her in the right size.

"Here, make yourself useful, and hold this." Handing him the black purse she had unstrapped from her shoulder, Rachel removed the woolly parka from its plastic hanger and slid her arms into it. The parka proved a perfect fit once she had engaged the front zipper and pulled it up to her neck, freeing her long off-black ponytail from it as she did so.

"What do you think?" she asked Felix, turning in the floor and modeling for him, her arms extended at her sides.

Felix noticed the way the bulky material falling to just below her hips morphed the curves of her figure out of sight and his sexy slender-lipped mouth pulled into a frown of disapproval.

"Where are you under all that?"

Rachel's own luscious medium-lipped mouth puckered in a frown at the impertinent question. "Will you be serious, and tell me what you think of it?"

"Is it warm?"

"Yea, it is," Rachel agreed; at the same time accustoming herself to the inviting warmth of the thick wool covering her arms and body.

"Then, let's get it, girl," Felix said.

"Yea, I think I will." Nodding, she quickly unzipped the parka and slid out of it, at the same time replacing it on its plastic hanger.

"Now, come on, let's go find you a camera and some film." Handing her black bag to her and waiting for her to slide the strap back onto her shoulder, Felix led her away from the coat area, the proprietorial claim he took of her hand again sending a warm pleasure dancing up Rachel's arm.

Over in the electronics department, Felix quickly led her to an assortment of cameras lined up along a couple white shelves. "How much can you afford to pay for one of these things?"

"On a kindergarten teacher's salary . . . ? Not much," she said, briefly flashing her gaze away from the cameras to fix him with a mocking look.

"Yeah, how much does a kindergarten teacher make a year, anyway?" Felix asked curiously.

"Chump change, compared to what you probably make . . . !" Rachel averted her long-lashed gaze away from the cameras to fix him with another mocking look. "Which reminds me—while we're on the subject, George tells me you've been on this soap opera for six years now. What was the name of it, again—*As The Stomach Turns?*"

Felix burst into outright laughter at the wrong name she had deliberately given his soap, the attractive sound of it falling pleasantly on her hearing.

"It's called *As The Star Shines*, and George is right: I've been on it for six years, and am a major player."

"You must be, in your Emmy award-winning role of a man presently sleeping with his boss, her daughter, and her stepdaughter," Rachel repeated observantly.

Again Felix showed his pretty teeth in a laugh beneath the boldly mocking look she had turned on him. Then he sobered, becoming serious.

"Here, let's find you a camera. Here. How's this?"

Pulling a Samsung automatic 35mm from the shelf, he showed it her, only for Rachel to frown at its too-high price.

"Sorry, too expensive," she said.

"Then, how about this one . . . ? No, on second thought, it's probably too expensive, too." Lowering the $180.00 Canon Sure Shot 35mm camera he had pulled from the shelf back onto it, Felix let his deep brown gaze pore over a number of others, as was Rachel beside him. "Hey, how about this one?" he asked of the next one he pulled from the shelf. "It's also a Canon Sure Shot 35mm, with power zoom, and three-point auto focus for sharp pictures every time. It includes accessory kit with case, film and batteries. And look, it's on sale, and costs just over a hundred bucks!"

"I'll take it." Not needing to be sold any further on the inexpensive camera, Rachel snatched it and the attached accessories out of his hand in a blur.

"Of course, you're going to need more film, but you can get that at the checkout counter. Come on—let's go see what they've got up there."

Aware that she stood with her black bag strapped to her shoulder and the mud brown parka hanging from the hanger in her hand, Felix took the camera and accessory kit away from her to carry in his own hand. Rachel wondered if his intention had been that of giving her more freedom of movement or one of a more personal reason as he again claimed her hand in his larger one.

However the warm pleasure that had again begun to slide up her arm was regrettably short-circuited when they approached an Elvis Presley cassette display to one side of one of the checkout counters.

"Oh, my God, it's Elvis!" Felix exclaimed, at the same time excitedly letting go of Rachel's hand to pick up one of the cellophane covered cassettes, which Rachel was doing beside him with equal excitement. "Oooh, you know, I've got this one on CDs," he said of the cassette he held in his hand, which was a collection of Presley's Top Ten Hits. "Recorded from 1956 to 1958, and it's got all my favorites on here—*All Shook Up, Don't Be Cruel, Heartbreak Hotel, Jailhouse Rock, Return To Sender,* and of course, *Love Me Tender.* And you know, my father had this one on 8-Track," he went on of another cassette he had taken into his hand, entitled *That's The Way It Is.* "Do you remember those things?" Felix laughed. "No, that was probably before your time. Anyway, the whole album had to be good, because if you wanted to hear the song again, you had to drive around the block until the track came around again. I got my father CDs of all those albums of Elvis's that he used to have on 8-Track. It simply blew his mind. Because all you have to do is stick the CD into the machine and it goes right to the song! Isn't that a marvel?" Felix laughed.

"It's all I've ever known, honey," Rachel replied, equally amused by his excitement over the latest device for playing recorded music. "And anyway, while we're standing here talking about the King's music, are you into anybody that's current?"

Felix's laugh sobered into a smile as he placed the cassette back into the display behind the other one. "I like Ruben Studdard, Beyoncé Knowles, Erykah Badu, Faith Hill, R. Kelly, Ludacris, and Alicia Keys. But baby, there's nothing like the classics . . . ! Sometimes, I think I was born too late. I should have been born in the forties, and then, I would have been around during Elvis's heyday, not to mention a lot of those other fabulous singers, such as Sam Cooke, Tammy Terrell, and Otis Redding, who have since passed on."

"I see." With the blank nod of her head, Rachel placed the Elvis Presley cassette tape she held in her own hand back into the display behind Felix. She had heard of Otis Redding—Mr. *Sitting By The Dock Of The Bay,* but she had no idea who the other two singers were that Felix had mentioned.

Following his lead then, she began to select out of an assortment of film displayed on a lower shelf three boxes of Kodak color print 35mm ISO two-hundred speed for daylight, one box of ISO four-hundred speed for nightlight and one box of ISO one hundred black and white for stills. Playfully Felix told her that she would not need the four-hundred speed film, as according to him, it didn't get dark during the Alaska summer months until midnight, anyway, but Rachel ignored his jeering remarks equally playfully as she put all up on the checkout counter along with the camera and accessories and parka. She was going to be broke come next month, but she tried not to think about that as she charged the large amount to a favored

MasterCard. For now, she was going to have fun in Alaska, and she wasn't going to think about the dent doing so would make in her pocketbook at all!

Finally, with everything bagged up by the friendly checker, Rachel and Felix picked the bags up off the counter and prepared to leave the department store. Or so that was what they'd hoped, except that three steps away from the checkout counter Felix was mobbed by four women, three black and one white. Felix wasn't annoyed—quite the contrary, with his award-winning fame, popularity and good looks, he expected it, he anticipated it. For that reason, he turned his most charming smile on the quartet who was his adoring fans, who were busy throwing papers and pens and soap opera magazines in his face for his signature.

"Well, hello, there, Mr. Latham!" said the first one.

"How're you doing, baby!" said the second one.

"May I have your autograph, Mr. Latham?" said the third one.

"You want mine, and my phone number?" said the forth one.

All the time the four women were gushing, Felix managed a tolerant smile as he signed the various magazines and papers they had thrust at him, along with the pens they had given him as well.

"Oooh, baby, you are so fine!" praised the first one.

"So, are you really the cad you are on the show in real life?" asked the second one.

"Because if you are, I'd like to be your caddie . . . ! And I'm not talking about golf! Or am I!" hinted the third one.

"Felix, the Cad, you are! Or should I say Felix the Cat!" hinted the fourth one.

Rachel turned a bemused look on Felix as he stood equally bemused by their come-ons amid autographing their various materials while at the same time trying to keep the too aggressive women at arm's length.

"Oh, you like this sort of thing, do you?" she teased him with a dry laugh.

However, before he could shake the four women off, three men, two black and one white, sidled up to Rachel, bent on coming on to her the same way.

"Ooh, baby, you are so fine, I want to make you right now!" said the first one.

"Are you a soap star, too? Because if you are, I'm going to quit my job, and start watching your show tomorrow!" exclaimed the second one.

"Please, tell me you're not his wife, because I'd like to make you mine! God, you're the finest woman I've ever seen!" praised the third one.

"Yes, she is, isn't she?!" Felix's ready agreement echoed the opinion of the white man as he used his compliment as a means to provide a much-needed escape for both him and Rachel. Picking up the bag he had lowered to the floor, Felix curved a possessive arm around her waist. "Let's get out of here, quickly!" he urged smilingly between his perfect teeth.

And in complete and smiling agreement to his suggestion, Rachel let him hustle her quickly out of the department store and away from the three fawning men and four equally fawning women gushing all over them.

Chapter Three

They laughed about it all the way back to the hotel. The way those four women came on to Felix and the way those three men came on to Rachel. Being the well-known soap star that he was and a gorgeous one at that, Felix expected such fan worship; after all, he had spent the whole week there being paraded around by adoring women—both the black and the white—trying to get next to him and who knows what else after that. But the funny thing was discovering that Rachel anticipated it, too. After all, with her beautiful dusky looks, long hair and hourglass figure, she had spent the last nine years since hitting puberty rejecting come-ons like that from interested men. Slick lines invested in an attempt to get them—both the black and the white—next to her and who knows what else after that. But she did not know then that it had just started for the evening.

They arrived back at the Amber Heights just in time to take Rachel's bags up to her suite and freshen up in their respective ones before going down to the Continental Room on the second floor for dinner. They were all there: Stacey and George, Diane from the front desk, and Martin Rolf and Flip Hart, a black and white duo that were two of George's groomsmen. As Rachel and Felix sat down at the table and George introduced her to the two men, they sized her up like she was a piece of food they were about to consume on their plates. Yet they somehow managed to keep their wayward thoughts to themselves—at least for the time being.

The meal started out easily enough with the seven of them feasting on an assortment of appetizers, such as onion rings, escargots Bourguignon, crabmeat Gratinee, fresh mushrooms, fresh sea scallops, fried calamari, smoked Alaskan halibut, and the classic shrimp cocktail, to be followed by salad, entrée, dessert, coffee and wine. Naturally, as the most prominent one at the table, Felix started the conversation, laughingly telling best friend George about the experiences that he and Rachel had had with the fawning men and women in the effort of trying to get out of Wal-Mart a while ago. He said that while that kind of adulation came with his name and career it had bowled him over to see her have to go through the same experience, leaving everybody at the table rolling with laughter, Rachel included.

And then, Felix's amusement turned into excitement. "Man, why didn't you tell me Rachel was into Elvis!" he demanded laughingly over his shrimp cocktail, changing the subject. "Not only does the girl like his music, but all his old movies, as well! Can you believe that?!"

"Yea, man, who are you kidding . . . !" George laughed from his seat two chairs away from him around the round white-clothed table, where he sat nibbling on some fried calamari, his bemused brown gaze sliding to his kid sister. "She stole several of his old records from Mom and Dad years ago, and she watched half his old movies from a cable channel when she was a kid!"

"Yea, I see that!" Felix continued to laugh. "A woman after my own heart!" he finished, still amazed, and eyeing Rachel incredulously from his seat at the table to the right of her.

Using that as his cue to move in on her, Martin turned his dull brown-eyed gaze on her. "So, you like Elvis, do you?" he asked her in his low resonant voice. "Yeah, I liked him, too. Elvis was the King in his day. He was truly a beautiful man. But he was nowhere near as beautiful as you."

Rachel looked away from the shrimp cocktail she was consuming along with Felix to turn an amused look on the black man sitting at the table to the left of her. He was an ugly man by anyone's opinion, possessing too short black hair around a too long face with too small brown eyes, a too wide nose, too full lips and a too long prominent chin to go with them all.

"Really?" she forced a smile in response to his last remark.

"Really, baby," Martin insisted over the fried calamari he was eating, as was George. "You know, you're just too damned fine! Oooooh, what you must look like with your hair down and wearing a low-cut mini-dress!" he schmoozed.

"Hey, man, that's my kid sister you're talking to!" George warned the thirty-year-old man, who sat ogling her shapely body from the long off-black ponytail hanging down her back all the way down what he could see of the frontal curve of her breasts above the table.

But Martin ignored his friend and so did Flip Hart, who chose that moment to join in on Martin's schmoozing of her as well.

"Yeah, Rachel, you know, there's a shortage of women in Alaska," the Alaskan Native began informatively over the sea scallops he was nibbling from his own plate.

"Is that a fact?" Rachel mused with an equally amused eye on the equally thirty-year-old man who was white, with light brown hair surrounding an oval face possessing only slightly softer features than his black friend.

"It's a fact," Flip went on smoothly. "As a matter of fact, Oprah did a show several years ago about a number of us—Alaskan men looking for women from the lower 48 in the hope of finding wives."

"Is that right?" Rachel went on with only faint interest, knowing she must have been a child in grade school when that episode of the talk show aired.

"It's right!" Flip went on in the same informative demeanor. "As a matter of fact, there was even a show on a couple of years ago showing women who were interested in coming over here to take Alaskan men as husbands. Anyway, the reason I'm telling you all this, darlin', is because if you ever decide to relocate over here from your home state, look me up. Or maybe even down!" the white man finished with the suggestive lowering of his hazel eyes over her figure.

"I'll give that thought some consideration," Rachel replied, smiling to herself at the suggestive way the Native Alaskan was looking at her and averting her brown gaze away to a distant corner of the restaurant. The Continental Room was arrayed in muted shades of the same blue hue that carried throughout the hotel, came with its own bar, and boasted a wine cellar of at least ten thousand bottles.

Thankfully, the friendly black waiter brought their meals to the table then, giving Rachel something else to focus on. Her eyes settled almost gratefully on the plate the short-afroed man placed in front of her. She had chosen the Veal Amber Heights, which consisted of veal filet mignon topped with foie gras and black truffles, served with potatoes au gratin, sautéed spinach and Medeira sauce, Caesar salad tossed with croutons, and the meal came with a roll, all of which she would top off with Tiramisu for dessert, espresso and a Riesling white wine. And she knew that she would be forever grateful to George for floating her bill on this trip, because she would never have been able to afford to eat at a restaurant as fancy and expensive as this on her teacher's salary. In fact, the glance Rachel turned on her brother relayed her sentiment, but George brushed her gratitude off as nothing as he smilingly began to dig into his own plate. He and Stacey had settled on the most expensive thing on the menu—the Chateaubriand for two, the plate consisting of prime hickory-grilled tenderloin served with a choice of mushroom or béarnaise sauce, came with a bouquetière of vegetables, roasted garlic mashed potatoes and a dinner roll, they had selected the tossed green salad, and they were topping their meals off with espresso, a California merlot, and Bananas Foster for two as well. To the right of her, Felix had selected the roasted salmon filet, which was topped with olive and sun-dried tomato crust, served with saffron rice, French green beans with red wine butter sauce, a dinner roll, he had selected the house spinach salad, and he was topping his meal off with espresso, a California Chardonnay and crème brulée for dessert. Rachel didn't care what the others were eating as she picked up her fork and began to dig avidly into her meal after already having finished her shrimp cocktail.

However just because the meals had come didn't mean the come-ons had stopped, for as soon as Rachel had raised the veal filet mignon to her lips, Martin started on her all over again.

"Oooh—oooh, baby, you are so fine!" he repeated over the strip sirloin he had just started in his own plate, forcing her again to fix him with a mocking look, which the bold man misconstrued as interest. "You know, you have the sexiest teeth," the black man went on amorously. "I've gotten excited just sitting here watching you chew. If you take one more bite out of that meat, you're going have to take me upstairs, and take a bite out of me!"

"Yea, and then, you can take one out of me!" added Flip meaningfully over the Oysters Rockefeller in his own plate.

"Didn't I tell you two to shut up? That's my baby sister you're hitting on!" George warned his friends yet again over the grilled tenderloin he was raising to his own lips.

And so it went for the entire meal—Martin and Flip were all over her, giving her blatant compliments, and expressing wayward thoughts of things they'd like to do with her—not to mention to her—not to mention things they'd like for her to do with them, not to mention to them—to the complete ignoring of George and Stacey's constant warnings for them to leave Rachel alone. To the right of her, Felix was being given the treatment by three of the hotel's off-duty employees that he had skirted around earlier in the week who were interested in picking up where they'd left off with him, to the complete ignoring of employers Stacey and George as well.

He put up with the trio falling all over him for about twenty minutes before he suddenly curved a golden brown hand around Rachel's darker-skinned wrist, aware that she needed a rescue from Martin and Flip also.

"Let's get out of here, quickly!" he told her smilingly between his perfect teeth. Rachel didn't need to hear him say it twice as she gratefully let him pull her to her feet, what food left on their plates forgotten as they sped from the restaurant without once looking back over their shoulders.

They laughed about it all the way down the hall and in the elevator—about their misfortune in being two beautiful people that everybody wanted to get next to—no matter how stupid or corny they had to sound or be while trying to go about it. In fact, they were nowhere near sobered upon arriving on the eleventh floor moments later.

"I'm sorry!" Felix exulted as they arrived outside Rachel's suite down the stripe-papered hall a not too far distance from the elevator banks. "Is it like that with you all the time?"

"Uhm-hmm," Rachel laughed in agreement, "same way I see it is with you."

He tightened his hold on the hand clasped warmly in his in a meaningful squeeze. "I guess I'm going to have to stay close to you to keep all these jerks away from you over the next few days," he said.

"As I see I'm going to have to do the same for you," Rachel reciprocated.

Dropping his brown gaze from her own sobering look, Felix glanced at the gold watch encircling his left wrist. "It's only eight thirty. What are you planning on doing for the rest of the night?"

"I'm going to bed," Rachel laughed. "It was a long flight from Georgia, and my jet lag is trying to lag back."

"I see." Understanding gleamed in the long-lashed dancing eyes as Felix continued to look at her. "Well, you have a good night. I'm going to get back with

George—although not anywhere near that Continental Room, I'll tell you that!" he half laughed, to which she did the same. "Anyway, meet me down in the cafeteria at eight-thirty for breakfast in the morning, and I'll take you for your first day of sightseeing. And by all means, don't forget what I said about dressing warmly, preferably in layers. And put some thermal underwear on under your clothes. You said you have some."

"Don't worry, I'll be fine, and I'll see you at eight-thirty." She smiled appreciatively as he prepared to turn away from her door. "And while we're on the subject of dressing warmly, thanks for taking me shopping for the parka and camera," she said gratefully.

"Don't mention it. I'll see you in the morning. Goodnight, Rachel."

"Goodnight, Felix." She bid him one last smile proffered with a wave as he moved back in the direction of the elevators down the hall.

The sun was high up in the sky when Rachel awoke the next morning, eager for what the day would behold. She glanced at her silver-toned watch on the French Provincial nightstand, which showed the time to be eight-fifteen. Felix had told her the evening before to meet him for breakfast in the cafeteria at eight-thirty. Quickly throwing back the covers, Rachel crawled out of the bed, piled her long off-black hair up into a shower cap pulled from a dresser drawer and ran into the bathroom to take a shower.

Having finished with a quick but thorough one minutes later, Rachel wiped herself down with a thick white towel and then wrapped a second dry one around herself before coming out of the bathroom and back into the bedroom of the two-room suite. Moving back to the six-drawer dresser across the large room, Rachel quickly donned a fresh bra and underwear from another drawer and slid her feet into a pair of thick black socks. She remembered how Felix had told her to dress in layers because not only did the summer mornings in Alaska tend to be on the cool side, but they had been especially so in the week or more that he'd been there, so Rachel piled into a pair of thermal underwear and then dressed in jeans, a blue flannel shirt, a blue V-neck pullover and the brown ribbed wool-lined parka she had bought the night before. Lastly, a pair of black ankle boots went onto Rachel's feet, suitable for hiking/biking through the Alaskan wilderness or walking the city streets in search of history of the area.

Turning her attention to her hair then, Rachel removed the dried off shower cap from her head, combed the snarls out of her long off-black hair, pulled it back into a ponytail, and then pulled a white skull cap over her head. This made it easy for her to brush her teeth without her hair falling all into her face, not to mention the wet basin. Then once the minty paste had been rinsed away, Rachel applied some berry lipstick to her medium lips. Nature had made it unnecessary for her to use much makeup because her facial features were so symmetrical, but she applied the lipstick so she wouldn't look fourteen. It seemed ironic however, that

Rachel should choose to use it at all, as she was only going to end up eating it off and reapplying it throughout the day.

Two last orders of business remained before she could meet Felix for breakfast, and that was the retrieving of her silver-toned watch from the French Provincial nightstand, where Rachel had put it upon taking it off the night before. With the blue carpeting muffling her steps as she crossed the bedroom to get it, she noticed that the time was eight-thirty five. Rachel hoped Felix wouldn't penalize her for being five minutes late. Then grabbing up her black bag and room key, which she slid into the black bag as well, and the Wal-Mart bag holding her camera, film and accessories, Rachel left the lavishly furnished blue-themed two-room suite to meet up with her tour guide on the first floor.

As Rachel had suspected, Felix was already waiting for her when she entered the blue, brown and gold-themed cafeteria. They all were. Stacey was there drinking a cup of coffee, as was George. Apparently they had been determined not to begin eating until Rachel had arrived.

When Felix had agreed with that white man at Wal-Mart the night before that she was fine, that had been high praise coming from such a sexy man, and she had felt herself being drawn to him like cheap metal to a magnet ever since. Rachel felt that sensation now as she prepared to take the seat in the chair next to him and he sat watching her with such marked interest.

"Good morning," Rachel said, greeting him with a smile that included George and Stacey. "I apologize for being late, but I didn't wake up until eight-fifteen."

"Yeah, I see you took my advice and dressed warmly," Felix reciprocated in his attractive tenor, smile on his own mouth as his dancing brown eyes perused her from head to toe with bold appraisal.

"Yeah, girl, you look like you're going on a trek through the wilderness on a wintry day!" George laughed at her state of dress.

"But you've dressed exactly as you should have. It's only thirty-eight degrees outside," Stacey said over her coffee. "So, be glad you took Felix's advice."

"Yeah, that, I am." As Rachel set her camera bag to the floor and shifted the strap of her black bag on her shoulder, she noticed that Felix had also taken care to dress warmly, in jeans and brown walking boots with a large white cashmere sweater pulled on over a woolly brown tunic. His head was bare, however, his short black afro glittering with moisture from his shower. Another parka was slung over the back of his chair, a black one not too much unlike her own.

"Come on, let's go get some breakfast," Felix said then, pushing back his chair.

"Okay," Rachel said as he moved to his feet.

Because George and Stacey remained seated, Rachel turned a perplexed look down at them upon rising to her own feet. "Aren't you guys coming with us?" she asked.

"We've already eaten," Stacey said as she downed another sip of her coffee.

"Oh, okay, I hadn't noticed. Then, we'll be back in a moment." Nodding, Rachel moved off to the food counter behind Felix.

He selected rice, scrambled eggs, toast, bacon, milk and orange juice, all of which she selected for herself. Once done, they paid for their meals and returned to their table, just in time to see George and Stacey moving to their feet.

"Hey, where are you guys off to?" Rachel asked George as she set her food tray to the brown table.

"Where do you think, Kid Sister? It's another day of work for us," George said with mild amusement.

"Yeah, it's time to put in another eight-hour day," Stacey said in a soft tone that stultified George's abrupt one. "Anyway, you guys have a good time sightseeing, and we'll see you this evening."

"Yeah, take care of her, man," George told Felix, who also had set his food tray to the table.

"Don't worry, man, she's in good hands," Felix said with bold amusement as he saw Rachel into her seat and himself into his.

"See you later, George," Rachel said, turning a saucy wink on her brother.

"See you later, Rachel," said George as he and Stacey left the cafeteria.

"So," Rachel began as she began to stir her pat of margarine into her hot rice, "what are we going to do today?"

"Everything," was the non-committal comment as Felix likewise stirred his pat of margarine into his own hot rice. "So, eat up, because you're going to need all the stamina you can muster."

Taking the command at face value, Rachel raised a forkful of rice to her mouth, as did Felix next to her.

They finished their breakfast in a half hour, returned their emptied food trays and dishes to the kitchen and then Felix led Rachel to the passenger side of the tan Pontiac Grand Prix in the self-parking lot outside. Apparently he, Diane and Stacey had not lied about the Alaska summer mornings being cool. The thirty-eight-degree temperature *was* cold. But thankfully in the layered clothing Rachel wore beneath the wool-lined parka, she didn't feel it. She settled into the car and slid onto her seatbelt, which although grateful for the warm sun shining from the clear blue sky, she ignored as she watched Felix slide behind the wheel to the left of her.

"So, where are we going?" she asked, naturally curious as she watched him clasp his own seatbelt in the lock to the right side of his bucket seat after closing shut his door.

"We're going to the Log Cabin Visitor Information Center, on Fourth Avenue," Felix explained in his attractive tenor amid sticking the proper key in the ignition and starting the engine of the car.

Not knowing where that was, Rachel shrugged indifferently as the quiet sound of the engine came to life beneath her. "Well, wherever that is, with any luck, it's far away enough for me to figure out how to use this camera."

Felix eyed her briefly as he pulled the car out of the parking spot after turning the heat on to a low temperature. "You mean to tell me you've been in your suite since eight thirty last evening, and you haven't figured out how to use that thing, yet?"

Rachel ignored the demeaning note in his seductive voice as she busied herself studying the silver-toned 35mm camera that she had pulled out of the Wal-Mart bag she had set on the floor along with her black purse.

"Well, I got it out of the package, and got the batteries in it, I just haven't figured out how to get the film in it, yet."

Again Felix turned a short glance on her amid steering the car out of the parking lot and onto the street. "That shouldn't be too much of a problem. Just open the back flap, and put the film in it."

"If you just give me a minute, I'm fixing to do it, now." Her tone was as short as his as she sent him a brief denouncing gaze before turning her eyes back to the instruction sheet that came with the camera that she held in one hand. "Now, let's see—what does this thing say about this camera, anyway? It's a Canon Sure Shot with 38-76mm power zoom with three-point auto focus—whatever that is." Rachel scowled ignorantly at the instructions in her hand, completely missing the brief amused glance Felix turned on her. "Let's see—it has automatic film-speed setting, automatic flash with red-eye reduction, and automatic film rewinding. Oooh, thank God for that. Why, I remember, I once had a 126mm camera. Do they even make those, anymore?" She turned a bewildered look on him that did not expect an answer. "I remember, I had to put that flash attachment on it, and you had to wind it forward by hand every time you took a picture. Do they even make those, anymore?"

"Anyway, what else does this thing say about how to set up this camera?" Rachel rambled on absently, her eyes back on the instructions she held in her hand. "Okay, this button unlocks the door where you put the film in and you pull this up, and you wind the film onto this spool, and you advance this knob until it moves the film into the first position." Leaning forward in her seat, she pulled out a roll of thirty-six exposure color print 35mm Kodak film from the Wal-Mart bag she'd set on the floor, removed it from the box and its protective covering and black holder and began loading it into the camera per the instructions she had placed on her lap. A moment later, the camera was in her hands ready to shoot.

"There!" She turned a triumphant smile on Felix, the 35mm camera raised to her face as if to take his picture.

"Good!" The smile Felix directed at the camera was equally triumphant as he flashed her with another brief glance. "Because we're here . . . !" And pulling the car into the nearest parking space, he shifted it into Park and extinguished the quiet engine.

The Log Cabin Visitor Information Center at Fourth Avenue and F Street was exactly that—a Bush-style log cabin with a sod roof festooned with hanging flower baskets and a giant jade boulder on the front yard. Quickly Rachel discarded the emptied Kodak box, plastic covering and plastic black film holder into the

Wal-Mart bag, an amazed look to her eyes as she placed the camera instructions into her black bag along with another couple of boxes of film. That amazement showed on her face as Rachel stepped from the car with an assisting hand from Felix a moment later, black strap of her bag on her shoulder, the silver-toned 35mm camera in her hand.

"My, what a pretty little place!" she exclaimed delightfully as Felix escorted her away from the car and toward the door of the one-story building. Raising the camera to her face Rachel snapped off a couple of shots; taking one of the giant jade boulder and one of the cabin itself. "And what's this?"

Felix smiled as he followed the direction of her eyes. "As you can see, Anchorage calls itself 'Air Crossroads of the World'—it's a stopping point for cargo jets en route to Asia. That signpost marks the miles between international destinations," he said.

"I see." Taking a picture of the red multi-directional signpost as well, Rachel averted her brown gaze to a marble statue of a building set amongst a colorful garden of flowers next door. "And what's that?"

"That building is Old City Hall, also known as Historic City Hall, which was built in 1936, and houses the Anchorage Convention and Visitors Bureau," Felix said informatively. "That statue honors William Seward, the secretary of state who engineered the purchase of Alaska from Russia—you know, who Stacey told you about in George's penthouse suite, yesterday."

Rachel had a vague recollection of Stacey telling her something about that as she raised the camera back to her face to take a picture of the marble statue.

"I've got to take a picture of that, too," she said.

"You're going to have to use the telephoto lens. You're not close enough to shoot it clearly at this distance."

"I don't need to use the telephoto lens. I'm close enough to it, as it is."

"You're going to have to use the zoom lens. If you try to shoot it at this distance, you're not going to get it all in the picture."

"I don't need to use the zoom lens. It's only next door. I'm close enough to it, as it is!"

"Just put the zoom lens on—"

"I don't need to put the zoom lens on! If I do, the whole picture will be out of focus!"

"Would you just put the zoom lens on—?"

"Don't touch that button! If you push that, you'll dispatch the batteries!"

"Well, then, what's this one!"

"Don't touch that one, either! It opens the back door of the camera! If you touch that one, you'll expose the entire roll of film to the sun!"

Felix dropped his hands from the camera and laughed at the good-natured argument they were having over taking a picture of a statue of a man who had been dead for years.

"You know, you're a lot of fun," he said.

"Just let me take the picture," Rachel insisted with equal amusement before turning her gaze back to the camera in her hands.

Beside her, Felix's laugh softened into an amazed smile as he watched her snap the marble statue in the distance. Telling her she was a lot of fun was a true compliment coming from him. With the command of his good looks and award-winning fame, he was not used to women being that natural around him. It was a strange feeling.

Turning her away from the statue a second later, Felix led her into the door of the Visitor Center cabin. Racks of brochures lined the walls out back, and the place was teeming with friendly volunteers ready to answer every question. And indeed friendly was the right word, for whether the women there recognized Felix from his soap opera or remembered him from an apparent last visit there or not, they were all over him like fleas on a dog at the command of his good looks. Felix grabbed a couple of colorful brochures that he thought Rachel would find interesting and got them the hell out of there quickly!

After that, they moved along Fourth Avenue, where some of Anchorage's original structures dated back to 1920, when Anchorage was incorporated as a city. One of those claimed Rachel's attention—the 4th Avenue Theatre. Registered as one of Anchorage's Historic Places, it was something like a comfortable movie palace, which to hear Felix tell it dated back to circa 1947—and set amid the assortment of modern hotels that sprang up in the area. Again the auto flash of the Sure Shot Camera came in evidence as Rachel took several pictures of all of these to reflect on after her visit to the forty-ninth state. Cater-corner from Old City Hall and just ahead of the 4th Avenue Theatre stood the Alaska Public Lands Information Center; one of four in the state that provided information on all of Alaska's public lands. Having said the day before that he was going to take her there, Felix quickly escorted her into the information center in the grand white Depression-area structure better known as the old Federal Building.

It was a great one-stop source of information on all of Alaska's public lands alright, including national and state parks, national forests and wildlife refuges. Rachel stared in amazement as a couple made reservations for a state ferry while other visitors watched nature videos, where they learned about plants and animals, and still others headed to the theatre for films highlighting different parts of the state. There was a trip-planning computer for public use, plus maps and guidebooks for sale, and there were excellent exhibits—even though Rachel wasn't exactly into backpacking and/or camping. And she was surprised to see that among the wildlife displays, a series of monitors showed videos on topics ranging from glaciers and salmon in the Kenai River to Inuit whaling.

After that, with half her roll of film dispensed and loaded down with a number of maps and brochures, Felix guided her to the Anchorage Museum of History and Art, the largest museum in the state, also a place he'd expressed a desire to take her to the day before. The museum, which was graced by a red metal sculpture out front, contained a fine collection of historic and contemporary Alaskan art and exhibited wonderful dioramas and displays on Alaskan history and village life as well. Again the flash of Rachel's camera came into play as she snapped shots of Native dancers performing in the first-floor atrium of the building. Informatively Felix dropped the news to her that in 1984, the museum was expanded to triple its original size, which explained why it occupied the whole block between Sixth and Seventh Avenues. It also held the Alaska Gallery, a 15,000 square-foot art gallery featuring work by regional, national and international artists, which traced the history and people of that land, Eskimos, Aleuts and Indians, in three-dimensional exhibits. Not to mention topics including exploration and settlement by the Russians, the Gold Rush era, World War II, and statehood.

Rachel found herself moving around the various exhibits upstairs on the second floor when a certain picture depicting the last great North American Gold Rush in the Canadian Yukon claimed her eye from a side wall. It took place in 1896, when news from the Klondike set off a wild stampede of the 40- to 50,000 thousand gold-seekers who came up the Inside Passage by steamer to Skagway, over the Chilkoot or White Passes by foot carrying a ton of supplies, and down the lakes and the Yukon River by homemade flat-bottomed boats in search of such. In this reproduction, they were all men standing in such small wooden boats and one of the three men in one of the boats was proudly displaying the U.S. Flag. The black and white picture was so stark that Rachel knew she had to have it in her collection.

"Oh, I've got to have this," she said unnecessarily to Felix standing beside her, a load of brochures and maps on the floor at his feet. "But I don't know if I'll be able to get the whole picture in the shot," she said as she held the 35mm camera squarely up to her eye. "Well, maybe if I turn the camera this way." Angling her head, Rachel turned the camera to the left so that she could observe the rectangular black and white picture through the viewfinder from a side angle. "You know, this would look good in black and white," she said on second thought, lowering the camera from her face. "I wonder if I put that black and white film in my purse."

"Oh, would you just take the picture?" Felix demanded with forced annoyance. Snatching the camera from her hands just when she was about to look into the black bag hanging from her left shoulder and see, he took a shot of the picture himself, his impatience so comical as to send Rachel into peals of laughter.

"Man, you are a trip!" The exclamation was a mock-demeaning one as Rachel continued to gaze up at his attractive sexy features. "Are you mad at me?"

Felix purposely ignored both the question and remark as he leaned down to pick up all the maps and brochures on the floor at their feet after pushing the camera back into her hands.

"Come on, I have something else I want to show you," he said in a softer tone amidst turning to lead her from the gallery.

They found some Cokes in the Museum Café on the first floor and then they returned to the car, where they dropped off all the various maps and brochures and Rachel loaded a new roll of film into the camera. Then with both of them having finished their sodas, Felix turned her in the direction of F Street North downhill toward Second Avenue. Here, the downtown area showed how it could quickly go from the familiar to the unusual, from the modern to the historic, from the metropolitan to the rustic, within the space of a couple blocks. The houses in that neighborhood were original town-site homes built by the Alaska Engineering Commission, who also built the Alaska Railroad in the early 1900's. Rachel took pictures of several of the modest homes as well as that of a neighborhood-marker telling of Anchorage's first mayor and the start of the Anchorage Women's Club and included photographs from the city's early days along the banks of Ship Creek.

From there, they walked east along Second Avenue, past the Eisenhower Memorial to a set of stairs leading down to the Alaska Railroad Depot at the bottom of the hill, which, Felix explained, played an important role in the city's growth. Again Rachel's camera went into overdrive as she took pictures of the monument in front of the depot relating the history of the railroad, where totem poles, a locomotive built in 1907 entitled Engine No. One could be seen outside and historical photos and a railroading gift shop could be viewed in the railroad's lobby. Turning just north of there, they approached the Ship Creek Viewing Platform, where Rachel snapped salmon that could be seen visibly running up the creek. Felix also showed her the Cadastral Survey Monument on the corner of West Second Avenue, which noted the original 1915 Anchorage town site survey and held four etchings tracing the city's development from the first auction of public land to a current city map.

Felix was swift to tell Rachel that the beautiful thing about getting around Anchorage was the simplicity of the street layout, especially in the city center, where numbered avenues ran east and west and lettered streets north and south. This Rachel was quickly made to see as they turned north on E Street, which became C Street and then right on Whitney Road in the direction of Christensen Drive. Finally, they turned onto the Tony Knowles Coastal Trail, which began west of Second Avenue and curled along Cook Inlet's edge. This being what Felix had really wanted to show her, he quickly curved a guiding arm around her waist to lead her down the recreational trail.

As he then began to tell her about the scenic paved trail, which was named after a former Alaskan governor and which followed the coastline from downtown Anchorage eleven miles to Point Campbell in Kincaid Park beyond Ted Stevens International Airport, Rachel stared at him in surprise.

"Felix, how do you know all this about this town? You've only been here for little over a week, and yet, you sound like a native!"

"Hey, what can I say? I had some very talkative and very friendly escorts," Felix replied carelessly, smiling at her. "Besides, it's all in the Anchorage Visitor's Guide you left in the car!"

Rachel decided to ignore the insinuations behind the remark that had followed his question in her preference in responding to his exclamation.

"I guess I'd better read that thing when we get back to the hotel!" she exclaimed with equal carelessness, shrugging her shoulders and returning her attention to the camera in her hands.

"I guess so," Felix agreed.

The walking trail was beautiful, providing tree-shaded terrain and panoramic views that were a photographer's dream. Again the Sure Shot camera came into play as Rachel took pictures of these as well as Mount Susitna (known locally as Sleeping Lady) and the huge snow-capped 20,320-ft. Mount McKinley, the highest peak in North America, always seen in the distance. She shot the vast blue waters of Knik Arm and Cook Inlet to the right of her, where white beluga whales could be seen rolling off the shore beyond mud flats Felix had warned looked innocent enough, but could quickly take the life of the unwary. And every now and then someone would whiz past them, either running or riding a bike rented from the shop at the beginning of the trail.

"You ought to see this place in the evening, when it's sunny like this, and it really gets crowded," Felix said.

"I'll bet," Rachel agreed as she snapped a jogger then speeding past them in a white parka and a gray running suit.

She stopped off about a mile down the trail to view the woods at the north end of Elderberry Park. Unbeknownst to her, the Oscar Anderson House Museum was there, it being Anchorage's first permanent frame house, built in 1915 by city butcher, Oscar Anderson. Taking a couple pictures of the house and woods, Rachel turned to take a couple of Felix, who had followed her into the wooded area.

"Might as well get a couple of you," she said needlessly, the camera still held to her eye. "After all, you won't exactly break the camera, will you? You've been in front of enough of 'em!"

Felix ignored the arty remark as he stared beyond her, an expression of terror spreading over the sexy features of his golden brown face.

"Put the camera down, quickly," he ordered immediately while at the same time trying not to frighten her.

"What's wrong?" she asked, lowering the camera from her eye and staring at him in surprise.

"Rachel, listen to me," Felix urged in a voice not to be disobeyed. "Do not collect two hundred dollars, do not pass go. Just get down on the ground and play dead, because there's a four-hundred-pound grizzly bear right behind you!"

"*What!*"

It was a weak scream that came from her lips as Rachel remembered the warning George had given her the day before about being unable to outrun the deadly animal. Without another word she dropped the camera from her hands and fell to the ground, only to become further shocked when Felix ran forward and fell to the ground on top of her to shield her from the approaching animal. Her heart jumped in her chest at the feel of the sexy man's body weight crushed against her and she cupped her arms around his head in a wooden gesture meant to keep him from seeing her expression, which she knew had to be one of utter terror at that. Yet it became a gesture to shield him as well as the bear stopped at his side. For ten tense seconds Rachel was held in suspended animation as the grizzly sniffed Felix's head before finally moving off after finding him non-threatening. She heaved a sigh of relief and heard his equal one as he sensed rather than felt the bear's departure away from them.

"Is it gone?"

With the question breathed desperately against her brown-clad shoulder, Rachel found the strength to supply an answer to it without sounding like the nervous wreck the feel of his weight pressing her into the hard ground had turned her into.

"Yeah . . . !"

However, sensing her effort, Felix raised his head to look at her, only then realizing by her still petrified expression that his gentlemanly gesture in covering her with his body like that may have unsettled her.

"I'm sorry." The seductive tenor voice seemed to mock her as it sounded unusually natural in her ear. "I didn't mean to make you uncomfortable by falling on top of you like that.".

"You didn't make me uncomfortable," Rachel replied, thinking the way her heart was thudding in her chest at their intimate closeness utterly ridiculous and recovering her composure with a lie.

Not knowing that, Felix took the disclaimer at face value and fixed her with a mocking look. "Oh, you have that many men falling on top of you, do you?"

Rachel fell silent as she stared up at the handsome face hovering so close above hers, not knowing how to handle the teasing question. After all, she couldn't say yes, because that would be an outright lie, and she couldn't say no, either, because she would come off sounding like a prude. Instead, she decided to parry the question by adopting an old-world sophistication she was nowhere near having, aware that he awaited her response.

"Well, you know what they say—the best way to get over one man is to get under another one!"

Felix pounced on the flip response with the theatrical narrowing of his eyes down on her. "Who do you want to get over that you want to get under me?"

Rachel laughed ridiculously as the unanticipated question pierced through her façade, barely able to withstand the intent way Felix lay gazing at her.

"Okay, the jig is up! It's just something I heard on a TV show once! I have no experience in that area, okay?"

Felix laughed too despite the fact that even though he'd seen the way those jerks had schmoozed all over her at the hotel the evening before, he couldn't help wondering how the hell a woman as lovely as she could still be a damned virgin at twenty four.

"George's friend would like that," he said after a moment.

Rachel stared up at him in surprise of the response she hadn't understood. "George's friend would like what?"

"That part about you getting under." Felix's chest heaved against her breasts as he laughed at the thought of the man she had yet to meet. Then aware that Rachel lay staring up at him in deepening confusion, he moved off her and pulled to his feet, at the same time extending a hand and pulling her to her feet also. "Come on," his gaze remained an amused one as he watched her retrieve her camera from the ground where she had thrown it, the black strap of her bag still attached to her shoulder, "let's get out of here, quickly!"

Rachel didn't have to hear him say it twice as she forgot all about the cryptic remark he had made to her and laughingly let him lead her from the wooded area.

Chapter Four

They got away from there in a hurry, raced all the way back up the trail and to the tan Pontiac Grand Prix still parked in the Log Cabin Visitor Information Center parking lot on Fourth Avenue. Rachel needed a drink, and she didn't drink often. Yet she needed something to calm the nerves that that close call with the grizzly had completely frayed. Not to mention the added shock she had experienced at the too devastating feel of Felix's body lying against hers as he had thrown himself atop her to protect her from the deadly animal.

Curiously Rachel gazed at his nearly straight profile as he backed the car out of the parking spot, quickly moved away from the Visitor Center and in the direction of the street. He ought to want to get drunk, considering how closely the grizzly had come to eating off his ear. Yet the man was as calm as the William Seward statue standing in front of Old City Hall that they were moving away from as he turned them right onto C Street. Rachel guessed it was his theatrical training that kept him so at ease and forced a composure to her own expression as she averted her brown gaze to the sun swept scenery passing outside her window, more hotels in addition to restaurants and a number of other places offering entertainment and shopping.

She wondered where he was taking her as they rode smoothly down C Street for almost two miles. Then she decided not to care as long as a drink was at the end of it. Picking up the camera she had lowered into her lap along with her black bag, Rachel decided to take a picture of a man and woman pushing a baby in a blue stroller to one side of the busy street, knowing it was going to be the blurriest picture she had taken all day, yet nevertheless shooting it, anyway.

She stared at Felix in surprise when he swore suddenly as they approached W. Thirty-First Avenue not much later. "What is it?" she asked, dropping the camera from her eye.

"I just missed my turn," Felix said, flashing her with a brief look from behind the wheel.

"Yes, where are we going, anyway?"

54

"You'll see." The brief response was all he chose to offer as they turned left onto A Street a short distance beyond W. Thirty-Second Avenue.

"Oh, good Lord—is that another Wal-Mart?" he demanded suddenly as they approached the world-renowned department store. "Are they everywhere? That Sam Walton died one rich mother! His great-great-great-great-great-grandchildren will never have to work!"

Rachel laughed at his expression of annoyance as he swung the car around in the crowded parking lot. "Do you know where you're going?"

"Yeah, I just missed my turn."

Her laughter sobered into an amused smile that mirrored the sudden one on his own lips as Felix steered them north back onto A Street toward W. Thirty-First Street and then left on W. Northern Lights Blvd. once back up at the intersection.

He took her to the Alaska Bagel Restaurant not too far down the street, where friendly service awaited them in a relaxing atmosphere. Felix had hoped she would be glad he had brought her there and Rachel was, suddenly realizing that she was starved as he settled her at a side table not too far from the door.

She was equally glad to see that the airy restaurant served wine as the friendly white waitress handed her an expansive menu once she had settled at the table across from Felix. She quickly told the woman to bring her a glass of any kind available, deliberately ignoring the flirting blue-eyed gaze the brunette turned on Felix as she moved away to do her bidding.

Ignoring the obvious look the waitress had turned on him also, Felix gazed across the table at Rachel and showed his perfect teeth in laugh.

"Do you want to get drunk?"

Rachel regarded his amused look with one of her own as she slid out of her brown parka and lowered it onto the back of her chair along with the strap of her purse.

"Don't you? That bear came close to biting your ear off! I'm a nervous wreck!" Deliberately she didn't tell him the other cause of her jangled nerves as she removed the white skull cap from her head as well and set it to one side of the table in front of her.

Across from her, Felix regarded her shot reaction with barely a nod, considering the terrifying experience they had gone through moments earlier as something that had happened ages ago.

"Yea, that was a close call, wasn't it?" He admitted that much despite himself as he began to slide out of his own black parka. "What was a grizzly bear doing over at the Tony Knowles Coastal Trail that close to the heart of downtown Anchorage?"

"I don't know," Rachel said as she watched him settle his parka over the back of his chair as she had done hers. "But somebody's going to get chewed up over there today if they don't look out! Do you think we should call somebody?"

"I don't know." Now it became Felix's turn to voice the three-word response. "I guess the people here are used to 'em. They say they be around here, everywhere."

I wouldn't be surprised if we walk out of here and see a moose going down the street!"

The infectious laugh that slid through his lips inspired Rachel's own as the waitress returned to the table with her glass of white wine. Accepting it with a thank you, Rachel raised it to her berry lips and took a quick sip.

Lowering it to the table then, Rachel picked up her menu and began to pore over the offerings the restaurant offered. She was glad she liked bagels, and in fact the restaurant offered every kind she'd ever heard of and then some more. They came in bakers' dozens, half-dozens, single bagels and mini bagels. They came in sandwiches, with shmears, with cream cheeses, with soup, and there were specialties. They were accompanied with salads, side orders, and there were breakfast bagels—although they were too late to order those since they were served till noon on weekdays and it was now one thirty. There were also cookies and ice cream for dessert and a number of beverages in addition to wine, such as beer, coffee and espresso, to name a few.

"My God, they have some of everything here! I'll never be able to make up my mind!" Rachel exclaimed as she continued to peruse the expansive menu she held in her hands.

Across the table from her, Felix smiled as he busied himself poring over his own menu. "Might I make a suggestion?"

"Yes," she said with a grateful smile. "But just remember, I don't have deep pockets like you!" she warned.

His lips broadened into a laugh as he gazed at her over the top of his menu. "Well, do you want a bagel & shmears, or a bagel sandwich?"

"Actually, I want a bagel sandwich, and a salad," she said. "I'm starved."

"Then, try the Denali. It's named for Mt. McKinley, referred to by most Alaskans by its traditional name, Denali, meaning 'The Great One.' And order the Green Salad. That shouldn't offend your wallet."

Rachel ignored the teasing remark as she decided that she would indeed order the Denali with a Green Salad and a tall Iced Tea. Felix settled on all for himself, except that rather than select the Denali bagel sandwich, he settled on the Pipeline, for Trans-Alaskan, of course. He would choose the most expensive one on the menu, Rachel thought dryly upon noticing its over ten-dollar price.

His dancing brown eyes settled purposely back on Rachel after he had given their waitress their orders and the white woman had moved away from the table, taking their menus along with her. Rachel was glad she had something to do as the intensity of his direct gaze unnerved her and reached for the white wine she had discarded to the table and took another sip.

"So, tell me, Rachel Hardison, what's it like being a kindergarten teacher?"

Rachel smiled over the white wine she had still raised to her lips. "It's great. Kids are so precious at that age. They're around four, and they're so innocent, they say anything that comes to their minds."

"Yea, I know. I remember that movie that came out a few years back—*Kindergarten Cop?* I swear that when that little boy told Arnold that boys have a penis and girls have a vagina, I thought I was going to die!"

Although Felix laughed at the innocence of the child's response, Rachel's own laugh was one of embarrassment at the subject matter. "I'm sorry I never saw that movie."

"You're a kindergarten teacher, and you never saw *Kindergarten Cop?* With Arnold Schwarzenegger, the *Terminator* . . . ?" Felix persisted, staring at her incredulously. "But then, I guess you wouldn't have. You must have been a kid when that movie came out. I was a teenager, myself at that time. I think I must have gone to see that movie with my brother. Anyway, *Kindergarten Cop* was a great movie. Arnold's partner, a woman who was also a cop, was supposed to have taken over the class, but she developed food poisoning, so Arnold had to take over the class. It was the sweetest movie. I'm going to have to get it for you. That is, if I can still find it in print!"

"Yea, thank you, I wouldn't mind seeing it." Her thoughts were on the class she'd had before school had turned out for the summer as she smilingly lowered her half-emptied wine glass to the table. "There was this one kid in my class last year, he was so precious. Kids do say whatever's on their minds. He came up to me and said, 'Miss Hardison, guess what I saw last night?' And I said, 'What, honey?' And he said, 'I saw my daddy doing it to my mama on the sofa!' I like to died . . . !" Rachel laughed, aware that Felix sat across from her doing the same. "Oh, they do say some of the most precious things!"

"Yes, they do."

Her amusement sobered somewhat at his ready agreement with her last statement. "I had this little girl in my class, name of Wanda Wajehao," she went on after a moment. "She was an adorable little girl, four years old, a transplant from Spain. Long strawberry blond hair, and looked like a china doll. Poor girl couldn't speak a word of English."

"How'd you communicate with her?"

"Luckily, I took Spanish in high school, and made it my second language requirement in college."

"You can speak Spanish?" The surprised query held a note of reverence as Felix continued to gaze across the table at her. "Say something in Spanish to me."

Rachel fixed him with a bold regard, knowing he would never know what she was saying, anyway. "Como las mujeres dijo en el almacén; usted es una especémen fina de un hombre."

"Tell me something I don't know, honey," Felix replied with an arrogant laugh.

"You know what I said?" A grin of embarrassment pulled at her lips as Rachel averted her shocked gaze away from the sexy features turned on her. Now the man knew that like the women said at Wal-Mart the night before, she thought he was a fine specimen of a man! "When did you learn Spanish, anyway?" she demanded with forced annoyance to cover her utter embarrassment.

"Same way you did. I took it in high school, and made it my second language in college."

"I see," Rachel replied as she raised her wine glass to her lips to steady the nerves that he had again jangled by knowing what she had said about him in Spanish.

Thankfully, the friendly white waitress returned to the table with their meals then, placing each respective plate and iced tea before them. Rachel knew this would give her a much more engrossing thing to do than sit there holding her near emptied wine glass. Thanking the blue-eyed brunette as did Felix, Rachel raised the Denali bagel sandwich to her berry lips. It was 'great', alright; in fact, it was huge, and she knew she wasn't going to be able to finish it all. Yet she determined to give it her best effort.

"So, what school did you go to, anyway?" Felix asked after a moment of biting into his own bagel sandwich, the Pipeline.

"I went to Georgia State University," Rachel answered amid chewing the bite she had taken out of her own sandwich, thereby missing the surprised look Felix had raised back to her.

"You went to Georgia State University? I went to Georgia State!"

"Yeah, I know." She took another bite out of her bagel sandwich. "George and you both went there."

"Yea, we did!"

"Yea, I know that." Rachel took another bite of her sandwich, its taste momentarily lost on her as her lips curved into a reminiscent smile. "You know, I remember the first time I heard your name," she went on informatively. "I must have been eleven that year, and it was the first week after George came home from Georgia State during his freshman year. He came busting into the house that weekend and said, 'I done hooked up with this dude in my math class named Felix Latham! You ought to see him, he is crazy! Lives up there somewhere in Chamblee! Wait until you see him. He is a nut!' And yet we did not see you until you two's senior year. You came out to the house with George that January weekend to see where he lived and meet his family. Devon had been home from West Georgia College that same weekend and you walked into the house behind George, took one look at Devon, and fell madly in love with her. And you must have been mad to drive all the way from Chamblee to Villa Rica to come see her the way you did!"

Felix's own smile was reminiscent as he took another bite of the Pipeline sandwich he had half eaten and watched her do the same to hers.

"Yea, I guess I was, wasn't I?"

There was another reason behind the subtle agreement that he must have been mad for driving all that distance to date Devon, and Felix was about to make Rachel privy to that information.

"You know, looking back, I realize that I was more infatuated with Devon than she was with me," he said over the iced tea he then raised to his lips. "She was a good looking woman, and being the good looking man that I am, my looks suited her. So, she dallied with me for those few months or so, but I don't really think I meant all that much to her, despite the fact that I was never more than a gentleman with her. Anyway, like you and George said, she put up with the relationship for the four months, three days and seventeen hours, or however long it lasted. But when it got too thick, she ran. Relationship was over just like that. She dumped me for another man, who, knowing Devon, she dumped for another man."

"You're probably right," Rachel agreed as she took a sip of her own tea after having taken another bite out of her sandwich. "Anyway, I'm sorry things didn't work out with you two." She offered the apology sympathetically as she saw his expression sadden over the tea still raised to his lips.

"Don't worry about it, I have to accept the fact that it's over." Shrugging his shoulders indifferently, Felix averted his gaze to the lively Green Salad set on the table to the right of him. Piling on some Ranch dressing from a packet on his plate, he dug his fork into it and raised some of it to his attractively carved mouth.

"So, what made you decide to be an actor?" Rachel changed the subject amid pouring her own Ranch dressing on her own Green Salad from the packet on her own plate and raising a forkful to her lips in tune with him.

"I've always wanted to be an actor," Felix replied as he chewed on his mouthful of salad. "Took it in junior high, took it in high school; took it in college."

"I never knew that," Rachel said.

"Yea, when I left Georgia State University, I went to New York City with the sole purpose of becoming a dramatic actor. I enrolled in Julliard, where I did some serious studying for four years. And while there, I did a number of plays—you know, just like I did in high school and college, but my intention after that was to go to Hollywood, and try breaking into movies there. As a matter of fact, three days after I graduated from Julliard, I was on my way out west, when I met this agent on the street. He took one look at me, and said, 'Look man, forget about pounding the pavement out there trying to break into the movies, or waiting around for pilot season on TV. With your looks and body and sex appeal, I can have you on a soap opera in a week. Here, take my card, come by my office tomorrow and see me, and I'll see what I can do for you.'

"Well, it wasn't vanity that made me take the man's advice, I mean, he was right—I'm a good looking man," Felix said somewhat modestly over the bagel sandwich he had taken another bite out of. "So, I went to the agent's office the next afternoon, and he sent me to this soap opera called *As The Star Shines*. The soap had been on for about seventeen years, your age at the time, yet despite that I'd never heard of it, but when I told them that, they didn't even care. Instead, they told me, 'Man with your looks, we can make you a star.' So, I auditioned with another current actor on the soap, and got the part just like that," he snapped the fingers of one hand. "The part was for the character of Joe Murray, who I'm still portraying after six years. And I'll admit that I was green at first—you know, having to adjust to the long hours, not to mention getting up around six every morning and being on the set at seven. Plus, I had to get used to learning forty pages of dialogue a day. But I got into it real quick, I'll tell you that."

"You must have," Rachel agreed over the bagel sandwich she was surprised to find herself finishing. "The way you're sleeping with your boss, her daughter, and her stepdaughter."

Felix smiled at the arty response over the bagel sandwich he was finishing from his own plate. "Yeah, I figure I'll go out to Hollywood to try and get into movies eventually, but for now, the soap's keeping me very comfortable. Not to mention that my character of Joe Murray has really boosted the show's ratings over the last six years."

"It must have," again her voice sounded in agreement, "considering you've won three Daytime Emmys playing that character."

"Yea," Felix nodded. "Best male newcomer five years ago, supporting actor three years ago, and best male pairing in a couple with my boss last year."

"Amazing . . . !" Rachel lowered her gaze back to her sandwich as she wondered where she had been while he was going through all his success. "So, what's a typical day like in the life of a soap opera actor, anyway?" she asked after a moment.

"Well, the way we do on my soap is arrive at the set at seven, enjoy some breakfast if you want, then, we get with the costars we're going to work with that day, and run lines during the morning. We go to lunch, come back and go to hair, makeup and wardrobe, do blocking in the afternoon, and tape later in the evening. Sometimes you can get kind of tired waiting around between tapings, and there are times when we do remote scenes where we might be taping as late as midnight. But it's a great job, and we're always off doing various things, such as autograph signings, auctions, visiting kids at hospitals, visiting schools, theme parks where fans gather to meet us, and so on. As a matter of fact, I was even lucky enough to do Broadway for a brief run amid working on the soap a few years ago."

"That must have been interesting," Rachel said with a smile.

"It was, indeed," Felix agreed.

Intently Rachel watched him as he bent his head to the salad he was finishing along with his tea, unaware as she did so that she was admiring his well-shaped head with its attractive frame of neatly groomed short kinky black hair. The man was truly impressive as an actor playing the juicy role of a philanderer sleeping with the boss he had just mentioned, her daughter and her stepdaughter all at the same time. And Rachel wondered how he could possibly have applied his brain to the learning of a script for a Broadway show after having to memorize forty pages of dialogue a day in order to play that role on the soap he had just mentioned. Dropping her gaze back to her own plate, she concentrated on finishing her own salad.

"So, speaking about these forty pages of dialogue you have to memorize a day," she began curiously over the tea she was raising to her lips then, "how do you do that?"

"I've always had a good memory, that's why I wanted to act," Felix explained. "You saw that in the way I remembered all the facts and information about all those places I showed you this morning. As a matter of fact, I remember that time I came to see Devon, and you crawled into my lap, and tried to kiss me!"

Rachel flushed from her head to her toe at the thought of putting her lips on his, her heart jumping into her throat. "I—I did not! No, I didn't! I did not kiss you! I don't remember that! I never kissed you!"

"Oh, yes, you did!" Felix insisted with a grin.

"No, I didn't!" Rachel screamed, glad she had finished her tea or she would have choked on it in her excitement. "You kissed me on the cheek that time when I came between you and Devon, but that was the only exchange of—of—that was the only exchange between us! I don't care how bratty I was in following you and Devon around, trying to get into your business! I did not kiss you! Not one day; not one time! I never kissed you! I did not kiss you! I did not kiss you!"

Felix's grin broke into a shameless laugh at the utter embarrassment he had brought her. "I'm only kidding you!"

"Wha . . . ! I'm going to kill you!" Rachel screamed while trying to keep her voice low, shocked that she had let him pull her in with a boldfaced lie. "I'm going to kill you, man! I'm going to kill you, Felix, for doing that to me!"

Again Felix laughed as he moved out of his seat across the table and settled his well-built frame into the chair to the immediate left of her.

"Was it that bad?" he teased.

"Worse!" Rachel tried not to let him see the utter pleasure that shot up her arm from the sudden possessive claim he took of her hand.

Unaware were both of them that a man sat observing them from a distant table. He was not looking at Felix, who he did not recognize as a soap opera star, but Rachel, who was plainly the most beautiful woman he had ever seen. He wondered if her date was anyone serious, and realized he must be by the sudden possessive hold he took of her hand after moving out of his seat and settling in the chair to immediate left of her. Rising out of his seat, the man moved across the floor toward them.

"You have a beautiful wife, man," the stranger said.

"I think so, too," Felix agreed.

As the man moved past their table, Rachel tried to cover the fact that the intent way Felix sat watching her had completely unnerved her, in addition to the feel of his hand still claiming hers so possessively.

"Why didn't you correct that man's assumption that I'm your wife?" she asked in a low insistent tone.

"... Because he was right about you. You turned out to be as beautiful as your sister. As a matter of fact, while we're on the subject of kissing, I wonder if you taste like her."

The equally intent way Felix's gaze dropped to her mouth unnerved her even further in the wave of sensation that shot down her spine, although Rachel tried to hide this behind a show of nonchalance.

"I guess you'll have to taste me, and see," she said audaciously.

Bent on doing just that, Felix leaned toward her and planted his sexy slender-lipped mouth against her luscious medium-lipped one in a claim that although firm, was tentative; at best. However, the kiss meant simply to see what she tasted like served only to excite her, sending a wave of sensation knocking through her brain in tune with the one already shooting down her spine. Yet this too Rachel hid beneath a show of nonchalance when he at last moved his face away from hers.

"What do you think?" she asked coolly.

Felix glided his tongue over his lips as if to identify the flavor he had tasted on her, only to find it too inconclusive to give him an answer.

"I don't know. I'll have to get another taste." And leaning over, he claimed her lips in a kiss that was far more invasive, exciting Rachel so completely that she actually had to restrain herself from yielding to the immediate urge she felt to respond. Yet she somehow managed to withstand the sensuous kiss, which Felix ended a second later, his tongue still scourging his lips as he sought to identify the elusive taste of her.

"What do you think?' Rachel repeated as he pulled gently away from her, still savoring her taste on his lips.

"Naw," Felix shook his head. "Devon is more like a Now or Later. You're more like a Sweet Tart."

Rachel stared in shocked surprise at the man still holding her hand so warmly in his larger one. Did he say Sweet Tart, or Sweetheart?

"You ready to go?"

"Uh-hmm."

"Then, come on. Let's pay our bill. Maybe if we're lucky, when we get outside, we'll see that moose I was talking about earlier."

Indulging a laugh that Rachel shared and moving out of his seat in tune to her moving out of hers, Felix let go of her hand to retrieve his parka from the back of the chair he'd occupied during their meal, Rachel pulling hers and her purse from her chair as well.

Outside in the warm sunshine that did not necessitate them sliding back into the wooly parkas or Rachel her white skull cap after they had paid their tab and left the restaurant a moment later, they did not see a moose. But what they were surprised to see was a black-haired flashily dressed Elvis Impersonator moving toward a blue car in the not too far distance away from them.

"Oh, my God, it's an Elvis Impersonator!" Rachel cried needlessly, the man having already captured Felix's attention. "What's an Elvis Impersonator doing in Alaska . . . ?"

"I don't know, but let's go follow him," Felix suggested excitedly. Equally excited, Rachel let him escort her over to the Pontiac Grand Prix, where he quickly saw her into the passenger seat and himself behind the wheel.

They turned right out onto W. Northern Lights Blvd. right behind the blue sedan the Elvis Impersonator was driving, followed him until the street became E. Northern Lights Boulevard and were surprised when he soon turned into The Mall at Sears, where he quickly parked his car toward the front of the Mall and extinguished the engine. Doing the same, Felix stepped quickly from the tan Pontiac and saw Rachel from the passenger side and they hurried inside the Mall behind the Impersonator. The flashily dressed black-haired man drew a lot of attention as he passed through the one-story Mall past a number of stores, but Felix and Rachel didn't approach him. Instead they followed stealthily as he led them all the way to one end of the Mall and into Sears, where he promptly disappeared in the men's department.

"Oh, no . . . ! Where'd he go . . . ?" Rachel cried regretfully, staring after the man who had seemingly disappeared into thin air.

"I don't know." Felix's resigned tone held equal regret.

And then the two of them looked at each other and burst into laughter at their insistence on chasing after a man who was only a carbon copy of the once Great Man who had been dead for decades.

"For God's sake, girl," Felix began through his last dying chuckles, "can't we at least waste our efforts in chasing after somebody who's alive?"

Rachel laughed all over again at the silly question, every attractive tooth in her head bared in her amusement.

"Hey, girl," Felix began then, "since we're in a department store, you want to go shopping?"

"Well, we might as well do something while we're here!"

Nodding at her laughing agreement, Felix began to guide her away from the area.

Inside the world-renowned department store, they browsed around, went everywhere and bought nothing. Again Felix had a proprietorial hold on Rachel's hand, having let it go several times as they had moved here, there, only to end up claiming it again seconds later. And deliberately she tried to ignore the pleasure that danced up her arm whenever he touched her, knowing his repeat claiming of her hand was just his way of keeping her at his side.

She was surprised when Felix stopped them in the TV department suddenly, where a number of televisions were turned on to a soap opera.

"Oh, look, *As The Star Shines* is on!" Felix's cry was one of delight as he recognized some of his coworkers in the scene playing at present.

But the scene quickly changed to that of a man and a woman, and Felix's delight thickened when he realized that the man in the scene was him.

"Oh, my God, it's me!" he said unnecessarily, grin broadening on his slender lips at the passionate clinch he was in with his coworker.

And passionate was hardly the word to describe it. As Rachel's brown eyes settled on one of the TV screens, she was shocked to see that it was indeed Felix in the scene kissing the black woman in it with him, and he was fairly consuming her, having slammed her up against the wall in his utter lust gone out of control.

"Oh, God . . . !" Rachel cried in a mixture of shock, embarrassment and disgust as the two of them went flying madly away from the wall and into a nearby bedroom, where they fell madly onto the bed in a heated embrace. Beside her, Felix stood with a rather pleased look on his face at the work he had done more than a month before.

"Not bad, huh?" he asked, turning a smug smile down on her.

Rachel's shock and disgust was reflected in the look she turned on the sexy rectangular golden brown features, having pulled her hand free of his automatically.

"Who's that woman in that scene with you?" she demanded.

"Her character name is Marjorie Young," Felix replied with a smile. "She's my boss."

"I see." Despite the two-word acknowledgment, Rachel wondered that if Felix could carry on like that with his boss, what must he be like with the daughter and the stepdaughter . . . ?! "And how old is that woman, anyway?"

"Fifty three, I think," Felix replied. "Looks good, doesn't she? She's been happily married for thirty two years, and to her college sweetheart at that, and together they have three grown kids."

"You're kidding!" Rachel didn't even try to hide her shock as she continued to gaze up at the attractive man. "And she can put on a performance like that? And you can, too? I mean, how do you display that—that—that kind—kind of—of passion for somebody that—that—that— You're not emotionally involved with her, are you?"

Felix laughed at her inability to conceive his ability to show such passion for someone with whom he was not emotionally involved. "Look, Rachel, it's just a job, like everybody else's. I think that Ellie and I—that's her name in real life—rehearsed that scene about seventeen times before we taped that day. And when we finally did, and I threw her up against the wall like that, I think I was thinking about what I was going to have for dinner that night."

"Oh, Felix, that's awful!" Rachel turned a half snort of disgust on him in the face of his abject nonchalance on the subject. "Oh, well, hey! I guess you are an actor, huh! I guess you deserve every one of those three Daytime Emmys you've won!" Her demeaning tone was one of equal nonchalance.

"I guess I do!" The laughing agreement was nowhere near an offended one as Felix again took claim of her hand, again sending that strange wave of pleasure skittering up Rachel's arm.

"Come on," he smiled down at her, "let's get out of here, quickly!" And pulling her away from the area, they did just that.

Piling back into the tan Grand Prix minutes later, Felix quickly started the engine and steered them off the Sears lot and turned left out onto the street in the direction of W. Northern Lights Blvd., bent on showing Rachel more of the city. As they approached C Street not much later, Rachel was shocked to discover that the Alaska Heritage Library and Museum was housed in the Wells Fargo Building there on the corner of the intersection. How many times had they passed by it anyway that day—one as Felix passed by it after missing his turn, two, as he retraced his tracks to the intersection and then turned left past it and then three, when they went flying past it in their pursuit of that Elvis Impersonator who had led them to The Mall at Sears? Knowing she had to see it, Rachel was relieved when Felix parked the car at the building, extinguished the engine, slid out of his seat and raced around the front of the car to help her from her passenger door, pocketbook and camera in hand.

It was a small museum located in the lobby of the first floor of the building, established in 1968 by the National Bank of Alaska, yet despite that, it was well-organized and peaceful. Native Alaskan artwork was presented, such as baskets, artifacts, dolls, paintings, photos, and rare books were on display, including a twenty-six hundred volume reference library of books on Alaska subjects. The museum featured an impressive collection of Native American tools, costumes and weapons, original paintings, including several by Sydney Laurence; and lots of Native scrimshaw. There was even a three-quarter size stagecoach present that showed Wells Fargo's role in the Alaskan Gold Rush. In fact, much of the carved ivory there was from the Gold-Rush days in Nome, and was purchased by miners as proof that they had been in Alaska, despite not bringing any gold home.

Piling back into the tan four-door Pontiac after exhausting another several shots of her camera, Rachel watched with interest as Felix drove them smoothly down W. Northern Lights Blvd. past the Alaska Bagel Restaurant where they had lunched earlier and toward tiny Earthquake Park just two miles past Minnesota Drive. Rachel was shocked upon learning that it was located at the halfway mark on the Tony Knowles Coastal Trail—especially when it brought to memory the grizzly they had encountered there earlier in the day—yet she tried not to show it as Felix began to tell her about the roadside park situated across from the northern runways of Ted Stevens International Airport. To hear him tell it, in 1964, five years after Alaska became a state, North America's largest recorded earthquake struck there, measuring 9.2 on the Richter scale. He said the structural damage to Anchorage was so bad that a school fell thirty feet, the Turnagain neighborhood dropped into the inlet, street-side buildings topped onto parked cars, and the brand-new J.C. Penney building downtown lost a corner of its building.

"Of course, time has so well healed the devastating ruin caused by that quake that there is virtually nothing left of its destruction now," Felix finished informatively.

"Yea, I can see that," Rachel replied, incredulous as she tried to imagine that much devastation.

Her eyes strayed reluctantly away from the small park as they headed farther west toward Point Woronzof, where great views could be seen of Cook Inlet, Mt. Susitna, the towering Mt. McKinley two hundred miles in the distance, in fact, the entire Alaska Range. Again the flash of Rachel's camera came into play as she took pictures of all of these after having stepped from the car so that her shots wouldn't be marred by movement or the glaring constrains of the windshield.

Sliding back into the car a moment later, her camera was still poised to the scene as Felix turned them left out of the parking lot and then back east along W. Northern Lights Blvd. a mile and a half to Aircraft Drive. A right there and traveling south and east along roads enabled Rachel to see two large lakes there—Lake Spenard and Lake Hood. To her surprise Lake Spenard had a beach where several souls were daring to take a swim in the too cold waters! And Rachel was surprised to see geese and floatplanes taking off and landing along Lake Hood.

Not much longer than that the Alaska Aviation Heritage Museum overlooked the south end of the lake, and to hear it, the museum held more than thirty vintage aircraft. Rachel got to photograph several of these as they stopped there for a moment before piling back into the car and taking the first left out of the parking lot. Taking care to watch signs to avoid the airport traffic, Felix steered the car east onto International Blvd. to Minnesota Blvd., which they traveled south about nine miles (it became O'Malley Road and crossed Seward Hwy.) to the Alaska Zoo, which was a wilderness setting with shaded trails spread out over twenty five acres. They decided to make this their stopping point, parking the car and getting out, paying the entrance fee and walking around for about an hour.

The zoo was home to Siberian tigers, musk oxen, seals, caribou, reindeer, elephants, snow leopard, walrus, alpacas, and a variety of Alaskan birds. Again Rachel's camera came into play as she took pictures of all of these. However, she stared at Felix's nerve in pointing out to her Oreo, a brown bear, who he claimed was one of the star attractions at the zoo, as it again brought to mind the grim memory of that grizzly that they had encountered on the Tony Knowles Coastal Trail earlier in the day. Yet Rachel snapped a picture of Oreo, anyway, as well as one of Ahpun, another bear, a polar one and another star attraction at the zoo, both of which, also according to Felix, were orphaned as cubs and grew up together at the zoo.

Then finally with all of her rolls of film spent—including the black and white one she had bought for stills, they returned to the car and circled around until they had arrived back on W. Fourth Avenue at Stewart's Photo Shop across the street from the Log Cabin Visitor Center in the heart of the downtown district. Stewart's Photo Shop—better known as Stewart's Jewel and Jade, was Alaska's largest photo shop, where every photographic job under the sun could be done. Dating back to 1921, it had its own pressed tin ceiling, resident reindeer (a great photo opportunity), and jade—Alaska's state gem—could be bought there by the ton or by the pound; in fact, it was Stewart's who supplied the huge jade boulder across the street at the Log Cabin Visitor Information Center. Rachel thought that interesting as she moved around the photo shop, where Alaska color slides, movies, photographs, and postcards were sold along with a myriad of photo equipment and accessories—including cameras. Having had enough of looking around, Rachel dropped off her four rolls of film to be developed as well as bought more on hand there for her next picture-taking session the next day. Then aware by a glance at the silver-toned watch on her left wrist that it was pushing six o'clock, Rachel directed her brown-eyed gaze up at Felix. Her look was a mixture of gratitude and regret for a day well-enjoyed yet nevertheless having come to its end.

"Well, thanks a lot for giving me a most enjoyable day, Felix," she smiled. "You're a very good tour guide, and I'm looking forward to our next day sightseeing together. But I think it's high time we got back to our hotel, now. George was probably expecting us ages ago."

The deep brown eyes danced mockingly in the sexy rectangular golden brown face as Felix blew off both her mention of the time and that of her brother.

"Not yet. I have somewhere else I want to show you."

And smilingly taking her hand back in his, he led Rachel from the shop, leaving her wondering what he wanted to show her now.

Chapter Five

He took her to the Captain Cook Hotel located not too far from the photo shop at Fifth Avenue and K Streets—in fact, how could Rachel miss it? After all, the three-towered multi-floor hotel took up a full city block and was visible from practically every direction, providing a fabulous view of the Chugach Mountain Range in the distance. Yet what was Felix doing bringing her to the Captain Cook Hotel, she wondered, when they were staying at the Amber Heights Hotel, which was comparable to this one? Or so that was what Rachel had thought until they stepped into the hotel's lobby. The interior was finished in warm teakwood paneling and polished brass, with marble tiles and columns in the foyer and furniture that was so out of this world that it left her eyes bugging out of her head in amazement.

"It's something else, isn't it?" Felix asked then, smiling down at her, having anticipated her incredulous look, his hand again holding hers. "It's named after Captain James Cook, the discoverer of Cook Inlet. I'll bet you didn't know that, did you?"

"No, I didn't." Although the smile meeting the one he'd turned on her was bright enough, Rachel couldn't help mentally kicking herself for not having put the two names together.

"Yea, it was built in 1964 to demonstrate prosperity in Alaska," Felix went on informatively. "It's one of Alaska's preferred hotels, rising twenty floors above Anchorage, one of the towers of which is capped by the Crow's Nest Restaurant, the repeat recipient of the AAA Four Diamond Award, and is the most pleasurable dining experience in Alaska. The hotel comes complete with Captain's deck featuring its own lounge, and while it was renovated in 1995, the dark décor recalls Captain Cook's voyages in the South Pacific. And you ought to see the guest rooms, Rachel; the nautical theme is continued there. Come on, I'll show you around," he said.

And tightening his hand around hers, Felix began to pull her through the lobby, leaving her no choice other than to follow after him, reluctant though she might be.

However, her eyes lingered on his confident profile in a demeaning look more so than one of impatience as they arrived at the elevator banks not much later. Who in the world had Felix been with at this hotel to know what the guest rooms looked like, she wondered, not to mention so many details about its past and present? Immediately Rachel checked her jealousy as one of the elevators opened up and a number of women stepped out and gave him the eye which he acknowledged with a nod. After all, it was none of her business who he had been sleeping with, knowing the women had to be numbered in the thousands at the command of his good looks, award-winning fame and popularity. Purposely she curbed her curiosity as she followed him into the waiting elevator and gave herself up to his will to show her around the hotel, named for the discoverer of Cook Inlet.

Rachel had to admit even to herself that the place was fabulous, possessing close to 550 rooms and suites on twenty floors comprised of three towers. Like Felix had said, there was the romantic and elegant Crow's Nest Restaurant at the top of one of the towers, which offered French cuisine amid a sophisticated candlelit setting; there was Fletcher's, an English-style pub that offered light Italian cuisine and various beers, wines, scotches and cognacs. There was The Whale's Tail, a mid-sized dance club located on the main floor with a full-sized cocktail bar, which offered fresh baked pastries, salads and sandwiches and 'mini-entrees' in a cozy comfortable setting; and there was The Pantry, an indoor sidewalk café located in the main lobby that featured an American fare. There was also the lounge on the Captain's Deck that Felix had mentioned nestled high up on the secured floor; in fact, the hotel even had its own jewelry store! Yet even though it was taller than the Amber Heights Hotel by five floors and was comprised by three towers instead of one main building, in no way was it better than the smaller hotel, for they had basically the same amenities—twenty-four-hour front desk, room service, meeting/banquet facilities, laundry/valet services, etc. So what if the Amber Heights Hotel didn't have a barbershop/beauty parlor! In Rachel's opinion, George had nothing to worry about.

"What do you think?" Felix asked once having arrived back on the first floor, breaking into her thoughts.

"Not bad," Rachel's berry lips forced a considering smile, "for good ol' Captain Cook."

"Not bad at all," Felix agreed as he walked beside her, his hand again holding hers, sending that crazy pleasure skittering up her arm. "Of course, it has nothing on the Trump Tower in New York. Now, that's a hotel," he said.

"I'll bet." Rachel's lips curved in another smile, this time one of agreement as she thought of the fabulous Manhattan hotel named for its owner, Donald Trump.

They had just been taking another last look around Fletcher's mahogany and stained glass interior when someone suddenly tapped Felix on the shoulder. Rachel turned around at the same time he did and heaved an inner sigh of relief upon discovering that the person that had approached him was a man.

"Felix!" began the interchange as the friendly white man greeted him with a smile. "I didn't know you were still here! I haven't seen you in a while! How're you doing . . . ?"

"Just great, Loge," Felix grinned, warmly shaking the hand the attractive oval-faced man had extended. "And yeah, I'm still around, and will be until Sunday—you know, after my best friend's wedding here on Saturday."

"Oh, I see," Loge smiled understandingly, relinquishing his hand and dropping his arm back to his side. "So, what are you doing, here, anyway?" he asked, his smooth alto voice rushing in over other talking and laughing going on in the popular locals' loaded pub. "Out to get drunk, or pick up new ladies, you hound dog, you?"

Felix intercepted the arty look the blonde man turned on Rachel and blushed mildly in the floor. "No, actually, what I'm doing is showing an old friend around this fabulous hotel," he flashed his perfect teeth in a smile. "This is Rachel Hardison, and Rachel, Loge Ingram."

"How do you do, Mr. Ingram?" Rachel smiled, a hand extended to shake his.

"How do you do, Miss Hardison? Or is it Mrs.?" asked Loge with a grin, warmly taking her hand in his.

"It's Miss, but you may call me Rachel," she corrected, her berry-colored smile lingering.

Although the white man's glimmering blue gaze indicated that he would like to do more than that, Rachel thanked God he had the grace not to say it to her face.

"Very well, Rachel, then," Loge replied instead, relinquishing her hand and dropping his arm back to his side, causing her to do the same.

"Loge is a close friend to one of the owners of the hotel. Or so that's what I learned when I first met him here last Monday. The couple of times I've been in here since, he's been right here, sitting over there at the bar trying to get drunk," Felix continued for Rachel's benefit, his smile on Loge having become mock-disparaging.

"I see." Rachel's own smile lingered kindly on the man who appeared to be in his early forties. Yet inwardly she fumed as she wondered who Felix had been in there hound dogging with for those three days, finding it no wonder he knew what the guest rooms looked like.

"Rachel is the younger sister of the groom, and is also going to be in the wedding as a bridesmaid," Felix went on smilingly to the white man, forcing her smile to become more engaging as his brown gaze lingered on her. "We haven't seen each other in ten years! Can you believe that, man—?!"

"Is that a fact—?!" Again Loge's blue eyes glimmered on her in a look that indicated to Rachel exactly what he was thinking. What must she have looked like ten years ago for Felix to have forgotten all about her considering what she looked like now! Yet again Rachel was relieved that the tactful man didn't have the indecency to voice his thoughts out loud as his flirting long-lashed gaze slid away from her and settled back on Felix in an enquiring look.

"So, how're you doing, Felix?" Loge beseeched, repeating the question he had asked before with a smile. "You know, I saw you on *As The Star Shines* today. When are you going to dump that old broad, Marjorie Young? That slut belongs in a pound with the rest of the dogs! She's slept around on you with half the men on the show!"

"I know that, man." Felix laughed at the derogatory remarks he'd made about his main love interest on the show. "That's why I'm getting back at her, by sleeping with her daughter, and her stepdaughter!"

"I see!" Loge indulged a laugh as well, although one of slight embarrassment at his shameless confession of resigned infidelity on his equally disloyal lover on the show. "So, what's eventually going to happen with you two? Have the producers let you know yet?"

"Yea, it's been worked up in the breakdown given us for the next six months. But I can't tell you what's going to happen with us, Loge; you'll have to watch the show!"

The man sighed doom at his inability to gain a little inside information about the show from the source himself. "Oh, well, like you said: I guess I'll just have to watch the show!" The sad look that had been in the blue eyes brightened considerably as Loge gazed at him with new interest. "Anyway, Felix, now that you and Rachel are here, why don't you stick around for dinner? Have a beer, and enjoy some oysters, a pizza, or even a fajita?"

Loge's hopeful smile turned into a pardoning one as he moved quickly away from Felix to respond to a favored local who had called out his name farther in the bar.

Behind him, Felix's smile was one of a relief that Rachel immediately translated as she gazed up at him with a smile of her own, albeit one of amusement.

"So what *is* going to happen with you and this Marjorie person on the show? Can you tell me?"

The smile broadened on the sexy slender mouth as Felix relegated himself to telling her the truth. "Her husband's going to walk in in two weeks and find us in their bed together."

Rachel indulged a loud shameless laugh after a moment of shock. "What? She's married? Oh, no! Felix, what kind of animal are you!" She screamed the remarks in her excitement, yet even then her girlish shrieks were hardly audible over the loud talking and laughing and drinking going on in the lively bar. "And here I'd never thought to consider the possibility that Marjorie is married! I thought she was divorced, or maybe even widowed! And you mean to tell me you're having an affair with a married woman whose husband is soon to find you lain up with her in *their* bed? Felix, you ought to be whipped! And I'm not asking for the job!"

Rachel laughed infectiously as she voiced that last exclamation so that Felix had to laugh himself as he recalled asking her that when she'd told him the afternoon before that he ought to be whipped. Then sobering, he reached out and curled his hand around hers in a gesture meant to sober *her* amusement.

"Come on, let's get out of here," he said. "I'm hungry, and I want something considerably more filling than an oyster, a pizza, or a fajita."

Rachel had to admit that she did too as she smilingly let him lead her from the Pub.

He took her to the Sourdough Mining Company on Juneau Street, about an eight minute drive south of the downtown area. The restaurant, which was a gold mine fit into a replica of an old millhouse that overlooked a creek, was naturally gold themed, offered American fare, such as baby-back barbecued ribs, blackened and fried seafood, enormous steaks and chops, and came with a choice of Korn fritters with whipped honey butter, steak fries, baked beans, corn on the cob, baked potato and naturally sourdough bread, plus dessert—not to mention beer served up in massive ice-chilled urns from a full-service saloon. Felix had not lied when he'd said he was hungry, for he downed a huge selection of the baby-back barbecued ribs as well as a steak, steak fries, baked beans, the sourdough bread and Korn fritters and a dessert, washing all down with a domestic beer there on tap. Across the table Rachel ate just as heartily, selecting steak and baked potato, corn on the cob, sourdough bread, and a 'build your own ice cream sundae' for dessert, though she passed on the beer in preference of washing her meal down with a light cocktail. And in spite of the attentiveness of the waitresses to Felix at the command of his good looks, naturally the food was quite good. In fact, Rachel determined to make Felix aware of that fact once they were back out in the sunshine almost an hour later.

"Well, it may not have been the most pleasurable dining experience in Alaska, but it sure worked in a pinch!" Rachel told him with a laugh.

"Yea, the food was good, wasn't it?" Smiling at her mention of the praise he had given the Crow's Nest Restaurant at the Captain Cook Hotel, Felix saw her back into the passenger seat of the tan Grand Prix.

Her brown eyes settled on him in a look of her earlier gratitude and regret as he slid in beside her behind the wheel of the car a moment later.

"Well, Felix—thanks for bringing me to this place for dinner, but I think we should be getting back to the hotel now. After all, it's pushing eight o'clock. George has probably long since missed us."

Felix turned a mock offended look on her amid starting the six-cylinder engine of the car. "Do you find me so hard to take that you're in that much of a hurry to get back to your brother?" he demanded with a laugh. "Come on, I have somewhere else I want to show you."

And quickly putting the Pontiac in gear he steered them off the lot, leaving Rachel staring after him in stunned amazement as she wondered where he wanted to take her now.

She found out about five minutes later, or two-and-a-half miles or so down the street, when Felix stopped them at the Dimond Center located on the southern tip of Anchorage at the corner of East Dimond Blvd. and Old Seward Hwy. As Rachel stepped from the car with the black strap of her bag attached to her shoulder, she tried to ignore the mocking smile that was on Felix's lips as he locked her door behind her and began to escort her into the center. After all, she didn't know what to expect—that is, until she had entered it a second later. The Dimond Center was a combination hotel and huge mall—the largest shopping center in Alaska, in fact and sold everything from candles to clothes, moose nugget swizzle sticks to pretzel sticks, fine jewelry to forget-me-nots. It came with two-hundred-plus known name stores, a Wells Fargo Bank was there, and there was even a public library and a post office, although both were closed at present. There were professional offices and a Lost And Found area, there were eating places, and the Center came complete with a video arcade, a bowling alley, an athletic club, a kick-boxing gym, and even a nine-screen movie theatre! But what Felix had really wanted to show her was the ice skating rink around the corner from the cinema on the Center's second floor. There, he gazed with increased mockery at Rachel in anticipation of the question he was about to put to her, certain she wouldn't be able to do it.

"Can you skate?" he asked.

Rachel regarded his mocking look with a proud smile. "I sure can!"

Felix recovered from the surprise brought on by her admission with a delighted grin. "Well, come on, girl," he began excitedly, "let's rent some skates, and get out on the ice!" And quickly running over to the rental office, they did just that.

They threw offf everything in a hurry—walking boots and woolly parkas that they had slid back into to shield them from the dropping temperature outside, Rachel took off the cap she had replaced as well, the two of them setting them all to the side along with her black purse, interested only in lacing the skates onto their feet. Then together, they moved onto the ice, where a number of skaters were already gliding around the perimeter of the floor. Rachel was glad she had kept up on the sport as she quickly moved away from Felix to glide across the ice in a number of figure-eights and free-form pirouettes. Straightening back to a full standing position, she showed off for his benefit, gliding farther around the ice around other skaters and doing a double-toe loop with the grace and skill of an Olympic skater, long off-black ponytail slicing through the air. Then aware that Felix had only gotten halfway across the rink in a simple glide, she returned to his side, her brown eyes twinkling with mockery at the deeply surprised look he was showering on her.

"Hey, girl, how'd you learn to skate like that!" he demanded with a laugh as he glided toward her, a hand automatically reaching out to clasp hers.

"How much time have you got?" Rachel grinned while trying not to mirror that crazy sensation of pleasure skittering up her arm!

"How much time do you need?"

"About twenty minutes, to tell this story!" Rachel laughed.

"So, tell me. I've got time," Felix said.

And to prove it, he dropped his hand from hers, curved her arm around his and began to lead her out of the way of a rush of oncoming skaters, bent on hearing all of her story. Rachel's smile was a mixture of delight at his genuine interest and relief that he had let go of her hand, as she found his arm-in-arm gesture far less distracting than the feel of his hand on her hand and his flesh on her flesh!

"Well, it all started when I was in the seventh grade," she began quietly as they slowly began to skate together around the perimeter of the floor to the sound of other skaters pounding the hard ice around them. "I remember my phys-ed teacher somehow got the whole class excused from P.E. for a week to attend that hour every day at a local roller skating rink. Now, I have to warn you that I had tried to roller skate before that, but I could never get my right foot off the floor. And it really showed when I got to that skating rink, because I was pathetic!" Rachel managed a reminiscent laugh. "Anyway, as badly as I was skating without being able to lift my right foot off the floor, I was doing pretty good gliding around the rink—at least, I wasn't bumping into anybody! All of a sudden this particular day, I thought I'd make a half turn around the rink—you know, just for fun—when Jock Whitman, the one boy in the class who could skate better than anybody, came flying down the center of the rink out of nowhere, and slammed into my side! Well, I just knew I would be gone when I hit that hard floor. But instead, Jock somehow got his arms around my waist, and he pulled me into him, lifted me off my skates, and spun around on his back wheels for several seconds before he finally steadied himself, stopped spinning, and set me back on my feet. To hear the kids in the class tell it, in those ten seconds, we looked like we were whirling in a wind! I am never going to forget that day."

"I don't imagine," Felix said in his seductive tenor, understanding as they continued to glide around the floor behind a number of other skaters moving in front of and behind them.

"Anyway, that's when Jock took pity out on me," Rachel went on smilingly after a moment. "He caught up with me after the hour was over, and said, 'Look girl, you can't skate. You don't belong on a pair of skates. You don't belong anywhere near a skating rink. However, I think you're cute, so, I'm going to teach you how to skate!'" She couldn't help laughing at the memory. "And believe me that was high praise coming from Jock, because he was a very adept skater. Not only could that jerk roller skate, but he could rollerblade, ice skate, and ride skateboard. He took me under his wing and taught me how to roller skate until I got so good that not only was I able to lift my right foot, but I could turn around the corners as if I was steering a scooter. And then, he took me to an ice skating rink, and got me into that. Well, I didn't think I'd be able to do that—I mean, after all, I was used to skating on four wheels—how did one go from that to sliding across some ice on a single blade? But Jock worked with me until I got that too, and I've had it ever since."

"Yea, I see that." The smiling tone indicated how deeply she had impressed him with her skills as Felix continued to glide her around the floor on his arm. "So, what ever happened to jerk Jock?" he derided after a moment.

"He dumped me a couple years later for a serious involvement with a fourteen-year-old girl who had a DD-cup, and a butt to match."

"I see." The two-word response was thick with amusement as Felix's dancing brown gaze lowered over the provocative swell of her breasts beneath the blue V-neck pullover she wore over a blue flannel shirt. "He should have stuck around. You would have surprised him."

"I guess so," Rachel agreed, although with no intention of telling him she was not that big. "Anyway, getting back to old Jock, there are times when I still think about him. I mean, that boy had skills on wheels. Not only could he skate both forward and backward, but he could do forward and backward flips both on roller skates and ice skates, and whirl up in the air and land on his feet. In fact, he used to be so good that they used to tell him that he should go into the Olympics. I don't know whatever happened to him. We simply got out of touch after he hooked up with Miss DD-cup. But I will be forever grateful to him for the time he took to teach me how to both roller and ice skate, because I really enjoy it. So, as a result of that, while I was still living in Villa Rica, I kept up my skating skills at a rink in Douglasville. And in the few years since I've been living in Atlanta, a girlfriend and I frequent an ice skating rink there. And I may be no Oksana Baoul, no Michelle Kwan, can't do a triple-toe loop or a triple Lutz, but I think I'm pretty good, even if I do have to say so, myself."

"Uhm-hmm, I think so, too," Felix agreed, still gliding her around the floor on his arm. "But it's a shame you're no Oksana, or Michelle. I'm every bit Victor Petrenko, and Brian Boitano, myself."

Rachel turned a surprised look on the attractive sexy golden brown features at his mention of the Olympic skaters. "What are you talking about, Felix?"

"See, you tried to show off on me before I could get in here good," Felix said staunchly, pointing a finger on his free hand at her. "Well, let me show you something, girl."

And quickly letting go of her, Felix began to skate swiftly backwards away from her, skillfully avoiding oncoming skaters in his glide around the large rink. Rachel stood in the middle of the ice where he had left her, her hands covering her mouth as she watched as if transfixed as he flew into a figure-eight, did several pirouettes and attempted a back flip, landing expertly on his feet on the other side of the rink. She prayed to God he wouldn't attempt to do a triple-toe loop or a triple Lutz as he picked up speed at the far end of the ice in preparation of a leap into the air. Her heart jumped into her throat as he maneuvered his well-built frame to do a triple Lutz, knowing he was too old for such a jump, only to end up covering her face with her hands when he suddenly threw his body up into the air, spun three times, crossed one leg over the other and landed perfectly on his left foot. A triumphant look was on the sexy rectangular face as he glided on around the rink back in the direction of her while Rachel stood petrified in the ice floor, knowing she was going to kill him for putting her through such terror.

"What did you think?" Felix asked as he stopped in front of her, the smug self-satisfied grin on his slender lips indicating he knew he had literally thrown her for a triple-toe loop.

She snapped at his careless demeanor, a hand swatting at him so forcefully that it sent him flying backward on his skates. "Felix, don't you ever do anything like that to me! You're not twenty years old, anymore! You're thirty one years old! You're too old for that! You could break a leg!"

Felix laughed slightly amid skating back toward her and taking her into his white cashmere sweater-clad arms. "Are you frightened for me?"

"What do you think—!" Rachel demanded furiously, withstanding the rush of sensation that shot through her at the closeness of his body against hers and pushing roughly out of his arms. "Felix, don't you ever scare me like that, again! You're too old to be skating like that! I'm twenty four! I'm going to have to quit skating like this myself in a few years! How'd you learn to skate like that, anyway?"

"Same way you did. I learned as a kid. When I lived in Chamblee, I attended a rink that wasn't too far away from my home, even though it did have an Atlanta address. I started out roller skating, and then, graduated to ice skating. It's something I've kept up ever since. And with being in New York for the past ten years, that's been a breeze, because Rockefeller Center, a huge ice skating facility, is right in the center of Manhattan."

"I see." The simple two-word response was uttered dryly over the sound of other skaters pounding through the ice around them before Rachel laughed suddenly, its sound an equally dry noise cackling from her throat. "What is this?" she demanded, turning an amazed look up on his sexy handsome features and meeting his similar look. "Why do I have so much in common with you?"

"I don't know. I guess I should have been trying to talk to you all those years ago when I was coming to see Devon. Not that there was anything there to you to talk to—skinny little flat-chested thing you were in those days. Of course, nobody can say that about you, anymore," Felix finished meaningfully, his dancing brown eyes lowering over the seductive curves of her figure in the V-neck pullover, flannel shirt and jeans she wore in a too approving look.

"Oh, please!" Rachel managed a laugh beneath his intently arrogant gaze—after all the man did speak the truth—before spinning away from him over the ice, an action that served only in inspiring him to spin away after her.

They played chase for fifteen minutes, Rachel fleeing, Felix pursuing, both of them grinning gloriously, having the time of their lives. They skated around the rink past less adept skaters in forward glides, backward glides, weaving in and out, moving skillfully across the ice, making half turns across the large rink. They did pirouettes and free-form figure-eights; they hugged the rink's perimeter and glided thoroughly down through its center. Racing; racing. Felix never had a chance of catching her. That is, until a less skilled skater suddenly pulled out in front of Rachel, forcing her to slow her speed just as she was about to cut halfway across the large rink again. Felix slipped up behind her from nowhere and had her quickly in his grasp, those strong white-sweater-clad arms pinning Rachel hopelessly to the rock wall of his torso and chest.

"Let me go!" she ordered with a laugh, arms flailing the air in front of her as she tried yet again to withstand the intimate closeness of his body.

"No way, kiddo . . . !" Felix laughed similarly as he pulled her from his front and settled her at his side, where the feel of his hard thigh brushing against the soft curve of her hip did other things to her libido. "So, tell me," he began to guide her out of the center of the rink with a strong manly arm curved around her waist, "who else has been in your life since jerk Jock Whitman dumped you all those years ago?"

"Would you believe no one special?"

"Not with your looks," Felix argued, gazing disbelievingly down at her beautiful round face, dusky features and long off-black ponytail trailing down her back.

Rachel resigned herself to telling him the truth as they began to glide slowly back around the rink behind a number of other skaters, the arm he had curved around her waist prompting her to do the same to him.

"Okay, there was my first date, at sixteen. The boy took me out for a hamburger, and drooled all over me all evening. The date couldn't have passed fast enough for me. End of seeing him. There was my second date. The boy took one look at me, and drooled all over me before he could even get his head in the door. He was simply too fast, and was out of there in five minutes. End of seeing him. There was my third date. The boy came over to study with me for a history test we were having later in the week, but the only history he was interested in studying was me. He was gone before the evening was out. End of seeing him. There was my fourth date. The boy came to take me to my junior prom, got drunk; threw up all over me in the car. End of seeing him. There was my fifth date. The boy was my best friend's boyfriend, but after taking one look at me, he dumped her to chase after me. He took me to the movies and tried to move me—if you know what I mean. I dumped him at the theatre, and had to call my father to come all the way from Villa Rica to get me. End of seeing him. There was my sixth date. The boy picked me up with sex so on his mind that he didn't even attempt to get us alone somewhere, but pulled his member out in the car halfway down the road. Unfortunately, he hadn't washed in days, and he smelled so of body odor and funk that it filled the car immediately, and we had to get out of it. And we couldn't get back in it for fifteen minutes waiting for it to air out, either. And when we finally could, I had him take me back home, and I never saw him, again. End of seeing him. There was my seventh date. The boy came to take me to my senior prom, but ended up taking me over to his older brother's apartment, where he spent the entire evening trying to lure me into having sex with him. I dumped him and walked all the way back from Douglasville to Villa Rica in my white prom dress and shoes at two o'clock in the morning, completely having missed the prom. And it didn't get any better when I got to college, because all any guy whoever looked at me wanted to do was the same thing. Men take one look at me, and all they want to do is get me into bed. As a matter of fact, in the three years that I've been out of school, I don't think I've had four decent dates. So, it's just as well that I've been too busy working to meet someone, because I'm suspicious of the motives of the men I date, because again, like I told you, all guys my age and even those not my age are interested in is a quick one-night-stand. They don't want a lady, they want a slut. And I have no intention of answering their nature calls."

"Uhm-hmm." Although amused yet somewhat saddened at her lousy date history, Felix's reluctant nod was an understanding one as they continued to glide around the rink arm-in-arm. "And I saw that last evening in the way those men came all on to you at Wal-Mart, not to mention how Martin and Flip slobbered all over you back at the hotel at dinner. Well, now, I see why you say you're content with just living single. Sounds like you've been meeting a lot of jerks out there that are not exactly gentlemen."

"Not at all," Rachel agreed before going on to clarify her meaning. "I mean, don't get me wrong. I'd love to find somebody that I could love and somebody who would love me. But how am I ever going to find that when most men who look at me can't get past this face and this body long enough to want to fall in love with me?"

"Yeah, you do have a point, seeing as you come in a very distracting package," Felix agreed.

"And there you have it. I have no choice other than to be single. . . . And loving every minute of it."

"I guess so," Felix agreed.

Taking the subject off herself at his ready agreement to her last statement, Rachel turned it onto him, completely mindless to the lot of skaters gliding noisily all around them.

"So, tell me, who else has been in your life since jerk Devon Hardison Lavery McClintock dumped you all those years ago?"

"Would you believe no one special?"

"Not with your looks," Rachel argued, gazing disbelievingly up at his sexy golden brown rectangular face and well-groomed short nappy black hair.

Felix indulged a worn sign as he resigned himself to telling her the truth. "Okay, there've been a number of women," he began quietly. "I mean—what the hell—they follow me everywhere I go. I mean, in the two days you've been here, you've seen how they've been all over me, the same way all the men have been all over you. But I'm tired of the one-night stands, leading them on, and later on dumping them by the wayside. I'm tired of the find 'em, feed 'em, fool 'em and forget 'em routine my friends and associates live by. Besides, I still had feelings for Devon that I was trying to deal with. And because of that, I've thrown myself into my work for the last six years. And the ladies simply can't stand to see that my dedication to my craft is more important to me than going out and bedding them down. Sure, I don't mind skirting the beautiful women around on my arms—I mean, after all, part of that comes with the job. However, in the last six years of my life, I doubt if I've had six decent dates. So, it's just as well that I've never been in the right place at the right time to meet someone, and as yet haven't had to work with anyone who floats my boat, so to speak, because all the women I meet want to do is get me between their legs. They don't want a gentleman, they want a stud. And I have no further intention of answering their nature calls."

"I see." Although surprised and yet somehow saddened by his lousy date history, Rachel's reluctant nod was an understanding one. "Now, I see why you say you're just content with being single. Sounds like you've been meeting a lot of floosies out there that aren't exactly ladylike."

"Not at all," Felix agreed before going on to clarify himself. "Oh, don't get me wrong. I'd love to find somebody that I could love, and somebody who would love me. Not just play with my emotions for a few months, and then, dump me, like Devon did. But how am I ever going to find that when most women who look at me can't get past this face and this body long enough to want to fall in love with me?"

"Yea, you do have a point, seeing as you come in a very distracting package," Rachel agreed to the tune of an endless number of skaters whizzing past them.

"And there you have it. I have no choice other than to be still single. . . . And loving every minute of it."

"I guess so," Rachel agreed.

Her tone was sympathetic, yet despite that, her eyes were playful as she pulled from the circle of his arm, moved in front of him and then began to skate swiftly backward down the rink away from him. Warmed to the thrill of another chase by the encouraging grin on her berry lips, Felix began to skate quickly after her, his own eyes playful as he weaved skillfully in and around and past slower skaters in a pursuit that lasted another fifteen minutes. Around and around the perimeter of the ice skating rink he chased while she fled, gliding across the ice in front of him forward, backward, weaving adeptly in and around and past slower skaters, making complete and half turns around the large people-filled rink in an ever lengthening attempt to flee while he chased. Racing; racing. In an endless ride that carried her around the ice rink many times with him riding right after her. Rachel flirted with him outrageously 'Come, get me, big boy!' And Felix was right back at her, grinning 'I'm going to get you, girl!'

Unaware were the both of them that three men stood watching them from a distance. They did not know who Rachel was, but they did recognize her date. Felix Latham, actor, worked on the soap opera *As The Star Shines*. They wondered what he was doing all the way over there in an Anchorage, Alaska ice skating rink seemingly having the time of his life with a long-haired woman they had never seen him with before. Could it be serious? Could long-time confirmed bachelor Felix Latham, actually be losing his heart and head over a woman, many though they'd seen him with over the last six years? With eyes riveted, they watched as he careened around the perimeter of the rink in hot pursuit of his date—pretty though she was—until he finally caught her. Curling an arm around her waist, he yanked her against his body with a playfulness that left them both laughing in the middle of the skating rink floor.

"You're the best fun I've had on a pair of skates in ages, girl," Felix said.

"You're the best fun I've had on a pair of skates in ages, too, boy," Rachel teased, again pushing out of his arms as the intimate closeness of his body against hers sent a strange sensation shafting through her.

Suddenly a skater passed by too closely and too fast and careened into Felix, knocking him off balance and sending him sprawling backward onto the hard icy floor. The strange sensation caused by the intimate closeness of their bodies was immediately forgotten as Rachel turned a concerned look down on him, knowing that lick had to hurt, as he had landed directly on his behind.

"Are you okay?" she asked as she knelt down at his side, where another skater went flying by too close to her, sending her sprawling on top of him. A whole new wealth of sensation knifed down her spine at this much too intimate closeness of their bodies, leaving Rachel able only to stare down at him with her mouth open.

Yet despite her obvious shock, Felix was completely at ease as he lay sprawled out under her. "Now, you're on top of me!" he said with a faint tone of amusement, his eyes gently mocking.

The reminder of their similar position in the woods off the Tony Knowles Coastal Trail earlier in the day was the cue for her to pull up off him, but Rachel was too stunned by his male virility and raw sex appeal to move. Which was just as well, because before either of them could do anything about rectifying their sprawled positions on the hard floor, a number of lights flashed as cameras went wild to print the moment for posterity's sake.

"Oh, my God . . . !" Felix said in a disgruntled tone while Rachel could only stare down at him, her arms flung woodenly around his head. "I can't believe somebody's been in here watching me for a whole hour! Now, it's going to be all over the press that Felix Latham, soap opera star, was seen sprawled all over the floor in an Anchorage, Alaska ice skating rink, with a gorgeous woman sprawled all out on top of him. Well, baby, let's give them something to photograph!"

And quickly cupping his hands to her head, Felix pulled her face down to his and ground his lips against hers in an ardent display, completely ignoring the number of lights that continued to flash against his closed eyelids. Rachel was not prepared for the sensuous kiss, which was far more invasive than the couple he had given her at lunch and served in sending that sensation already knifing down her spine traveling all the way down to the soles of her skates. In harmony with that, her throat threatened to close up as blood began to flow into her neck, leaving her face flaming, a strange heat rushing over her skin. And with these effects so stupefying her senses, not only did Rachel forget that they were being photographed, but she could hardly speak when Felix ended the potent kiss a moment later.

"Oh, ah—" was all she could manage to say, so complete was her disturbance. Gazing back at him, she was shocked to see the same mirrored in the gaze he had turned up on her.

Yet to her added shock and surprise, Felix recovered his composure with a grin, the amused light having flashed back into his dancing brown eyes.

"Let's get out of here, quickly!" he instructed between his perfect teeth.

And scrambling to their feet, they skated off the ice, while cameras flashed endlessly after them as the photographers went wild.

They slid out of those skates and back into their boots, parkas, and Rachel her white cap, grabbed up her black bag and got out of there in a hurry. Rachel was shaking like a leaf on the inside, never in her life having been so affected by a kiss, and she wondered if it had had the same effect on Felix. She also wondered what he was thinking as they sped quickly to an exit. Yet the man appeared as cool and collected as if he were going to collect another Daytime Emmy Award. And no wonder, when he had made it quite clear by his quick recovery of his composure after the kiss that he was not interested in a romantic entanglement. And neither for that matter, was she. Rachel quickly got the point and gained control of her physical reactions, telling herself that they were simply normal responses from a woman to a very good looking, very virile, very sexy man.

In fact, she was even able to brush the kiss off as nothing once they were outside the Center and on the way to the car a moment later, where Felix suddenly reached out and curved a hand around hers as usual.

"I'm sorry," he said in his seductive tenor, smiling apologetically down at her. "I didn't mean to embarrass you in front of all those crazy photographers back there by kissing you like that."

"You didn't embarrass me," Rachel replied, smiling up at him, having completely recovered her own composure and again answering with a lie. "I've been kissed before." Even though it wasn't like that!

Felix didn't doubt that for a minute as he recalled her lengthy confession about all those teenage jerks and others in her life who had tried to kiss her and get her into bed.

"Come on," he said, "I'm going to take you back to your brother."

And settling her into the passenger seat of the tan Pontiac they approached in the still sun swept parking lot, he moved quickly around the car to slide in behind the wheel.

By the time they arrived back at the Amber Heights Hotel twenty five minutes later after stopping at an ATM machine to replenish their cash and a filling station for a fill-up of gasoline on the way there, Rachel was practically able to laugh about the whole thing. In fact, it was with much amusement that she watched Felix instruct a hovering bellboy to take all the brochures and maps and film and camera she carried in her arms up to her room on the eleventh floor ahead of her.

"Now, get a good night's sleep tonight, because you're going to need to be well-rested for where I'm taking you tomorrow," Felix said from his position beside her in the lobby just beyond the reservation desk.

"Yea, where are you taking me?" Rachel asked curiously.

"To Chugach State Park, site of that huge mountain range visible from every side of this city," Felix answered.

"Okay," Rachel smiled.

"Yeah, I'm going to have the concierge gather up some carry-along supplies for us. It's the real wilderness out there, baby, and we're going to need everything we can get our hands on to come out of the experience alive."

Her eyes narrowed on his handsome face in a sudden frown of disbelief as she tried to imagine a place so terrible. For a moment, she actually found herself rethinking her desire to explore as much as she could of this untamed Alaska, North America's last frontier.

"I see," Rachel said.

"So, do like you did this morning, and dress warmly," Felix urged, "and meet me in the cafeteria for breakfast at eight thirty tomorrow morning. I'm going to go work out in the gym for a while."

Rachel deliberately hid the moment's disappointment she felt at the thought that he was leaving her to ride up in the elevator to her floor alone beneath a show of surprise.

"You're going to go work out after all that exercise you got back at the ice skating rink?" she demanded.

"Hey, how do you think I keep this body?" Felix insisted with bold innuendo, eyeing her with an incredulity that made her look away from him in amused embarrassment. "Anyway, you get that sleep, and I'll see you in the morning."

And smilingly taking her hand back in his he raised it to his lips in a gentlemanly gesture, leaving her staring after him in renewed surprise as he strutted across the swanky lobby away from her.

Chapter Six

They were splashed all over the front page of the Anchorage Daily News the following morning. Rachel got to see that the instant she stepped into the cafeteria at eight fifteen and George bolted from his seat with a swiftness that nearly sent it falling backward to the floor.

"What the hell is going on with you two!" he demanded furiously, raised voice flying out over those of everyone else in the blue, brown and gold cafeteria, newspaper upraised in one hand.

Rachel somehow managed to recover her composure from his attack on her as she lowered her black bag and camera to the brown table across from him and slid her wooly mud brown parka over the back of the chair in front of her.

"Hello, Stacey," she smiled.

"Hello, Rachel," Stacey greeted in her soft-spoken way, smiling also. "I see you had a pretty interesting day, yesterday."

"Yea, I guess I did, didn't I?" Deliberately Rachel's gaze lingered on the white woman sitting at George's side, knowing her refusal to let him inveigle her into an argument would infuriate him further, which it did.

"Look, girl, don't you ignore me!" George exploded in a predictable act of growing rage, thrusting the newspaper in his hand toward her. "What is this?"

Resignedly Rachel took the paper from his hand and let her chocolate gaze settle reluctantly on the article her brother was bent on showing her. There to her horror and dismay was a large too revealing black-and-white photo of her and Felix sprawled out kissing on the Dimond Center ice skating rink floor, her long off-black ponytail having been thrown askew from his assault on her mouth. Equally worst was the caption printed in large bold capital letters above the incriminating photo, which read: WHO'S THIS WOMAN CONFIRMED BACHELOR FELIX LATHAM, EMMY-WINNING ACTOR ON THE SOAP OPERA *AS THE STAR SHINES* IS LAID OUT KISSING ON THE FLOOR OF AN ANCHORAGE, ALASKA ICE SKATING RINK????!!!!

"Okay, what can I say? You caught me." With continued resignation, Rachel lowered the newspaper to the brown table beside her camera and settled into the chair in front of it, an action which prompted George to resettle in his chair across from her as well. "Just like what you see in the paper, Felix kissed me. We did a lot of things, yesterday. He took me to that Visitor Center, showed me Old City Hall, that Public Lands place, and various other places downtown, ending up at that Tony Coastal Trail. Then, we went to lunch. He took me to this bagel place, and we followed an Elvis Impersonator to Sears. You know how crazy Felix is about Elvis . . . ," Rachel couldn't help interjecting impertinently despite her brother's still implacable look. "After that, we did more sightseeing, wound up at the Alaska Zoo, and then, he took me to this photo shop to drop off all the film that I'd used up taking pictures all day.

"Well, it was pushing six o'clock, so, I thanked him for a lovely day and told him it was high time we got back here, but the man's crazy," Rachel went on. "Instead, he said, 'Not yet, I have somewhere else I want to show you.' So, then, he took me to the Captain Cook Hotel, showed me that fabulous place, and then, he took me to dinner. We ended up eating in a gold mine—can you believe that?" She laughed, her uneasy gaze including Stacey, who sat beside George, intently listening, quietly sipping on a cup of coffee. "Anyway, by the time we came out of the restaurant, it was pushing eight o'clock, so, I thanked him for taking me to dinner and told him again that it was high time we got back here. But the man's crazy! Instead, he said, 'Not yet, I have somewhere else I want to show you!' So, that's when he took me to the Dimond Center—the largest mall I've ever seen anywhere, I believe, where we ended up on the ice skating rink. And George, you know how much I love to ice skate," Rachel said, and watched her brother acknowledge that with a nod.

"Anyway, Felix surprised the hell out of me, because I didn't know the man could skate!" Rachel went on excitedly. "Anyway, we were having an absolutely glorious time, when all of a sudden somebody careened into him, sending him falling backward to the floor. Well, I knelt down to ask him if he was okay, when another skater went flying by, and knocked me on top of him. All of a sudden, before we could get up, they started taking pictures. So, Felix said, 'Well, baby, let's give 'em something to photograph!' And that's what you see here." Rachel ended her uneasy rambling by fixing George with an imploring look that begged him to forgive her for her indiscretion and watched his face soften as resignation planed across his own mannish features.

"Okay, fine, Felix made the most out of a bad situation," George said over the nearly finished coffee he was raising to his well-hewn full lips. "But let me tell you something, Kid Sister, that lady killer has had at least twenty five women on his arms in the past week. Don't let him suck you in with his charm and good looks."

A sigh slid through Rachel's berry-colored lips as she gazed at her brother, an equally attractive man, though not with the devastating raw sex appeal of Felix. And she wondered why Felix hadn't told George that all those women he skirted around on his arms were just for show, as he was not bedding any of them down, that he wasn't in fact the least bit interested in a romantic entanglement.

"Don't worry, George, you know how cool I am. I won't lose my head. Felix and I are old friends, we go way back. You know I'm not interested in him, and he's not interested in me. Besides, he's still hung up on Devon, anyway."

As Rachel had hoped, that last response served in appeasing George's anger, as he emitted another sigh over his coffee, this time a relieved one.

"Where is he, anyway?" George asked, as Felix had not yet put in an appearance in the large cafeteria.

"He's not due yet. He told me to meet him here for breakfast at eight thirty. I came down early because I wanted to talk to you two before your workday started and Felix and I wound up back into the street." She included Stacey in her gaze, the long-haired brunette still sitting there quietly lingering over her coffee, as George was. "How're things coming with the wedding? Did you finally settle on a caterer?"

A line wreathed George's suntan oval face on either side of his well-hewn full-lipped mouth as he broke into a delighted grin at her mention of his favorite subject these days, that of talking about his wedding.

"Oh, yes, we got a caterer," George said, including his fiancée in his excited brown-eyed gaze. "He is exactly the right price, and we're going to have a spread fit for the president! We're going to have pies, we're going to have cakes, we're going to have beef, we're going to have filet mignon, we're going to have shrimp, truffles, caviar, and a number of other delicious delicacies. And there's going to be champagne! In fact, by the time we get to the Riviera, we're going to be drunk, aren't we, baby!" George exclaimed to Stacey, a blue-sleeved arm curling affectionately around the stout woman's equally blue-clad shoulders, nearly making her drop the coffee she still sat sipping from a white china cup.

"Just as long as you're sober enough to perform your husbandly duties when we get there," Stacey told him with heavy inflection.

Rachel didn't think the innuendo-laced remark fit the soft-spoken older woman and looked quickly away from the too obvious small-toothed grin she had turned on her brother, her berry-colored medium lips pulled up in an expression of disgust.

George saw her embarrassment and sobered immediately, dropping his arm from Stacey and straightening up in his chair.

"So, while you're on the subject of you and Felix getting back into the street," George said then, "where's he taking you today?"

"We're going to go to Chugach State Park," Rachel smiled.

"What does that fool know about Chugach State Park?" George exploded, again predictably. "He's only been up there once! Even if he was there all day, and with some very willing escorts . . . !"

Rachel didn't get a chance to respond to that as Stacey joined in the conversation again, her soft-spoken voice again softening George's abrupt tone.

"You'd better be careful up there. That's the real wilderness up there. People have lost their lives up there from exposure, hypothermia, falling; avalanche in winter, drowning in summer, disorientation, or even by being shot by a hunter. And you may have the misfortune of running into a grizzly," she said.

"Yea, so, I hear."

While those other things Stacey had mentioned concerned her, Rachel deliberately didn't tell the brown-eyed freckle-faced woman that she and Felix had encountered a grizzly off the Tony Knowles Coastal Trail the day before. She knew George would freak if he were to know his sexy friend had been on top of her the same way she ended up on top of him at the Dimond Center ice skating rink, as evidenced by the glaring photo in the folded paper on the table in front of her.

Fortunately Felix saved her the necessity of a response as he entered the cafeteria, saw them, and strutted over to their table. Beneath her long black mascara-coated lashes Rachel's brown gaze slid over the six-foot-one-inch length of him, sexy as ever in brown walking boots, tan Levi's and a brown sweatshirt pulled on over a brown and tan plaid shirt.

"Good morning, all," he greeted in his attractive tenor, lowering a tan wool-lined jacket onto the back of the chair beside Rachel. "How're you doing, girl?" he asked her smilingly, to which she smiled back in return. "And how're the newlyweds? You know, you two are going to be tying the knot in three days!" Felix finished delightfully, twinkling brown-eyed gaze flashing onto George and Stacey respectively.

"Which reminds me," George began to his best friend, "now that you bring it up, while you've been doing all this running around with all these different women for more than the past week, have you given any thought to what you're going to say at the reception as my best man?"

"Hey, man, don't worry about it." Rachel watched Felix brush George's concern off as nothing as he settled indolently into the brown chair next to her. "You know how spontaneous I am, I'll think of something. It'll be very flattering. You know I'd never say anything bad about you. You know I love you like a brother."

"Which also reminds me—since you've brought up the subject of siblings, explain how you wound up on the floor of the Dimond Center Ice Chalet with my sister last night."

George pushed the paper placed on the table in front of Rachel toward him and watched him take it into his hand. Intently Rachel watched Felix peruse the picture and caption on the front page, his eyes finally slicing onto her in a mocking shimmer.

"You mean we did make the paper?" he asked her.

Needlessly Rachel bent her head in a nod, brown eyes taking in all of his golden brown handsome sexy features and short kinky black hair.

"Apparently so," she said with wry amusement.

"I told you! Shoot!" Felix laughed the article he had anticipated off as inconsequential as he lowered the paper back to the tabletop, his dancing eyes sliding from Rachel back to his best friend. "Hey, what can I say, man? I took her to the ice skating rink. Why didn't you tell me the girl could skate! She skates as well as I do! Anyway, we had a great time there last night. I mean, we had big fun, didn't we, girl?" Felix's glimmering gaze settled briefly back on Rachel in a deeply amused look. "We chased each other all over that rink, didn't we, girl! Until things got kind of out of hand. . . ."

"Obviously," George said as his brown gaze lowered back to the paper discarded to the table in front of his friend with heavy meaning.

"And why didn't you tell me the girl went to Georgia State University?" Felix went on with an excited grin, completely overlooking the belittling look George had turned back on him. "She went to our same school! She went to my alma mater! And why didn't you tell me also that the girl could speak Spanish! Rachel spoke Spanish to me! We have a lot in common. Of course, I'm not going to tell you what she said!"

"Thank God for that!" Rachel managed with a grin of her own, albeit an embarrassed one.

George watched the way his sister flushed beneath the toothy grin his friend had turned on her and did not like what he saw. "What time did you two come dragging back here last night, anyway?" he asked caustically. "Stacey and I waited around for you two all evening, and you never showed up!"

Felix's chocolate gaze lingered on Rachel's beautiful dusky features in another deeply amused look. "What time did we get in here last night?" he asked her. "Ten? Ten thirty?"

"Actually, I didn't look at my watch," Rachel said.

Across the table, a frown marred the attractive mannish features of George's oval face as he watched the two of them indulge a private laugh.

"Rachel tells us you're taking her to Chugach State Park today," George said to his best man.

"Yea, I'm going to take her into the wild. That is, if I can remember how to get there." Felix brushed his own statement off as unimportant as he turned a sobering gaze back onto his friend. "So, how're things coming with the wedding?"

"We're having another wedding rehearsal Friday afternoon at two o'clock."

Rachel's eyes lingered on her brother in a curious look, as she was not aware that he and Stacey had had such before her arrival two days before.

"When did you guys have a wedding rehearsal?" she asked.

"We and all the friends in the wedding party had a run-through with the wedding coordinator here on Saturday afternoon. But the rehearsal scheduled for Friday should be better, for all the families will have arrived by then to participate in it."

"Of course. . . ." After all, that made sense, Rachel thought as she dropped her self-belittling gaze back to the table. Indeed, she thought herself silly for not having expected him and Stacey to have attempted one before that time, especially when they had been in the throes of planning the wedding for weeks.

"Anyway, we'll have to try and remember to be there, man," Felix's unconcerned half laugh brought her back to the present.

George busied himself downing the last of his coffee before lowering the white china cup back into its saucer. "Well, we've got to go; it's time to get to work." Pushing back his chair, he rose to his feet, prompting Stacey to do the same beside him. "Anyway, you guys have fun sightseeing today," he wished, including Rachel in his hopeful gaze. "And try and get her back here before ten o'clock tonight," George said, eyes slicing back to his handsomer, sexier friend. "I'd like for my sister to see more of me while she's here than you."

"I'll see what I can do, man."

The careless chuckle that bubbled from Felix's throat was completely ignored as George sliced a parting gaze onto Rachel. "See you later, Kid Sister," he said.

"See you later, George. Stacey." Rachel's parting smile prompted Stacey's own to her and Felix as she moved away from the table behind her fiancé, her white hand clasped in his brown larger one.

Left alone with Felix behind their exit from the cafeteria, Rachel turned a curious look on the man's too handsome rectangular face and sexy features.

"Are you okay? You're a little fired up today. Is this what working out at the gym does to you?"

"Hey, I'm great." Deliberately Rachel did not react to the congenial arm he curled around her shoulders in accompaniment to the charming grin he'd turned on her. However, her eyes did roll at the intent way his gaze slid over her, noticing the thick white sweater she wore with white Wrangler jeans, the gold-toned earrings spiraling from her lobes with white topaz stones, the relaxed off-black ponytail hanging from a white knit band tied at the crown of her head. Rachel had left off with putting a cap on in preference of letting her head go bare, her hair hanging long and unrestrained down her back.

"I've had the concierge gather up some supplies for us to take with us to the Park. I've had him put them in the car," Felix said.

"Okay," Rachel said with a nod.

"So, how long have you been in here? Have you eaten yet?" Felix asked.

"No, I was waiting for you," Rachel replied.

"Come on, let's get some breakfast. Talking to your crazy brother's worked up my appetite."

And Rachel had to admit to herself that she was famished too as she rose to her white Nikes clad feet to follow Felix over to the food counter.

They selected a breakfast of rice, eggs, bacon, toast, juice and coffee and had just about downed it all when one of the hotel employees sidled up to the table next to her.

"Hi, Rachel," grinned the hotel employee, a thirty-year-old brown-skinned man with fat cheeks in a too oval face framed by too short black hair.

Rachel tried but failed to remember the name of the man George had introduced her to two days before. Was he a waiter, a bartender, a fitness instructor?

"Hello, ah—umh—" she began uneasily, unaware that his presence at the table had captured the attention of Felix as well.

"Linc." He supplied his name with ease, already having expected her to have forgotten it. "I'm one of the meeting planners that your brother, Mr. Hardison, introduced you to on Monday."

"Oh, I see. Well, how are you, Linc?" Rachel smiled; thinking herself way off in the positions she had assumed he held at the hotel.

"Just fine, Rachel, how are you?"

"The same," she said over the coffee she had half finished.

"I saw you in the paper this morning," stated Linc, getting to the subject uppermost in his mind and grinning at her. "Or so I think that was you by your hair. Was that you?"

"Hmmm, I'm afraid so," Rachel smiled, aware that the man stood staring at the incriminating length of ponytail hanging long and straight and off-black down her back.

"Yeah...." Linc's roving brown eyes lowered onto the revealing picture of her and Felix on the paper pushed to one side of her breakfast tray and his grin broadened lasciviously. "What I wouldn't give if you were laid out on top of me, like that!" he finished to her faint amusement.

However, before Rachel could respond tactfully to the crass remark, another of the hotel employees, a tall redhead, sidled up to the table to the left of Felix.

"Hello, Mr. Latham, Felix," she purred in a husky voice.

Blankly Felix stared up at the short-haired woman he had skirted around on his arm less than a week ago, like Rachel, trying unsuccessfully to remember her name.

"Hello, er—"

"Marjorie," she said. "Like the name of one of your love interests on *As The Star Shines.*"

"Oh, yes." Felix managed a smile at the white woman, wondering how he could have forgotten her same name.

"I'm one of the reservationists who work here at the hotel," Marjorie reminded him smilingly.

"Oh, yes. How are you, Marjorie?" Felix continued to smile likewise at the reasonably attractive woman, who like Linc wore the hotel uniform of blue jacket over black slacks.

"Just fine, Felix," Marjorie said, still smiling at him likewise while still addressing him by his first name. "Saw you in the paper this morning," the redhead went on, like Linc, getting to the topic uppermost in her mind. "What I wouldn't give to have you stretched out under me, like that! Why don't you let me refill that coffee for you?"

Although Felix was hardly surprised by her bold nerve in telling him indirectly that she wanted to climb on top of him, he still couldn't help staring at her disbelievingly.

"Yes, why don't you do that?" he suggested after a moment, smile back in place as he pushed the half emptied coffee cup he held in his hands toward her.

As Marjorie moved away from the table to replenish his cup, Felix curved a hand around Rachel's wrist to claim her attention, aware that she needed an escape from Linc also, as the man still stood drooling all over her like a bull mastiff.

"Let's get out of here, quickly!" he instructed smilingly between his perfect teeth.

And quickly gathering up her black bag, camera and jacket, as did Felix his, Rachel let him pull her from the cafeteria.

They laughed about it all the way down the hall, through the lobby and out to the parking lot. The nerve of those two hotel employees, telling them that they wanted to get over them, under them, or whatever! Well, they were just going to have to get over it! Sobering her amusement as Felix did as well, Rachel let him see her into the passenger seat of the tan Pontiac Grand Prix before he strode around the back of the four-door car to slide in behind the wheel.

It was another beautiful day for sightseeing, the sun shining brightly in a clear blue sky, a repeat of the day before. Yet despite that, just like the day before, it was cold, the temperature hovering somewhere around thirty nine degrees. This made Rachel grateful for the warm woolly brown parka she wore over her clothes, not to mention the added heat flowing into the car at a low temperature that Felix had turned on after starting its engine and pulling them away from the hotel. Hence it was in much comfort that Rachel sat back to see if he would get them lost, as he had implied to George that he might not remember how to get them to Chugach State Park.

Actually, the way there was nothing to forget. All they had to do was get on Seward Highway and drive south for twenty miles or so. To hear Felix tell it, it was one of America's National Scenic Byways, and indeed it was—the winding two-lane highway providing panoramic city and mountain views. There were the beautiful waters of Turnagain Arm on one side, where those same beluga whales that Rachel had seen in the waters of Knik Arm were spotted plowing unusually early in the season through bore tides at Beluga Point. On the other side of the highway beyond Chugach State Park Headquarters in the Potter Section House was Turnagain Arm Trail, formerly called the Old Johnson Trail, which paralleled the coastline and the Seward Highway from Potter to Windy Corner. It was a 9.4-mile trail that led through spruce trees, birch and alder groves and flower-filled meadows and which, according to Felix, got its name from Captain James Cook, who sailed up Cook Inlet in 1778 hoping to find the Northwest Passage but had to 'turn again,' leading him to name the water body River Turnagain. Rachel found that interesting as they continued to move smoothly down the trail, where spotting scopes and viewing decks provided scenic views of the Chugach Mountains to the north and the Kenai Mountains across Turnagain Arm.

When she unexpectedly spotted beautiful Dall sheep on the cliffs at Windy Corner, her first impulse was to jump from the car and access the not too seemingly difficult sloping trail, which also according to Felix, was the mail and transportation route in the old days before there was a road from Anchorage to Seward. But no, of course, he had somewhere else he wanted to show her! Moving farther down Seward Highway, he showed her Bird Ridge along Turnagain Arm, which elevated about four-thousand feet into the air, and then Falls Creek, where they entered a beautiful alpine valley, where more Dall sheep could be spotted on the high escarpments and brought Rachel's camera into action as she took her umpteenth picture since entering the wooded mountain area. Then, turning around, Felix steered them all the way back down the trail, where he turned right to show her something on a side road and promptly got lost. Rachel couldn't help laughing in a mixture of amusement and relief when they wound up at their starting point after seemingly driving around for five minutes, as apparently that exceptional memory Felix claimed having was not as infallible as he'd have her believe.

"Look, honey, why don't we just go on back to Turnagain. Trail?" she teased when they wound up at the Glen Alps access point parking lot a moment later. "And isn't that Flattop Mountain in the distance? We can start our exploration here."

Felix shook his head at the huge murky mountain range standing at an elevation of over thirty five hundred feet spread out a mile and a half beyond them that Rachel was shooting with her camera.

"Naw," he said, "it may be the city's most-climbed mountain, but it's not a cakewalk. It is quite steep, particularly at the summit, and I hear that people have died on its flanks. Besides, it's not what I want to show you, anyway." And turning away from her with his usual smirk, Felix steered them off the lot, leaving Rachel snapping Wolverine Peak, another mountain rising above forty four hundred feet across the valley in the distance, with equal regret.

He somehow managed to get them out of there and onto Glenn Highway, where the Chugach Mountain Range rose to an impressive eight thousand feet to the right of them beyond a small cropping of trees. There after a quick right down the rolling two-lane road which he had originally intended, Felix began to tell Rachel more about their scenic location. He said that Chugach State Park, created in 1970, was Alaska's most accessible wilderness, nestled beyond the foothills at Anchorage's edge and comprised of a half-million acres, the third largest state Park in America. He said that the nearly thirty trails that cut through the Park provided for hiking, skiing, camping, wildlife viewing, snowmobiling, rafting and climbing in Alaska. And Rachel didn't doubt that as they approached the Eagle River Campground, one of three in the Park, where early morning visitors were already gathering at the Eagle River Nature Center for a day of activity.

Still she wondered where Felix was taking her as he drove them all the way up to the northeast end of the Park before turning finally off at the Eklutna Lake exit at Mile twenty six. Once done, he carried them two quick rights down a frontage road and then left onto Eklutna Lake Road where Rachel was surprised to find another campground several miles down the road and into the wilderness. The Campground, named for Eklutna Lake, was the third one in the Park along with Eagle River and Bird Creek and came with fifty campsites, water, latrines, picnic tables, and fire pits. And there were interpretative displays and a telescope for viewing wildlife and lake activities in the busy trailhead parking area Felix steered the tan Grand Prix into then.

They were nestled in the Eklutna Lake Valley, a cottonwood, spruce and birch woodland, where the turquoise waters of Eklutna Lake flowed along the steep canyon walls of the towering Chugach Mountains. Rachel couldn't help but be overwhelmed by the scenic beauty of the area as she stepped from the car, strap of her black bag slung over her shoulder, silver-toned 35mm camera in her hand.

"Oh, wow!" She exclaimed her delight of her location, the camera raised to her eyes to knock off a couple of shots of the busy campground and beautiful blue waters of Eklutna Lake flowing placid and peaceful between the towering Chugach Mountain walls in the distance.

Behind her, Felix smiled at her excitement as he busied himself removing a red skullcap from a large backpack on the tan Pontiac's tan back seat.

"Here, put this on," he said.

Rachel frowned at the knit cap he was bent on handing her. "Why do I have to put this on?" she demanded.

"So that a hunter will see its red color and won't shoot you, just in case one might be in the area," Felix answered.

Although Rachel remembered Stacey saying something earlier that morning about people being shot by hunters there and knew that the cap was a protection she'd best make use of, she wasn't exactly warmed by the idea of putting somebody else's dungy cap on her pretty hair.

"Darn! The one time I decide not to wear a cap, and you mean I have to put this silly thing on? Darn! It's going to mess up my hair!"

"And lovely it is," Felix praised, his eyes on her long off-black tresses amid watching her take the cap from his hand. "Since when have you had all this hair, anyway? Or at least it doesn't look like a weave."

Rachel ignored that last mocking taunt as she lowered her camera to the roof of the car and pulled the cap onto her head, knowing it wouldn't exactly overheat her considering the coolness of the morning temperature.

"I've always had hair. You just never noticed because I always kept it cut."

"Really?"

"Uhm-hmm. As soon as I would cut it, it would grow right back. Well, I finally decided to stop cutting it, see how long it would grow. And I've managed to luck up on a good beautician who keeps it in good condition for me."

"I see." Felix slid a red skull cap over his own short-cut black hair, unaware of how ridiculous he looked in the thing, as Rachel imagined she did in hers as well. "Well, all I can say is if you'd had it like this when you were twelve, maybe jerk Jock Whitman wouldn't have dumped you for Miss DD-cup, with the butt to match."

She smiled at his recollection of the tale she had told him the night before about losing her roller and ice skating boyfriend/teacher to a more endowed girl at fourteen.

"I'm surprised you remembered that," Rachel said.

"Hey, I have a good memory," Felix said immodestly.

"Yea, so, I see, from the way you got us lost back down there at the beginning of the Park," Rachel said observantly.

Felix ignored her teasing tone as he busied himself pulling a string of bells from the backpack he had opened and sliding them down around her neck.

"What are these for?" Rachel asked in surprise.

"To keep the grizzlies away. Some say they work, some say they don't," Felix said, turning away from her with a shrug.

"Yea, you know, Stacey said this morning that we might encounter a grizzly up here, and I don't think I could go through that, again."

"Don't worry; if we run into one, I'll just throw myself on top of you, like I did yesterday."

Rachel ignored the teasing grin Felix had turned on her amid sliding a string of bells around his own neck. He wasn't getting on top of her again in any way, shape, form or fashion! Not when such close proximity to his fine virile body shook her up the way it did!

"Anyway, I just hope we don't run into one," she said.

"Probably not." Turning back to the backpack on the car's back seat, Felix pulled out a pair of dark sunglasses and slid them over Rachel's eyes, taking her completely by surprise.

"What—What is this!" Rachel demanded, black mascara-lashed brown eyes squinting against the opaque darkness of the shades she had not been prepared for.

"To protect your eyes from the sun. It can be glaring at some of these elevations."

Nodding, she watched as Felix turned away from her again to pull another pair of shades out of the backpack and slide them over his own eyes. Rachel was surprised to see how stunning he looked in the dark glasses, which gave him a detachment as attractive as the rectangular shape of the lens frames enhancing that of the equal shape of his equally attractive face.

Assuming his ministering of her was over, Rachel retrieved her camera from the roof of the car, only for Felix to take it from her hand and put it back where it was. She turned a look of surprise on him, a surprise that deepened when he suddenly slid the backpack over her arms, its weight nearly sending her sprawling to the ground.

"Hold on!" he laughed, a steadying arm lowering around her waist.

Rachel was glad she had the thickness of her wooly jacket to protect her from the intimate closeness of his arm as she sought to accustom herself to the weight of the backpack he had slid onto her back.

"What is this!" her response came predictably.

"First aid kit, water, matches, fire starter, bug spray—the mosquitoes can be murder around here—gloves, a compass, a knife, a map, food."

"Oh." Rachel was surprised she hadn't thought of that as Felix dropped his arm from her waist to reach into the car and slide a similar backpack onto his own tan-clad shoulders. "When did you have a chance to have the concierge get us some food?"

"This morning, before I joined you for breakfast. That's why I wasn't in the cafeteria when you got there."

"Oh." Rachel digested that with a nod before allowing a curious frown to mar her beautiful round face and dusky features. "Who've you been up here with anyway, to know all this basic emergency and survival stuff?"

Felix shrugged amid clasping the straps of the backpack across his chest, the same of which she stood doing to her own in front of him.

"I don't know—a couple of the hotel employees that were off duty last week. Neither one of them was Marjorie, I'll tell you that."

He flashed his perfect teeth in a laugh at the memory of how the reservationist had come on to him that morning and watched Rachel do the same.

"You just don't have luck with women named Marjorie, do you?" Rachel teased.

The smile lingered on Felix's slender lips at her reference to the character name of one of his love interests on his soap. "I guess not," he agreed.

"Anyway, getting back to this survival business of yours, you know, I was just thinking at that Lands place we went to yesterday that I'm not exactly a backpacking kind of girl, a camping kind of girl. I'm more a city girl. But I guess I'm going to have to be a backpacking kind of girl today, aren't I?"

"Uhm-hmm. And you're going to need it, because we're going to be up here all day." Felix's long-lashed dancing brown eyes narrowed on her in a curious look. "What kind of physical shape are you in?"

She stared at him in her usual amusement at the prying question. "What kind of physical shape does it look like I'm in?"

"There are approximately thirty miles of trails in the Eklutna Lake Valley. They go from easy to easy-to-moderate to moderate-to-difficult, and sometimes very difficult," Felix qualified his question with a simple answer. "And they can go anywhere from a mile to thirteen, such as the Lakeside Trail, which takes at least, six hours hiking on foot one way."

Rachel stared up at him in a shock that left her mouth hanging open. Although she considered herself in pretty good shape, she couldn't see herself trekking on a twelve-hour round trip through the wilderness, no matter how much of Alaska she wanted to see on her visit there.

"I—I don't think I'm up to that Lakeside Trail," she said.

"Then, we'll start out on the one they took me on, better known as the Twin Peaks Trail. It's rated moderate-to-difficult because of steepness in places, but it's only two and a half miles one way. Hiking time is about two hours going up, and one hour coming down."

"Yea, I think I can handle that," Rachel agreed.

Taking the camera from the roof of the car and handing it to her, Felix slammed shut the back passenger door and locked all with the automatic door-locking device that came with his keys. Sliding all into the back pocket of his tan Levi's, he saw Rachel into the building of the trailhead, where he paid the small parking fee for the day. Then leading her back out into the sun, Felix escorted her across a footbridge to the mouth of the Twin Peaks Trail leading north of the parking lot and away from Eklutna Lake.

As they began to move up the trail, Rachel was relieved to see through the darkness of her shades that it was well-maintained, as according to Felix, it was popular because of its easy access to good views of the entire Eklutna Valley. However, she couldn't help realizing all over again that they were in the wilderness! A dense forest of spruce and birch trees towered each side of the trail, where ferns, mushrooms, and a number of wildflowers covered the forest floor. In fact, Rachel determined to tell him that not long after they had set foot five feet on their hike down the moderate-to-difficult trail.

"Felix, baby, we're in the woods! We're in the wilderness!" she said.

Felix laughed at the distressed note in her tone as he curved a comforting arm around her waist. "If you think this is bad, you ought to see Kachemak Bay State Park to the northeast. Talk about being in the wilderness, that place is so inaccessible by car that you have to hire a bush plane or a boat to get you out there."

"I see." Rachel's reply was an incredulous one as she tried to imagine a bush denser than this one.

However, she decided that if she was going to be in this bush, this wilderness, she was going to be able to see it without the muting shade provided by her dark glasses. Taking the silly things off, she lowered them into her purse.

The ring of those silly bells tied around her neck sounded through the air as Rachel raised the camera back to her eye just in time to see a large moose sprint out of the woods a distance in front of them.

"Oh, look, a moose!" she cried needlessly, briefly lowering the camera from her eye to see the brown animal.

"Yea, they're plentiful around here. I'm surprised we haven't seen one before now." Having stopped in the trail beside her, Felix watched as she took a couple snapshots of the large antlered animal before it had just as quickly darted into the woods on the other side of the trail. He initiated the resumption of their leisurely hike then, the arm he had curled around her waist lowered back to his side to give her freedom of movement.

"So, tell me, Rachel Hardison," Felix began then, string of bells ringing around his own neck, "what made you decide to become a kindergarten teacher? You never told me that."

Rachel smiled over the camera she still held raised to her eye to take a picture of a dwarf dogwood growing at the edge of one side of the trail.

"Actually, the truth about that is very interesting," she said amid lowering the camera from her eye. "I had a babysitting job for one of our neighbors during the summer that I was seventeen. The woman's granddaughter was visiting her that day, a most adorable girl of six. Well, my neighbor got called away on business, asking me if I would come over and watch her granddaughter for a while. She also asked me if I would try to work with her on her reading, said she'd had trouble with it ever since being enrolled in kindergarten a couple years before that. Well, I did that, and I couldn't help noticing that while the little girl had an excellent vocabulary for a six-year-old going into the first grade, she paused and stumbled and stammered over those same words on the printed page. That's when I realized that her problem was not that she was illiterate as her grandmother had thought, she could use the words in a sentence, but she didn't yet know what they meant, and I told my neighbor that when she got home later on. Anyway, that's when my neighbor realized that that was exactly the problem and told me that I had a gift. She said I had a way with young children and should devote my life to working with them. Well, I was going off to college in the fall and I knew I had to take something, especially when I'd had no idea before that what I wanted to do. So, when I got to the University, I applied for young children education. And I guess I'm pretty good at it, because I absolutely love working with those kids, because as I told you, they are positively adorable."

"I see." Felix's red-capped head bent in a nod as he absorbed everything she had said. "So, working with that little girl that day brought out your maternal instinct. Well, I guess it came with your maturation process. Still it's hard for me to see that in you, Rachel Hardison, because you were such a brat yourself the last time I saw you at fourteen. And it's equally impossible for me to imagine you as somebody's mother."

"Hey, I can't exactly see you as somebody's dad, either!" Rachel pounced on his deliberate words and blasted him with the remark. Gorgeous one that he would be at that!

Felix laughed again at the insulted look she had lowered over his physique, a hand reaching briefly out to curve around her neck. "So, what part of Atlanta do you live in, city girl?"

"I live in an apartment not too far from the Georgia Dome. The car I drive is two years old, and with all my other bills, I'm terribly in debt. But I'll get over it."

"I see." Again came the two-word response, although this time accompanied with a smile as Felix watched her take yet another shot of a distant porcupine, one of several small mammals living in the area along with fox, lynx, porcupine, ground squirrel, rabbit, vole and a number of others.

"So, what part of New York do you live in, city boy?" Rachel asked, applying the question he had asked her to him.

"I live in an apartment not too far from Central Park. The car I drive is two years old, and with all my other bills, I'm terribly in debt. But I'll get over it."

Rachel dropped the camera from her eye and stared at his nerve in daring to mock her, knowing the dancing brown eyes had to be dancing all the more behind the dark glasses.

"You are yanking my leg!" she snapped.

Felix dropped his gaze from her demeaning look and let it lower onto the white Wrangler jeans snugly covering her legs from thigh to white Nikes-clad feet.

"And while we're on the subject, I wonder what they look like!" Felix remarked curiously, his smile teasing as he raised his face back to hers.

"Oh, please!" Rachel fairly laughed as usual beneath the mischievous look she knew he had turned back on her behind the dark glasses before her expression sobered, her tone becoming serious. "And anyway, while we're on the subject of New York, about this 9/11 thing—I mean, I saw that on TV. What must that really have been like for you, what with living there at the time?"

Felix's own eyes became serious behind his black-rimmed shades. "It was awful," he answered in a reminiscent tone. "I—I must have been on the set when it went all over the air that those planes had crashed into the World Trade Center. I—I mean, it was incredible, the way both buildings just burst into flames, and then, just tumbled to the ground like a pile of ashes. Blood and dust and soot were all over Manhattan for weeks. I had two friends who were on the seventy-ninth floor of the North Tower that morning. I lost both of them in that tragedy."

Rachel didn't need to see his eyes behind the dark glasses to know the pain he was going through, as she saw by the expression on his face that he had become very saddened by the memory.

"I'm sorry," she said, a hand reaching out to claim his sympathetically. "That must have been very hard for you."

"Yeah." Felix's resigned nod was absent, as he was still reflecting on the bad memory. "The World Trade Center was a twelve-million-square-foot complex built between 1968 and 1973 and resembled a miniature city with 430 companies representing a variety of commercial activities from twenty eight countries. Its daytime population included 50,000 employees and 100,000 business and leisure visitors. The two 110-story towers were New York's tallest buildings, and while some say they were a design fiasco, others say they were an engineering marvel, and at night when they were lit up from within, they were a beautiful site to behold. Lower Manhattan's famous skyline was permanently altered after those terrorist attacks in 2001. Five outlying buildings were destroyed along with the Center and two towers, not to mention the North and South pedestrian bridges and an underground mall, where the subway ran through several train stations. And I didn't think they would ever rebuild any of it, although they have since reconstructed it in the new 7 World Trade Center project, which although only 52 stories tall to the Twin Towers' 110, has shown the resilience of man's capacity to bounce back from disaster while at the same time imbuing Lower Manhattan with a new vitality borne of the historicity of its impact. And they even capitalized on the vitality that came with the new development with the release of the World Trade Center movie that came out last year. Not that any of it will ever make up for the 3,000 lives that were lost in those terrorist bombings of the original World Trade Center of September 11, 2001, including the lives of my two friends."

Rachel didn't think so either, judging by what she had seen on the TV. Yet she declined from commenting that as she hiked quietly down the trail beside him deliberately trying to ignore the crazy pleasure shooting up her arm from the feel of her hand holding his.

Fortunately there was no more talk about sad things after that. Instead it required all their concentration to negotiate that trail. It quickly went from moderate to difficult in their trek up toward East Twin Peak, making Rachel grateful for the prominent switchback at the mile-and-a-half point. There, the vegetation opened to a rest area that provided a picture-perfect view of Eklutna Lake and the massive Bold Peak in the distance, a ptarmigan roosting nearby, Dall sheep grazing in the nearby Goat Mountain Bowl as the trail continued around the mountain's west side. In fact, Felix told her that the Twin Peaks Trail was once only used for sheep hunters. The Canon Sure Shot 35mm was raised to her eye as Rachel took several shots of all of those.

Then, they were on the move again, requiring Rachel to hold Felix's hand again not to comfort or derive an inner pleasure, but to drag her screaming up over the dirt terrain with its unsteady footing, which just as Felix had said, became quite steep in places. And as Felix laughingly dragged her after him toward the alpine tundra with those crazy bells around their necks ringing to warn bears in the vicinity of their approach, Rachel hoped to God that it would be worth it when they got to the end of the two-and-a-half mile trail. For she was going to need a nap for weeks after such strenuous activity—especially when she was not accustomed to it!

Chapter Seven

It was worth it. As the trail dead-ended just above tree line, they descended a footpath to the left, crossed a creek, and climbed tundra slopes to the northeast until they ended up on a barren one in the upper valley below East Twin Pass. The location enabled Rachel to look down on a view so much more panoramic than the one she'd had at the trail's switchback that it left her sighing in disbelief. Below her in the distance against the backdrop of a clear blue sky lay Eklutna Lake Valley, the turquoise waters of Eklutna Lake cutting through the Chugach Mountain Range. In fact, the view was so scenic that even Felix had to take his own sunglasses off to admire it without the muting effect produced by the dark lenses, even though he had seen it a week before.

"It's beautiful, isn't it?" he couldn't help asking incredulously, his attractive tenor sounding soft and seductive in Rachel's ear. "Eklutna Lake feeds a power plant, and provides drinking water for the Anchorage area. It is a mile wide and seven miles long, was created by glacial and freshwater streams flowing into the valley, and in fact, extends to Eklutna Glacier, one of fifty in the Park. Also, in fact, Eklutna Glacier carved the lower valley as it retreated, which explains the horizontal scarring on rock formations as evidence of its passage."

"I see," Rachel replied with some distraction, as she was busy taking pictures of the scenic view. In the two or more hours that it had taken for them to climb up from Eklutna Lake Valley, more visitors had arrived at the Park, and men could be seen fishing from the lake shore while a number of canoes and kayaks dotted the turquoise water. Felix explained the reason for the non-motorized boats she was seeing in the distance, as boats with electric motors were not allowed on Eklutna Lake. Nodding her acceptance of that, Rachel continued to take pictures of the panoramic view, catching more Dall sheep high up on a distant steep ridge as well as a golden eagle soaring in flight, like before, using the camera's telephoto lens to bring all up close. And at their elevation of more than fifteen hundred feet in the air, she was able make a 360-degree turn and snap the vast blue waters at the opposite end of Eklutna Lake Valley, which she was both delighted and surprised to hear Felix tell her, comprised the Knik Arm River beyond Cook Inlet.

"Incredible!" Rachel cried her amazement, so high up in the air that she felt she could just have been standing on the top of the world. "I—I've never seen anything so breathtaking! This beats Stone Mountain in Georgia any day!"

"Yes, it is impressive, isn't it?" Felix agreed, still standing quietly while she dispensed a roll of film, her second one since arriving at the Park over two hours before.

Rachel took advantage of her running out of a second roll of film by using it as a stopping point, lowering the camera to the slope along with her black leather purse and sliding out of her backpack. The cool early morning temperature had heated up to at least fifty two degrees, making the brown ribbed parka and red cap she wore no longer necessary. Removing both, she lowered them to the ground to the left of her, aware that Felix stood to the right of her discarding his own backpack, skull cap and tan lined parka as well.

Settling her white Wrangler jeans-clad hips to the barren ground along with her things while Felix did the same beside her, Rachel took one last look about her surroundings. The dense spruce and birch, ferns, mushrooms and wildflowers such as dwarf dogwood, fireweed and broomrape forest floor coverings that had dominated the lower elevations had been replaced with nootka lupine, Indian paintbrush, spotted saxifrage and cut-leaf anemone, mosses of the tundra. In harmony with that, the highbush and lowbush cranberries, currants, raspberries, and watermelon berries that had grown along the lower trails had been replaced by blueberries, bearberries, and crowberries along the higher trails up there as well, all of which would provide much berry picking delight in late summer and early fall.

"Incredible!" Rachel couldn't help repeating one last time as her amazed gaze lingered over the sun-kissed area. Then bringing her gaze up close, she let it settle onto the brown backpack she had pulled into her lap to see what the concierge had packed them for lunch, just then realizing that it was twelve thirty and she was starved from her almost three-mile trek up from the lower Eklutna Lake Valley.

Beside her, Felix uncovered the meal the hotel employee had provided for them as well. There were thermoses of ice water and Gatorade—the heaviness of both of which explained why Rachel's pack had been so unwieldy on her trek up, there were cheese snacks in a cellophane package, fried potato sticks in another, seedless raisins in carry-along boxes, dried apple wedges for dessert. And there were thick ham slices, thick chicken breast slices and an endless array of fresh lettuce arranged on French bread, providing a most delightful and filling submarine sandwich for her enjoyment.

And as Rachel bit into it in tune to Felix biting into his in sync with her, she knew she was going to enjoy it, indeed. The six-inch sandwich was sluiced with Ranch dressing, its tangy flavor adding to her taste buds' delight.

"God, this is delicious!" she exclaimed amidst also raising some of the tasty fried potato sticks to her mouth. "That concierge is worth every cent Stacey pays him."

"Yes, he is," Felix agreed over the sandwich and cheese snacks he too was biting into.

Removing the top from the thermos of ice-filled water, Rachel raised it to her lips and downed a long-lengthy swallow, only then realizing just how thirsty she had been made by her trek up. Then returning her attention to her sandwich, she took another bite, bent on quickly sating her hunger as well.

Beside her, Felix downed a lengthy sip of the Gatorade to wash down the huge bite of sandwich he had just eaten as well, his dancing brown gaze pensive on the panoramic view in the distance.

"You know, while we're on the subject of Eklutna Lake, there's a historic park named for it on the other side of Glenn Highway off the exit," he said.

Rachel stared at him in surprise over the sandwich she had taken another bite out of, not having known that. "Really . . . ?"

Felix nodded over the sandwich he himself had bitten into. "Yea, it was established around 1990 by Eklutna, Inc., an Alaskan Native Corporation, to preserve the heritage and traditions of the Athabascan people, and to portray the rapidly disappearing lifestyles of the Dena'ina Athabascan Indians in South-central Alaska. In case you may have forgotten from our visit to the Alaska Gallery at the Anchorage Museum of History and Art yesterday, the Dena'ina people first encountered the white man in the late eighteenth century with the explorations of Vitus Bering and Captain James Cook."

Rachel smiled her amusement over the cheese snacks she was munching on at his mention of the name she was fast becoming familiar with. "It's amazing how that man's name keeps coming up in the conversation," she said finally.

"Yea, apparently Captain Cook was all over the place in his day," Felix agreed over the sub sandwich he had half eaten. "Anyway, Eklutna dates back to 1650, is the oldest continually inhabited Athabascan site in the Anchorage vicinity, and is located at the junction of several traditional Indian trails. Now, of course, the Russian Orthodox missionaries came in the early 1800's, bringing their religion and western influences. And you can see that when you enter the park, because Russian merchandise is sold in the Eklutna Village Heritage House there, and they have a cemetery that holds what they call 'spirit houses' over the graves of dead loved ones. Isn't that gross? This custom comes from the melding of Athabascan and Russian Orthodox beliefs and practices—and in fact, you will even see an Orthodox cross on the graves of members of the Orthodox Church. And the St. Nicholas Church there, originally built in the 1830's, is the oldest standing building in greater Anchorage, and like the 4th Avenue Theatre and Alaska Public Lands Information Center, is also listed on the National Register of Historic Places."

"I see." The smile Rachel turned on him amid taking another bite out of her sandwich was one of amazement at his vast knowledge of the history of the area and guilt at her knowledge of little. "You know, notwithstanding the Alaska Gallery you just mentioned us visiting at the Anchorage Museum of History and Art, after all those maps and guidebooks and brochures I picked up at the Visitor Center and that Public Lands place you just mentioned that we also went to yesterday, I probably would have more knowledge about some of these things. Except that you kept me away from the hotel all day, and I never got a chance to read up on any of them."

Over the sandwich Felix had bitten into yet again, his dancing brown eyes rolled with amusement at the accusing note he'd heard in her attractive medium tone.

"And with any luck, I'm going to keep you away from there all day today, too," he teased over the ice-chilled Gatorade he was raising back to his smiling lips. "For instance, for starters, after we climb down from here, I'll take you over to Eklutna Historical Park, show you around."

"I think I'd like that," she said.

Returning her attention to the cheese snacks she was downing along with her half eaten sandwich, Rachel tossed a couple of the tasty morsels back into her mouth, her gaze again pensive as it settled back on Felix.

"So, when do you have to be back on the set?" she asked curiously.

Felix's brown gaze again turned pensive as he busied himself downing his own cheese snacks in harmony with the sub sandwich he had half finished.

"Well, I fly back to New York on Sunday, and have one last week to kill before returning to work. I have to be back on the set bright and early Monday morning after next."

"Wow!" Rachel couldn't stop the pang of sorrow she felt for him as she took another bite out of her own half finished sandwich. "I don't have to be back to work until late August. I've got the whole summer free."

"Why don't you fly up, and see me one day?" Felix suggested with a smile, to her mild surprise. "I'll show you around the set. I'll introduce you to Marjorie, one of my character's love interests on the show—not to mention her daughter, and her stepdaughter," he finished wickedly.

"That should be interesting," Rachel replied with a smile.

"Indeed," Felix agreed.

Taking another bite out of her dwindling sandwich, Rachel fixed him with another curious look. "How're they going to explain your three-week hiatus from the show?"

Felix concentrated on downing another bite out of his own disappearing sandwich, which he followed with a lengthy drink of iced Gatorade from a brown thermos.

"Well, after Marjorie's husband finds the two of us in their bed together, he's going to put a contract out on me, so, I'm going to flee to Kansas, get a job as a farm hand there for a while. Unbeknownst to me, throughout all this, Marjorie's daughter has found out about my infidelity to her as well, but she's so in love with me she doesn't care. So, she's going to come looking for me, and she is going to leave no stone unturned in her desperate need to find me. Her trek is going to carry her all the way from New York City through several upper central states and down to the lower mid-western states, when she is finally going to find me working at the Kansas farm three weeks later. Well, after all that effort she has put out to find me, I realize that it's her whom I really love; and we spend we spend two glorious weeks at the farm making out in our newfound love. Then, her father, Marjorie's husband, who's been looking for me since I fled New York as well, shows up breathing bloody murder, forcing me to hit the road again, only with the daughter accompanying me this time. We go all the way out west to Arizona, where I am met by the stepdaughter, who's also become privy to my infidelity to her and demands to know what I'm doing sleeping around on her with her stepsister and her stepmother.

"Well, just like her stepsister, the stepdaughter is in love with me, too, so it doesn't take too much to assure her of my love, and pretty soon, we end up back in bed," Felix went on humorously over the crisp potato sticks he was munching on. "That's when the daughter, who I've been sleeping with for the past two weeks, comes in and finds me in bed with her stepsister. Well, I somehow tell her that I love them both, and pretty soon the three of us are in bed together in a ménage à trois. And that's when Marjorie's husband catches up with me in Arizona, and finds me in bed with his daughter and his stepdaughter, after already having found me in bed with his wife."

"Oh, no . . . !" Rachel nearly choked on the seedless raisins she had raised to her mouth from a carry-size box, laughter bubbling from her throat. "You mean to tell me that not only is Marjorie's husband going to find you in bed with his wife but he's going to make a cross-country trek in pursuit of you, only to find you at the end of it in bed with his daughter and his stepdaughter! Man, you really ought to be whipped!"

"Oughtn't I . . . !" Felix managed a shameless grin in the face of Rachel's outright laughter. "Yea, what I've just given you is a preview of what's going to happen with my character over the next couple of months. In the breakdown, it's called Devil On The Run. It's going to be a mess. And a lot of fun," he laughed.

"I'll bet," Rachel agreed, own laughter sobering. Her eyes settled on him in another curious look after having finished her sub sandwich and turning her attention back on her half emptied packet of cheese snacks. "So, what's going to happen when Marjorie's husband finds you in bed with his daughter and his stepdaughter? Is he going to kill you?"

"I can't tell you that, you'll have to watch the show," Felix laughed. "But let me tell you something—my character of Joe Murray is real slick and a major player on the show. And as a result of that, the writers have some stuff planned for him that is going to bind him to the daughter and the stepdaughter in a way that's going to drive Marjorie crazy. It is going to be a mess, and a hell of a lot of fun to play."

"I see," Rachel replied with a smile that became a tickled one as she observed the amused grin that lingered on Felix's attractive lips. She wondered what the writers could possibly have in store for his character that was going to bind him to his lovers in a way that was going to drive their mother crazy. Could it be possibly that both the daughter and the stepdaughter were going to become pregnant? Rachel had to force herself not to choke at the thought as she deliberately checked that laugh and turned her attention to finishing the bag of cheese snacks she held in one hand.

"So, what do you do in Atlanta, Rachel Hardison?" Felix asked over the sub sandwich he too turned his attention to finishing then.

"Hang out with my friends, mostly," Rachel said over the ice water she was drinking from her brown thermos. "I have three of them, all teachers from the school. We have great times together, enjoying recreational activities when we have the time, and spending an occasional night out on the town. Of course, two of them have expressed a desire to get married and settle down, but as yet no one special has come along. So, in the meantime, we're choosing to let the fates fall where they may. You know—living single. . . . And loving every minute of it."

"I see," Felix smiled after having finished his sandwich. Picking up his own half emptied bag of cheese snacks, he concentrated on finishing them as well.

"So, what do you do in New York, Felix Latham?" Rachel asked him after a moment.

"Hang out with my friends, mostly," Felix said over the last of the Gatorade he was raising to his lips. "I have several of them, some actors like me, others holding down normal jobs. We have great times too, enjoying recreational activities when I have the time, and spending an occasional night out on the town. Of course, two of them are married, and three more have expressed a desire to get married and settle down as well, but as yet, no one special has come along. So, in the meantime, minus our married buddies, we're choosing to let the fates fall where they may. You know—living single. . . . And loving every minute of it."

"I see," Rachel said, this time choosing to smile at his nerve in daring to mock her again. Dropping her twinkling gaze back to the cellophane bag in her hand, she concentrated on downing the last of her cheese curls.

Putting the emptied bag to the side then, Rachel turned her attention to the rest of her fried potato sticks, finishing them as well. She also finished the last of her ice water and drank her ice chilled Gatorade. But she didn't want the dried apple slices and put them back into her backpack, bent on leaving them for another day.

Moving into her black purse then, she pulled out a 36-exposure roll of Kodak color print 35mm film and put it in the 35mm Canon Sure Shot Camera after emptying its silver body of the spent roll and sliding it into her purse along with another spent one and another unused one. Then Rachel raised the camera to her eye, snapping another ptarmigan—Alaska's state bird—flying overhead, a windsurfer visible in the distance on the blue waters of Knik Arm. And then with the camera aimed in his direction anyway, Rachel knocked off several shots of Felix. Like her, he had finished his lunch and sat there looking sexy as ever with the afternoon sun shining down on him and tinting the short black hair framing his attractive face brown in its yellow rays.

Having finished with shooting him a moment later, Rachel was surprised when he suddenly took the camera from her hands. Snapping several shots of her, Felix at last pushed it back into her hands.

"And when you get it developed, I want copies of all of them," Felix said.

She practically flushed beneath the intent way he sat looking at her, surprised he wanted a picture of her that badly. "Okay," she smiled.

Replete from his lunch now, Felix gathered up all his empty food wraps and thermoses and placed them back into his backpack, aware that Rachel sat beside him doing the same thing. He also placed his discarded red knit cap and dark sunglasses there as well. Then moving to his feet with the backpack and tan lined jacket held in one hand, he curled his free one around Rachel's wrist and pulled her to her feet with him.

"Come on," he said, "let's see what else we can get into around here."

Nodding acquiescence, Rachel let him escort her farther up the slope and onto East Twin Pass, straps of her backpack and purse slung over one shoulder, brown jacket carelessly slung over the other one, silver-toned camera in her hands.

She jumped when the loud plaintiff cry of an animal pierced the air suddenly, nearly sending the camera falling from her hands and the brown ribbed woolly jacket from her shoulder.

"What's that!" she cried.

"I'm afraid it's a wolf," Felix answered.

" . . . A what?"

" . . . A wolf."

"A wolf—?"

"Yea, they're plenteous around here, too. Just consider yourself lucky that you haven't run into one yet."

Rachel ignored the teasing smile Felix had turned on her. She didn't find the fact that she had not yet run into a wolf a fit recommendation for her to remain calm at all.

However, her fear deserted her as they continued down East Twin Pass. To the north of them were views of the town of Palmer and the closer Matanuska Valley. To add to it: Dall sheep were gathered there in large number, providing such beautiful sights that Rachel's camera again came into play as she took several shots of both the white woolly animals and Valley.

"Beautiful!" she exclaimed, eyes still focused through the camera viewfinder.

"Indeed," Felix agreed.

She suddenly became aware of a pair of moose fighting in the Matanuska Valley bowl not too far from where the sheep were grazing. "Look, Felix, dueling moose!" she cried excitedly, a hand extended to lead him in the direction of her gaze. "Look, moose fighting! Or is it mooses? Or is it meese! Or is it meeses! Well, whatever they are, I've got to get a picture of this!"

She raised the camera to her eye to get a quick couple of shots and was surprised when Felix suddenly stalled her, his free hand curling around her upper arm.

"Honey," Felix began quietly, not wanting to startle her, "they're moose. And they're not fighting; they're jousting over a female with which they want to mate. Which is weird—, because—it's not mating season."

Rachel averted her gaze away from the two large apparently male animals rutting antlers head to head in the distance and onto Felix in surprise.

"Well, when is mating season?"

". . . For a moose, September."

"I see," Rachel said, her gaze back on the two male animals jousting in the distance. "Oh, well, I guess they wanted to get a jump on the season, not to mention a jump on each other, huh!" she laughed.

"Girl, you are a trip!" Felix just did manage to sober his amusement after laughing along with her. "Come on—let's see what else we can get into up here."

Continuing on East Twin Pass, they turned left in the direction of East Twin Peak. The mountain, which stood at a distance of about four miles ahead of them with West Twin Peak to the left of it, rose to an imposing four thousand feet and appeared to be imploding. Felix explained the reason behind its eroding slopes—it was made of a crumbling, fragmentary rock called greywacke, as was West Twin Peak and most of the other mountains in Chugach State Park. And because of that, East Twin Peak was too dangerous to climb—at least one hiker had died from a fall after becoming lost on the steep slopes toward its summit. Yet despite that and the fact that it and its twin West Twin Peak were among the ugliest in the Park, they were both somehow compelling—the closer East Twin Peak vividly offsetting the grace and symmetry of Eklutna Lake. Sufficiently warned, Rachel passed on the idea of advancing on the peak and let Felix guide her back off the loop toward the straightway of East Twin Pass and through gentle terrain leading southeast to the nearby Pepper Peak.

Suddenly Felix's idea of finding out what else they could get into up there stalled when they ran into a swarm of mosquitoes. Rachel wondered why they hadn't encountered them before, what with Felix having told her earlier that they were murder in the Park. Well, he certainly had not been kidding, for they were suddenly so thick there that they actually had to get off the muddied section of East Twin Pass and move into the surrounding woods to get around it. More mud was there—whether left over from a recent rain or a form of ground thawing—and Rachel went rock stiff in her white Nikes when Felix's face went as still as the frozen Eklutna Glacier at the end of Eklutna Lake in the distant Eklutna Lake Valley.

"What is it?" Rachel asked as she continued to observe his frozen stillness.

"We've got to get out of this area," Felix answered in his attractive tenor. "There is a bear or bears here."

"A—A what?" she stammered.

"There's a bear or bears around here," Felix repeated, brown eyes lowered to the ground. "See this mud? There are bears tracks here, and scat."

"What's scat?" Rachel asked curiously.

"What do you think?" Felix asked, turning an incredulous look on her that met her equally incredulous look. "What's the matter, haven't you ever seen bear doo in the woods?" he grinned.

"I—I—I—Okay, so, there's scat here!" Rachel cried, finally getting his message. "Why don't we do the same thing—scat!"

"Why don't we—?!" Felix agreed frantically, a hand curving impulsively around her wrist. "We'll just move a little farther into the woods, and move down just long enough to escape that swarm of mosquitoes on the Pass, and then, we can get back on track."

That was the plan, but it didn't work. As Felix began to lead Rachel away from the muddied area and through the woods across a wildflower and moss covered floor, and with those silly bells around their necks ringing to warn bears in the vicinity of their presence, her sneaker got caught up under a hidden tree root. She tripped, sending the ribbed parka sliding from her shoulder, the backpack flying into a tree where it caught on one of the tree's lower branches, and the camera falling from her hands. Felix saw her lose balance, his own parka and backpack falling from his hands as he tried to steady her, only for her weight to send him sprawling backward to the moss-covered forest floor. In her off balance position she fell in an undignified heap atop the length of him, her face hovering mere inches away from his, her arms thrown somewhere about his head with his thrown about her waist.

However, before Rachel could react to the strange sensation she always experienced at being in such close proximity to his virile sexy body, her backpack slid from the tree's lower branch and landed on the back of her neck. The dancing brown eyes became serious as Felix registered yet another intimate closeness between them as well before a glint of terror slid into their depths that left Rachel staring at him in surprise. She stared in deepening surprise when that terror transferred to his mouth, which gapped open as his gaze slid above her, a terror she too felt at the feel of something tearing at the hair flowing long and off-black behind her neck from the white knit band at the crown of her head. Except that it wasn't after her hair, it was after the backpack. It was a grizzly! As Rachel realized that they had roused the animal from its hiding place—and in fact, that had probably been his tracks that Felix had seen in the mud—despite the bells they had worn to alert him to their approach in the vicinity, she went rigid as a board the length of Felix, her mouth widened in a terror that mirrored his as the animal tore through the backpack in the hopes of finding food there. For endless tense seconds Rachel held her breath, her heart racing, aware that Felix's was doing the same as he lay holding his breath as well—while the four-hundred-pound brown animal proceeded noisily to rip the backpack to shreds, scattering first aid supplies, survival gear and empty food wrappers all over her, thermoses around her. Then finally having found the dried apple slices she had not eaten for lunch, the grizzly loped off with the carton snared between its teeth, leaving her stunned and literally too shaken to move.

Yet somehow out of her terror she managed to gaze down at Felix, who lay just as petrified as she, shocked expression mirroring hers, dancing brown eyes having narrowed on her despairingly.

"Let's get out of here . . ." he began.

". . . quickly . . . !" They screamed the word at the same time. And scrambling to their feet, they grabbed up their gear minus the thermoses, moved out of the woods and back onto the Pass.

They got out of there in a hurry, which wasn't easy, because in his haste to get them all the way back down East Twin Pass to the mouth of Twin Peaks Trail, Felix got them lost twice. Not to mention that three black bears crossed their paths on their descent down the dirt trail, forcing them to stop and stand frozen like statues until the large equally four-hundred-pound animals loped away in the distance. In fact, a hike that was only supposed to take them one hour going down and one that had gone from two and a half miles to five naturally took two. Rachel was terrified as she raced behind Felix, his hand holding possessively onto hers, her footing seemingly even more unsteady on the moderate-to-difficult trail than it was coming up in her equal haste to get away from the memory of that grizzly tearing that backpack to shreds on her neck. All-terrain vehicles whizzed past them as other people visiting Chugach State Park took advantage of the lovely day, people came riding by on horseback, and they encountered a number of other hikers and bikers and climbers bent on trekking up toward East and West Twin Peaks and East Twin Pass on the way to Pepper Peak. But Rachel and Felix saw very little of any of them in their haste to get to the tan Pontiac Grand Prix in the Eklutna Lake trailhead. Once in the car heading away from the trailhead, Felix did not take Rachel to the Eklutna Historical Park as he had told her; quite the contrary, he turned left onto Glenn Highway, carried them all the way down to the base of the Park, and got them the hell out of there quickly.

In fact, it wasn't until they were on Seward Highway heading back in the direction of downtown Anchorage that Felix started to breathe from their ordeal. Rachel, on the other hand, was a nervous wreck.

"I need a drink. I need a drink!" she cried. "I don't drink often, but you're going to turn me into a drunk!" A demeaning glance turned on his attractive profile accompanied the accusation. "And then, I'm going to need a nap. I'm literally going to have to go into hibernation like that grizzly that was on my neck after all the walking and running you've put me through today!"

Behind the wheel, Felix turned a brief amused look on her, like the day before, already having considered their experience with the grizzly something that had happened ages ago.

"You don't need a drink. You had one yesterday after our encounter with Mr. Grizzly. Therefore, I'm not going to take you to get one, today, because as you said, I have no intention of turning you into a drunk."

"Well, then, fine! Then, take me back to the hotel. I want to see George. I want to see my brother. I want to tell him how close that animal came to snapping off my neck!"

"Calm down, girl," Felix urged, reaching out and curling a steadying hand around hers. "I have somewhere else I want to show you, and you're going to find it very relaxing."

Deliberately Rachel ignored the usual pleasure that slid up her arm from the feel of his hand holding hers amid turning a surprised stare on his sexy profile, wondering where he wanted to take her now.

She found out a few minutes later when he steered them into a parking lot at the University of Alaska at Anchorage off Lake Otis Parkway and Providence Drive. With its multi-buildings, multi-parking lots, couple of creeks, numerous walking trails, lake and a nearby hospital, the University was huge, far more than Georgia State University. Again Rachel's brow furrowed in surprise as she watched Felix step from the car to come round and help her from the passenger side.

"Felix—Felix, what are we doing at the University of Alaska at Anchorage?" Rachel asked as he saw her from the car, black strap of her bag curved over her shoulder, his hand holding hers in a gentlemanly gesture. "It's pushing four o'clock. Most classes are over for the day. Not to mention school's out for the summer, anyway!"

"Not summer school, which is not the reason why I've brought you over here, anyway. Here, let's take these off."

Removing the string of bells she still wore around her neck away from her face and long hair, Felix removed the string of bells he still wore around his neck as well, discarding both to the back seat, where they hit the tan leather beside his backpack, her camera, and their parkas with a loud jingle.

Rachel's chocolate gaze narrowed on him in deeper surprise as he locked all doors with the automatic lock device attached to his key ring.

"Then, why've you brought me here?"

"There's a showing of local and well-known talent going on at the Wendy Williamson Auditorium here, sort of like a folk festival they have here every year," Felix explained easily, his hand again claiming hers after having lowered the keys into the front pocket of his tan Levi's. "They told me when I was here on Monday that it would be lasting all week. I hope it's still going on."

Rachel hoped it was too as the thought of being entertained by some local talent and even some not so local did sort of calm her nerves somewhat.

"But Felix—how do you know about this place?" she couldn't help asking curiously as he began to lead her away from the tan Pontiac. "I mean, what were you doing over here on Monday?"

"I sweet talked a couple of off-duty barmaids at the hotel—two very friendly women and naturally fans of the soap—into bringing me over here with them when they mentioned their plans to come over here to see some friends of theirs who were slated to be in the show. Unfortunately, once we got here, they introduced me to two other fans, who turned out to be the two women I was skirting around on my arms when I arrived back there."

"I see," Rachel replied with her usual amusement, thinking the man shameless, although quite remarkable in his ability to leave the hotel with two women and return there with two others. Well, she hoped the stylishly sophisticated long-haired black-and-white duo she remembered wouldn't be there today to try and hook up with him again. Especially when Felix had confided to her that he wasn't romantically interested in them in the least. No more than he was in the barmaids he had picked up at the hotel that had introduced them to him.

"They tell me this place is home to the Seawolves Hockey Team," the attractive tenor said to her then.

"I see," Rachel commented, naturally not having known that.

Fortunately, it didn't appear that her dread of running into his black-and-white fan duo from Monday was going to come through. As they found seats in the back of the large well-lit auditorium after relieving themselves in the rest rooms moments later, no one seemed to notice that he was indeed Felix Latham, actor and star of New York City-based soap opera *As The Star Shines*. And as long as Rachel kept from calling out his famous name, no one would be able to associate it with the article that had come out on him in the Anchorage Daily News that morning. And if she were lucky, no one would recognize by her hair that the woman sitting quietly next to him in the crowded auditorium was in fact the very one sprawled all out on top of him in that incriminating photo in said paper.

They had arrived just in time to hear the Baha Men, a black band of mostly today, doing their barking hit *Who Let The Dogs Out*—in fact, they had even heard their loud music blaring from the outside before they had entered the auditorium. And as Rachel lowered the strap of her black purse from her shoulder and settled it in her lap, she wondered what were the Baha Men doing performing at a free concert at the University of Alaska at Anchorage? Then she decided not to care as she settled back in her seat to enjoy the reggae/hip-hop/rock/R&B music from the multi-member band.

As the driving sound of *Who Let The Dogs Out* continued to blare from the stage, Felix leaned over to whisper in her ear.

"You know, despite their recent popularity in the United States, this group has been around for a while," he said.

"Really . . . ?" Rachel mused, briefly turning her gaze away from the band to eye him curiously.

"Yeah, they went by another name for years before taking on that of Baha Men a few years ago—Baha being short for Bahamas, where they are originally from," Felix went on informatively over the loudness of the music.

"Oh, I didn't know that," Rachel replied, turning her attention back to the band playing in the distance.

She slowly forgot all about her terrifying experience with the grizzly at Chugach State Park as she relaxed amid the Caribbean flavor behind the band's music. The Baha Men played a number of their hits; including *Move It Like This (Shake It Like That Mix)*, a lively tune from the CD of the same name. And as they finished playing and cleared the stage of their instruments some time later, Rachel wondered who would possibly be able to succeed a veteran band of such following?

She found out a moment later when Bon Jovi hit the stage along with a new partner he had acquired over the last couple of years. Jon Bon Jovi? *What was Bon Jovi doing playing for a free concert in Alaska,* Rachel couldn't help asking herself with knitted brows? Then she decided not to care as she let herself—like with the Baha Men—become swept up in the sexy white man's music.

She was sitting there rocking her head to the latest tune the brunette/blond/strawberry blond/whatever man was singing when Felix again claimed her attention with a golden brown hand curved over her white-sweater-sleeved arm.

"Feeling better?" he asked over the loudness of the pop/rock tune, sexy mouth curved in a smile. "Have you gotten over that grizzly at the Park bearing down on your neck yet? Scared me to death, girl."

Rachel ignored the attractive half amused laugh that followed the remark as she stared at him in surprise. He had been so calm on the drive to the University that she had half wondered if he had been affected by the frightening experience at all.

"Who are you kidding!" she demanded in response to the question he had put to her. "I still need a drink!"

Again the attractive laughter bubbled in Felix's throat before he returned his attention to the tune long-time rock music veteran Bon Jovi was singing, leaving Rachel to do the same.

Apparently he and the Baha Men were the only well-known talents due to grace the stage for a while, for a number of local names followed after that. There was a black-and-white male and female quartet who sang Black Eyed Peas' *Don't Phunk With My Heart*, there was a white guy—another Alaskan Native—who sang Justin Timberlake's *(I Got My) Sexy Back* which was very good for a laugh, and there was a brown-haired Shania Twain wannabe who complemented *Sexy Back* by singing her country hit *Man! Feel Like A Woman*. Then a black woman around her mid-twenties performed Sade's *No Ordinary Love*. And with her too round face, double chins and two spare tires around her middle Rachel wondered how she would ever get any love at all.

Felix thought the same thing as he sat beside her, staring at the too fat singer in amazement. "That woman is never going to get no exceptional love, much less no ordinary love!" he told her with a laugh.

"Hush up!" Rachel ordered with a rivaling laugh that belied her agreement with his vocalization of her own unspoken thought.

After that, to their delight, they were regaled with music from Jessica Simpson, another current artist of the day who sang title track *A Public Affair* and *You Spin Me Round (Like A Record)* from her recent CD. Then the mood turned old school as a band of at least ten 'brothers' took center stage and performed Kool & The Gang's *Jungle Boogie*. Rachel's black mascara-lashed brown eyes narrowed on them in amazement, as they were playing that song to a T.

Beside her, Felix stared at the ten-piece black band with similar amazement. "Good Lord! Is it real, or is it Memorex?" he demanded over the loudness of their music, causing her to turn a smile on him. "I haven't heard that song played that well since Kool & The Gang wrote it! When did it come out, anyway, the '60's? Seventies . . . ?"

"I don't know," Rachel shook her head, sending her long off-black ponytail waving from side to side behind her back. "All I know is I haven't heard that song played that well since my parents bought a CD of The Best Of Kool & The Gang when I was a kid!"

Yet despite not having heard *Jungle Boogie* played in its entirety in at least fifteen years, Rachel remembered every bit of it and so did that ten-piece band. They played every rift of the guitar, every bang of the drum, every toot of the horn, every nuance of lead singer J.T. 'Kool' Bell's equally cool voice. In fact, when they at last finished the jumping soul tune, all Rachel could do was stared after them incredulously. That was one local Alaska band that was soon to be discovered. Those 'brothers' were going to be rich someday.

She was still staring after the departing band when Felix claimed her attention by curving a hand around her arm again. And Rachel wished he would stop that, as his touch was doing its usual thing in sending that mad pleasure shooting up to her shoulder.

"You know," he began smilingly once she had turned to look at him, "now that I think about that song, I think your brother's been doing a little jungle boogie."

"I guess so," Rachel agreed, smiling also, "considering that 'jungle love' thing he and Stacey's got going on."

"No, what you're thinking about is 'jungle fever,'" Felix corrected, still smiling, "based on the movie *Jungle Fever* that came out several years ago, starring Wesley Snipes and Annabella Sciorra. However, there was a song called '*Jungle Love.*' Who put that song out, anyway? Morris Day & The Time?"

"I don't know. That was before my time," Rachel said.

"Of course, it was," Felix agreed, knowing she had barely been born then. "Nevertheless, if they can pull a song out of their repertoire as old as *Jungle Boogie*, I'm telling you that if anybody sings Elvis in here, it's going to be all over."

"It'll be '*too much*' for you, huh?" Rachel asked, putting the old Presley classic into the form of a question with a smile. "Leave you all weak and dangly, like a '*puppet on a string?*' Turn this into an '*oh happy day?*'"

"You said it, girl." Felix's smile rivaled hers in his delight of her knowledge of/and mention of the old Elvis tunes he so loved. "After all, you know he's '*always on my mind.*' I will be in '*t-r-o-u-b-l-e.*'"

"Well, *'don't cry, daddy,'* I think you'll be alright," Rachel said.

The smile broadened on Felix's attractive slender lips at her continued mention of an Elvis Presley tune. "What kind of *'witchcraft'* are you working on me?"

Another classic Presley tune put in the form of a question. Rachel looked away from his deeply flirting look, not knowing how to answer that one.

Unfortunately, no one sang any Elvis Presley tunes, but it was still an Oh happy day. They were regaled with old school, new school, black music, white music, pop/rock, R&B, soul, country, even one heavy metal tune. And as the many different performers took stage, Rachel wished she had brought her camera with her to record the memories instead of leaving it in the car. That is, it remained an Oh happy day until around five-twenty when some Fat Boys wannabes hit center stage and started to rap. The fast words spouting from their mouths over the stillness in the auditorium was such noise that all Rachel could do was stare at them in shock, feeling a complete letdown from the high she had been on since arriving there nearly two hours before.

Beside her, Felix, a professed lover of the classics, also reacted in disgust at the new age form of musical expression he had yet to understand or get used to.

"What is this?" he demanded over the gibberish spilling from the black trio's mouths. Yet even then his attractive tenor was barely audible over the loud rapping.

"I don't know," Rachel answered quietly, turning an equally stunned look on his handsome sexy features. "We've sat here for the last couple of hours and heard some old school, new school, nice music sung to us. This is just noise!" she exclaimed softly over the continued rapping. "And even though it's all I've heard all my life, I can't help wishing I had been born back in my parents' day. You remember those old groups like the O'Jays, the Dramatics, Earth, Wind & Fire, the Chilites, and even Kool & The Gang, you know, with the *Jungle Boogie* that that band did a while ago? Those old groups made songs that still sound good to this day! But can you imagine these guys getting together for a reunion in thirty years? They'll come strutting out on the stage, except that they won't be able to walk because arthritis will have set in, leaving them to take baby steps instead of those large strides. Run-D.M.C. can't run no mo' . . . !" she laughed. "They'll get ready to rap all this fast talk, but their dentures will come flying out of their mouths. *'Whoomp, there it is!'* Or in their case, whoomp, there they go!" Rachel laughed.

Felix joined in her ridiculous laughter at the thoughts that her exclamations and mention of the title of the old Tag Team rap tune brought to mind, a golden brown hand curving over her arm, a brown-sleeved arm curving congenially around her white-sweater-clad shoulders.

"Girl, you are a trip!" he exulted, falling half over her.

"Tell me about it!" Rachel agreed, doing the same.

Unwittingly their outrageous laughter attracted the attention of a woman sitting in a seat in a side aisle. She did not know who Rachel was, but she recognized the man laughing beside her immediately. Felix Latham, the most gorgeous black thing she had ever seen on legs, actor on the soap opera *As The Star Shines*, where he portrayed the popular, although slick character of Joe Murray. Yea, that was him, alright. In fact, he had even been in the paper that morning sprawled out over the Dimond Center ice skating rink floor with some long-haired woman sprawled out the length of him. Possibly the one sitting beside him, laughing with him so shamelessly. . . . Forgetting all about the three baggily dressed youths rapping from the stage the woman watched him intently, her smoky brown gaze figuratively eating up his attractive sexy features and short well-groomed black hair.

Felix's laughing gaze slid absently away from Rachel and in the direction of the short-haired black woman seated in the distance, saw her smoking him with her intent gaze as if he may as well have been a cigarette between her lips, and froze in his seat.

"Oh, no!" he said in a dreaded tone, grin falling from his lips. "I've been recognized."

Rachel saw the defeated way he hung his head as if to hide from his adoring public and turned a confused look on her surroundings as if to somehow find the person or persons who had identified him.

However, before she could look back at him, a woman seated in the aisle behind them reached forward and tapped him on the shoulder.

"Excuse me," she began in an uncertain tone, causing Felix to turn around and look at her and Rachel beside him as well, "but I've been sitting here for the past hour or so listening to your voice, hearing you laugh, and watching the back of your head. "Aren't you Felix Latham, actor on that soap opera *As The Star Shines?*"

"Uhmm, I'm afraid so," Felix replied over his broad brown-sweatshirt-clad shoulder, smiling reluctantly at the black woman who had claimed his attention.

"Well, honey, let me get your autograph! Oooh, Lord, I can't believe a man as foxy as you have been sitting here in front of me for a whole hour!"

With forced patience Felix watched as the drooling fan fumbled through her purse for a pen and a piece of paper with which to get his autograph, aware that Rachel sat watching him intently, a tickled smile on her berry-colored medium lips. Accepting the pen and paper she handed him a second later, Felix lowered it onto his tan-Levi's-clad thigh, and signed his name on it in a very masculine black scrawl.

However, before he could give the signed paper and pen back to the woman, four more of each were thrust into his face as women—the black and the white—who had been seated nearby came rushing over at the calling out of his famous name. Having no choice other than to honor their requests, Felix accepted their pens and papers and began again to sign his coveted name.

Predictably, before he could autograph the first paper, the come-ons started.

"Oooh, baby, when did you hit town? Because I sure want to hit you!" the first woman said.

"You know, I watch your show all the time. Are you as hot in bed in real life as you are with your three costars?" asked the second one.

"You know, while she's on the subject of bed, it gets mighty cold over here at night in Alaska. Would you like to warm mine? Because I sure would like to warm yours," the third one said suggestively.

"If I give you my name and phone number, will you call me? I won't hang up on you. Because I'm already hung up on you, not to mention that I want to get hung up *with* you!" the fourth one asserted brazenly.

Rachel had to laugh outright at the outrageous boldness of the four women, the attractive girlish sound sliding with barely veiled amusement from her throat. After all, Felix had said it himself: *As The Star Shines* had a huge following all the way over there in Alaska, and as a result of that he was used to, anticipated and expected such idol worship and fan adulation. And this showed in the tolerant smile that was on his lips as he autographed the women's various slips of paper with the pens they were handing him. In fact, Rachel couldn't help noticing that the brief look he turned on her flashed a mockery in further evidence of that, the intensity of which left her staring back at him with heightened amusement.

Across the auditorium on the stage, the three Fat Boys wannabes had been replaced with another trio bent on performing another current rap tune. Rachel was not interested in the black threesome and so completely ignored the thrust of their voices sounding loud and forced through the air. Neither were the four women who scrambled back to their seats with their eyes lowered to the autographs in their hands, nor for that matter was Felix, who Rachel could tell by the relieved look he'd turned on her had lost interest in the whole thing and was only interested in getting out of there. In fact, Rachel was hardly surprised when he took advantage of the departure of his fans by reaching out and curving an impulsive hand around her wrist.

"Let's get out of here, quickly!" he instructed smilingly between his perfect teeth.

Again Rachel laughed at the predictable response as she moved to her feet in tune with him moving to his own, her free hand guiding the black strap of her bag back onto her shoulder.

"That seems to be a catch-phrase with you, isn't it?" she teased playfully.

"Only with you," Felix answered. And returning her look with equal playfulness, he quickly hustled her from the aisle, bent only in getting the two of them away from his cloying fans in a hurry.

Outside the Auditorium a moment later, Rachel pulled her hand from the disturbing clasp of his and fixed him with a mocking grin.

"You know," she began as she walked beside him to the parking lot, a finger pointed at him to emphasize the suggestion she was about to make to him, "I have the perfect solution for you. Instead of having all these women coming on to you everywhere you go because of your looks, why don't you do like that guy I remember seeing on several reruns of The Gong Show on the cable Game channel did years ago? He went around with a brown paper bag on his head, and you could do the same. You could cut out the holes for your eyes and mouth, just like he did. He was the Unknown Comic; you could be the Unknown Soap Opera Star!"

She laughed so ridiculously after voicing her last statement that Felix had to laugh himself as he gazed down at her, her long off-black ponytail dancing around her face, her body half bent over in her amusement.

"You are beautiful, girl," he said.

And in harmony with that thought, Felix slung an arm around her waist, pulled her against him, and lowered his lips onto hers in an ardent display that stopped Rachel from laughing immediately. The kiss was as sensuous and invasive as the one he'd given her at the ice skating rink the evening before and in fact, her physical reactions were the same—sensation knifed down her spine all the way down to the soles of her sneakers, her throat threatened to close up as blood flowed into her neck, her face flamed, heat rushed over her skin. Yet before she could respond to the immediate urge she felt to kiss him in return, Felix had broken away from her to respond to something another fan said to him in passing. And as he did so Rachel stared after him in shock, wondering if he had any idea as to just how completely his unexpected assault on her mouth had devastated her.

Chapter Eight

    She didn't know how she managed to make it to the car, except to say that she found herself safely strapped in the passenger seat a minute later. Rachel was a nervous wreck all over again. She was no fool, nor blind. Beneath the white sweater and Wrangler jeans she wore with white Nikes sneakers, she knew she had a figure, for she had a D-cup bust-line with the hips to match and long shapely Beyoncé legs that most men couldn't take in one sitting. To add to these considerable assets: she was an attractive woman, a beautiful woman, with long straight relaxed off-black hair pulled back from a perfect round face with dusky features that included large long-lashed luminous deep brown eyes beneath perfectly arched black brows, she had high cheekbones and a gently flaring nose. Equally so, she had perfect Halle Berry teeth behind medium lips that most men she met wanted to kiss all day every day of the week, even though she often didn't let 'em. However, of the men who had kissed her in her life, she had never met one who'd ever had the nerve to kiss her in broad daylight on a college campus parking lot as Felix had just done. Nor had any of their kisses ever affected her all the way down to the soles of her feet as his had done for the second time in two days, either. And that was what terrified her.

    As Felix slid into the car and started its six-cylinder engine after strapping himself into the driver's seat, Rachel had to fight the urge to scream. She wanted to run. She wanted to go back to the hotel. She wanted Felix to take her back to the hotel so that she could hide behind George's skirts, beg him to make it better—stop that crazy shaking that had erupted inside her body from his best friend's unexpected assault on her mouth with his. Yet contrarily, instead of telling Felix to take her back to the Amber Heights Hotel, she heard herself smilingly agreeing to his suggestion that they go pick up the pictures she had dropped off for developing at the photo shop the evening before, as well as drop off for developing what film she had spent taking pictures that day.

    Her smile sobered as again like the evening before, she stared at Felix from the corner of her eye as he began to steer them away from the University and on to a connecting street. Again like the evening before there was that indomitable calmness to his expression, as if having kissed her hadn't affected him in the least. But then, why should that bother her? After all, Felix had made it quite clear the evening before that he was not interested in a romantic entanglement. Again getting the point Rachel quickly gained control of her inner shaking and terror, attributing the kiss Felix had planted on her a normal response from an all-American red-blooded man to an equally all-American red-blooded woman that he himself had said was beautiful.

In fact, she was completely composed when they arrived at Stewart's Photo Shop downtown several minutes later. Rachel prided herself on her ability to keep her head under tense situations and in fact, nothing gave away the momentary disturbance Felix's kiss had brought her as he strode around the front of the car to see her from the passenger side. Nor was there the slightest reaction from the feel of his hand curving around hers in his usual gentlemanly gesture in seeing her into the photo shop, however disturbing she still found his touch. Instead, like Felix, Rachel was the picture of cool and calm as she stepped up to the counter to buy another couple rolls of film for use for the next day, picked up the pictures developed from the film rolls she had dropped off the day before, and dropped off the rolls she had shot that day for developing to be picked up the following day as well.

Having paid for the new couple rolls of Kodak 35mm color print film as well as the four packets of developed film a moment later, Rachel opened the first one and began to pore through the color prints. Again she prided herself on the calm she exuded as she opened the first packet and Felix moved in to look through it with her, his closeness distracting her as usual. And as she did so, she couldn't help wondering yet again how the man had been so unaffected by a kiss that had practically devastated her. Taking her mind off him altogether, Rachel turned her attention to the 35mm prints she was pulling from the packet in her hand.

However, her intention to ignore him wasn't going to be as easy as she'd hoped as the first color print came up into her hands. It was the third picture that she had taken the day before, that of the William Seward statue in front of Old City Hall, the one that she and Felix had gotten into a good-natured argument over as to whether to use the zoom lens or not. Well, Rachel should have listened to him. In her determination not to use the telephoto lens and her inexperience in handling the new camera, all she had managed to get of William Seward in the shot was the top of his head and one of his ears.

Despite her intention to play it cool, Rachel laughed at her blunder, a laughter Felix joined in as he saw it at the same time.

"You mean to tell me that after that whole argument we went through to get you to take this shot, you missed it, altogether?" he exulted.

"I guess so!" Rachel howled similarly amid gazing regretfully at the ruined picture in her hand. "Anyway, good-bye, William Seward . . . !"

"I guess so!" Felix agreed amid struggling to get hold of his own amusement. "See, I told you to use the zoom lens!"

Deliberately Rachel ignored the mocking note that lingered in his attractive tone as she gazed up at him to find him smiling down at her gently. The man was so damned sexy that she found herself responding to him despite herself. Her heart raced in her breast at the disturbing proximity of his too virile body standing on brown walking boots in the floor next to her.

She decided to counter yet another physical reaction to his closeness by returning her brown gaze to the pictures in her hands. Both to hers and Felix's delight, they all looked good—including the black and white ones Rachel had taken at the Alaska Zoo after running out of color film the afternoon before. That is, they all looked good with the exception of one, and that was the color picture she had taken through the car window of the man and woman pushing the baby carriage as they had sped past them on C Street. Rachel had expected that shot to be blurred and in fact, it was so out of focus that she asked the cashier to discard it into the trash behind the counter along with the shot one of William Seward.

The pictures she had taken at the Anchorage Museum of History and Art were exceptional, those of the Native dancers that she had shot performing in the auditorium there, those of other historic contemporary Alaskan art, including the shot of the Gold Rush that Felix had snapped after taking the camera from her hands in a feigned act of annoyance in the Alaska Gallery. And in fact, Rachel was surprise to see just how well the shot of the Gold Rush had come out in color when considering how she had longed to take the stark black and white reproduction in the same monochromatic tones. The pictures she had taken off the Tony Knowles Coastal Trail were exceptional as well, those of Cook Inlet's edge, the vast beluga whale-filled waters of Knik Arm, the grand vistas of Mount Susitna and Mount McKinley and the Alaska Range seen in the distance—all of which she had also taken at Point Woronzof at the Trail's end. And there were the fabulous shots she took at the Alaska Aviation Heritage Museum, those of an historic Fairchild American Pilgrim, a 1944 Noorduyn Norseman, and a 1928 Stearman C2B, the first plane to land on Mt. McKinley back in 1932—not to mention a number of others of the thirty vintage aircraft explaining Alaska's unique aviation history.

Rachel found herself staring at one particular photograph she had taken of Grant McConachie, aviation pioneer who built CP Air, later known as Canadian Airlines, and a furrow knitted her perfect brow.

"You know," she began to Felix, still standing aside her also poring through the packets of pictures, "now that I think about it, this guy looks like a boy who was in my archery class. Boy, I wonder whatever happened to him!" Rachel looked away in consternation, brows still knitted as she reflected on the old classmate she hadn't thought of in years.

Unaware was she that Felix had turned a surprised look down on her at her mention of the word archery. "When did you take archery?" he asked curiously.

"During P.E., when I was in the tenth grade."

"You took archery in the tenth grade? I took archery in the tenth grade!" Felix exclaimed.

Rachel turned an incredulous look on the attractive sexy features that met the similar look he'd turned on her. "You took archery, too?" she demanded, shocked that they had yet another thing in common.

"Yeah . . . ! I've kept it up ever since! I'm a pretty good aim!"

"Really . . . ? I've kept it up, too! I'm a pretty good aim, myself!"

"No kidding!" Felix mused.

"No kidding!" Rachel insisted, still pinning the golden brown face with her incredulous look.

However, Felix's look of disbelief was slowly beginning to morph into one of his usual amusement. "I wonder if there's a bow hunting shop around here, somewhere. We can get some archery equipment, go to a park, and put your little butt to the test!"

"I wouldn't do that if I were you," Rachel said in dissuading tones, incredulous look becoming serious on his handsome, sexy features. "You may be able to ice skate better than me, but like I said, I'm a pretty good shot with a bow and arrow. If I'd have had a set with me at Chugach State Park today, that grizzly we encountered wouldn't have had a chance. I'd have shot that sucker at a hundred yards. You give me a bow and arrow, and I'll shoot it right through your heart."

"I've a feeling you're going to do that, anyway," Felix said to her surprise, softening the remark with a smile. "Come on," he slid the color prints back into their packets in tune with her, "let's get out of here. I'm hungry. Let's go find some dinner."

And sliding the packets into the bag with the newly purchased rolls of color film that she held in one hand in tune with her doing the same with hers, Felix took her other hand in his and led her from the shop, his touch sending a wave of pleasure dancing up Rachel's arm as usual.

He took her to the Sweet Pink Pepper restaurant on South Bragaw Street. It was located in the midtown area and was Korean. Rachel had never been to a Korean restaurant in her life, and she wondered who had brought Felix there in the week that he had preceded her arrival in Anchorage to know of its existence. Yet as he settled her at a table in the sparsely furnished place which she could see for herself was one of the city's local hot spots, she decided not to care who Felix had been cavorting with in her delight of her discovery of the tab size. Like the restaurant's name, the prices were sweet and Rachel knew they wouldn't exactly break her pocketbook. And she needed that after all the money she'd had to shell out at the photo shop in order to pay for all her processing, not to mention buy new film for the next day's picture taking.

She settled on the Won Ton Soup followed by the Mongolian Beef Plate while Felix tried the Hot and Sour Soup followed by the Sweet and Sour Pork. No alcohol was served there, so Rachel followed her meal with a Coca Cola while he followed his with a Sprite. Oh, well, Felix had said he'd had no intention of taking her anywhere where she could get a drink! Rachel guessed he had been serious!

By the time they left the restaurant sometime later, it was pushing seven twenty. The look Rachel turned on the good looking sexy features as they walked slowly side-by-side to the parking lot was a mixture of her usual gratitude and regret.

"Well, thanks again for a lovely day, Felix," she said with a smile. "It got kind of rough in places, considering that close call we had with the grizzly at Chugach State Park, but it had a rather nice ending. But it's time we got back to the hotel, now. I've got tons of pamphlets and brochures that I have yet to read over about this place, not to mention you told George this morning that you were not going to keep me out late."

The usual smile slid onto Felix's attractive slender mouth at her mention of George. "You know I'm not studying about your brother," he said.

Her heart jumped into her throat when his somewhat mocking gaze lowered from the outraged look that had slid into hers and settled on her mouth. It was a look so intent that Rachel couldn't miss it, sending a sensation knocking down her spine that nearly stopped her in the slow approach they were making on the car. And as a strange heat began to suffuse her face in harmony with that equally strange sensation, Rachel looked abruptly away in the distance, determined never again to let that man kiss her. Not when his kisses shook her up the way they did while barely leaving him fazed.

To add to her disturbance was the feel of Felix's hand as it suddenly curved around hers, sending a sensation in tune with the other two dancing up her arm.

"Come on," he began in his attractive tenor, "I have somewhere else I want to show you." And guiding her over to the tan Pontiac Grand Prix a short distance down the parking lot, Felix saw her into the passenger seat.

He took her across town to the Bear Tooth Theatre Pub on W. 27th Avenue, where the parking was terrible, though he somehow managed to steer the Pontiac into a spot toward the back of the lot. Rachel's brown eyes were narrowed in their usual surprise as she watched Felix slide from the driver's side and then come around the front of the car to help her from her passenger's seat.

"Felix," she began curiously as she stepped from the car with his assistance of a gentlemanly hand, black strap of her purse already slung over her shoulder, "what is this place?"

"Exactly what the name implies—it's the Bear Tooth Theatre Pub. It's a theatre that comes complete with a Pub that offers beer and wine and a full menu in addition to popcorn and candy."

"I see." Confusion still clouded her eyes as she watched him close the passenger door behind her and then lock all doors with the automatic locking device on his key ring. "But Felix, we just came from eating at a restaurant. If you wanted to go see a movie, why didn't we just go to a more conventional theatre like those we saw at the Dimond Center last night?" Not that Rachel needed that memory!

"They play second-run Hollywood fare, classic movies and art films here," Felix explained as he dropped the key ring into the lower front pocket of his tan Levi's.

"Oh, I see." Rachel fell silent as he began to lead her hand-in-hand past a number of parked cars and SUVs toward the theatre in the near distance. She should have known the place would appeal to him, being a lover of the classics as he was.

"This place opened here a few years ago in what was formerly the old Denali Theatre," Felix said informatively.

"Really . . . ?"

"Yes. Its owners also operate a brewing company and pizzeria in town—called I think, the Bear Tooth and Moose Tooth. Both the Bear Tooth and Moose Tooth are named for peaks in the nearby Alaska Range."

"Oh, I didn't know that." Rachel felt stupid and wondered how that apparently fabulous brain of his could retain so much knowledge about an area and places that he had only learned about little over a week earlier.

Inside the Bear Tooth Theatre Pub at the ticket box office just beyond the entrance, Felix paid the small fee for two tickets to see the classic showing for the evening, a time during which Rachel glanced about her surroundings. The lobby was quite spacious, had an Alaskan theme and came complete with a seventy-seat casual dining area and a full-service kitchen. Felix had not lied when he'd said the movie house provided a full menu, for they offered pizza, burritos, tacos, salads, appetizers, homemade desserts, espresso, smoothies and draft sodas, in addition to the more traditional popcorn and candy. And with the exception of pizza by the slice, most food items were prepared fresh on order. Not that Rachel was hungry for anything, although she wouldn't have minded having a slice of carrot cake only if her already sated appetite were more obliging.

Inside the main floor of the theatre after showing their tickets and ID, Rachel's surprise increase was considerable. Unlike the conventional theatre with row after row of cramped movie seats, every other row was occupied with tables, providing the perfect place to stretch out your legs, eat or set a red or white wine or one of an assortment of Moose Tooth beers on tap at the bar there. A single screen dominated the movie house, which was far smaller than Rachel was used to, what with a main floor space of only two hundred and seventy five seats. However, an attractive balcony offered additional seating of one hundred and twenty five, giving the theatre a seating capacity of four hundred altogether. A section of the auditorium was for under-21 seating, and to hear Felix tell it, the theatre also featured live entertainment as well.

Her amazement was reflected in the look she turned on him as she settled in one of the spacious movie chairs that he was guiding her to and himself in the one beside her.

"This place is great!" Rachel exclaimed softly over other children and people talking and eating and/or drinking in the family-friendly theatre. "How'd you ever find this place?"

"Another couple of the hotel's employees brought me here my first day here after I casually mentioned my love for the classics," Felix explained in his attractive tenor. "I think we saw *A Farewell To Arms* from 1957 starring Rock Hudson that evening. Or rather, that was my intention. All my new friends had wanted to do was to get me in the dark and see how fast they could have me stretched out over one of these tables."

Rachel looked briefly away from the joking grin that had accompanied his last remark, her expression one of dry amusement. Well, he wouldn't have to worry about that from her.

"Which reminds me," she began instead, turning back to look at him, "barring the wedding rehearsal you were at last Saturday, have you been at the hotel any in the eleven days since you arrived here Sunday before that?"

"Hey, what can I say? I'm just like you. I want to see as much of this Alaska as you do. And as a result of that, aside from that day, I've barely seen the place. Besides, I was there this past Monday when you saw me," Felix half teased.

"Uhm-hmm." Unlike his mouth which was still curved in a grin, Rachel's own was only a tolerant line as for the second time that day she recalled the two groupies that had been on his arms upon his return to the hotel. Abruptly she changed the subject. "So, what are we going to see here tonight, anyway?"

"Fortunately, the offering doesn't go all the way back to the fifties or behind. Instead, they're having a showing of *Sophie's Choice*, from 1982. You're going to love it. It takes place in 1947 Brooklyn, and stars Meryl Streep. The movie won a Golden Globe Award for best picture, which garnered Streep an Academy Award for best actress in a drama."

Rachel didn't doubt that for a minute as she sat there amazed by his memory of the facts about such an old movie as well as being personally aware of the white star's skills as an actress.

"You know, I saw her a few years ago with Clint Eastwood in *Bridges Of Madison County*. She was good in that movie. My girlfriends and I rented it out on one of those 'let's go rent some videos, and go home and binge until we heave' Saturday afternoons!" Rachel laughed.

Felix laughed softly as well at the funny remark, an arm curling around her chair back in a deliberate proprietorial action. "Girl, you are a trip!" he said before his laughter sobered into a smile. "But it was a good movie, wasn't it?" he agreed, mind reflecting back on the subject. "I saw that movie when it came out in the theatre all those years ago. As Meryl and Clint started slow dancing in the kitchen, the whole theatre fell silent as everybody sat waiting—waiting—for something to happen between them. I mean, you could literally have heard a pin drop on the carpeting behind the sexual tension flying off the screen between the two actors. Yea, you're right, Streep is good. She's had a stellar movie career, with the exceptions of three movies she did that I couldn't adapt to—*Adaptation*, last year's *Prime*, and a particular dud she starred in with Goldie Hawn called *Death Becomes Her*. The movie was a basic black comedy with Streep playing a woman who discovered an immortality treatment and then tried to outdo her rival, Hawn, who along with lover Streep's husband, then schemed to kill her, but she came back to life. And even though it got a good rating, and showed Streep's stretch as a comic actress, when her head spun around on her neck after it stretched eerily up away from her shoulders like that, in addition to all that water pouring out of the massive hole in Hawn's gut, I'm telling you, I didn't like it."

"I see." Again Rachel fell silent at his worn sigh as she imagined such a sight. Although she knew who Goldie Hawn was and was acquainted with some of her works, she had not seen the movie he had just mentioned her starring in with Streep, nor did she know in her young life when it had come out. "So, who else is in this movie, *Sophie's Choice?*" she returned to their former subject.

Felix's lips curved back into a smile beneath the one she had turned on him to coax him out of his sudden despondency. "Well now, let's see—Peter MacNichol is in it. You may have seen him on the current TV drama *24*, as well as the recent drama *Numb3rs* and the less recent drama, *Ally McBeal*. And Kevin Kline makes his screen debut in this movie, which garnered him a Golden Globe nomination for best new male film star. He's gone on to do countless movies since then, such as *The Pirates of Penzance, The Big Chill, I Love You To Death, Consenting Adults, As You Like It, The Hunchback of Notre Dame I & II, French Kiss, Life As A House, The Pink Panther—*"

"Kevin Kline was in *French Kiss?*" Rachel stared in surprise at his mention of the one movie title she took exception to. "You, know, I saw that movie. Meg Ryan was in that movie, wasn't she? My girlfriend Sydney is a Meg Ryan freak! She's seen everything the woman's done!"

Again Felix showed his perfect teeth in a laugh as he derived amusement from her last couple of remarks. "You have some weird girlfriends, don't you!" he teased.

"I guess so!" Rachel agreed, showing her own perfect teeth in a laugh.

Silence ensued between them as the lights lowered then, indicating the start of the movie. The story of *Sophie's Choice* takes place in 1947 Brooklyn just as Felix had said, and is told through the eyes of aspiring writer Stingo, Peter MacNichol's character. Stingo is a Virginia-born writer who moves into a New York City boardinghouse and strikes a friendship with Sophie Zawistowska, Meryl Streep's character, and her boyfriend Nathan Landau, portrayed by Kevin Kline, Stingo's upstairs neighbors. Nathan is a biological researcher, Sophie is a recent immigrant to the United States, and Stingo meets them during one of Nathan's violent lashings-out against Sophie, which plays out on the main staircase of the apartment. As soon as Rachel learned that Sophie was a survivor of WWII concentration camp Auschwitz by the serial number tattooed in her forearm and the slash scars on her wrists, she knew immediately that she was going to hate the movie. But as it quickly evolved into an eccentric and intense love triangle between the three characters, Rachel couldn't help but sit transfixed by Meryl Streeps' carefully shaded performance and perfect accent as a Polish woman. And as she shows through sincere and occasionally heartbreaking flashbacks the pain Sophie went through during her time in Auschwitz, including her servitude in a German Admiral's house, Rachel knew she was going to love that movie forever. In fact, in accord with that, all she could do was sit staring at the screen with a whole new appreciation for the Holocaust once the movie finally came to an end two and a half hours later.

"Ba-Baby," she began to Felix as she moved to her feet to follow him from the theatre along with the rest of the departing audience, "that was good. That woman was worth every ounce of that Academy Award she won for that performance! And Peter MacNichol—whom I've never seen—was charming in his role of the writer who sees her first as a source of literary material and then, falls in love with her! And Kevin Kline was positively evil in his undisciplined performance as Streep's enraged lover! Now I see why he got that Golden Globe nomination as male newcomer that year. He was such a bastard compared to the character he played in *French Kiss*—! He was positively sweet in the gentleness he showed to Meg Ryan's character, talking to her on the plane where they first met, deliberately getting her angry so that she forgot about her fear of flying, and then spending the rest of the movie trying to help her get over the stupid fiancé who jilted her for another woman and who she was flying all the way to Paris—Kevin's character's birthplace—to try and get back, by the way—only to end up falling in love with her himself and her with him. The man was positively sweet! His range between the two movies is incredible!"

"See, what'd I tell you?" Felix smiled at her awe and appreciation of the white man's acting ability as they crossed the lobby behind a number of other people likewise talking amid filing out of the theatre. "Kline is a truly versatile actor. In fact, he's even done Shakespeare. And he showed that in his portrayal of Bottom in Shakespeare's *A Midsummer Night's Dream* that he did several years ago. But then, you know how popular the Bard's become these days. You remember that movie *Shakespeare In Love* that came out years back starring Joseph Fiennes and Gwyneth Paltrow, not to mention Romeo and Juliet that came out also starring Claire Danes and Leonardo DiCaprio? And Denzel Washington was positively wonderful in his portrayal of the lovingly charming and self-assured Prince Don Pedro in *Much Ado About Nothing*. Lawrence Fishburn did Shakespeare's *Othello;* in fact, even Keanu Reeves of *Speed* and *The Lake House* fame was in the same Shakespearean piece of *Much Ado About Nothing,* as Washington where he portrayed the evil-plotting character of Don John. And despite the fact that while some say he played John like a real movie villain, some critics panned him as the worst actor ever to portray a Shakespearean character. But you know who I think was the best actor to play a Shakespearean character? Barring Lawrence Olivier, Richard Burton, Kenneth Branagh, and his recent trouble of late, was Mel Gibson in *Hamlet.*"

Rachel didn't even try and hide her surprise as they spilled out into the slightly cooling evening, luminous brown eyes wide on the attractive features turned down on her in the lingering daylight.

"Mel Gibson did *Hamlet?*" she demanded. "Mel Gibson from *Bird On A Wire* with Goldie Hawn whom you just mentioned, a movie which came out a hundred years ago and which has been played frequently over the air ever since? Mel Gibson, who played comedy to perfection in that movie portraying a man who was in the Witness Protection Program, but then, had to run for his life along with Goldie when his true identity was found out, did Shakespeare?" Rachel was incredulous as they began to move slowly away from the building. "You know, I couldn't get with that *The Passion Of The Christ* that he did a couple years ago, but I saw him in *What Women Want* with Helen Hunt. He played comedy to perfection in that movie also, portraying—what was it—an advertising executive who had an accident with a hair dryer in the bathtub that enabled him to read women's minds. And believe me, every woman he passed by thought something raunchy about him, too—including Loretta Divine, the black actress most recently of Boston Public fame who portrayed the door attendant of Mel's apartment building in the midst of hailing him a cab in the movie. And I will never forget that scene between Mel and Helen in her office, where she says to herself: *'Oh, my God, I'm looking at his chest! Oh, my God, I'm looking at his crotch!'*, or words to that effect, anyway. And Mel just stood there and grinned because he had read her mind! Anyway, Mel was positively charming in his pursuit of Helen—until he wound up in bed in that silly sex scene with Marisa Tomei. For me, the movie went downhill after that." Rachel sighed wearily, unaware that her lengthy critique of the Mel Gibson vehicle had stopped their leisurely walk before they could get one-eighth way down the parking lot.

"Yea, I guess all actors have their duds," Felix agreed in his attractive tenor, gazing respectfully down at her. "Mel's done some good movies, though. Did you ever see *Mad Max* and *Mad Max Beyond Thunderdome* that he did with Tina Turner back in the day? And then, there were all those *Lethal Weapon* installments he did with Danny Glover—another renowned actor in his own right. But like Meryl in her comedy portrayal in *Death Becomes Her*, Gibson showed his stretch as a dramatic actor in his rendition of the movie *Hamlet*. He put a spin on the Old Danish prince, giving him a fullness and clarity and delivering his famous soliloquies with a naturalness and emotion that the critics are still talking about today. Mel literally became Hamlet in that movie in the way he enabled the audience to completely comprehend each scene. These days, Gibson's doing it all, writing, acting, and directing."

"That's for sure!" Rachel agreed, although the smile she turned on the handsome face of the Daytime Emmy Award-winning soap actor was more of amazement than amusement. "You know, you must really want to go to Hollywood to know so much about all these actors' careers, both past and present," she said.

"Hey, it's like I told you, it's all I've ever wanted to do. As a result of that, I've followed their lives ever since I was a kid."

"I guess so," Rachel agreed, still smiling up at him and staring in amazement.

"As a matter of fact, while we're on the subject of Shakespeare, I'm reminded of one of his characters that I played on Broadway three years ago."

Although she tried not to show it, Rachel's gaze turned curious as she continued to walk slowly beside him down the parking lot. "Yea, you did tell me yesterday that you've done Broadway."

"Uhm-hmm." Felix's black-short-haired head bent in a nod. "The play ran for nine weeks. I performed it nights while working on the soap days—you know, just like I told you. As a matter of fact, I still remember some of the dialogue. *'O, she is ten times more gentle than her father's crabbed; and he's composed of harshness!'*" he said with dramatic license, showing off for her benefit. *"'I must remove some thousands of these logs and pile them up, upon a sore injunction. My sweet mistress weeps when she sees me work, and says such baseness had never like executor. I forget; but these sweet thoughts do even refresh my labors most busy least, when I do it—'"*

"'Alas, now pray you work not so hard! I would the lightning had burnt up those logs that you are enjoined to pile! Pray, set it down and rest you. When this burns, some thousands of these logs and pile them up, 'twill weep for having wearied you. My father is hard at study: pray now rest yourself. He's safe for these three hours.'" Rachel gazed up at Felix with an amused grin as she filled in the response that followed his partial delivery, already having anticipated the shocked look he turned on her.

"You know Shakespeare's *The Tempest?*" he demanded with a surprise that had stopped them in their tracks.

"I'm afraid so," Rachel affirmed smilingly to his increased shock.

"When did you learn Shakespeare's *Tempest?*"

". . . During my senior year in college. My English professor was a Shakespeare nut. But rather than do the usual stuff such as *Othello, Romeo and Juliet, King Lear* and *Macbeth* and *Julius Caesar* and *Hamlet* that I studied in high school, he thought he'd work us out on one of Shakespeare's later works, *The Tempest*. It's sort of a tragicomedy that takes place in of course, seventeenth-century England. That dialogue that you and I just had took place in Act Three, Scene One of the play, between Ferdinand, your character, and Miranda, my own, with Prospero looking on unseen. I know that because for weeks, my English professor grilled it into my head that Prospero, the former Duke of Milan who had lost his throne through an act of betrayal by his brother Antonio, had commanded Ferdinand, Alonso's son the King of Naples, to pile firewood for him, unaware that Miranda would attempt to assist him. Miranda and Ferdinand are young lovers and Prospero, whose plan is to regain political power through a dynastic marriage between their two ruling families of Naples and Milan, watches with delight as Ferdinand and Miranda's affection for one another grows and they proclaim their love. The man was on my case for weeks. I had to learn the entire Act and Scene, and then do a dissertation on the whole thing. If I forget everything else in my life, I will never forget that Act, which closes with Miranda pushing Ferdinand to answer to the promise of marriage directly, a deal that they seal with a handshake—not a kiss—a symbol of the purity of their love."

Felix blinked his long-lashed eyes at her in deepening surprise at the staggering accuracy with which she had nailed the entire scene. "Let me get this straight—at the same time I was performing this play on Broadway three years ago, you were studying it as a college senior? Why have you done everything I've done?"

"I don't know, honey," Rachel laughed, equally amazed as he at yet another thing they had in common. "But one thing I do know is we need to get back to the hotel." A brief glance at her watch confirmed the time. "It's ten thirty five. I'd like to show George the pictures I took yesterday, and if we get back to the hotel now, we just might catch him before he goes to bed. And with any luck, he won't be furious with the both of us for staying out way past ten, yet again."

"Uh-uhh . . . !" Felix shook his head in a bold negation. "That's it. Forget George. I'm taking you dancing with me, girl. I want to see if you're as good on the dance floor as you are at everything else I do!"

And pointedly curving a hand around her wrist, Felix began to pull her speedily the rest of the way down the parking lot to the car, leaving her hair and black purse strapped to her shoulder barely able to keep up with her. Again Rachel stared after him in surprise as she wondered where he was going to take her now.

He took her to a midtown nightclub called Club Oasis on Old Seward Highway, where Rachel had already noticed that a number of clubs stretched out over a short distance. However, this club was different, in that it came with an on-site ATM machine plus its own liquor store! There was a pool table, there was a pinball arcade, and there was golf and an area sealed off to play darts. Plus the club—which to hear Felix tell it opened in 1981 and was the coolest hot spot in Anchorage—was filled to the brim with locals—the black, the white and the Indian—in proof of that. In fact, Rachel wondered what all those people were doing in a nightclub as late as ten forty five on a Wednesday night while at the same time wondering if they worked during the day.

Some fast Kelly Clarkson was rocking through the house as a disc jockey threw down from a concealed area. Curiously Rachel turned to Felix to speak over the loud playing of the tune by the former American Idol winner.

"How do you know about this place?"

"Your brother George brought me here last Wednesday," Felix explained softly over the white woman's singing. "I somehow managed to talk him away from that 'jungle fever' thing he's got going on with Stacey long enough to take me somewhere where we could get into a little 'dance fever'!"

"I see." Rachel's smile lacked the amusement in his, as she had not understood his reference to an old TV show that had come on before her time.

With the smile dwindling from her lips and one hand clutching her purse strap to her shoulder, Rachel let Felix escort her over to the full-sized bar, an act that surprised her, as he had been so against the idea of her having a drink earlier in the day. Yet her surprise was short-lived as he simply ordered a Coke, forcing her to do the same. Rachel laughed at his intention of keeping nothing alcoholic from hampering her coordination when he put her dancing skills to the test.

Having paid for the couple of sodas a moment later in a gesture that renewed her surprise, Felix led her away from the bar and over to a vacant table they just managed to find not too far away from the dance floor. As Rachel settled at the table and Felix to the right of her, she took a sip of her Coca Cola and gazed about her surroundings. Again she was reminded of the oft-claimed shortage of women in Alaska as a number of men occupied several tables to the right of her. Plus three of them had noticed her—black men whose leering eyes were taking her in from the top of her swept up off-black hair all the way down to what they could see of her figure over the top of her table. Already having expected her good looks to stand out in the attractive dimness of the nightclub, Rachel forced a smile over her drink and looked away, not in the least bit interested in being a pick-up.

However, the fact that she had not yet seen any women nearby didn't mean none were there, for they wore. As her black-mascara-lashed gaze swept around the club in the opposite direction, it showed her three black women staring from an equally nearby table. But they were not looking at her, they were looking at Felix, possibly the sexiest black man in America that they had ever seen, in their opinions, Rachel guessed. Plus, a white woman stood watching him from a side wall as well, a big mama, eyeing him as though he were a generous piece of steak that she was undoubtedly more than used to having on her plate. Rachel wondered if the four women had recognized him from his soap opera or were simply responding to an attractive man seated near them in the short distance.

She laughed suddenly when Felix spun around from the opposite direction, saw the big platinum blond woman eyeing him as though he were a meal she were about to consume, and quickly turned around in his seat, shock sliding over his handsome features.

"You know, when you get to Hollywood, I think you'd best put that brown paper bag I told you about over your head and go as the Unknown Movie Star," Rachel teased over the half drunk Coke she held to her lips.

"I guess so." Felix managed a smile of agreement as he raised the half drunk Coke he held in his hand back to his own lips. "And you know I couldn't handle all that, no matter how much woman she thinks she might be for a man."

The lip of her cup hid the smile that still played about hers as Rachel watched him down the rest of the Coke in his own cup. "Well, don't get too relaxed, there are three more behind us looking at you the same way."

Felix's dancing brown eyes slid in the direction she had gestured with the cool angling of her head, saw the three black women eyeing him with the same intensity of the big white woman behind him and the smile curving his lips became a sheepish one.

"Oh, yeah, they are looking at me, aren't they?" Felix asked unnecessarily, lowering his empty Coke cup to the white napkin placed on the table in front of him. "So, put that silly drink down, girl," he grinned, "it's time for you to show me what you can do." Having moved to his feet, he curled a hand around hers and pulled her to hers, causing her to do just as he had ordered. "Besides, you promised me that you were going to keep close to me in order to keep all these women away from me. You saw how they were at the Auditorium at the University of Alaska at Anchorage this afternoon."

"So long as you promise to keep those three men over there away from me . . . !" Rachel reminded him laughingly as did Felix the same amid drawing her away from the table.

A fast techno tune by Pink was sounding through the nightclub from concealed speakers, one of two that had followed the Kelly Clarkson song that had played upon their arrival. As Felix found them a place on the dance floor that had thinned slightly during their presence there, Rachel slung her black purse crosswise over her breasts and let herself come swept up in the new wave tune. She determined to show Felix exactly what she could do as she flailed her arms to the side, did the bump and grind and gyrated her body in every current dance she could think of, her long off-black ponytail bobbing prettily over her shoulders. And she was surprised to see that Felix was not a bad dancer, himself, twisting his six-foot-one-inch well-built frame in a number of attractive gyrations that easily kept up with her. The soap actor could move. He had definitely been in some dance clubs in New York.

Rachel was doing something between the hustle and the rock when Felix suddenly leaned forward in the space between them and tapped her on her white sweater-clad shoulder.

"Hey, girl," he began with a grin, himself doing something between the skate and the bump, "with only those four decent dates you've had in the last three years, how'd you learn to dance like that?"

"I've always been able to dance," Rachel said over the sound of the loud music without stopping one second in the floor. "Before I started dating, I would go downstairs and dance to whatever music my parents had in their collection, not to mention the latest tunes I'd managed to get them to buy for me. It's something I've kept up ever since. These days, my girlfriends and I hit the clubs often on Saturday nights. We pick up a hundred men in those places. They teach us the latest dance crazes. Of course, we realize they're only after one thing. Leave 'em at the door on our way out."

The grin broadened in the attractive rectangular golden brown face as Felix derived amusement from her shameless last remark. "You're just a tease!" he said.

"I guess so!" Rachel agreed.

"Anyway, like the song says, girl, I like *'the way you move'*," he said with an impressed smile.

"You're not so bad, yourself," Rachel praised, while at the same time smiling her delight at the way he had praised her with his usage of/and mention of the OutKast tune.

And the fast tunes came on—a mixture of hip/hop, pop, rock, and R&B that kept them on the floor for at least forty five minutes. They did the 'bootylicious' to

Beyoncé, they 'work'ed it' to Missy 'Misdemeanor' Elliott, they 'got low' to Lil John & the East Side Boyz, and then they 'dipped it low' some mo' to Christina Milian. They 'got busy' to Sean Paul, they 'rocked their bodies' to Justin Timberlake, they 'got it twisted' to Mobb Depp and they 'got it together' to Seal. They got 'dirrty' to Christina Aguilera, got 'dirrty again'; and then they 'shook their tailfeathers' to Nelly and P. Diddy. They even danced to a fast Paul Oakenfold remix of Elvis Presley's *Rubberneckin'*. In fact, Rachel thought Felix was going to have a stroke in his delight at hearing the remake of the old King's tune.

Then the hot dance mixes came to a stop as the disc jockey slowed the pace in the nightclub by putting on a slow romantic ballad by Tamia. Rachel went smilingly into Felix's arms, grateful for the slow dance; for she needed it in order to cool down from her exertion brought on by the long rush of hot dance mixes. Yet predictably her blood pressure and pulse rate shot up while her heart knocked in her chest in immediate response to the sensation that tore through her at this too disturbing proximity of his virile sexy body supporting hers. Rachel determined to ignore all of those as she lowered her chin against his broad brown shoulder and let her brown gaze fan out over the number of couples moving in the floor around them.

Incredibly, Felix was a smooth ride as a slow drag partner. He carried her easily around in his arms, his lack of command lulling her senses away from his raw sex appeal until she found her blood pressure and pulse rate slowly beginning to return to normal along with her respiration. And Rachel needed that, for he made no effort to let go of her. Instead, Felix continued to twirl her around to the number of slow ballads that followed the Tamia tune. And with a continued lack of demand on his part, Rachel became so relaxed that pretty soon a strange sense of euphoria began to envelop her, sapping her of every inhibition she normally kept in place in order to keep men at a safe distance.

In harmony with that, about twenty minutes into the set and to a slow romantic tune by Ashanti, Rachel started to do something she hadn't expected to do. She started noticing things about Felix in response to the sensation still racing along her nerves. For instance, the way the hard line of his body fit against the soft curve of hers from the wall of his chest pressing against her breasts all the way down to his tan Levi's clad thighs rubbing against her white Wrangler clad ones, the cozy warmth of his embrace, the feel of his strong arms holding her, his equally strong hands moving gently to and fro across her back in tune to the slow beat of the sultry tune they were dancing to. By the same token, her hands were moving over him, exploring the work-out tautened lines of his waist and back, the broad ridge of his shoulder, the inviting warmth of the flesh at the back of his neck just above the collar of the brown and tan plaid shirt he wore beneath his brown sweatshirt. And she wondered how a man with all he had going for him could still be unattached at thirty one. In fact, that thought was on her mind as she raised her face away from his shoulder and let her brown gaze pore endlessly over his too good looking rectangular face with its too good looking features and too good looking short kinky black hair.

"You know, you are just too gorgeous for your own good," Rachel said after a moment, smiling up at him. "Forget all that stuff you said at the Park today about living single, and forget about all those hussies coming all onto you at the University of Alaska at Anchorage this afternoon—why hasn't some lucky woman snatched you up somewhere?"

Felix smiled over her shoulder at the question she already knew the answer to. "So, now you think I'm gorgeous, as well as a fine specimen of a man?"

"Why not . . . ?" Rachel asked carelessly in response to the teasing question. "Every other woman does. Besides, you think I'm beautiful."

"And a fine specimen of a woman, like every other man does," Felix added, smiling down at her. "But let me tell you something, beautiful, fine specimen of a woman, if you don't stop groping me like you've been doing for the last ten minutes, I'm going to be all over you in about three seconds. And I'm not talking about that silly scene with the grizzly at the Park this afternoon, for he's not going to be anywhere around, and I am going to be all over you."

"Really . . . !" Rachel maintained the careless tone as she smilingly returned the long-lashed dancing brown gaze twinkling down at her. "Well, let me tell you something, gorgeous, fine specimen of a man, if you don't stop groping me like you've been doing for the last ten minutes, I'm going to be all over you in four. And I'm not talking about that silly scene with the grizzly at the Park this afternoon, for he's not going to be anywhere around, and I am going to be all over you."

The smile broadened on Felix's lips in amusement at her bold nerve in applying every word of the teasing threat he'd made to her back to him, a threat he wondered if she meant beneath the smile of equal amusement that had broadened on hers.

And so it went throughout the duration of the slow set, which lasted at least another twenty minutes. They touched and stroked and caressed and groped and felt each other up. And no one dared intrude on them as they watched their shameless display from the sidelines of the dance floor and surrounding seating area.

They stayed in that nightclub until two fifteen in the morning, when they finally left, arriving back at the Amber Heights Hotel around two thirty. The wooly ribbed brown parka was pulled back on over Rachel's sweater-clad shoulders to protect her from the chill that had returned to the early morning summer Alaska air, the tan lined jacket that matched Felix's Levi's having been pulled back on over his sweatshirt-clad broader stronger ones as well. Rachel faced him with an expression of delight mixed with her usual gratitude and regret once he had seen her safely to the door of her eleventh floor suite.

"Well, thanks a lot, Felix, for a most elongated day," she smiled, black strap of her purse hanging from its usual perch from her left shoulder. "It's been a pleasure. But just like every good thing, I guess it, too, must come to an end."

"I guess so," Felix agreed, smiling softly down at her.

"I hope the concierge doesn't become too riled when he learns that that backpack and everything in it was lost to that grizzly after all the careful effort he put into preparing it for us," Rachel couldn't help interjecting reminiscently.

"Don't worry, he gets paid for his understanding and discretion," Felix said.

"I guess so," Rachel agreed, knowing he would know more about such things than she did in her limited knowledge about the discretionary capacities of employees at a hotel of the Amber Heights' caliber.

"Anyway, you won't have to worry about a grizzly being anywhere around tomorrow," Felix said. "I'm going to drive you out to meet a nice old Native Alaskan. He's sort of like a historian of the area."

Rachel stared in surprise at his mention of this old man, whose name he had yet to divulge. "How'd you meet this man?"

"Your brother introduced me to him."

The smile returned to the soft curve of her lips as Rachel took new pleasure from his mention of yet another activity enjoyed with George.

"I'm glad you and George have been doing some things together while you've been here," she said.

"Of course," Felix agreed smilingly before sobering slightly. "Anyway, since we're getting in so late, why don't you sleep in, and meet me for breakfast in the cafeteria in the morning at ten? We'll spend another day hiding from your brother."

"Man, you are a trip!" she laughed. Then thinking the joking remark a nice way to say goodnight, Rachel turned to unlock the door of her suite with the blue-tagged key she had pulled from her purse, only for a detaining hand to curve around her wrist, sending a wave of pleasure skittering up her arm all over again. Rachel hoped this didn't show as she turned curiously in the floor to gaze back at Felix, who still stood smiling down at her gently.

"Hey, girl," he began softly, "before you turn in, I just want to say that I, too, think that our most elongated day has been a pleasure. And I had a lot of fun with you at the club tonight. I really enjoyed what took place between us on the dance floor amid dragging to all those slow songs. Whatever the hell it was," Felix added in bewildered afterthought.

"You mean our touching, groping, flirting, playful banter, blatant compliments of each other and sex threats?" Rachel dared with a laugh.

"Uhm-hmm. But I think I'm going to enjoy this better."

Before Rachel could shrink back from realization of his intention, Felix had already pulled her against him, his hand having dropped hers as his arm sought the more intimate circle of her waist. She froze in the floor as his lips descended on hers in a most invasive kiss, for she knew it was going to shake her up, and it did. Indeed, it produced the usual physical reactions—a whole new wave of sensation went knocking down her spine all the way down to the soles of her feet in tune to the one that had been sliding up her arm, her throat threatened to close up as blood flowed into her neck, her face flamed, heat rushed over her skin. To make matters worse, the sound of her own blood threatened to deafen her as it pounded in her ears, having rushed speedily to her head.

Yet as the kiss lingered sensuously, all Rachel's physical reactions found expression. The frozen stiffness melted from her body, which then began to mold itself pliantly to the harder line of his, her arms slid around his neck in tune to the feel of his sliding around her waist along with his other one, her lips moved in sync with his as she satisfied an immediate urge to yield to his possession. And as her answering response deepened what was a very dizzying kiss, Rachel felt as if she were back at the nightclub being twirled around in Felix's arms. In fact, it was with much effort that she struggled to regain her equilibrium when he ended the kiss a second later to burrow his hot mouth amid the curve of her neck, an action that served only in upsetting her equilibrium further.

"Well, that wasn't bad," Rachel somehow managed over his shoulder while at the same time trying to keep the breathlessness out of her voice. "Or at least, I hope you didn't find it repulsive."

"Uh-uhh." Felix's head bobbed a negation against her neck. "I like kissing you."

"You do?"

"Uhm-hmm. As a matter of fact, ever since I kissed you at the restaurant the other day, I've wanted to kiss you ever since. Oh, I've tried to fight the desire," Felix went on amid raising his face from her neck and meeting her surprised stare, "as a matter of fact, when I kissed you at the ice skating rink the other night, I blew it off as inconsequential. I did the same thing when I kissed you at the University yesterday afternoon, telling myself I was only doing it to silence your silly laughter. But should the truth be told, I've spent the past four and a half hours after learning we have something else in common yet again fighting that same mad desire to kiss those lips of yours the way I just did. And just like I knew, I did enjoy it."

"I see. Well, I don't exactly feel insulted by your action," Rachel confided with a smile.

"I'm glad to hear that," Felix answered, smiling similarly. "Because girl, there are no grizzlies around, and if you don't hurry up and get in that suite, I'm going to be all over you in about two seconds."

And to give her an idea as to exactly what he meant, Felix lowered his lips against hers in one last invasive kiss before raising his face away from hers and dropping his arms from her body, forcing her to do the same.

"Anyway, you get some sleep, and I'll see you in the morning," Felix said, smile back on his lips as he strutted down the hall away from her.

And as Rachel stared after his departure a moment later, an amazed smile slid onto her own lips still tingling from his parting kiss. And here she'd thought the kisses between them had had no effect on him, when in fact, she'd had him the whole time.

Chapter Nine

She was roused out of her sleep several hours later to the sound of loud knocking coming from the door of her suite. Lazily Rachel glanced at the AM/FM clock radio set on her French Provincial nightstand, the earliness of the time succeeding in pulling her to full consciousness. She was not expected to meet Felix until ten, and yet, it was only eight o'clock! Who would be dropping by to see her at an hour as early as this—especially when she didn't manage to fall asleep until around five a.m., anyway! Then realizing it might be George stopping by to catch her before she and Felix got into the street again, Rachel rushed out of the bed, sped from the bedroom and quickly into the living room. She knew George was going to be furious at her for having allowed Felix to keep her away from the hotel for the entirety of the day before! As a result of that, she phrased several words in her mind that she could ply like a balm to his frayed nerves as she crossed the swanky blue-themed living room and curved her hand around the brass doorknob.

Yet incredibly, the person who stood on the other side of the white door once Rachel had opened it a second later turned out to be the cause of her delayed fall asleep.

"Good morning," he greeted in his attractive tenor, turning a cheery smile on her.

Rachel ignored both as well as the sudden quickening of her heartbeat as she unwittingly took in the length of him, sexy as ever in a navy lined parka and bib overalls pulled on over a navy and red plaid shirt.

"Felix, what are you doing here?" she asked in surprise. "I wasn't expecting to see you until ten o'clock. I thought you were in your suite sleeping!"

"Who could sleep? I may have told you to get some sleep, but all I did was lie in bed thinking about you all morning, along with a couple other things. Besides, I'm used to being up early. I have to be on the set at seven."

The entire response was absent as Felix's gaze had dropped to the length of her legs, the dancing brown eyes taking in the shapely curving dusky-colored limbs with a fascination that filled Rachel with faint embarrassment. And she wished she had slid on the white terry guest robe that came with the suite rather than arriving at the door in the simple blue thigh-length nightie she wore.

"Not bad!" Felix praised, smiling gaze returning to her face, surrounded by a long mass of tousled relaxed off-black hair. "You really grew up, Little Sister. But then, I noticed that, three days ago."

And cupping his hands to her face, he pulled her into a heated kiss which he ended a second later to gaze down at her. "Go wash up and get dressed so we can go get some breakfast," he ordered, dropping his hands from her face. "I'm about to starve."

And as he moved away on blue, black and white Reebok sneaker-clad feet to settle on one of the blue padded French Provincial loveseats across the lavish living room, Rachel couldn't stop the chord of surprise that struck through her. Barring the fact that Felix had confided earlier that morning that he liked kissing her after doing just that, for the first time in three days, Rachel saw the reason why. He was no longer hiding the fact that she disturbed him just as much as he did her, as it had flashed clearly from the dancing brown eyes as he had ended the kiss to look at her. The realization of that both delighted and terrified Rachel at the same time.

She didn't know how she managed to make it out of the living room with him sitting there watching her, except to say that Rachel found herself showering in the lavish tub and steam bath a moment later. And to think that she had spent almost three hours lying in bed unable to fall asleep that morning for remembering the couple invasive and very sensuous kisses Felix had given her before leaving her at her door. Now, he had just zinged her with another kiss, a most heated one, her mouth still throbbing from the force of it.

She pulled a fleecy denim heather sweatshirt and matching pants on over her underwear and her white Nikes sneakers on over heather blue crew sock-clad feet. Then Rachel turned her attention to her hair, carefully combing the sleep-snarled tangles out of its long straight off-black length and then sweeping it up into its usual ponytail, although she chose to pull it to the side for a change, letting it hang down over her breast from a knit navy band. The brushing of her well-aligned teeth with a minty paste followed, the sliding of gold hearts dangling from blue jeweled posts into the lobes of her ears, rich navy shadow over black mascara-lashed eyes, a burgundy blush over her dusky cheeks. Rachel didn't know why she was bothering with putting on lipstick, for she was either going to end up eating it off, or Felix was going to kiss it off—whatever. Yet she applied the raspberry color to her medium lips anyway, blotting the excess off with a white tissue from a box set to one side of her French Provincial dresser.

Moving to one side of the king-sized blue-print spread-covered bed a second later, Rachel picked her silver-toned watch up off the French Provincial nightstand and slid it onto her left arm, at the same time noting with regret that it was twenty minutes till nine. George and Stacey had started the day's work ten minutes ago. What must they be thinking about her and Felix, after not having seen them since yesterday morning at eight thirty, Rachel wondered? Realizing that she was simply going to have to go searching her brother out in the penthouse, she gathered up her purse, bag of camera, film and accessories, and parka and returned to the living room, aware that Felix awaited her there.

However, when Rachel put the idea of going in search of George to Felix upon joining him in the living room a second later, he regarded her with his usual nonchalance.

"You know I'm not studying about your brother," he said carelessly through one side of his slender mouth.

Rachel stared stealthily up at him from beneath her lashes as they took an elevator down to the first floor. He was holding her free hand in his as usual, its snug claim sending that warm pleasure sliding up her arm. Yet her regard for the confident sexy profile was not one of appreciation, but debasement. He was as crazy as George had once said he was in his complete disregard for the best friend whose wedding he would be standing in as best man in only two days. And Rachel realized that maybe she had gone a little too far in groping and petting and bantering with him at Club Oasis the night before the way she did—even though she did enjoy it, herself. Yet still the thought that he wanted to be with her to the complete neglect of his long-time friend staggered Rachel, as not only had she not expected to get under his skin—much less under it so thickly—but she had not expected to do it in such a short time.

However, in proof that she had done just that, Felix didn't even take her to the cafeteria once they had arrived on the first floor. And indeed, Rachel stared at him in confusion as he steered her quickly down the stripe-papered hall past it and in the direction of the lobby.

Her eyes remained on him in surprise once they had arrived in the chandelier and lamp-lit French Provincial outfitted lobby, swanky as ever in sophisticated shades of blue, brown, rust and autumn gold.

"Felix, where are we going?"

"I don't know, somewhere where we can be alone," Felix said carelessly amid escorting her through the large lobby and out the door held open by a red-uniformed doorman.

Outside despite the sunny weather, the temperature just like the day before hovered at thirty-eight degrees, making Rachel grateful for the thermal underwear she had pulled on under her clothes. But that was the last thing on her mind as she fixed Felix with a belittling glance as he slid in behind the wheel of the tan Pontiac Grand Prix after having seen her in on the passenger side.

"You know, you are crazy," she denounced him in mocking tones.

Felix's own tone was mocking as he slid into his seat belt in tune with her. "You know, I think Patsy Cline did that song," said the attractive tenor.

And as he looked smilingly away from her to start the engine of the car, Rachel's glance on him became another one of amazement. She should have known he would associate her description of him as *'Crazy'* with an old tune that came out in the sixties, what with being the lover of the classics that he was.

They wound up at the Sweet Basil Café on E Street not too far downtown from the Amber Heights Hotel. It was a colorful up-beat eatery and coffee shop across from the Anchorage Hotel—possibly the oldest in the city—with a somewhat metallic décor and pots of flowers and works of local artists displayed on its walls. Once there, Felix downed a huge breakfast of large waffles dolloped with fresh berries, scones, orange juice and coffee while Rachel enjoyed a three-egg omelet, also with a scone, orange juice and coffee. To add to her enjoyment: Felix paid for her meal for her. Rachel guessed she really had gotten under his skin, although she had yet to wonder how as they left the café hand-in-hand yet again some time later.

Then Felix drove her to the house of the man he had said he was going to take her to see earlier that morning. He lived in a residential trail-filled area with wide yards and quiet streets beyond the Dimond Mall Shopping Center in Anchorage's South district. Pockets of businesses dotted this residential area, one of several in the district that circled bodies of water such as Campbell Lake, which was also a floatplane runway. In fact, Rachel was surprised to see that many of the area's residents parked their floatplanes in their back yards there, and raised her camera to her face to take several attractive pictures of the area.

Her thoughts swayed instantly away from the floatplane-riddled runway of Campbell Lake as Felix suddenly appeared at her door. Discarding her camera to the carpeted floor beneath her feet, Rachel let him see her from the car, black bag strapped to her shoulder.

"So, who is this man, this old sort-of historian you've brought me here to meet? You haven't yet told me that."

Felix smiled over his shoulder at the curiosity underlining her composed tone amid pulling her from the white driveway and up to the white brick and wood frame two-story home.

"His name is Thacker Muldoon," he told her. "Your brother brought me here to meet him personally. He's just like you said—a historian of the area. George has even invited him to the wedding. Wait till you meet him, Rachel, he's crazy. He's eighty-eight years old and his wife's forty."

"Oh, my God . . . !" Rachel tried unsuccessfully to stifle a laugh as she thought of the yet unmet Thacker. The man must be quite robust to marry a woman less than half his age, especially when her sexual needs would be much more than a man of his declining years could handle.

However the amused laugh on her lips softened into an amazed smile when the owner of the house responded to Felix's knock against the carved wood door a second later. The black octogenarian who answered the door was not robust—quite the contrary—he was a small-boned wizened little man with short nappy gray hair framing an oval face creased in age lines. Although thankfully he still had all his own teeth, the white color slightly tinged with age providing a contrast to the dark tone of his skin as he grinned in recognition of his company.

"Felix!" the man began with unexpected exuberance, taking him into red-sleeved arms. "I wasn't expecting to see you until George's wedding on Saturday! How've you been doing since he brought you out here to meet me last week . . . !"

"Just great, Thacker!" Felix grinned equally as he dropped Rachel's hand to return the shorter man's hug. "And how have you been doing!"

"The same," said the man in a low-range voice that just like his exuberance, somehow did not match his age, its strength reverberating through the large house he busied himself seeing them into then. "So, what gives me the pleasure of having a man of your esteem come to visit me on a nice June Thursday morning?"

"I have someone here that I want you to meet." Having dropped his hands from the man's shoulders, Felix turned to face Rachel with a smile, curling an arm around her own shoulders to pull her forward. "Thacker, this is Rachel Hardison, and Rachel, Thacker Muldoon. Rachel is George's kid sister and will be a bridesmaid in his wedding on Saturday," Felix finished for Thacker's benefit, dropping his arm from her shoulders.

"How do you do, Mr. Muldoon?" greeted Rachel with a smile, extending a hand to shake his.

"Oh, Thacker, please!" insisted the octogenarian, his brown eyes twinkling on her in a look of flattery and incredulity as he took the hand she had proffered forward. "My God, you are George's sister, aren't you . . . ! You are as attractive as he is! Looks must run in your family!" The grin broadened on the old wrinkled face as he dropped her hand and let his twinkling gaze lower over her long hair, the provocative swell of her breasts beneath the ribbed wooly mud brown parka she wore over her denim heather pullover, the curve of her legs in the matching pants, all of which complimented her good looks. "Look Rachel," he said pointedly, "I'm eighty-eight years old, and I've been married four times. Do you want to be my fifth wife? Naw, on second thought, I'd better leave you alone. I don't think I could handle all of you. You'd be too much for me. You'd probably give me a heart attack. And I've already got one foot in the grave!"

Rachel managed a relieved laugh at the facetious last remark, which softened the blatant compliments underscoring the ones that had preceded it.

"That's terrible!" she said.

"Isn't it!" agreed the octogenarian. Laughing at his own wit, he saw her and Felix out of their wraps, which he hung into a guest closet just inside the front door.

"Rachel and I haven't seen each other in ten years," Felix told Thacker informatively as he led them into a large living room that branched off the wide foyer. "Can you believe that, man? The last time I saw her, she was a fourteen-year-old kid!"

"Well, she ain't no fourteen-year-old kid no more, man!" Thacker said, meeting the incredulously amused look Felix had turned on her in turn.

"Yea, I noticed that," Felix agreed, having told her that earlier.

Rachel fairly blushed beneath the intent look Felix turned on her before seeing her into a plush velvet Queen Anne chair to one side of a tan-brick fireplace and him into the one to the left of her. Gratefully she dropped her gaze to the black purse she was lowering to the floor beside her chair as she struggled to get a grip on the sudden heat suffusing her face. Raising her head then, she let her gaze return to their host, who had moved past the matching Queen Anne coffee table and settled on the plush matching Queen Anne sofa on its other side, which put him directly across from her and Felix.

"Felix tells me you're sort of like a historian of the city." A raspberry smile accompanied the statement as Rachel's gaze lingered on the wizened wrinkled face in a desperate need to change the subject.

"Yea, I guess you could say that," Thacker's somewhat age-tinged teeth flashed in a smile. "Anchorage isn't old enough to have a sharp identity as a city yet—in fact, it started as a tent camp then known as Knik Anchorage on the banks of Ship Creek for workers mobilized to build the railroad in 1915. Of course, I came several years after that, but to hear my parents tell it, back in 1914, hot on the wheels of President Woodrow Wilson's authorization to build the railroad out of federal funds, two thousand Americans flooded to Ship Creek valley looking for federal employment. Yet, ironically when the first white pioneers got here, they needed little encouragement to stay. Back then, Anchorage was a massive, undeveloped territory that was rich in resources, but lacked transportation. I mean, it was nothing but a wilderness. So, to alleviate the problem of inaccessibility, the legislature allocated funds to build a 500-mile-long railroad stretching from Seward, 126 miles south of Anchorage, through the coal fields of Interior Alaska, to the gold claims near Fairbanks, 358 miles to the north, with the midpoint construction headquarters in Anchorage, in doing so serving as a catalyst to the city's growth."

"Yea, you know, I remember Felix telling me something about that the other day. Didn't you tell me something yesterday about Turnagain Trail serving as a mail and transportation route in the old days before there was a road from Anchorage to Seward?"

Felix nodded at her probing look, unaware that Thacker sat on the plush velvet sofa across from them, bending his own gray head in a nod.

"I'm afraid he's right, Rachel," Thacker showed his age-tinged teeth in a smile. "If you will allow me to go back with my history a little bit, I have to tell you that in 1725, Czar Peter The Great of Russia wanted to find out whether Asia and North America were connected by land. So, he commissioned Vitus Bering, a Danish sea captain, to explore the North Pacific. Bering and his men discovered Saint Lawrence Islands, now part of Alaska in 1728, but they did not see the North America mainland because of fog; hence, their return to Russia and Czar Peter The Great. Well, in 1741, he, and a Russian explorer named Alexei Chirikof led a second expedition to the region. This time, they proved that the two countries were connected by land, sighting Mount Saint Elias in Southeastern Alaska as they came upon the mainland at Kayak Island. And they were soon followed by explorers sent by Spain, England, America and France, most of whom were looking for a route between the Atlantic and Pacific Oceans so that they could cash in on the rich fur trading in the Orient, including Captain James Cook, who arrived in 1778 with funding from the British Admiralty, intent on its search for the elusive Northwest Passage to China. So, he sailed up the inlet, later to be known for him, in the hopes of finding that passage through the Arctic, but had to 'turn again,' leading him to name the water body River Turnagain. Anyway, in 1903, the Alaska Central Railway began building a railroad from Seward to Fairbanks, but the company went bankrupt in 1910. That's why the U.S. Government bought the railroad in 1915, and just like Felix said, they improved the trail along the arm to handle the horse and wagon traffic needed for railroad construction. And just like Felix said, the trail was also used to deliver mail between Anchorage and Seward. Well, in 1917, telegraph lines were laid along the Turnagain 'road', and by 1918, the railroad extended from Seward to Anchorage, with flag stops at Bird Creek, Potter, Indian, and Rainbow, coming to completion in 1923. And also like I said, with the railroad's midpoint construction headquartered in Anchorage, it served as a true catalyst to the city's growth—particularly during World War II and the Cold War, when it brought large profits from hauling military and civil supplies and materials, not to mention that by 1962, railway cars could ship anything from any railway point in the Lower 48 to any point along the Alaska Railroad. Serious money, honey," Thacker said. "Well, remnants of the construction camps remain along the Turnagain Trail, but are barely discernible, today. Also, part of the original trail was covered by Seward Highway, which was completed in 1950 and paved in 1954."

"I see," Rachel said thoughtfully, not having known that last point. "Oh, well," she smiled, "although Felix had not told me that during our drive down Turnagain Trail yesterday, he did tell me all about the financial advantage of the railroad and its important role in Anchorage's growth during our walking tour on Tuesday, something I got to see for myself when he showed the Alaska Railroad and Depot to me shortly thereafter."

"Yea," the wrinkled lips in Thacker's dark-toned face were also still curved in a smile. "These days, the Alaska Railroad is the overall best railroad in America, not to mention its last full-service rail line. And I say that, because you can take the train on a pleasure, scenic sightseeing, romantic—whatever—day trip all the way up north if you want—for a price. Too bad Secretary of State William Seward is no longer around to see this traveling marvel, though, which provides transportation from his name city of Seward to Fairbanks in the north. Bering's voyage to Alaska back in 1741 ended up in Russia's rule over the Natives for more than a hundred years, and they killed practically everything with fur on it along the Pacific Coast for the wealthy China trade, but by the mid-1860's, they began to view the land they had stripped of most of its natural bird, seal, and sea otter resources as a purgatory and left as soon as they could. So, as a result of thinking the colony of Alaska no longer profitable, the departing Russians saw a political advantage in doing their American allies the favor of selling it to them. But Congress bawked at the amount of money Seward had negotiated for it, considering it a worthless waste of ice and snow. In fact, one reason Congress relented after more than a year was partly out of fear of offending the Russian Czar at that time, who sold Alaska to Seward on October 18, 1867 in Castle Hill in Sitka, a small town about a hundred miles southwest of Juneau off the Pacific, and which was the Russians' very capital at that time for only $7.2 million, or about two cents per acre. As another matter of fact, Americans even called his purchase of the land 'Seward's Folly,' or 'Seward's Icebox.' That is, until the gold discoveries came a couple of decades later—including the one in Turnagain Arm in 1888."

"I'll bet!" Though Rachel hardly found the latter part of Thacker's last statement surprising because of knowing about Alaska's Gold Rush years of the 1880's to the 1900's, she couldn't help staring at the octogenarian in more absorption with the new information of Russia's sale of Alaska to the U.S. that he had just so smilingly divulged to her. "So, barring this discovery of gold in Turnagain Arm in 1888, what you're saying is the only reason Russia sold Alaska to the U.S. in 1867 is because after more than a hundred years of stripping the Natives of mostly what they lived on, they considered the land no longer profitable and saw a political move in dumping it onto the Americans? And that's why William Seward only paid $7.2 million or two cents per acre for it because they considered the land here a worthless waste of ice and snow? I didn't get all that at the Museum yesterday!"

"Isn't that amazing?" Thacker's laugh intercepted the incredulous look she had turned on Felix and the equally incredulous one that he'd turned on her. "Well, the Americans don't call it 'Seward's Folly' no more, Rachel, not only because sea otter hunting was outlawed in 1912, and the Natives have since recouped their losses in fur in lumber and gas, but for the other reason I just mentioned, the gold. It was first found in Juneau around 1880, which became our capital in 1906 when the seat of government was transferred from Sitka, one of our three significant towns along with Kodiak and Unalaska, and which is now Alaska's third largest city; with Fairbanks, where like I said, gold claims were also made—and in fact, that's where the famed Fort Knox was found in the early 1900's—now Alaska's second largest city; and with Anchorage, now the state's largest."

Rachel didn't doubt that last fact that she was also already acquainted with, yet despite that, she couldn't help staring at the octogenarian in another expression of surprise. She'd had no idea that the famed Fort Knox Gold Mine was discovered in Fairbanks, Alaska, an ignorance that was reflected in the gaze she again turned on Felix, which met his equally reflective look.

"That's amazing!" Rachel exclaimed finally, luminous brown gaze slicing back to the elderly man as she voiced the agreement with his earlier-spoken claim.

"Isn't it . . . !" Thacker's own agreement came with a grin in his own continued amazement at Alaska's prosperity during its years under U.S. control. "Yea, the Americans have really put their stamp on this place since Seward purchased it from Russia all those decades ago. But you can still see the Russians' presence in Sitka's many historic places, as in everywhere else in Alaska, including Anchorage, where you can see it in our historic churches and a couple golf course names, for example. But that railroad is what's really helped our city grow, paving the way for government construction of roads, two army bases, Merrill and Elmendorf, an airport, housing, real estate, health care, and companies that run the gamut from natural gas to utilities to finance to oil," Thacker went on informatively with his age-tinged smile. "Yea, 1915 was truly a year for Alaska's largest city, now the state's center of commerce. To think back then, Knik Anchorage hadn't even been heard of until the Alaska Railroad was cut through here. As a matter of fact, when that railroad was being built back then, we didn't have but one hotel. And that, I think, was the Historic Anchorage Hotel built the same year of 1915 downtown on E Street. Well, look how many we have now, in addition to everything else here."

Rachel digested that yet new information with a nod of her head, her mind sliding onto the fabulous Historic Anchorage Hotel that had been across the street from the Sweet Basil Café that she and Felix had enjoyed breakfast at that morning. She turned another look on his attractive features that again met his own reflective look, aware that he was sitting there thinking the same thing.

"And speaking of hotels, how do you know my brother, George, Thacker?" Rachel finally asked after a moment.

Thacker sighed at her change of subject, Rachel guessed because he was grateful for something new to talk about.

"I met him at the Amber Heights Hotel four years ago," said Thacker in his strong low-range voice, smiling at the memory. "Friends of mine threw me an eighty-fourth birthday party over there, where I happened to make George's acquaintance. He had only been living in Alaska for a year then, and he was green about everything. Anyway, we somehow ended up making conversation, during which I told him everything I knew about this place. We ended up talking for three hours, long after everybody had moved off to get drunk, get screwed, or whatever. I met my present wife over there that night. And because of that, we're always over there celebrating in memory of the occasion."

"I see." Rachel had to force herself not to laugh at the man's mention of the words 'get screwed', although she couldn't keep a tickled smile from sliding onto the soft curve of her lips. "Felix tells me she's rather young for you. She must be out working to not be here with you this morning, by the way."

"Yea, well, somebody's got to keep me in the style to which I've become accustomed!" Thacker laughed.

"Aw, don't listen to him!" Felix urged her in dissuading tones, laughing also. "In proof of those oil companies he mentioned a while ago, Thacker is richer than J. Paul Getty! He's an oil man from way back!"

"I see," Rachel repeated, her smile broadening. And she saw that in the way the living room was laid out, with its plush blue velvet Queen Anne furniture, matching tables, glass lamps, plush carpeting and various other attachments, all fit into a sophisticated blue-green and greenish-blue setting that was to die for. No wonder the forty-year-old woman had married him.

"Yea, I'm afraid I was a part of the development of the Prudhoe Bay oil fields back in 1968," Thacker went on with his information about the city's growth. "The first year's production totaled $900 million dollars in oil lease sales from the North Slope off the Arctic Coast alone, and within two years, gross product had doubled for Alaska. Then came the completion of the 800-mile Trans-Alaska Pipeline from Prudhoe Bay to Valdez six years later, followed by other development projects around the state, including oil fields that had already been discovered in Cook Inlet and Kenai Peninsula. And there have been tremendous outpourings of oil fields ever since, even though we did have that infamous debacle of the Exxon-Valdez Oil Spill in 1989," Thacker frowned in dismal reflection. "Nevertheless, we'd needed that boost of oil to our economy after the $750 million dollars in damage caused by the devastating blow of that Good Friday earthquake Anchorage experienced on March 27, 1964."

"Yea, you know, Felix told me about that the other day, too. As a matter of fact, he showed me some park—I think named after that quake the other day." Rachel smilingly brushed off his mention of that most infamous Exxon-Valdez Oil Spill of 1989.

"Yea, that would be Earthquake Park on the northernmost part of Anchorage, in the Government Hill area. That quake was the largest recorded one ever experienced by North America at the time. It centered in Valdez, as a matter of fact, a tiny waterfront town on Prince William Sound about seventy five miles southeast of Anchorage, measured 9.2 on the Richter scale, and released ten million times more energy than an atomic bomb. Lasted about five minutes, and was felt in all of Alaska, parts of Canada, and as far south as Washington state. It completely destroyed Valdez, when huge landslides caused the whole town to be sucked under the tsunamis that flooded in from Valdez Harbor. Water, water, waves everywhere. Hundreds of people drowned in that mess. And over here in Anchorage, which was hardest hit, just like you said, in Earthquake Park, it was a mess. Tsunamis, waves everywhere, landslides, more people died. I'm telling you, structural damage was so bad over there that when four hundred feet of its bluff collapsed in a huge landslide, it destroyed a school, a neighborhood dropped into Cook Inlet, and our nice new railroad yard and ship yard fell by thirty feet. Of course, to a tourist, or a newcomer to the area, the damage caused by that quake is barely visible, now. But to anybody who had lived here back then and knew what that area looked like before that quake hit, you can still see signs of the huge subsidence and damage caused by the high tides and movement of the land, which was shifted two thousand feet into the sea."

Rachel fell silent as she digested this added information caused to Anchorage by the 1964 earthquake, something she was aware that Felix was doing also as she gazed at him again and saw his pensive look.

"I'll tell you something else that quake tore up," Thacker went on informatively. "To show you just how bad it was, the downtown area of Anchorage was hard hit, too. Thirty blocks—thirty blocks of stores, office buildings and apartment buildings were destroyed. For instance: the J.C. Penney building, irreparable. As was the Four Seasons apartment building, totally gone in that mess. Other schools were damaged in the rumble, streets were torn up. To give you an example of one, if you go downtown and cross E Street, notice how all buildings are modern on the left side of Fourth Avenue. That's because everything on that side from E Street east for several of those same blocks I was telling you about collapsed in that same 1964 earthquake. The street split in half lengthwise, with the left side ending up a dozen feet lower than the right. Of course, the Corps Of Engineers got in there and braced the street up somewhat, but that slope remained because they didn't want to risk any further earthquake damage. Well, fortunately, they found a way to make use of the damage there. That stretch of Fourth Avenue is where the Iditarod Trail Sled Dog Race takes place each year."

"I see." The two words repeated by Rachel came from Felix at the same time. She turned a curious gaze on his handsome features at the coincidental occurrence, all the while wondering if he had noticed the additional earthquake damage brought on Fourth Avenue or whether he like her, a person new to Anchorage and not looking for any, had failed to pick up on it at all.

"So, how've you guys managed to see Earthquake Park, Turnagain Arm Trail, and take a walking tour of the city, including the Museum of History and Art, so far?" pumped Thacker with a smile. "Has George being showing you two around?"

"Quite the contrary, my friend has been so busy running the hotel and preparing for Saturday's wedding that we've hardly had any time to do anything together," Felix answered, again taking control of the conversation before Rachel could reply. "Luckily, I've had a number of friendly escorts show me around. For the same reason, George hasn't been able to show Rachel around, either. So, as a result of that, since she arrived here on Monday, I've been showing her around. And we've had a great time, haven't we, girl?" Felix flashed her with a brief teasing grin. "I took her shopping for a parka and camera, showed her the Visitor Information Center downtown, Old City Hall—you know, which honors William Seward that you mentioned a while ago, the Anchorage Museum of History and Art you just mentioned, Turnagain Arm Trail, Earthquake Park, and also like you mentioned—various other places on the walking tour. We've been all over the place, haven't we, Rachel? I even showed her that fabulous Captain Cook Hotel down on West Fifth Avenue, named also for the famed British explorer you mentioned a while ago."

"Oh, now, that's a place," Thacker said, fixing him with a smile of appreciation and agreement. "I remember when former governor Walter Hinkle built that hotel shortly after the quake in order to demonstrate continued prosperity in Anchorage. We were only a small population then, having just joined the Union as the 49th state on January 3, 1959, but we grew in leaps and bounds between the '70's and the '80's, when investors blew in from everywhere serious about the future, and with money for development. And catering to that cash-rich and predominantly male group of transients, the red-light district of Spenard flourished, becoming home to massage parlors, brothels, escort services, and streets littered with girls in skimpy outfits. Of course, that district has been reformed now, and other hotels have blown up that are comparable to the Captain Cook, such as your brother's Amber Heights. But I will never forget good ol' Captain Cook Hotel. We used to party serious in that place. As a matter of fact, I met my second wife there. I can't remember where I met my first wife. Don't want to remember my third."

Rachel laughed as the old man fell silent again in reflective consternation, aware that Felix sat besides her doing the same. But at least Thacker telling them about the many cash-rich and male investors that had poured into the state between the '70's and the '80's explained the shortage of women in Alaska that Native Flip Hart had been so swift to tell her about over dinner at the hotel on Monday.

"So, how many children have you managed to produce out of these four marriages of yours?" she asked Thacker after a moment.

"I had six children from my first wife, seven from my second, three from my third. My present marriage has produced none, but then, I don't want anymore, anyway. Too old and too tired to do all that running around behind some little natty-nosed kids," Thacker half laughed, and watched Rachel and Felix do the same. "Besides, I'll leave that to my children. They've been long grown, have had children of their own, and they have had children of their own. As a result of that, in addition to my sixteen children, I have forty-three grandchildren, twenty-eight great-grandchildren, and a number of great-greats. And they're all over the place," the wrinkled old black man went on proudly. "One of my daughters works as a producer at local adult Top Forty radio station KMXS 103.1 FM, one works on the staff of Alaska Magazine, and another of my daughters co-owns a hardware store with her husband in Nome. And I have two sons who run wilderness lodges up near Denali State Park along with their families. Two of my sons work for a touring service near Wrangell-St. Elias National Park and Preserve taking people on day trips to view glaciers and enjoy camping in the wilderness by kayak. And then, I have three more sons who work for a major cruise line taking people on sightseeing tours in the most-recovered Prince William Sound."

"Wow!" Rachel looked away from the proud smile Thacker had turned on her to fix an amazed one on Felix, aware that he sat in the chair beside her as equally impressed by everything the man had said as she. "You've been very blessed to have so many kids, and with so many great jobs," she finished, her eyes back on her host.

"Yea," Thacker agreed, nodding his short-haired gray nappy head. "And I mean, my folks are all over the place," he repeated sprightly. "I have two granddaughters who are curators for a couple of museums here, and three grandsons who fly floatplanes for an air taxi service located on Lake Hood. As a matter of fact, my grandson Dicky has devoted his time specifically to flying visitors on wildlife and bear-viewing excursions in Katmai National Park, Homer, the aforementioned Kodiak, Juneau, and the also aforementioned Wrangell-St. Elias."

"Now, that's an interesting subject to bring up," interjected Felix with a laugh, turning a brief conspiratorial look on Rachel and watching her answer it with an equally furtive look. "Rachel and I had the displeasure of running into a grizzly on the Tony Knowles Coastal Trail the other day," he informed their aged host in his attractive tenor. "The thing came this close to biting off my ear. Scared Rachel to death—in fact, she wanted to go out and get drunk, after that!" he went on with a smile, pinning her with another amused look. "Scared me, too, but I brushed it off. But can you believe that, man? What was a four-hundred-pound brown grizzly bear doing over there on the Tony Knowles Coastal Trail that close to downtown Anchorage?"

"Oh, that was nothing." Like Felix, Thacker brushed off their terrifying experience as inconsequential with the indolent lift of his red-clad shoulders. "I had just come out of the Club Paris Restaurant about thirty, thirty five years ago—right there on West Fifth Avenue in the middle of downtown, when this equally four-hundred-pound brown grizzly bear came waltzing down the street out of nowhere and went straight for a tourist. Attacked the man, tore his clothes from his body in two minutes. All I could do was stand there transfixed as the deadly grizzly cleaned the man's flesh from his bones in another five. It was the most horrifying and disgusting thing I had ever seen. I threw up right where I stood."

Rachel turned another stare on Felix that met his equal stare, her mouth like his hung open in stunned shock at the graphic turn the conversation had taken. What would the old man do were he to know of their second experience with a deadly grizzly at Chugach State Park the day before—an experience that they had yet to disclose, Rachel wondered, at the same time grateful that the animal had moved away from her and Felix when it did.

The shrill sound of the phone ringing through the large house then brought her attention back to her host as it broke in on her troubled thoughts.

"I'd better get that," Thacker said, rising to brown mule-clad feet, the color of the slacks he wore with his red shirt. "I don't have the answering machine on. And it might be my wife. Or one of my exes. Or one of my children. Or one of my grandchildren. Or my great-grandchildren. Or my great-great grandchildren—I have so damned many of them to keep track of!" he finished with a parting laugh amid excusing himself from the sophisticated living room.

Behind him, the composed smile had returned to Rachel's raspberry-colored lips. "He's something else, isn't he?" she asked Felix.

"Yes, he is," Felix agreed deceptively. "Anyway, now that that man's gone outta here, why don't you give me a heart attack?"

Rachel turned another stare on the handsome, sexy features in her surprise of the sudden seriousness that had taken over his attractive tenor.

"What?" she half laughed.

"Why don't you crawl into my lap, and try and kiss me, and I'm not kidding this time?"

Rachel's long black mascara-lashed navy shadowed gaze remained leveled on the attractive face turned on her in a look of growing astonishment. Surely he couldn't be serious about her giving him the heart attack Thacker had said she'd probably give him at their introductions any more than suggesting that she crawl into his lap and kiss him like he had falsely teased her about doing to him when she was a fourteen-year-old kid at the Alaska Bagel Restaurant two days ago! And yet as Rachel continued to behold his good looking features, there was a look burning behind the dancing brown eyes that beckoned her despite herself. Moving quickly out of her chair, she did just as he had instructed, settled in his lap and curled her arms around his neck. She didn't know a damned thing about how to seduce a man, so the claiming of his lips with hers was tentative, at best. Yet Felix quickly grabbed hold of her inexperience, curling his arms around her body to pull her more fully against the wall of his chest while his answering response succeeded in eating all the lipstick off her mouth, turning the kiss into a wild thing that left the blood hammering in her ears while an equally wild fire raced through her veins. And with those increased sensations so new to her, all Rachel could do was stare over his broad navy and red plaid-clad shoulder when Felix ended the kiss after a moment to look at her.

"Uhmm, that was very nice," she managed in a voice almost devoid of breath.

"Uhm-hmm," Felix agreed. "In fact, it deserves another taste."

And cupping her face in his hands, he pulled her into another kiss, his arms pinning her back to his chest and inspiring an immediate response from hers, which quickly retightened around his neck, his lips moving over hers with a slow seductive mastery that inspired her equal response and left her head spinning while her heartbeat tripled in her breast. In tune with this, the sound of its quickened rate coupled with that of the blood pounding in her ears, both of them threatening to deafen her. In fact, Rachel was so left disturbed by this second assault on her mouth that she was robbed of what little breath she'd had left when Felix at last ended the dizzying kiss to look at her again.

"Uhmm, yea, very nice," Rachel somehow managed to repeat over his broad shoulder.

She jumped guiltily when Thacker reentered the living room and found her huddled shamelessly in Felix's lap. Intent on rectifying the situation, Rachel moved to push immediately out of his arms, only to remain right where she sat when Felix made no effort to let go of her.

Fortunately, Thacker didn't even notice their incriminating positions as he resettled on the blue velvet sofa across from them and started to talk more about his beloved native state of Alaska. But Rachel was no longer listening to the historian nor paying attention to his lengthy discussion about a subject he had brought up only moments before, that of the Iditarod Trail Sled Dog Race, an eleven-hundred-mile race which wound from Anchorage across two mountain ranges to the city of Nome that had been held annually since 1973. Instead, Rachel was looking at Felix. Noting his smooth golden brown skin, his unlined forehead, the straight black line of his brow, his deep long-lashed dancing brown eyes, the shape of his nose—strong yet gently flaring, the sexy slender-lipped mouth that had just moved so sensuously and so seductively over hers, the short kinky black hair that framed the gorgeous rectangle of his face, the strong chin which was equally rectangular. The way his head—well-shaped that it was—seemed to fit within the curve of her arm. . . . The feel of his strong warm body under hers, his arms still curved around her waist, his well-muscled thighs supporting her hips as she remained cuddled in his lap. And Rachel recalled the smooth way he had finessed her into giving him a goodnight kiss earlier that morning when she had turned smilingly away from him in preparation of unlocking the door of her suite and turning in for the night. And as Rachel considered all those things about Felix, she wondered how her sister Devon could have been so stupid as to let a man like him go all those years ago—especially when considering that dog Dustin Lavery she ended up marrying. And all as the result of a meaningless one-night-stand!

About ten minutes into Thacker's conversation and onto another subject—something about the Alaskan Mardi Gras, a Fur Rendezvous Festival and Trading Event that started in 1936, Rachel realized that Felix was no longer listening to him either, as he suddenly pulled up and claimed her upper lip in his teeth. The seductive action sent an electric current knifing through her with a force that left her able only to stare over his shoulder with her mouth open. It was as though an earthquake had struck through her with ten million times more energy than the atomic bomb Thacker had mentioned a while earlier. And yet the old man didn't even notice their inattention, so busily was he discussing facts about his beloved Native state—Alaska, from the Aleutian *Alyeska*, meaning 'Great Land,' North America's last frontier.

Felix tolerated the octogenarian's endless rambling for about five more minutes before he gazed up at Rachel and whispered in her gold heart-shaped and blue bejewel-ringed ear.

"Let's get out of here, quickly!" he suggested quietly between his perfect teeth.

And begging Thacker's pardon and telling him that they would see him at George's wedding on Saturday, Felix hustled Rachel up off his lap, waited for her to pick her black bag up off the floor, saw her to the foyer with a smiling Thacker following regretfully after them, grabbed their wraps from the guest closet and got her the hell out of there quickly.

Outside in the tan Pontiac Grand Prix amid sliding into her seatbelt, Rachel fixed the handsome features with a mocking smile. "I like that man," she said, "but he is long-winded."

"Very!" The smile of agreement that slid onto the sexy slender lips rivaled hers as Felix slid into his own seatbelt and then started the engine of the car.

They drove around the quiet residential neighborhood for about fifteen minutes before winding up at the Dimond Center Mall. Why not? They were in the area. Seeing Rachel from the car, Felix escorted her into the shopping center, the largest one in Alaska, his hand holding hers as usual. And of course, that mad pleasure was gliding insanely up her arm. Somebody was having a serious birthday party at the Dimond High Score Arcade there, though Felix took little notice of it as he led her in the direction of the ice skating rink on the second floor. There he stopped at its edge and watched the number of skaters glide around the perimeter of its ice floor while Rachel stood beside him doing the same.

"Hey, do you remember all the fun we had here—when was that—just two days ago?" Felix asked with a laugh.

"I'm afraid so," Rachel replied, meeting his look with similar amusement.

"What are we going to do if somebody comes out of the woodwork and starts taking pictures of us, again?"

"Well, baby, I guess we'll just have to give 'em something to photograph!" And slinging her arms around Felix's neck as she repeated the response he had given her at that time, Rachel pulled him into a kiss, his arms finding her waist at the same time. And of course the feel of his sexy lips moving against hers sent that mad pleasure that had been gliding up her arm on a quick U-turn all the way down her spine and to the soles of her feet. Leaving her barely able to stand or walk on either of them when he at last let go of her.

However, another kiss planted on her lips in the parking lot a few minutes later insured that Felix would have to carry her the rest of the distance to the car as it left her literally weak-kneed.

"I do like kissing you," Felix said against her lips, repeating the claim he had confided to her amid their goodnight kissing earlier that morning.

Oh, hell, she liked kissing him, too. Curling a hand over his cheek to lengthen the kiss, Rachel gave herself up yet again to another most disturbing possession of his lips.

They left that Center and went everywhere—to Resolution Park, where Rachel snapped the bronze Captain Cook Monument, which honored the 200th anniversary of the English Captain's sailing into Cook Inlet standing on a large wooden viewing deck gazing out to sea; they went to the Alaska Botanical Gardens, a wooded 110-acre site on Campbell Airstrip Road, where a one-mile nature trail left the garden and proceeded to Campbell Creek, where Rachel snapped several shots, as well; they lunched on fish and chips and grilled teriyaki at the Stuart Anderson's Cattle Company Steakhouse on West Tudor Road in mid-town; they observed the Three Ships Sculpture between Fourth and Fifth Avenues, which depicted the voyages of Captain James Cook in the South Pacific—another dedication erected by the city to show its respect for the sailor's impact on Anchorage's history; and they visited the Cabin Fever Gift Shop and Trapper Jack's Trading Post—a couple shops located back on West Fourth Avenue, where they noticed the difference in the modern-ness or lack of it of the buildings on each side of the street but had never attributed it to earthquake damage and where Rachel took new pictures as well. And everywhere they went they were kissing, kissing, and kissing . . . each one carrying Rachel to higher dizzying heights of distraction. And she knew she was going to have to slow them down, because Felix was taking her much too fast. . . .

She was in the process of snapping a couple boys playing slingshot in Delaney Park between West Ninth and West Tenth Avenues an hour and a half later when Felix suddenly pulled her into their thirty-twelfth kiss for the day, nearly sending the camera falling from Rachel's hands. And her response to the demanding kiss was predictable—the camera in her hand was forgotten as it and her other one curled speedily around his neck, her lips moved immediately against his, sensation swept through her with a force that left her feeling as though a tornado had twisted through her. And because of that, Rachel went against her own desires and strained to push out of his arms. Yet Felix made no effort to let go of her, although his mouth did pull away from hers to burrow sensuously along the sensitive cord of her neck.

"You are delightful, you are delicious; you are delectable. And a number of other d's," Felix said in his attractive tenor.

Rachel wondered how many other women he had given that line to as he busied himself blazing a flaming trail of kisses over her neck while she gazed from a daze over his broad shoulder.

"Am I?"

"Uhm-hmm," Felix insisted against her soft quivering dusky flesh. "Downright damned divinely devastating and disturbing . . . !"

And you are downright dangerous, Rachel thought, *not to mention deleterious to my continued state of mental health.* And she would be *delirious* to continue with this whirlwind romance thing they had going on and not stop it before something erupted between them that she was not yet ready, nor had the experience to handle. Aware of that, Rachel moved yet again to push out of his arms, relieved when they set her free. But an outstretched hand mocked her attempt to get away from him as it curled unexpectedly around her wrist, detaining her before she could have moved two feet away from his side.

"Hey," came the soft tenor behind her, "do you realize that you have a thousand pictures on that camera, but not yet one of us together? And I definitely want one of me with you."

At the somewhat desperate note in his seductive voice, Rachel turned to gaze back at him, only to see the same glimmering from the depths of the deep brown eyes meeting her searching look.

Turning away from her, Felix suddenly reached out and claimed a boy passing by them with a basketball in his arms by his shoulder. "Hey," he began to the boy, about fifteen, "will you take a picture of us? Here. Just push the button, right there. Shoot off the whole roll of us."

"No problem, Mister!" grinned the brown-skinned youth, setting his basketball to the ground and taking the camera he was showing him how to use into his hand.

Forcing calmness to her expression that she was nowhere near feeling, Rachel curved her arm around Felix's waist in response to the one he slid around hers, struck a pose against his side and smiled for the camera, as did he beside her. And as the youth did as Felix had ordered and shot off the entire roll of them, she hoped that the troubled look in the darkened depths of her brown eyes would not show up on the film.

She somehow managed to get out of that park—only for Felix to take her to another one—the expansive flower-filled one fronting the stone and glass building comprising the Alaska Center for the Performing Arts on West Sixth Avenue three blocks over. But then, Rachel had wondered when he was going to get around to taking her there, especially when they had passed by it a number of times over the last couple of days and with Felix being the Performer of the Arts that he was.

Six women rushed over to him at the command of his good looks and soap opera fame before he and Rachel could set three feet inside the multi-million-dollar complex.

"Oh, my God, it's Felix Latham!" the first one cried.

"I can't believe it's you!" the second one said.

"You know what you need? You need me! You want to make my 'star shine'?" suggested the third one.

"Because I sure would like to make yours shine!" assured the fourth one.

"Good God, man, you are just too good looking, and gorgeous!" the fifth one asserted.

"Can I have your autograph, your phonograph, your photograph, your telegraph, and your constant digraph, whatever the hell graph you've got!" the sixth one screamed.

For once grateful for the women's intrusion, Rachel moved away to look around the lobby while Felix regarded their pandering to and requesting him of his autograph with his usual tolerant smile.

From a distance, she watched as Felix somehow managed to get the six fawning fans away from him in order to purchase a couple of tickets for the two of them to see the offering of the day. Indeed, it was the third offering of the day, as it was pushing five o'clock and the program had already aired at eleven a.m. and two p.m., to be played a fourth and last time in an eight p.m. evening showing. Then another couple volunteers—more women fawning all over him—escorted him and Rachel to the Sydney Laurence Discovery Theatre, where other people awaited the start of the next showing of the movie. Settling into a seat in the 350-seat theatre and Felix beside her, Rachel waited the few minutes for the intermission to be over.

Actually, the movie turned out to be quite interesting once it had started. It was called Sky Song's Aurora Borealis 'Alaska Gallery of Light,' was played to some of the world's most beautiful music, and told the story about the mysterious aurora borealis, the northern lights—and other Alaskan sky phenomena. The flashes of color were breathtaking, the movie showing spectacular scenes of the aurora from space, the Hale-Bopp Comet, starfields, other comets, the aurora over Lake Eyak, and constellations such as Orion the Hunter. The awesome, brilliant colors of light flashing over a midnight sky and which could only be seen in the north and usually during the cooler months, because it does not get dark in Alaska in the summer, were amazing. And Felix was equally impressed by the vivid flashes of color across the sky. He sat in the seat beside her and was all over her, just like he'd said he would be after kissing her good morning in the middle of the night and leaving her to see herself inside her suite. And even though inwardly Rachel enjoyed the extremely good looking virile sexy man's attention, outwardly, she was looking for a grizzly! And there was not a one around.

Outside the theatre complex an hour later, a chill had filled the air as the temperature had dropped by several degrees, making Rachel long for the ribbed mud brown parka she had taken off ages before and left in the car. In harmony with the colder temperature, the sun had gone down and hidden in a cloud, the sky having turned overcast. Rachel wondered if rain was in the forecast as Felix stepped from the Center behind her and curled his hand around hers, sending that crazy pleasure dancing up her arm as usual. Even though she didn't want it to . . .

"That was some movie, huh?" he smiled, gazing gently down at her.

"Yea, it was." Rachel's raspberry-painted lips curved in a smile of agreement. "I don't think I've ever seen anything as awesome or as breathtaking in my life as the aurora borealis, the northern lights. With the exception of being on that uphill slope below East Twin Pass at Chugach State Park yesterday, looking down on everything below from an even more breathtaking vantage point."

"Yea, the two experiences are comparable," Felix agreed. "But like you, I did enjoy the northern lights." Glancing at his watch, Felix saw that it was a quarter till six. "Come on," he said, tightening his hand around hers to guide her toward the street, "let's go pick up the film you dropped off for developing yesterday, as well as drop off the film you took for developing, today."

Nodding against the staggering chill in the air, Rachel let him escort her the couple blocks to Stewart's Photo Shop back on West Fourth Avenue.

Once there, she quickly dropped off the rolls of film she had spent that day and placed in her black bag after removing them from her camera, for developing. Then picking up yet another three rolls of film for next day's use, Rachel paid for it as well as the film she had dropped off the day before to be processed for picking up that day.

Outside the photo shop with the bag of new film tucked in the black purse slung over her heather denim shoulder, Rachel took a moment to open one of the packets and look at the new prints. The pictures she had taken of Eklutna Lake and Valley were spectacular, the Dall sheep in the Goat Mountain bowl and Matanuska

Valley, the moose who had crossed their path down the winding Twin Peaks Trail, as well as those that she had snapped of the two male moose jousting over a female with which they wanted to mate in the aforementioned Matanuska Valley. And the pictures Rachel had taken of Felix were fabulous. As were the ones he had taken of her. Aware that he stood besides her eyeing the 35mm Kodak prints with equal fascination, Rachel handed him the three prints he had taken of her, recalling how he had expressed a desire to have a copy of all of them after having snapped her.

"Girl, you are lovely," Felix praised after a moment of admiring the pictures of her that he had taken into his hand.

Then curling his free arm around her waist, he lowered his lips against hers in what—their forty-thirteenth kiss of the day. The deeply ardent kiss sent a sensation shooting through Rachel that shook her to the core, leaving her clinging to him despite the fact that her hands were full, pictures in one hand, packets of not yet seen prints in her other, both encircling his neck in an urgent need to satisfy the quaking going on inside her.

Yet incredibly just as Rachel prepared to devour him in an insane need for more, Felix pulled out of the kiss and looked away from her. "Oh, God, I'd better stop this," he said, turning back around to smile at her. "I felt that 'way down'."

Rachel did, too. And that was the problem.

She shook visibly at the realization as to just how accurately the old Presley tune applied to her, as that last kiss had stirred something inside her way down . . . that she had never felt before.

Beside her, Felix observed her distress with the narrowing of his long-lashed dancing brown eyes over her. "You're shaking," he said, curling his arms around her as if to protect her from the cold. "But then, it has gotten cold out here, hasn't it? Come on, let's go back to the hotel."

Rachel thanked God he had misconstrued the cause of her shaking as she let him lead her stiffly away from the photo shop and in the direction of the car.

Chapter Ten

She went into a meltdown on the drive back to the hotel as thoughts whirled through her head. For instance, the one of how even as a fourteen-year-old girl, she had always thought of Felix as a handsome man. And she supposed that it was because of that that from the moment he had taken her hand in his on Monday, a warm pleasure had slid up her arm in a natural reaction to his good looks and male virility. Rachel also supposed that was why just the thought of his lips on hers was enough to send strange sensations through her, sensations she had felt in earnest from the first moment he had laid his lips on hers only two days ago. And in the two days since Felix had first kissed her those sensations had doubled, tripled, quadrupled, intensified, ballooned, tripped over the other and a number of other things so that every time he had kissed her that day she was reduced to a quivering mass of sensation. In fact, Rachel had spent the last few days enjoying his company too much for her own good, even when she hadn't wanted to. After all, why not?! The man had more in common with her than any that she'd ever met in her life when considering the fact that she hadn't seen him in ten years. Well, that was just too bad, because she had no intention of falling in love with him—certainly not in as little as three days—she didn't care how good looking and sexy he was. Rachel didn't care how much he'd confided liking kissing her or even how much she liked kissing him in return. Rachel had no intention of falling in love with him—she didn't care how intimately he had confided his self-imposed celibacy to her, that he was not getting any from any other women. She had no intention of falling in love with him. Not Felix Latham, lady-killer, who drew them like flies everywhere he went? Felix Latham, Daytime Emmy Award-winning actor on a soap opera, who could slam a woman up against the wall and kiss her with no feeling in proof of it? He had been all over her all day, just like he'd hinted upon kissing her good morning at her door last night in the middle of the night. Rachel had actually started looking for a grizzly! She knew he was setting her up for a boody call, just like all the others before him. After all, her looks and body commanded attention from the opposite sex, also. Felix had even told her that she was beautiful, lovely,

155

delectable, devastating, delightfully divine, and a number of other d's. Well, Rachel had no intention of answering his boody call any more than any other man's. But how did she stop Felix from making a move on her when the touch of his hand curling around hers amid the process of seeing her out of the car sent a sweet pleasure dancing up her arm that was so intense that she wanted to scream?

She somehow managed to accompany him past the red-uniformed doorman and into the hotel without pulling her hand from the disturbing claim of his, her gaze deliberately lowered to the bag of camera, film, prints and accessories she carried in her other hand. She had no intention of letting Felix see the terror in her eyes, a terror Rachel struggled to mask immediately at the sight of George standing in front of the reservation desk talking to Diane Mortemberg. He turned automatically in the brown-carpeted floor as she and Felix entered the sophisticated table-lamp and chandelier-lit lobby, the snort sliding through his well-hewn full lips one of delight and outrage at their delayed return.

"Where in the world have you two been since yesterday morning?" George demanded, eyeing them with immediate suspicion.

"Everywhere, man . . . !" Felix laughed amid ignoring the shorter man's suspicious look, the delight in his attractive tenor seeming to crash in on Rachel's petrified senses. "Just like I told you yesterday, I took Rachel to Chugach State Park. We had a great time up there, didn't we, girl? We stayed up there half the day. And then, we left there, and I took her to that Wendy Williamson Auditorium over at the University of Alaska at Anchorage, where we relaxed listening to some local and not-so-local talent for a couple hours. We have something else in common. Rachel hates rap just as much as I do! And then, we went to pick up her pictures from the photo shop, where she just so happened to mention that she loves archery. Can you believe that, man? We have something else in common. Rachel is an archer! She loves archery as much as I do! She's as good a shot as I am! Of course, that remains to be seen!" Felix went on laughingly while Rachel stood beside him simply staring, her hand still encased in the warm claim of his. "And then, we went to dinner, and took in a movie at the Bear Tooth Theatre Pub, after which she just so happened to recite the response to a Shakespearean character that I was delivering—you know, just to show off for her benefit. We have something else in common. Rachel knows Shakespeare's *The Tempest!* She was studying it in college at the same time I was doing the play on Broadway three years ago! Can you believe that, man? Anyway, after that, I said: uh-uhh . . . ! I'm taking this girl dancing with me. I want to see if she's as good on the dance floor as she is at everything else I do! So, I took her to Club Oasis—you know, the nightclub you took me to last week—or rather the one I begged you to take me to. And she can dance, George, can you believe that, man? Rachel and I danced all over that club! We turned that place out last night. Stayed practically till closing before we finally left to get back here! And boy, did we slow dance. Felt each other up, too. Not to mention a couple other things!" Felix finished wickedly, the hand warmly holding hers pumping it in a meaningful squeeze.

George watched the way his friend's excited gaze traveled from him to Rachel and then back to him and he pulled his lips to one side in an expression indicating he wasn't yet ready to let the subject drop.

"Okay, fine, so you two hung out all day yesterday and topped your evening off with dancing at Club Oasis," George said reluctantly after a moment. "What time did you two come dragging in here, anyway?"

Like yesterday morning, Felix's gaze was mocking as it slid away from George's suntan attractive mannish face and onto Rachel's beautiful dusky features.

"What time did we get in here last night? Two . . . ? Two thirty?"

"Actually, I didn't look at my watch!" Rachel wondered where her sudden flippancy came from as she repeated the exclamation she had given to his very same question of the morning before. *Please, let go of my hand,* she thought desperately.

"So, I take it that by the fact that you two didn't come dragging in here until two thirty last night that that explains why Stacey and I missed you at breakfast this morning?"

"Actually, we left out of here about a quarter till nine this morning. We just didn't want to see your ugly face," Felix said with sudden carelessness.

"Uh-huh." George's brown gaze lingered on the two of them with new suspicion after venturing the simple response, doubtful that it was. He had not missed the possessive way the taller, sexier man stood holding his baby sister's hand. Nor had he missed the way Rachel stood deliberately avoiding his gaze. "So, where'd you two drag off to at a quarter till nine this morning?"

"Where do you think, man? We went out and got us some breakfast. You know how hungry I stay all the time," Felix answered with a growing carelessness that deepened the suspicion shimmering in George's brown eyes. "Anyway, after that, I drove Rachel out to meet Thacker. And after that, we just kind of hung around. And we saw a movie about the aurora borealis, the northern lights, over at the Alaska Center for the Performing Arts. As a matter of fact, we'd probably still be in the street if Rachel hadn't started to shiver from the dropping temperature outside."

Rachel hoped George would accept Felix's last remark for what it was as she stood with her brown gaze lowered to the black slacks covering her brother's legs. Deliberately she refused to look at him so that he would not see the terror in her eyes—a terror that had increased considerably at Felix's refusal to let go of her hand.

"So, where's Stacey, man?" she heard Felix ask George then.

" . . . At the bridal shop; having last minute dress fittings. You know the wedding is in two days," George said.

"Yes, I'm aware of that."

Rachel heard Felix's dryly forced response a bit late as she averted her gaze onto Diane Mortemburg behind the reservation desk. However, before she could respond to the smile the brunette turned on her, George stepped forward and curved a blue-sleeved arm around her brown-parka-clad shoulders, claiming her attention. Still Rachel did not meet his gaze, unaware that George hadn't noticed, as his own gaze had strayed away from her and back onto his best man.

"Anyway, I have a surprise for you, Felix. Come on up to the penthouse, and I'll give it to you."

As George had anticipated Felix's gaze widened on him in a mixture of curiosity and delight at his mention of the word surprise. "What is it, George?"

"Just come on up in the elevator with me, and I'll give it to you."

Rachel heaved an inner sigh of relief as George turned her away from Felix, thereby breaking her hand free from the possessive claim of the taller man's. Yet she knew it was a relief that wouldn't last long in her acute awareness of the sexy man following their lead across the swanky sophisticated lobby.

"So, you started getting cold out there, and that's why you two decided to come back to the hotel?"

Rachel forced a smile to her lips as they entered the sophisticated blue, rust, brown and gold stripe-paper-walled hall moving away from the lobby.

"Yea," she nodded, still not looking at him. "It's really cooling off out there. I didn't want to stay out there longer lest I caught a chill and wound up in bed sick with flu two days before your wedding."

"I know that's right." George included Felix in his smiling gaze as they stopped at the elevator banks around the corner. Once there, George pushed the 'up' button on the panel and guided Rachel into the one that opened immediately, Felix stepping in beside her.

Pushing the proper button on the inner panel, George waited for the elevator doors to close and the elevator began to ascend from the first floor. His probing brown eyes settled back on Rachel then, aware that something was troubling her, as she had not yet met his gaze.

"So, barring this chill you've managed to avoid by coming in out of the cooling weather, how're you're really doing, Kid Sister? You alright . . . ?"

Rachel had to force her gaze to meet his gaze, aware that her refusal in having done so up till that time had prompted the questions indicating his suspicion that something was troubling her.

"I'm fine, George," she smiled. "You know, just prodding on along."

If George suspected her of lying, Rachel was thankful he didn't say anything about it, unaware that his eyes had flashed briefly away from her and onto Felix before resettling on her in a look of continued curiosity.

"This man been treating you alright?"

"Of course, George . . . ! After all, you know how gentlemanly he is." Rachel forced a second smile to her lips as she voiced the compliment, aware that Felix stood beside her having heard every word she had said.

In proof of that, his hand curved back around hers in his delight of the praise she had given him, causing Rachel to recoil from yet another heady wave of sensation that went floating up her arm. And in fact, if George hadn't had his arm still curved around her shoulders, she would have bolted from the elevator on the eleventh floor and run screaming back to her suite. Instead she had no choice other than to remain nestled between the two men as the elevator sped past her floor on its ascension to the penthouse on the fifteenth.

Yet again if George had sensed her desire to bolt out of the circle of his arm, he didn't say anything about it as he continued to gaze down at her with a look of new interest.

"Felix said he drove you out to see Thacker, today, our city's old and most famed historian," George told her with a smile in his abrupt alto voice. "How'd you like that?"

"I liked it. Thacker's very likable," Rachel said, again forcing a smile up at her brother. "The man really knows this state's history. And he's had a lot of wives and a lot of children, not to mention too many grandchildren, great grandchildren, and great-great-grandchildren. He told me and Felix all about this place, how he met you, everything. And I think the eighty-eight-year-old man absolutely ridiculous in marrying a woman less than half his age! However, like I said, he's very likable. Even if a bit long-winded. . . ."

"You've got that right!" Felix agreed with a laugh.

Yet Rachel barely heard his agreement, so busy was she trying to ignore the feel of his hand holding hers. By the same token, she was deliberately trying not to think back on the passionate kisses they had shared during their visit with good ol' Thacker, knowing she didn't need the memory as to how they had devastated her as well.

To the left of her, a laugh burst from George's own throat as he too derived amusement from her rather mixed praise about the octogenarian he had met a year after arriving there in Alaska.

"Yea, that Thacker Muldoon is something else," George agreed. "I had the pleasure of meeting him four years ago, when friends of his threw him an eighty-fourth birthday party here at the hotel. The man met the woman who would become his fourth wife at the party that evening. You ought to see her, Rachel. Felix saw her when I drove him out to meet Thacker the other evening. The woman don't look like nothing. But then, neither does Thacker, for that matter."

Rachel tried unsuccessfully to stifle a laugh that came out over that of the two equally laughing men as she tried to imagine a woman that ugly.

"That's awful!" she cried amid turning an almost accusing look on Felix, as he had not told her that.

However, she forced her twinkling gaze away from his handsome features as the elevator arrived on the fifteenth floor. Rachel knew she had to get away from him. He was doing things to her that she neither understood nor had the experience to handle. As a result of that, she pushed away from both him and George and into the lobby foyer, her terrified gaze sliding unseeingly over its rich varying shades of red and gold. By the same token, Rachel saw very little of the large sophisticated penthouse with its French Provincial furniture, deep red sitting areas and carpeting and multi-lamps and two offices that she followed George into a moment later. Instead, she lowered her black bag and camera and accessories bag onto a French Provincial side table and sped quickly off to the guest bathroom down the wide red-walled hallway.

Inside the lavish brass and white themed bathroom a second later, Rachel leaned against the hardwood door in desperation, her terrified gaze slicing wildly through the air. *Oh, George,* she began silently to her brother, *I need help, George. I—I've lost my cool. I've lost my head. I did just what I didn't expect to do. I did what you warned me not to do. I've been sucked in. Felix has sucked me in with his charm, good looks and male virility! I mean how could I not have been?! The man is so damned fine! Plus, we have so much in common. And he's been kissing me all day, and I've liked it. I've liked it! Even though I know I shouldn't have. And now he's got me aching with this—sensation—I don't know what it is except that I'm shaking! I'm shaking! Oh, God, George, please, help me!* Forcing herself to get a grip, Rachel moved away from the door to use the toilet and wash her hands.

She had just managed to gather her composure when Felix's sudden scream through the large penthouse scattered it to smithereens all over again.

"Man! Oh, man!" Rachel heard him exclaim in his soft tenor before she could get three-quarter-ways back down the red hallway. "Where in the world did you find this, man—?"

"Don't thank me, man, Stacey found it for you at Borders Books," Rachel heard George reply in his abrupt alto. "We were going to give it to you yesterday, except that you stayed out with Rachel all evening."

Rachel saw Felix completely blow off George's last remark as she arrived back in the living room, her gaze flying onto his good looking sexy features in immediate curiosity.

"Oh, man, Elvis Presley! I haven't seen this in years! Man! *Tickle Me!*" he went on excitedly over the video cassette he held in one hand. "I'm surprised this is still in print!"

Felix's dancing brown gaze espied Rachel's return a short distance from where he stood in front of the French Provincial desk and his grin broadened.

"Look, Rachel, look what your brother's got me! Elvis Presley! *Tickle Me!*" he grinned excitedly, displaying the video cassette in his hand. "Have you ever seen this movie? Oh, come on, girl!" Fixing George with one last grateful look, Felix moved away from him to approach her across the large red-themed living room and curve an impulsive hand over her wrist. "Oh, come on, girl, you've got to go see this movie with me. We'll go down to my suite, call up room service! Oh, you're going to love this movie! You're going to love it!" He was busily pulling her to the door of the suite. "Oh, thanks, again, George! I'll see you later, man!" he threw the words over his navy-parka-clad shoulder. Rachel just did have a chance to grab her black bag from the side table at the door in his haste to pull her from the penthouse.

Back out in the lobby/foyer amid waiting for an elevator, Rachel's long-mascara-lashed brown gaze lingered on him in a mixture of surprise and bewilderment. His hand was still curved around her wrist, its clasp sending that crazy pleasure up her arm, having completely wrecked her nerves again! But Felix wasn't even aware of her disturbance in his continued excitement over the old movie cassette he held in his other hand.

"Oh, God, I think I'm going to have a stroke!" Felix half laughed after pushing the elevator 'down' button with a forefinger. "I haven't seen this movie in years! Oh, girl, this is so good!" Pulling her into the elevator that opened up to them then, he punched the button for the twelfth floor. "Oh, Rachel!" he screamed excitedly as the elevator doors closed and they began to descend to his floor. "Elvis Presley! *Tickle Me!* . . . Nineteen sixty five. Elvis Presley, Jocelyn Lane, Julie Adams! Elvis plays Lonnie Beal, an unemployed rodeo star who gets a job working at an all women health ranch. He tries to put the moves on Jocelyn Lane, the fitness instructor while Julie Adams, his boss and an older woman, tries to put the moves on him . . . !"

That last exclamation came as they stepped off the elevator on the twelfth floor. But Rachel wasn't listening to his synopsis of the old movie she had seen on the AMC cable channel years ago. Instead, all she could think about was that they were going to his suite. And there was no way Rachel was going to be alone with him in the intimate confines of his suite for two hours—not when he would more than likely try and put the moves on her!

She jumped in the floor when Felix actuated that intention by suddenly leaning over and kissing her excitedly.

"I have to go!" Rachel said quickly, wrenching her wrist out of his grasp and pivoting away on her heel.

However, a detaining hand curved over her arm, sending her black purse flying from her shoulder as it yanked her back before she could move two feet down the hall.

"Are you running from me?"

The voice seemed to come from all the way down the corridor, when in reality, it was right behind her. She turned curiously to look at him at the querulous undertone that had sounded behind his question.

"What?" Rachel asked in surprise.

"What is this ill luck I have with Hardison women—?!" Felix demanded furiously, dancing brown eyes glowering down at her. "First, Devon leaves me, now you? Well, let me tell you something, *Little Sister, don't you! Little Sister, don't you! Little Sister, don't you kiss me once or twice, say it's very nice, and then, you run . . . ! Little Sister, don't you do what your big sister done . . . !*"

Rachel's luminous brown gaze narrowed on the handsome features in deeper surprise as he both named the old classic Elvis Presley tune and quoted part of its lyrics. Blood pounded through her brain as her own need to succumb to the beckoning look in his eyes overwhelmed her.

"Okay, fine! I won't run! Now, what . . . !"

"I'll tell you in a minute!" Felix said in his attractive tenor, one hand holding the Elvis tape, the other arm curling around her waist as he lowered his lips back on hers. The driving demand of the kiss gave expression to all the sensations he had roused in her since laying his lips on hers two days before. Raising her arms to his neck, Rachel gave in to all the hot passion flooding into her veins, the soft curves of her body molding themselves to the hard lines of his, her nostrils flaring with his scent, her lips moving against his hungrily. Yet just as she was about to eat him up, Felix ended the burning kiss and pulled out of her arms.

"What?" Rachel demanded in a voice riddled with equal disturbance and confusion.

Felix stood staring incredulously at the blue-carpeted hallway floor, a hand having curved around one of her wrists in a detached manner.

"It's you!" he said, turning back to look at her. "I never felt when I kissed Devon the way I feel when I kiss you. And I never felt so jealous over a woman as I did sitting there listening to those two fools drooling all over you like slobbering dogs at the dinner table Monday evening. Why do you think I told you when we got back from the club last night how much I liked kissing you?"

Confusion deepened in the navy-shadowed eyes as Rachel continued to stare up at the golden brown handsome, sexy features turned fitfully down on her.

"What?"

"Why do you think I've been all over you, today? Don't you get it, girl after my own heart? I think I'm falling in love with you, if such a thing makes sense. I mean, is it possible for a man to fall in love with a woman in three days?"

"Well, I guess there's only one way for you to find out," Rachel said with a boldness that surprised her.

"What do you suggest?" Felix asked curiously.

"Well, for one thing, you can kiss me like you did your costar!"

"That's not a problem!" Felix rushed out quickly, immediately getting her meaning and slamming her bodily against the richly elegant stripe-papered wall. Rachel did not crash through it—quite the contrary, as his lips moved hotly onto hers, she responded in turn—returning his kiss with equal fire, her body straining against his as he crushed her buttocks into the wall, her arms and hands moving heatedly all over his face, back, shoulders and neck, wildfire racing through her veins. And as the kiss lingered fervently, Rachel knew exactly what she had been feeling for him every time he touched her, looked at her, put his lips on her. This man she could talk about school with, talk about Elvis with, flirt with, play with, speak Spanish with, ice skate with, go hiking with, discuss her dislike of rap with, run away from grizzlies with, play archery with, talk Shakespeare with, go dancing with, kiss. . . . This man she wanted to . . . make love with. . . .

The realization as to just how badly she wanted to do that reverberated in her brain as Felix ended the passionate kiss to blaze a trail of hot fire all over her face and the sensitive cord of her neck while his free hand slid over her curves with equal heat. In fact, Rachel was so excited by the thought of climbing into his bed that in her mind she called on God, or any deity that had ever been given the name of a god. She didn't even know her mouth had translated her inner need until she heard her own voice sound out into the corridor over that of the blood pounding in her ears and hammering wildly through her brain.

"Felix . . . !" Felix . . . !"

Felix's mouth hardened on her neck at the hot passion he heard underscore her quaking tone. "Let's get out of this hall, quickly!" he instructed huskily between his perfect teeth.

They were in his suite down the hall in two seconds, silence filling the two lamp-lit rooms, the white door closed behind them. Hotly Rachel threw her black bag to the blue-carpeted floor and slid out of her brown parka in tune with him sliding out of his navy-lined parka after having lowered Elvis carelessly onto a side French Provincial table near the door.

"You'll have to forgive me," Felix began amid discarding the parka to the floor and moving to lift her up in his strong arms, "but I don't feel very gentlemanly right now."

"I'm sorry to hear that," Rachel said as he carried her out of the living room and into the bedroom, her arms tight around his neck, "because for the first time in my life, I feel like a natural woman!"

"Hey, that's Aretha!" Felix said amid lowering her roughly onto his blue-print king-sized bed.

"Who . . . ?"

"Aretha Franklin." Felix stared down on her in surprise as she busied herself pulling him on top of her. "You've never heard of the Queen of Soul?"

"Who hasn't heard of the Queen of Soul?" Rachel asked at his silly mention of the renowned black artist that had practically started the soul/R&B movement, although not realizing she had just vocalized the thought behind the singer's hit 1967 tune *You Make Me Feel Like (A Natural Woman)* that Candace Bergen had practically made one of her theme songs on her late '80s-to-late '90s TV show, *Murphy Brown.*

"We'll talk more about her, later!" Felix rushed out dismissively before lowering his mouth hard back onto hers.

And as another fervid kiss began, Rachel allowed herself to become swept up on the flaming waves of his possession, her arms curved around his precious head while his were thrown under her shoulders, her head flying feverishly up off the firm quilt-covered bed to meet his hot descending mouth. And as an answering need throbbed inside her, Rachel wrapped her legs hungrily around his, never in her life having ever thought she would feel this for a man. In fact, Rachel not only acknowledged that thought but she reveled in it as Felix's lips left hers to blaze an insistent trail of hot fire all over her face, neck and flaming throat while a careless hand swept her long hair out of his way.

"Your brother asked me up in his penthouse suite what was going on with you and me," Felix told her breathlessly between kisses he was raining over her quivering flesh. "I told him you've blown my mind. And that I can't keep my lips off you."

"So long as you don't keep them off me, now . . . !" Rachel cried in his ear, equally breathless.

"No way . . . !" Felix husked against the curve of her neck before his hot mouth slid across the curve of her jawbone and resettled on hers. The kiss took in all of her mouth, its driving force sending her pulses into overdrive while her heartbeat seemed to come from her throat. To add to her disturbance: her own breathing was suddenly loud and rushed and ragged in her ear. And with the sound of both of those threatening to deafen her, Rachel held on and didn't let go, reasoning that she didn't need her sense of hearing anyway as her lips and arms and hands communicated to him in American Sign Language the exact burning need for him that he was displaying hotly for her.

The kiss was endless—taking in all of her mouth, possessing it with a primal fury that demanded her equal response and left her mind reeling with incredulity. When did she fall in love with this man she had no intention of falling in love with and with whom she was all wrapped around, Rachel wondered as she lay all wrapped up in Felix's arms and hands? Three days ago? Ten years ago when she was a fourteen-year-old kid? Is that why she used to follow him and Devon around so relentlessly whenever he dropped by to see Devon? Aw, but that was as nonsensical as Felix telling her that he was falling in love with her in only three days after not having seen her in ten years! And yet as he continued to kiss her senseless, Rachel realized that she did indeed love him, a man after her own heart as well, the thought leaving her head spinning, her mind reeling. In harmony with that, as his lips left hers to blaze yet another trail of fire over her face, ear, neck and throat, Rachel felt herself whirling . . . whirling . . . like a leaf blowing in the wind. Yet the whirling came to an abrupt stop when Felix suddenly pulled his mouth away from her skin. She stared at him in surprise when he suddenly pulled his body away from her also.

"What?" Rachel demanded impatiently, heart pounding in her chest, her pulses still racing from his hot dizzying kisses.

"Somebody's at the door," Felix answered incredulously, reality crashing in on the passion she could still see burning in his deep brown gaze.

"Well, don't answer it," Rachel said reasonably as she saw his reluctance to leave the dream world she too was still floating in.

"But I have to. I didn't put the do not disturb sign out. Besides, it might be your brother," Felix said in his attractive tenor.

Rachel's flesh cooled immediately at the idea of them being intruded on by George. As far as he was concerned, she and Felix were supposed to be in the living room watching an Elvis Presley video. She knew George would freak were he to come in and find out they were in Felix's bedroom making out! Even though Felix did tell him that she had blown his mind and that he couldn't keep his lips off her!

Felix laughed softly as her suddenly petrified expression translated the thoughts running through her mind. "Don't worry," he said, "I told George that I'm gone on you. It is not going to shock him to come in here, and find you in my bed."

Her face flamed all over again at his mention of the word bed. Rachel turned away from him, not wanting him to see her embarrassment.

A hand curved over her chin, forcing her gaze back to meet the sudden tenderness in his. "You are precious, girl," Felix said. Leaning over, he planted another quick kiss on her before straightening and rising off the bed.

As he sauntered out of the bedroom in response to the knock coming yet again at the door, Rachel stared after him in amazement. Considering how terrified she had been upon arriving at the hotel with him thirty minutes earlier, the events that had taken place between them in the last ten were a shock. Rachel closed her eyes as she lay stretched out the length of Felix's bed, still wondering what George was going to do when he found out his baby sister had lost her heart to his best man.

However, the voice that sounded from the door a moment later wasn't George's, or even masculine. In fact, Rachel's flesh turned to stone from her head to her toe as she recognized the female voice that wafted into the suite in a delighted shriek.

"Felix, darling, it's good to see you! You are as good looking as you ever were!" praised the excited female voice.

"Devon . . . ? Oh, my God, it is you! It's good to see you! Why, I haven't seen you in ten years! How in the world are you doing these days . . . ?" Felix recovered from his surprise with ease, unlike Rachel, who lay on his bed wondering what the hell her sister was doing there all the way from Atlanta, where she was supposed to be in the midst of getting a divorce!

"I'm doing just fine, darling!" Devon's composed voice came intruding on her thoughts then. "How are you?!"

"The same . . . !" Rachel heard Felix reply in his attractive tenor. "Anyway, what are you doing over here? Rachel told me you were in the midst of getting a divorce!"

"I was, but I had my attorney wrap that mess up yesterday," Devon replied airily. "So, since I already had the time scheduled off from work, I went home, packed my bags and jumped on a plane for here. I just landed at the airport twenty minutes ago. Had a cab drive me straight here. This is not a bad little place George's fiancée has here. Anyway, Dad told me that he had asked you to be his best man, so, as soon as I checked in, I had the front desk clerk give me your suite number. They put me on the seventh floor, in Suite 758. Well, as soon as the bellboy got my bags in there, I came on up here to see you. I haven't even seen George yet nor Rachel for that matter, and I know she's here somewhere because if she weren't, she wouldn't have been able to tell you I was getting a divorce, not to mention that she told me when I talked to her last Saturday that she was coming in on Monday, anyway. As a matter of fact, I haven't even seen Mom and Dad yet, and I know they've got to be around here somewhere, too."

"No, they haven't gotten here, yet. I think Rachel said something about them arriving here possibly tomorrow—you know, after driving in all the way from Villa Rica," Felix said.

"Aw, well, that's my dad. Rachel told me he wanted to try out that silly RV he bought last year. The man must be crazy to think of driving all that distance, considering his age, and all."

"Your dad is what—sixty? Sixty one, now . . . ? That's hardly old," Felix contradicted.

"I guess not," Rachel heard Devon agree smoothly. "Anyway, you certainly don't look any older. The years sure have been kind to you! How are you doing, really? You know, it took you so long to answer the door, I thought I had missed you."

"I was busy," Rachel heard Felix respond quickly.

"Uhm-hmm. You've a woman in here, don't you?"

"What makes you say that?"

"There's a woman's purse on the sofa, not to mention two parkas. And it doesn't take a rocket scientist to realize you can't wear both of them at the same time."

"Okay, you caught me. I've a woman here. She's in the bathroom. We were just getting ready to watch Elvis," Rachel heard Felix lie smoothly.

"Are you still hung up on that man? That hunky's been dead for thirty years, now! When are you going to get over him—!"

A brief silence ensued in the exchange between them, Rachel guessed Felix was debating whether to respond to the inflammatory remark or ignore it altogether.

"So, how have you been doing, Devon? How have you really been doing—since you dumped me all those years ago?" Felix asked, leaving Rachel to assume that he had chosen to do the latter.

"I guess you can see by my track record that I haven't been doing that great. Two divorces in eight years."

"Yea, so I hear."

"So, how are you doing, darling?" Rachel heard her sister ask with renewed excitement. "George tells me you're an actor on a soap opera!"

"Yes, I play Joe Murray on *As The Star Shines*. It's only been on the air for twenty four years, but it has a huge following—even all the way over here."

"Yea, well, you definitely have the looks and body for it," Rachel heard Devon say admiringly. "But you know, I never really believed you when you told me you wanted to be an actor all those years ago. I guess I should have listened to you, shouldn't I?"

"I guess so."

"So, tell me about this woman, this Stacey Lumas, that my brother's marrying," Rachel heard Devon change the subject matter. "Is she tall, is she pretty, is she built, flat-chested, straight-hipped, light-skinned, dark-skinned, young, old, is she fat, what?"

"Well, let me put it this way—she's young," Felix said.

"What are you trying to tell me—is she even black?"

"Well, let me put it to you this way—she's Alaskan."

"Are you trying to tell me George is marrying a short fat out-of-shape white woman? And after all the fine 'sisters' he dated back in Georgia? Oh, good Lord . . . !" Rachel heard her older sister flare up in disgust. "But then, I shouldn't be surprised. After all, there aren't that many 'sisters' owning hotels like this one." Same thing Rachel had thought. "Anyway, I guess it's like they say—love is blind. It certainly was in my two cases. Anyway, whatever the hell she looks like, it's going to blow her mind when she finds out I can be a bridesmaid in her wedding, after all!"

"As I'm sure it's going to please George, also."

"Oh, I know it is," Devon agreed. "And while we're on the subject of him, go tell that silly woman you have in here—who hasn't come out after all this time because she hears me in here talking to you that you've got to go. You can see Elvis later. I want you to take me up to the penthouse and see George, meet this fiancée of his. Plus, you've got to take me and see Rachel. They tell me she's somewhere on the eleventh floor. She's probably around here somewhere vamping some damned man, even though she has no intention of ever giving it up to anybody," Rachel heard Devon say disparagingly. "And then, you and me have got to go somewhere and talk, baby. We've got a lot of catching up to do!"

A brief silence ensued after that exclamation, again Rachel didn't know whether Felix was contemplating answering it or ignoring it altogether.

"You know," he began after a moment in his attractive tenor, "it's interesting that you should make that remark about Rachel being somewhere around here vamping some man—well, she definitely has what it takes to do it. The last time I saw her, she was a fourteen-year-old-kid. She's not exactly fourteen years old anymore, is she? She really grew up, didn't she?"

"Uhm-hmm," Rachel heard Devon's somewhat suspicious response to Felix's laughingly uttered last couple of questions.

"Anyway, give me a minute, and I'll take you up to see George."

And as the lively conversation ground to a halt, Rachel imagined that Felix was returning to the bedroom to speak to her. As he did a second later, the same amusement she had heard in his voice in the dancing brown eyes as usual.

"I guess you heard that your sister's here," Felix said unnecessarily, a half laugh cracking in his quiet tone as he settled his well-built navy-clad frame on the side of the bed.

Rachel's demeanor lacked the lightness of his as she pulled herself up to a sitting position beside him. "Yea, so I heard," she replied equally unnecessarily, equally quiet tone thick with annoyance. "What's she doing here?"

"I guess it's like she said—the divorce came through yesterday. So, since she already had the time scheduled off from her job, she hopped a plane and flew over here to be in the wedding."

"I see." Rachel forced herself to see the good behind her unexpected arrival rather than reflect on the insulting remark Devon had just made about her, even though Felix did make a quite adequate response to it. "Oh, well, at least that is going to make George happy. He was quite sad when I told him on Monday that Devon wasn't going to be here because of that divorce. He's going to be really pleased upon learning that not only is she here, but she will be able to be a bridesmaid, after all."

"Yea, I guess that's true," Felix agreed lightly before the dancing brown eyes glimmered on her with new intensity, a hand curving over her arm. "You know, what she said about you running around here somewhere trying to vamp some man with no intention of giving it up, what would she do were she to know that the man you had vamped was me, and as a result were in here about to give it up to me?" Felix dared with an outrageous laugh to Rachel's mild amusement before leaning over and kissing her meaningfully. "Anyway, I'm going to go on and take her up to see George, like she asked. Stacey should be getting back pretty soon. George and I can introduce Devon to her, also. And why don't you come up to the penthouse and get with all of us after a few minutes, and meet your sister? Devon's already asking for you, anyway."

"Yea, so, I heard." Warmed by the loving smile on his lips, Rachel watched as he pulled away from her and sauntered back out of the room.

She sat there for a long moment reflecting on just how deeply she loved that man before she got up, gathered her purse and parka from the living room and then returned to her eleventh floor suite, where she quickly hung her parka up in the closet. Then she settled in the make-up chair of the French Provincial dresser and gazed at her appearance. The reflection in the mirror showed long relaxed off-black hair hanging in a ponytail from the side of her head—however, all mussed, navy eye shadow in need of repairing, raspberry lipstick long having been eaten off her mouth from Felix's passionate kisses. Removing both lipstick and shadow from her black bag, Rachel took quickly to repairing both as well as touching up her black mascara and refreshing the burgundy blush Felix had kissed off her cheeks as well. Then replacing all makeup in her bag, Rachel pulled out a wide-toothed white comb and ran it several times through her long hair.

Satisfied that she had removed all the love-clench-induced snarls from its length then, Rachel slid the comb back into her purse and took one last look at her reflection. The newly refreshed makeup was perfectly applied, the gold hearts dangling from blue bejeweled posts hanging prettily from her ears, and her off-black ponytail hanging from a knit navy band now lay long and smooth and straight down over her breast. And thankfully the fleecy denim heather sweatshirt and matching pants were still as fresh as when she had put them on that morning. Moving to her white Nikes sneaker-clad feet, Rachel squared both, her admiring gaze lingering over the provocative swell of her breasts behind the V-neck styled sweatshirt. Then secure in the fact that the curve of her hips was as equally provocative beneath her denim heather pants, Rachel slid the strap of her bag onto her shoulder, left her suite, and returned to the elevator banks down the elegantly stripe-paper-walled corridor, stepping into the one that opened immediately.

A glance at the silver-toned watch confirmed the time as six fifteen when she stepped off the elevator onto the fifteenth floor seconds later. Rachel moved quickly through the lobby/foyer, her heartbeat quickening at the thought of seeing Felix again, her almost lover and the object of her love. He was not the only cause of her excitement, for her anticipation of both seeing Devon and George's delight at her unexpected arrival there was equally great. Raising her knuckles to the red penthouse door then, Rachel swept her appearance with one last look, hoping only that Devon wouldn't notice that the black bag strapped to her shoulder was the very one she had seen in Felix's suite just moments earlier.

Predictably, George answered her knock a second later, his eyes fixing on her in a conspiratorial look as he saw her just inside the door.

"How're you doing, Kid Sister?" he asked her with a smile, his voice low as he slung a brotherly blue-sleeved arm around her heather denim shoulders. "Look who's here asking for you."

Rachel feigned an immediate act of surprise when Devon turned around on the deep red sofa she was sitting on and saw her moving away from the door with their older brother.

"Devon, what are you doing here!"

Devon ignored the demand as she jumped from the sofa to approach her across the large red-themed living room. "Rachel! It's about time you showed up! Where the hell have you been since I got here!"

Rachel kept up her act of surprise as she moved from beneath the circle of George's arm to curl her own around Devon's shoulders in response to the pink-sleeved ones Devon was curling around hers.

"And just how long have you been here?" she demanded, even though she well knew.

"Oh, I don't know, I guess it's been about thirty minutes since I arrived at the airport," Devon replied carelessly, hazarding a guess.

"But—But what are you doing here!" Rachel persisted with the stupefied tone as she pulled her face away from her shoulder to look at her. "I mean, you're supposed to be in Atlanta in the middle of getting a divorce!"

"Well, I was, dear, but luckily, my attorney came through in a way that enabled me to wrap that mess up, yesterday," Devon replied smoothly, her arms loosening slightly on her heather denim shoulders. "So, as soon as I left court, I went home, packed my bags, and hopped a plane here. 'Done knocked George for a serious loop, seeing that I'll be able to be a bridesmaid in his wedding, after all!"

"I'm sure!" Although Rachel kept up her act of surprise, the eyes that settled on her brother glimmered with delight, the same of which she saw shimmering from the depths of his own brown eyes. And Rachel did not need to see that to know how glad he was at having her there, already having anticipated his pleasure at their sister's unexpected arrival. "Your showing up here like this has probably made his day!"

"Of course . . . !"

With her pink manicured hands moving onto her shoulders, Devon pushed her gently away from her to give her the once-over with a sweep of her equally pink-shadowed black-mascara-lashed eyes, same thing Rachel was doing to her. The woman older than her by five years was exquisitely dressed, wearing a smart pink zippered jacket over matching pink slacks, pink ankle boots on her feet, an ensemble that made Rachel think she was going out on the ski slopes. They had the same full figure, except that Devon was a size larger, a twelve, same five-feet-eight-inch height, same dusky coloring. But that was where the resemblances fairly stopped, for Devon's long relaxed off-black hair was several inches shorter than Rachel's and worn in a sexy fluffy curly do flowing prettily down over her pink-clad shoulders. Rachel was an attractive woman, a beautiful woman, with her perfect round face, high cheekbones and other symmetrical features, her long relaxed off-black hair flowing down over her breast from her side ponytail. Yet next to Devon, she was plain. Devon was truly the beauty in the family, for though her features were equally as symmetrical, her face was more of a wide oval, the shape producing higher, more prominent cheekbones and equally prominent jawbones, giving her a sensuality that was almost potent—something Rachel lacked. Plus there was a glow about Devon, a radiance—that impacted every man she met. Truly, the woman was dazzling. And Rachel hoped Felix would not take notice of that all over again as a brief glance across the large living room showed him sitting on the second sofa watching the interchange between the two of them with interest.

"You look great!" Rachel told her sister then, flashing her Halle Berry smile.

"So do you!" Devon remarked with a pink-medium-lipped grin that exposed her own perfect teeth. "Although you know, you need to do something about that purse, because it does not go with those shoes."

Rachel bent double in the floor as she laughed in response to the funny remark, sending the black purse strapped to her shoulder falling to her elbow. She should have known her fashion-conscious older sister would attack her dress sense, and was glad Devon had noticed its color didn't match that of her sneakers rather than that it was the same color of the one she had seen in Felix's suite a while ago.

Beside her, George stood laughing at the funny retort their sister had uttered also, although he sought to quell it amid curling a blue-sleeved arm back around Rachel's shoulders.

"Come on over here, Rachel, Devon's been telling us about the divorce. You have got to hear this."

Rachel somehow managed to stifle her own laughter as her navy-shadowed eyes resettled on her older sister in a curious look. "Yea, what did your attorney do to get your divorce wrapped up so soon?"

"Oh, honey, you are not going to believe this."

Settling her curving pink-clad frame on the deep red sofa she approached then, Devon waited until George had settled beside her, Rachel in the deep red French Provincial chair to the left of George. Felix occupied the deep red second sofa directly across from Rachel, the dancing brown eyes flashing amusement as usual. Setting her black bag to the French Provincial coffee table alongside Devon's pink leather clutch purse, Rachel met his gaze in a furtive look before directing her own on her sister, just then beginning to speak.

"Well, you remember that most regrettable talk we had on the phone last Saturday, when I told you I simply would not be able to be here for George's wedding?" Rachel nodded at Devon's question. "Well, after that, I felt so bad that I called my attorney on his cell, and said, 'Look, Angel, I do not have a whole week to listen to weak testimony trying to prove Richard's adultery. I've got to go to Alaska. My brother is getting married there next Saturday. I need to be out of here by mid-week. So, get something on those two silly women I found him in our bed with that will confirm that they were actually there than my word.' Well, Angel did better than that. He didn't even have to touch those two bitches, because he went out and found something better. Guess what it was."

"What?" Rachel included George in her curious gaze. Having already heard the story, he was not listening to Devon but sat watching her intently; the same conspiratorial look in his eyes that had shimmered in their brown depths when he had greeted her at the door. Rachel knew immediately that George knew something had been going on between her and Felix—that is, before Devon had shown up and intruded upon them.

"Would you believe that that bastard Richard was such a dog that those two women I found him in our bed with were not the only two he'd been with during our marriage?" Devon demanded then, causing Rachel's gaze to flash back on her in shock. "Well, on Tuesday, two days ago, three women came walking into court—one single, one married, one divorced—each with kids, and each claiming that Richard was their father. The oldest one was five, and the youngest one was two. Six kids, and three of them looked just like him! Well, naturally, paternity tests were ordered, which came back yesterday, and proved that Richard was the father of all six of them! Can you believe that—?!" Devon demanded to Rachel's deepening shock. "That son-of-a-bitch . . . ! Been screwing around on me from the beginning of our marriage! Adultery proved! Divorce granted right there! Now, Richard's going to have to pay alimony, palimony and child support, and he's going to pay it on the street and on his feet, because I'm taking the cars, the house, and everything in it. And with any luck, I'll never have to set eyes on that bastard for the rest of my life!"

"I know that's right!" Rachel stared at her older sister in utter disbelief at all she had said. She could not believe that the husband she had found in their bed with two women three months ago had been playing around on her the whole time. "Well, I guess you deserve to take him for everything he's worth after all that. And be grateful that at least your marriage to him did not produce any children from you."

"Oh, you know that's right!" Devon half-parroted in agreement.

Beside Devon George sat, a smile sliding onto his well-drawn full lips at the new look of outrage flitting over her. "You know, I think after this, you need to stay single for a while. You just don't have any luck with men. Richard's been doing this to you for the past six years? And then, there was that guy you married when you were twenty one? What was his name, again?"

"Oh, don't even mention him! Dustin Lavery . . . !" Devon turned her snorting gaze on Felix and then realized he didn't know who they were talking about. "That resulted from a one-night stand. I met Dustin at a bar; he took me back to his place and took me. We tried to turn it into a relationship. We got married two months later, the marriage lasted six. Ended when I came home one evening and found him in our bed with a woman he'd met through another one-night stand."

"Oh, good Lord . . . !" Rachel saw Felix try unsuccessfully to hold back a laugh as he continued to sit on the deep red second sofa looking at her. "How have you managed to make such bad choices of men for husbands?"

"I don't know, honey," Devon answered dismissively. "All I know is that you were always so good to me. You never did anything to hurt me. You were never anything more than a gentleman to me. Why did I leave you?"

Despite the amused smile that remained on Felix's attractive slender lips, his dancing brown eyes turned on George in a conspiratorial look that he returned and that Rachel couldn't miss. Her made up eyes slid back to her sister; determined that if she was going to make a play for Felix, she wasn't going to get him that quickly!

"But Devon, look here," she began, bent on getting her off his scent, "how did your attorney find those three women who showed up in court with all those kids that proved Richard's adultery beyond the shadow of a doubt?"

"I don't know, Rachel," Devon repeated impertinently. "All I know is that that man is worth every cent I pay him. I was so happy for the divorce to be over, I almost screwed him! And you know I couldn't do that to old Angel, because I would have given that old dog a heart attack!"

At her mention of the words heart attack, Rachel fell over in her seat and exulted.

Chapter Eleven

She laughed for ten minutes. Rachel couldn't stop it. Every time she thought of the words 'heart attack,' she exulted all over again. Rachel was hysterical. The memory of Thacker Muldoon telling her that morning after asking her if she wanted to be his fifth wife that he'd better leave her alone, that he didn't think he could handle all of her, that she'd be too much for him, that she'd probably give him a heart attack, and he already had one foot in the grave, sent her into peals of hysteria! She screamed. Rachel almost fell out of her seat. She literally laughed until she cried. Tears rolled out of her eyes, causing her mascara to run, leaving it streaking down all over her cheeks. And yet still she could not get a handle on her laughter. Rachel was beside herself. She was hysterical!

On the deep red sofa to the right of her, George stared on at her in tickled amazement. He did not understand the apparent inside joke that had caused her to crack up, and he even asked her in fact what was wrong with her. To the right of him, Devon didn't understand the cause of her hilarity either, although she laughed herself, imagining Rachel had cracked up because of the cleverness of her last remark. Only Felix knew that it was not the cleverness of Devon's last remark but the memory evoked by it that had triggered her. He sat on the deep red sofa adjacent to Devon and George and across from Rachel laughing himself while at the same time telling her: 'Calm down, girl!' Yet Rachel could not get control of her laughter. Finally after about another minute and with the running mascara beginning to sting her eyes, Rachel laughingly excused herself to go to the guest bathroom down the hall while George and Devon stared after her in tickled amazement.

Inside the lavish brass and white themed guest bath, Rachel tried to pull herself together, but that was impossible. The more she thought of her twenty-nine-year-old sister giving her seventy-year-old attorney a heart attack, the more she laughed. Removing a white monogrammed washcloth from a brass rack of three, Rachel moved over to one of the tan-and-white marbled sinks, her laughter doubled at the realization that she was going to have to remove all the attractive makeup that she had just so carefully reapplied from her face.

She had just gotten the water running in the sink when Felix suddenly appeared at the double vanity beside her. Rachel wondered how he had managed to follow her into the bath without Devon catching on to the fact that something was afoot between them.

"Look, girl," he began in his attractive tenor, smiling at her, "for the genuine surprise you showed when you arrived here and saw your sister; you deserve an Academy Award for that performance. But you're going to blow your nomination if you don't stop all this ridiculous laughing. Am I going to have to kiss you in order to shut you up?" he threatened her playfully.

Aware by the three Daytime Emmys the actor had been awarded for his own performances that he must know what he was talking about, Rachel turned her eyes on Felix, imagining she must look like something out of the worst freak show ever with all that black mascara streaking down her face.

"She said she was going to give her attorney a heart attack, the same way Thacker said I'd probably give one to him!" she squeezed out through her teeth, falling against him and laughing hysterically. The water running briskly in the sink was forgotten as Felix cradled her in his arms and joined in her ridiculous laughter.

She somehow managed to pull out of Felix's arms and wash all the makeup off her face with some nonirritating pearly liquid soap dispensed from a brass container to one side of the lighted mirror. Then clean-faced she returned to the living room, where she settled on the second sofa to the left of Felix, who had returned there before her. And both to George and Devon's amazement, she was still hysterical.

She was still laughing when Stacey returned from the bridal shop five minutes later. The short brunette came into the suite accompanied by George, took one look at her half huddled over on the sofa next to Felix, tears still streaming down her cheeks, and the brown eyes narrowed on her immediately.

"What's the matter with you?" asked the soft-spoken woman curiously.

"Apparently, our sister said something that cracked her up. Some kind of inside joke, I imagine." George laughed as he stood beside his fiancée, a blue-sleeved arm around her equally blue-clad shoulders. "And while we're on the subject of our sister, I'd like for you to meet her." He turned her toward the flashy woman sitting on the first sofa to the left of her, Devon having already caught the brunette's attention. "Stacey," George smiled, "I would like for you to meet Rachel's and my sister, Devon McClintock. She's the apparent producer of the inside joke that's got Rachel in stitches. Devon somehow managed to get out of her divorce and arrived here just in time for our wedding on Saturday. And Devon, this is my fiancée, Stacey Lumas."

Even at a distance of three feet, Rachel could tell exactly what Stacey was thinking as she sized up the older woman who had risen smoothly to her feet at George's mention of her name with a quick sweep of her brown lashes. So this was the one who dated Felix for four months, three days and seventeen hours when he and George lived in Georgia all those years ago before dumping him on his duff, eventually marrying two other men! Rachel guessed Stacey found it small wonder Felix had fallen for Devon at the command of her dazzling good looks—although thankfully Stacey did not show that as she proffered a blue-sleeved hand forward to shake hers.

"How do you do, Devon? George has told me so much about you. It's good to finally meet you," Stacey smiled innocently, showing her pretty little teeth.

"And it's good to meet you," Devon said with only the slightest hint of insincerity, showing her own perfect smile. With the quick sweep of her own black mascara-coated lashes Devon took in the stout semi-attractive Alaskan Native, noting her oval-shaped face, same color brown eyes, freckles across her nose, long brown hair flowing down her back, short five-foot-four-inch height. "So, you're the young filly who's lassoed my brother's heart," she said.

Rachel wondered where her sister had gotten that metaphor as she watched Devon drop her hand back to her side after having shaken that of the white woman.

"I guess so," Stacey said in reply to Devon's last remark, also still sizing her up in her innocent look.

"This is not a bad little hotel you have here," Devon said, letting her pink-shadowed eyes sweep around the circumference of the large red-themed living area of the penthouse suite.

"Not at all," Stacey agreed.

"Anyway, like George said, I somehow managed to wrap things up with my divorce and arrived here just in time for you two's wedding on Saturday. So, if you still need a bridesmaid in that procession, I'm here, ready, and available."

"I'm glad to hear that. I still have the shoes, and dress in your size—twelve, isn't it? Well, then, come on, Devon," smiled Stacey. "Let's go down to my suite on the tenth floor, and try on those shoes and dress."

"Lead the way," Devon smiled equally, and moved to follow her as the shorter woman pushed out of the circle of George's arm.

Rachel did not miss the brief conspiratorial look in the brown eyes Stacey had flashed onto Felix before she moved away from George across the deep-red carpeted floor, Devon following her. Rachel knew by that look exactly what the white woman had thought. She hoped Devon wouldn't rope him in again with her staggering beauty, especially when their breakup all those years ago had left him vulnerable. Except that Stacey didn't yet know that that was no longer the case, Rachel thought as she sat there on the deep red sofa beside Felix, tears of laughter streaming endlessly all down her face.

Any further thoughts Stacey may have had on the matter were forgotten as she pulled open the penthouse door a second later just as a man standing there along with a woman had raised a hand to acknowledge their presence with a knock.

"Daddy . . . ! And Mama! So, you guys finally made it up from Ketchikan!" Stacey screamed, taking the couple into her arms.

"Yes, dear, at last!" grinned her father, returning her excited embrace along with her mother. "And look who just caught up with us in the parking lot!"

Dropping his arms from his daughter, the man turned to pull a man standing behind him and her mother in front of her.

"Rick! So you finally got in from Hawaii!" beamed the soft-spoken Stacey in deepening delight, taking him into her arms.

"How're you doing, girl?" asked the man named Rick amid curving his arms around her. "What the world's wrong with this weather? It's cold as hell over here!"

Stacey laughed as she dropped her arms from his shoulders at the same time he dropped his from hers. "You haven't been living in Hawaii so long that you've forgotten what the Alaska summers can be like sometime?"

"Well, it has been a while," smiled the Alaska-born Hawaiian, a smile that broadened into a grin when his eyes strayed away from Stacey and onto Devon standing patiently two feet away from her. "Oooh-oooh-oooh-oooh! Who-who-who-who are you!"

To the right of her, George smiled. He had followed Stacey to the door to greet her parents and had already anticipated the man's interest in his attractive younger sister. Stacey stood quietly in front of George, likewise having expected Rick to take notice of her.

"Rick, this is my sister, Devon McClintock," said George, making introductions. "And Devon, this is Stacey's brother and my brother-in-law-to-be, Rick Lumas. Like Stacey, Rick owns a hotel comparable to this one in Honolulu."

"How do you do, Devon?" greeted Rick charmingly, extending a hand to take hers.

"How do you do . . . ?"

Immediately Rachel saw the reason behind her sister's cool response as she extended a dusky-skinned hand to shake that of the white man. Despite his apparent wealth in owning a hotel comparable to the Amber Heights, Devon could never go for him. His name was too close a derivative of her ex-husband, Richard. And she certainly didn't need that memory! However, unaware of that, Rick continued to hold her hand in the clasp of his until Devon pulled away predictably, leaving him staring at her wistfully as she remained standing within the circle of George's arm.

Assuming their brief interchange to be over, George turned a smile down on Devon. "Anyway, while you're over here, why don't I introduce you to Stacey's parents?" Turning her away from Rick while she acquiesced, he moved her in the direction of the couple standing just inside the door beside Stacey. "These," George went on smilingly to Devon then, "are my future in-laws and Stacey's parents, Al and Dora Lumas. And Mr. and Mrs. Lumas, my sister, Devon McClintock."

Although Dora Lumas shook the hand Devon had smilingly extended in greeting naturally enough, her husband when she raised her hand to him stared at her in shock, something he had been doing from the moment he had first laid eyes on her.

"Good God, woman, you are gorgeous!" Al Lumas cried, like son Rick, sizing her up from her hair to her feet. "And you say this is your sister?" persisted the Alaskan Native to George, grinning suddenly. "Do looks run in your family or what . . . !"

"Hold on, Mr. Lumas," smiled George. "I have another one to introduce you to."

As he then began to lead the couple over to meet her along with Rick and Stacey, Rachel forced a smile of interest to her medium lips. She hoped they would not be able to tell that she had been sitting there laughing herself silly as she wiped what tell-tale traces of tears remained on her cheeks off with a brush of her hand.

She sized the approaching pair up in the space of two seconds. The man named Al Lumas was tall, at least six feet, had gray hair, blue eyes, an oval face and was semi-attractive as was Stacey, had an average build and appeared to be in his early sixties. His wife Dora Lumas was a taller version of Stacey, graying brown hair flowing down from an equally semi-attractive oval-shaped face, she was also heavy-set, had Stacey's same brown eyes and appeared to be in her early sixties, as well. And unexpectedly, Rachel's brown gaze slid also onto Rick. About thirty, he had the same six-foot height and average build as his father, blond hair, same blue eyes. And like his parents and Stacey he was only semi-attractive, for though the oval shape of the face he had also inherited from his parents was symmetrical enough, there was some puffiness to his features, a thickness that was much too unbecoming to be appealing. Small wonder Devon had rebuffed him.

Her eyes were forced away from him as George stopped at her side with his future in-laws and Stacey looking on expectantly. "Mr. and Mrs. Lumas, this is my kid sister, Rachel Hardison. And Rachel, Al and Dora Lumas, Stacey's parents," George smiled.

Rising automatically to her feet as her brother made introductions, Rachel proffered a hand forward to shake the one Al Lumas had extended.

"How do you do, Mr. Lumas? It's good to meet you at last," she smiled.

Like with Devon, the Native Alaskan sized up the curving length of her with a quick sweep of his blond lashes. "And it's good to meet you, Rachel. My God, you are as beautiful as your sister!"

Indifferently Rachel shrugged. After all, the man did speak the truth! But damnit, she felt naked without any makeup on. And she remembered Stacey saying something on Monday about him having a brother. What must he be like, Rachel wondered, if Al Lumas was this obvious? And was he coming to the wedding?

"Thank you," Rachel acknowledged the man's appraisal with a last polite smile before dropping her hand back to her side.

George introduced her to his future mother-in-law next, Dora Lumas greeting her with the same naturalness and warmth with which she had greeted Devon a while ago. Then George introduced her to Rick. Like with Devon, Rick made the same overture to her as she extended a hand to shake his in greeting. And Rachel knew immediately by the glint in the blue eyes that Rick was going to make a play for her, already having realized Devon was out of his league. Well, not if she could help it, Rachel thought with a sigh of relief as he at last let go of her hand.

"And last but not least, you guys, I'd like for you to meet my best man, and my best friend, Felix Latham," George went on excitedly with his introductions.

Warmly Al Lumas shook the hand of the man who had risen to his feet next to Rachel, as did Rick on the other side of his mother. Dora Lumas, on the other hand, stood staring at his gorgeous sexy features, all her composure having deserted her as she stood having gone stiff in the floor.

"Oh-oh-oh-oh . . . ! Wait! Wait! I know you! I know you! I've seen you! I've seen you!" repeated the Native Alaskan woman amid shaking the hand Felix had extended in greeting. "You—ahm—you're on that soap—*As The Star Shines!* I watch it every day during my afternoon break! You play that character—ah—uhm—what's his name—? Joe Murray! You're Joe Murray!"

"I'm afraid so." Although flattered by her recognition of him, Felix's smile was apologetic, as his unexpected presence there had completely decimated the woman. His dancing brown eyes were kind as he let go of her hand, while she remained standing in the floor, staring at him disbelievingly.

On the other side of the first sofa, Devon turned a curious look on Felix at Dora Lumas' apparent absorption with his presence and soap character.

"Honey, are you that hot on the show?"

"Who are you kidding . . . !" The incredulous response came from George, who laughed at her complete lack of knowledge of Felix's character's doing on the soap. "Felix has won three Daytime Emmys for his portrayal of Joe Murray, a character who is so slick that he is presently having an affair with his boss, her daughter, and her stepdaughter, with none of them knowing of the others!"

"Really . . . !" Devon fixed her ex-flame with a renewed look of interest at her brother's mention of Felix's award-winning status and portrayal of his character of Joe Murray as a man presently having an affair with three women, all of them related, yet none of them knowing of the others. Crossing the red-carpeted floor toward him, she stopped at his side. "Well, come on, honey, why don't you come with me to try on this silly bridesmaid's dress, and you can tell me all about this Emmy Award-winning character of Joe Murray that you say you play on the show? Besides, we've got a lot to talk about, catch up on, anyway. So, come on, Stacey, let's go down to the tenth floor, and try on that silly dress! And after that; me and this man have got to go somewhere, and talk!"

Curling a dusky-skinned hand around Felix's larger golden brown one, Devon began to pull him speedily away from Rachel's side, giving him no chance to look back as she hustled him quickly across the floor away from the sitting area. Rachel no longer found anything to laugh about as she watched Felix sail out of the penthouse with her older sister, unaware that Stacey too was suspicious as she followed after them.

She was on him from that moment. She kept him down in Stacey's tenth-floor suite trying on her bridesmaid's dress and shoes for forty-five minutes before the three of them returned to the penthouse suite. Once done, the eight of them went down to dinner in the fabulous blue, green, gray and white Mediterranean Room on the second floor. Devon even managed to wangle a seat at the white-clothed table for eight to the right of Felix while Rachel somehow wound up all the way around on the other side to the left of Al Lumas. Rick Lumas sat to the left of her. As she had seen in his eyes when George had introduced them that he was going to make a play for her, that was exactly what he had done, in fact, he had spent the last forty-five minutes since Devon and Felix had left the penthouse trying to hit on her. He did that now, although Rachel fairly ignored him, as she wasn't interested in anything the thirty-year-old white man had to say to her.

What she was interested in was the conversation going on across the table between Felix and Devon as appetizers were served and consumed. They all were, as a matter of fact—with the exception of Stacey. The stout freckle-faced brunette sat to the left of Felix chattering her excitement over the fact that Devon's bridesmaid's dress and shoes had fit her perfectly along with other details about the upcoming wedding to her mother who sat across the table to the left of Rick, though Dora Lumas barely heard her, as she was too absorbed in the fact that a man of Felix Latham's eminence and star-status was sitting at her table to respond. George sat to the right of Al Lumas naturally listening to Stacey who sat to his right; after all, she was his fiancée and the one to whom he was getting married in the aforementioned wedding in two days. Yet like everyone else George was doing it with only half an ear, aware by the intense interaction between his best friend and his older sister that something suspicious was going on.

She had said they had a lot to catch up on, a lot to talk about, yet incredibly, all Devon wanted to do was talk about him. She sat smiling all in Felix's face, rose-blushed cheeks radiant, perfect teeth showing behind medium-pink lips, large luminous pink-shadowed and black mascara-lashed brown eyes fluttering; fluffy curly off-black hair flowing all down over her pink shoulders. Rachel nearly choked on her crab cake at Devon's nerve in telling him how fine he was, how good looking he was, how kind the years had been to him, how much better looking and sexier he was since she had last seen him ten years ago—how she found it no wonder he had been awarded three Daytime Emmys for his portrayal of Joe Murray on his soap, a man presently schtupping three women all at the same time, because as she had just mentioned, with his better sexier looks and body, he didn't belong anywhere but in a bed—*why did I leave you?* Was she insane, Rachel wondered? It was just as she had read on Stacey's mind when she had flashed a brief glance at Felix an hour before hoping that he would not let Devon rope him back in again with her dazzling good looks—that was exactly what Devon was trying to do. She was making a play for him before everyone at the table! Yet whether Felix had picked up on that warning look Stacey had sent him or not, Rachel thankfully realized Felix was aware of Devon's intention, as his regard of her—an equally good looking and sexy woman—outrageous flattery was one of amusement as usual.

"And while we're on the subject of you leaving me—what do you do, Devon?" he asked in his attractive tenor, smiling over his shrimp cocktail at her. "You know, you haven't gotten around to telling me that, yet. What did you decide to major in after graduating from West Georgia College all those years ago? What have you been doing in a work field since we've been out of touch?"

Devon smiled over her own shrimp cocktail at the smooth way he had brushed off her praises of his physical attributes. "I'm surprised George and Rachel haven't told you. You know I was studying journalism in college, and as a result, I'm an editor for a beauty magazine. But then, why shouldn't I be? You know I have the looks and body for it."

"Uhm-hmm." Felix ignored both her last remark and her reference to George and Rachel as he continued to stare at her. "And what did your ex-husband do that enabled him to leave you the house and everything in it, more than one car plus be able to pay alimony, palimony and child support?"

"Oh, don't talk to me about that son-on-a-bitch! That son-of-a-bitch . . . !" Devon screamed over her shrimp cocktail. "Let me tell you what that son-of-a-bitch did!"

She went into a long lengthy discussion about bastard ex-husband Richard McClintock, investment banker, who screwed around on her with other women during their entire six-year marriage and had the kids to prove it, that was still going on when the meals were served ten minutes later. Rachel was amazed at her going power as she dug into her roasted garlic chicken, and Felix's as well as he sat there aside her lapping it up. Truly the man could act, Rachel thought. He deserved another Emmy, an Oscar, an Academy Award, for his performance. To think that only two hours before, he had kissed her, slammed her up against the wall, spun her into his suite and almost made hot passionate love to her, yet he had not looked her in the eye since leaving the penthouse with Devon an hour earlier. And even though Rachel knew his act was to keep Devon in the dark as to his involvement with her, Felix's deliberate indifference to her still hurt her. And Rachel hoped that didn't show in her eyes when a fleeting glance at George showed him gazing at her with a similar concern in his own brown eyes, aware again that Devon's unexpected arrival there had caused something to go terribly awry between them.

Her eyes slid quickly away from George and settled onto Stacey sitting to the right of him and the left of Felix. The short stout brunette had long since stopped talking as she had become absorbed in the bantering going on between Devon and Felix. The expression on the semi-attractive freckle-faced Alaska Native again translated to Rachel exactly what she was thinking. Was this good looking black woman, Rachel's and George's sister, George's sister, her fiancé's sister, a woman who was going to be her sister-in-law, who dumped Felix ten years ago and then married two other men, the second of whom had apparently fooled around on her with other women in affairs that had produced children outside of the marriage and a man that she had just divorced, this crazy? And now that that was over she was here bantering with Felix—her good looking sexy actor ex-flame, praising him for his award-winning portrayal of Joe Murray on his soap, smiling all in his face and trying so blatantly to get him back? Trying to rope him back in when their breakup all those years ago left him vulnerable? *Why did I leave you?* Stacey was shocked at Devon's boldness and utter nerve. All she could do was stare, stunned, staggered and stupefied.

Unaware was Rachel that to the right of her and in complete opposition to the rage she and Stacey were feeling, Al Lumas sat amused by the floor-show being put on by the soap actor and his apparent ex-girlfriend. Rachel had just dropped her eyes back to the zucchini she was about to lift off her plate when the Native Alaskan suddenly leaned over and spoke in her ear.

"Your sister's gorgeous, but she's outrageous, isn't she?" asked the gray-haired man with a laugh.

"I guess so," Rachel agreed.

She took another look at her older sister as she and Felix began to reminisce about some Keith Sweat concert they went to when they went together back in the day. Al Lumas had not lied when he had said she was gorgeous, for Devon was dazzling, she was exquisite. With her wide oval face with its higher, more prominent cheekbones and prominent jawbones, Devon was a shiny new nickel, reducing Rachel—a woman whose round face was similarly as beautiful though lacking in such potent sensuality—to the slug she knew she was. Next to Devon, she felt like a dull penny, a dud dropped in the mud.

She suddenly became aware that Rick was speaking to her as she took a sip of her white wine. The blond man had been talking to her from the moment they had sat down at the table, although Rachel had ignored him as she sat watching Felix macking with his ex-girlfriend. What all had the Alaskan-born Hawaiian said to her, anyway, Rachel wondered as she lowered her wine glass back to the table? Hadn't he said something about Hawaii being the Aloha State, its capital of Honolulu and its resort annex of Waikiki being on the island of Oahu, Hawaii itself being more commonly known as the Big Island? Something about his hotel there that he had inherited from his Uncle Raj, the Kaikilani, being named for a beautiful princess that the fertility god Lono fell in love with in Waipi'o Valley? Something about Kona winds, the world's most active volcano Kilauea, something about King David Kalakaua, Kings Kamehameha I, II, III, IV and V, Kahuna Falls, Kapi'olani Park, Kaunala Trail, Kahalu'u Beach, what? What? The names spun around in Rachel's head as she concentrated on eating her wilted spinach without screaming out of frustration!

"Girl, Rachel, baby, I'm telling you, you should come and let me take you to my hotel, the Kaikilani, and stay there for a week," the thirty-year-old wealthy man flirted with her then, claiming her attention. "I'm telling you, the place is exquisite. Unlike this cold place, in Honolulu it doesn't get any colder than sixty, or hotter than eighty five, which makes for a much milder climate than over here. So, come, and let me put you up for a week. The hotel's fabulous, and it's bigger than this place. You can have your hair done in the beauty parlor, have your toenails cut, your elbows pumiced, your body wrapped in seaweed in the spa. And on the south side, you can look out the window and watch the kanes and the wahines eating poi, pua'a and pupu while strolling or sunbathing on Waikiki Beach. And if that's not enough for you, you can take a cruise; fly—depending on how fast you want to get there—to Kealakekua, on the Big Island. Once there, you can hike to Kealakekua Bay, go snorkeling in the spinner dolphins and coral-filled waters, or observe the obelisk monument on the north side of the Bay of Captain James Cook."

    Quickly Rachel averted her gaze from the roast chicken she had returned her attention to and back onto Rick's thick features in her surprise of his mention of the familiar name.

    "Wait a minute!" She blinked her eyes at him. "Are you talking about Captain James Cook—Captain Cook, Captain James Cook—the English discoverer for whom the Three Ships Sculpture depicting his voyages in the South Pacific was erected between what—Fourth and Fifth Avenues? The man who named—what is it—Cook Inlet, namer of Turnagain Arm Trail, and the man for whom the Captain Cook Hotel was named also? What was he doing in Hawaii?"

    "Are you kidding?" Rick turned an incredulous grin on her despite his obvious delight in having gotten her interest. "Why do you think that sculpture depicts Cook's voyages in the South Pacific? The English were the first known Europeans to set foot on Hawaiian shores. British Captain Cook spent most of a decade exploring and charting that South Pacific before chancing on Hawaii as he searched for a northwest passage to the Atlantic. The man spotted the islands of Oahu, Kauai, and Ni'ihau on January 17, 1778. His ships sailed into Kauai's Waimea Bay on the 20th. Captain Cook named the Hawaiian archipelago the Sandwich Islands, in honor of the Earl of Sandwich."

    Rachel blinked her eyes in amazement at this newly revealed information about Captain Cook as well as Rick's vast knowledge of the history and discovery of Hawaii, considering he was a fairly new transplant to the fiftieth state. The half-eaten food on her plate was momentarily forgotten as she watched him take a bite out of the pan-seared tuna in his own half-emptied plate.

    "I don't believe this," she shook her head.

    "Hey, what can I say? Like you said, Captain Cook was an explorer. He was all over the place in his day," smiled Rick amid swallowing the food in his mouth. "Unfortunately, he never did find the fabled Northwest Passage—possibly because he found it too damned cold going through the Arctic. So, on January 17, 1779, practically a year to the day of its first sighting, Cook returned to Hawaii, where he happened on the remaining Islands. He sailed into Kealakekua Bay on the Big

Island, where ten thousand curious onlookers and a thousand canoes carrying Hawaiians in the midst of celebrating the annual Makahiki festival sailed to greet him. When Cook went ashore, he was met by High Priest Kalaniopu'u and led to a temple lined with skulls. Everywhere he went people fell face down in front of him chanting 'Lono,' god of peace, agriculture and fertility for whom the festival was named, and recognizing him as his incarnation. And Cook and his crew became enamored with the islands' erotic exoticism and hospitality, which included food, drink, shelter, and in those days, sex.

"Unfortunately, on February fourth of that year, 1779, Cook and his vessels sailed north out of Kealakekua Bay and ran into a storm," Rick continued. "One of his ships broke a foremast, forcing him to return to Kealakekua to repair the mast. With the festival of Lonoikamakahiki then over, Cook's return was unexpected on the part of the Hawaiians whose observance was now on the main god Kunuiakea and as such, tensions rose with the unwelcome 'Lono' and a number of quarrels broke out among the two camps. Anyway, a whole mess erupted when a boat was stolen from Cook's flotilla. Captain Cook blockaded Kealakekua Bay and set off to capture the High Priest Kalaniopu'u with the simple intention of holding him hostage until the cutter was returned. But Cook released Kalaniopu'u at the request of his wife, only for a stomach ailment and increasingly irrational behavior on his part to lead to an altercation with the Hawaiians gathered on the beach when he went ashore to retrieve his goods. The villagers, also angered at hearing that another British search party had killed Hawaiian Chief Kalimu, began to attack with spears and stones. Shots were fired at the Hawaiians, but their woven shields protected them, forcing Cooks men to retreat down the beach. The Hawaiians closed in as Cook turned his back to launch his boats, and he was struck in the head. The blow stunned him and he staggered into the shadows. I think it was around February fourteenth of that same year, 1779. Cook ended up dying a most violent death."

"Oh, no . . . !" Rachel frowned at the unexpected news. "So, what are you saying—that Cook was killed by a bullet?"

"No, what killed him was the Hawaiians. When Cook's men abandoned him after he was hit, the Hawaiians both clubbed and stabbed him. Beat him to death in ten minutes. Angry attackers continued to stab his lifeless body, which it is rumored they then dismembered and ate."

"Oh, God . . . !" Rachel was almost put off her own eating of the zucchini she had returned to in her plate as she gritted her teeth at the thought of such a violent end. She wondered if Felix knew about this as she sliced a glance across the table only to find him still deep in reflection with his ex. "Poor ol' Captain Cook . . . !"

"Yea, he was," Rick agreed over the chickpeas that he was finishing eating from his own plate. "That's why that monument is erected on the north side of Kealakekua Bay, to mark the spot where Captain Cook was killed at the water's edge. But you know, Cook did some good things for Hawaii. He and his crew altered the course of its history. They introduced advanced weaponry, brought diseases to which the

Hawaiians had no immunity, and sired the first mixed-blood generation. They even named a small town after him just above the bay where Cook met his untimely end. And all that in addition to what he did for Alaska."

"Wow!" Rachel stared over the half emptied wine glass she was amid raising to her lips in amazement. "That's incredible!"

"Yeah."

She supposed it was because she had shown interest in the famed Captain Cook and his impact on Hawaii that Rick started to tell her about another famous person who had made an indelible mark on the Aloha state. Rachel was silent as she finished her meal, something Rick was doing also. She was not really interested in Ka'ahumanu, favorite wife of King Kamehameha I's twenty one, that he was discussing as she sat intently watching his face. Sure, the features of his oval face were rather thick and unbecoming, but they were symmetrical, providing just the right distance between his vivid blue eyes. He had a nice nose, nice lips. Indeed, they were medium and rather kissable. Rachel wondered if she would get a reaction out of Felix were she to suddenly kiss—kiss him—kiss Rick on his medium lips. No doubt it would get a reaction out of Rick, she thought! Deciding against it, Rachel dropped her eyes back to the roast chicken she was finishing on her plate.

Inevitably, her chocolate gaze returned to Felix still sitting across the table from her reminiscing with Devon about a day they spent walking hand-in-hand around Fernbank Science Center a thousand years ago. Rachel had been so terrified when she had returned to the hotel with him that she had wanted to run from him. She admitted to herself—she liked it when he would hold her hand, because a pleasure would go up her arm that she had never felt with another man. And she liked kissing him—an action that would imbue her with a whole new wealth of pleasures. Unfortunately, with each kiss, those pleasures had ballooned into feelings and sensations that had not only delighted her but terrified her. She had not known how to handle all those new feelings and hot sensations quaking through her body. Rachel had wanted to run from Felix. She had bolted off the elevator on the penthouse floor away from him and George and run straight to the bathroom once inside it. There, she had leaned against the door and given in to her terror. *Oh, George, I need help, George. I—I've lost my cool. I've lost my head. I did just what I didn't expect to do. I did what you warned me not to do. I've been sucked in. Felix has sucked me in with his charm, good looks and male virility!* And Rachel had known he was going to suck her in all the more when they had gotten off the elevator on the twelfth floor, for as soon as he had kissed her yet again on the way to his suite, she had literally jumped in her shoes.

'I have to go!' Rachel had said amid wrenching her wrist free of his hand and pivoting away on her heel. And yet it was Felix who had freaked at the thought that she was abandoning him the same way Devon had done him all those years ago, grabbing her by an arm and pulling her up short before she could move two feet down the corridor. *'Are you running from me?' 'What?' 'What is this ill luck I have with Hardison*

women? First Devon leaves me, now you? Well, let me tell you something, Little Sister, don't you . . . kiss me once or twice, say it's very nice, and then, you run . . . ! Little Sister, don't you do what your big sister done . . . !' 'What?' 'I never felt when I kissed Devon the way I feel when I kiss you! Why do you think I told you when we got back from the club last night how much I liked kissing you?' the memory rolled around in Rachel's head. *'What?' 'Why do you think I've been all over you, today? Don't you get it, girl after my own heart? I think I'm falling in love with you, if such a thing makes sense. I mean, is it possible for a man to fall in love with a woman in three days?'* Well, Rachel guessed it wasn't, for Big Sister had blown in from the South just in time to catch him before he hit the ground, or as she had read on Stacey's mind, roped him back in. Rachel lowered her eyes back to her plate, not wanting anyone to see the utter pain she knew must be reflected in their brown depths.

Her heart sank several inches farther down to the soles of her feet when the meal finally ended and Devon reached out and claimed Felix by an arm while picking her pink clutch purse up in her other hand.

"Come, darling," Devon began, "you've been at this hotel for a while. Why don't you show me around this fabulous place?"

Felix shook her hand off his arm with a smile. "Sorry, no can do," he said in his attractive tenor. "It's been real talking to you, seeing what you're up to these days, and I enjoyed our little trip down memory lane. But I have to go. I have a woman waiting for me, and she's beautiful. We have a date to watch Elvis, remember?"

Although Felix kept his dancing brown gaze directed intently on Devon in his refusal of further offer of her company, Rachel could not stop the intense pleasure that showed on her face at his mention of their earlier broken date and reference of her as beautiful. Apparently Big Sister having blown in from the South to catch him before he hit the ground wasn't exactly the case after all, Rachel thought! *Too bad, Stacey, Felix did not let Devon rope him with her shameless play for him, though you did not know yet that the woman he had dumped her for and with whom he had a date to watch Elvis was me!* Rachel thought happily as she watched the brunette stare at Felix in total confusion. *Your fiancé knew, though.* One glance at George and Rachel could see the same delight flashing in his deep brown eyes as he too knew exactly who Felix had been talking about.

Devon however, did not appreciate Felix's abrupt brush-off of her as she stared at his good looking sexy features in offense. " . . . Not this evening, you don't!" she flashed.

And quickly curling her hand over his arm again, and with her pink clutch purse still held in her other one, Devon moved to her feet, pulled him to his, and spun him resisting all the way out of the restaurant.

Behind them, Rachel's gaze resettled on her brother in amazement, the same of which she could see in George's eyes as he continued to gaze past Al Lumas at her. They were going to have to play the game of keep-Devon-in-the-dark-as-to-their-involvement-with-each-other until the wedding was over on Saturday!

In the seat to the right of her, Al Lumas leaned over to speak in her ear again. "Your sister's gorgeous, but she's bold, isn't she?" asked the gray-haired Native Alaskan with a laugh.

"I guess so!" Rachel agreed. *Not gorgeous enough,* she thought to herself with a laugh!

In the seat to the left of her, Rick leaned over to speak to her again as well. "Yea, he really told her off, didn't he?" asked the blond Alaska-born Hawaiian, laughing similarly.

"Uhm-hmm!" Rachel agreed.

Wiping his mouth on a white napkin the same way Rachel was doing hers, Rick pushed back his chair and moved to his feet. "Come on," he said, "let's get out of here. Let's you and me also take a walk around this fabulous place."

Rachel couldn't help smiling at the thought that he reminded her of Felix as she rose in response to the hand he had curved around hers to pull her to her feet.

He took Rachel all over the hotel, refreshing her memory of the two large meeting rooms, game room and lounge on the first floor, the kitchen, guest laundry/cleaning service and housekeeping department on the ground floor, large indoor pool and twenty-four-hour unisex Nautilus fitness gym not too far from it, the men's fitting/dress room on the third floor, women's fitting/dressing/powder room, also on the third floor. They talked to the concierge, a couple of bellboys; a couple of waiters, one of the fitness instructors, a bartender and one of the reservationists at the front desk. And just like from the moment they had first been introduced, the white man was all over her—especially after the interest she had shown in his tale of the legendary Captain James Cook. But Rachel did not care that Rick was misconstruing her secular interest as sexual interest in her utter delight of Felix's confession—although indirectly—of his complete absorption with her to her sister.

He had said he thought he was falling in love with her. Apparently he was. He had said she had vamped him. She guessed she had. He had said he was gone on her. Well, he must be, because he did not fall for Devon's gorgeous good looks, seductiveness and outrageous play for him. On that same note, Felix had said Rachel was beautiful. She was beautiful! More beautiful than Devon! Well, apparently he was falling for her, the same way Rachel had fallen for him. All six-foot-one gorgeous attractive good looking sexy well-built inches of him! Rachel was delirious. She was delirious!

Rick noticed her smiling to herself like a Cheshire Cat as they arrived in an elevator back on the first floor close to an hour later and laughed.

"Hey, Rachel, what I just said about Prince Jonah Kuhio Kalanianaole can't have been that damned funny," Rick said. "What in the world are you thinking about?!"

Rachel turned a laugh on the thick-skinned white face. She had been so wrapped up in her delicious thoughts that she hadn't heard a word he had said about Hawaii's first delegate to the U.S. Congress.

"I guess I'm still thinking about how Felix cut my sister down after dinner tonight," she said, after all, it was not a total lie. "Devon's not used to that kind of dismissal from a man!"

"I don't imagine she is!" Rick agreed with a laugh.

They hadn't gotten twenty five feet away from the elevator banks when George came striding down the hall from the direction of the lobby. Four blue-clad bellboys accompanied him carrying a number of luggage belonging to the couple he had his arms around. Rachel jumped in the floor in added delight at the realization that the black couple was their parents.

"Oh, Mama!" she cried as the threesome approached her. "So, you guys finally got here!" Rachel took her into her heather denim arms.

"Yes, we finally made it!" her mother agreed, stepping from the circle of her son's arms and smilingly curling her own arms around her youngest daughter despite the tan leather clutch purse she carried in one hand. At the same time, George gave the key of their suite to one of the hovering bellboys and sent them on ahead of them. "How are you, Rachel?"

"I'm great, Mama!" Rachel laughed, knowing that had never been so close to the truth as in that moment of her pulling her face from her shoulder to see her mother's own face. Sephora Hardison was exquisite, possessing the same dusky coloring as she and Devon, her facial shape the same wide oval as Devon's, features equally as symmetrical as Rachel and Devon's, same long straight relaxed off-black hair—barely grayed—curling down to her shoulders. And beneath the long stylish brown wooly midi-coat she wore over tan slacks, she had their same full figure except that she was a size larger than Devon, a fourteen. And at fifty eight years of age, Sephora looked thirty nine. She did not look in any way as if she'd bore three children. "You look great!" Rachel exclaimed then, brown gaze sliding back to her mother's face.

"So do you!" Sephora grinned, own brown eyes lowering over her blue-clad figure and long straight relaxed off-black hair flowing down over her breast.

Yet Rachel did not see her mother's admiring gaze as hers slid to her father standing beside her in a smart black woolen midi-coat pulled on over navy slacks. At sixty-one years of age, Marshall Hardison was an extremely good looking man, possessing short salt-and-pepper hair around a suntan brown face shaped in a perfect oval, features as equally symmetrical as his five-foot-seven-inch wife. And despite the fact that he was only five-eleven, he had a bearing that implied a much taller height. In fact, he looked like Harry Belafonte. George looked just like him.

"Daddy . . . !" With equal happiness Rachel walked into her father's arms, black purse strapped to her shoulder banging gently against the curve of her hip. "So, you guys finally got here! How was the drive all the way from Villa Rica?"

"Long!" exclaimed Marshall with a laugh as he held her to his chest, his voice the same brusk alto timbre as that George. "We just got on the road and drove. 'Been rolling ever since bright and early Monday morning!"

"I'll bet!" Rachel agreed over his broad black-coat-clad shoulder. "I'm sure George is glad you guys finally made it here! We weren't expecting you until tomorrow! How was the drive in the RV?"

"Great!" her father grinned over her heather denim shoulder. "That thing drives like a dream! I should have bought it twenty years ago, instead of just last year!"

"I'll bet!" she agreed. Only absently did Rachel realize she was repeating herself as she pulled her face from her father's shoulder. Her eyes were as bright as her Halle Berry smile as she turned to introduce him and her mother to Rick, who stood aside her eyeing them expectantly.

"Mom, Dad, I'd like for you to meet Rick Lumas," she began, "and Rick, these are George's and my parents, Marshall and Sephora Hardison."

"How do you do, Rick?" greeted her parents warmly, extending their hands to shake his.

"How do you do!" asked the white man amid shaking their hands and staring incredulously. "My God, I guess my father was right! Looks do run in your family! As you can see, they ran away from mine!" Rick half laughed.

"Hush up, man! I happen to think your sister's pretty enough!" George censored him, laughing also as were his parents and Rachel.

"Rick is George's fiancée Stacey's brother," Rachel smiled. "Have you met her yet?"

"Not yet," George said. "She's currently tending to some business with a guest up on the sixth floor. She'll be down in a little bit. I'll introduce the parents, then."

"Oh, I see. Well, you're going to love her. She has long brown hair, freckles across her nose, she's soft-spoken. She looks much better than Rick!" Rachel turned a laugh on the blond man, whose own face reddened in amusement of her praise of his sister's looks and putdown of his.

"Like Stacey, Rick owns a hotel in Hawaii," Rachel continued. "He's been telling me all about the state. A whole lot of names with a whole lot of k's—you know, that naturally I can neither remember, nor pronounce."

"Yeah, you'll have to come to my hotel," Rick offered with a smile. "It starts with—of course, another K. It's called the Kaikilani, and it's in Honolulu, on Oahu. You'll have to come see the place," he repeated. "It's fabulous."

"I'm sure. Well, we'll have to keep that in mind," Marshall said.

"Consider it for your next anniversary. The city has great make-out places, not to mention great wedding chapels from which to renew your vows. You should try and remember that, Rachel," Rick said suggestively.

Rachel turned a laugh on the thirty-year-old wealthy man flirting despite being all business. "Hush up!" She sliced her twinkling luminous brown gaze on her mother who, like her father and George, stood listening to their interchanges with interest.

"And while we're on the subject of states, how've you been enjoying this one since you got here on Monday?" Sephora asked. "Have you been able to do any sightseeing since arriving here in Anchorage?"

"Boy, have I ever!" Rachel practically flushed in the floor at the excitement brought on by her mother's question. "Well, I mean, George couldn't take me around because of being busy tending to his wedding and the running of this hotel. So, he asked Felix to take me around. He's seen pretty much of the city, what with having arrived here Sunday before last."

"Now, that's an interesting thought, Felix showing you around," Marshall inserted with a laugh. "You know, the last he saw you ten years ago, you were just a little kid. It must have bowled him over to see what you look like now!"

"Boy—did it, ever!" Rachel laughed, her eyes sweeping past his shoulder onto George and meeting his knowing look. "Anyway, he's been a great tour guide. He's taken me everywhere, and we've done everything. And we've had the best time."

"I see." Sephora's brown gaze rolled over her observantly, for she had not missed the excitement underlining her quiet tone.

"And while we're on the subject, where is Felix, anyway?" asked Marshall curiously.

"I don't know. . . . Somewhere running around here with Devon. She's here, by the way."

"Yea, so George's told us," Sephora replied in a look that indicated her initial surprise at the discovery. "What's she doing over here? She's supposed to be back in Atlanta amidst getting a divorce from Richard!"

"Well, let me put it in a nutshell. She told her attorney, Angel, that her brother was getting married on Saturday here, and that she needed to be out of court by mid-week. Find some way to prove that Richard had been in bed with those two women she had found him with and that he had lied about, and them, too. Well, Angel found something better than that. On Tuesday, just two days ago, three women other than the two she found him in bed with came into court, possessing six kids between them, claiming that Richard was their father, three of them looking just like him. Paternity tests proved that Richard was the father of all six of them. Adultery proved. Divorce granted right there. The youngest child was two, and the oldest one was five. You figure it out." Rachel fell silent as she rendered that last remark and watched the realization dawn on her parents' faces.

"Wait!" The order came incredulously from Sephora. "What are you trying to tell us—that Richard has a five-year-old child, and he and Devon had only been married for six? What are you trying to tell me—that Richard got a child from another woman before he and Devon had even been married a year?" Sephora lowered her distressed face into her hand after Rachel's affirming nod. "Oh, God . . . ! Devon must be a mess! How is she handling this?"

"Hey, she's handling it," Rachel said dryly. *If that was what you could call it,* she thought.

"I have got to talk to her," Sephora said. "She must be destroyed."

Rachel determined to change the subject as she watched her mother pull her face from her palm. "So, what suite number are you guys on the way to?"

"They've put us in Suite 1224. That is, if we ever make it to the elevators, and get there!" Sephora laughed. "How long have we been standing here in the corridor talking anyway, about ten minutes?"

"I guess so!" Rachel agreed. "Anyway, you'll be down the hall from Felix. He's on the same floor."

"I see." The simple response was Sephora's.

As if summoned by mental telepathy, Felix came speedily down the richly elegant sophisticated stripe-paper-walled hall at just that instant from the direction of the lobby. Devon was hanging all over his arm, although thankfully, Rachel could see, he was busily resisting her touch.

Predictably, a grin curved his lips as he stopped at George's side and turned an amazed look on her parents. "Oh, my God, look who's here! It's Mr. and Mrs. Hardison!" he exclaimed in his attractive tenor. "How in the world are you two?!"

"Just great!" smiled Sephora, responding to the embrace Felix had taken her into and curling her arms equally over his broad navy-and-red-plaid shoulders. "And how are you, Felix?"

"The same . . . !" Felix loosened his hold on her coat-clad shoulders to turn another look of amazement down over her smiling features. "My God, you look the same as you did ten years ago! You haven't changed a bit! You're just as gorgeous as ever! And you know, I always wondered all those years ago how you could have a twenty-one-year-old son, when you were only eighteen!"

"Flatterer . . . !" Sephora practically blushed beneath the grin the attractive man had turned on her as she pushed the rest of the way out of his arms. "I see the years have given you more charm, along with even better looks, huh!"

"So they tell me!" Despite his laugh of agreement, Felix fairly brushed off her similar flattery amidst turning his twinkling brown gaze on her husband. "And Mr. Hardison . . . ! God, you look as great as you ever did! It's good to see you, again! How in the world are you!"

"I think the question here is: How are you!" Marshall laughed amid breaking gently out of the embrace Felix had taken him into. "George tells me you're an actor now!"

"Yes, I play Joe Murray on the soap *As The Star Shines*, a role which has won me three Daytime Emmy Awards over the last five years," Felix smiled, dropping his arms from his shoulders.

"Really . . . ! I had no idea you were so talented!" Marshall stared at the younger man, impressed by his obvious ability as an actor. "In any case, you definitely have the face for an actor, whatever you want to work on," Marshall went on smoothly in his brusk alto, bold brown long-lashed gaze sizing him up from his short well-groomed black hair all the way down to his black, blue and white Reebok-sneaker-clad feet. "And you know, that's one thing I've always hated about you. You look better than me!"

"Oh, don't tell that lie!" Felix turned a blushing laugh on the shorter although equally attractive suntan-skinned man twice his age. "So, what are you guys doing here tonight?" Felix asked Marshall and Sephora, briskly changing the subject. "Rachel told me you weren't going to get here until tomorrow!"

"Actually, we've been on the road since Monday morning, and just drove straight in," Marshall explained in his brusk alto. "Which reminds me—what's with this weather—? George told us that the summers were cool here, but it feels like its twenty degrees out there! It's like going through culture shock, when considering the fact that it was eighty degrees when we left Georgia Monday morning!"

"Yea, the difference in temperature here does take some getting used to."

"That's the truth!" Rick agreed, intercepting the conspiratorial smile Felix turned on George still standing behind his father smiling quietly.

"And I'm going to tell you right now, Mr. and Mrs. Hardison," Felix went on, "you're going to have to get rid of the heavy coats. They don't wear them over here, they wear layers and parkas. As a matter of fact, when Rachel got here Monday saying that she'd brought sweaters and a coat, I said look, girl, that's not going to work. You're going to have to get a parka. So, I took her out to get one, didn't I, girl?" Felix turned a grin on Rachel that sent her flushing in the floor. "Anyway, I guess I'm going to have to take you two out and get you ones, too!" Felix finished to her parents with a laugh.

"And while we're on the subject of Rachel, you know you haven't seen her since she was a kid," Marshall said then, mind back on a thought he'd voiced earlier. "It has to have blown your mind, seeing what she looks like today!"

"Boy—did it ever! As a matter of fact, I was just telling Devon when she arrived this evening that Rachel's not fourteen anymore! She really grew up, didn't she . . . ?"

Rachel flushed deliciously beneath the meaningful assessing look Felix lowered over figure, her heart thudding ridiculously. "Fresh!"

She was almost relieved when Felix diverted his smiling eyes away from her after a moment and back onto her parents. "So, what suite have you guys been assigned to, tonight?" he asked in his attractive tenor, dancing brown gaze slicing from Marshall to Sephora.

"They've put us in Suite 1224. That is, if we ever get up there. George sent the bellboys ahead of us thirty minutes ago. We've been standing here talking for the past three hours!" Marshall laughed.

Felix laughed too at the exaggerated remark; dancing eyes settling briefly back on his friend. "Well, I think that's amazing. As a matter of fact, I'm in Suite 1202. I'm right up the hall from you."

"Yea, so, Rachel tells us. Is that where you two were heading anyway?" Sephora took control of the conversation, her smiling brown gaze slicing meaningfully from Felix to Devon still standing quietly to the right of him, pink leather purse still clutched in her hand. "And while we're on the subject—how are you doing, anyway, baby?" She curved a motherly arm around Devon's pink-clad shoulders, brown eyes having become probing on the dusky-skinned made-up face that she had inherited from her. "Rachel told us the divorce was a mess. That Richard—to put it in a nutshell—has produced six children from three women other than the two you caught him in bed with, and that the oldest one is five."

Devon's head bobbed a nod in front of the coat-clad arm curled around her shoulders. "Mama, I'm telling you, it was a mess," she repeated sourly. "That swine has been messing around on me since the first year of our marriage. I don't know where Angel found those three women! He's worth every cent I pay him! Anyway, it's over, I'm out of there, and I'm here to be in George's wedding, after all."

"Well, at least, I know he's glad for that!" Sephora turned a smile on her eldest child amid consolingly patting Devon's arm. "And we're glad to have you over here with us."

"I'm glad to be here, too."

"So, I take it that now that that's over, you two are going to get back together after all these years?" asked Marshall of Devon and Felix, having noticed their close standing positions in the floor and eyeing the two of them artily.

"With any luck," Devon said hopefully, curving her free hand over Felix's arm.

"Oh, no, I'm sorry," Felix shook his head. "I have a woman waiting for me. I've been trying to shake this one for the past hour!"

"I see!" Marshall laughed at the funny response despite wondering if Rachel weren't that woman as he watched her literally melt beneath the conspiratorial grin the attractive younger man had turned on her.

"You know, I told you that in order to keep all those women from chasing after you because of your good looks to put a brown paper bag over your head, and go as the Unknown Soap Opera Star!" Rachel teased him with a laugh.

"Hush up, girl!" Felix ordered despite flashing his perfect teeth in a laugh at the memory as well.

A grin curved Rachel's lips as the feel of his left hand suddenly curving over her wrist sent that giddy pleasure sliding up her arm as usual. She was delirious!

George was the only one who saw the murderous glare Devon slid over her and Felix as she stood there wondering what the hell was going on between the two of them.

Chapter Twelve

They moved to the elevator banks, climbed into the first one that opened, and rode it up to the twelfth floor. All of them with the exception of Rick, that is, who got off on the eighth floor in search of his parents in Suite 828. Which was just as well, as Rachel no longer wanted him around, anyway—certainly not after they got off the elevator on the twelfth floor. They had just approached Suite 1202 down the hall when Felix suddenly reached out and curved a detaining hand over her wrist, pulling her away from the others. Rachel was glad that George, the only one who saw his friend's intention, smilingly hustled Devon and their parents on down the hall and around the corner to Suite 1224 as she turned to face Felix, smile on her own mouth, that wave of pleasure skittering up her arm again.

"Hey, girl," Felix began in his attractive tenor, smile on his own lips, "I'm sorry our evening got messed up like this. I never dreamed tornado Devon was going to fly in from Atlanta and blow it all over the place."

"Well, maybe if we're lucky, we can put it back together," Rachel suggested with a boldness that surprised her. "Because like you said after dinner, we still have a date to watch Elvis, remember?" she half grinned.

"Uhm-hmm. Although I'm afraid not this evening," Felix shook his head regretfully. "What is it—ten o'clock? I'm going to jump out of these clothes—literally speaking—" he forced a laugh, "and turn in for the evening. I'm tired, we got in late last night, and I couldn't get any sleep after that for thinking about you, anyway. Besides, you need to get with your parents, help them get settled in after their long drive in from Georgia. So, I'll see you in the morning at eight thirty in the cafeteria for breakfast. Your parents will probably be there, as well as Stacey's parents, Devon, and Rick. We can spend the whole time there hiding our feelings for each other from all of them. And maybe if we're lucky after that, we'll be able to go somewhere and get away from all of them before the wedding rehearsal starts at two o'clock."

"Now, that's not a bad idea, the thought of getting away somewhere with you."

"I should hope not."

Rachel couldn't hold back the gurgle of pleasure that sounded in her throat as Felix tightened his hold on her wrist and pulled her into a kiss that sent a wealth of delicious sensations shooting through her. She was thoroughly delirious when he ended the goodnight kiss after a moment to look at her.

"Go catch up with your parents, let me catch up on that sleep, and I'll catch up with you later," he said.

Rachel knew he meant every word of that promise by the meaningful way the dancing brown eyes rolled in his head in accompaniment to the sexy smile he'd turned on her.

"Okay," Rachel responded breathlessly, smiling also, that gurgle sounding in her throat again.

Leaning forward, Felix lowered his lips against hers to get one last taste of her before finally raising his face away from hers and dropping his hand from her wrist. Completely breathless, Rachel turned away from him with a smile at the same time he unlocked the white door with the key poised in his hand and disappeared into his suite.

She floated all the way down the hall to Suite 1224, where her parents were in the process of emptying an assortment of luggage sprawled atop the king-sized bed and surrounding floor in the large bedroom identical to hers. George and Devon moved around the room helping them. Rachel had to force the giddy smile from her lips as she lowered her black bag onto the bed and picked a tweed Pullman of the same color, one out of a six-piece set of luggage by American Flyer, up off the floor at one side of it. Or so she thought she had as she unlocked the Pullman with the key attached to its carrying handle.

"So, how was the drive up?" Rachel heard herself asking as she opened the luggage and began emptying it of its contents. "Did you drive into any bad weather?"

"Actually, it wasn't too bad," Sephora contradicted, like her, emptying a black tweed Pullman of the same set of luggage, although a larger one. "I mean, we were only on the road for what—four days. And the weather held up pretty well everywhere we went, I mean, after all, it is summer. But we did have our moments. I mean, when we got to St. Louis, it rained. And when we passed through Des Moines, it rained. And whoever said it never stopped raining in Seattle didn't lie. After driving for forty one and a half hours, we hit there when—early yesterday morning, and it rained, rained, and rained! We were on our way north up Interstate Five, and I didn't think we were ever going to get to BC-97 in Prince George, British Columbia, Canada, it was such a slow nerve-wracking drive through the slush!"

"Yea, but when we hit Mile 320 on the Alaska Highway past Fort Nelson and began the climb to the top of Steamboat Mountain, it was sunny and beautiful," grinned Marshall over the carry-on bag, one of three red-and-black tapestry-patterned luggage also of the American Flyer label that he stood emptying on the bed next to his wife. "Large groves of poplars, the Highway lined with wildflowers, while off in the distance to the south, you are rarely out of sight of the equally snow-capped Rocky Mountain peaks. Okay, so the narrow turns and gravel patches slow you down a bit, but the higher you get, the better the view. And then, as you begin heading down Steamboat Mountain around Mile 350-352, the view down through the Muskwa River Valley and over to the Rockies is exquisite. And does that Alaska Highway go on forever, or what! Called by at least eleven names that I can remember, it not only goes up and down and loops around as I just said, but twists north, south and west, and it especially became so as we entered Stone Mountain Provincial Park at Mile 375, because the next hundred-mile section of road has got to be the most hazardous on the entire Highway. But thank God, once we hit the Canadian Customs at Mile 1203 just outside Beaver Creek, like the information the travel agency gave us, the actual border to the U.S. is marked by a clear-cut strip of trees that extend in a perfectly straight line for 740 Miles. Another 92 miles to Mile 1314 at Tok way with the Mentasta Mountains to the left and it was practically smooth sailing in that RV all the way through the Tetlin National Wildlife Refuge down Alaska Route One South for the next hundred twenty two miles or so, down AK-1/AK-4, and then back to AK-1 another 146 miles to Glen Allen, where the Glenn Highway also turns right, beginning another thirty five or so miles down AK-Route One South to Anchorage situated at the foothills of the equally beautiful towering Chugach Mountain Range. Twenty seven hundred miles from Atlanta to Seattle in forty one and a half hours, and then, 2,275 more miles from Seattle to Anchorage in thirty five and a half hours for a total of what—seventy seven hours in four days? How many miles did we travel altogether, Sephora? About 4,980 . . . ?"

Devon's long curled off-black hair fanned over her pink shoulders as she shook her head in amazement at her father's most detailed description of his and her mother's convoluted and lengthy cross-country trek.

"You guys are crazy for taking all that time and driving all that distance at your age," she denounced both of them amid lowering a pair of folded slacks that she had removed from one of the same red-and-black tapestry patterned luggage her father was emptying into a bottom French Provincial chest drawer. "I hopped a plane out of Hartsfield-Jackson International last night, and was here at five thirty this evening!"

"Yea, but it was fun, baby," Marshall laughed, deriding her similarly in his brusk alto voice as he bent beside her to place more clothing items into one of the French Provincial chest drawers. "Besides, I'm not dead, yet!"

"I know what you mean, Dad!" Although George agreed with his father as he busied himself placing some clothing items in one of the French Provincial dresser drawers alongside his mother, his smile had not been meant for him, but for Rachel. Completely unaware was she that from the moment she'd begun emptying the black tweed Pullman luggage she had placed on the king-sized bed and throughout their father's entire discourse, she had been doing it inattentively with a delicious smile on her face. "Yea, that Alaska Highway is something else," George agreed with his Dad then. "Nicknamed the Alcan Highway for Alaska-Canada Highway, it was cut through the bush during WWII after the bombing of Pearl Harbor, a muddy, twisting, single-lane trail fit only for trucks and bulldozers that was designed to provide a military supply route to threatened America, also to provide a supply line to a series of Air bases—the Northwest Staging Route—which stretched in a chain from Edmonton, Canada to Fairbanks here in Alaska. In fact, it's because the surveyors had worked from the tops of the bulldozers and partly to protect convoys from enemy aircraft in a pioneer business that was so tiring that convoy drivers were changed every forty five to ninety hours, resulting in the Highway being crooked every which-a-way it is," George added informatively. "It's about fifteen hundred miles long, passes from Delta Junction east through Alaska toward Dawson Creek, British Columbia; extends about six hundred miles to Lower Post, where it enters Canada's Yukon. Stacey and I drove all the way up there through all that twisting through mountain and bush during a week vacation last August. We must have been insane!"

"You traveled what—1,400 miles from Anchorage up into Canada's Yukon when your Mother and I just traveled 5,000 miles to here from Villa Rica, Georgia? What could have been so bad about so short a trip . . . ?" Marshall derided with a laugh.

From a love-struck daze Rachel heard her father brush off the implication in George's last remark that his and Stacey's drive had been as equally difficult as his and Sephora's.

"With two flat tires as soon as we reached Whitehorse, and with Stacey driving?" George demanded of his father with an incredulity that immediately translated his fiancée's obvious lack of the muscle and manpower necessary in a tire changer.

"Yea, but still, I'll bet it was fun!" Marshall continued to laugh.

Although Rachel heard the lighthearted response their father had repeated with only half an ear, she knew that George like her would accept it as just another indication of his adventurous nature.

"Anyway, while we're on the subject of my fiancée, it's only what—ten fifteen? Why don't we put off setting all this clothing aside for a while?" Rachel heard George suggest to his parents with a smile. "Come on, I want you to meet her. She ought to be finished with business on the sixth floor and back in her tenth-floor suite, by now."

Abandoning the black tweed Pullman she had barely been paying attention to emptying onto the cluttered blue-print spread-covered king-sized bed anyway, Rachel slid the black strap of her bag back onto her shoulder amid moving to her feet to follow her brother out of the suite behind their parents and Devon.

As George had hoped, Stacey had returned to her tenth floor suite when they arrived there a couple minutes later.

"Darling, it's about time I caught up with you!" George laughed.

The softly-spoken woman smiled her surprise upon seeing him into the suite after a brief greeting kiss. "How long have you been looking for me?" Stacey asked amid opening the white door to see him on into the suite.

"Well, let me put it this way. I have someone else I want you to meet. They arrived here from Georgia about a half hour ago while you were handling business with a guest on the sixth floor."

As Rachel followed George into the large elegant living room of the suite behind him, her parents and Devon, she came out of her daze long enough to see that it was deceptively clean and neat, for everything was in its place around a number of furniture pieces in the same French Provincial design of her own suite. For that reason, she wondered if Stacey's bedroom was in the same sloppy disarray that it had been in when she had last seen it on Monday, and was glad the woman had no cause to take her parents in there as George turned in the floor to make introductions.

"Dad," George began smilingly to Marshall, a blue-sleeved arm still curved around Stacey's waist, I'd like for you to meet Stacey Lumas, owner of this hotel, and my fiancée. And Stacey, this is my father, Marshall Hardison."

If her father was shocked upon discovering that George was marrying a white woman, he thankfully didn't show it, Rachel was at least glad to see as he gazed down at the short Native Alaskan standing and eyeing him expectantly.

"How do you do, Mr. Hardison? It's good to meet you at last," smiled Stacey, proffering a blue-sleeved arm forward to shake his hand.

"And how do you do, Stacey!" grinned Marshall, showing perfect teeth, all his own as he extended his own hand to shake hers. "It's good to meet you!"

"And it's good to meet you at last," repeated the softly-spoken woman, smiling despite staring at him in amazement. "I see where George gets his good looks. You look like a movie star!"

"You don't look so bad, yourself!" Marshall shrugged off her praise of his good looks with a smile as he took her other hand in his. Raising her arms out to her sides, he slid a bold assessing gaze over her long flowing brown hair and stout figure in the blue jacket and black slacks she wore before returning it to the semi-attractive features of her oval face. "Look, Sephora, Rachel was right! She has freckles!" Marshall turned an amazed stare on his wife upon noticing the spots across Stacey's nose that his younger daughter had mentioned but that he had missed at first glance. "Isn't that the most precious thing you've ever seen?!"

"Adorable!" Sephora agreed, like her husband staring at the rich white woman in amazement.

"And this," George went on excitedly, an arm curving around Sephora's tan-clad shoulders, "in case my dad didn't give it away, is my mother, Sephora Hardison."

"How do you do, Mrs. Hardison?" Stacey grinned upon taking the hand the taller woman had extended to her. "It's good to meet you, at last, too! I see where

Rachel and Devon get their looks, as well! You look just like them! Or rather, they look just like you! Well, I guess there was no way they could have turned out ugly with a mother who looks like you!" For once, Stacey had lost all of her composure as she stared at the fifty-eight-year-old shapely black woman with the same amazement with which she had regarded her husband.

Sephora brushed off her fawning praise as if used to it, which she was. "Welcome to the family, dear," she smiled, dropping her hand and taking her warmly into her arms.

As George took Stacey back into his arms just as she dropped her arms from their mother's shoulders, Rachel realized just what he felt for her. Damn, this was potent, she thought, this thing called love.

"Is she precious, or what!" she heard George insist lovingly down at Stacey, her arms curved around him also.

Sephora smiled at the attractive couple they made standing embracing in front of her. "Adorable!" she repeated.

"Yeah, and you know it won't be bad, knowing we're going to have some money in the family!" Marshall exclaimed.

Rachel wondered why her father would say a corny thing like that as everybody laughed at the jocular remark except for her. She knew that the last thing that man would ever need was money.

Recovering her composure, Stacey turned a sobered smile on her in-laws-to-be. "Anyway, now that I've met you two, why don't I take you down to meet my parents on the eighth floor? It's only ten thirty. I'm sure they'll still be up. Besides, it doesn't get dark in the summer here until midnight, anyway."

"Yea, so, we've heard. Anyway, lead the way, dear," Sephora smiled. At the same time, Marshall turned in the blue-carpeted floor so that she could lead them out of the suite. Rachel did not miss the knowing look George turned on her as he followed his fiancée past her in front of her parents and Devon.

Back in a daze, she followed the quintet to the elevator banks, where they took the first one that opened down to Stacey's parents' suite on the eighth floor. Rick was not there when they arrived at Suite 828, where he had stopped off to see his parents some time ago. No doubt he had returned to his own sixth-floor suite, Rachel was relieved to see as Stacey saw them into the living room as soon as her parents had opened the door.

With the same naturalness and warmth that Dora Lumas had greeted her and Devon with up in the penthouse earlier she greeted her parents, the woman in her early sixties star-struck by the presence of Felix long having recovered her composure. Al Lumas, on the other hand, just like with Rachel and Devon upon meeting them earlier, took one look at their parents and stood staring in stunned shock.

"Good damn!" he exclaimed once his daughter had introduced him and his wife to her fiancé's parents, the vivid blue eyes in the face of the tall gray-haired white man sizing the handsome black couple close to his same age up from their heads to their toes. "Now, I see where George and your daughters get their good looks! You two are good looking people! Do all black people in Georgia look like you two do?"

If Marshall Hardison thought that a racist remark or simple awkward flattery coming from a less attractive man, Rachel was glad that her father had the good grace not to show it as he smilingly shook hands with the Native Alaskan.

"Don't worry, you had what it took to get a wife," Marshall said jokingly to the white man, dropping his hand back to his side. "I see you got two kids along with it," he said in his brusk alto. "As a matter of fact, Rachel introduced me to your other kid a while ago. I believe his name is Rick, isn't it?"

"Yes, it is," Al Lumas smiled, completely impressed with the salt-and-pepper haired black man shorter than him by an inch.

"I see he looks just like you," Marshall said.

Al Lumas looked away in a blush, not quite knowing how to take that remark. "I don't know whether to take that as a compliment, or an insult," he said.

"Don't worry; whichever way you take it, it'll still get you there!" Marshall said.

Devon leaned in to speak to the white man as everyone laughed at the funny remark he had uttered with the exception of her and Rachel. "You'll have to excuse my father, he's a little outrageous," she said, pink clutch purse again tucked in her hand.

"I see it runs in the family!" Al Lumas smirked.

Devon turned a demeaning look on the Native Alaskan as he again sized up her curving figure from her head to her toes with a quick meaningful sweep of his blond lashes.

"So, come on in here, you two, and tell us about yourselves." Turning, Al led the six of them away from the white door and into the lavish elegant sophisticated living room of the two-room suite. "George tells us you're a contractor for a home building corporation, and that you and your wife live in this town—what is it—Villa Rica?"

"Yes." Marshall settled his strong navy-clad frame onto the plush blue velvet French Provincial loveseat next to Sephora, a position that put them directly across from Al and Dora on a second blue velvet French Provincial loveseat. Stacey and George cuddled on a blue velvet French Provincial sofa with Devon settling to the right of them. Rounding out the sitting area, Rachel settled in a blue velvet French Provincial chair, one of two directly across from George and Stacey, black purse curled up in her lap. "It's a small town to the west of Douglasville, the county seat, both Douglasville and Villa Rica being west of Atlanta. The homebuilding corporation I contract for is based in Atlanta, where Sephora is a design engineer there also. As a matter of fact, that's where I met her thirty two years ago, when she came to the firm five years out of college to work as a design drafter. I took one look at her and have had designs on her ever since."

"I see," smiled the white man while Sephora slapped his navy sweater-sleeved arm in a gesture delivered to silence her gushing husband.

"Hush up, Marshall, you're giving away my age," Sephora said with a laugh.

"Nothing could give away your age," Al Lumas said with a wicked blue-eyed meaning as he saw the ageless black woman's slight embarrassment.

"Now, you hush up!" Dora ordered her husband in a voice delivered to silence his own gushing demeanor.

Al Lumas plainly ignored his less attractive wife as he turned his blue-eyed gaze back on the rich looking salt-and-pepper-haired black man sitting on the loveseat to the left of the ageless black woman.

"You know," Al began to Marshall, "while we're somewhat on the subject of building, you know, my brother Raj was kind of into that."

"Is that right?"

"Yes. He acquired a number of properties which he liquidated in order to buy two hotels—this one, and another in Hawaii. Unfortunately, he died of pancreatic and liver cancer six years ago, so, he willed his hotels to my children, his nephew and niece. Stacey, as you can see owns this one, while Rick owns the one in Honolulu."

"I see," observed Marshall reflectively, as that explained how Stacey and Rick were both millionaires at barely thirty and had been for years. A quick glance at Sephora, and he could see the same thought being reflected in her own observant luminous brown eyes.

"And while we're on the subject of that, why did your brother Raj will his hotels to your children, instead of to you and your brother?" Marshall asked curiously.

"My brother's two marriages produced no children, so, he had no natural heirs," Al explained informatively. "And as his brothers and closest relatives, Raj did offer the ownership of the hotels to me and Stevan, but for the same reasons, we didn't want 'em. Too many worries! Too much time doing business! Too much time making deals, breaking deals, too much overhead involved in keeping the places going. Too many hassles arranging banquets and meetings with this group or that group, or whatever conventioneers are attending some function, or other! And there're too many employees to have to deal with, not to mention a thousand problems with housekeeping on a daily basis, with the maids not being able to get into the rooms or guests lacking discretion and not checking out on time. For instance, George, tell your parents about that situation you had at the hotel here with a guest two months ago."

A reminiscent smile slid onto the well-hewn full lips of George still cuddling with Stacey on the loveseat to the right of his father-in-law-to-be.

"Boy, that turned out to an interesting day," began George with a laugh, Stacey smiling too at the memory, Devon sitting to the right of Stacey staring suspiciously at Rachel occupying one of the French Provincial chairs across from them staring from a glass-eyed state. "It all started on a chilly April evening, when a man visiting the hotel sat in the lounge downstairs quietly having a drink," George said in his abrupt alto. "He had to be at least seventy. All of a sudden a thirty-year-old woman, a guest registered at the hotel, sidled up to the bar next to him. She asked him to buy little ol' thing 'her' a drink, which the man did. She proceeded to get him drunk, at which point, she took him up to her suite, where she then screwed him, injected him with a drug that knocked him out, took all his clothes—including his shoes and underwear, and checked out." George paused while everyone around him stared in anticipation and disbelief with the exception of Rachel, who sat in the chair mind barely on what her brother was talking about.

"Well, the next day, the do not disturb sign was hanging on the door, so the maids didn't bother with the suite until check-out time at twelve o'clock," went on George brightly. "Except that the do not disturb sign was still hanging on the door at one. Well, that's when they started getting worried, because the check-out was not registered on the housekeeping report, and as far as they were concerned the hotel guest was still in the suite, having ignored the stated check-out time. Well, they went and got Stu, the assistant manager to come see what the problem was, because they did not want to intrude on possibly a sexual situation with the guest, especially when the do not disturb sign was still on the door. Well, it must have been what—about one thirty when Stu finally got up there and saw the blue do not disturb sign still hanging on the door. Anyway, ignoring the sign, Stu rapped briskly on the door, only to get nothing. There was not a sound coming from the inside of the suite. Problem number two: Stu decided to try the door. He put his passkey in the knob, but it wouldn't go in. The lock had been jammed from the other side. So, that's when Stu called a locksmith to come take the knob off the door, the lock of which had been jammed with a fork tine. Guess what the maids found after he did that."

"What?" demanded Marshall and Sephora simultaneously, Devon staring curiously; Rachel in dreamland.

"The seventy-year-old man that the guest had picked up in the lounge the evening before lay the length of the bed naked; stretched out dead. The guest was no where in sight."

"Oh, my God!" cried Sephora, like Marshall, not knowing whether to cry or laugh. Devon had sliced her made-up eyes away from Rachel and onto her brother in shock.

"Don't worry, it gets better," George reassured, like Stacey, laughing at the memory. "Anyway, the maids were screaming stone cold death, not knowing whether the man had been murdered or died naturally. Nor did they know what to do, and neither did Stu. So, he brought the situation to my attention. I don't know where Stacey was that afternoon, possibly having gone off on an errand," George flashed a brief dismissive gaze on his fiancée sitting next to him quietly, listening intently.

"Anyway, in order to keep the murder, or death—whatever it was, from other hotel guests, I went quietly to the suite to see for myself, see if I could find some graceful way to get the man's dead body to the morgue without alerting the entire hotel staff along with the guests what was going on. I walked into the bedroom big as you please, and sure enough, the white man was laid out fully naked stretched out dead on the bed. Well, to make sure, I checked his pulse, only to find that he wasn't dead, he was in a drunk, drugged-out stupor. Anyway, that was a relief. Well, I somehow got word down to the kitchen to bring me a pot of strong coffee, which I then proceeded to slowly pour down the man's throat. He slowly came to after a moment of being revived by the strong coffee. Can you believe that?" asked George with a laugh at his parents. "A seventy-year-old dried up man, came to still drunk and with a hangover! Yet when he saw himself lying there naked with everything of his gone out of the suite including all of his money—not to mention the woman who had picked him up the evening before, he knew exactly what had happened. That's when he proceeded to tell me the story of the thirty-year-old woman who had picked him up in the lounge the evening before, got him half drunk, brought him to her suite, fucked him, drugged him, and then, apparently left with all his belongings and money. The man came to well enough to see that he had been scammed, and he yelled bloody murder at me to find that damned woman who had occupied that suite the day before, because he was going to kill her! Well, I only considered that the ramblings of a drunk old man, although I did check on the roster to see who had checked into that suite the day before. And I did give her name to the old man upon tactfully having some clothing and shoes brought over for him from a nearby store and seeing him home in a cab. Well, three weeks later, the man found the woman, alright. Guess what he did?"

"What?" burst out Marshall, Sephora and Devon simultaneously, Rachel, simply staring.

"Married her the next week . . . ! Brought her here for their honeymoon! They occupied the same suite on the fifth floor where she had scammed him a month before!"

"Oh, no . . . !" Sephora screamed, like everyone except for Rachel, laughing hysterically along with George. "That's awful! That's awful! That's truly awful!"

"Wasn't it . . . !" Dora laughed while husband Al bent double doing same on the sofa next to her.

"It was a day!" George agreed, sobering and smiling in reflection of the memory.

"Now, you see why Stevan and I did not want our brother's hotels," said Al Lumas after the laughter had died down, including his own. "So for the last thirty seven years, Stevan has worked as a pharmacist—a position he was trained for, for a drug chain that has him presently living in Juneau. He'll be here for the wedding, too, although he won't be able to get here until possibly tomorrow, or early Saturday," Al went on informatively. "And as for me, for the last forty years, I've worked in our hometown of Ketchikan for the Convention and Visitors Bureau there. As a matter of fact, I met Dora there thirty five years ago, where she's been working at the Greater Ketchikan Chamber of Commerce for the last thirty."

"I see," said Marshall in his brusk alto. His brown eyes settled on the equally brown-eyed smiling white woman sitting to the right of Al. Quietly he deduced by what Al had said that they had been married close to thirty five years to his and Sephora's thirty two. And he wondered what his brother must be like, this Stevan, Stacey's uncle, this pharmacist presently residing in Juneau. He swept the white woman sitting at George's side in a brief look before letting his bold brown gaze slide back to her parents. "So, where is this Ketchikan?" he asked curiously, his eyes probing from Dora's face to Al's.

"Its location is 679 miles north of Seattle and 235 miles south of Juneau, where it sits on the western coast of Revillagigedo Island, near the southernmost boundary of Alaska off the Pacific Ocean."

"I see," Marshall observed quietly while at the same time wondering if they had passed that Ketchikan on the drive up the coast from Seattle toward Juneau on the way to Anchorage.

"Yea, you ought to see it," the tall gray white man smiled as he perceived his interest as well as that of Sephora sitting quietly beside him looking on intently. "I mean, Ketchikan is a small area—only about three miles of land and one square mile of water, but it's a nice place to visit. It sits up kind of like on a steep hillside, with sections of the town built right over the water on pilings with rustic boardwalks, such as you would see on Creek Street in the city's historic area. It's Alaska's First City, actually, and it dates all the way back to 1883, where two men started a salmon cannery on the banks of Ketchikan Creek. As a matter of fact, because of that, it's called the Salmon Capital of the World. Fishing started there, mining activities, and timber operations. But the logging industry has nearly disappeared now to tourism."

"I see." Marshall slid a quiet gaze on Sephora which she met, both of them deducing by the man's last revelation that it was small wonder both he and his wife held jobs in the tourism industry.

"Yea, it's great," Al went only smilingly, warmed to talking about the hometown he knew so much about. "Ketchikan comes from the name Katch Kanna, which means 'spread wings of a thundering eagle', and you can see that in the many eagles that are often perched on the waterside. Yet would you believe that as small as Ketchikan is, Ketchikan Airport is on its own island?"

"Really . . . ?" Marshall asked curiously.

"Oh, yeah . . . !" Briskly Al nodded his gray head. "It's called Garvina Island, located in the heart of the Tongass National Forest, and if you arrive there at Ketchikan Airport, all you need is a short ferry ride across Tongass Narrows to the city of Ketchikan. And guess what you'll see when you get there?"

"What?" Marshall asked at his deliberate pause.

"Cruise ships," Al replied with a smile.

"Oh, really . . . ?"

"Oh, yeah . . . !" Al insisted with a grin, claiming all their attention. "Katch Kanna is Alaska's first port-of-call for northbound cruise ships. Didn't you ever see that old show back in the eighties called *The Love Boat?* When Captain Stubing used to moor the Pacific Princess into Ketchikan Harbor, it was a real place. Cruising is big business there. On a busy day between May and September, you can see as many as six cruise ships tied up at the docks or anchored in the Tongass Narrows, not to mention Alaska State Ferries nearly every day. You ought to think about bringing your wife on your next vacation on a cruise up the Pacific Coast to Ketchikan. We must have at least twenty different cruise lines coming through there!"

"I see," smiled Marshall, impressed by all he had heard. "Well, my wife and I might just have to take you up on that idea. We might just take a cruise up there. And you know, I guess you do work for the Convention and Visitors Bureau of Ketchikan! You really know your city!"

"Oh, yeah . . . !" Al repeated with a grin.

As the Native Alaskan started to talk more about his home city, Rachel's mind soared back into dreamland. She wasn't thinking about Katch Kanna, she wasn't thinking about Ketchikan. She was thinking about *katching* a man! Felix! The thought of him put a smile on her lips that was wider than the Pacific Ocean. God, she loved that man, she thought. All six-foot-one gorgeous sexy well-built good looking golden brown inches of him!

A hand curved over her arm suddenly, breaking her out of her reverie. Imagining it the man of her thoughts, Rachel was surprised to find that the hand belonged to George, who had settled his sturdy frame quietly into the French Provincial blue velvet chair to the left of her.

"Hey, Kid Sister, when are you going to come down off that cloud you've been on for the past hour?" George asked laughingly in her ear in a voice that only she could hear. "That man kissed you, didn't he? I know he did. That's why he pulled you aside. And that was why you were late getting to Mom and Dad's suite behind us earlier. But must you wear your heart on your sleeve? Because you look like you're about to float away any minute over here . . . !"

Rachel managed a sheepish smile as she continued to stare at her brother, shocked that her inattention had been that apparent. "Am I that bad?"

"Uhm-hmm." Despite the reproof, George's eyes were full of understanding as he slid the hand clutching her arm down to her wrist. "Come here and let me talk to you." And rising to his feet, he pulled her to hers, giving her just enough time to slide the black strap of her bag onto her shoulder as he led her out of the suite.

He didn't stop until they were halfway down the hall, where he let go of her hand and propped his five-foot-ten-inch blue-and-black-clad frame up against the stripe-papered wall and Rachel in front of him.

"Look, honey," George began in his abrupt alto, smile curving his well-hewn full lips, "I know you're happy Felix came around. I am, too. I mean, after what all he had told me, I knew something was happening between you two, or was going to. I also knew when Devon showed up unexpectedly that she might possibly have interrupted a moment between you two. And after all Felix had told me, I especially wondered that at dinner tonight. The way Devon sat there and chewed the scenery in the restaurant and came all onto him, and he sat there and laughed it up and lapped it up! Even went down memory lane with her! I said to myself something's going on wrong here! I looked at you, and I saw the pain in your eyes, and I looked at him, and I said to myself what the hell is he doing! Is he out of his mind! But when Felix then turned down Devon's offer of showing her around the hotel while at the same time rejecting any further offer of her company saying he had to go, that he had a woman waiting for him, that she was beautiful and that you had a date to see Elvis, I thought I was going to have to excuse myself!" George grinned excitedly. "I looked at you and I saw that look of pleasure that came on your face, and I said to myself that's my boy! I guess he's back on track! I guess he did mean every word of all those things he said about you!"

Rachel returned the delighted smile George had turned on her, the same of which was reflected in her large luminous brown eyes. "Yea, what all did he say about me, anyway?" she asked, aware by all George had said to her that she had only partial knowledge of the conversation Felix had confided having with him earlier.

"Well, before I answer that, I must first go back to what I saw happening with you two yesterday." George assumed a reminiscent look as he stood with one hip propped against the wall as did Rachel in front of him. "Do you remember how enraged I was at you after seeing that article in yesterday's paper of you and Felix kissing at the Dimond Center ice skating rink?" Rachel nodded. "You waltzed into the cafeteria all nonchalant and composed and rambling on about how the kiss just resulted because a skater passed by and knocked him off his feet, another passed and knocked you down on top of him, and he just took advantage of the situation when photographers started taking pictures of the two of you. Said he'd said, 'Well, baby, let's give them something to photograph!'" George laughed, showing his well-aligned teeth. "Then he walked in all nonchalant and flying all over the place! I'd never seen that man like that in my life! Plus you two had this kind of conspiracy thing sort of going on. Well, I said to myself: something's going on here! But I didn't have a chance to pursue it further, because it was time for Stacey and me to go to work." George paused briefly, round brown eyes narrowed in his suntan-brown face in reflection.

"Anyway, come this evening, you two come waltzing in after practically having been away from this hotel for a whole day and Felix was higher than he was yesterday. I mean that man was flying all over the place. Talking about what all else you two had in common. 'Rachel loves archery! She hates rap as much as I do! Rachel knows Shakespeare's *The Tempest!*' That man was flying all over the place. He was holding your hand and wouldn't let go and speaking all excitedly, I mean Felix was higher than a kite! You, on the other hand, were morose. Looked like you were going to jump out of your skin any minute. . . . You would not look at me, you would not meet my gaze, and you were barely speaking to Felix. Well, I said to myself:

something's going on here! That's why I pulled you away from him and pumped you all the way up in the elevator as to whether you were alright, having known by your unusual silence and refusal to look me in the face that something was going on here! And then you jumped away from both of us as soon as the elevator doors opened up on the fifteenth floor, not to mention bolted straight down the hall to the guest bathroom once we'd entered the penthouse. Well, I said to myself: something's going on here! So, I pulled Felix over to my desk and I said to him, 'What's going on with you and Rachel?' And this is exactly what he said:

"'Your sister's blown my damned mind. I can't keep my lips off her. As a matter of fact, ever since I kissed her at the restaurant the other day, I've wanted to kiss her ever since. She's so luscious, and she's so sweet and innocent. Plus, she's done everything I've done. I've never met a woman in my life that I have so much in common with when considering we haven't seen each other in ten years. And in those ten years, she's grown into a very beautiful, very shapely, very seductive woman. And she's more fun than I've ever had with any woman. We have the same likes and dislikes. And we can do everything, and we can talk about everything! I'm totally gone on her!'

"Well, I said to him understandingly, 'I see. So, what about Devon . . . ?' Felix looked at me disinterestedly and asked, 'Who's she?' 'I see,' I repeated. 'So, you're over Devon for good and onto Rachel for better?' And Felix said with a nod of agreement, 'With any luck. But you really want to know what got me onto her? It was discovering all the way back on Monday that she loves Elvis. And you know how much a fan I am of that man.' Well, I said, 'Boy, do I ever! As a matter of fact, that's the surprise I have for you!' That's when I pulled the video cassette of Elvis' *Tickle Me* out of my desk drawer and handed it to him. All that, my dear, took place while you were in the guest bathroom, and you returned to the penthouse living room just in time to hear him scream with excitement."

"I see." The response was an amused one as Rachel derived pleasure from these new feelings Felix had confided having for her that her brother had just so smilingly revealed to her. So Felix thought she was luscious, did he, she wondered? He thought she was sweet, did he? He thought she was shapely? But then, Felix had made that point to her on Monday, when he told her up in George's suite that her body was out of this world! And then to add to that, he thought she was seductive? Oh, well, Rachel thought, small wonder the man had grabbed her down the hall and told her he thought he was falling in love with her.

"And now, you see why I'm floating on a cloud," Rachel answered after a moment of smiling incredulously. "For all the reasons Felix mentioned, I feel the same way about him. I mean, he's right. I haven't seen him in ten years. I have not heard of him, I have not thought of him, I had forgotten him; I had no idea what he was doing these days! I mean, for God's sake, I was fourteen years old the last time I saw him! And I had nothin', you know what I mean? There has been no communication between us, neither physically, nor even by mental telepathy!

And yet, it's like he said: I've done everything he's done! I've never met a man in my life that I have so much in common with! And I know it's only been three days since we've seen each other after not having done so in ten years, but because of all these things we have in common, we've got this thing going on that is hotter than the sun. And you know this is ridiculous, my brother! I mean: How long can this heat wave last—!"

George laughed sympathetically. "I'm sorry, honey. Three days or no, this might just be it for both of you. This is how it was with me and Stacey."

Rachel did not tell him that she had already suspected the heat between him and his fiancée nor the fact that Felix had said he thought he was falling in love with her. Neither did she mention the fact that she'd realized by all the heat Felix brought out in her that she'd already fallen for him.

"But the two of you'd better be careful," George said as she fell thoughtfully silent, "because there's a fly in your ointment."

Rachel's luminous brown eyes swept the handsome suntan mannishly-featured oval face of her brother curiously, as she did not know how to apply the remark, to pardon the pun.

"What do you mean?"

"Devon, who else . . . ? She's already suspicious of you. Oh, you should have seen her when Felix brought her up to the penthouse to surprise me this evening," George said with a laugh. "She had just said something about Felix telling her that Mom and Dad hadn't gotten here, yet, when I said, 'I'm afraid not, they're driving in cross-country. According to Rachel, they should be arriving tomorrow.' That's when Devon said the nastiest thing. She said, 'Yes, where the hell is Rachel? Around here somewhere trying to vamp some damned man she has no intention of sleeping with?' That's when Felix laughed and said, 'Will you get off her?' You should have seen the look she turned on him. Devon sliced a look on Felix that demanded to know why he'd spoken in such quick defense of you by telling her to get off you like that. It was a look that said, 'Could it possibly be because you want to get on her?' Well, I somehow managed to get Devon off your scent by suggesting that she tell me all about her divorce, and you can see after arriving at the suite a while later how into that she was. But I'm telling you, the woman's suspicious. You should have seen the way she looked at you before we rode up in the elevator here from the first floor. Felix had just dumped her again by telling Dad that it wasn't going to happen between them, he had a woman waiting for him, and that he had been trying to shake her off for the past hour! That's when you said something to Felix about putting a brown paper bag over his head—something silly," George laughed, "in order to keep women from chasing him because of his good looks. Something about going as the Unknown Soap Opera Star or something . . . !" George laughed again despite failing to get the joke. "Anyway, Felix told you, 'Hush up, girl!' Yet in the midst of doing that, he turned a grin on you that was so hot, I thought I would have to excuse myself, again!" George laughed. "You two shared a laugh, he reached out and curved a hand over your wrist, and you just blushed. You literally went to putty in the floor! You didn't even try to hide the fact that the touch of his hand on your flesh left you soaring in the clouds. Devon noticed, though. She turned a murderous glare on you and Felix as if demanding what the hell is going on with those two! I'm telling you, you'd better watch out!"

Rachel was too delighted by the memory of the moment to heed her brother's astute warning. "I don't care about her," she responded carelessly, how else? "Felix said it himself. He told you—he's over her for good, and onto me for better. And in harmony with that, he told me before he kissed me goodnight tonight to meet him in the morning at eight thirty in the cafeteria for breakfast, where my parents will probably be as well as Stacey's parents, her brother Rick, and Devon. He said we'll spend the whole time there hiding our feelings for each other from all of them. And he said that maybe if we're lucky after that, we'll be able to go somewhere and get away from all of them before the wedding rehearsal starts at two o'clock. And my brother, I don't find that a very bad idea."

George observed the shameless smile Rachel had turned on him and the one that slid onto his own lips was a mixture of sympathy and amazement.

"Oh, my God," he said in his abrupt alto, "you are gone."

"I'm delirious," Rachel confided, smiling deliciously, "and a very tired delirious, at that. Felix was right. He turned in more than an hour ago," she said as a glance at the silver-toned watch on her wrist confirmed the time as eleven twenty. "We had a very late night out last night, and I'm beginning to feel it, too. You need to get back to Stacey, anyway, who's probably wondering where you've run off with me. But I don't think I could make it back there even if I weren't tired. I don't think I could stand another word of Al Lumas going on about Katch Kanna, Katch-Katch-Ketchikanna, Ketchikan . . . !" Rachel laughed; showing her even teeth and watching him do the same. "So, give my apologies to Mom and Dad, and tell them I'll see them in the morning. I'm going to float on my cloud back up to my suite on the eleventh floor, and go to bed."

Again George laughed at the deliberate way Rachel drew out the word bed. "Well, you have a good night, Kid Sister. And maybe, if you're lucky, you'll have sweet dreams of Felix in the process."

"Now, that, too, I don't find a very bad idea."

Reciprocating the hug and kiss he planted on her cheek, Rachel bid him a goodnight and stepped out of his arms. The strap of her black bag was still curved over her shoulder as she floated all the way to the elevator banks around the corridor to ascend the first one that would open on the eleventh floor.

It was raining when Rachel awoke the next morning, the sound of it thrashing against the windows concealed behind the closed drapes across the large blue-themed bedroom. Not just a mild rain, Rachel noticed, but it was really raining. It was just as her mother had said it had done last night when she and her father had hit Seattle two days ago—raining, raining, and raining. Rachel should hardly have been surprised by it—after all, its imminent arrival had shown itself in the way the sky had clouded yesterday and the temperature had dropped considerably. Still she knew that it was going to be a disappointment to her parents to have to be met by another heavy rain their first morning after arriving there in Anchorage.

With another dim realization, Rachel glanced at the AM/FM clock radio on the French Provincial nightstand to the left of her bed, seeing that it was seven fifty nine. She and Felix would not be able to get into the street today, get away so they could be alone. Instead, they were going to have to play the game of keep-everyone-in-the-dark-as-to-their-involvement-with-each-other—especially Devon—all day there at the hotel. Rachel wondered how they were going to do that, especially when her delirium had been so apparent that George had lovingly chided her the night before about wearing her heart on her sleeve?

She recalled his last words to her before she had stepped out of his arms to float on her cloud back up to her suite on the eleventh floor to go to bed. George had told her that maybe if she were lucky, she would have sweet dreams of Felix after falling asleep. Yet though Rachel had slept peacefully, she had not dreamt of her almost lover and the object of her love. In fact, if she had dreamt of anything, the formless images had already been swept from her mind.

Yet despite not having dreamt of Felix, Rachel's mind remained on him as she recalled the events that had taken place between the two of them just the day before. Felix had shown up at her door at that very time—eight o'clock, surprising Rachel, as she had not expected to see him until ten. Felix had lowered his eyes over the length of her long shapely dusky colored legs in an admiring look that had embarrassed her in its intensity before the dancing brown eyes had swept back up to her face. "You really grew up, Little Sister. But then, I noticed that three days ago," he had said in his attractive tenor. And then, he had cupped her face in his hands and pulled her into a heated kiss that had been the start of many that they would share throughout the day. Rachel determined to get out of the bed to wash up and get dressed so that she could meet Felix for breakfast in the cafeteria at eight thirty so they could play their game of let's-keep-everybody-in-the-dark-as-to-our-feelings-for-each-other.

The shrill ringing of the multi-line phone on the nightstand sounded into the suite before Rachel could throw back the covers and get out of the king-sized bed. Wondering if it might be her parents calling to enquire of her somehow, Rachel reached over to lift the blue receiver to her ear on the second ring.

However, both to her surprise and delight, the caller turned out to be the object of her thoughts. The man who thought of her as luscious. . . .

"Girl, girl, girl," began the attractive tenor once Rachel had placed the receiver to her ear and said hello, "guess what! There's an Elvis Presley movie marathon on ENC that started at seven thirty this morning and is going to run until seven thirty tomorrow morning! Can you believe that? Elvis, Elvis, Elvis! So, get up here quick, quick, quick! Come and watch some of these movies with me! Besides, it's raining. We can't go out this morning, anyway."

Rachel laughed at the excitement behind his seductive tone. "Honey, you know I can't come up there with you," she declined his offer regretfully. "My parents are here. You said it yourself last night: they'll be expecting me to join them for breakfast in a little while. As a matter of fact, I was just about to move out of this bed to wash up, get dressed and join you in the cafeteria so that we could play our game of pretend we don't like each other with them, Devon, Stacey's parents, and Rick. And after that, because as you just said—it is raining, I thought I would come back up here and have the laundry/valet service clean some dirty clothes of mine that are beginning to pile up. And after that, I was going to wash my hair, which incidentally, I haven't washed since last Sunday."

"Forget your parents, forget Devon, forget Stacey's parents, forget Rick, forget the dirty clothes, have them cleaned later," Felix said. "Just bring your dirty hair and the rest of your gorgeous body up here. We can eat breakfast here. I'll have some sent up by room service. *Harum Scarum's* playing presently. By the time we eat breakfast, we'll be just in time for Elvis' next installment, *Girls! Girls! Girls!* So, get up here, girl. Get your clothes on, and be up here in thirty five minutes!"

Rachel couldn't help laughing all over again at the excited voice sounding so insistently in her left ear. How could she turn down an invitation like that?

"I'll be there in thirty four," she heard herself saying smilingly before hanging up the phone and sliding out of her bed.

Chapter Thirteen

She was there in thirty three. Raising her luminous brown gaze from the silver-toned watch on her left wrist, which showed the time as eight thirty five exactly; Rachel let it sweep her appearance in one last assessing look. She wore simple black stretch denim jeans with a black woolen long-sleeved sweater, the two form-fitting garments up-playing the provocative curves of her figure, the black pumps she wore on her feet over beige knee-highs and that she had worn on Monday matching the black leather bag she usually carried strapped to her left shoulder. The same color carried over in the black onyx stone earrings held to her lobes by silver posts, an added provocation that was clearly in evidence, as her off-black hair had been swept away from her face and up into its usual ponytail, which flowed long and straight down her back from a black knit band at the top center of head. Rachel didn't need a mirror to know that her face was equally as provocative, as she had applied her usual black mascara to her long lashes, rose blush to her curving cheeks and wine lipstick to her medium lips—although she didn't know why, as Felix was only going to kiss off what of it that she wouldn't eat off. And that was for sure, she knew in the way he had insisted that she get up there to the complete neglect of her own parents having arrived at the hotel just the evening before. Raising a hand to rap on the white door of his suite, Rachel prayed her parents wouldn't come waltzing down the hall from Suite 1224 at just that time only to find her standing there in anticipation of trysting with a man.

As if having been standing by the door in anticipation of her arrival, Felix opened it immediately. The sight of the good looking man smiling down at her sent her heart thudding with equal swiftness.

"Get in here, girl!"

Curling an arm around her black shoulders, Felix swept her into the large blue-themed suite identical to hers, his lips briefly touching her cheek in a greeting kiss. Rachel turned automatically to meet the lips touching her skin, but Felix had moved away from her to hang the blue do not disturb sign on the brass knob before closing the self-locking door. Rachel couldn't help noticing that he slid the secondary lock in place at the same time, which displayed the words do not disturb in a second expression to the outside world not to intrude.

Her eyes swept him in a furtive look as he turned away from the door. The man was sexy as ever, a fetchingly attractive sky blue knit sweater and white dungarees covering his manly frame, the white Nikes sneakers he had worn earlier in the week pulled on over feet covered in white crew socks. Deliberately Rachel sliced her gaze to a distant lamp so he wouldn't sense she had been observing him as he moved forward at the same time to curve his arm back around her black-clad shoulders.

"So, how're you doing, kiddo?" Felix asked as he then began to lead her briskly away from the door.

"I'm fine, honey, how are you? How'd you sleep last night?"

" . . . Very well, as a matter of fact."

"How long have you been up?"

"Since around seven thirty. . . . I called you as soon as I got out of the shower."

"I see." Rachel guessed that was the truth, as she noticed upon second glance that his short groomed kinky black hair was still somewhat damp from that shower.

Dropping his long-lashed gaze away from her, Felix settled it onto a white clothed food cart holding an assortment of covered food dishes he led her to halfway across the lavishly appointed large living room.

"I had them send up some of everything. I didn't know what you had a taste for."

Rachel couldn't help smiling at the loaded statement as Felix dropped his arm from her shoulders to begin lifting several stainless steel lids from the various food dishes. If only he knew that what she had a taste for right now wasn't on the menu.

Yet she forced her gaze onto the many breakfast dishes spread out on the cart sent up by room service that Felix was then showing her. He had ordered everything, alright. There was toast, there was dry cereal, there were waffles and pancakes, both dolloped in margarine, berries and syrup, there were omelets, and there was milk and juice—both orange and grape. There were ham slices and crisp bacon slices, and an assortment of other condiments with which to round out the meal. And Rachel wondered what all that must have cost Felix in added charges to his hotel bill, reasoning that he must be richer than the President, which he probably was in his juicy career as an award-winning actor playing a character on a soap that was presently sleeping with his boss, her daughter, and her stepdaughter.

"How long has it been since this got here?"

" . . . Only about two minutes. That's why I answered your knock at the door so quickly. I was standing there anticipating your arrival. I knew you'd be here in another couple of minutes, or so."

"I see." Despite the smile on her own wine-painted lips, Rachel deliberately ignored the smile on his as her gaze lingered over the many breakfast items on the cloth-covered food cart. It had been there for only a short time, alright. The pot of black coffee that accompanied the meal evidenced that, as it was still hot and steaming from its long trip up from the kitchen on the ground floor.

Picking up one of the fluted white china plates stacked to one side of the large food cart then, Rachel began to fill it with an omelet, a ham slice, and a couple of pancakes dolloped in berries while Felix filled a second plate with two bacon strips, a ham slice, an omelet, and three large waffles drizzled in syrup. In the four days that she had been with him, Rachel hadn't been able to help noticing that Felix had a huge appetite for food, and found it no wonder that the six-foot-one-inch man was as built as he was.

Pouring a glass of grape juice while Rachel settled for orange, Felix led her over to one of the blue velvet French Provincial loveseats in the center of the large elegant living room, where he settled her on the right of it and himself on her left. *Harum Scarum* was still playing from the hardwood TV across the blue-themed room, its low volume just loud enough not to be drowned out by the heavy rain that could be seen thrashing against the large picture window between the heavy print linen drapes Felix had opened. Rachel had never seen the movie *Harum Scarum* before, yet as she settled her orange juice to the French Provincial end table and her black bag to the right side of her on the sofa, she recognized Elvis' frolicking partner as Mary Ann Mobley. Rachel recognized the brunette because she had seen her in another movie Elvis had done—*Girl Happy,* she believed it was.

"You know, I've never seen this movie," Rachel confided amid starting on her pancakes. "What's this one about?"

Felix concentrated on downing a forkful of the three large waffles he had started in his own plate. "Oh, you know, the usual fare—Elvis singing and dancing, Elvis singing and prancing, Elvis singing and romancing," he finished with a wicked grin.

"I guess so!" Rachel agreed with a laugh at the clever way he had rhymed the three activities.

"So, how'd things go with your parents after I turned in last night?" Felix asked the question over the waffles he was still lighting into in his plate. "Did they get settled in well?"

"Actually, they had already started unpacking when I got to their suite, so I joined in and asked them how was the drive up, and if they had encountered any bad weather. Anyway," Rachel went on after downing another forkful of the pancakes she was eating in her plate, "Mom said that the weather held up pretty well wherever they went—I mean after all, as she said, it is summer. Except that when they got to St. Louis, it rained. And when they got to Des Moines, it rained. And then, when they got to Seattle, it rained, rained, and rained! And you know, I was just thinking upon waking up awhile ago how unfortunate my parents were going to find it their first morning after arriving in Alaska doing the same thing. Raining, raining, and raining!"

"That's the truth!" Felix agreed with a laugh, its sound in evidence as it thrashed madly against the window behind them.

"Anyway, we must have stayed there unpacking for maybe twelve minutes, when George decided for them to put off their unpacking for a while so that he could take them down to see Stacey," Rachel went on after downing the forkful of omelet she had raised to her mouth. "Now, one thing I can say about Stacey after having known her for the last four days is that she is very calm, very composed, very level-headed; soft-spoken. But when George introduced her to our father, Stacey stared in amazement. She told Dad, 'Well, now, I see where George gets his good looks! You look like a movie star!' And then, when George introduced her to our mother, all Stacey's composure deserted her. That soft-spoken voice of hers became shrill as she gushed to Mom, 'Well, I see where Rachel and Devon get their good looks! You look just like them! Or rather, they look just like you! Why, there's no way they could have turned out ugly, after having a mother who looks like you!'" Rachel laughed at the memory she had managed to retain through her love-struck daze of the evening before.

Beside her, Felix laughed too over one of two bacon strips he had started on in his plate. "Yea, your parents do look good," he agreed in his attractive tenor. "They haven't changed a bit in the last ten years. Your mother is as gorgeous as she ever was. And after inheriting her genes, I'm hardly surprised that you ended up turning out the way you did."

Rachel smiled his praise of her to the back of his short-haired head, as Felix had turned away from her to pick his juice glass off the French Provincial end table to his left and take a long sip of its grape contents.

"Oh, here comes the best part." Rachel paused briefly over the orange juice she had lifted from her own side table and raised to her lips, downing a quick sip. "George and Stacey then took Mom and Dad down to meet Stacey's parents on the eighth floor. You remember how meeting you yesterday evening shook Dora Lumas up?" Rachel watched a smile shape the corners of Felix's attractive mouth as he nodded at the memory. "Well, she had gotten all her composure back and greeted my parents with the same naturalness and warmth with which she'd greeted Devon and me earlier in the evening. Al Lumas, on the other hand, did the same thing he did after being introduced to Devon and me at that time. He took one look at our parents—and stared in stunned shock.

"He said, 'Good damn!'" Rachel laughed at the memory of the white man's shock, nearly dropping the tall juice glass she still held in her hand. "He said, 'Now, I see where George and your daughters get their good looks! You two are good looking people! Do all black people in Georgia look like you two do?' Is that a racist remark or what . . . !"

Felix laughed at the same time she did. "Does sound like it could be misconstrued as one!" he agreed finally.

"Anyway, you know my Dad," Rachel said after a moment of calming down and taking another sip of her orange juice. "He somehow managed to gloss over the moment and turn the man's awkward flattery back onto him. And I mean, my Dad did it so well that pretty soon, Al had him engrossed in the lengthiest of conversations. I mean, you may not believe that a man that unassuming at first glance could be so long-winded, but that Al Lumas can talk. He told my Dad all about this place they're originally from, he, his wife, Rick and Stacey, called Ketchikan down on the southern tip of Alaska off the Pacific Coast. He said it's like 230 miles west of Juneau, which puts it maybe 130 miles west of Sitka—you know, where Thacker told us yesterday was the Russian capital and actual site of William Seward's purchase of Alaska from the Russians back in 1867. Derived from the words Katch Kanna, which means 'spread wings of a thundering eagle,' Ketchikan is the Salmon Capital of the World, and a tourist hot spot. In fact, Al and his wife Dora, both of whom work there in the tourism industry, said Ketchikan is Alaska's first port-of-call for northbound cruise ships and as an added fact, at least twenty different cruise lines come through there between the months of May and September every year. Not to mention the same for Alaska State Ferries nearly everyday." Rachel was surprised by the extent of her memory as she relayed to Felix all she had retained through the love-struck daze she had been during Al Lumas' entire discourse about his hometown.

"Does sound like a place," Felix smiled over the second bacon strip he was starting on, not having missed her quick thoughtful calculation of the city's location from that of Alaska's sale to the U.S from Russia all those years ago.

"And I'll tell you something else," Rachel continued over the orange juice glass she still held in her hand. "Meeting Al Lumas yesterday evening reminded me of something Stacey said to me on Monday. He has a brother. Al confirmed it last night. His name is Stevan, who's worked as a pharmacist for the past thirty seven years, and for a drug chain that has him presently living in Juneau. To hear Al put it, Stevan's coming in for the wedding either today or early tomorrow. Can you believe it? Al Lumas has a brother! What must he be like for Al to be as blunt and obvious as he is—?"

"You tell me!" Felix suggested with a laugh over the bacon strip he was still munching on.

"If only I could!" Rachel exclaimed with a rivaling laugh. Sobering, she returned her attention to the partially eaten food beginning to cool on her plate.

She finished her meal in about twenty minutes, as did Felix, and then she poured a cup of black coffee, which she both creamed and sugared while Felix went back for a second large glass of juice—this time orange. The coffee had started to cool, but it was still hot enough to warm her up. Settling against the back velvet cushion of the sofa with the coffee in her hands, Rachel turned her attention to the TV to watch the old Elvis Presley movie *Girls! Girls! Girls!* coming on then.

The movie, filmed in 1962, stars Elvis, Stella Stevens, Laurel Goodman, Jeremy Slate. Elvis plays Ross Carpenter, a struggling tuna fisherman in Hawaii (oh, well, Rick would find that interesting, Rachel thought), who was forced to sell the boat he and his deceased father built, the 'Westwind'. The Stavroses, who bought it, have to move to Arizona, and their fleet is up for sale. To make enough money to buy it back from the new owner, Wesley Johnson, played by Jeremy Slate, Ross has to take up nightclub singing while using the Westwind as a hired fishing boat for obnoxious tourists. Meanwhile, Ross is besieged with girls, Laurel Goodman's Laurel, fiery little rich girl spending the summer by the shore and going incognito as a nobody who Ross takes to, and Stella Stevens' dull-as-nails Robin, tough entertainer at the town nightclub, who doesn't care for Ross lavishing so much attention on her, two, for example. Finishing her coffee a few minutes later, Rachel lowered her emptied cup and saucer to the French Provincial end table and settled against the back sofa cushion in smiling anticipation to see how Elvis would extricate himself from his situation with too many girls.

They had gotten about twenty minutes into the movie when Felix suddenly reached over and curved a hand over her wrist, sending a dizzying wave of pleasure dancing up Rachel's arm.

"Come here, luscious," he said in his seductive tenor, moving to his feet and pulling her to hers, "I want to see if I can *ketch* you if I can!" Felix forced that last expression out smilingly between his perfect teeth, leaving Rachel laughing at his play on the word *'ketch'* with those of *'I-can'* as in Ketchikan, the very hometown of the Lumases that she had previously mentioned—as he led her from the living room.

He took her to his bedroom where he lowered her into his disheveled bed and then himself in on top of her. Rachel stopped laughing immediately as the feel of his fine hard gorgeous sexy body sprawled the length of her and pressing her into the firm mattress aroused her and in fact, the teasing light had gone out of the dancing brown eyes as Felix gazed down at her with a look of equal disturbance. Because of that, his gaze barely strayed away from her as he used the remote control device on the French Provincial nightstand to turn the TV across the large bedroom on to the same Encore cable channel as the one in the living room, where Elvis continued to frolic with a number of girls. Rachel was hardly surprised when Felix then cradled her head in his hands and lowered his mouth on hers, turning what started as a simple kiss into an ardent display that left the blood pounding in her ears while her stomach muscles convulsed in a spasm.

However, Rachel's surprise was genuine when Felix pulled his face away from hers suddenly, as she was unaware that he had felt the explosive spasm that had convulsed through her torso.

"Are you okay?" Felix half grinned the question at her despite the concern behind his attractive tone.

"Yeah." Rachel forced a smile despite the lie, not wanting him to know just how completely his ardent kiss had excited her.

"Good, because I haven't got started yet," Felix said before lowering his mouth to her neck in a series of kisses that moved easily up over her sensitive cord, black onyx stone-bejeweled ear and curving jaw in the direction of hers.

Yet this time Rachel was ready for the lips that closed over hers, her own fervently matching their ardent claim. The rain thrashing against the window behind the drapes Felix had yet to open was drowned out by the sound of her heartbeat as it hammered against her breast; in fact, Elvis too was momentarily forgotten as her arms tightened around Felix's neck in heady submission. Yet just as Rachel was beginning to acclimate to the searing temperature of the wildfire racing through her veins, Felix again pulled his face away from hers to stare over her shoulder strangely.

"Oh, God!" he cried in amazement. "I can't believe I'm hung up on George's kid sister!"

"Hey, I can't believe I'm hung up on George's old friend either; and I do mean old!" Rachel teased him with a laugh.

"Hey, girl, I am not old," Felix laughed back challengingly. "I'm just well-seasoned."

"Like the beefcake you are?" Rachel continued in the same teasing vein, taunting him playfully.

"That's right, cheesecake," Felix replied with similar playfulness amid lowering his mouth back to her neck.

"Well—look here, beefcake," Rachel went on laughingly against his golden brown cheek, "we need to stop this. Elvis is still on. By the time we get through here, *Girls! Girls! Girls!* will be gone, gone, gone, and will have moved on, on, on! They'll have become Hags! Hags! Hags!"

"Oh, who cares?" The question was laced with disinterest as Felix rolled over onto his back and pulled her over on top of him, his arms encircling her waist while he raised his head to shower a number of searing kisses over the quivering sensitive cord of her neck at the same time. "I've got my own girl. Besides, I hear Elvis is dead, anyway!" he finished with a jocularity that made them both laugh.

However, Rachel stopped laughing when he did the same suddenly and lay with his head pressed into the pillow staring up at her strangely.

"What is that?" Felix asked curiously.

"Hmmm . . . ?"

"That sound."

"What sound?"

"That sound that you just made in your throat. You made that same sound in your throat when I kissed you last night. Is that a laugh?" Felix asked, grin sliding onto his slender lips, long-lashed eyes dancing up at her. "It's sort of like a-a gurgle—*ur-ul! Ur-ul!*" His whole face pulled into a frown as he forced the sound from his throat. "It's sort like a-a cat's meow—*eow! Eow!* A-A mouse squeak—*eak! Eak!* A sing-song *hmmm! Hmmm . . . !*" He continued to form the sounds in his throat. "It's adorable! It's precious! Does this sound mean you're dizzy?" Felix asked, perfect teeth flashing behind the grin that slid back onto his lips. " . . . Because my head is reeling. I'm spinning like a top."

"I'm whirling in a wind." A smile accompanied the confession, which Rachel was delighted to see brought more of what she was already beginning to see of the same to Felix's own handsome sexy features. "But I need to come down off this high I'm on, because I have family here. They're probably wondering where in the world I am."

"George knows where you are."

Deliberately Rachel did not reveal that she was aware George knew she was with him as she beheld the knowing look that had crept into his dancing gaze.

"Maybe so," she agreed quietly, "but I do need to go find my parents. They must be going insane wondering where am. After all, not only have I not seen them since last night, but I didn't even get a chance to finish helping them unpack or say goodnight to them, because George had to get me out of there."

Felix's eyes narrowed. "What do you mean George had to get you out of there?"

Rachel laughed at the curious note that had crept back into his attractive tone, at the same time realizing she was going to have to tell him the truth after all.

"Like you said, I was dizzy," she began forthrightly, arms thrown about his head. "After you kissed me goodnight last night, I walked around in a daze for a whole hour, thinking about you. Anyway, we were in Stacey's parents' suite on the eighth floor, and Al Lumas was going on and on and on about Ketchikan, and I was barely listening because like I said, I was thinking about you. Anyway, that's when George suddenly came over, sat down beside me, and said quietly in my ear in a voice that no one else could hear, 'Hey, Kid Sister, when are you going to come down off that cloud you've been on for the past hour? . . . Because you look like you're about to float away from here any minute . . . !'" Rachel laughed while Felix lay gazing up at her indulgently. "Anyway, he got me out of there, took me halfway down the hall, and talked to me. Said he knew I was happy you'd come around. He said he was happy you'd come around, too. He said he thought you had lost your mind the way you sat there at dinner and laughed it up and lapped it up with Devon while she chewed the scenery in the restaurant and came all onto you—especially after all you had said to him about your feelings for me earlier—most of which you'd told me and which George made me privy to, by the way. So, you think I'm luscious?" Rachel asked, smilingly getting off the subject and voicing one of those things George had made her privy to.

"I believe I told you that a while ago," Felix answered, slim-lipped mouth curved in a smile at her, brown eyes dancing up at her.

"And you think I'm sweet?"

His well-shaped head moved in a nod against the blue encased pillow, his hands gently stroking her waist. "Uhm-hmm."

"And you think I'm seductive?"

Again the brown eyes danced in definite affirmation of that thought. "Uhm-hmm!"

"And you know I'm innocent," Rachel went on with the things he had told George about her and that George had made her privy to. "As a matter of fact, that's why I tried to run from you when we got back here yesterday evening. George said you were flying all over the place, speaking all excitedly, talking about what all else we had in common. He said you were flying all over the place. You were higher than a kite! I, he said, on the other hand, was morose. . . . Looked like I was going to jump out of my skin any minute. And he was right, because I was scared to death. I mean, hey, I'll be honest with you—practically from the first moment you took my hand in yours on Monday, I've felt this warm pleasure sliding up my arm—I didn't know whether because it was good seeing an old friend again after all these years, or what. But then, when you kissed me at the restaurant on Tuesday, you aroused a sensation along with it that I spent the next more than twenty-four hours trying to hide from you—especially when you brushed off the couple kisses that took place between us after that as inconsequential! But then, you shocked me when you told me early Thursday morning after kissing me yet again that you liked kissing me, and we've been kissing ever since! I mean, how many times did we kiss yesterday, about a hundred and ninety seventeen? And I enjoyed all of them. I mean, you know I liked them! I mean, hey, are you kidding? Unfortunately, just like the others we'd shared earlier in the week, each one brought with it sensations upon sensations until they built up inside me a need for something that I had never before felt for a man and as a result, did not understand nor had the experience to handle—you know, just like I told you. Anyway, I was shaking in my shoes. I was scared to death. I wanted to run from you! I bolted off the elevator away from you and George, flew into the penthouse, ran straight to the guest bathroom, and freaked! I was literally going out of my mind! I was shaking in my shoes!" Rachel rambled on frantically while Felix lay gazing up at her intently, understanding glimmering in the dancing brown depths of his eyes.

"Yet I somehow managed to get a grip on myself, when you grabbed me by the arm and said let's go down to my suite and watch this Elvis Presley movie, *Tickle Me*," Rachel went on after pausing for a brief moment. "I was terrified at the thought of being with you any longer. That's why as soon as we stepped off the elevator on this floor and you kissed me in what—our hundred and ninety eighteenth for the day, I said I had to go, and bolted. Or so, that was my intention. Except that that's when you freaked. Grabbed me by the arm, yanked me back, and asked me if I was running from you. You quoted those lyrics from Elvis Presley's hit tune, *Little Sister*, telling me not to kiss you once or twice, say it's very nice, and then, run like my big sister done. So, I said, fine, I won't run, now, what! But I still didn't understand what was going on with me—that is, until you pulled me into another kiss—our hundred and ninety nineteenth of the day, at which point I realized exactly what it was that I was feeling for you. As I'm sure you know by what happened between us after that."

"Uhm-hmm." Taking one of the hands she had cradling his head into his, Felix raised it lovingly to his lips, sending a predictable wave of pleasure skittering up Rachel's arm, even though she knew that had not been his intention for the gesture to do.

"Anyway, getting back to George and what he said about you and Devon in the restaurant yesterday evening," Rachel returned to her former subject, "he said he actually thought he'd have to excuse himself when you ended up dumping her the way you did!" She laughed at the memory of George telling her that, a laugh Felix shared with her. "Anyway, George and I talked for a long while in the hall, after which point I just floated on my cloud back up to my suite, and went to bed. So, you see, I never saw my parents again to say goodnight. And I know they've got to be going out of their minds wondering what's going with me after not having heard from me since eleven o'clock last night. Not to mention Devon, who's already suspicious that that woman you said you had waiting for you is me."

Again the long-lashed dancing brown eyes narrowed on her face in a curious look. "What makes you say that?" asked the attractive tenor. "I gave that woman no hint whatsoever yesterday that there was anything going on between you and me."

"Certainly not at dinner," Rachel agreed. "You were brilliant, darling, you were truly deceptive. You deserve another Emmy, an Oscar; an Academy Award for that performance. As I sat there watching you interact with Devon, I was just like George. Just like he said, you were laughing it up and lapping it up while she chewed the scenery and came all onto you. Just like George, I said to myself: what the hell is he doing! You would not look at me, you would not look my way, and I thought I heard vacuum noises as she sucked you in, again. And that made no sense in light of what you had said to me and what almost happened between us what—? A couple hours before . . . ? Stacey sat to the right of George and the left of me, just like George and me, watched you eat up Devon's attack on her ex-husband and outrageous come-ons to you in a rage that had actually stopped her from talking. She turned a glance on you on the way from George's side yesterday in preparation of taking Devon from the penthouse down to her tenth-floor suite to try on her bridesmaid's dress and shoes as if to say 'Don't let her rope you in with her good looks, again.' And who knows what went on, after that. And then, Stacey had to sit there at the table in the restaurant watching as Devon did just that, roped you back in, coming all onto you like a freight train. I'm telling you, the look I afforded her showed her utter rage at Devon's boldness and utter nerve. All she could do was sit staring, shocked, staggered, stunned and stupefied. I, on the other hand, sat heartbroken, helpless, horrified and hurting the way you completely ignored me like that. I had to keep my head down because I didn't want anyone to see the utter pain in my eyes—although George saw it, and felt for me. So, naturally, when you turned down Devon's offer for you to show her around the hotel by telling her you had a woman waiting for you and that she was beautiful, reminding her that we had a date to watch Elvis, like George said, I could have glowed. I looked at George and I saw the delight in his eyes, because unlike Stacey who was relieved that you did not let Devon rope you back in and yet baffled because she didn't know who you were talking about, just like me, George knew exactly who were you talking about. My brother said there was nothing but pleasure on my face, although you didn't see it, because you had those gorgeous brown eyes of yours directed intently upon Devon in your refusal of further offer of her company. So you gave her no reason to be suspicious about us at dinner. But you messed up two times. You want to hear the first time?"

Again the brown eyes in Felix's sexy rectangular face were narrowed on her in a curious look far removed from the amused one Rachel had turned on him. In the time she had been relaying her own perspective of last evening's events, his expression had gone from droll amusement to sympathy and regret that let her know immediately how sorry he was for having put her through that pain. And he was going to have to do some tall explaining to Stacey, that is, if George hadn't already done so, since as Felix had told Rachel, George knew where she was by what he'd confided to him yesterday as to what was going on between them and also by what George had seen quietly going on between them the night before—the going's on of which Rachel had just said George had confided his awareness of to her not much later after that. Bent on rectifying at least one of those situations, Felix continued to tenderly kiss the fingers of the dusky-colored hand he had taken into his golden brown one, the touch of his lips on Rachel's flesh sending that wave of pleasure dancing up her arm as usual.

"What?" Felix asked in final response to her question.

"It was when you took Devon up to the penthouse to surprise George yesterday evening," Rachel said. "George said she had just said something about you telling her that our Mom and Dad hadn't gotten here, yet, when he told her that I'd said they'd be arriving today after driving in cross-country. George said that's when Devon said the same thing she'd said to you after interrupting us here yesterday. George said Devon said, 'Yea, where the hell is Rachel? Around here trying to vamp some damned man she has no intention of sleeping with?' Well, that's when George said you laughed and told her, 'Will you get off her?' George said Devon sliced a curious look at you that demanded to know why you'd spoken in such quick defense of me by telling her to get off me like that. George said it was a look that said, 'Could it possibly be because you want to get on her?' Suspicion Number One. Do you want to hear the second time you messed up?"

The light had returned to the brown eyes as Felix gazed up at her with his usual amusement. "When . . . ?"

"George said it took place, also last night, just when you, our family and Rick were about to ride up in the elevator here from the first floor," Rachel continued.

"To hear George put it, you had just dumped Devon again by telling Dad when he asked if you two were going to get back together that it wasn't going to happen between you, that you had a woman waiting for you, and that you had been trying to shake Devon for the past hour! You remember when you said that?"

"Uhm-hmm." A smile accompanied the memory.

"That's when I reminded you about putting that brown paper bag over your head in order to keep women from chasing after you because of your good looks and go as the Unknown Soap Opera Star! Do you remember that?"

Again Felix smiled at the memory. "Uhm-hmm . . . !"

"Do you remember what you said to me after that?"

"Uhm-hmm. I said, 'Hush up, girl!'"

"Yes, you did," Rachel agreed. "And to hear George tell it, in the midst of doing that, you turned a grin on me that was so hot that he thought he'd have to excuse himself, again! Do you remember that?" Rachel asked with a laugh.

"Uhm-hmm . . . !" Felix agreed, own smile broadening into a laugh.

"To hear George tell it, we shared a laugh, you reached out and curved a hand over my wrist, and you did do that, remember?" Felix nodded. "Anyway, to hear George tell it, I just blushed. He said I literally went to putty in the floor. He said I didn't even try to hide the fact that the touch of your hand on my flesh left me soaring in the clouds. And you know, I don't think I did, I think I just stood there and grinned. Anyway, George said Devon noticed, though. He said she turned a murderous glare on the two of us as if demanding what the hell was going on with the two of us. Suspicion Number Two. And you know she's going to come here looking for you, because my sister does not take rejection well. You saw that last night, in the way she pulled you from that restaurant despite the fact that you had just rejected her."

The sexy mouth pulled into a snarl as Felix indulged another rejection of his ex-flame. "Well, if she comes up here and can't read the meaning behind those two do not disturb signs on the door, I know a good optometrist in New York I can take her to," he said in his attractive tenor.

"That's awful!" Rachel laughed.

"Uhm-hmm." Felix laughed too, both hands holding hers out to the side, playing with her fingers.

"I have another reason for getting out of here. Rick Lumas is probably walking around here looking for me, as well," Rachel said after a moment.

Felix frowned again at her mention of Stacey's older brother. "Yea, what were you doing with him last night, anyway?" he demanded. "I saw him flirting with you at dinner, and I didn't like it. But I couldn't say anything because I was too busy playing my game with Devon."

"Oh, who are you kidding—?!" Rachel's own lips twisted in a snarl as she heard the jealousy behind his attractive tone. "I knew from the first moment George introduced me to him yesterday evening that that man was going to make a play for me by the way his eyes gleamed at me in the process. And I knew the reason why—he had tried to hit on Devon but she rejected him, and he had realized she was out of his league. And that is exactly what Rick did. As soon as you left with Devon and Stacey to go down to her suite so that Devon could try on her bridesmaid's dress and shoes, that man was all over me like wallpaper. As he was at dinner—no doubt what you saw in a quick glance. The man told me everything he knew about Hawaii, the Aloha State, although I paid him very little attention for sitting there watching you macking with your ex!"

Felix's perfect teeth flashed in his golden brown face as he indulged just as equally an amused laugh as she at her use of the slang word meaning to pimp.

"Anyway, Rick had just started on me again by telling me to come and let him take me to his hotel in Honolulu, on Oahu, the Kaikilani, I think it is, and stay there for a week," Rachel went on after a moment, having sobered her amusement, as had Felix. "He said the hotel is bigger than this one. He told me I could have my hair done in the beauty parlor, have my toenails cut, my elbows pumiced, my body wrapped in seaweed in the spa!" A smile shaped Rachel's lips again as she recalled the exact words Rick had said to her. "And then, he said something about me going to some place on the Big Island—Kakika—Kakeala—no, I think it was Kealakekua, something like that. Rick said that once there I could hike to Kealakekua Bay and go snorkeling in the waters, or—and this is going to kill you—observe the obelisk monument on the north side of the Bay of Captain James Cook."

Rachel's eyes widened on the handsome sexy face in playful anticipation of the surprise that mention of the familiar name brought immediately to his.

"W-hat—What do you mean, Captain James Cook?" Felix demanded predictably in his attractive tenor, dancing brown eyes having narrowed on her beautiful dusky features. "Are you talking about Captain Cook, Captain James Cook—the English discoverer, who has a monument dedicated to him at Resolution Park, a sculpture erected in his name between Fourth and Fifth Avenues, and who I showed you Cook Inlet was named for, not to mention Turnagain Arm Trail and the Captain Cook Hotel, all this over here in Alaska? What was he doing in Hawaii?"

"Oh, boy, do I have a story to tell you!" Rachel's perfect teeth flashed in a grin in her complete excitement over the subject matter. "Do you remember telling me when you took me to the Captain Cook Hotel that its dark décor recalled Captain Cook's voyages in the South Pacific, which also is depicted in that sculpture—the Three Ships Sculpture that you just mentioned?"

Felix nodded his well-shaped head against the blue encased pillow. "Uhm-hmm."

"Well, get this! That's why that sculpture depicts Cook's voyages in the South Pacific. According to Rick, the English were the first known Europeans to set foot on Hawaiian shores. He said that Captain Cook spent most of a decade—a decade, baby, a decade—exploring and charting that South Pacific before stumbling on several Hawaiian Islands as he searched for a northwest passage to the Atlantic on the way to China in Asia just like Thacker said, and just like you said. This took place in January 1778, the same year that he sailed up Cook Inlet here, in search of that Northwest Passage, but had to 'turn again', therefore leading him to name that body of water River Turnagain—you know, also just like you told me and Thacker told us!" Rachel went on with the same excited grin. "Anyway, Rick said that Captain Cook never did find that fabled Northwest Passage—possibly because he found it too cold going through the Arctic. So, he turned again and wound up back in Hawaii the next year, 1779, where he discovered other Hawaiian Islands. He sailed into Kealakekua Bay on the Big Island of Hawaii in the same month, January, 1779, where ten thousand onlookers and a thousand canoes carrying Hawaiians in the midst of celebrating the annual Maka—hiki—that's right, Makahiki festival sailed to greet him. When Cook went ashore, he was met by the High Priest—let me see if I can get this name—Kalaniopu'u—yea, that's right, and led to a temple lined with skulls. The Hawaiians sort of deified Cook with Lono, god of peace, agriculture and fertility for whom the Makahiki festival was named and fell down chanting Cook's name everywhere he went, thinking him the god Lono's incarnation. And Cook and his crew became enamored with the islands' erotic exoticism and hospitality, which included food, drink, shelter, and of course, sex!" Playfully Rachel drew out that obvious last word as she grinned down at Felix, who smiled up at her with equal interest in the subject that had her so animated.

"Anyway, come February fourth of that same year, 1779, Captain Cook and his ships sailed north out of Kealakekua Bay and ran into a storm. One of his ships broke a foremast, so, he had to return to Kealakekua to repair the mast. Well, with the Makahiki festival now over and Cook's return unexpected on the part of the Hawaiians whose observance was now on their main god Kunuiakea, tensions rose with the unwelcome 'Lono' and quarrels broke out between the two camps. Anyway, a whole mess erupted when one of Cook's boats was stolen. Captain Cook blockaded Kealakekua Bay and set off to capture High Priest Kalaniopu'u with the simple intention of holding him hostage until the ship was returned. But Cook released Kalaniopu'u at the request of his wife, only for a stomach ailment and increasingly irrational behavior on Cook's part to lead to an altercation with a large crowd of Hawaiians on the beach when he tried to go ashore to retrieve his goods. Also, the villagers, angered after learning that a British search party had killed another Hawaiian chief—Kalimu, I think his name was, began to attack with spears and stones. And in the melee, shots were fired, but the material that the Hawaiians' shields were made of protected them, forcing Cook's men to retreat down the beach, abandoning him. When Cook turned to launch his boats, he was struck in the head. The blow stunned him, and he staggered into the shadows. The Hawaiians followed him, where they proceeded to both club and stab him. Beat him to death in ten minutes. Angry attackers continued to stab his lifeless body, which it is rumored they then dismembered and ate. According to Rick, Captain Cook met this most violent end on February 14, 1779, just ten days after he and his crew attempted to sail out of the site of Cook's death, Kealakekua Bay."

Felix stared up at Rachel for a shocked moment after hearing the most gut-wrenching news, the amused light having completely fled from his dancing brown eyes.

"Oh, God, that's awful!" he exclaimed finally, shock still ringing in his attractive voice and gritting his teeth. "It's like I told you—I knew the man was all over the place in his day, but I never dreamed he was met with such a terrible demise in Hawaii."

"Isn't that awful?" Rachel agreed, herself sharing his look of shock. "That's why according to Rick, that obelisk monument is erected on the north side of Kealakekua Bay, to mark the spot where Cook was killed at the water's edge. He said that Cook and his crew altered the course of Hawaii's history. In harmony with that, Rick said they even named a small town after him called Captain Cook just above the bay where he met his untimely death. And all that, in addition to what he did for Alaska. Those were Rick's exact last words."

Despite the confirming nod that accompanied Rachel's last statement, Felix was speechless for a long moment as he tried to recover from the utter shock and disbelief he felt from all he had heard.

"That—That—That's incredible . . . !" Felix stammered finally.

"Isn't it?" Rachel agreed. "Rick said it too: apparently, Captain James Cook was all over the place in his day. The man had a fascinating career as a discoverer. I'm telling you, I spent half the dinner ignoring Rick trying to hit on me, until he started talking about Captain Cook. He had my interest, after that."

The dancing brown eyes lingered on her for a thoughtful moment as Felix reflected on her last statement. "Well, he's not going to have it this morning. You're not getting out of here."

"Oh, yes, I am. I've got to go find my parents—"

"Uh-uh."

"George—"

"Uh-uh."

"Stacey—"

"Uh-uh."

"Devon—"

"Uh-uhh! You're going to stay here with me, and we're going to watch every Elvis movie that comes up until we have to leave for that miserable wedding rehearsal at two o'clock this afternoon. Besides, I haven't even begun to 'tickle you' yet!"

Rachel laughed at his teasing mention of the Elvis Presley movie *Tickle Me* that she had not long mentioned and that Felix had intended for them to watch yesterday and which they had not yet seen because they had gotten too busy *literally* 'tickling' each other not much later. That is, before Devon had shown up unexpectedly after that.

"But baby, we haven't even gotten around to watching *Tickle Me* yet, not to mention we're not even watching Elvis now. I mean, is that still *Girls! Girls! Girls!* on over there, or what, what, what?"

"Who knows? Who knows? Who knows? I stopped paying attention ages ago!"

"But I've got to get out of here. You need to open that door, anyway. You need to take the do not disturb signs off and let the maid get in here, because you are a slob!"

Felix laughed. "Right now, I'm going to slob all over you!" he threatened. And rolling her back over onto her back and himself back over on top of her, he lowered his lips to hers. And both to Rachel's relief and delight, there was not a bit of slobber to his possession.

And the rain continued to thrash against the window outside while Elvis played from the large wood-grained TV across the equally large swanky bedroom. Eventually *Girls! Girls! Girls!* ended and was succeeded by *Follow That Dream*, from 1961, where Elvis plays Toby Kwimper, an innocent Georgia boy living on government subsidies and disability pension for a bad back strained in the army, who has to find a way to get his hillbilly-type family who have run out of money and gas and have set up their mobile home on a Florida Beach next to a highway soon to be dedicated by the State Governor, on the road again. The movie also stars Arthur O'Connell as Toby's widowed father, Alan Hewitt, who plays state supervisor H. Arthur King, and Joanne Moore as nosy welfare worker Alisha Claypoole, who is first turned on by Toby's raw sexuality and then determines to destroy him after he spurns her. After that followed *Clambake* from 1967, where Elvis stars as Scott Hayward, millionaire playboy, who swaps places with a water ski instructor at a Miami Beach resort to find out if people will like him for himself and not his money. He sets his eye on hotel guest Dianne Carter played by Shellie Fabares, who is out to marry rich and has no interest in poor Scott, setting her sights rather on millionaire J.J. Jamison played by Bill Bixby, who signs up for a boat race and tries to win the young Dianne over. So Scott sets out to build his own boat, join in the regatta and make gold-digger Dianne fall for him before she finds out that he's loaded. But Rachel and Felix barely saw either of them because they were too busy kissing, kissing, and kissing . . . each one leaving them floating higher in the clouds from the dreamlike states they were already in. And how appropriate that the next movie scheduled after *Clambake* was *Kissin' Cousins*, though they would sadly have to miss that one because it started at one fifty and the wedding rehearsal was at two o'clock. Equally unfortunate, Rachel realized that she would have to miss the end of *Clambake* as well as with smiling regret, she pulled away from Felix at one thirty to pull herself together, comb her hair and touch up all the attractive makeup he had kissed off her face. And all the time she wondered how she would possibly be able to keep a straight face as with one last delicious kiss, she bid Felix a laughing goodbye and got out of his suite quickly.

Arriving at the elevator banks down the corridor with her black leather bag strapped to her shoulder a moment later, Rachel stepped into the first one that opened and took it up to the penthouse to see George. He answered her knock on the red door immediately, the deep brown eyes in his suntan face settling on her in a mixture of welcome and curiosity. Rachel couldn't help noticing that he was not wearing his usual hotel uniform of blue jacket pulled on over black slacks, but wore a beige knit sweater and equally beige slacks on his sturdy five-foot-ten-inch frame. Rachel guessed the reason George was dressed so casually was because he was getting married the following day and was thus taking this one off to relax before the nuptials.

"Hey, Kid Sister," George greeted with a smile, a brotherly arm gliding around her shoulders as he saw her into the large well-lit red-themed penthouse suite. "Have you been where I think you've been—or do I need to ask? Because if my suspicions are correct—"

"Yes, have you been with Felix, Rachel?" Having been standing in front of a nearby desk, Stacey approached them across the large carpeted floor, grin on her red-tinged lips as she cut off her fiancé's last remark. Like George, Stacey was in casual attire of green slacks and a white sweater, her long brown hair flowing down over her shoulders. Rachel deduced by the way she had answered her own question that George had cleared up the confusion she had felt upon watching Felix dump Devon after dinner last evening with the claim that he had a woman waiting for him, that she was beautiful, and reminding Devon that they had a date to watch Elvis by making Stacey privy to the fact that the woman Felix had been talking about was Rachel. Hence, the stout white woman's present knowledge of the romantic goings-on between her and Felix, George's best friend and best man.

"I'm afraid so," Rachel replied finally in answer to the question the Alaska Native had asked her, despite not being able to keep a straight face and blushing in the floor.

"Been holed up in his suite watching part of the Elvis Presley movie marathon that came on on the Encore Channel this morning at seven thirty?" asked Stacey with a knowing grin equally shared by George as he moved away from Rachel to come to stand at his fiancée's side, sending Rachel's straight face crooking even further as she flushed all the more.

"I'm afraid so," Rachel repeated guiltily, her soft brown gaze sliding from that of George to the same color gaze of Stacey standing several inches shorter to George's right.

"George tells me its all this crazy stuff you have in common, more of which you learned having yesterday, and that because of that, you've got this thing going on that's hotter than the sun," persisted the soft-spoken Stacey with a smile.

Rachel didn't think her mockery of her and prying into her business seemed to fit the normally composed, quiet-natured woman who had not only just teased her so unexpectedly but practically quoted word-for-word her confidence to her brother George the night before.

"I'm afraid so." Again Rachel repeated herself guilt-faced despite going on to take the woman into her confidence, as had she George. "And I know it's ridiculous for something to happen like this in only three days when considering Felix and I haven't seen each other in ten years, but what can I say? It's so big that I actually let the man talk me into spending the morning locked away with him in his suite watching part of that Elvis Presley movie marathon on ENC that you just mentioned, when George's and my parents got in last night and I haven't seen them since. As a matter of fact, I didn't even get a chance to say goodnight to them because in case George hasn't told you, he had to get me out of your parents' suite last night, because the whole time they and you were getting acquainted with my parents, I was sitting there dreaming about Felix. Is that ridiculous, or what?"

Stacey's laugh acknowledged her relief that Felix did not let Devon rope him back in as well as her own awareness of Rachel's inattention in the hour or so of being in her parents eighth-floor suite the night before that she had just mentioned, although Stacey had not been aware of the cause of it being Felix at the time.

"Well, ridiculous or no, hot as this thing is that you and Felix have got going on, you'd better not let Devon see it," Stacey warned in her soft-spoken way.

"You've got that right," George agreed.

"Yea, we've already come to the conclusion that we're going to have to play the game of keep-Devon-in-the-dark-as-to-our-feelings-for-each-other until the wedding's done tomorrow." Again Rachel drew the woman who would be her sister-in-law in little over twenty four hours into her confidence, as she'd already done her brother George. "As a matter of fact, what you saw at dinner last evening with Felix completely ignoring me amid laughing it up and lapping it up as Devon chewed the scenery in the restaurant and came all on to him like that, was part of that game."

"So, George also told me. Which, while we're on the subject of such dinner, must have been a horrendous experience for you to have sat through, watching the outrageous play Devon made to get him back, especially when as you just said, Felix completely ignored you amid laughing it up and lapping it up in his game of playing up to Devon like that," Stacey said with a smile of her red-tinted lips.

A smile slid onto Rachel's own wine-painted lips at the soft-spoken woman's perspicacity in having deduced the experience the dinner must have been for her to have sat through.

"It was horrendous," Rachel agreed as she recalled telling Felix just earlier that morning the heartbreak, helplessness, horror and hurt she had felt watching as he completely ignored her amid laughing and lapping it up in his pretend game of play back to Devon's play up to him. "And while we're still on the subject of such dinner, I would like to apologize for my sister's ruining it the way she did," Rachel told Stacey on a note of deeper regret. "I saw by the look on your face just how absolutely shocked you were by her behavior."

The smile on Stacey's red-tinted lips became a poised one as she sought a polite way to respond to her last remark without sounding supercilious.

"I'm just glad she's here to be in the wedding tomorrow," Stacey said finally. "Her arrival here yesterday evening couldn't have given George a better gift."

Rachel thought she couldn't have found a more fitting reply as she gazed delightfully at George and saw the equal delight he had derived from his fiancée's tactful answer.

"So, how's Mom and Dad doing?" Rachel finally got around to asking George, changing the subject. "Have they missed me this morning?"

"I haven't given them a chance to," George said. "I know my boy, Felix. Two things I knew when I woke up this morning and found out it was raining. One: When Felix woke up and found out the same thing, he would suggest that you stay huddled up in his suite all morning. And when Stacey and I discovered that Elvis Presley movie marathon playing from seven thirty this morning till seven thirty tomorrow morning on ENC, I knew what you two would be doing once he locked you into the suite with him—watching Elvis Presley movies, amongst other things!" George hinted with a laugh, returning to their former subject. "So, Stacey and I took our parents, her parents and Devon and Rick out for breakfast, and then we sort of drove them around town. Rick enjoyed it. It gave him a chance to refresh his memory of the hometown he hasn't seen in a while."

Rachel ignored those last two remarks in her preference of responding to the one that had preceded them, all mention of Elvis, Felix and *other things* George had hinted at forgotten.

"You took our parents and Stacey's parents around in this rain?" she asked in surprise. "And after all the rain our parents had to go through on their cross-country drive here through St. Louis, Des Moines, and Seattle?"

"Hey, just like as in Missouri, Iowa, and Washington, if we let the rain stop us in this state, we'd never get anything done," said George with a laugh. "Alaska is known for its wet summers, or at least, I'm beginning to think so. You and Felix just happened to arrive here during a long and fortunate dry spell."

"I see," Rachel answered thoughtfully, thinking how interesting a drive that must have been for Devon—to think of her one more time—knowing of her dislike of Rick the way Rachel did. "So, what'd you guys go out in? Your Ford Contour is not exactly an eight-seater."

"We went out in Dad's RV. I drove. Dad was right when he said that thing handles like a dream," George grinned. "Anyway, we just got back about an hour ago. Told our parents and Devon and Rick to rest up from their sightseeing for a while. They should be meeting us in a few minutes for our wedding rehearsal at two."

"I see." Rachel gave little regard to George's last statement as her brown gaze slid curiously back to the equally brown gaze of Stacey. "So, I take it by your lack of mention of seeing your Uncle Stevan in that last hour that he hasn't arrived here from Juneau, yet?"

Stacey showed her teeth in a second smile of pleasure at Rachel's polite inquiry of the pharmacist brother her father had discussed during her family's visit with him and her mother in their eighth-floor suite the night before. She hadn't expected her to have any recollection of Al's mention of her uncle—especially from the inattentive state Rachel had been in the entire time he had been talking about his brother—much less for her to inquire of him.

"Not yet," Stacey said in response to her question. "But Dad said he'll get here somewhere between this afternoon and early tomorrow morning."

"I'm sure. I'm sure that seeing him is going to make your father's day. Not to mention yours and Rick's—seeing as he can't possibly see his uncle much with living in Hawaii these days."

"Yea, it's going to be a nice visit for all of us." The long-haired brunette swept her with a new look of purpose as she returned to the subject her fiancé had mentioned only a moment ago. "Anyway, now that we've got all this out of the way, why don't you come with us down to the wedding rehearsal, which is due to start in what—twenty minutes?" suggested Stacey with another smile, this time curving a congenial arm around her black-clad shoulders. "You're in the wedding, and will have to be there, anyway. We were just getting ready to leave for the first floor before you arrived."

"Exactly what I came up here to do," Rachel said. Smiling equally, she picked the camera and accessories bag she had left on the French Provincial side table the evening before up into her hand and let her and her brother escort her from the penthouse suite.

Chapter Fourteen

Apparently George had known what he was talking about when he said the wet Alaska summers didn't keep anyone from getting anything done. Rachel saw that when they arrived on the first floor minutes later. The hotel was buzzing with activity as guests undaunted by the downpour checked in from various locations while maids, porters and janitors were all over the floor cleaning suites, throwing out dirty linen, vacuuming the corridor, cleaning the game room, lounge, cafeteria or lobby off the end of the hall. To add to the hustle and bustle: caterers were bringing in food storage units while florists brought in flowers in preparation for the wedding that would take place the following day. In harmony with that, a number of them were in the large meeting/banquet room they approached then, turning the drab businesslike blue, gray and brown-themed interior into an elaborate church.

Rachel's gaze swung away from the large purple ribbons a couple of florists were stringing from one row to another of padded blue chairs on the left side of the aisle and onto two men standing halfway toward the front of the large meeting/banquet room. The pair of men, one black and one white, were both around thirty, both married, who Rachel recalled as two friends that George had introduced her to back on Monday, also in the wedding party. George had to introduce her to them again. The tall black man was named Damon Evans, while his equally tall white partner was named Vic Dalene. It seemed George didn't have any short friends, Rachel noticed. Smilingly shaking hands with the two men, she averted her brown eyes just as Martin Rolf and Flip Hart entered the meeting/banquet room and stopped at her side.

"Hey, baby, Rachel, where have you been, girl?" asked Martin with a grin after a brief acknowledgment of his two married friends.

"Yea, baby, where have you been?" asked Flip after doing the same, forever parroting everything Martin said.

Rachel didn't get a chance to answer either of those questions, for Devon suddenly walked in and ran straight to her side as well. "Hey, Rachel, how come you weren't with us this morning?" asked the twenty-nine-year-old dusky-skinned

231

woman, off-black hair curling long and fluffy and sexy down around her perfectly made-up sensually-featured beautiful wide oval face.

"Hey, I've already seen this town. I had no intention of going out in the rain this morning, so, while you all were going out, I was turning over."

Rachel sighed in relief that Devon didn't press the issue as she dropped the subject with the sardonic twisting of her medium red lips.

"These are my friends, Damon Evans, Vic Dalene, Martin Rolf, and Flip Hart," George made introductions with a smile, brown eyes encompassing his four friends. "And Damon, Vic, Martin and Flip, this is my sister, Devon McClintock."

"How do you do?" asked Devon, sending the four men staring at her a cursory look, unaware that Damon and Vic were already married as she quickly placed the quartet out of her league and moved to pass by them all.

However, Martin curved a detaining arm around the circle of her waist before Devon could walk two feet away from them. "Ho-Hold on, baby," he said to her in his low resonant tone, reclaiming her attention with a grin, "come over here, and let me talk to you!"

"Yea, and let me talk to you, too!" added Flip, who moved off down the brown carpeted aisle toward the front of the room at the same time behind Martin and Devon, Damon and Vic following.

Rachel's gaze was bemused at the swift way the two single men had forgotten her as she lowered the black leather bag and camera and accessories bag she still carried on her shoulder and in her hand to the blue padded seat in the row behind her.

"Stacey," she began smilingly amid turning back to face the white and shorter woman still standing at her side, "do you have any women friends in this wedding party?"

Stacey laughed over the sound of the four men and Devon talking farther up the aisle at the front of the large meeting/banquet room. "Diane and Rochelle should be here any minute," she said in her soft tone, satisfying Rachel for the moment.

Stacey's gaze was diverted from the beautiful features of Rachel's dusky-colored face by a hand that suddenly curved over her arm. She looked around and was surprised to see that she had been approached by her parents.

"Hi, Mom, and Dad," she greeted with a smile, taking them both into her arms.

"How're you doing, baby?" asked Al Lumas with a grin, which he then turned on George standing next to his daughter. "'You looking forward to that wedding tomorrow . . . ?"

"You'd better believe it, Dad-to-be!" grinned George, curving an arm around the white man as well as one around the shoulders of Dora Lumas, quiet as usual.

Yet the Native Alaskan woman in her early sixties who was an older version of Stacey managed to fix Rachel with a smile. "Hello, Rachel," Dora greeted in her warm friendly tone, Native-styled brown purse held in one hand.

"How are you, Mrs. Lumas?" Rachel greeted the long-haired graying brunette in hers. "And how are you, Mr. Lumas?" Her eyes swung away from the brown eyes of Dora to the blue ones of Al. "I see your brother Stevan hasn't gotten here yet," she offered with a smile.

"Don't worry, he'll get here," assured the fully grayed tall Alaska Native man. "You're going to love him! He's just like me!"

"Oh, good Lord . . . !" Rachel turned away from the broad grin the white man had turned on her with a laugh. She was afraid of that!

And of course Rick was there. After greeting Stacey with a hug, the wealthy white man raced straight to her side, where he was then all over her.

"How're you doing, girl, Rachel, baby?" he greeted with a grin, an arm snaking around the circle of her waist, the same way Martin had claimed that of Devon.

"I'm fine, Rick, how are you?" Rachel smilingly asked the Alaska-born Hawaiian, who in his position behind her missed the conspiratorial look that passed between her and Stacey.

Ignoring the anemic response Rick made to her, Rachel let her brown-eyed gaze stray away from the same color one of Stacey as another black man walked into the large meeting/banquet room and stopped at George's side.

"Oh, hey, A.J., it's about time you got here," George said to the man who appeared to be around his same age of thirty-one. "I'd like to introduce you to my sister. Rachel," he began with a smile, "this is my good friend, A.J. Over, and A.J., this is my sister, Rachel Hardison."

". . . A.J. Over," the black man smilingly repeated his name as he took into his the hand she had extended to greet him. "My nickname is Over/Under—you know, as in the rifle, Over/Under? And right now, I want to live up to that name, because I want to get over you, and get you under me!" the man leered, deep brown eyes lowering suggestively over the curves of her body.

"Hold on, man, that's my baby sister you're talking to!" George warned his friend, not having failed to miss the look he had lowered over Rachel. Nor had Rachel, who stood with a bemused grin on her wine-colored lips as she continued to eye the dark-skinned oval-faced man. She knew exactly who he was. He was the man Felix had referred to on Tuesday when he had told her about the friend George had who would like that part about her getting under.

But A.J. barely saw her amusement or even heard the warning George had given him for having noticed Devon standing up front talking to Martin, Flip, Damon and Vic.

"Hold on, man, I want to get over that babe!" A.J. brushed him off with a smile, Rachel forgotten as he moved off in the direction of the quintet.

Rachel stared after the tall black man in amazement, unaware that George, Stacey, her parents Al and Dora Lumas and Rick stood doing the same. In fact, the white man's voice was thick with it as it cut in on her thoughts.

"Good God! I wish I'd come up with that line!" Rick said.

Rachel's attention was diverted from the quintet they were all staring at by the sudden movement of Al and Dora as they moved away to settle in a couple padded blue seats in the aisle to the right of them. They were replaced by Diane Mortemberg, who suddenly appeared at George's side, black zippered bag hanging from her shoulder, having entered the large room both unseen and unheard.

"Hi, Stacey, hi, George," greeted the reservationist Rachel had been introduced to on Monday and seen briefly the day before.

"Hi, Diane," smiled Stacey while George stood smiling down at her from his taller height in an equal look of greeting. "So, you finally made it through the rain, did, you?"

"Hey, it's no problem, it's beginning to slacken up out there," Diane said.

"That's good to hear," Stacey replied, sharing her relieved tone.

Rachel watched the attractive brunette acknowledge Rick with a nod before the hazel eyes—the color of which Rachel had just noticed—settled on her in an interested look.

"Hi, Rachel," began the twenty-six-year-old woman, teeth again bared in a smile. "How are you?"

"The same as you, Diane," Rachel replied, flashing her own Halle Berry smile. "And how are you?"

"I'm doing okay. Anyway, how are you?" Diane repeated in a friendly tone. "I haven't seen you in a while, not since you joined us for dinner on Monday. Of course, with the exception of yesterday evening, when I just did manage to catch your eye while you were standing in the lobby talking to George, Mr. Hardison, after having just gotten back to the hotel from having gone out with Felix, Mr. Latham."

"Yea, we had just come back from the Alaska Center for the Performing Arts, where we saw that film—Sky Song's Aurora Borealis' Alaska Gallery Of Light, I believe it was—you know, about the northern lights." Rachel hoped her response was innocuous enough as she continued to return the white woman's smile; aware that Diane's prying comments—however innocent—could put her secret involvement with Felix in serious jeopardy. Especially with Rick standing there aside her, having heard every word she had said.

As if somehow sensing her faux pa, Diane quickly changed the subject. "I see your and George's sister Devon got here yesterday." The hazel eyes flashed briefly onto Devon still talking with George's friends in the distance. "I guess she somehow managed to get herself out of her mess of a divorce after all and got here, and will be able to be in the wedding after all, huh?" she went on with a smile. "I was on duty last evening when she got here, and checked her in."

"Yes, it was a surprise twist that really delighted George," Rachel continued to smile equally, her gaze however uneasy as it slid onto George and met the unease in his. As the woman Rachel was beginning to see could be quite talkative was about to put her foot in her mouth and embarrass everyone.

Rachel heaved a sigh of relief when Diane's rambling was silenced by the arrival of another black man who had approached their group accompanied by a black woman.

"Hey, Ray!" George greeted, turning a hearty grin on the taller man, Rachel guessed that he too was glad for a reason to stop Diane's talking and change the subject. "How're you doing, my man?"

"How're you doing, old man?" the man named Ray grinned, the arm George had curved over his shoulders prompting him to do the same to him. "You ready to tie that knot tomorrow?"

"Been ready . . . !" George turned an affectionate look down on Stacey before his deep brown gaze settled back on Rachel with purpose. "I have someone I want to you to meet, Ray," he smilingly began introductions in his abrupt alto. "This is my kid sister, Rachel Hardison. And Rachel, meet my dear friend, Ray Marlboro."

Rachel didn't bother to extend a hand to Ray Marlboro, because he stood watching Devon in the distance with the other men, not even having noticed her. In fact, Rachel was hardly surprised when the black man at least Devon's same age moved off in pursuit of her before Rachel's name was barely off George's tongue.

Thankfully, the furor she felt at the way the man had brushed her off didn't last long. As Stacey then turned to introduce her to the black woman who had accompanied Ray Marlboro into the meeting/banquet room, Rachel was surprised to find her staring at her admiringly.

"Rochelle," Stacey began in her soft-spoken way, "I have someone I want you to meet. This is Rachel Hardison, George's kid sister. And Rachel, this is my good friend, Rochelle Loring."

"Hey, you're pretty," grinned Rochelle before Rachel could greet her, the twinkling brown eyes in her made-up round face lingering over Rachel's beautiful equally made-up dusky looks and pulled back off-black hair.

"You're not so bad yourself, Rochelle," Rachel smiled back at the less attractive woman, though she found her smile quite engaging.

As if sensing her lack of looks compared to hers, Rochelle then showed those engaging teeth in a shameless laugh. "Hey, I use what I got," she said through red-painted full lips.

And she had a lot, Rachel thought. Sharing her height of five-feet-eight and about a size sixteen, she had big breasts, but she was stylish. . . . Big hips—although straight—but she was stylish. And she had big legs to go with them, but she was stylish. Wearing a double-breasted color-blocked woolly knee-length dress in hues of red, white and green, the colors matched her purse and shoes and the earrings dangling in her ears behind the shiny curtain of off-black hair that curled to just below her cheeks. In fact, she carried her weight with a grace and presence that reminded Rachel of her friend Sydney, the Meg Ryan freak. Rachel decided that she was going to adopt Rochelle as her new best friend for the next couple days as she continued to smile at the amber-skinned woman, who Stacey had just told her was twenty six.

"And that woman up there charming all the men is our sister, Devon," George smilingly informed the younger woman before moving off in the direction of her, Stacey and Diane following him.

Left alone with Rick and Rachel, Rochelle turned a surprised stare on the latter. "That's your sister?" Rochelle asked her with a half grin. "What's she doing here? Stacey told me when I talked to her on the phone on Tuesday that she wouldn't be able to make it for the wedding, because she was in the process of getting a divorce!"

"She was." A smile accompanied Rachel's nod of affirmation. "But she somehow managed to get her attorney to wrap it up on Wednesday, so, she hopped a plane and arrived here yesterday evening just in time to be a bridesmaid in George and Stacey's wedding, after all."

Rochelle's eyes fixed back on the flashy black woman centered at the front of the room around George's friends in amazement. "Well, I guess that's all good for George, but personally, I don't like her." She shook her head, directing her dismissing gaze to the color-blocked leather purse she was dumping into the padded blue seat in the row to the left of the aisle in front of Rachel's. ". . . Looks too artificial."

"You've got that right!" Rick agreed.

Rachel laughed at the two disparaging remarks the pair had made about her older sister, causing Rochelle's green-shadowed brown-eyed gaze to settle back on her with a new look of interest.

"Stacey tells me that you live in Georgia, where George is originally from," ventured the woman with a smile of her red lips.

"Yes," Rachel replied with a wine-colored smile of her own. "Devon and I live in Atlanta while our parents still live in Villa Rica, where we're originally from. As a matter of fact, they should be here any minute." Rachel wondered why they hadn't gotten there yet as a brief glance at the silver-toned watch on her left wrist showed the time as five till two.

"What do you do in Atlanta?" Rochelle asked.

"I'm a kindergarten teacher at one of our premiere schools there."

"You're a kindergarten teacher? With little kids . . . ?"

"Yea, they're around four—four-and-a-half—something like that."

"Really . . . ? That's amazing!" By the broad grin that continued to curve Rochelle's full lips, Rachel knew immediately that the last occupation she would ever have placed on a woman with her looks was the teaching of natty-nosed four-year-old kids.

"Yea, one of my neighbors told me I had a knack for it before I went to college, so, I made young children's education my major once I got there. And of course, the pay is ridiculous and I'm going to be broke next month for expending my entire this month's check on this trip over here for George and Stacey's wedding, but I really love those kids."

"You can come back with me to my hotel in Honolulu, on Oahu, let me put you up there, and you'll never have to worry about being broke, again," Rick told her.

Rachel deliberately ignored the suggestion the wealthy white man had put to her and thankfully so did Rochelle as her gaze settled back on her face in continued interest.

"Do you have any kids of your own?"

"No, I'm not married."

"That's incredible!" Rochelle muttered the two words half under her breath, as if finding the idea of a woman as beautiful as she still single impossible.

"I can change that," Rick said.

Again Rachel deliberately ignored the suggestive response the Native Alaskan had whispered in her ear. "So, what do you do, Rochelle?"

"I'm a dental hygienist. You've got some pretty teeth. You have a movie star smile," Rochelle observed.

Rachel blushed beneath the older woman's flattery as she continued to show her own teeth in a smile not unattractive itself, as Rachel had thought previously.

"Yea, I'm afraid it's all in the genes," she said. "My parents have good teeth."

The smile on Rochelle's lips broadened back into a grin. "I can't wait to meet these parents of yours that produced kids that look like you and George and that one up there."

Rachel showed those teeth Rochelle thought so pretty in a ridiculous laugh at the barbed reference she had made of Devon with the demeaning tilt of her head.

"So, how've you enjoyed your stay here in our famous city?" Rochelle asked, again changing the subject.

"I've loved it," Rachel replied, laugh sobering to a grin. "Well, I mean, I've only been here five days—or is it four—? What I mean is I arrived here on Monday, and I've seen a lot of the place. I've been to Chugach State Park—that was an experience. I've seen the Tony Knowles Coastal Trail—also an experience; and I've been to that fabulous mall, the Dimond Center. I've seen Cook Inlet, Turnagain Arm Trail, the Captain Cook Hotel, the Three Ships Sculpture, and even the Captain Cook Monument over at Resolution Park. And you know, last night, Rick told me the most interesting tale about this explorer for whom all these places here in Anchorage are named over dinner. For instance, did you know that Captain Cook lost his life in a most violent death off the—what is it, Rick—? The Kealakekua Bay off of a Hawaiian Island, one of which comprises the whole state of Hawaii, where Rick has been living for the last six years . . . ?"

"Yea, I knew that." Rochelle smiled at her incredulous look.

"Well, I didn't. I'd never heard of the man until I got here. I mean, I've lived in the Lower 48 all my life. So, I find the story of the man's life fascinating. His career's got to be the most incredible I've ever heard!"

"Yea, that Captain James Cook was all over the place in his day," Rochelle said.

"Yea, I see that," Rachel agreed.

The flow of their friendly conversation was interrupted by the sound of Devon's laughter filling the room as she responded to something one of George's friends said to her then. Rachel fell silent as she watched her sister flirt, as did Rick and Rochelle standing either side of her. . . . A.J. Over was using the trademark line derived from his nickname Over/Under by telling Devon the same thing he'd said to her, that he wanted to get over her and get her under him; Ray Marlboro was saying that he wanted to roll over her and bowl her over too; Martin wanted to roll over her as well as did Flip who had literally flipped over her; even the two married men Damon and Vic were playing up to her more beautiful older sister. They were schmoozing her smoothly and she was smoothly schmoozing them right back. Even Rick, who didn't like Devon, was absorbed as he too stared at her in amazement.

"You know, your sister's damned twisted, but she's a serious babe!" he told Rachel then, having to give the black woman her props despite his loathing of her.

Rachel didn't have much to say about that as she continued to watch her sister work, as did Rochelle in front of her.

In the padded seat he occupied in the row to the right of the aisle next to his wife Dora, Al Lumas watched the floor-show being put on by the sexy black woman and George's groomsmen and leaned over to speak to Rachel with his usual amusement.

"Your sister's gorgeous, but she's aggressive, isn't she?" asked the white man with a laugh.

"I guess so," Rachel agreed. After all, what else could she say?

Her attention was diverted from the Native Alaskan when Felix suddenly strode past her as if he didn't know her. Cut through the room as if he owned the hotel. The tall good looking black man quickly caught Rochelle's attention, her brown-eyed gaze lowering over his sky blue-sweater-clad back and white-dungarees-clad derriere in womanly appreciation.

"There goes that fox, again, Felix Latham, the best man!" she said in a voice that only Rachel and Rick could hear. "I hear he's an actor on a soap opera; playing a character that's presently sleeping with three women at the same time. Well, I can certainly see that, because he is a serious fox! That man doesn't belong anywhere but in a damned bed!"

Rachel recalled Devon's similar words of the evening before and tried unsuccessfully to stifle a laugh at the simultaneous recollection of being in serious fox best man Felix's damned bed a half hour ago!

Devon noticed Felix coming up the aisle toward George and dumped all George's friends to run to her ex-flame's side. Rachel's amusement deepened as she saw the smile Felix forced down at her older sister, aware as she was that the man couldn't stand her.

Her luminous brown gaze was diverted from the pair when a hand suddenly closed over her upper arm, claiming her attention. She turned out of the circle of Rick's arm and was delighted to see that they had been approached by her parents.

"Mama . . . ! And Daddy . . . !" Rachel exclaimed with an excited grin of her wine-colored medium lips. "It's about time you two got in here!"

"Hey, baby!" grinned Marshall amid taking her into his arms at the same time Sephora took her into hers. "How're you doing this afternoon?" asked her father in his brusk alto.

"I'm fine, Daddy! And how're you two doing today?" Rachel pushed out of their embraces to regard both him and her mother with a curious look. "George told me he and Stacey took all of you out for breakfast in the RV this morning, and then took you out driving around in this miserable rain!"

"Yea, he did," spoke up Sephora, smiling in agreement. "Where were you to not have been with us?"

Deliberately Rachel ignored her mother's most pointed question, aware that Rick stood aside her no doubt wanting an answer to that as well. Instead she diverted her gaze to Rochelle, who stood eyeing her mother and father with interest.

"By the way, Mom, Dad, this is Rochelle Loring, and Rochelle, this is my mother and father, Sephora and Marshall Hardison," Rachel made introductions smilingly. "Rochelle is a friend of Stacey, and also a bridesmaid in tomorrow's wedding."

"Oh, I see. How do you do, dear?" Sephora smilingly extended a hand to shake that of the stylishly dressed black woman larger than her by a size and who had been staring at her ever since she had entered the room.

"Yes, how you do, Rochelle?" Marshall's well-hewn full lips were also curved in a smile of greeting as he extended a hand to shake hers along with his wife.

"How do you do . . . ? And how do you do!" Rochelle's smile broadened into a grin as her gaze slid from Sephora and settled back on Marshall, a hand extended to shake his after having shaken that of his wife. Her eyes lingered on his attractive oval features and short salt-and-pepper hair in a look that told Rachel exactly what she was thinking. No wonder George, she and that other one back there were so good looking when they had such good looking parents—especially this daddy here! You want to be my daddy? My sugar daddy . . . ? Rachel thanked God Rochelle didn't have the indecency to voice her thoughts out loud as her brown eyes lingered over the sixty-one-year-old man more than twice her age long after Marshall had dropped her hand and lowered his back to his side.

Sephora barely noticed Rachel's relief as she returned to the subject she had brought up earlier and which her daughter had smoothly evaded.

"So, why weren't you with us this morning?"

"Hey, I've already seen this town. I had no intention of going out in the rain this morning, so, while you all were going out, I was turning over." Deliberately Rachel kept to the lie she had given Devon and hoped her mother would buy it—which she didn't.

"Uhm-hmm," Sephora said doubtfully, again curving a dusky-skinned hand over her arm, the tan clutch purse she had carried the night before clutched in the other. "Come here, and let me talk to you."

Rachel stared after her mother in surprise as she pulled her quickly away from Rochelle and Rick, not stopping until they were at the back of the large meeting/banquet room. Once there, Sephora turned to face her, her hand still curved around her arm as the same luminous brown gaze Rachel had inherited from her peered over her face closely.

"What's with you today?" Sephora asked quietly over the sound of other loud talking and laughing, a half smile curving the russet tinted medium lips Rachel had also inherited from her. "You're glowing, flowing, and blowing. You have the look of a woman who's been kissed by a man, and a lot. Who have you been kissing? Is it Felix?"

Rachel stared at her mother in shocked surprise that she had assumed that she had been kissing the attractive man. "What?" she demanded in stunned outrage.

"Girl, don't mess with me!" Sephora said with an unconvinced laugh that showed her own perfect teeth, dropping her hand from Rachel's arm. "We haven't seen you since last night. Not only were you not with us this morning when George and Stacey drove us around, but then, neither was Felix, nor were you in your suite when we dropped by to see you when we got back over an hour ago. By the same token, two do not disturb signs were on Felix's door when we passed by it on the way to our own suite. You been laid up with that man all morning?"

Every tooth in her head showed as Rachel stared at her mother in open-mouthed shock at her astuteness in having guessed her whereabouts. Rachel wondered if George knew that all the time he and Stacey had spent driving their families around in the rain in the RV in order to cover her absence, its location in Felix's suite had not only been suspected at her mother's departure but confirmed as the location of her presence at her return.

"What?" Rachel repeated in deepening shock at her obvious transparence.

"Look, girl," Sephora began, her free hand curving back over her arm, "you think your father and I are stupid? The man told Marshall when he asked him last night if he and Devon were going to get back together that he was sorry, that he had a woman waiting for him, and that he'd been trying to shake Devon for a whole hour. And then, he looked at you—and grinned! The look told your father and I right away that you are that woman, so, don't lie to me. Tell me the truth. What's going on with you and Felix?"

A forced sigh escaped Rachel's throat as she gazed at her father, who had returned to his wife's side just in time to hear the question Sephora had asked her. With deep resignation, she realized she was going to have to do just as her mother had told her. Tell her—and her dad who stood there expectantly awaiting an answer to the question as well—the truth.

"Okay, it's like this." Rachel spoke quietly so as not to be overheard in the distance. "You remember that guy Jock Whitman, and how he taught me both how to roller skate and ice skate when I was twelve?" she asked her parents. They nodded. "Felix learned both how to roller skate and ice skate as a kid, too. You remember how I took Spanish both in high school and in college?" They nodded. "Felix took Spanish in high school and college, too. You remember how I took archery in the tenth grade?" Again they nodded their well-shaped heads. "Felix took archery in the tenth grade, too. You remember how I used to dance downstairs all to myself when I was alone, and have kept it up ever since? Well, Felix can dance, too. You remember how I had to learn Shakespeare's *The Tempest* in my senior year in college three years ago?" Again Marshall and Sephora nodded. "Felix did the play on Broadway the same year—three years ago, as a matter of fact. As a second matter of fact, I still remember the dialogue to his Ferdinand, and he still remembers the dialogue to my Miranda! We both hate rap, we went to the same University. And here's the clicker—we both love Elvis. And you know that, because I stole half of those old records of yours that you used to have of Elvis', and watched half his old movies on the cable channel when I was growing up. I have not seen this man in ten years, and yet, I've done everything he's done! I have more in common with him than any man I've ever met in my life. He says the same about me. And he says I'm more fun than any woman he's ever been with, and I feel the same about him. We can talk about everything, and we can do everything. So, how do you go from having all that in common without becoming romantically involved in some way?"

"Yea, well, I guess that's true," Sephora said after a moment while Marshall stared in amazed wonder at all those incredible coincidences surrounding her life with that of a man that just as she said, she hadn't seen in ten years. "And it doesn't help that Felix looks like a made-up bed ready to be turned down and crawled into—or in this case, under."

"Yeah, and you know I've always hated him for that, because he looks better than me!" Marshall added with an affected laugh, repeating the remark he had voiced to Felix the evening before.

Rachel's luminous gaze was leveled on her parents in deepening shock, as not only was her good looking father's continued play of envy over Felix's good looks unwarranted, but her mother by her last response, sounded just like Rochelle and A.J. Over of only a while ago!

"Are you two serious?" she demanded.

Sephora gave little thought either to the impertinence of her husband's shameless exclamation or the boldness of her own statement as she brushed off the look of embarrassment that Rachel had turned on them with a look of unconcern.

"So, why are you two playing this game with her?" Sephora gestured Devon hanging all over Felix up at the front of the large room with the angling of her head, sending her straight relaxed barely grayed off-black hair gliding gently over her shoulders.

"Because, dear, mother," Rachel went on, keeping her voice low, "your daughter doesn't take rejection well. Felix tried to dump her after dinner was over last evening. Well, you saw how Devon was hanging all over him when you arrived later on last night. Besides, she's on the rebound, anyway. She's just gone through her second divorce from a terrible husband, and now she's over here with the one man in her life who did not treat her like a dog and who moved on with his life after she dumped him all those years ago. She wants him because he's managed to move up in the world and is now a famous Emmy Award-winning actor on a soap opera playing a character who is currently sleeping with his boss, her daughter and her stepdaughter all at the same time. Devon wants him for that same reason, the reason she mentioned at dinner last evening and for the very reason you mentioned a while ago—Felix has bed appeal. But according to Felix, that nerve ending stopped functioning ages ago. And we're playing this game because just as you were able to pick up on last night, obviously there's something going on between us, as Devon's already suspicious of me being the new woman he's having a fling with here at the hotel. And you know she's not about to give up her better looking sexier ex-flame to a kid sister who has no experience whatsoever in that area."

"Yea, well, that may be true," Sephora agreed thoughtfully, gazing regretfully at Devon climbing all over Felix up at the front of the room despite the inner relief she felt that as yet Rachel—her single daughter—had no experience in 'that area.' "Well, she needs to sit down, because she's making fool of herself. Marshall, you go up there, get your daughter off that man, and bring her back here and sit her down."

A smile slid onto the well-hewn full lips so like George's as Marshall derived amusement from his wife's order. "Quite the contrary, I'm going to sit down, and watch her performance," he replied to Sephora's shock and disappointment, at the same time seating himself in the blue padded seat in the aisle to the right of them. "Devon always could work a room."

Rachel had to agree with that as she continued to observe her older sister while her mother slid resignedly into the seat in the right aisle to the right of her father. She literally had George's friends worked into a lather—including the two married men just as before—as they watched her work her charms on Felix, flashing her perfect smile, batting her black-mascara-coated lashes at him, throwing her long fluffy off-black hair over her shoulders and firing off a battery of blatant compliments about his charm, good looks, sex appeal, bed appeal, whip appeal, etc., to Felix's usual amusement. Only George and Stacey knew by the quick glance they flashed her all the way at the back of the room that they like Rachel, knew Devon was wasting her time.

The wedding rehearsal got underway then as the preacher and wedding coordinator arrived. The preacher was a tall black Alaska Native—did George know any short men, Rachel wondered? He was in his early fifties and went by the name of Reverend Adomi Claymon while the coordinator, also a man, a white one and tall—of course, was named Trend Renolds. Gathering them all up front, Trend quickly set up the seating arrangement: who would sit where, who would seat who, who would accompany whom on the walk down the aisle. Damon and Vic—the two married friends—were assigned to be the two groomsmen who would seat everyone. Dora Lumas, mother of the bride, would be seated on the front row on the left side of the aisle along with Rick, brother of the bride. Marshall and Sephora would be seated on the front row to the right of the aisle, parents of the groom. George would stand before the preacher with best friend and best man Felix standing to the right of him.

And then would enter the succession of bridesmaids and groomsmen. Diane as Stacey's maid of honor, would enter first on the arm of Ray Marlboro, the black man who'd barely noticed Rachel for drooling all over Devon. . . . Too bad for Ray. Devon would follow on the arm of Flip Hart, who literally flipped further at the thought of having the sexy black woman at his side. Rochelle would follow them on the arm of Martin Rolf, his bad luck, as well. And Rachel was shocked to see that the groomsman who would bring up the rear with her would be A.J. Over, who still wanted to get 'over' her, having seen, like Rick, that Devon was out of his league. Well, Rachel thought, he would just have to get over it.

After all the bridesmaids filed to the right of the Reverend Claymon and all the groomsmen to his left and to the right of the best man, Stacey would then be escorted up the aisle by Al Lumas, who would stop her at George's left side and then take a seat on the front row of the left side of the aisle, also to the left of Stacey. Trend Renolds then took a seat while Reverend Claymon went into a long spiel to George and Stacey that would include vows that they had already personally prepared to say to each other. Then finally after the Reverend's preaching, after which he would pronounce them as husband and wife, they would kiss, and it would be all over.

After the rehearsal was over, Devon moved from her side on the bridesmaids row and raced right back to Felix's side across the aisle while Rochelle, as if never having seen such a fine black man in her life, looked on in amazement. By the same token Rachel was horrified to see, Rick returned to her side. Despite the fact that Rachel was giving him no encouragement, the wealthy white man was all over her, telling her the same as did A.J. Over that he wanted to get her under him. Rachel laughed. Well, he'd just best get over it.

Rachel's luminous long-mascara-lashed brown eyes flashed onto the face of Martin Rolf when he suddenly suggested to his buddies that they throw George a bachelor party that night to celebrate his last night as a single man.

Seated two rows up the right aisle of Martin, Felix's equally long-lashed brown eyes flashed in delight of that idea. "Yea, I hear there used to be some serious places of ill-repute over in the Spenard District that we can take him to!" he said with a laugh.

"Chill out, man, those places aren't over there, anymore," Martin said, unaware as was Rachel that Felix had been joking, knowing from what Thacker had told the two of them just the day before that fact also.

"But whatever place we take him to, it's going to be hot!" A.J. chimed in from the right fourth row of blue padded seats. "There will be women, there will be strippers, there will be a woman coming out of a cake, and there will be booze everywhere!"

"Yeah, and we're going to get him drunk, so that by the time the wedding takes place tomorrow, he won't be able to stand up, he'll have to be propped up!" Felix went on in his attractive tenor, grinning excitedly at George seated in the row behind him next to Stacey.

Both Rachel and Felix's gazes were averted to Stacey as she turned a warning laugh on her husband-to-be quietly smiling at the suggestions being put to him by his friends on how to spend his last night as a single man.

"Don't you let these guys take you out and get you drunk," the stout brunette said in her soft-spoken way.

"Don't worry, darling, you know I don't drink," George reassured her with a laugh.

Seated next to Rachel in the fourth row to the left of the aisle, Rick was also all for throwing his future brother-in-law a bachelor party.

"Yeah, and I'll be your official photographer at the party," the rich white Alaska-born Hawaiian told George with a grin. "I'm pretty good with a camera. I'll have every memory recorded of you walking around with a lampshade on your head while one stripper binds you in chains and another one forces you to drink out of her shoe!"

"Now, that, I definitely want to see!" Flip Hart laughed from his fourth row seat in front of Rick and Rachel. "Come on, Rick, you, too, A.J. Let's go set this baby up!" Moving quickly to his feet, the white man waited for Rick and A.J. to move to their feet as well before leading them excitedly from the room.

Expelling a breath on a sigh of relief at no longer having to bear the drooling Rick's presence, Rachel thought she'd take advantage of her own picture-taking skills since she'd brought her camera with her down from the penthouse. Moving to her own feet, she strode down the aisle to pick it up from the eighth row seat where she had placed it beside her black bag upon arriving there some time earlier, pulled it from its plastic bag and raised the silver-toned Canon Sure Shot 35mm camera to her eye. She took pictures of everybody—Damon and Vic, George's two married friends, Martin, Diane, George and Stacey, her parents Marshall and Sephora displaying their mature smiles, Al and Dora Lumas displaying theirs, Rochelle mugging at her, Felix with his gorgeous sexy self—and even Devon sitting next to him drooling all over him, Trend Renolds, the wedding coordinator still standing talking to George and Stacey, and even Ray Marlboro, the 'brother' who had brushed her off without even bothering to look at her during George's process of introducing them earlier. Rachel even took a couple of pictures of two florists still busy draping the blue, brown and gray outfitted meeting/banquet room with a myriad of flowers and ribbons in preparation for tomorrow's wedding. Then finally having dispensed a roll of film and feeling a need to relieve herself, Rachel placed the camera back into the blue padded seat next to her black bag and accessories bag and left the large room to go to the ladies room down the corridor.

She had gotten halfway down the corridor when she was stopped by a maid wiping at a spot against the blue, rust, brown and autumn gold stripe-papered wall with a bottle of spray and a blue cloth. Rachel recalled the stout black woman as one of the housekeeping staff that George had introduced her to on Monday, although she had long since forgotten her name.

"You're Miss Rachel Hardison, aren't you?" asked the short-haired aging woman with a smile. "I'm Shereen Akison. Your brother, Mr. George Hardison, introduced you to me after your arrival here on Monday."

"Oh, yes, that's right. How are you, Miss Akison?" Rachel was relieved that the woman had supplied her name to her failing memory, as she wore no name tag that would otherwise have reminded her as to what it was.

"Shereen, please," suggested the brown-skinned woman, who wore a blue uniform, the main color of the hotel, with a smile. "Mr. Hardison and Miss Lumas are getting married, tomorrow. You must be very excited about that."

Rachel showed her own teeth in a smile as she paused to talk to the friendly woman. "Yes, we're looking forward to it," she said. "Stacey's very nice. Her parents and brother are here. And my parents delighted George by arriving here from

Georgia last night, and even my sister Devon surprised him yesterday by showing up unexpectedly from same place when George had thought she would not be able to make it here to be in his wedding."

"Mr. Hardison's got to be delighted about that," agreed the aging woman, busy wiping away a shadow on the richly elegant papered wall.

"Yes," Rachel agreed.

She stared at the maid in surprise when her brown gaze slid past her suddenly. Rachel didn't have a chance to turn and see what Shereen was looking at as a hand suddenly curved over hers in a furtive action. Snarling at the thought that Rick had slipped up behind her, Rachel lowered her gaze to the hand that had closed over hers only to find that it was not white but a delicious golden brown. The realization that the hand belonged to Felix left a heady pleasure gliding up her arm while a giddy smile slid onto her wine-painted lips. In fact, so intense was that pleasure that even Felix felt it as he leaned over her shoulder to whisper in her ear.

"Calm down, don't float away on me," he said in his seductive tenor.

Rachel wondered if the maid had recognized him as soap opera actor Felix Latham as she quickly deduced that something was going on between them. Yet whether Shereen did or not, she walked discreetly away, leaving Rachel to turn just in time to meet Felix's lips as they descended on hers. It was a secret kiss that she moved into immediately, her arms finding his neck while at the same time he pinned her to the wall with his gorgeous body, his arms encircling her waist, both actions serving only in making her hotter. The kiss steamed—igniting her body with a fire that left her holding him heatedly, her lips devouring him feverishly while his devoured her with equal fervor. And it was a heat that left her sweltering, as for a long scorching moment she remained swept up in the searing flames of his possession. Yet just as Rachel felt herself beginning to incinerate seconds later, Felix dropped his arms from her body and pulled out of hers, a hand finding her chin in one last stoking action before it dropped to his side along with his other one.

"That ought to hold me for a while," he said in his attractive tenor, smiling down at her. "Anyway, I'll see you, later, senorita."

And walking down the hall away from her, Felix left Rachel to turn dizzily down the hall after him on her way to the ladies' room.

Once there, Rachel somehow managed to regain her equilibrium and control over her accelerated heart rate amidst relieving herself in one of a number of facilities. Then zipping her black stretch denim jeans back in place around her curving hips, she moved across the blue and white tiled floor to the blue and green marbled quadruple vanity to wash her hands. Her reflection in the well-lit mirror that stretched the length of the wall left Rachel frowning dismally as it reminded her of what had just happened between her and Felix down the hall. The sexy man's devouring kiss had eaten all the lipstick that she had so carefully reapplied to her mouth off of it and no doubt onto his, tell-tale signs of its occurrence showing in the smears outside her lip line and way past its outer corners. Quickly Rachel used the pearly pink soap dispensed from a silver metal container and several tissues from one of three boxes to remove all traces from her medium lips, all the while hoping that when she returned to the meeting/banquet room her mother wouldn't guess from the sudden absence of the wine color that Felix had been kissing on her again.

If Sephora noticed the sudden absence of color from her medium lips when Rachel returned to the meeting/banquet room moments later, she couldn't say anything about it, for she was too busy talking with George and Stacey about the wedding. Rachel was grateful for that. Returning to the side of new best friend Rochelle, who grabbed her as soon as she had stepped back through the door, Rachel let the bigger woman engage her in a talk about a past boyfriend. Some puny guy who wanted a little bit of her lot, while she told him that with what little bit he had, he couldn't handle her. Well, Rachel could certainly relate to that. After all, Thacker Muldoon had told her just the day before that he didn't think he could handle all of her, that she'd probably give him a heart attack. As only she knew she would!

There was no one around to intrude on their private girlish conversation. Rick had not returned to the room, neither had Flip Hart nor A.J. Over, the three of them undoubtedly still out making arrangements for George's bachelor party for that evening. Rachel was grateful for that also. Felix had not returned to the room, either. And even though Rachel couldn't help noticing Devon's absence from the room as well, she didn't give much thought to her older sister. For all Rachel knew, she could be out somewhere flirting with Ray Marlboro, another man absent from those remaining of George's friends along with Diane, Trend Renolds, Al and Dora Lumas and her, Devon and George's parents, Sephora and Marshall.

Her gaze was diverted away from her parents and back onto Rochelle's amber-skinned made-up face as she began a smiling commentary about some current boyfriend named Vern. Rachel listened with similar amusement despite the embarrassment she felt as it grew lengthy and turned rather intimate. Yet it wasn't as though she couldn't understand where the woman was coming from as she became quite explicit in her bedroom goings-on with this man she had met at her dental office when he had come in for a teeth-cleaning a month before. Certainly not after the fire Felix had lit under her that past week, leaving her with little thoughts other than getting him in the same place—as she had literally been all morning—in a manner of speaking.

Rachel decided to counter the sudden heat suffusing her face at the thought of climbing into Felix's bed in all manner of speaking by getting Rochelle off the subject as well and showing her the pictures she had taken during her visit at Chugach State Park on Wednesday. She started out with photos of the Dall sheep she had taken at Windy Corner and then followed those of the waters of Turnagain Arm and the rising Kenai Mountains across Turnagain Arm, followed by the woods of Turnagain Arm Trail. The alpine valley of Falls Creek, Bird Ridge Mountain, Flattop Mountain, Wolverine Peak.... The Eklutna Lake Campground and

Trailhead, the dwarf dogwood, moose and porcupine she took along Twin Peaks Trail, the ptarmigan roosting in the vegetation and the Dall sheep in the Goat Mountain bowl. The Chugach Mountains and Eklutna Lake Valley and the turquoise waters of Eklutna Lake cutting through the Chugach Mountain Range that she had taken on the barren slope in the upper valley just below East Twin Pass.... The golden eagle in flight that she had taken there as well and those taken of the windsurfer on the vast blue waters of Knik Arm.... Those taken along the Pass of East and West Twin Peaks, those of Matanuska Valley, more Dall sheep, the dueling moose there, as well, the distant Pepper Peak. And even the wilderness, for God's sake! Rochelle was impressed. She stared at one of several pictures taken of the serene waters of Eklutna Lake cutting between the Chugach Mountain Range in Eklutna Lake Valley and grinned in amazement.

"Girl, this is beautiful!" Rochelle exclaimed over the scenic picture she held in her hand. "You really captured Eklutna Lake. Who'd you get to take you to Chugach State Park?!"

"George got a tour guide for me." Which was not a lie; Rachel just didn't tell her that it was Felix. For that reason, she kept the pictures that she had taken of him during their lunch on the uphill slope below East Twin Pass hidden from Rochelle's eyes. And she was glad she did when Rick suddenly appeared at the side of the blue padded seat she was sitting on, the footsteps of whom would have alerted her to his return to the room had they not been muffled by the plush brown carpeting.

"Hey, how'd it go?" Rachel began smilingly to the thirty-year-old man standing in front of her. "Did you, Flip and A.J. make arrangements for George's bachelor party?"

"We sure did!" The somewhat kissable medium lips in the puffy white oval face of the blonde curved in a grin. "We've got it set up at a very private place! George is not going to know what hit him!"

Rachel didn't think she liked the sound of that as she returned the vivid blue-eyed gaze twinkling down on her. "Don't you guys do anything that's going to hurt my brother," she warned in a concerned tone similar to Stacey's of moments earlier.

"Don't worry about it, girl, Rachel, baby, it's going to be great!" Rick grinned.

He suddenly became aware of the color 35mm prints that Rochelle held in her hands. Rachel wondered if it weren't a deliberate ploy to get her off the subject as she sensed a hidden meaning behind his sudden quick lowering of his eyes from hers.

"Girl, where'd you get such beautiful pictures...!" Rick exclaimed then, leaning down and taking several Rochelle still held in her hands into his.

Though Rachel thought his excitement over the glossy 3 x 5 inch photos taken by her amateurish hand a bit much, she hid it beneath a pleased smile.

"I took them at Chugach State Park the other day."

"They're beautiful!" Rick repeated the excited response as he continued to admire the shiny scenic pictures of Eklutna Lake Valley and the Chugach Mountain Range that he had taken into his hands. "Are you a photographer on the side?"

Again Rachel smiled at the white man's flattery of her photographic prowess. "Actually, these are just a little something I've taken to reflect on after my visit here to Alaska. I've taken them everywhere I've gone this week. As a matter of fact, I have some I need to pick up at the photo shop today. That is, if I can find a way to get there." She pulled her luscious medium lips up into a frown, just then realizing Felix couldn't take her because of the game they were playing with Devon.

"What photo shop do you need to go to?"

". . . Stewart's, on West Fourth Avenue."

"I'll take you there!"

Rachel stared in surprise at the broad toothy grin the Alaska-born Hawaiian had turned on her. "You will?"

". . . Yeah! I know how you must want to get your pictures. I dabble in photography, too. As a matter of fact, I just offered to be the official photographer at your brother's bachelor party tonight, remember—?"

"Yea, I guess you did, didn't you?" Rachel agreed, staring at him studiously and only then recalling that moment.

"Anyway, go get your coat, and let's go!"

Her lips curved in a considering smile on the white face beaming down at her. "Well, you know, actually, I would appreciate that, because I need to go out. I need to go shopping. It suddenly occurred to me that of all the places I've been this week, I haven't been anywhere to buy a wedding present for Stacey and George." She had not bought anything for them yet because everywhere she and Felix had been that week, everything they had seen had had an Alaskan and Russian theme, and why would she buy a gift for a Native Alaskan and an Alaskan resident that was both Russian-themed and Alaskan?

Unaware that she was thinking that, the brown-eyed gaze Native Alaskan Rochelle turned on her reflected her considering look. "You know," she began then, full red-painted lips curved into a grin, "while I think about it, I don't have a wedding present for George and Stacey, either. I could use a drive out to do a little shopping, myself! And I don't exactly relish the idea of going alone!"

"Well, then, come on, ladies, go grab your coats, and let's hit the road!" Rick grinned.

The more Rachel thought about it, the more she warmed to the idea despite the fact that she did not want to lead the equally Alaskan Native on.

"Okay! Just let me go and let Mom and Dad know where I'm going. And maybe while I'm at it, I'll leave them these pictures to look at that you think are so beautiful!"

Rising to her black pump-clad feet, Rachel moved quickly out of the row of seats. The grin on her lips matched that of Rochelle and Rick as she led them in the direction of her mother still talking with George and Stacey toward the front of the room.

Chapter Fifteen

He had her at Stewart's Photo in twenty minutes. Rochelle accompanied them. Per the request of the larger amber-skinned woman to tag along with them, Rick had happily seen her into the back seat of a white Acura Legend rental car. Rachel had naturally sat in the front passenger seat. And even though it had not been like being in the tan Pontiac Grand Prix with Felix, Rachel had forced herself to get used to it. After all, what else could she do?

There really had been nothing for her to do before leaving the hotel but inform her mother and father of her intention of going to pick up some pictures from the photo shop and afterwards do a little shopping. She had left the pictures that she had shown Rochelle with them for their viewing pleasure as she'd done so. Again and with deliberation Rachel had left out the pictures she had taken of Felix, lowering the three attractive prints stealthily into her purse. After all, she couldn't chance Devon coming upon the glossy prints, knowing her sister would flip for sure at the suspicion implied behind them that something was indeed going on with her and her sexy ex-flame.

After that, all Rachel had had to do was run up to her eleventh-floor suite and pull out her heavy coat, the burnished tan leather providing all-weather protection through sun, rain or snow. Naturally Rochelle had accompanied her. Having slid into the smart white leather coat and white leather hat of her own that she had left with the coat-check attendant on arriving at the meeting/banquet room for the wedding rehearsal earlier, she had settled on one of the loveseats to await her return from her bedroom while Rick had been pulling a black leather coat from his own sixth-floor suite. Yet just as when Diane had said upon her arrival for the wedding rehearsal that the rain had started to slacken, the three of them had found that to be exactly the case upon leaving the hotel minutes later—in fact, the heavy downpour had stopped completely. Well, they didn't call them all-weather coats for nothing. After all, the rain had left a slight chill in the air, making Rachel, Rochelle and Rick all grateful for the warmth of such all-weather coats, as they were fully-lined and just as appropriate for cold sunny weather or rain.

During the short drive from the hotel, Rachel had asked Rick what kind of camera he used in his practice of photography on the side, since she had told him that the pictures she had taken and that he had so admired were shot with a Canon Sure Shot 35mm. Rick had confided that while he had a couple of Minolta Digital 35mms that he favored, he had absently left them at his Honolulu, Hawaii hotel. Hence, he was grateful that she had expressed a need to go pick up her pictures and go shopping, because he had to get out to go visit an old friend and see if he could borrow a camera with which to take pictures at George's bachelor party that evening, anyway. To hear Rick tell it, this friend worked as a photographer for a portrait studio, had a hundred cameras, not to mention boxes of film to go with them—and in fact, because of that, since knowing this friend, he hadn't had to buy film for his own picture-taking in years. Rachel thought some people had all the luck as Rick dropped her off at Stewart's with the order to wait for him at the Downtown Deli and Café down the street while he pulled briefly off to go seek out that old friend in his North Anchorage neighborhood.

The smile lingered on Rachel's lips as she entered Stewart's Photo a second later, an expression of relief at being granted a respite from the white man who had been fawning all over her for most of the afternoon. Rochelle accompanied her into the photo shop. Having been impressed with the pictures Rachel had shown her back at the Amber Heights Hotel, she stood waiting in eager anticipation as Rachel stepped up to the service counter to drop off for developing the roll of film she had taken that day, buy new film for the next day's picture-taking, as well as pick up the film she had dropped off for developing the day before. In fact, the larger woman's grin brought a blush of embarrassment to Rachel's dusky cheeks as she moved away from the cashier with the three packets of prints in her hands seconds later.

"What'd you take?" Rochelle asked excitedly.

Seeing that she would not be able to curb the Native Alaskan's curiosity, Rachel lowered a quick stealthy glance into the first packet of prints she held in her hands. Relieved that they were not those that she and Felix had taken at Delaney Park, Rachel handed them to her. The woman larger than her by three dress sizes grinned admiringly at the number of prints she pulled out of the packet, which Rachel had taken during her and Felix's visit to the Alaska Botanical Gardens the day before. The glossy color pictures of the hundred-plus-acre spruce and birch woodland were quite attractive, the two perennial gardens where hundreds of hardly species flourished along with more than a hundred native plants in a riot of colors, the formal herb garden, the alpine rock garden, the vivid purples and greens lined by white stones alongside the graveled Wildflower Walk. Those taken during her and Felix's half-hour walk down the one-mile Lowensfeld Family Nature Trail off the East Fork of the Botanical Gardens down to the North Fork toward Campbell Creek. Even Rachel was impressed with her amateur photography as she gazed with equal admiration at a couple of pictures she had snapped of the Chinook salmon making their summer run beneath the blue waters of Campbell Creek.

She was just about to point out a picture that she had taken along the dog-mushing trail when in her effort to juggle her black purse on her left shoulder, the small bag of new film in her right hand and the two unopened packets of prints in both, one of them slipped from her hands. It fell to the floor, where it slipped open, its contents half spilling from it. Anticipating another display of attractive prints, Rochelle bent down to pick it up while Rachel froze in the floor at the realization that she had dropped the packet of prints taken at Delaney Park that she had intended to keep hidden from her. The two boys playing sling-shot, the man flying a kite, two others playing horseshoes, the basketball court, the tennis court, the steam engine and that of a man sitting on a bench eating a hot dog near the small gym quickly gave way to the endless number that Felix had had the fifteen-year-old boy carrying a basketball snap of them. The repeated and most incriminating shots of Rachel standing there sharing a smiling and intimate embrace with the sexy black man broadened the grin on Rochelle's red-painted lips as she immediately perceived that there was something going on between them.

"Oh, so, it's like that, huh? You got a hot thing going on with Mr. Fox!" Rochelle exclaimed in an excited voice as she continued to eye the chummy photos of her and Felix. "So, why are you letting your sister hang all over your man?"

Rachel's frozen stance melted out of existence as she indulged a laugh beneath the intent gaze Rochelle had turned on her, which indicated to her exactly how aware she was of having watched Devon do just that to Felix back at the hotel.

"She doesn't have a chance with him," she said. "That boat has sailed, and sunk!"

"I see. So, what are you trying to say—that Miss Artificial and Mr. Fox once had a relationship since he is not only George's best man but his best friend and has been for years according to Stacey, and as a result of that, has to have known Miss Artificial along with you and your parents when both he and George lived in Georgia?" continued the twinkling gaze.

"That's exactly what I'm saying." After all, Rachel could hardly be surprised Rochelle had guessed all that; as it didn't take much to deduce from what Stacey had said that George and Felix's close friendship would have resulted in Felix knowing George's family from its Georgia origin years ago also.

"But George has lived over here for the last five years, and according to Stacey, Mr. Fox has lived in New York for the last ten. When did he and Miss Artificial have a relationship?" Rochelle asked.

". . . That very same year."

"Miss Artificial and Mr. Fox had a relationship ten years ago?"

". . . Uhm-hmm. The very year we all first met."

"What?" Rochelle stared.

Aware that she couldn't go into the details in the too open atmosphere of the photo shop, Rachel slid the packet of prints she held in her hands into the black bag strapped to her left shoulder. Rochelle, knowing the same thing, slid the prints she still held in her hands back into their packet just as Rachel reached for both of them, slipping them into her black bag as well. Then, curving a dusky-skinned hand over the white sleeve of the leather coat covering Rochelle's amber-skinned wrist, Rachel quickly pulled her from the shop. It was still cool once they'd arrived back on Fourth Avenue—the temperature hovering somewhere around forty-eight degrees—but like Rochelle, Rachel at least had the protection of her fully-lined all-weather tan leather coat to keep her warm along with the added realization that she would be able to speak to her privately.

"The very year we all first met," Rachel repeated quietly as they stood just under the photo shop sign, cars whizzing past them down the street. "George asked Felix to be his best man in their wedding because just like Stacey told you, they have been best friends for years," she went on informatively. "They met during their freshman year at Georgia State University in Atlanta thirteen years ago, although we did not meet Felix until their senior year—ten years ago, when George brought him to the house one weekend to meet his family, introduce us to the guy he had been ranting about for three years. I was a fourteen-year-old kid then, nowhere near puberty—if you know what I mean. Devon was an exquisite nineteen-year-old sophomore attending West Georgia College in Carrollton, a small town near the Alabama border. Devon had been home from West Georgia the very weekend that George, then twenty one, brought Felix to the house to meet us. Also twenty one, Felix entered the house behind George, the cutest thing you could ever hope to set eyes on walking on two legs, took one look at Devon, and fell madly in love with her. The man was a serious doll. Even as a fourteen-year-old girl I noticed that, and as a result of that, I practically followed him and Devon around whenever he came to see her. Devon dated him for four months, three days and seventeen hours—to be exact, before she dumped him for another man, whom she then dumped for another man, eventually marrying two others. Felix never got over her."

"You're kidding!" Rochelle was incredulous as they stumbled into the door of the Downtown Deli and Café they approached then, where Rick had instructed them to await his return. "But if he never got over her, how'd he end up cuddled up so lovey-dovey with you at Delaney Park yesterday?"

"Actually, there's an interesting story behind that." Quickly seeing her away from the entrance, Rachel led her to a booth near the windows and saw her into a seat to one side of it and herself in the seat across the table from her, both of them placing their purses on the table in front of them, Rochelle the white leather hat from her head there, Rachel her small bag of new film there also. She gazed briefly around the busy restaurant as she did so, recalling that Felix had told her that just like the Coastal Trail named after him, the Deli was owned by former governor, Tony Knowles. Though she found it ironic that she should now be there with Rochelle in await of Rick's return for her rather than being there with Felix, Rachel hid it behind an interested look as a waitress came over and asked for their orders. Telling her to bring her a Coca Cola as did Rochelle, Rachel waited for the blond woman to move away from the table before settling her luminous brown gaze purposely back on Rochelle.

"After Felix and Devon broke up all those years ago, I forgot all about him," Rachel said finally, while Rochelle sat all ears. "The following year, I proceeded to grow into this face and this body, and went on with my life, just like he did. I forgot all about the man. I never heard his name again. I thought I'd never see him again. I had no idea what he was doing these days. Anyway, like I said, I arrived on Monday, the first of the family to get here for George's wedding. I had to give him the news that Devon sadly would not be able to be here, because she was in the midst of finalizing her divorce. It almost broke George's heart that his older sister would not be able to be here for his wedding. Yet we somehow managed to change the subject, at which point, I remember expressing my desire to see as much as I could of this wilderness, this state he called Alaska, North America's last frontier. George, who was too busy running the hotel and getting his and Stacey's wedding together to show me around and wasn't exactly into the idea of me sightseeing alone, said he would supply me with a tour guide to take me where I wanted to go, said that out of the six men who were his groomsmen in the wedding that he would be able to find one who was just right for me. And that's when George asked me to guess who was standing in as his best man. I asked him who, at which point, he proceeded to tell me Felix. Now, like I said, I had forgotten him, hadn't heard his name in ten years, and didn't even know that George had kept in touch with him since they went their separate ways after graduating from Georgia State University all those years ago. Yet I somehow managed to play off my shock and ask how he was doing, when George told me he was fine and an actor on a soap opera taped in New York City. Well, that surprised me, because I never knew the man wanted to act. And I'd certainly never heard of the soap opera *As The Star Shines* that he was working on either, even though George said it had been on the air for over twenty years and that Felix had been on it for the last six. I remember saying, 'Wow!' Felix Latham, a soap opera actor! And didn't he date our sister Devon for a while?' George said, 'Uhm-hmm.' And then, he brought up the part about them dating for the four months, three days, and seventeen hours—you know, that I told you about, adding after all these years that Felix was still in love with her. So, I told George to be glad she wouldn't be here to play on his emotions. That's when George said the reason he had mentioned Felix was because he would make a fitting tour guide for me, what with having been here for more than a week and having seen quite a bit of Anchorage in that time. Anyway, George gave me Felix's suite number and suggested I go visit him. Said he was sure Felix was going to get a kick out of seeing how I'd turned out after all these years."

"As I know he did," Rochelle agreed, engaging teeth showing in a laugh, "judging by those lovey-dovey pictures I just saw of the two of you at you know where."

"Oh, yea, Felix noticed, alright." Rachel laughed as she raised the tall frosty Coke glass the waitress had set in front of her to her lips to take a quick sip of its cool contents, Rochelle laughingly doing the same to the icy Coke the blond had set in front of her. "Though it was several hours when he finally arrived back at the hotel with two women on his arms, he quickly forgot all about them as he stood there looking at me, smile of recognition sliding onto his face." Rachel's own smile was reminiscent as she lowered her Coke glass to the white napkin the friendly waitress had placed on the table, the same of which Rochelle was doing to hers. "Felix said, 'Rachel—? Oh, my God, it is you! Little Rachel Hardison! George's kid sister! Only you're not so little anymore, are you!' You know, grin, grin, hug, hug . . . !" Again, Rachel laughed at the memory. "And then had come the dreaded, 'So, what about the rest of your family? What about Devon? Is she coming to the wedding?' Well, I sadly had to tell him no, that she was in the midst of getting a divorce and wouldn't be free to travel until next week when it would be too late. Rochelle, Felix reacted to the bad news the same way George did when I told him the divorce was going to keep Devon from being in the wedding: his face fell. Can you believe it? It was just as George had said—after ten years, Felix was still in love with Devon. Anyway, that's when George mentioned his idea to Felix about being my tour guide over the next few days. And thankfully, Felix had not been averse to that, saying that he would be happy to be my tour guide, we had a lot of reminiscing to do, a lot to talk about. And I'd agreed with him amid standing there smilingly checking him out while thinking to myself how good looking he was. The man as gorgeous as ever, as sexy as he ever was. And I say thankfully he had not been averse to that, because asking Felix to be my tour guide these last four days is the best thing George could ever have done for that man."

"I guess so!" Rochelle grinned over the lip of the Coke she had raised back to her lips, already having guessed that Felix was the tour guide who took her to Chugach State Park that she didn't mention when she asked her earlier who she got to take her there on Wednesday. "As I keep mentioning, we've already seen evidence of that!"

"Yea, it's been an interesting four days," Rachel agreed with a laugh over the lip of the Coke glass she had raised back to her own lips. "Not only did Felix agree to be my tour guide, but he took me to buy a parka, film, and my camera, a ride during which we got reacquainted. He asked me why a woman as beautiful as I was still single, and I told him I'd been too busy working to meet someone, not to mention that most men my age were only interested in quick one-night-stands. And I told him that I did not want to find myself getting divorced for the second time at twenty nine as Devon was presently. Well, I shouldn't have said that, because that's when Felix asked me to tell him about her—tell him how she came to find herself twice divorced at twenty nine."

"Yes, how did Miss Artificial find herself divorced from these two men you say she married, and at the young age of twenty nine, anyway?" Rochelle prodded curiously of the sister previously revealed to her as being five years older than her.

"That's easy enough to answer. Her first marriage at twenty one resulted from a one-night-stand. They tried to turn it into a relationship, got married two months later; the marriage lasted six. Ended when Devon came home one evening and found Dustin in their bed with a woman he had met through another one-night-stand. And who knows how many there'd been before that," Rachel suggested with dry inflection. "Anyway, her second marriage of six years, which climaxed in the divorce on Wednesday, ended when she came home three months ago and found Richard in their bed with two women. That's what I'd had to tell Felix, which had broken his heart further, as he'd said, 'The poor dear. She would have been so much better off if she'd stayed with me.'"

"Oh, God, Mr. Fox had it really bad for Miss Artificial!" Rochelle observed with a regrettable smile. "So, how did you get him off this woman?"

"Well, I changed the subject, quickly," Rachel went on over the Coca Cola she was slowly downing. "I asked him why a thirty-one-year-old man as good looking as he was still single, he said he guessed it was a matter of never having been in the right place at the right time to meet someone, plus, he hadn't yet had to work with anyone who floated his boat, so to speak. He asked me about my job and I told him, and I asked him about his job and he told me about it. And then, I asked him how Elvis was doing these days. Felix is an Elvis Presley freak," Rachel told Rochelle with a laugh, "a fan of the man from way back. Devon never liked him. Anyway, it blew Felix's mind that I remembered his love for the King from all those years back, and we discussed Elvis for the rest of the way to the store. It simply blew Felix's mind that I, too, was a fan of the man, having watched half his old movies on the cable channel while I was growing up, not to mention that I stole several of his old records from my parents' music collection years ago. Well, we got to the store, I bought the parka, film, and camera, and we were on the way out when Felix suddenly got mobbed as four women and fans of his soap, threw soap opera magazines and pens in his face for his autograph. They started coming all onto him. Yet before he could get away, three men came up to me and started coming onto me the same way! Anyway, Felix got us out of there and we laughed about their come-ons all the way back to the hotel, where the same situation was awaiting us there. We joined George and Stacey for dinner in the Continental Room, as did Stacey and your friend Diane from the reservation desk, and George's friends, Martin Rolf and Flip Hart, also in the wedding party. Martin came onto me all through the dinner, as had Flip, while to the right of me, Felix was given the treatment by three off-duty hotel employees that he had skirted around on his arms during the last week. Well, he put up with it for about twenty minutes before grabbing me by the arm and getting us out of there, again. We laughed about it all the way up to my suite. And that wouldn't be the first time; as a matter of fact, in the next few days, Felix would find himself in situations where I would have to rescue him from women coming onto him, and he would have to rescue me from men coming onto me."

"I can certainly believe that," Rochelle grinned over her Coke, "the way you two look and are built."

"Tell me about it!" Rachel laughed agreement over the Coke glass she had raised back to her own lips. "Anyway, those were two things that started making Felix lose interest in Devon. And they just kept on coming."

Again the green-shadowed brown eyes flashed curiosity from the fleshy face possessing the same round shape as hers. "How so . . . ?"

"Well, from the moment Felix started showing me around Anchorage on Tuesday, my first day of sightseeing, there's been this connection between us," Rachel confided quietly amid lowering her Coke back to the white napkin on the table. "Felix is the adventurous type, always has been, Devon never was. And there I was—George's kid sister, a woman he hadn't seen in ten years, who in Felix's own words was 'such a bratty kid at fourteen,' but was now a full-grown twenty-four-year-old woman who shared his love for adventure. In Felix's own words when I asked him barring the wedding rehearsal you guys had last Saturday if he'd been at the hotel in any of the time since arriving here—what—Sunday before last, he said, 'Hey, I'm just like you. I want to see as much of this place as you do.' And he proved that over the next couple of days. He took me all over the place. Unfortunately, in our quest for adventure, we experienced a little terror. But it, too, turned out to be conducive to our hot thing."

Rochelle's brown eyes narrowed on her in surprise of her last couple remarks, finding them incongruent, not making sense. "How is that?" she asked with continued curiosity.

"Remember how I told you at the wedding rehearsal that I'd seen the Tony Knowles Coastal Trail, named for the same former governor who owns this restaurant, and now you know with whom and who told me that, Felix, of course, and that it was an experience?" A smile indicating her impression of Felix's apparent acquirement of knowledge of her home city of Anchorage and in such a short time accompanied Rochelle's nod at Rachel's question. "We met a grizzly," Rachel answered over the lip of the Coke glass she had raised back to her own smiling lips. "I had just stepped off the Trail to take a picture of some museum, I think it was. Felix followed me into the woods. I had just turned to take a picture of him when the grizzly came out of nowhere. Felix ordered me in the calmest tone he could muster to get down on the ground and play dead, which I did, at which point, he then raced forward and threw his body on top of mine to protect me from the deadly animal. We lay holding our breaths for a tense ten seconds as the deadly grizzly stopped at Felix's side and sniffed his head before seeing him as non-threatening and finally moving off.

"You remember how I told you I'd been to Chugach State Park, also with Felix, and that it was an experience?" Rachel asked, to which again Rochelle nodded, understanding replacing the shock that had crept into her brown eyes. "We met another grizzly. Felix and I had not long moved down East Twin Pass in the direction of Pepper Peak. All of a sudden, a huge swarm of mosquitoes forced us off the muddied section of the Pass and into the woods, where tracks and scat in the mud warned Felix that there was a bear or bears there and that we had to get out of that area. But in our frantic attempt to do just that, I tripped on a hidden tree root, and Felix, making an attempt to catch me, teetered off balance and fell to the ground, while I, equally off balance, fell on top of him. That's when the second grizzly, whose tracks Felix had seen in the mud and who we had obviously roused from its hiding place despite those silly bells we had worn around our necks to alert bears in the vicinity of our presence, came out of nowhere and went straight for my backpack. Felix and I lay with our eyes bugging, our mouths open, our hearts racing, holding our breaths in utter terror for tense endless seconds as the four-hundred-pound deadly animal then proceeded to noisily rip the backpack on my neck to shreds in its search for food, scattering first-aid supplies, survival gear, and emptied food wrappers all over me, empty thermoses around me, before it finally loped off with the carton of apple slices that I had not eaten for lunch snared in its teeth."

"Oh, God . . . !" Rochelle stared, understanding having turned back into shock as she considered their encounters with the two deadly animals too close calls; Rachel guessed. "Girl, I can't believe you and Mr. Fox went through that kind of terror twice in a couple of days! Well, no wonder he's forgotten about Miss Artificial! Those two experiences did turn out to be conducive to you two. They've bonded Mr. Fox to you!"

"Tell me about it!" Again Rachel laughed agreement over the Coke she had raised back to her lips before lowering the glass back to the napkin on the table. "There was the initial reaction: this warm pleasure that had slid up my arm practically from the first moment Felix had taken my hand in his on Monday—I didn't know whether it was from seeing an old friend again, or what. It hasn't stopped since. And he held my hand a lot. There was the physical attraction. I mean, how could there not be? Not only is he good looking, but the man has such raw sex appeal and male virility. Every time I as much as brushed up against that well-built body of his, sensation. Like the two instances off the Tony Knowles Coastal Trail and Chugach State Park, where I either fell on top of him or he fell on top of me? Sensation . . . !"

"I'll bet!" Rochelle agreed with a dreamy grin as she again reflected on the good-looking, virile, sexy man.

"And then, there were the kisses that we shared. Starting with the one in the restaurant on Tuesday, where Felix had kissed me after telling me that I had turned out to be as beautiful as Devon and wondered if I tasted like her. . . . The man kissed me twice just to see what I tasted like—each one arousing those pleasures and sensations I had already started to feel, exciting me so completely that I'd actually had to fight the immediate urge I'd felt to respond. And another one would soon add itself to the growing number. I say that, because we both love to roller skate and ice skate, both of us having learned as kids. In harmony with that, like I told you, I've been to that fabulous mall, the Dimond Center. Felix took me there to the ice skating rink Tuesday evening, where he asked me if I could skate and where I surprised him by telling him I could. I got out on the ice and showed off for his benefit, skating speedily away from him, doing a number of pirouettes, figure-eights and a double toe loop, unaware that Felix could outdo me until he showed off on me, skating swiftly backward away from me, doing a number of pirouettes around the rink, figure-eights, a back flip and a triple Lutz, leaving me standing in the middle of the ice staring after him in terror, certain that he was going to break a leg or even worse his neck when Felix glided smugly back in front of me, laughing at my shock!" Rachel laughed while Rochelle stared across at her in amazement doing the same. "We shared facts about our personal lives that we had never told anyone else and were all too similar, between which we skated around that rink in a game of hot pursuit, where Felix chased, while I fled. We literally had the time of our lives. We flirted with each other all over that place. We tore that rink up for at least an hour before a skater passed by too closely and knocked Felix flat on his back, while another passing by too close to me knocked me on top of him! Sensation! So powerful, in fact, that I was too stunned to pull off him. Which was just as well, because before I could move, a number of photographers started taking pictures of us, at which point, Felix went nuts! He said, 'Oh, my God! I can't believe somebody's been in here watching me for a whole hour! Now, it's going to be all over the press that Felix Latham, soap opera star, was seen sprawled all over the floor in an Anchorage, Alaska, ice skating rink with a gorgeous women sprawled all out on top of him. Well, baby, let's give 'em something to photograph!' Sensation all over again as the third kiss came, a very ardent one that shook me from my head all the way down to the soles of my feet. However, sensation stalled when Felix brushed the kiss off as inconsequential, leaving me shaken and frustrated. And just like he'd said, one of those most incriminating photos of us wound up on the front page of the Anchorage Daily News the next morning, along with a lengthy article and a caption that read: WHO'S THIS WOMAN CONFIRMED BACHELOR, FELIX LATHAM, EMMY-WINNING ACTOR ON THE SOAP OPERA *AS THE STAR SHINES*, IS LAID OUT KISSING ON THE FLOOR OF AN ANCHORAGE, ALASKA ICE SKATING RINK????!!!!"

"Are you kidding?" demanded Rochelle with an incredulous grin over the half-drunk Coke she had raised back to her lips.

"Naw, I'm dead serious! We were all over the paper Wednesday morning!" Rachel persisted with a laugh over the half-drunk Coke she had raised back to her own lips. "Just ask Stacey, she'll tell you. George—George had a fit! When I walked into the cafeteria that morning where he and Stacey sat lingering over a cup of coffee, George jumped up in a rage, paper in hand, demanding to know what the hell was going on with that article of Felix and me on the front page, which I somehow managed to blow off. And then, George jumped all over Felix when he sauntered in a few minutes later. Threw the paper in Felix's face and demanded to know the same thing from him, which Felix, already having anticipated the article just as I said, laughed it off, as well. And then, just as we were about to finish our breakfast a while later after George and Stacey had moved off to start their workday, we had an experience with a couple of the hotel's employees who had seen the article in the paper about us. He, some man named Linc, who George had introduced me to on Monday and whose name I had naturally forgotten, came up to the table and said to me, 'What I wouldn't give if you were laid out under me like that!' However, before I could respond tactfully to that, she, some woman named Marjorie, who Felix had skirted around on his arm last week and whose name he had also forgotten, came up to him and said, 'What I wouldn't give to have you stretched out under me like that! Why don't you let me refill that coffee for you?' Can you believe that? Now, is that brazen or what!" Rachel demanded with a laugh that Rochelle sat across the table from her duplicating. "Well, Felix somehow got us out of that cafeteria, at which point we laughed at those two hotel employees' utter nerves in telling us they wanted to get over/under us down the hall, through the lobby, out of the hotel and all the way to the car. All that took place before we got to Chugach State Park, where we were going that day. And remember what an experience I told you that turned out to be."

"Does sound like the aftermath of that kiss Mr. Fox brushed off as nothing between you two served only in bonding you further, considering the way you ended up laughing yet again after another shared experience with people coming on to the two of you like that!" Rochelle agreed.

"Tell me about it!" Again Rachel's agreement echoed hers as she raised the Coke back to her lips before lowering the glass back to the napkin on the table. "Then, there are all those other things we have in common when considering we haven't seen each other in ten years. For instance, we both took Spanish, both in high school and in college. We both took archery in the tenth grade. I went to Georgia State University, Felix's alma mater years after he and George did. We both know Shakespeare's *The Tempest,* Felix having done the play on Broadway three years ago at the same time I was learning it in school as a college senior. We learned at a concert being put on at the University of Alaska at Anchorage by local and not-so-local talent that we attended after fleeing out of Chugach State Park late Wednesday afternoon that we both hate rap. Plus, the man dances as well as I do. He took me to Club Oasis Wednesday night, where again, I had to rescue him from four women leering at him, and he had to rescue me from three men leering at me. We laughed about it all the way to the floor, which we then tore up fast-dancing and slow-dragging, where we proceeded to feel each other up and flirt outrageously, giving each other blatant compliments and sex threats, both of us saying that we were going to be all over the other in few seconds if each or the other didn't stop. We stayed in that club until two fifteen in the morning before finally leaving, returning to the Amber Heights at two thirty. I have not seen this man in ten years, and yet I've done everything he's done. And then, there's the clicker—we both love Elvis."

Rochelle's green-shadowed brown-eyed gaze lingered on her dusky face in a long amazed stare before she looked away in resignation. "Oh, well, hell, girlfriend, no wonder Mr. Fox forgot about Miss Artificial after all that. With the two terrifying experiences you two had with the grizzlies bonding you, the laughter you shared from five more experiences with people coming all onto the both of you, or at least looking at you like they want to again forging a bond with you, and with all those incredible things you have in common with him when considering just as you said—you haven't seen him in ten years, you had him all the time."

"Oh, yea, I had him," Rachel agreed with a laugh as she watched her down another sip of her dwindling Coke, "but I didn't know it at the time. It was the kisses. Like I said, we were at the University of Alaska at Anchorage Wednesday afternoon attending a free concert. We had a great time there, enjoying well-known talents while laughingly putting down some of the locals. We even got into the most scintillating conversation where we used Elvis Presley song names to flirt with each other—that is, until Felix zinged me with one that was too thick and I had to back out of it!" Rachel continued to laugh. "All of a sudden, Felix noticed a woman watching him intently from a distance and realized he'd been recognized. He tried to shrink down in his seat while I glanced away to see who the person was, but before I could turn back to look at him, a woman in the row behind us had recognized him as well. She called out his name, called him a fox—you know, just like you did, asked for his autograph, and gave him a slip of paper and a pen with which to sign his name. But before he could give it back to her, four more women who had heard her call out his famous name were in his face with paper and pen, also demanding his autograph. They came all onto him, leaving him able only to sit there smiling in amusement, while I sat next to him laughing outright at the women's utter brazenness.

"Anyway, by that time, Felix had lost interest in the concert, as had I," Rachel went on smilingly. "So, taking advantage of his fans' departures back to their seats, he took my hand in his and again, got us out of there. Well, just like I told you, practically from the first moment Felix took my hand in his on Monday; I've felt that crazy pleasure go up my arm. So, I tolerated his disturbing touch until we were outside the Auditorium, where I quickly pulled my hand from his and told him I had the perfect solution for him to keep all those women from coming on to him. I told him to do like that guy I saw on a rerun of the Gong Show on the Game Channel did all those years ago—you know, the Unknown Comic, by putting a brown paper bag over his head and going as the Unknown Soap Opera Star! I laughed at him. I laughed in his face. Felix laughed too before telling me I was beautiful and pulling me into kiss Number four. Sensation everywhere as it shook me from my head all the way down to my toes again. Yet again, sensation stalled as he brushed it off as inconsequential for the second time! Turned me back into a nervous wreck that wanted to scream and run from him at the same time. I don't know how I let that man talk me into going to pick up my pictures at Stewart's after that—I was so frustrated with him for being so unaffected by a kiss that had practically devastated me. And then we went to dinner, took in a classic movie at the Bear Tooth Theatre Pub, afterwards which we critiqued the actors that had starred in it at length along with a couple of others in related movies before we ended up at Club Oasis—you know, where he had to rescue me and I had to rescue him and where we did all our fast-dancing and slow-dragging, during which point, we proceeded to flirt outrageously and feel each other up. Yet despite that, I was determined never to let that man put his lips on me, again. That is, until he finessed me into giving him a goodnight kiss after we returned from the Club late Wednesday night, early Thursday morning. Sensation everywhere as the kiss again shook me to my shoes, although I tried to cover my disturbance by telling him it wasn't bad and that I hoped he hadn't found it repulsive. That's when Felix admitted that he liked kissing me, that in fact, ever since he'd kissed me at the restaurant, he'd wanted to kiss me ever since—although he'd tried to fight that desire, which was why he had brushed off our kisses before that as inconsequential. And then, he kissed me again before saying he'd see me later on in the morning for a late breakfast and strutted smilingly away. And as I stared after his departure with an amazed smile on my own lips still tingling from his parting kiss, I realized the same thing you just said. There I'd thought the kisses between us had had no effect on him when in fact, I'd had him the whole time."

Pausing over the dwindling Coke she had raised back to her own lips, Rachel slid her gaze around the circumference of the busy deli/café in a quick sweep before letting it resettle on Rochelle sitting across the table from her. The Alaska Native sat staring at her in smiling amazement, totally enthralled with her apparent ease in having snared the attention of a man like serious fox Felix Latham in as little as a couple of days.

"That's amazing!" Rochelle said finally, vocalizing her thoughts.

"Isn't it . . . !" Again Rachel laughed agreement amid lowering her Coke glass back to the napkin on the table. "To think that what started out as an initial reaction became a physical attraction that would now turn into a sexual thing that would scare me to death."

The green-shadowed eyes in Rochelle's face narrowed quizzically in her lack of understanding of the latter part of her response. "How do you mean?"

"Like I said, I had him. And I found that out for sure yesterday evening at the hotel. We had a showdown. Felix had told me earlier that morning that he liked kissing me, and he proved it yesterday, because he kissed me everywhere. I mean, we kissed all day. Everywhere we went we were kissing, each one igniting all those sensations I'd already felt, carrying me to higher dizzying heights of distraction, while like I said, scaring me to death at the same time. And because of that, I knew I had to slow that whirlwind romance thing we were on down, because Felix was taking me too fast. In fact of that, when that boy took those pictures you saw of us at Delaney Park, I had already gone against my own desires and tried to pull away from Felix in a desperate need to do just that. As a second matter of fact, I'm surprised that the troubled feelings I had been experiencing at that time didn't show in my eyes. As a third matter of fact, when six women jumped out at him at the Alaska Center for the Performing Arts, I let them have him. I needed a break. Still, another kiss came—exciting, igniting, and arousing those sensations to such intensity that even Felix felt them. He pulled out of the kiss with a smile, saying he'd better stop this, he felt that *'way down.'* Elvis. . . . Well, I'd felt it way down, too. And that was the problem."

Again Rachel let her mascara-coated long-lashed luminous brown eyes sweep the noisy Deli as she indulged a deliberate pause. Across the table from her, Rochelle stared in further enthrallment as she wondered what Rachel had meant by that last remark.

"So, what happened after that that led up to this showdown between you and Mr. Fox that you mentioned?" prodded the Alaska Native over the still dwindling Coca Cola she had raised back to her red-painted full lips.

"Like I said I'd wanted to do before, I tried to run from him," Rachel laughed simply, staring incredulously and aware that she was about to tell the woman who was practically a stranger to her and yet who had confided the intimate details of her relationship with boyfriend Vern earlier at the hotel that not only was a woman as beautiful as she still single and with no kids at twenty four, but she was still a virgin on top of it. "The man had scared me," she began, her low tone becoming intimate. "I didn't know how to handle all those new sensations he had awakened inside me that I had never before felt for another man, which explains why I was never interested in all those quick one-night-stands most men I've met have wanted to get me into. I was simply not in love with them, and just didn't feel that way. And for a number of reasons, I had no intention of falling in love with Felix, either. I didn't care how good looking or sexy he was. I didn't care how much he had confided liking kissing me, or how much I liked kissing him in return. I had no intention of falling in love with him! Certainly, not in as little as three days!

"Anyway, some funny twists happened when we got back to the hotel," Rachel went on in the same low intimate voice as Rochelle sat across from her totally enthralled, green-shadowed eyes intent on her face. "George turned away from the reservation desk just as we stepped through the double doors, saw us and exploded in a rage, as he had not seen us since breakfast Wednesday morning, where he had chewed us out about being on the front page of the *Anchorage Daily News*—you know, like I told you. Felix was flying off the ceiling with excitement over all the places he had taken me since that time, as well as going on and on about all the new things we had in common. I, on the other hand, wouldn't look at him or George, because I was terrified and did not want either of them to see it in my eyes. For that reason, I directed my gaze at George's legs, wanting only for Felix to let go of my hand so I could stop that crazy pleasure from sliding up my arm! Felix managed to calm George's rage down, at which point, George curved a brotherly arm around my shoulders and told Felix at the same time to come on up to the penthouse, that he had a surprise for him. George turned me away from Felix, thankfully breaking my hand from his, and led me to the elevators. Felix followed us naturally, curiosity piqued, the three of us stepping inside the first one that opened. We ascended to the penthouse, a ride during which George spent the whole of it pumping me as to how I was doing, asking if I was alright, if Felix was treating me alright—you know, because he knew something was troubling me, as I had neither spoken to him nor looked him in the eye since we'd arrived at the hotel. Well, I managed some monosyllabic responses about being okay—you know, just plugging on along, and Felix being nothing but a gentleman while I'd forced a couple of smiles up at George, but I just couldn't look him in the eye. All I had wanted to do was get away from Felix, because he was doing things to me that I didn't understand. As a result of that, as soon as the elevator stopped on the fifteenth floor, I bolted away from both him and George and headed straight for the guest bathroom once inside the penthouse, where I then proceeded to freak quietly for half a minute. Then finally, I managed to get a grip on myself, use the bathroom, and wash my hands.

"Anyway, I was what—three-quarter ways back down the hall toward the living room when all of a sudden Felix screamed, shattering what composure I had managed to restore in the bathroom," Rachel went on in the same quiet intimate tone while Rochelle sat in the booth across from her still totally enthralled, listening intently, having completely left off finishing the last of her Coke. "It was because of the surprise George had had for him. A video cassette, entitled *Tickle Me*. Elvis. Felix was screaming his excitement abut the movie that Stacey had apparently found for him at Borders Books on Wednesday, and he saw me standing there, and he went nuts. He screamed, 'Oh, girl, look what your brother got me! Elvis Presley! *Tickle Me!* Have you ever seen this movie? Oh, come on, girl, you've got to come watch this movie with me. We'll go down to my suite! We'll order room service! You're going to love this movie! You're going to love it! Oh, thanks, George! I'll see you later, man!' He'd approached me, grabbed me by an arm and was busily pulling me from the penthouse, at the same time throwing his last words over his shoulder at George. Well, he flung me into the elevator with him, his hand on my arm having wrecked my nerves again, but Felix wasn't even aware of that as he pushed the button for the twelfth floor in his excitement of the old movie. He was telling all about it, but I wasn't listening to his synopsis of the old movie I had seen on cable years ago. All I could think of was that we were going to his suite! A place where we would be alone together for two hours and he would more than likely try and tickle me? Oh, no, I wasn't about to let that happen! In fact, Felix actuated that very intention once we'd stepped off the elevator on his floor by leaning over and kissing me excitedly.

"And this is where the showdown came down: the instant his lips touched mine, I jumped in the floor. I said, 'I have to go!' and wrenched my arm out of his grasp with the intention of bolting. However, Felix curved a hand over my arm, sending my pocketbook falling from my shoulder as it yanked me back before I could get two feet down the hall. He said, 'Are you running from me?' The man's voice had seemed to come from all the way down the hall, although when I was forced around by the detaining hand he had curved back over my arm, I saw that he was right behind me. I said, 'What?' He said, 'What is this ill luck I have with Hardison women? First, Devon leaves me, now you? Well, let me tell you something, *Little Sister*...,' Elvis, who else? '... *don't you kiss me once or twice, say it's very nice, and then, you run...! Little Sister, don't you do what your big sister done...!*' Those are lyrics from the same Elvis Presley tune, *Little Sister*. And I had done that yesterday after a couple kisses he had given me had blown me away and left me breathless by saying, 'Uhm, that was very nice,' or words to that effect," Rachel went on informatively and with low intimacy while Rochelle sat thoroughly absorbed, listening intently. "Now, is that slick, or what—him using that line in the song to tell me, Little Sister, Rachel, not to do to him what Big Sister, Devon done?" she asked rhetorically and with her previous incredulity. "Anyway, I felt the blood pound through my brain as a need to succumb to that beckoning look in his eyes overwhelmed me, so, I said, 'Okay, fine! I won't run! Now, what...?' Felix said, 'I'll tell you in a minute!' And then, with the Elvis tape in one hand, he slung his other arm around my waist and pulled me into another kiss, a very hot one and a very devouring one that let me know immediately what all those sensations had been building up to all day, maybe even all week. So, I grabbed him in tune to the hot passion flooding into my veins, molded my body to his, and began to kiss him back with equal hunger. Yet just as I was about to devour him as well, Felix ended the burning kiss and pulled out of my arms."

Rachel paused to slide a glance around the busy restaurant, which showed her other patrons eating, drinking and thoroughly absorbed in their own conversations, completely oblivious to the confiding tone her own had taken.

"Anyway, I stared at Felix in confusion and disturbance," she continued with the same quiet intimacy; brown eyes back on Rochelle's absorbed features. "I said in frustration, 'What?' And now, this is where it's going to kill you. Felix said to me, 'It's you! I never felt when I kissed Devon the way I feel when I kiss you! And I never felt as jealous over a woman as I did sitting there listening to those two fools'—that would be Martin and Flip—'drooling all over you like slobbering dogs at the dinner table Monday evening. Why do you think I told you when we got back from the club last night how much I liked kissing you?' Well, in my surprise, I said, 'What?' And this is the clicker. Felix said, 'Why do you think I've been all over you, today? Don't you get it, girl after my own heart? I think I'm falling in love with you, if such a thing makes sense! I mean, is it possible for a man to fall in love with a woman in three days?' Well, it was just like we both said: I had him. The man had just told me he thought he was falling in love with me! So, I said boldly, 'I guess there's only one way for you to find out!' Felix said, 'What do you suggest?' And I said, 'Well, for one thing, you can kiss me like you did your costar!' Well, Felix knew exactly what I'd meant by that, because we were in the TV section at The Mall At Sears the other day—where we had followed an Elvis Impersonator—who else—who had given us the slip, and a scene was playing from Felix's soap opera *As The Star Shines*, where Felix slammed his costar up against the wall in a most heated kiss before they whirled into a nearby bedroom and fell madly onto the bed in each other's arms. So, in answer to my response, Felix rushed out, 'It's not a problem!' and he slammed me up against the wall the same way. And as the kiss burned quickly out of control, I realized exactly what I had been feeling for him every time he had touched me, looked at me, put his lips on me. It was like I said: I had more in common with him than any man I had met in ten years. I could do everything with him. I could talk about Elvis with him, talk about school with him, speak Spanish with him, play with him, have fun with him, go skating with him, go hiking with him, run away from grizzlies with him, discuss my dislike of rap with him, play archery with him, talk Shakespeare with him, dance with him, kiss him. . . . Well, that wasn't all I wanted to do with him. . . ."

Leaving Rochelle to figure that out, Rachel paused to raise her Coke glass back to her lips and down the last of its icy contents. Then she lowered it back to the white napkin on the table. In the booth across from her, Rochelle sat tensed in anticipation. She'd figured it out alright; in fact, she was too titillated by the insinuation behind her last statement for her to stop there. Yet she lacked the indiscretion to tell her to go on with her most personal subject.

"The realization as to just how badly I wanted to do that other thing with him reverberated in my brain as Felix ended the passionate kiss to blaze more of the same all over my face and neck while his free hand slid over me with equal heat," Rachel went on to sate her curiosity in the same low intimate tone after a moment, eyes deliberate on Rochelle's face, the woman totally enthralled. "In fact, I was so excited by the thought of climbing into that place with him that in my mind, I called on God, or any deity that had ever been given the name of a god," Rachel said. "I didn't even know my mouth had translated my inner need until I heard my own voice sound out into the corridor over that of the blood pounding in my ears and hammering through my brain. Felix heard me passionately cry out his name and suggested that we get out of that hall quickly. We were in his suite down the hall in two seconds, where Elvis was discarded to the side along with our parkas and my purse. Felix picked me up in his arms, carried me into his bedroom and lowered me swiftly onto his bed, where I then proceeded to pull him swiftly down on top of me. Slight variation from the soap opera. . . . And we had the craziest conversation, where Felix said to me, 'You'll have to forgive me, but I don't feel very gentlemanly right now.' I said, 'I'm sorry to hear that, because for the first time in my life, I feel like a natural woman!' Felix said, 'Hey, that's Aretha!' I said, 'Who?'

He said, 'Aretha Franklin. You've never heard of the Queen of Soul?' I asked, 'Who hasn't heard of the Queen of Soul?' Felix rushed out, 'I'll tell you more about her, later!' before the kissing began again and he was all over me and I was all over him. What had started out as an initial reaction and become a physical attraction had now turned into a sexual thing that had my arms and hands and legs all over him, my lips devouring him, kissing him passionately. My heart was racing, my body aching with that inner need—the same of which Felix was displaying hotly for me, my blood was pounding in my ears as well as through my brain, both sounds threatening to deafen me, wildfire racing through my veins. I never thought I'd feel that kind of passion for a man in my life, and I reveled in it. Felix ended the kiss after a long hot moment, searing more of the same all over my face, ear, neck and flaming throat, while an impatient hand swept my hair out of his way.

"He was entirely breathless as he mouthed against my flesh, 'Your brother asked me in the penthouse suite what was going on between you and me. I told him you've blown my mind. And I can't keep my lips off you.' Well, I told him in the same breathless vein, 'So long as you don't keep them off me, now!' Felix husked out, 'No way!' And then, another heated kiss began that demanded my equal response and left my mind reeling with incredulity. I'd lain there all wrapped in Felix's arms asking myself when did I fall in love with this man who I had no intention of falling in love with, and with whom I'm all wrapped around, as well? Three days ago? Ten years ago, when I was a fourteen-year-old kid? Was that why I used to follow him and Devon around so relentlessly whenever he came to see her, I'd wondered? But that was as nonsensical as Felix saying he was falling in love with me in only three days after not having seen me in ten years! And yet as he had continued to kiss me senseless and in a kiss that had been endless, I'd realized that that was exactly the case," Rachel continued in the same confiding tone. "My sexual thing was borne out of a love thing! I loved Felix—a man after my own heart, as well, the thought leaving my head spinning, my mind reeling. And as his lips left mine to blaze another hot trail of kisses all over me, my mind whirled with the increased realization that I actually had him. And I was about to have him—do that other thing with him, you know what I mean—when the whirling came to an abrupt stop as Felix pulled away from me in a passion-struck daze to answer a knock that had sounded at the door. He said he had not put the do not disturb sign on, not to mention that it might be my brother. The thought of George intruding on us had cooled all the hot blood still racing in my veins. As far as George was concerned, Felix and I were supposed to be in the living room watching an Elvis Presley video. I'd known George would freak were he to come in and find us in Felix's bedroom making out, even though by Felix's own admission, he had told George that I had blown his mind and that he couldn't keep his lips off me. Felix read my petrified expression, smiled and said, 'Don't worry; I told George that I'm gone on you. It is not going to shock him to come in here and find you in my bed.' The mention of the word bed had so embarrassed me that I had looked quickly away in a gesture that Felix had thought was precious; in fact, he had even called me that before kissing me yet again and then rising off the bed to go answer the door. I'd stared after him in amazement, thinking the events that had taken place between us in the last several minutes a shock when considering the terror I'd felt upon our return to the hotel what—a half hour earlier. And I couldn't help thinking as well what was George going to do when he found out his baby sister had lost her heart to his best man. I lay there expecting it to be George when Felix answered the door a second later, only for my flesh to turn to stone from my head to my toes. The voice that sounded through the suite wasn't George's, or even masculine. It was Devon's! She had blown in unexpectedly from Atlanta, having had her attorney wrap her divorce up on Wednesday, and the first thing she did after arriving at the hotel—even before going to look up George—was come seeking out her ex-flame with the apparent plan of picking up with him right where they left off ten years ago!"

Deliberately Rachel averted her gaze from that of the older woman as she let the impact of all she had quietly said to her hit her. The green-shadowed brown eyes in Rochelle's face lingered on her half-turned profile in a long stare of stunned stupefaction before finally twinkling with the same amazement that showed in the grin that suddenly curved her red-painted full lips.

"Girlfriend," she began with a laugh, reclaiming Rachel's attention, "this has got to be the most fascinating story with a couple I've ever heard in my life. Forget my thing with Vern—this is some serious heat you got going on with Mr. Fox and all this Elvis Presley business! I guess you were right when you said George asking him to be your tour guide was the best thing he could ever have done for that man. To think that when you showed up here on Monday, Mr. Fox was still hopelessly in love with Miss Artificial . . . ! Yet now that he's fallen long-overdue out of love with her and is falling for you—a woman who apparently has more in common with him than he ever did with her—Elvis, especially—and even if it is in just three days—that's when she showed up, yesterday? Just as you and Mr. Fox were about to get busy? And that was going to be your first time, too?"

". . . Uhm-hmm." Rachel nodded affirmation to all three questions, appreciative of Rochelle's look of incredulity. "I mean, I'm glad she showed up for George's sake—you know, just like you said, her arrival is for his good. And I succeeded in diverting her attention from Felix when she started coming onto him by telling him that he was always so good to her, he never did anything to hurt her, he was never more than a gentleman with her—why did I leave you? But the mess didn't really start until George went to introduce Stacey's mother to Felix when she, Al, and Rick Lumas arrived a few minutes later. Dora Lumas stared at Felix in startled recognition of him, telling him she knew him, she'd seen him, that he was Joe Murray from the soap opera *As The Star Shines* that she watched every afternoon on her work break. Devon saw the woman fall apart at the command of his good looks, presence and eminence as a soap actor and said, 'Honey, are you that hot on the show?' And that's when George laughed and said, 'Who are you kidding? Felix has won three Daytime Emmys for his portrayal of Joe Murray, who is so slick that he is presently having an affair with his boss, her daughter, and her stepdaughter all at the same time, and with none of them knowing of the others!' Devon's been on him seriously ever since."

Rochelle's brown gaze lingered on her face in an expression of disgust, just then realizing the untenable situation her sister's unexpected arrival there had put her in.

"That's awful," she sympathized after a moment over the rush of voices still coming from other patrons visiting the busy Deli/Café.

"Isn't it?" Rachel agreed. "And in answer to the question you put to me back there as to why I'm letting her hang all over my man like that, we're playing a game with her."

Again the green-shadowed eyes in Rochelle's fleshy round face narrowed on her curiously. "Why?"

"We have no choice. Devon's trying to get him back, and she doesn't take rejection well. You should have seen the way she came all onto Felix at dinner last evening and the way he lapped it up and laughed it up with her. Dora Lumas stared in fascination that a man of Felix's star eminence and award-winning status was at her table; Al Lumas watched the floor-show they put on with amusement; Stacey, who had sized Devon up from the instant George had introduced them up in the penthouse an hour before as the one who had dated him for the four months, three days, and seventeen hours before dumping him for another man all those years ago when he and George both lived in Georgia, eventually marrying two other men, Dustin and Richard—in fact, had been sitting right next to George in that very penthouse when he and I had teased Felix mercilessly about the shortness of their affair and voiced our suspicions that he was still in love with her, doubted if he'd ever gotten over her to this day, that being like I said, shortly after I'd arrived here on Monday; and who after having flashed Felix a warning look not to let Devon rope him back in with her good looks—especially when she'd thought he was still vulnerable, had sat staring in a rage that had actually stopped her from talking, shocked, stunned and stupefied at Devon's shameless display and terrified that Felix was going to let her do just as Stacey had feared and rope him back in; Rick Lumas barely noticed either of them for coming all onto me the same way; George and I sat staring in shock and confusion as Felix played up to her throughout the whole dinner before turning the tables at the end of it and dumping her before everyone, telling her he had a woman waiting for him and that they had a date to watch Elvis. Devon didn't get the point. Nor did she get it when my father asked them upon their arrival here last night if she and Felix were going to get back together. Devon said hopefully, 'With any luck,' but Felix said he was sorry, he had a woman waiting for him, and he had been trying to shake Devon for a whole hour! So, we're playing this game with her. Devon doesn't take rejection well. Were she to find out that Felix has a thing going on with her kid sister, Devon would not like it. I know it, Felix knows it, George and Stacey know it, and even my parents know it, because they sensed by the hot grin Felix turned on me when he mentioned that new woman he had waiting for him that she is me. Although George says Devon is suspicious of me, because she saw that grin, as well. In fact, George has even told me to watch out for her."

Rochelle stared at her for another long silent moment, shaking her head at her. "That's incredible!" she exclaimed finally. "Well, I guess I was right about your sister. She is artificial if she can make this kind of play for a man she dumped ten years ago and hasn't thought of since."

". . . Uhm-hmm." Rachel completely blew off the disparaging tone of Rochelle's last remark as she bent her head in an affirming nod. "I'm telling you—the woman's insane."

". . . Uhm-hmm." Rochelle's own head bent in an affirming nod. "And while we're on the subject of insane, and before we get completely off mention of him, where is Stacey's brother?" she demanded after a moment, just then noticing his delayed return. "Where is Rick? Where the hell is Rick! Has he left us here without a way to get back to the hotel?"

Rachel stared in surprise at her mention of the tall blond thirty-year-old man, herself just then noticing his delayed return.

Chapter Sixteen

She had just confided where she had spent her morning and partial afternoon—locked away in Felix's suite upon his call for her to join him in watching part of an Elvis Presley—who else—movie marathon on ENC—which they had missed mostly for being too busy kissing in his damned bed—to Rochelle's further shock and amazement when Rick entered the Deli/Café and saw their heads bent over in shameless laughter. The gaze Rachel turned on the thick-skinned face once he'd appeared at their table was one of innocence and dual relief—that he had at last returned for them and that he had given her a chance to relay the details of her hot thing with Felix in-depth and whereabouts before the wedding rehearsal to Rochelle before doing so.

"Where'd you go?" Rachel asked the white man curiously, aware by a quick glance at her watch that it was four twenty five, fifty minutes since he had dropped her and Rochelle off at Stewart's Photo Shop down the street.

The medium lips curved as Rick smiled at the question, already having anticipated her concern over his delayed return. "I'm sorry, Rachel, baby," Rick began apologetically, aware that Rochelle sat expectantly awaiting an answer as well, "but my friend got held up. When I got to his home, he was in the process of trying to photograph a couple and their quints. The three-year-olds were crawling all over the place. . . . Took him fifteen minutes just to get them settled down, and then another ten to photograph all of them!"

"I see." Rachel's luminous brown gaze met the green-shadowed brown one of Rochelle in an amused look, finding it no wonder Rick was late getting back to them—what with having to wait almost a half hour for his friend to tend to him, much less the time expended in doing so and that spent in driving back and forth. "There're not very many couples with quintuplets. He must truly have had his hands full in trying to control five three-year-olds at the same time," she said.

"He did!" Rick agreed with a smile that showed his appreciation for her understanding of the situation.

Rachel's eyes turned away from the similar twinkle in Rochelle's to settle on the white man in another curious look. "Did you get a camera?"

"Boy, did I ever . . . !" Rick grinned. "Makes that thing you got look like a toy! Come on, I'll show it to you."

Sliding his vivid blue gaze on Rochelle in a look that encouraged her to follow, Rick curved a hand over Rachel's and pulled her from her seat. Grateful that she had long paid her tab for the Coke she had consumed—as had Rochelle—Rachel gathered up her black bag and small bag of new film and let him lead her ahead of Rochelle out of the Deli/Café.

Arriving back at the white Acura Legend moments later, Rick let go of Rachel's hand to unlock the trunk with the key he had pulled from the pocket of his black leather coat.

"I had my eye on a Nikon D2H Digital SLR," Rick said as he pulled the truck open. "Thing delivers eight pictures per second, and features Nikon's exclusive new JF-ET imaging sensor. Thing costs $3200 dollars. But my friend didn't trust me with that one; said it was too expensive and far exceeded my simple need to take stills at a bachelor party. So, he settled on letting me have this one."

Sliding the key out of the lock and back into his front coat pocket, Rick leaned into the trunk he had opened to pull it from its carrying case, unaware that Rachel stared in amazement as she tried to imagine a camera that cost that much money. Rochelle shared her amazed look as Rick turned away from the trunk with it in his hands.

"This is also of the Nikon series," Rick said as he showed it to her. "It's a D70 Digital SLR. Has 18-70mm IF-ED Nikkor zoom lens, built-in speed light, takes three frames per second, and has a buffer that lets you capture up to 144 shots in sequence," he grinned. "It has auto mode, can snap portrait, landscape, close-ups, sports, night photos and night landscapes, and is designed for both experienced and amateur photographers, as well."

"I see," Rachel said as she looked over the black body of the expensive compact camera and large zoom lens he showed her. "So, what's this one cost?"

"This one's only about $1500 dollars," Rick explained as he continued to gaze admiringly at the camera in his hands. ". . . Comes with a Lexar compact flash memory card that costs an additional $1500."

Rachel turned a mock-outraged glare on the white man at the ridiculous idea of spending $3,000 dollars for a simple camera and attachment.

"Look, honey," she began with a laugh, "for my Canon Sure Shot, that toy you were talking about, I only paid just over a hundred bucks for it at Wal-Mart. Wal-Mart, baby! Wal-Mart . . . !"

Like her, Rick showed his teeth in a laugh. "What do I need with such a cheap camera?" he asked, also mockingly. "I'm rich! Besides, I didn't have to pay anything for this one, anyway. Here, let me take a picture of you." And raising the Nikon D70 Digital 35mm camera which was all ready to shoot to his eye, he snapped her standing there glaring at him in a lingering expression of outrage and amusement.

It was the first that Rick would snap of her, for he snapped several. He snapped Rochelle as well. In fact, Rick took pictures of the both of them posing and laughing all the way down to the Egan Civic and Convention Center on West Fifth Avenue a block over. There in front of its glass-walled exterior and with the colorful gardens of Town Square Municipal Park across the street from them, they were approached by two black men in loud garish women's clothing, stockings, heels and wigs, one wearing a long curly red one, the other wearing a short blond curly one, along with a white man whose black hair was cut in a Mohawk. Rachel gasped at the realization that they were two drag queens and an Indian. What were two drag queens doing in Alaska, she wondered? Were they everywhere, she asked herself as her wide-eyed gaze slid back to the pale-faced Indian, whose pointy breasts beneath the thick red sweater he wore over a white shirt clearly revealed that he was a transsexual, as well.

Her shocked gaze was diverted from the Native Indian as one of the drag queens slid his own over Rochelle, saw the size of her breasts beneath the white leather coat she still wore over her dress, and smiled.

"Look, m'lady," began the black man in the long elaborate red wig, who appeared to be in his early thirties, "you got some serious stuff upstairs. If I weren't a fag, it'd be just that quick I'd be trying to get on your bag!"

Rochelle's engaging teeth flashed in her amber brown face as she laughed at the way the dark-skinned man's well-made-up brown eyes roved suggestively over her.

"Then, it's just as well you are a fag, because you couldn't handle it!" she said, deliberately thrusting her large breasts at the thin man she could devour in five seconds.

Rachel's shock gave way to a similar amusement as the drag queen, equally amused by the way Rochelle had brushed him off, allowed his gaze to slide over the equally provocative curve of her breasts beneath the tan leather coat she still wore over her own clothes in the same suggestive manner.

"Well, don't look at me, because you couldn't handle me, either!" she laughed, knowing she was speaking the truth!

Rick reacted equally when the well-painted brown eyes of both drag queens settled on him and remained in manly appreciation of him as a member of their same gender.

"Well, don't look at me," he laughed, "because I don't want to handle either one of you!" Farther amused by his brush-off of him as well, the first drag queen proudly turned up his nose, while the second rolled his equally made up eyes in disdain, the Indian stared.

As the two of them sauntered off in the loud garish women's wear, stockings, heels and wigs along with the Mohawk-shaved Indian, Rachel grabbed Rick by an arm.

"Get the picture! Get the picture, baby, get the picture!" she urged him quickly.

"Hold on, Rachel, baby, I'm going to get it! I'm going to get it!" Rick assured, raising the Nikon D70 Digital SLR 35mm back to his eye.

However, his attempt to shoot the most precious picture of the two loudly dressed gays and transsexual walking away from them was shot as well at the discovery that he had already shot his last exposure on the roll.

"Oh, shoot, I'm out of film!"

"Oh, no . . . !" Rachel cried, laughing at the irony, as did Rochelle and Rick.

They laughed at the lost opportunity for five minutes, cars whizzing past them, people entering and exiting the Egan Civic and Convention Center behind them, the Westmark Hotel towering across the street just to the east of them. Then somehow managing to sober their amusement, the three of them returned to the car parked a block over on West Fourth Avenue. Once done, Rick replaced the expensive camera in the trunk and drove them the short distance back down D Street and up West Fifth Avenue to the Fifth Avenue Mall, which connected at the corner with A Street. As they stepped from the late model white Acura Legend after Rick had parked in the Fifth Avenue adjacent garage, Rachel couldn't help thinking that she had never been there, as Felix had not brought her there in the four days since her arrival in Anchorage. Not even despite the fact that the Mall was connected by a skywalk to the Alaska Center for the Performing Arts on West Sixth Avenue one block over, where he had taken her the day before. Nor could Rachel help recalling for the second time that day the fun that they had had at another Mall three days before—the Dimond Center—the largest in Alaska. Nor could she help noticing that not only was the Fifth Avenue Mall anchored on one side by Nordstrom's Department Store, but JC Penney & Company on the other. Rachel couldn't help hoping smilingly that they wouldn't have an earthquake as she remembered also how Thacker Muldoon had told her and Felix just the day before how the March 27, 1964 quake had decimated the original Penney Building.

Yet despite the fact that the Fifth Avenue Mall was not as large as the Dimond Center, it was comparable, Rachel saw as Rick led her and Rochelle into the flashy multi-level shopping venue moments later. With elevators and escalators leading everywhere, it had a Wells Fargo Bank and Lost and Found on Level One; there was a U.S. Postal Store on Level Three near JC Penney; a large food court on Level Four. And it had a variety of shops that sold everything from sunglasses to fake nails, from cell phones to film. In harmony with that, there was a Kits Camera on Level Two, same as she had discovered at the Dimond Center three days ago. The reminder that the shop offered one-hour photo developing along with a number of drug stores in the area barely fazed Rachel any more than it had then. After all, Felix had taken her to Stewart's Photo Shop for her film developing that same day—Tuesday—and though the Shop offered one-hour developing at a higher rate, she had determined to stay with it for that very reason. Besides, Stewart's was the largest photo shop in Alaska anyway, offering every photographic job that could be done under the sun.

Because of the many shops at the Fifth Avenue Mall, Rick had explained to her that that was why he had brought her and Rochelle there, as it offered a number of places from which to purchase that special wedding gift for that special couple, as Rachel knew Rochelle was already well aware. Hence, Rick showed her what he meant by taking her and Rochelle quickly to Katherine The Great—a Russian-based, what else—gift store on Level Three, where he spent $600 dollars on a Palekh Tea Party Lacquer Box for his sister and brother-in-law-to-be—a price that not only insulted Rachel but infuriated Rochelle, as just like with Rachel, it was way out of her league. Bent on getting back into their good graces after throwing his money around, the millionaire Alaska-born-Hawaiian then steered them smilingly and apologetically back to Level One, where gift shops that were more suited to their pocketbooks lie in an assorted number. However, of the three that they went to, to Rachel's disappointment, everything in each was either Russian-themed or Native crafted, although Rochelle was unaware of why she was proving so be so hard to please as she selected for Stacey and George a laser-etched crystal bridal champagne set for two for nighttime use that reflected the Alaskan northern lights from Walleen's Northlight Gallery. Wondering if she would be able to find something less theme-flavored in the bridal department of JC Penney, Rachel reluctantly let Rick escort her along with Rochelle back up to Level Two to A & H Hallmark so that they could make the necessary purchases of cards, ribbons, wrapping paper and cellophane tape, and was thankful to stumble on the perfect wedding gift for her brother and his wife-to-be—in fact, she chided herself for not having visited the non-themed universally known gift shop in the first place! Then with her purchases encased in shopping bags, as as were Rochelle and Rick's, Rachel happily let the wealthy white man escort her along with Rochelle back down to Level One. There rather than guide them to Sullivan's Steakhouse farther up the floor, where Rochelle longed to sate a certain urge for a nice prime rib, Rick guided them back to the car, where once with all their packages piled in the back seat, he drove them back down West Fifth Avenue past the Egan Civic and Convention Center and Westmark Hotel to Corsair Restaurant farther down the street. The four-star restaurant, which Rick said was established around 1979, catered to Continental and American cuisine with an emphasis on French haute cuisine and was far more expensive than Sullivan's Steakhouse, insisting on a reservation they didn't have. But the tuxedo-clad Maitre 'd gladly waived that aside as multi-millionaire Rick slipped him a bill, at which point, he quickly led the three of them to an empty corner fan-back wooden booth. Once seated in the cozy booth in the mahogany-walled restaurant crafted in the theme of a sailing vessel, Rochelle quickly lost her taste for steak in preference of rack of lamb, which she then ordered while Rachel ordered veal and Rick the King Salmon, each of them with an order of the Alaskan Bouillabaisse on the side. And all were to be indulged with the appropriate burgundy and white wines from a list of over 800 bottles and cellar of at least 10,000, to be followed with equally fancy liquor-lace d desserts, such as Bananas Foster flamed right there at the table.

Naturally, it only served that Rick was going to pay for all three meals, which he was plus the appropriate tip, Rachel guessing that all were going to cost him at least three hundred bucks. She was impressed. So was Rochelle. Halfway through her sumptuous lamb plate, she looked up at Rick and grinned.

"You know, this is fun, isn't it!" the larger woman insisted with a laugh. "Look at us. . . . The three R's. Rachel, Rochelle, and Rick . . . !"

"You got it, baby!" Rick laughed agreement in his seat in the booth across from her, where he sat downing his Bouillabaisse, Rachel in the seat to the right of him. He was hanging all over her, an arm slung around her shoulders, though Rachel tried her best not to notice as she busied herself emptying her own veal plate, as sumptuous as Rick's salmon and Rochelle's lamb.

It was pushing six thirty when they finished their meals close to an hour later; Rachel guessed that Rick was naturally going to drive the three of them back to the Amber Heights Hotel. Instead, it seemed he was intent on making up for the fifty minutes he had left them waiting his return at the Downtown Deli and Café a couple hours earlier. In proof of that, steering them away from Corsair Restaurant, he showed Rachel the mid-town office building where Rochelle worked as a dental hygienist—an action which delighted Rochelle—and then the apartment complex she lived in on the southern tip of Anchorage not too far from the Dimond Center Mall and Hotel as well—an act that delighted Rochelle even further. Heading north back toward the center of town on Arctic Boulevard then, Rick took them to Melody's Grocery Store, where they shopped through the aisles and bought nothing and then to Alaska Leather, Incorporated, a furrier where they tried on sumptuous mink coats and fox stoles to their hearts' content. Then Rick went from the sublime to the ridiculous by taking them to Moni & Gold Mine on East Tudor Road, a consignment and thrift shop where naturally nothing suited any of them. Improving, they moved on down the street where Rick stopped them at Silva Saddle, where they tried on western wear and yet again bought nothing and then to 2-Go-Tesoro, another grocery/supermarket where they shopped through the aisles and bought nothing yet again. Rick literally took them all over the place, leading them through a number of shops around a labyrinth of avenues and streets—until they ended up at a discount store near Merrill Air Force Base close to an hour later, where again they browsed through the aisles and bought nothing. And throughout all those places the white man was all over her, though Rachel gave him no encouragement, secure in her love for Felix and his equal attraction to her that she had no need for another man.

They were downing Cokes at a bar on G Street called Darwin's Theory another twenty minutes later, where Rick sat still hanging all over her. The bar, which he had told her had inspired the Indigo Girls' Amy Ray to write the group's 1995 hit tune *Cut It Out*, held an interesting clientele, a fun place with plenty of both young and old, the regulars and the tourists. Rachel wished she could remember what the song *Cut It Out* had sounded like as she wished also that Rick would cut it out, though she gave away nothing of her thoughts as she smiled in automatic response to another old song Rick was telling her the now defunct Indigo Girls had put out years ago.

She had just looked away in response to a more current tune by Genuwine beginning to play in the background when a hand suddenly curved over her wrist as Rochelle yanked her out of the circle of Rick's arm. Rachel stared at the older woman in surprise as she pulled her quickly away from their table, not stopping until they were halfway across the dimly lit floor of the lounge/nightclub.

"Look, girlfriend," Rochelle began over the noise of talking and drinking and music, "while we're on the subject of the Indigo Girls' old tune *Cut It Out*, you need to seriously cut it out with Rick," she insisted seriously. "That man is not being genuwine with you."

Although Rachel did not miss the meaning behind Rochelle's clever play on the Indigo Girls' old tune to *cut it out*, she was totally thrown by her equally clever play on the musical artist Genuwine presently playing in the background with Rick not being genuine with her.

"Come again?"

"Look, girlfriend," Rochelle went on in the same serious demeanor, "I know that man doesn't mean anything to you, but you need to stop letting Rick hang all over you. That man is not playing with you. He hasn't been hanging all over you all evening for nothing. He wants to get on you to the point where he might even be willing to do something to hurt you to get you."

While Rochelle had simply voiced the same thought Rachel had been having that Rick cut it out, Rachel brushed off her warning as nonsense as she shot a look over her shoulder at Rick, who still sat innocently sipping on the Coke he had half downed in his glass.

"Don't worry, I can handle him," Rachel said dismissively, thinking the thirty-year-old man aggressive but harmless. "He is going to cut it out, because he's not getting anywhere near on me. Besides, you know the only man I want on me, anyway is Felix Latham, Latham, Latham!" *Uh-uhm! Uh-uhm!* she thought dreamily.

Curving a hand around Rochelle's wrist, Rachel watched the disapproved line of Rochelle's full red lips curve in resigned appeasement before she pulled her back to their table, where she settled back in her seat beside Rick, Rochelle in hers adjacent to her. There, Rachel proceeded to handle Rick for another thirty five minutes as he drooled all over her before he finally cut it out and got up to drive her and Rochelle back to the hotel. After all, as official photographer at George's bachelor party, he had to be on his way, as it was pushing nine twenty and the party started at ten. Hence, he steered the white Acura Legend quickly off in the direction of that party after having dropped Rachel and Rochelle at said hotel along with their bags twenty minutes later, leaving Rachel heaving a sigh of relief at having ridded herself of the fawning man while at the same time hoping he and George's other friends wouldn't get her brother drunk.

Beside her, Rochelle echoed her sigh of relief at Rick's departure. "Thank God, he's gone." She said disparagingly. "That man can be a bit much at times."

"Yea, he can be a little overpowering, can't he?" Rachel agreed with a laugh.

Rochelle's freshly painted red full lips curved in a laugh of their own suddenly, although for a different reason as she continued to pin Rachel with her twinkling gaze.

"Anyway, just think! Tomorrow is George and Stacey's wedding day! I know she's been looking forward to it for the longest time. Although I wonder how she's been taking her last day of single-hood since that fool Rick kept us out all afternoon and evening and I didn't get a chance to talk to her."

"Yea, I know. As a matter of fact, while we're on the subject of single-hood, I was just thinking about George's. I was just hoping to myself as Rick drove off that he and the rest of George's friends wouldn't get him drunk. You know, at the bachelor party, the very private place of which Rick wouldn't make known to us."

"Yea, I know," Rochelle agreed.

"I've also been thinking about my parents," Rachel went on in the same confiding tone. "Since that fool Rick as you just mentioned kept us out all evening, I haven't seen them since we left here this afternoon at three fifteen. They have to be going out of their minds wondering what happened to me. And I missed Felix. I wonder how he's been doing with me having been gone away from here all this afternoon and evening. Although I can't go up to his suite to seek him out and find out, because it's nine forty five and he and George have to have been long gone out of here to attend that bachelor party at ten o' clock. You know; at the very private place that that fool Rick wouldn't make known to us."

Rochelle's head bent in a nod of agreement as she busied herself throwing her shopping bag and purse into the passenger seat of the late model red Mercury Cougar she had just opened from the driver's side, throwing her white leather hat in on top of them as well. She had pulled the white leather coat that matched it and that she had taken off earlier back over her figure as had Rachel her burnished tan one, both of them needing them to protect them from the slight chill that still remained in the air from the day's rain.

"Well, one thing I know is you won't have to worry about George overdrinking," Rochelle said after a moment. "He told Stacey after the wedding rehearsal this afternoon that he had no intention of letting his friends get him drunk."

"No, that, he's saving until tomorrow!" Rachel went quickly on to clarify herself as Rochelle turned a quizzical look on her in her misunderstanding of her exclamation. "George was telling me the other morning when I asked him at breakfast if he and Stacey had gotten a caterer that they had, and of all the fabulous food they were going to have. He said they were going to have pies, they were going to have cakes, they were going to have beef, they were going to have filet mignon, caviar, and a number of other things. And George said they were going to have champagne. In fact, he said they were going to be drunk by the time they got to the

Riviera. Well, Stacey said in her soft-spoken way, 'So long as you're sober enough to perform your husbandly duties when we get there!' Isn't that the most outrageous thing you ever heard?!" Rachel demanded with a laugh that Rochelle indulged with her. "I mean, I just couldn't help thinking at the time that the innuendo behind the remark didn't seem to go with her soft-spoken nature somehow!"

"Doesn't exactly sound like something Stacey would say," Rochelle agreed, her twinkling green-shadowed gaze indicating that she was impressed by her astuteness in having observed that about her long-time friend after having known her for only four days. "I guess that's what love does to a person, takes away their inhibitions." It certainly had taken away Rachel's, Rachel thought. "Anyway, tomorrow's going to be interesting for us all," Rochelle said. "Vern's going to be my date at the wedding. I want you to meet him," she said excitedly. "He's nowhere near your Mr. Fox. As a matter of fact, Vern's more like a cougar. But he has the hands of a wolf—do you know what I mean?"

"That must have been him I heard howling at Chugach State Park the other day!" Rachel's laugh followed the shameless hoot Rochelle had forced through the air.

"Anyway, let me get on out of here, so that I can get back to that apartment of mine and get some beauty sleep. Not that I need much of that, huh?" Rochelle asked with suggestive meaning.

Again Rachel laughed along with her as she returned the embrace the bustier woman had taken her into, knowing by that just what she had meant by the word beauty.

"Well, that being the case, I'd better go get myself some No Doz and stay up all night, huh!"

Rochelle pulled her arms away from her shoulders to hold them in her hands. The short pageboy she wore her straight relaxed black hair styled in curled just bellow her fleshy amber-brown cheeks presently upraised in a grin.

"Girlfriend," she began through engaging teeth, "it's been real meeting you. I really like you. And I'm looking forward to being in that wedding with you tomorrow. You're exceptionally beautiful without being stuck up about it, and you proved that today by confiding all those juicy details about your hot thing with Mr. Fox to me the way you did at that restaurant—even though I did kinda step on a limb and blab the same juicy details of my thing with Vern to you first," Rochelle added with a sudden comic pensiveness that made Rachel laugh. "Anyway," Rochelle went on with all seriousness, "because of that genuineness in you—and I'm not talking about the artist here, either, I can see how Mr. Fox is falling for you. Just be careful, do as your brother George said, and watch out for that artificial one related to you two."

Rachel didn't find the warning misplaced any more than she had her use of the word genuineness with the recording artist they had previously listened to at the Club as she pulled her own arms from her white coat-clad shoulders and watched as Rochelle slid into the red Mercury Cougar and quickly started the engine after closing the door and sliding into her seatbelt. A smile was on her lips as she watched her back out of the parking spot before pulling finally off the lot, a smile on her own full lips in a last statement of goodbye.

As Rachel turned on the pavement in the direction of the manned double doors of the hotel with the bags she had acquired at Stewart's and the mall and her black bag strapped to her shoulder, she wondered if that Artificial One related to her and George had tried to come on yet again to Felix while she had been away from the hotel all afternoon. Then she thought against it. After all, in Felix's words to George, he was off Devon for good and onto her for better. Rachel could hardly wait for another opportunity for him to be just that again, the thought leaving her floating dreamily all the way up the elevator to her eleventh-floor two-room suite.

She awoke with a start the following morning, a quick glance at the AM/FM clock/radio on the French Provincial nightstand to the left of the king-sized bed she lay in showing that the time was seven fifty eight. It was George's wedding day, Rachel thought with a smile, a day he had been awaiting for ages. Even better, it was a beautiful day, she saw as she crawled out of bed, crossed the bedroom and pulled open the frilly print blue linen drapes hanging at the large window stretching its length on the far side. The sun reflected brilliantly off the huge backdrop of Flattop Mountain in the Chugach Mountain Range buffering Anchorage's east side in the distance, its yellow rays shining from the cloudy one that had hovered over the city the entire day before thanks to the heavy rain that had fallen all through its morning and partial afternoon.

Moving back into her bedroom, Rachel pulled a ribbed cream sweater, matching slacks, same color socks and underwear from a couple of dresser drawers and then moved quickly into the bathroom, where she quickly slid out of her sleepwear and stepped under the hot spray of the shower. She was going to have to wash her hair today, Rachel thought—Felix's insistence in having her join him in his suite to watch Elvis Presley movies the morning before having stalled her intention of doing it then. Yet because she had the same intention—that of washing it later on in the morning, she did not do it during her shower, but donned the same shower cap she had used every morning since arriving in Anchorage on Monday. Coming out of the shower minutes later, Rachel removed from her well-protected head the wet plastic cap and let her still dry hair fall over wet shoulders that she then dried in a thick blue terry towel along with the rest of her provocatively curved dusky-brown body.

Quickly dressing in the fresh underwear, Rachel slid over the two pieces the ribbed cream sweater and slacks and then pulled the same color crew socks onto her feet. Then she took to the task of detangling her sleep-snarled off-black hair. The pink large-toothed comb that she pulled from her toiletry case matched the one she normally carried in her purse was just as effective in handling her long hair—and in proof of that, the relaxed tresses hung smooth and straight down below her shoulders in a matter of minutes. Then she swept it away from the circle of her face and up into her usual ponytail, letting it hang down her back from a cream-colored and cloth-covered elastic band.

Turning the water on in the sink then, Rachel brushed her teeth with a minty paste applied to a red brush before rinsing her mouth and brush and turning off the water after rinsing out the sink as well. Then she slid a pair of simple gold ball studs through the holes in her ears and applied an equally simple matte mauve tint from her toiletry case to her luscious medium lips. She didn't bother putting on any further makeup—after all, her facial features were so symmetrical that she didn't need it, not to mention it was only going to come off when she shampooed her hair later on, anyway. Then giving her attractive appearance little further thought, Rachel moved back into her bedroom, slid her feet into her white Nikes sneakers and tied the silver-toned watch she had left on the French Provincial nightstand the night before onto her left wrist.

She wondered how the bachelor party had gone the night before, how George was handling his last morning as a single man. The thought naturally brought to mind Felix as well. Rachel wondered if he had missed her since they had last seen each other the afternoon before as a lingering glance at her watch showed that it was eight twenty five, five minutes before their usual time to meet in the cafeteria for breakfast. Oh, well, she was determined to find out both. Picking her room key and black bag up off the French Provincial dresser, Rachel sailed from the suite in the direction of the elevator banks down the sophisticatedly elegant stripe-paper-walled hall.

Yet to her disappointment, neither Felix nor George was in the cafeteria after she had stepped off the elevator on the first floor and arrived there moments later. Her mother and father were there though, occupying a table toward the center of the blue-brown-and-gold-themed eatery along with Dora Lumas and Stacey. Rachel swallowed back the disappointment she felt as she crossed the floor toward them, a smile sliding automatically onto her mauve-painted medium lips. Besides, Felix and George were probably still sleeping from having gotten in from the party late last night, Rachel thought, as had Rick, whose presence she had also noticed was missing from the cafeteria. Rachel also noticed that Devon was missing from the cafeteria, though she gave little thought to her older sister as she stopped at the brown table directly across from the foursome.

"Good morning, everyone," Rachel greeted, smile broadening into a grin as she lowered her hips into the brown padded seat across from her mother, at the same time sliding the strap of her bag from her left shoulder and placing it on the brown table in front of her.

"Where were you all day, yesterday?" demanded Sephora, glaring at her over a forkful of egg she was amidst raising to her lips. We haven't seen or heard anything from you since you left out of here after the wedding rehearsal yesterday afternoon!"

The luminous brown eyes Rachel had inherited from her; were understanding as they lingered over the slightly lined dusky features she had also inherited from her, aware that her mother's question had been prompted out of maternal concern.

"I'm sorry, Mom, Dad, but what can I say?" Rachel's smile begged forgiveness from both her mother and her father, who sat eyeing her with equal concern over the slice of toast he had raised to his own lips. "It's like I told you: Rick offered to take me to pick up my pictures at the photo shop yesterday, and afterwards do a little shopping, and he did. And I offered a reason for him to do that, because he had to go out anyway to get a camera from a friend so that he could take pictures at George's bachelor party last night. You remember, he'd offered to be the official photographer there," Rachel said, and watched the expressions soften on both her parents' faces as they recalled the memory. "Unfortunately, when he got to his friend's studio, he had to wait about thirty minutes while he tried to photograph a couple and their three-year-old quints that were crawling all over the place. So, Rochelle and I sat up at the Downtown Deli and Café after I picked my pictures up at Stewart's Photo, where we waited for Rick to get back for close to an hour, when he then took us shopping, just like he'd said he would. Unfortunately, again after that, he took Rochelle and me to dinner, after which he then proceeded to take us around town. Rick took us all over the place. We wound up at some nightclub/lounge/bar called Darwin's Theory downtown, where we listened to music and drank Cokes for another close to an hour before Rick finally brought Rochelle and me back here around nine forty last night to go to George's bachelor party, which he, A.J. and Flip had arranged to start at ten. I'm sorry, Mom and Dad, I didn't intend to stay out all day, but what can I say? The man's nuts," Rachel rambled on uneasily, at the same time wondering why she was always explaining her whereabouts to her family when she was a twenty-four-year-old grown woman. First George and now her parents staring at her incredulously over the breakfast they were in the middle of consuming? "I'm telling you, Mrs. Lumas," Rachel went on then, her brown-eyed gaze sliding from Sephora to the same color one of Dora sitting to the left of her mother, "your son's crazy."

"I think my son is crazy in love with you!" Dora Lumas grinned over the cup of coffee she was raising to her lips.

Rachel knew Dora was the only one of them who did not know she was involved with Felix and therefore nowhere near interested in Rick. Her parents' eyes reflected that in the knowing looks that met the brief similar one Rachel had sliced onto them before letting her gaze dart past Dora and onto Stacey sitting to the left of her. Like her mother, Stacey sat drinking coffee from a white china cup, teasing demeanor of the afore-afternoon hidden behind her usual quiet, although her brown eyes did meet hers with the same knowing look as had that of her parents.

"Good morning, Stacey," Rachel repeated to her sister-in-law-to-be, mauve-colored mouth curving back into a grin. "Today's the big day! Today, you and my brother George take the big plunge!"

Stacey lowered the white china cup she held in both her hands to its saucer on the table in a huff. "I'm not going to marry that man! I'm not going to marry that man!" shrieked the soft-spoken long-haired brunette, voice raised over the sound of other hotel guests talking and eating in the large cafeteria. "What do I know about him, anyway? I've only know him for five years! How much time is that for a woman to get to know a man? Besides, I'm only twenty-eight years old! I'm too young to get married, anyway!"

Rachel's grin broadened as she indulged a laugh at the unexpected display of rage, which, although she had evidenced her capacity for it during Thursday's dinner, seemed another step out of character for the soft-natured white woman somehow.

"It's just jitters, honey!" she said, eyes still twinkling on Stacey's oval face and semi-attractive features.

"She's been like this all morning," Dora explained over the coffee she was raising back to her lips.

Stacey barely found her mother's observance of her as a cause to calm down as she flared in a new expression of rage. "Where is he this morning, anyway? Where is George? I've neither seen nor heard of/or from him all morning! I'll bet he's upstairs passed out! I'll bet they got him drunk! Felix said he wanted to get him drunk, anyway! And while we're on the subject, where is Felix? Where is Felix? He's not here, either! I'll bet he's upstairs passed out, too! And while we're on the subject of my brother, where is Rick! Where is Rick! I'm telling you, I'll bet they all got him drunk! I'm telling you—I'm not going to marry George! I'm not going to marry that man! Besides, he's probably only marrying me for my money, anyway!"

Rachel's surprised stare lingered on Stacey in amazement as she found her ravings unreasonable despite her inner understanding of them. She too had been disappointed upon entering the cafeteria only to notice the absences of George and Felix, though she had attributed them to them sleeping in after getting in late from the bachelor party the night before. Rachel had also noticed the absence of Rick as well, though she had the tact not to tell the woman her suspicions of her brother as she sat flying off the handle three seats down across the table from her.

Her thoughts were diverted from the bride-to-be and her older brother by the sound of her father's brusk alto voice as he began to speak to her then.

"And while we're still half on the subject, your mother and I saw the pictures you left us after the wedding rehearsal," Marshall began, lighthearted demeanor having returned as he smiled over the sausage patty he was cutting into in his white china plate. "They're very beautiful. You really captured the majesty of the Chugach Mountains to the east, while at the same time doing not too bad with the Alaska Range to the west. Much better than with that 126mm camera you used to have when you were a kid."

"They are impressive," Sephora agreed over the orange juice she had raised to her own smiling rose-tinted lips, earlier perturbance gone, "both your pictures, and the mountains."

"Wait till I show you guys the pictures I picked up at Stewart's Photo Shop, yesterday." Rachel smiled her delight of their praise of her for an added reason. She knew she wouldn't feel the panic she'd felt at the photo shop when Rochelle had stumbled on the endless number of photos of her and Felix sharing an intimate smiling embrace that Rachel had not intended for her to see. Quite the contrary, Rachel had no qualms about showing the cozy prints of her and Felix to her parents. After all, they'd known of him for years, had a personal relationship both with him and Rachel and as a result of that, had a personal awareness of their involvement as well.

Her luminous brown gaze was averted from her parents by the sight of Al Lumas as he suddenly approached her from the other side of the table, stopping at her father's right. He was accompanied by a man in his mid-sixties who had his same blue eyes, same gray hair surrounding same oval though slightly better looking semi-attractive face and same six-foot height and average build, with the exception that he carried a slight paunch around his middle. Rachel guessed the man to be Al's older brother Stevan as he looked just like him, the quiet acknowledgment causing her eyes to swing back to Al's delighted features in a look of bemusement.

"Good morning, Rachel, look who blew in from Juneau last night!" began Al to her with an excited grin, his quick greeting of her and disregard of his wife and daughter indicating he had eaten with them already. "This is my brother, Stevan! Stevan Lumas that I was telling you about! How do you like that! And Stevan, this is Stacey's fiancé George's kid sister, Rachel Hardison!"

"How do you do, Mr. Lumas?" Rachel greeted with a smile, doing the usual thing and proffering an arm across the table to shake his hand.

"Oh, Stevan, please!" the white man grinned, proffering forth his own hand and taking hers with the same excitement evidenced by his younger brother. "It's good to meet you, Miss Hardison, Rachel, if I may call you that!" the Alaska Native went on, blue eyes twinkling over her face, pulled back off-black hair and seductive curve of her breasts beneath the cream sweater she wore. "Good God, girl, you are as beautiful as your mother! Which, while we're on the subject, I'm sorry, Sephora," Stevan began in a demeaning aside to her mother, "you're too old, not to mention, you're married. Besides, I want to talk to this one here!"

"Hey, man, that's my daughter you're leering at, not to mention, my wife you've insulted!" Marshall both warned and demeaned with a laugh. His twinkling bold gaze intercepted the amazed one Rachel turned on her mother as she sat across the table to the left of her father briskly downing her half-emptied plate of breakfast. To think that it was Sephora from whom Rachel had inherited her own beautiful dusky looks and yet the man had the nerve to come on to her amidst putting down her mother's more mature equal luminous beauty. Apparently, Stevan was worst than his brother! And Rachel didn't think anyone could be as obvious as Al!

Al completely brushed off Marshall's lighthearted warning and mock-demeaning demeanor as he addressed his brother with continued excitement. "Wait until you meet Rachel's older sister. That woman is bold, aggressive and outrageous, but she's gorgeous!" he finished to his brother with a laugh.

Stevan couldn't imagine a black woman more 'gorgeous' than Rachel and ignored both his younger brother's praise of Rachel's yet unmet older sister and

Rachel's father's friendly warning as he continued to eye her with interest, larger white hand still holding hers, thin lips curved in a grin.

"Look, Rachel, have you had breakfast yet?" Stevan asked.

Rachel smiled at the question, which she guessed the white man in his mid-sixties had asked because there were no dishes whatsoever in front of her, indicating she might possibly not have eaten yet.

"Actually, I was just about to go and get some when your brother Al brought you over to the table and introduced us."

"Well, now that he has; why don't you let me treat you to a meal?" suggested Stevan, continuing to smile as he moved around the table and stopped at her side. "And while we're eating, I'll tell you all about this state Capital where I presently reside. It's called Juneau, you know?"

"Okay." A meek smile curved Rachel's lips as she let the large white hand still holding hers pull her to her feet. Yet despite that, the brief look she turned on her parents was conspiratorial, the same of which was reflected in their own brown gazes as Stevan began to escort her away from the table. After all, Marshall and Sephora like Stacey his niece knew there was nothing the aged Native Alaskan could do for her save her the cost of buying her own breakfast. All other things were the privileges of Felix Latham alone!

He said that Juneau is located 900 air miles north of Seattle (two-hour flight) and 600 air miles south of Anchorage (ninety-minute flight). He said that Juneau, the third largest city in Alaska, has Tlingit history and started out as a boomtown that grew out of gold mining operations. Rachel knew both, that Juneau was the state's largest city and that it grew from gold because of the stark black-and-white picture she had snapped at the Alaska Museum of History and Art depicting the thousands of prospectors that had arrived by steamer from Skagway and over the Chilkoot or White Pass to pan for it. He said that Juneau was in fact, named for gold miner Joe Juneau in 1881. Rachel didn't know that. He said that Juneau grew along the banks of Gastineau Channel on Douglas Island and the mainland and that it is located in the Inside Passage. He said in second fact, that Juneau is supported by state and federal employment and by tourists; cruising that Inside Passage. He said that Juneau was established as Alaska's State Capital in 1906, when the government was transferred from Sitka. Thacker told Rachel and Felix that yesterday. He told her more about the Channel—better known as the Gastineau Channel, the body of water between Juneau and Douglas. And then he told her about the Channel Channel—TV station with twenty-four-hour videos of the Gastineau Channel. He told her about the Glacier Gardens—fifty acres of rain forest eight miles north of Juneau, which is comprised of ponds, waterfalls and four miles of hiking trails, where roots of fallen trees turned upside down and buried in the ground act as planters that overflow with seasonal flowers and where a 580-foot-high overlook provides dramatic views across Mendenhall Glacier. And then he told her about Mendenhall Glacier, Juneau's drive-up attraction, which sits thirteen miles north of downtown five miles north of the Gardens, spans twelve miles, and is fed by the massive Juneau Icefield. He also told her about the Alaskan—a bar and hotel in downtown Juneau where an Alaskan—state resident—could have an Alaskan—a malt beverage brewed by the Alaskan brewery there. To sum it up: You could have an Alaskan with an Alaskan at the Alaskan. Stevan told Rachel everything he could think of about his present city of residence in order to impress her. Naturally, Rachel was flattered. Yet as she sat at her seat at her table eating the breakfast Stevan had bought for her in tune with him sitting beside her downing his own huge meal, Rachel knew she could never feel anything more for the middle-aged man who was going to be her brother George's uncle-by-marriage other than dim fondness for a distant relative. Aware of that also, Marshall attempted to get the drooling white man off his baby daughter by embroiling him in talk about the 1500-mile-long Alaska Highway. Rachel heaved a sigh of relief as she busied herself downing the food in her plate, grateful that her parents had chosen to remain in the cafeteria with her rather than leave after having finished their own breakfast minutes before her.

Her luminous brown gaze slid away from the eggs she was finishing and onto the semi-attractive countenance of Stacey still sitting in her seat to the left of her mother, surprised to find her staring at her intently. Unaware was Rachel that Stacey had watched the way her Uncle had practically salivated over her—a woman forty years his junior and a black one at that, recalled her father's earlier spoken compliments about her older sister Devon, not to mention Devon's similar reaction from her fiancé George's friends at yesterday's wedding rehearsal, and her brown eyes lingered on Rachel in a look of utter amazement.

"What's with you and your sister?" asked the soft-spoken woman curiously. "First, Devon gets George's friends all in a lather yesterday, not to mention my father—now, you've got my Uncle salivating all over you this morning, not to mention again my brother Rick, who's been hung up on you ever since meeting you on Thursday!"

"You've got that right!" smiled Dora Lumas in agreement, still sitting at the table indulging a second cup of coffee.

Like her own mother across the table from her, Rachel laughed at the question, at the same time glad her father had had Stacey's Uncle Stevan too heavily embroiled in conversation about another Alaska subject for him to have heard the uncomplimentary remark Stacey had just made about him.

"I guess it's the curse of the beautiful," Rachel said over the sausage patty she was finishing.

"That's right, dear, it's the curse of the beautiful," her mother smiled agreement. "Thankfully, this man came along thirty two years ago and rescued me from mine!" Sephora finished with a grin, excitedly curling an arm around Marshall's and nearly breaking him out of the involved conversation he was still having with Stevan Lumas.

"I'm still waiting for one to come along and rescue me from mine!" Rachel laughed over the orange juice she had raised to her lips.

"Judging from what I've seen over the last few days, I don't think you'll be waiting for much longer," Stacey said.

Rachel hoped that that would be the case and so did Sephora, who astute as ever, also picked up the hidden meaning behind the millionairess's veiled statement.

"Anyway, while we're on the subject of being rescued by men, I've got to go get ready for mine. I'm getting married in less than seven hours. I've got to go get myself beautified for my man. I've got a cosmetologist coming in here to give me a facial at ten thirty, a manicurist coming in to do my nails at eleven thirty, and a hairstylist coming to do my hair at one—and all so I can look my best for your brother George, who's rescuing me."

Rachel's lips curved in a smile as Stacey's brown eyes twinkled on her with deliberate meaning for the second time. "I'm glad to see you're beginning to feel better about the wedding!" she said.

"Yes, so am I, dear," Sephora smiled also, as had Dora Lumas.

"Of course . . . !" Pushing away from the table, Stacey moved to her feet as did Dora beside her, Al having long returned to his and Dora's eighth-floor suite to rest up for the afternoon's activities. "Anyway," Stacey said to Rachel then, "if I don't see you after that, just bring your dress and shoes to the women's dressing/fitting/powder room on the third floor at two. Rochelle and Diane will be arriving around that same time. They'll primp you all up for the wedding. I'll have a messenger sent up to Devon's suite to tell her since she's not down here, probably sleeping in, as is everybody else this morning. Not that Devon needs that much primping, a point I made a while ago," Stacey finished, again with heavy meaning.

Like Sephora across the table, Rachel laughed again over the forkful of egg she had raised to her lips after having seen Stacey's deliberate look.

"I'll have to remember to tell her that," she said, laugh sobering to a smile as she watched the white woman move away from the table and out of the cafeteria with her mother.

"Whew, now that she's feeling better about the wedding, I wonder how George is doing." Sephora got to the subject uppermost in her mind.

Rachel didn't doubt the reason for the concern behind her mother's wearily uttered question. After all, she had not heard from her eldest child all morning—he hadn't made an appearance in the cafeteria the entire hour that she and her father had been there. Was his absence there due to having gotten drunk last night and being passed out or sick, or both?

"Yea, you know, I've been wondering the same thing," Rachel said as she downed the last bite of her toast. In fact, what she had been wondering was how was Felix and if he was drunk or not, as she had missed him not being there for them to enjoy their meal together as they had, for example, up in his suite just the morning before.

"I'm going up to that penthouse and see if George is dead or alive," Sephora decided finally.

"I'll go up with you," Rachel offered, and downing the last of her juice, moved to her feet. Carrying her emptied breakfast dishes and brown tray to the service kitchen attached to the back of the large cafeteria, Rachel returned to her table. Sliding the black strap of her bag to her shoulders in tune to Sephora picking her own white bag up off the brown table, they said an I'll-see-you-later to Marshall on their way out of the eatery, who was still deep in conversation with Native Alaskan Stevan Lumas on a favorite subject of his own, that of another State Capital, Atlanta, Georgia's largest city.

Outside the cafeteria a moment later, mother and daughter stared at their surroundings in amazed wonder. A flurry of activity was going on as maids having started the day's work were cleaning suites with housekeeping supplies loaded onto large maid carts while porters fled from everywhere to pick up the dirty linen they were discarding to the sophisticatedly elegant four-color stripe-paper-walled corridor. Janitors were cleaning and vacuuming everywhere while florists brought in flowers and other assorted floral supplies along with caterers bringing in food, dishes and various other eating accessories in preparation for the wedding taking place at four o'clock. Party planners were moving furnishings in and out in their intent of turning the second meeting/banquet room into a ballroom, photographers were coming in to set up photo equipment and Stu Giddian, the assistant manager who would be taking over the running of the hotel during George and Stacey's honeymoon, could be seen talking to several musicians just outside the lounge door. All this Rachel and Sephora saw as they moved down the elegant hallway to the elevator banks around the corner to take the first one that opened back up to the fifteenth floor.

A workman stood high on a ladder to one side of the elevator banks replacing a shot bulb in the ceiling's attractive track lighting. The black man in about his early sixties gazed down from his vast height at just that moment, saw Sephora standing there all gorgeous and sexy for a black woman close to his same age though she looked forty, and smiled.

"Say, darling," he said to her in a low bass tone, "why don't you let me get down from here and take you someplace where you can really get high, and me with you?"

Sephora wondered if the dark-toned man were suggesting to her that she get high on drugs or him and laughed at his come-on as she stepped into the elevator that opened then, Rachel beside her.

As the elevator doors closed and quickly began to carry them away from the first floor, Sephora looked at Rachel and they both laughed. "It's the curse of the beautiful!" Rachel repeated her earlier words—words that had been spoken to Stacey—with a lingering laugh.

"That's right, Rachel, it's the curse of the beautiful!" Sephora agreed, a motherly arm curling around her shoulders in response to the one Rachel had slid around hers as her laugh lingered also.

Sephora fairly snarled when George opened the penthouse several minutes later in response to her and Rachel's repeated knocking on the red-painted door.

"Oh, my God . . . ! What did they do to you at that bachelor's party last night?" Sephora queried to her eldest child, her critical eye noticing his simple attire of crumpled blue pajamas, sleep-snarled face and short black hair all crushed in on the side he had slept on, all of which Rachel had stood quietly noticing, herself. In his professional position as General Manager and soon-to-be part-owner of a $200 million dollar hotel, it was just not like George to show up at the door as late an hour as nine forty seven in the morning looking so unkempt.

As if becoming aware of that as well, George jumped in the floor. "Which reminds me—what time is it?"

"About a quarter till ten."

George jumped again at the lateness of the hour. "Oh, good God, I got to get out of here! I got to get out of here! I've got to get washed up! I've got to shave! I got to get dressed! And I know the groom's not supposed to see the bride before the wedding, but I've got to call Stacey! She's probably wondering where I've been all morning. She probably thinks I'm up here passed out from having gotten drunk last night, even though I did tell her yesterday that I had no intention of letting those friends of mine get me drunk! Plus, I've got to call my best man. Felix is probably still sleeping, too! We got in here late last night! He asked about you yesterday," George said then, flitting gaze settling purposely on his kid sister. "Where were you all afternoon and evening?" George asked Rachel pointedly. "Felix missed you!"

Warmth flooded into her body at her brother's mention of Felix asking about her and having missed her that stultified any offense she may otherwise have taken at the accusing tone George had taken with her.

"Hey, what can I say? I was out with Rick. Like I told Mom and Dad yesterday, he offered to drive me up to Stewart's to pick up my pictures there. The only reason I accepted his offer was because I knew I couldn't ask Felix to take me because of the game we're playing with Devon." Rachel included their mother in her sweeping gaze, which indicated Sephora's own knowledge of that game Rachel and Felix were playing with her older daughter. "Rick was more than glad to take me out, said he'd needed to get out, anyway," she went on, luminous brown eyes back on her brother's attractive mannish features marred by rage as usual. "He said my needing to get out as well provided him with the perfect opportunity to go borrow a camera from a friend with which to take pictures at your bachelor party last night. And then Rick took me shopping, something else I'd needed to do. Rochelle accompanied us. Rick took pictures of us, he took us shopping and then he took us to dinner. And then he took us all over the place, including a downtown bar called Darwin's Theory where we lounged for close to an hour before he brought us back here around nine forty last night—just in time to turn around and serve as official photographer at your bachelor party, which according to him, started at ten. How was it, by the way?"

Rachel changed the subject smilingly; knowing her refusal to let George weaken her into starting an argument would perturb him further, which it did.

Yet realizing the nonsense behind pursuing such an unimportant thing at the moment, George sighed again. "I've got to call Stacey, see how my baby is doing this morning; assure her that I'm okay, as well. And I've got to call Felix. We have got a lot of running around to do before the wedding. We have got to get into the street."

"Well, one thing I do know is that you do need to call Stacey," Rachel agreed, "because your fiancée is screaming all over the place that she's not going to marry you!"

George stared at her resulting laughter in confusion, the same of which Sephora stood doing to his right. "What—?"

"I'll let Mama tell you all about it." Rachel reached smilingly up to kiss George's nearest manly suntan cheek while at the same time taking care not to bang him in the bare ribs with the hard edge of her black bag. "I've got a lot to do before the wedding, myself. I'll see you two later. Oh, and George, when you call Felix, explain to him why he missed me all yesterday afternoon and evening. And tell him that I missed him, too."

And leaving her older brother in the smiling care of their mother, Rachel pulled away from him, gave Sephora a parting hug as well and then left the penthouse to approach the elevator banks beyond the lobby/foyer.

As Rachel stepped into the first one that opened and pushed the button for the eleventh floor, she reflected on all those things she had to do before the wedding. She had to wash her hair as previously planned, wrap the wedding gift she had bought for George and Stacey the day before, and she had to gather up the clothes she had dirtied up that week and have them washed and dried by the guest valet/laundry/cleaning service provided by the hotel. After all, she would be flying back to Georgia the following day—no sense taking dirty clothes across five time zones back with her. And even though George had said that Felix had asked about her the evening before—even stating to George that he had missed her and there had not yet been anything said about the state of their relationship and its dependence on continued communication—especially when Felix would be flying all the way back to New York that same following day—Rachel determined to think positive about their situation. Besides, as Stacey had so aptly put it during her breakfast that morning, her rescue might be imminent. *So, what could possibly go wrong today*, Rachel thought, *when it was such a beautiful day, George and Stacey's wedding day? George's wedding day and a so Oh happy day?*

Chapter Seventeen

Rachel decided to tackle her chores in descending order once she had arrived back in her eleventh-floor suite. Quickly gathering up all the clothes she had worn that week, she called the guest valet/laundry/cleaning service down on the ground floor and a valet was there to pick them up in ten minutes. Then she tended to the wrapping of the gifts she had bought as a wedding set for George and Stacey. The first was a 'Happily Ever After' wedding memory book, white with pale floral detailing, that Rachel had been delighted to find at practically the last minute at A & H Hallmark at the Fifth Avenue Mall that Rick had taken her and Rochelle to the day before, and because the large-size keepsake wedding album had cost just under fifty bucks, Rachel had purchased along with it a romantic *Always And Forever* CD for another twenty, considering her brother at least worth making the small but thoughtful dent in her pocketbook. Wrapping the 'ever after' wedding memory book and 'forever' CD together in fancy colorful wedding paper and rainbow ribbons and a self-stick blue bow, Rachel set the set to one side of the French Provincial dresser in her bedroom. She included along with it a sappy wedding card that she had also found at A & H Hallmark Co., to which she added sentiments of her own to the loving couple before signing her name in her professional teacher's scrawl. Sliding it into the blue envelope that came with it then, Rachel addressed it to George and Stacey in the same blue feminine scrawl and then stood admiring both gift-set and envelope that she had sealed with a moistening wipe of her tongue over its back flap.

Moving into the bathroom then, Rachel tended to the washing of her hair—removing it from its cream-colored elastic knit-covered band and throwing it into the wide blue and white marble basin that she had filled with water running from both hot and cold taps. There with a bottle of a pearly white gentle shampoo/conditioner, she proceeded to shampoo every bit of its long relaxed off-black length, lathering it over several times for good measure. Repeat rinsing followed to remove all the creamy lather from her hair, which she then towel dried and detangled with the pink comb from her toiletries case until it hung practically weed straight below her shoulders and down toward her waist. She followed the shampoo/conditioner mix with a gentle leave-in conditioner from the same black hair company, applying a lavish bit of the red liquid to her hair and then combing it gently through the detangled tresses all the way down to their ends. Then wrapping all up into the large blue terry towel that was monogrammed with the letter AHH for Amber Heights Hotel that she had used to towel dry it with, Rachel returned to her bedroom to dry her hair completely with the hair dryer that came with the suite.

She was just about to set the portable appliance up on the French Provincial desk in the living room's work area when a knock sounded at the door of the suite. Checking her slightly damp sweater and matching slacks she still wore for dishevelment, Rachel moved to answer the door, wet hair still encased in the large blue terry towel tied around her head.

To her delight, Felix stood on the other side of the door she opened a second later. The sight of the tall attractive man, whose equally attractive physique was covered in tan Guess jeans and same color sweater, set her heart racing in her breast immediately. Yet despite that, Rachel was equally horrified that he had chosen that moment to arrive only to find her half damp from her hair washing, as evidenced by the equally damp towel wrapped around her head.

"Good morning," he greeted with a smile, the same delight in his attractive tone—and which Rachel had initially felt—seeming to mock her suddenly petrified senses. "Or should I say good afternoon? What is it now, anyway—twelve o'clock?"

Rachel guessed it to be at least that as she closed the door after seeing him into the suite, as she had removed her watch to wash her hair and so had no way of confirming the time.

"It must be at least that by now," she said after a moment of regaining her composure, the smile on her medium lips returning the similar one on his slimmer ones. "I've been doing so much since returning here after Mom and I saw George up in the penthouse. What time must that have been, anyway, about a quarter till ten this morning?"

"Yeah, I'm afraid George and I had a late night out last night," Felix apologized, a hand reaching out and curving around one of hers meaningfully.

"Yes, how was the bachelor party?" Rachel repeated the question George hadn't answered earlier despite deliberately trying not to mirror the intense pleasure sliding up her arm from the feel of his hand holding hers.

"Wild," Felix answered. ". . . A.J. Over lived up to his nickname and got over three women."

"Yea, you know, I kinda figured out he was the man you were telling me about at the Tony Knowles Coastal Trail the other day—you know, when you told me about George's friend who would like that part about me getting under. You hadn't arrived at the wedding rehearsal yet, but when George introduced me to him yesterday, that was the first thing he said to me. After repeating his name in greeting, A.J.

told me he was nicknamed for the rifle Over/Under and that he wanted to live up to that nickname by getting over me and getting me under him! Same thing he said to Devon five minutes later!" Rachel laughed.

". . . Uhm-hmm!" Felix laughed in agreement. "And I saw him run back to you after Devon dumped him after having classed him out of her league."

"Uhm-hmm . . . !" Rachel repeated the two-word affirmative with lingering amusement. "He came right back to me with the same line of getting over me and getting me under him, which naturally, I ignored. And then, I had the misfortune of landing him as the groomsman who would escort me up the aisle at the wedding this evening! And I know he's going to be giving me that same line the whole time. Well, he'll just have to get over it!"

"That's for sure," again the attractive tenor agreed with her, "because the only man I want getting over you is me!"

And in fitting punctuation to that claim, Felix tightened his hold on her hand and pulled her into a kiss that left a thousand exclamation points printing across the page of her brain in tune to more of the same printing from her every nerve ending. He would have to get over her, alright, Rachel thought. Because she definitely wanted to get under him!

Yet incredibly, the dancing brown eyes diverted away from her mouth as Felix ended the kiss to take further note of the terry guest towel bundled around her head.

"I see you finally got around to washing your hair," Felix smiled after a moment.

Rachel answered that a bit late, as she was too busy struggling to overcome her confusion brought on by his quick change of action and subject.

"Yes," she said finally, a composed smile having returned to the soft curve of the luscious medium lips he had just kissed. "As I also got my dirty clothes to the valet to have the guest laundry service here clean them for me. You know, both chores of which I had intended to do yesterday morning before you called asking me to come up to your suite and watch part of that Elvis Presley movie marathon being put on on ENC with you?" Rachel teased him playfully.

"And while we're on the subject of Elvis," continued the attractive tenor with new interest, "you know, after the wedding rehearsal, I had to go back to my suite and watch him all by myself for the rest of the afternoon and evening, because you were out running around with Rick. But I'll forgive you, because George told me after calling and waking me up this morning that Rick offered to take you to go pick up your pictures at Stewart's Photo, and the only reason you accepted was because you couldn't ask me to take you up there because of the game we're playing with Devon."

"I'm glad you understand," Rachel said with a pleased smile. Her free hand slid over the strong curve of his holding her other one in its possessive claim, knowing that if the man were to kiss her again, she'd probably melt like brown sugar in a hot pan. "But actually, I had another reason for accepting Rick's offer to take me to pick my pictures up yesterday. Did George tell you that?"

"Actually, I think he did." Felix nodded his well-shaped head, the short kinky black hair of which was still slightly damp from his usual morning shower. "George went on to say you said Rick had needed to get out anyway, that your need to do the same provided him with the opportunity he needed to go borrow a camera from a friend with which to take pictures at George's bachelor party last night. George said you said Rick then took you shopping, something else you'd needed to do."

". . . Uhm-hmm." Like him, Rachel bent her towel-wrapped head in the affirmative. "It had suddenly occurred to me that after all the places we went this past week, I never got anywhere to buy a wedding gift for George and Stacey. Everything I've seen here is either Alaskan and/or Russian-themed, and why would I want to buy a wedding gift for a Native Alaskan and an Alaskan resident that is both Russian-themed and Alaskan?"

"You've got a point," Felix agreed, laughing as did she. "After all, everything here is either Native-made or Russian-based, just as you said. That's why I had a nice wedding gift wired here for George and Stacey from New York two weeks ago that arrived here Tuesday before last, two days after I did. The Manhattan-based Bloomingdale's is nowhere near Russian. Quite the contrary, it's completely—American."

"It sure is!" Rachel agreed with a laugh as she thought of the expensive well-known American-made department store. "Anyway," she sobered after a moment, "Rochelle didn't have a gift for George and Stacey either, and so, had needed to go shopping, also. So, that's why I went with Rick, her as well. Anyway, she and I picked up the photos at Stewart's and then we waited at the Downtown Deli and Café down the street for about fifty minutes before Rick returned with the camera, which he then used to take pictures of us. And then just like he'd said he would, he took us shopping at the Fifth Avenue Mall, the same of which he did himself. He took us to dinner at Corsair's Restaurant and then he took us all over the place. We ended up at some downtown bar called Darwin's Theory before he finally got Rochelle and me back here around nine forty last evening, just in time to turn around and go take pictures at George's bachelor party as he'd offered, and which I believe he said started at ten. And baby, we had the weirdest experience last evening on West Fifth Avenue. We were approached by two black drag queens who hit on all three of us and an Indian transsexual with a Mohawk who simply stared. Now, I ask you: are they everywhere? Was that ridiculous, or what?" Again Rachel howled with laughter, to which Felix did the same.

"I'm sorry I wasn't there to see that," Felix replied after a moment of waiting for her to get a grip on her amusement and him a grip on his.

"And baby, I'm sorry that I wasn't here all late yesterday afternoon and evening and that you missed me—I missed you, too," Rachel confided finally, her tone like his earlier having turning apologetic. "But what could I do? Once away from the hotel, I was entirely in Rick's hands. Had I done anything to shorten the evening, he might have become suspicious. I mean, after all, we're playing the same game with him that we're playing with Devon."

"I guess you're right." Felix's sexy golden brown rectangular face pulled into a brief frown at the reminder. "And what do we have here anyway, another reference to a man trying to make a claim on you? Well, just like when you said A.J. wanted to get over you, and I said the only man I wanted over you is me, as far as this thing goes with you being in Rick's hands, one thing I know is that you're going to be in my hands in the next second."

And pulling his hand free of the claim of both of hers, Felix slung it and his other one quickly around Rachel's waist to pin the soft curves of her body more fully against the harder lines of his. The second kiss followed with a heat that sizzled, imbuing Rachel with the sensation of meat frizzled from the fire. Her arms scorched all over as they reached up out of the flames to curl around Felix's neck in heady submission, her lips moving against his in ready attention, returning his kiss with equal sizzle, downing him like a delicious swizzle. In fact, Rachel wondered if she weren't that brown sugar melting in the hot pan that she'd thought of earlier as she felt herself liquefying amid the lingering heat of his possession. She was literally in Felix's hands—not to mention all over them as her body turned to caramel, oozing all through his fingers and down over the backs of hands seductively stroking, sensuously stoking, leaving her seriously smoking as she flowed all down over his jeans and onto the blue carpeted floor at his white Nikes sneaker-clad feet.

She felt all the more like the sweet chewy gooey confection when Felix pulled his lips from hers to sear a trail of hot candy kisses onto her jaw, ear, and the sensitive cord of her neck. Rachel clung to him like the bubbling brown sugar he had reduced her to, though she was presently trying to stop the caramelizing process and return to her pre-liquid state by turning off the heat still racing like wildfire through her veins.

"Baby," she laughed in his ear, again becoming aware of the damp state of her sweater and simultaneously trying to push out of his arms, "I'm wet."

"You sure are, aren't you!" Felix laughed too when the heavy blue terry towel wrapped around her head suddenly loosed and fell to the floor, sending her dark damp hair falling in a disheveled disarray down around her face and below her shoulders and his. "Then, it's just as well," he sobered after a moment. "I've got to get going, anyway. George and I have got to get into the street. We've got to go meet the guys at the formal wear shop, pick up our tuxes and shoes, go to the travel agency and pick up George and Stacey's tickets to the Riviera—you know, so on. It's finally their wedding day, you know. In case you haven't figured that out yet by all this conversation we've been having."

"Yes, I'm aware of that." Rachel's delighted smile mocked the teasing one he'd turned on her. "As a matter of fact, you should have seen the way Stacey was going through wedding-day jitters down in the cafeteria at breakfast this morning.

She was screaming that she was not going to marry George, she was not going to marry that man, he was probably only marrying her for her money, anyway—you know—stuff like that!" Again Rachel laughed and watched Felix do the same. "Anyway, she'd gotten over them by the time she left the cafeteria with her mother Dora later with plans of beautifying for that man she's going to marry this evening. I think she really does love my brother."

"And he loves her. George proved that this morning. He practically went nuts with me before he finally reached Stacey to let her know he was okay and remind her that he does indeed love her. Anyway, like I said, we've got to go. I just dropped by to give you a belated kiss hello, and an 'I'll-see-you-later' kiss goodbye. So far, I've not only given you a belated kiss hello, but a let's-think-about-it-in-the-middle-of-it kiss!" Again Felix showed his perfect teeth in a laugh, to which Rachel did the same. "Well, guess which one this is."

And tightening the circle of the arms that had loosened around her waist slightly, Felix lowered his sexy slender lips against her luscious medium ones in one last claim, which though firm, was tepid, at best. Yet the kiss meant not to excite or arouse served only in doing just that, leaving Rachel's arms re-circling his neck heatedly, lips kissing him feverishly while his devoured hers with equal fire. And with this new heat of desire sparking a need to get under this man all over again, Rachel's head throbbed with a dull realization and the added insurance that the goodbye resulting after their most steamy I'll-see-you-later kiss was going to be a very reluctant one.

In fact, Felix expressed that same thought as he ended the kiss after a moment to gaze regretfully down at her. "A very reluctant 'I'll-see-you-later' kiss goodbye," he smiled, pushing slowly out of her arms. "Anyway, you do something about that hair of yours flying all over the place before it dries out like that. It'll be impossible to comb through then."

"I'll do that," Rachel promised, knowing he was speaking the truth and watching with one last smile as he curved a hand around the brass knob. Her smile broadened into a grin when he blew her one last smiling kiss before slipping out of sight on the other side of the door.

The grin remained on her lips as Rachel turned away from the white door Felix had closed behind his exit. He had said he'd see her later, which she knew he was going to do. Happily Rachel crossed the living room back to the work area, where she settled at the French Provincial desk and started the drying of her hair with the portable hair dryer she had set up there before Felix's arrival.

She had just turned off the hair dryer close to an hour later when the sound of knocking coming from the door alerted her to the fact that someone else was there to see her. Wondering if it was the maid having arrived to clean the suite while at the same time certain it couldn't be Felix again, Rachel removed the plastic bonnet from her head and let her fully dried hair spill somewhat tousled down over her cream shoulders as she moved to her feet to answer the knock.

Yet it was not the maid who stood on the other side of the white door she opened a second later but Rick, a black long-sleeved shirt and gray slacks covering his six-foot average frame, a smile curving his medium lips. Rachel smiled too—as his presence brought to memory her telling Felix a while before how she had been in Rick's hands the day before and Felix's response that she was going to be in his hands in the next second—which she had been literally.

"Hi, Rick," Rachel greeted the white man, smile on her lips broadening into a grin. "What brings you by to see me on this lovely wedding day of your sister and my brother?"

"I brought the pictures I took of you and Rochelle yesterday evening." The Alaskan-come-Hawaiian grinned too as he stepped past her on black-loafer-clad feet into the living room. "I thought I'd show you what that camera can do."

Rachel disregarded that last statement in her preference of responding to his first one as she closed the door behind the blonde's entrance into the suite.

"How'd you get that film developed so fast when you couldn't possibly have tended to it before this morning?" she asked curiously, her eyes on the couple of film packets he held in one hand. "Did you take it to a one-hour drug store, or a place like Kits Camera?"

"No, actually, I took it to my friend. He has a full darkroom at his studio. Besides, I had to take the camera back to him this morning, anyway. He only trusted me to keep it for twenty four hours."

"I see." An amused smiled shaped the soft curve of Rachel's lips at the irony behind the millionaire's implied lack of trustworthiness. Having followed him away from the door and back into the living room, she settled on the padded blue French Provincial sofa to the right of him. Her gaze lowered intently to the packets Rick held in his hand, her own raised to sweep a stray lock of long relaxed off-black hair carelessly over her shoulder and out of her way.

"You think that Sure Shot of yours is so hot?" Rick's mocking laugh forced her gaze to swing back to his face. "Here, take a look at these I shot with that Nikon D70 Digital SLR."

With her brown eyes narrowing on him in another curious look, Rachel watched as he slid the first set of 35mm prints from one of the two white packets he held on his lap. Rick handed them to her then, the glint in the blue eyes that had flashed back on her indicating his anticipation of her surprise.

And surprise was the right word. As Rachel took the prints into her hands and began slowly to flip through them, her eyes widened in amazement.

"See, what'd I tell you?" Rick prodded her with a smile as he admired the shots along with her. "It was cloudy after all that rain yesterday, yet see those colors? They practically jump out at you, don't they? And look at those images—not a blur in sight. Built-in speed light gives the perfect lighting for day or night shots at any film speed, whether portrait, sports, landscape, whatever. Automatic red-eye reduction, you can shoot anybody at any distance, plus with that camera's ability to shoot three frames a second and that buffer that allows you to shoot a hundred and forty four shots in sequence, it's almost like looking at a movie, isn't it, so fluidly does it capture the subject's movement."

"Yea, I see that," Rachel said as her gaze remained lowered to the prints in her lap. The pictures that slid through her fingers showed images that were sharp, hues that were clear, colors more vivid than a sunset. Plus the camera's ability to shoot sequence frames gave a movement to the still prints that was so realistic that it was just as Rick had said—as if you were looking at a movie. "Amazing!" she exclaimed as a word finally came to mind that expressed the incredulity she was feeling.

There was the first picture Rick took of her scowling at him in a look of disdain and amusement in the parking lot—amazing. Another one of her smiling in a gesture of amusement—this time a genuine one—exquisite. . . . A close-up of Rachel smiling yet again, showing every attractive tooth in her head—fabulous. . . . Rochelle displaying her own pretty smile—engaging. . . . Rachel holding opened the lapels of her tan leather coat in order to display the provocative curve of her breasts—seductive. Rochelle holding opened the lapels of her own white leather coat to display her bigger breasts—sinful. Rochelle throwing her matching white leather hat into the air Mary Tyler Moore style—every frame of its ascent and descent back into her hands. Rochelle leaning down in a pretense of pulling her stocking from her ankle all the way up one big leg and halfway up an even bigger thigh—every frame of the most sensuous movement captured by the fast-speed camera. Full-length shots of Rachel and Rochelle laughing—both together and apart—hilarious. . . . Shots of the two of them; sticking their tongues out at a stray dog that had wandered out onto the sidewalk. . . . Shots of them running in terror as the dog, the only animal that the Natives domesticated, an Alaskan Husky and incredibly an undomesticated unfriendly one at that, gave chase, not liking at all the way they had provoked him. Endless prints of Rachel and Rochelle snapped with them posing and laughing as they made their way running down West Fourth Avenue past a number of businesses—including Stewart's Photo Shop again—to the historic circa 1915 Wendler Building at the corner, where they looped right onto D Street past the Spelman Evan Downer North Pacific Mural juxtaposed across the street, the equally historic Kimball Building a block over and right onto West Fifth Avenue at the corner, where with the flower-filled lawns of the Town Center Municipal Park and the towering Westmark Hotel across the street from them, Rick ran out of film in front of the Egan Civic and Convention Center. And in all the color pictures made all the more vivid against their backdrop of cloudy weather, every frame—every frame taken of her and Rochelle—had been captured by the high-powered camera, leaving Rick admiring, Rachel staring.

"Amazing . . . !" Rachel repeated as she came to the last picture in her hands—a fetching full-length smiling color shot of her standing on D Street with the Chugach Mountain Range towering fabulously behind her in the distance. "I guess that camera is worth every penny of that $3,000 dollar price—including memory card and zoom lens!"

"I'm afraid it is!" Rick agreed with a laugh. "And by the way, before we get completely off the subject of your brother, let me show you how well that camera performed on the pictures I took at his bachelor party last night."

Lowering the last print in her hand to the stack on the sofa to the right of her, Rachel turned her gaze to the second set of pictures Rick was pulling from his lap.

"Girl, Rachel, baby, you are not going to believe the hijinks that went on at that place," Rick said amid sliding the prints from the white packet container they came in, as had the first set.

Rachel's gaze was momentarily diverted from the pictures Rick was about to show her and onto the thick features of his face as she picked up on the incredulity that had sounded behind his statement.

"The party wasn't that bad, was it?" she prodded with a smile despite already knowing that from what Felix had told her close to an hour earlier.

"Oh, yea, it got wild last night," Rick insisted with a grin that forced Rachel's gaze back to the prints he was displaying in his hands. "George got crazy! And so did Felix! He got really busy with your sister! I don't know how she came to be there, but she and her ex-flame got seriously busy in the bedroom! It appears that Felix still has a thing for her after all these years, after all!"

"Yea, I see that!" Rachel's lips curved in a smile of agreement as she continued to observe the prints Rick had pushed into her hands.

They were all there: Martin and Flip leering at a scantily-clad woman coming out of a cake, that same woman hanging all over George in the next picture, him laughing hysterically, George on the floor dancing the tootsie roll with another three. Martin and Flip; then cuffed in chains by two other skimpily-clad women. . . . Ray Marlboro doing the hustle with another and then drinking from the shoe of yet another: A.J. Over literally having sprawled over three other half-naked women stretched out on the floor in the next three; the two married men, Damon and Vic, fondling two others in the wrong places, all of them hookers, Rachel guessed. Last of all was Felix, all six-foot-one gorgeous inches of him stretched out on a bed in the bedroom, Devon in his arms all over him, him all over her.

"Amazing . . . !" Rachel prided herself on the control she maintained over her shock as she swept Rick with a second smile of agreement. After all, the thirty-year-old white man had no idea that she and Felix were secretly involved. She had no intention of reacting to the most incriminating evidence of Felix's disloyalty to her, choosing rather to blow it off as nothing. "That camera, I repeat: is worth every expensive cent your friend paid for it!"

"Isn't it . . . !" Rick agreed with a laugh. "But then, I told you it'd make that Sure Shot of yours look like a toy, didn't I!"

"I guess you did," Rachel responded to the teasingly uttered exclamation put in the form of a question in the same smiling manner.

The smile on Rick's own lips sobered as he patted her arm with a hand. "Anyway, I've got to get going, girl, Rachel, baby," he said regretfully. "My sister's getting married at four o'clock. What is it now—five after one?" A glance at the expensive gold watch on his left wrist confirmed the time. "That leaves us less than three hours to get ready. Besides, I've got to go see my Uncle Stevan. Dad told me he got in from Juneau last night—you know, when I wasn't here to see him."

"Now, that's a character," Rachel said as she recalled the white Native Alaskan older brother of Rick's father that Al Lumas had introduced her to that morning. "Your Uncle Stevan is something else. He bought me breakfast in the cafeteria and told me all about Alaska's capital city of Juneau where he's presently residing, and which you just mentioned." Deliberately Rachel did not tell Rick how his uncle had practically drooled all over her through most of the meal until her father had found it necessary to rescue her from the fawning man.

"Yea, it's been a while since I've seen the old man since I've been living in Hawaii." The smile meeting hers again turned regretful as Rick patted her arm a last couple of times before moving to his feet. "Anyway, I'm going to go visit Uncle Stevan for a while. Dad tells me he's down on the first floor." Rick began to cross the blue-carpeted living room floor away from her. "Anyway, I'll see you at the wedding. It's only in what—less than three hours!" he laughed from the door he neared then. "Okay, Rachel, baby?" he asked, turning back to look at her.

"Okay." Rachel returned his smiling look as he stepped through the white door he had opened with a last parting wave.

As she sat alone on the padded blue sofa with the door having closed behind Rick's exit a second later, her eyes lowered to the endless number of pictures of Felix and Devon that she still held on her lap, the smile falling immediately from her medium lips. Rachel did not think why Rick had left the most incriminating photos with her, nor did she wonder how Devon came to be at George's bachelor party the night before when no one had had previous knowledge of its location with the exception of Rick, A.J. Over and Flip Hart. Rachel did not think of how she and Rochelle had even called Rick a fool the night before for not having divulged even to them the most private location where the bachelor party was due to take place. Rachel did not even think why George would allow his own sister to be at his bachelor party, much less where he was while Devon was all wrapped up in the bedroom with his best man. All Rachel saw as she looked at the 35mm glossy color pictures was Felix. Felix kissing Devon.... Felix kissing her sister.... His mouth on her mouth, her face, her ear, her neck, her throat, his hands holding her hair out of his way.... Felix kissing her sister, his tongue practically down her throat, his hands all over her.... Devon's hands all over Felix as she kissed him back, both of them hugging. Hugging and kissing. Kissing, kissing. Felix kissing her sister—rolling Devon all over the damned bed.... With its built-in speed light, that sophisticated camera that Rick's friend had loaned him had provided just the right light to the dimly lit bedroom so that there was no mistaking the clear images projected on the pictures. Plus, with its three frame per second and sequence capabilities, the camera had captured every frame—every frame of Felix and Devon's most heated movements in sequence—until Rachel looked painfully away, unable to bear the thought of the obvious lovemaking that had resulted between them after that.

To think that Felix came to see her—what—an hour earlier—and yet he didn't say a word to her about having slept with her sister last night, Rachel thought. In fact, he'd actually mentioned the game that they were playing with Devon, a woman he had told her he was over. Yet apparently, that was not the case, for in the many pictures Rachel still held on her lap, Felix was all over Devon, alright, indicating just as Rick had said—that he was not over her, but still had feelings for his ex-flame after all those years after all. Rachel had not known how to handle all those new feelings and hot sensations Felix's kisses had roused inside her, never before having experienced them with another man, not even understanding what they were at the time. She had tried to run from Felix, too terrified by the intensity of them to remain in his company any longer. And yet Felix had grabbed her in the hallway, demanded if she was doing just that, reminded her that first Devon left him, now her, and then he had used an old tune called *'Little Sister'*, a classic from Elvis Presley—his favorite singer of all time—insisting that Rachel not do that. Employing the song title and part of its lyrics, Felix had called her Little Sister, told her not to kiss him once or twice, say it was very nice, and then run . . . not to do what her big sister done. He had told her he thought he was falling in love with her, that he was hung up on her; in fact, just an hour earlier, Felix had told her that he didn't want any other man getting over her, that the only man he wanted over her was him and that the only man's hands he wanted her to be in were his. Felix even kissed Rachel three times—each one heated in evidence of that fact—before leaving with the promise that he would see her later, even blowing her a fourth kiss—a parting one—from her door.

Yet Rachel would not be seeing Felix later. She could hardly stand the thought that all those new feelings and hot sensations his kisses had roused in her were born out of her intense love for the man. And yet Felix had lied to her, fooled her, duped her, almost used her, and it embarrassed Rachel to think how intently just a while ago, she had wanted to get under him in the same manner he had implied wanting to get over her. Well, Felix had best get over it, for he could not have both Devon and her at the same time, Rachel didn't care how well he was being paid to sleep with two sisters simultaneously on his soap—three as a matter of fact, if you added their mother. And small wonder Rachel had missed Devon at breakfast that morning—in fact, she had not heard from her older sister all day—no doubt because she was in her seventh-floor suite resting up after having slept in late thanks to her late night out the evening before literally sleeping with Felix. Well, now he could sleep with her all he wanted to, the thought as to just how completely the award-winning actor had performed with her leaving her numb all over as all the sensation drained from her body. The game was over, Rachel thought. Not as in A.J., but as in the one they had been playing with Devon. To think that Felix had even asked her himself if it were possible for a man to fall in love with a woman in three days. Rachel guessed it weren't after all, as apparently, just as she'd feared, Big Sister blew in from the South and caught him before he hit the ground. Felix was still hung up on her, Devon was still hung up on him, and she had chased him until they literally got hung up together. Well, now they could have each other, because as far as Rachel was concerned, it was over. Over. Over. Over. The game was over. . . .

She went through a vacuum as everything happened in a blur after that. The maid arrived ten minutes later, an Alaskan Native, an Aleutian woman, who chatted with her for the next forty minutes as she busied herself cleaning the large lavish, elegantly appointed blue-themed two-room suite. Yet Rachel barely heard what the friendly hotel employee said in her inattention and numbed state. She just did think to call a valet to come pick up her card and gifts for the bride and groom and take them to the meeting/banquet room where the reception would be held after the wedding about one forty five, and the dark-haired man arrived five minutes later. Then finally with the two o'clock hour having approached, Rachel left the maid to finish cleaning the suite while she took the elevator down to the women's fitting/dressing/powder room on the third floor, bridesmaid's dress and under slip slung over one cream sweater-clad shoulder, box of shoes tucked under one arm, removable strap of a beige leather clutch purse strapped over her other shoulder, having replaced the black one she usually carried for the occasion.

Diane Mortemburg was already in the large elaborate blue, beige and white themed combination women's sitting/fitting/dressing/powder room when Rachel arrived there seconds later. The attractive yet talkative twenty-six-year-old hazel-eyed woman embroiled her in immediate conversation. What did the woman say to her, Rachel wondered as she heard her speak through numbed ears? Something about being sorry for the blunder she made at yesterday's wedding rehearsal when she tactlessly blurted the private business surrounding Devon's divorce and unexpected arrival at the hotel to all and sundry, almost embarrassing everyone—including herself—in the process? And even worst: mention of that unexpected arrival, which had since put Rachel and Felix in the position of having to play a game with Devon in order to keep her in the dark as to their feelings for each other because Devon is Felix's ex-flame from ten years ago? And Diane knew that because she was standing right there at the front desk when you and Felix met for the first time in those ten years last Monday and Felix asked you if Devon was coming to the wedding, and you sadly had to tell him the same thing you told me—that Devon was in the process of getting a divorce and so wouldn't be able to fly out until next week, an affair Devon evidenced in the way she asked for Felix's suite number along with yours first thing upon her arrival last evening? And now, two days after the aforementioned divorce, she is trying to get him back? Something Diane saw with her own eyes in the aggressive way Devon came all onto Felix at the wedding rehearsal yesterday?

"Don't worry; you didn't blow anything between us, everything's still alright. Besides, everyone makes a mistake sometime or another. You were just being friendly and conversational, anyway. I guess that comes with your job in handling the front desk at a multi-million-dollar hotel the caliber of this one." Was that Rachel saying all that to her, already having expected the woman to put two and two together from what she'd heard and seen between Rachel and Felix on Monday, and Stacey to have filled in the blanks to her friend at the wedding rehearsal the day before about that very game Diane had mentioned, which Devon's unexpected arrival there on Thursday had forced them into playing with her? Well, apparently it was, as the tactful response she had smilingly uttered brought a pleased smile to Diane's own lips before the reservationist moved out of the sitting area and into one of six fitting rooms to change out of her street clothes and into her own bridesmaid's dress and shoes.

However, the smile fell quickly from Rachel's lips at the realization that she was going to have to keep up the lie she had just told Diane about everything being alright with her and Felix to Stacey, the bride-to be and her sister-in-law-to-be, as well as Rochelle, Rachel's new best friend. Her mind numbed all over again at the thought as to just how completely close-mouthed and dishonest she was going to have to be with the other woman when considering how completely open-mouthed and honest she had been with her at that restaurant just the afternoon before.

Rachel was just about to follow Diane into the fitting area when Rochelle came bustling into the sitting room carrying her own cellophane-wrapped bridesmaid's dress, under slip, box of shoes and her own beige leather purse and went straight for her. Dumping her load onto a plush velvet blue French Provincial sofa, Rochelle, who wore a stylish—what else—ecru pantsuit over her big-hipped—although straight—big-breasted figure, greeted her with a smile and a hug.

"How're you doing, girlfriend? This is the big day!" the amber-skinned twenty-six-year-old black Alaska Native said in her ear.

"Yes, it is." Rachel voiced the agreement with a somewhat wooden smile, as she couldn't return the older woman's hug because of the load she still carried in her own arms.

Aware of that, Rochelle pulled the cellophane-covered designer dress identical to hers from its slung position over her shoulder as well as the box of expensive shoes—also identical to hers—under slip and beige clutch purse from her shoulder, dumping all onto the sofa alongside her own.

"Come here, I have someone I want you to meet!" Curving a hand around her wrist, Rochelle pulled her in front of a man who had accompanied her into the large lavish sitting room. "Rachel, I'd like for you to meet Vern Denison," she introduced with a grin. "And Vern, I'd like for you to meet my new friend, Rachel

Hardison. She's Stacey's fiancé George's kid sister, and also a bridesmaid in the wedding—you know, like I told you."

"Ah, yes, how do you do, Rachel?" prompted Vern Denison charmingly, a hand proffered forward to shake hers in a friendly greeting.

Rachel couldn't help noticing that he had skipped the formality of addressing her by her surname as she proffered her own hand forward to shake his.

"How do you do, Vern?" greeted Rachel in turn, not needing to force an interest to her expression as she met the smile he had turned on her with her own. The man named Vern was tall, about six-three—were there any short men in Alaska—Rachel wondered for the second time in a couple of days? Dressed in a brown single-breasted suit a shade darker than his medium skin tone, a black shirt and a striped tie that contained both hues, Vern was a big man—but then, he had to be to fit up Rochelle—any smaller man and the voracious woman would devour him in five seconds. Yet though Vern wasn't wholly attractive—he had nice short-cut kinky black hair around an oval face, but his too strong nose, prominent cheeks and brow line seemed out of harmony with his too small drawn mouth and narrow brown eyes, his chin too angular. In fact, he looked like that cougar Rochelle had told her he resembled before they parted company the evening before. Except that he had the prettiest teeth, white, gleaming and not a filling in sight. Perfectly aligned with a gap—a baby gap between his two front central incisors. . . . The most precious gap Rachel had ever seen in a set of teeth. It was the most perfect smile she had ever seen—well, with the exception of Felix's. Rachel dumped thought of him immediately as in the space of two seconds she continued to smile at Vern, who she was quickly beginning to see also had the hands of that wolf Rochelle had told her about as he cupped his other hand over hers and pumped it in both.

"It's good to meet you," Rachel finished smoothly, pulling her hand from the cradle of both of his.

"It's good to meet you, Rachel," Vern repeated.

What all had Rochelle told her about Vern, anyway, Rachel wondered as she continued to return the man's charming smile? She had said she had met him a month ago when he had come to her dental office for a teeth cleaning. With his wolfish hands and perfect smile, Vern had quickly wangled a date out of her. He had taken her to dinner and a show, four hours during which he had been all over her, and they had barely been back at the door of her apartment before she had had him out of his clothes and in her bedroom, where she had had him, and she'd been having him ever since. Rachel didn't doubt the reason why as she continued to stare at the man who appeared to be about thirty, finding it no wonder Rochelle had been so explicit in her bedroom antics with him after the wedding rehearsal the day before and with a woman who was practically a virtual stranger to her.

"Rachel's got a hot thing going on with Felix Latham," grinned Rochelle, capturing both Rachel and Vern's attention then. "Felix is a serious fox and an actor on a soap opera, George's best man and best friend from the days they both lived in Georgia," Rochelle went on for Vern's benefit, the man smiling at her with new interest. "Of course, George and Rachel's sister Devon is here, too, also a bridesmaid in the wedding. Wait till you meet her, Vern, the woman's totally artificial. No offense, girlfriend," Rochelle said in a remorseless aside to Rachel.

"None taken," Rachel told her with a smile. After all, she could hardly expect the woman to be complementary about her older sister after all she'd told her the day before about her history with Felix and determination to get him back after having dumped him ten years ago. And she thanked God Rochelle possessed the tact not to go into the details of her whirlwind hot thing with serious fox soap opera actor best man Felix Latham, which she was unaware had become a cold thing due to Devon's determination to/and success in having done just that and gotten him back. Blood receded from Rachel's veins as the numbness returned.

"How are things with you and Mr. Fox?" Rochelle smiled then, unaware of the turmoil she was going through.

"Not bad!" Rachel forced a smile to cover up her total lie. *Oh, Rochelle*, she thought quietly, *Miss Artificial did it! She succeeded in getting back Mr. Fox, better known as Mr. Dog!* What was that hit tune the Baha Men performed when she and Felix were at that free concert at the University of Alaska at Anchorage Auditorium late Wednesday afternoon? *Who Let The Dogs Out? Who let that dog out?* Rachel continued to think silently to herself. *Somebody, come walk that dog!*

"I don't think I want to meet this Devon, this sister of Rachel that you say is so artificial," Rachel heard Vern saying disparagingly to Rochelle through dead ears then. Besides, you're the real thing, not to mention more thing than a man can handle. With the exception of me, of course," Vern finished with a roguish grin, wolfish hands going to the obvious places.

Rochelle pushed his hands away from her large bust-line with a laugh. "Get out of here, Vern. Rachel and I've got to get dressed. We've a wedding to be in in less than a couple of hours. Go down to the lounge, have a Shirley Temple, something nonsexual to take your mind off that outrageous sex drive of yours that I'll take care of later," Rochelle brushed him off with the dismissing wave of one hand.

"That's a promise I'm going to hold you to, baby." Assurance underlined his deep masculine tone as Vern turned smilingly away from her just as Devon entered the sitting room loaded down with her own cellophane-wrapped designer bridesmaid's dress, under slip, box of expensively-styled shoes, and purse. Vern slid only a cursory look over the dusky-skinned woman around his same age and who had a striking resemblance to Rachel, gorgeous as ever, but not enough woman for him. Dismissing her from his mind, Vern walked through the door past her, unaware that Devon stared after him in surprise, as she was not used to being brushed off by any man, whether out of her league or not.

Rochelle saw Devon's shocked look and thought her artificial as ever, knowing it was born out of vanity that a man such as Vern and a man she considered way out of her league had dismissed her—a woman as beautiful as her—considering her out of his league as well. Yet despite that, Rochelle's eyes flashed with interest as Devon came into the room, stopping finally in front of her and Rachel.

"How do you do, Devon?" Rochelle greeted with an engaging show of her teeth, proffering an ecru-sleeved arm forward to shake her hand. "We weren't formally introduced yesterday, but I'm Rochelle, Stacey's friend, also a bridesmaid in her wedding with your brother, George, along with you and Rachel. As a matter of fact, I'm in the line-up behind you and Flip Hart with Martin Rolf."

"Oh, yes." Devon forced a smile at the woman she had barely noticed at the wedding rehearsal the day before. "How do you do, Rochelle?" she asked smoothly, taking her amber-brown hand in her own, a darker dusky brown one. "And how are you?" Devon dropped Rochelle's hand immediately as her gaze slid curiously to Rachel. "Where were you all day yesterday afternoon and evening?"

And where were you all night, not to mention at breakfast this morning! Rachel demanded of her silently, though she darn well knew. Out sleeping with Felix at George's bachelor party, which explained also her absence from the cafeteria that morning. . . . She had skipped breakfast in preference of sleeping in—although Rachel hadn't known then that it was because of her late night out with said man. And Rachel couldn't help noticing that Devon's hair like hers was pulled up in a ponytail hanging from the top center of her head, all the curl that had been in it the day before gone out of existence. No doubt she had sweated that perm out last night humping the good looking sexy ex-flame she had been trying so blatantly to get back for the last couple days and finally gotten. Yet Devon did not know that her conquest of Felix had destroyed a hot thing going on between her and Felix. Or did she? Rachel wondered. After all, George had warned her. He had told her Devon was suspicious of something going on between her and Felix; in fact, Rachel had even told their parents that Devon was suspicious of her being the new woman Felix was having a fling with at the hotel. Yet again Devon did not know Rachel was aware of that. For that reason, Rachel forced a smile at her older sister, aware that Devon stood beside Rochelle patiently awaiting an answer to her last question.

"Rochelle and I were out with Rick," she said simply. Rachel knew that was a safe enough response. As far as Devon was concerned, Rachel liked Rick. After all, the man had been hanging all over her ever since meeting her two days ago. Not to mention that also, as far as Devon was concerned, Rachel thought Devon hated Rick. Hence, Rachel would certainly not suspect Devon of being out with him herself later on the night before in order to have appeared in all the pictures of Devon and Felix that Rick had snapped of the two of them at George's bachelor party. Aware of both facts as well, Devon forced a dismissive smile to her own lips before moving off to enter the fitting area with her armfuls, leaving Rachel standing in the floor feeling as hot as a volcano ready to spew molten lava.

Her eyes flashed onto Rochelle in surprise when she curved a hand around her arm suddenly, claiming her attention. She did not know that the turbulent thoughts she'd undergone throughout her entire confrontation with her sister had been seen clearly behind her large luminous brown eyes by her new best friend, who stood staring at her curiously.

"Hey, what's going on with you and Miss Artificial?" Rochelle demanded quietly.

Rachel pushed that sensation down immediately, determined to feel nothing. "Nothing," she said finally after having regained control of her outrage. "Come on, let's go get dressed. That wedding's not getting any farther away." And picking her dress, shoes and purse up off the padded blue French Provincial sofa, Rachel moved into the fitting area behind Diane and Devon, leaving Rochelle no choice other than to do the same.

A flurry of activity began as the time of the wedding drew closer. Rachel quickly slid out of her ribbed cream sweater, cream slacks, same color socks and white Nikes sneakers and into her beige under slip, designer bridesmaid's dress and beige vamped heels in one of the six cubicles, Rochelle doing the same in the one next to her. And there was the addition of beige pantyhose matching the color of the dress and shoes—a gift from the bride—to be pulled up the length of her long shapely dusky-colored legs. Another gift from the bride was diamond-studded earrings with three beige pearl drops dangling from their silver posts. Rachel thought them exquisite as she slid them through the holes in her ears, guessing they must have set Stacey back a couple hundred dollars—nothing to the multi-millionaire hotel owner. The earrings were accompanied by a matching necklace of glimmering diamonds and pearl drops arranged in the same sturdy silver setting that tied around her neck with an elaborate claw clasp; setting Stacey back another pretty penny—or in this case, at least five thousand of 'em, Rachel guessed. Stacey was there also, long brown hair having been swept up into a sophisticated chignon by the hairstylist she'd mentioned expecting to come see her at breakfast that morning, medium curving nails having been filed and painted a deep red by the manicurist whose arrival she'd also expected, face dotted with the same red lip color, moon rose blush, brown mascara and same color brow pencil; glittering white diamond eye shadow with a darker sand pencil shading the outer corners of her brown eyes giving her an ethereal beauty—all applied by the cosmetologist she'd expected also. And diamond-studded earrings with white pearl drops three sizes larger and probably that much more expensive than Rachel's own diamond-and-beige-pearl-drop arrangement shimmered from the holes in her ears and matched the equally larger, equally expensive and equally studded diamond-and-white-pearl-drop arrangement fitted into the same sturdy silver setting around her neck. Stacey was accompanied by three women attendants from the bridal shop who slid her into a long-sleeved white designer wedding dress with a V-neck and cinched waist, lace flower detailing all over it and a three-foot train flowing behind her from its flare ankle-length hem. And though the white woman was stout, every fleshy curve of her was poured seductively into that dress. George was going to have a feast when they got to—well, wherever they were going, Rachel thought absently, at present unable to recall the honeymoon destination Felix had reminded her of what—more than two hours earlier. Rachel quickly dropped him from her mind as she watched the three bridal shop attendants fit a long flowing white designer net veil that hung from a wide white satin beret fitted with the same flower lace detailing of Stacey's dress onto her head. Rachel did not want to think about him.

Stacey had told her at breakfast that morning that someone would be there to primp her up, as well as her other bridesmaids. Well, she had not lied, Rachel saw as two hairdressers, a manicurist and two cosmeticians—the manicurist and one of the cosmeticians that Stacey possibly may have employed earlier to tend to her own beautification—arrived five minutes later to make them up. Together the two women and man swept Rachel's long straight off-black hair up into a chignon as sophisticated as Stacey's, as did they Diane's shoulder-length brown hair and Devon's own slightly longer off-black hair while Rochelle's own short cheek-length straight black hair was filled with wispy curls all over. Black mascara was applied to all their lashes with the exception of those of Diane, to which the same brown color matching that of her own was applied, as was to Stacey's same-color brown lashes. For the same reason, brown pencil was applied to Diane's arching brows while a soft black defined the same-color arches of Rochelle, Rachel and Devon. An incandescent bronze shadow with a hint of glitter that brought out the beige color of their bridesmaids' dresses was applied to all their eyelids, a softer color outlining the shapes of their eyes while a coral pink blush was applied to their cheeks and a shimmering rose matching their eyeliner was applied to their lips. Finally, a glimmering rose just a shade darker was painted onto their nails as glossy and attractive as the shimmering-rose color brushed onto their lips.

Devon bubbled throughout the entire hairdressing, make-up arranging and nail painting like fizz rising from expensive champagne. She chatted endlessly about the similar preparations she and her bridesmaids underwent the mornings of her marriages to Dustin and Richard, smiling innocently all in Rachel's face and prompting her agreements. Rachel, having been a bridesmaid in both Devon's marriages somehow managed a monosyllabic response here and there, but she wasn't the least bit interested in anything her older sister had to say to her. Each excited utterance from her throat brought to Rachel's mind all those photos Rick had left her of Devon stretched out on that bed the length of Felix. Felix kissing Devon. . . . Devon kissing him. . . . Devon kissing Felix. . . . Felix kissing Devon. . . . All over him and him all over her! The two of them all wrapped up in each other's arms before they got hung up with each other in an even worst way, the final way. And while Rachel was at least grateful that Devon didn't go into the gory details of both husbands' philandering which had ended both marriages, she was so enraged at Devon that she could have spit on her! Again Rachel pushed that sensation quickly down, determined to feel nothing. Choosing to ignore her altogether, Rachel averted her bronze-shadowed eyes to the white-lace flowered satin shoes a bridal attendant was sliding on Stacey's beige stocking-clad foot while Devon chatted endlessly as Diane looked on in mere professional interest.

In front of her however, Brooke Dalene looked on at Devon in total fascination. At only five-four, the Alaska Native who was married to Vic Dalene shared the same long brown hair and short height as Stacey. But that was where the resemblances ended for unlike Stacey, Brooke's slender figure belied the fact that she had given birth to three children, the youngest of which was two and the oldest of which was six. In fact, it seemed that Stacey had another surprise—Damon Evans' two-year-old son Ortis who was in the large men's fitting/dressing room across the hall getting dressed for the wedding along with Damon, George and the rest of his groomsmen was going to be the ring-bearer in the wedding while Vic Dalene's six-year-old daughter Katarine would follow him up the aisle as flower girl. The girl named Katarine had just been helped into strapped beige shoes over lacy beige socks and a beige dress with the same beige net scarf detailing draped from the boat neck down to its cinched—although straight for her—waist as those of the bridesmaids by her mother, Brooke.

Yet Brooke could hardly tend to combing her daughter Katarine's shoulder-length same-color brown hair for watching Devon as she chatted. Noting the sexy figure that gave shape to the beige satin bridesmaid's dress she wore which flowed over the provocative swell of her breasts down to her cinched waist, around her curving hips and to the flare hem that stopped just below her beige stocking-colored shapely legs, one crossed seductively over the other, well-turned ankles supporting nice length of feet pushed into the beige vamped heels that matched her dress. Sliding back to her face, Brooke took in the diamond studs glimmering from Devon's ears with their triple beige pearl drops; two beauties in themselves. And then there was her relaxed long off-black hair presently pinned into a sophisticated upsweep, her black penciled brows, black mascara-lashed bronze-shadowed rose-lined large luminous brown eyes shining, coral-pink-blushed cheeks radiant, perfect teeth flashing behind shimmering rose lips, the prominent jawbones of her wide oval face giving her a sensuality that was potent. Brooke was amazed. Rachel was beautiful. But she knew exactly what the less attractive less endowed oval-faced white woman was thinking as she continued to watch her observe Devon out of the corner of her eye.

"Where do you and your sister get your looks?" Brooke then asked as her green gaze remained leveled on Devon's dazzling dusky beauty. "That woman is exquisite!"

Rachel forced a humorless smile to her shimmering rose lips before gazing quickly away at Rochelle seated in the blue padded makeup chair to the left of her. Hands manicured and polished with the same glimmering rose pink nail color as Rachel's draped over the chair's arms, eyes made up with the same incandescent bronze shadow, black brow pencil, black mascara and rose pencil liner as hers fixed on her intently, for though Rochelle made no bones about the fact that she did not like Devon, she had not missed Rachel's deliberate brush-off of Brooke's fawning flattery of her and her sister's good looks—especially those of Devon, artificial though she was—not even chancing a reply to Brooke's added praise of her as exquisite. Rachel knew immediately that just as before, Rochelle sensed an undercurrent going on between her and her sibling and was glad she looked away to laugh as Stacey spoke to her then, a sigh of relief sounding from Rachel's throat. Rachel knew also by that second suspicion of the bigger woman—although unspoken—that she was going to have to get control of her anger before she exploded and blew the entire day for Stacey—who thankfully just like Devon had been too busily and excitedly preparing for her and George's wedding in the time since her arrival at the fitting/dressing room to take note of Rachel's distress and distraction.

Yet inevitably, as Rochelle remained in joking conversation with Stacey and Diane, her gaze swept back to her older sister still chatting with the nail technician busy applying a top gloss coat to her medium-length curving rose-pink-painted nails. Felix had told Rachel that he never felt when he kissed Devon the way he felt when he kissed her; that in fact, he thought he was falling in love with her. But he hadn't kissed Devon in ten years. Felix was a twenty-one-year-old kid then. What did he know about love at such a young age? He was a thirty-one-year-old grown man now with experience in matters of the heart. And with what he must have built up in his mind after ten years of mourning the loss of Devon, he probably exploded when he kissed her, not to mention completely disintegrated when they made love. And Devon looked too complacent not to have given Felix the opportunity. Rachel knew she couldn't compete with that. Not when her looks—equally beautiful—were nowhere near as dazzling as her older sister's. Rachel looked painfully away as sensation returned, all the while cursing herself for having let Felix make such a fool of her.

She gladly looked up at the sight of Al Lumas entering the fitting/powder area, accompanied by his wife Dora. The tall white gray-haired Alaska Native in his early sixties who was dressed in a single-breasted black suit, white ruffled shirt, black bowtie and black shoes went straight for the center of attraction. His diminutive stout daughter stood resplendent in the long net veil, long-sleeved white V-neck wedding dress with its all-over lace flower detailing and three-foot train trailing behind satin heels in the middle of the blue-carpeted floor. The makeup and expensive diamond and pearl jewelry gave her a beauty and elegance Rachel could never have imagined the woman possessing upon her arrival in Anchorage five days ago. Small wonder George had fallen for such subtle beauty.

"Good afternoon; everybody!" Al Lumas grinned as he danced around the room. "The sun is shining, it's seventy three degrees outside; it's a perfect day for a wedding!" The six-foot man stopped dancing in front of his daughter, his grin softening into a smile. "Are you ready to marry this man?"

"Yes, I am, Daddy!" The exclamation came through slim grinning lips painted a deep red that Stacey had turned on her father.

Again Rachel noted with some delight that Stacey had completely gotten over the terrible wedding jitters she had displayed at breakfast that morning—in fact, they hadn't been in evidence in any of the hour and a half or so of her dressing and making up for the wedding along with her bridesmaids. Rachel noticed Dora Lumas was delighted also, as she stood smiling, face, hair and body likewise having been enhanced by attractive makeup and jewelry, her dress an exquisite lavender, the heels on her beige-stocking-clad feet a darker lavender that matched the clutch purse she carried under one arm.

"Then, let's go do it, girl," Al Lumas smiled, offering Stacey an arm.

"Let's do, Daddy!" Stacey agreed, proffering a moon-rose-blushed cheek forward for both parents to reward with a best wishes kiss while Rachel, Brooke, Katarine, Diane and Rochelle gave her hugs of best wishes and congratulations. Even the three bridal shop attendants, two hairdressers, two cosmeticians and nail technician proffered a hug for the bride-to-be. Devon, on the other hand, artificial as ever in Rochelle's opinion, stood smiling at a distance, too high-faluting to lower herself into giving her sister-in-law-to-be as much as a tepid handshake welcome into the family.

Chapter Eighteen

The grooms wore single-breasted designer tuxedoes of deep purple satin, a black bowtie pulled around the collar of an equally purple silk shirt under a black satin vest and purple socks pulled onto feet pushed into shiny black shoes. Rachel saw all that immediately as she, Rochelle, Diane, Devon, Brooke, Katarine and Dora preceded Al and Stacey from the women's sitting/fitting/dressing/powder room and into the stripe-paper-walled hallway. Trend Renolds and three other wedding coordinators waited to pair up each bridesmaid with her proper groomsman before lining them up in order of entrance and dispatching them to the wedding soon to start on the first floor. Already Damon Evans and Vic Dalene—George's two married friends—had been sent ahead of them—no doubt to seat the guests arriving for the wedding as Trend had quickly arranged for them to do the day before. George had been sent ahead as well—no doubt to take his place before the preacher to await his bride's entrance. Felix had been dispatched as well to take his place beside George as his best man, a realization Rachel was more than relieved to see because she didn't have to set eyes back on the lying dog! Rachel pushed that sensation of rage down immediately as she determined to feel nothing for the rest of the evening.

Two floral designers accompanied Trend Renolds and the three other wedding coordinators, a colorful array of flower bouquets and a blue basket of more flowers loaded onto two gray service carts, one of which was pushed by each of them. The bouquets—pastel arrays of ivory and peach roses, purple lisianthus, lavender statice, blue delphinium, pink carnations, yellow daisies and fern greenery—were wrapped in white ribbons which streamed down from a large bow. They were given to Rachel and the other bridesmaids while an even larger bouquet of same was pushed into Stacey's hands, the blue basket of flower petals of the same pushed into Katarine's. White carnations serving as boutonnieres were pushed into the provided buttonholes in the jacket lapels of the four remaining groomsmen, father of the bride and ring-bearer, Damon Evans' two-year-old son, Ortis. A purple satin-covered pillow on which set the most expensive set of gold-toned wedding rings Rachel had ever seen was given to the child as well. Despite determined to feel nothing, Rachel couldn't help staring as Ortis was quickly placed at the head of the line, not only because the adorable little boy was entrusted with such obvious wealth for his young age, but because she was utterly amazed that a suit, shirt, vest and tie equally identical and smartly designed as those of the groomsmen could actually be cut out and made to fit a child of his small size.

Damon Evans' wife Mariah, a tawny-skinned woman of medium height fussed endlessly over two-year-old Ortis, needlessly straightening his tie and smoothing his closely-shaved kinky black hair while Brooke did the same to daughter Katarine's own straight shoulder-length brown hair from her position in the line behind Ortis. With her white ribbon-wrapped bouquet of colorful and pastel ivories, peaches, purples, lavenders, blues, pinks, yellows and greens proudly displayed in one hand, Diane stood behind Katarine on the arm of Ray Marlboro, who barely noticed her for looking at Devon standing behind him bubbly as ever on the arm of Flip Hart, who barely noticed either of them for looking at Devon himself. Rochelle stood behind Devon and Flip on the arm of Martin Rolf, who barely noticed Rochelle for looking at Devon also. Last in line before Stacey on the arm of Al Lumas, Rachel stood on the arm of A.J. Over, who barely noticed her for gazing longingly at Devon equally!

Yet incredibly, as Trend Renolds and the other three wedding coordinators began to lead the lot of them to the elevator banks around the corner—including the two florists—the black man whose sex drive was bigger than the entire state diverted his attention away from Devon and onto her; Rachel guessed he'd decided settling for her as second best in the face of her dazzling older sister's more luminous beauty was better than nothing. For that reason, Rachel ignored him completely as he began to schmooze her as soon as they stepped into the elevator, one of three that had been called to transport the wedding party from the third floor—purposely aiming her gaze onto the emptied gray service cart still being handled by one of the florists occupying their elevator, wanting none of Devon's hand-me-downs, nothing from her sister. However, Rachel was hardly surprised when her indifference and lack of interest failed to get him off her; in fact, by the time they had arrived on the first floor seconds later, A.J. was as graphic in his come-ons to her as ever.

"You know, you look damned good in that dress—you look seriously good," A.J. was persisting with his flattery in a voice that only she could hear, brown eyes roving her curving figure in the beige designer bridesmaid's dress suggestively. "I can take you out of that dress in five seconds. In fact, after this miserable wedding and reception are over, why don't you take me up to your suite and let me get you out of that dress and everything under it? Then, let me get over you and get you under me?"

Rachel laughed at the oval-faced not unattractive purple-tuxedo-clad man despite herself as they pulled up down the hall along with the others behind Rochelle and Martin.

"Are you still on this over me/under you thing? From what I heard, you got over three women at George's bachelor party last night and certainly don't need to get over another one. So, will you please, get over me?"

Picking up on her last usage of the word in the vernacular, A.J. allowed his shameless gaze to slide away from her and longingly back onto Devon standing in front of Martin and Rochelle on Flip's arm.

"I want to get over your sister," A.J. said.

"Everybody wants to get over her," Rachel responded dryly, using the word in the same literal way he had intended. With the exception of Vern Denison, apparently. . . . And she wished the rest of them would get over it as she averted her own gaze away from A.J. and onto Stacey positioned behind them on the arm of Al Lumas. The white woman stood glowing, the light in her brown eyes thankfully too bright to notice the pain in the brown of Rachel's own eyes that she had deliberately blinded from her all afternoon.

The smile broadened on Stacey's deep-red-painted lips as she was kissed on one moon-rose-blushed cheek by Stevan Lumas, whose footsteps had been muffled by the rich blue carpeting covering the corridor floor, his approach on her unexpected.

"How're you doing, baby?" grinned Stevan as he pulled slightly away from her, though maintaining a hand over her arm, the hand of which was curved around the green floral-wrapped stem of her wedding bouquet. "You ready to marry this man?"

"Yes, I am, Uncle Stevan!" Stacey grinned in response to the same question her father had asked her before they all had descended from the third floor. Her twinkling glittery white-shadowed brown gaze lingered on her uncle, whose paunchy six-foot frame like her father's fitter one was covered in a white shirt, the collar supporting a black tie matching the same color of his smart single-breasted black suit and shoes.

Averting his blue gaze away from her, Stevan let it settle on Al in a look of equal delight, though threaded with slight regret.

"Well, I'm sorry, old man, but it looks like you're about to lose one!" Stevan laughed.

"Well, don't you think it's about time?" Al bit back with his own incredulous half laugh. "Your kids have been married with kids of their own for years now. You've been a grandpa forever. It's about time one of mine got married and gave me and Dora some grandkids of our own. Besides, I've been waiting for Rick to get married for the last ten. He's tall, he's healthy, and for the last six, he's been rich as hell. What the hell is he waiting on?!"

"I think she arrived on Monday!" said Dora Lumas with a rose-lipped grin from her position to the right of Al. Her lavender-shadowed brown eyes twinkled onto Rachel in a deeply meaningful look, although Rachel ignored it and her insinuation as her eyes remained leveled intently on Stevan. It had surprised her to hear Al say he was a grandfather. Though the Native Alaskan had flirted with her that morning, bought her breakfast and then told her everything he knew about his present residence of Juneau in order to impress her, he had not bothered to tell her whether he was married or divorced nor whether he had children or not, nor had she bothered to ask in her complete lack of interest in the man forty years too old for her. Although Rachel guessed he must either be divorced or widowed to be attending his only niece's wedding alone. She wondered how many children and grandchildren he had and where they were to not be attending their cousin's wedding along with him. Or were they already gathered in the meeting room in wait of it?

"I have three sons, two daughters, same number of daughters- and sons-in-law, two grandsons and two granddaughters, all of whom should have arrived for the wedding by now," Stevan answered with an anticipatory grin as he saw her look.

"I see!" Rachel's own lips curved in a grin as she slid a veiled gaze over Stacey and Al respectively. She thought the six-foot blue-eyed gray-haired man obvious and often too talkative for his own good, yet in the two days since meeting her and despite the excitement he had displayed in anticipation of introducing her to his older brother, the Native Alaskan had not once said a word about his marital status nor number of children and/or grandchildren. Nor had Stacey in the week she had known her mentioned a word herself about having so many cousins, cousins-in-law and second cousins.

"Of course, my wife left me five years ago," Stevan's somewhat self-mocking tone reclaimed her attention then. "I guess I wore the bitch out!"

Rachel laughed outright at the joking slur he had made about his ex-wife, especially with Trend Renolds and the three other wedding coordinators in hearing distance still fussing over them.

"That's terrible—!" she exclaimed, again finding him more obvious than his younger brother.

"Isn't it . . . !" Stevan agreed, dropping his hand from Stacey's arm to step forward and curl a black-clad arm around her beige-clad shoulders. "You want to be my woman tonight?" asked the white man with a grin.

"Sorry, man, she's my woman!" negated A.J. to the white man, slapping his arm off her shoulders with his right hand and tightening the hold his left arm was maintaining on her right in a proprietorial action.

Rachel diverted her eyes away from the suggestive grin the black man had also turned on her and onto Rochelle standing in front of her arm-in-arm with Martin. The knowing look that met her cursory one told her exactly what the larger amber-skinned woman was thinking. Rachel was not Stevan's woman, A.J.'s woman nor Rick's woman, as Dora Lumas had so insinuated a while ago. She was Felix Latham's woman, Mr. Serious Fox! Rachel looked purposely away from Rochelle, sensation again dead, not wanting to think about Mr. Serious Dog!

Unaware was she as she did so that Devon had turned around at Stevan's mention of the word bitch, claiming his attention immediately. Moving away from Rachel's side, Stevan neared her older sister, mouth hanging open in shock.

"And who's this!" Stevan demanded in a voice ringing with equal shock, question claiming the attention of Brooke and Flip, both also having turned around at his mention of the word bitch.

Rachel reacted somehow out of her numbness and dead paralysis, not wanting that bitch to steal Stacey's thunder on this: her most special day, certainly not when she didn't want to blow up and steal it herself, sending it crashing down from the sky in every direction. Pulling her arm from the tight clinch of A.J.'s before Al Lumas could step from behind her and gush all over her sister as he had done to his brother in the cafeteria that morning, Rachel moved quickly forward and slid her arm over Stevan's black-clad shoulders, bouquet of flowers still held in her left hand.

"Stevan, this is my older sister, Devon McClintock," she began with a forced smile at the woman who shared her same full figure and dusky coloring, although more sensual looks. "And Devon, this is Al's older brother and Stacey's Uncle, Stevan Lumas."

"How do you do, Mr. Lumas?" Devon's own smile was genuine as she raised the free arm she had pulled from under Flip's to extend her hand to shake that of the white man, already having anticipated his shock at her commanding beauty.

"Holy Father . . . !" Stevan exclaimed as he continued to stand staring at her in amazement while in front of Diane and Ray Marlboro, Brooke still stood fussing over Katarine's hair, doing the same. "Or should I say Holy Mother! My God, Al was right. You are the most gorgeous creature I've ever seen!" the man went on, a slow grin beginning to slide onto his face as he raised his hand to shake hers. "Oh, and please, by the way, call me Stevan! And how do you do, Miss McClintock? Or is it Mrs.? Well, whatever it is, may I call you Devon? Look at that—you're Devon, I'm Stevan! We're Devon and Stevan! Our names rhyme!" the aged Native Alaskan gushed as if the thought had never occurred to him despite earlier mention of her name to him by the brother he had just referred to. "Forget your sister—why don't we see what else we can make together tonight, such as time?"

Devon's shimmering rose smile saddened as she continued to return Stevan's suggestive blue-eyed gaze in a look that translated to Rachel exactly what she was thinking. Although she was flattered by the man's interest, Devon knew there was nothing she could do for the grayed man in his mid-sixties except the same thing she could do for her seventy-year-old attorney Angel and that was give him a heart attack. Rachel dropped her arm away from Stevan's shoulders immediately, no longer finding anything amusing in the thought.

The gaze she had flashed away from both him and Devon settled in surprise on Thacker Muldoon as he suddenly approached her group from the men's room down the elegantly blue, brown, rust and autumn gold stripe-paper-walled corridor. Rachel forced a smile back to her lips as the octogenarian stopped at her side after having given Stacey a congratulatory hug, smile having broadened on his own lips in delighted recognition of her.

"Hi, Rachel," Thacker greeted in his low-range exuberant tone, at the same time curving black-sleeved arms around her shoulders in a congenial hug while taking care not to crush the colorful bouquet of ribbon and flowers she held in her left hand. "How's George? Like Stacey, in there standing in waiting anticipation for the wedding?"

"I guess so." Rachel matched her tone to the friendliness of his as she watched him gesture the meeting/banquet room just in front of them.

"How're things with you and Felix?" persisted the dark-toned man with a smile.

"Not bad," Rachel lied, smile on her own lips becoming uneasy, as she hoped Devon had not overheard the old man's casual mention of Felix's name.

However, her smile became forced again as Thacker's gaze slid away from her and onto Devon, as her attractive laugh in response to something Ray and Flip had said to her claimed his attention then.

"Oh, my God, who is this woman?!" Thacker demanded in the same exuberant voice that did not quite match his age.

With Stevan Lumas apparently having moved graciously off into the meeting room after Devon's rejection of him, Rachel stepped numbly forward to introduce her to Thacker. Rachel knew she was going to reject him in the same way. After all, the only man Devon was interested in was Felix Latham! Rachel tried not to think about that as she tapped her sister on a dusky arm while at the same time fighting back the wave of revulsion she felt at having to touch her.

"Devon," she began after having reclaimed her attention, smile back on the same shimmering-rose-painted medium lips identical to hers, "I have someone else I want you to meet. This is Thacker Muldoon, a historian of the area and friend of George and Stacey. And Thacker, this is mine and George's sister, Devon McClintock."

"How do you do?" inquired Devon dryly, unaware that Thacker was married as she rejected him the same way she had done Stevan and returned her attention to the joke she had been sharing with Ray and Flip.

Yet despite that, Thacker continued to stand beside Rachel staring after Devon in amazement. "Oh, good God, is that your sister?" came the predictable response from the old man. "Well, I guess looks do run in your family! That woman is gorgeous! I'm eighty eight years old! I don't think I can handle this! I feel a mild cardiac infarction coming on! I'd better go find my wife!"

Rachel stared in utter rage as she watched Thacker's black suit-and-tie-clad wizened little body move in the direction of the meeting/banquet room a short distance beyond her. Only two days ago, he had told her during her and Felix's visit to his South Anchorage home after asking her if she wanted to be his fifth wife that he'd better leave her alone, that he didn't think he could handle all of her, that she'd probably give him a heart attack, and she knew he had been speaking literally because with her looks and body, she could. Felix hadn't forgotten hearing him say that; in fact, only moments later in that visit with Thacker, Felix had suggested that Rachel crawl into his lap and give *him* a heart attack. Yet Thacker had just told her that her more beautiful older sister *was* giving him one, literally speaking. And to think how Felix had been speaking to her in the figurative sense, yet it was Devon who was giving him one in the literal sense, jealousy returning as memory of all those incriminating photos taken at George's bachelor party showed Felix in the heated throes of her doing just that! Again Rachel pushed that sensation down immediately, determined to feel nothing for the lying man!

With the sound of background music coming from the meeting/banquet room indicating the start of the wedding, Rachel moved back into her position in the line behind Rochelle and Martin, linking her right arm around A.J.'s left at the same time. The sex-crazy thirty-one-year-old black man was all over her, but Rachel fairly ignored him as she faced front in waiting anticipation of the wedding that was due to start in a few minutes. A glimmer of guilt flashed immediately from the brown of her glittery incandescent bronze-shadowed eyes as her straight-forward gaze settled on Rochelle who had turned around in front of her, her own incandescent bronze-shadowed brown eyes fixed on her curiously. Rachel knew then that she had witnessed her quiet rage upon being forced to have to introduce Stevan Lumas and Thacker Muldoon to her older sister, a quiet rage which had heightened into utter fury when the two old men had insulted her by gushing over Devon's more sensual beauty with Stevan telling Devon that she was the most gorgeous woman he had ever seen and Thacker saying the same thing to Rachel in a matter of seconds. But that shouldn't have bothered Rachel when considering she wasn't the least bit interested in those two old men any more than Devon was. So gorgeous Devon must have done something to come between her and the man she was interested in, Felix Latham, Mr. Serious Fox! But Rochelle had a high opinion of the good looking Daytime Emmy Award-winning soap actor. That explained why Rachel had become saddened at the realization that she was going to have to keep up the lie she had told Diane two hours ago about everything being alright between her and Felix to both Stacey and Rochelle, her mind numbing all over again at the added thought that she was going to have to go through the entire wedding practically close-mouthed and dishonest to the woman like a close friend to her that she had been so open-mouthed and honest with about that everything-that-was-alright between her and Felix at that restaurant the day before. Rachel had no desire to lessen Felix's esteem in Rochelle's eyes by confiding the fact that everything was no longer alright between her and Felix because he had lied to her; that in fact, Miss Artificial had chased him until she caught him; that Mr. Fox was in second fact, a dog, a son-of-a-bitch, an asshole, a mutha! Quickly she averted her gaze away from Rochelle and onto a distant wall display, leaving Rochelle no choice other than to turn around and face front herself, again linking her arm around the purple-sleeved one of Martin Rolf.

Trend Renolds took center stage along with the three wedding coordinators as they began to talk to them about the timing of their imminent entrances into the meeting room. Ortis the ring-bearer would be dispatched promptly at four o'clock and given ten seconds to walk down the aisle and file in line to the right behind the best man. Katarine would follow him, taking another ten seconds to walk slowly down the aisle dropping her flower petals before filing to the left at the preacher's right. Diane and Ray would follow an additional ten seconds later to be followed by Devon and Flip five seconds later, Rochelle and Martin an additional five seconds later, Rachel and A.J. a last five. Each bridesmaid would file to the left behind Katarine at the preacher's right and each groomsman to the right behind the ring-bearer—all of same of which Trend Renolds had shown them at the rehearsal the day before. And then ten seconds later Stacey would enter on Al's arm and the two would file down the aisle, where Al would stop her at George's left and take a seat on the front row along with Dora Lumas. With the nearness of the wedding imminent, Dora gave Stacey one last smiling hug and a kiss on her cheek before leaving to enter the meeting/banquet room, as did Mariah Evans and Brooke Dalene after doing same to their children and moving off behind her.

With the playing of the Wedding March on a piano at four o'clock promptly five minutes later symbolizing the start of the wedding came the dispatching of Ortis Dalene into the meeting room by one of the three wedding coordinators accompanying Trend Renolds, some white woman named Arian. Katarine was dispatched ten seconds later, also by Arian, and then Diane as Maid of Honor with her ribbon-wrapped floral arrangement held proudly in front of her followed ten seconds later on the arm of Ray Marlboro. Devon and Flip followed five seconds later dispatched by another wedding coordinator, a black man named Crusoe, Rochelle and Martin following five seconds later, also by Crusoe. Rachel followed on the arm of A.J. a last five seconds later by the third wedding coordinator, a white man named Tehran. The large blue, brown and beige meeting/banquet room had been turned into an elaborate church, with ribbons of purple and white having been strewn from one attractive row of blue padded seats to the next down either side of the aisle; floral sprays matching the bridesmaids' bouquets had been woven into the threads of ribbon from every other end seat and flowers covered the raised stage at the front of the room, where a black male pianist continued with his playing of the Wedding March. The room was filled to the brim with well-dressed guests, at least more than a hundred—but then Stacey had said the wedding was going to be a small but elegant affair. And indeed it was, Rachel thought as her incandescent bronze-shadowed gaze glittered over her mother and father sitting on the right front pew proudly watching her come up the aisle with A.J., same way they had undoubtedly just watched Devon on the arm of Flip. And photographers were busy taking pictures; in fact, that was why Rachel had not thought to bring her camera—she knew there would be plenty of picture-taking by the photographers George and Stacey had hired in no small quantity. Yet as Rachel continued to saunter slowly up the white-covered aisle on A.J.'s arm to the most beautiful arrangement of the Wedding March by the male pianist, she deliberately did not look at Felix. Deliberately she did not allow herself to see how the stylish cut of the designer deep purple satin tuxedo up-played the tapering lines of his manly physique. Deliberately she did not allow herself to notice how terribly good looking and sexy he was—wanting to remember nothing of the hot passionate kisses they'd shared earlier in the afternoon, determined to feel nothing for the man. Instead, Rachel shifted her eyes onto George standing before the Reverend Adomi Claymon. George looked positively resplendent in the designer purple satin tuxedo, a proud smile on the well-hewn full lips so like their father's, which he had probably displayed when Devon walked up the aisle on the arm of Flip Hart ten seconds sooner. Dropping her arm from the curve of A.J.'s as they stopped in front of him, Rachel forced the numbness from her lips long enough to return her brother's smile before filing to the left to take her place behind Rochelle, A.J. filing to the right to take his behind Martin.

And then the attractive playing of the Wedding March by the black pianist became an even more elaborate arrangement, causing all guests in attendance to move respectfully to their feet as the bride-to-be then entered on her father's arm. Stacey looked as resplendent as George in the long-sleeved V-neck form-fitting designer wedding dress with its all-over flower lace detailing, flare hem and three-foot train dragging gracefully across the white-runner-covered aisle behind her. The equally lacy net veil that fell below her hips had been pulled over her face, although its sheer coverage in no way concealed the glittering majesty of her expensive diamond and white pearl drop necklace glimmering in a circle around her throat. The white of her wedding gown, shoes and jewelry made a stark contrast against the black of Al Lumas' suit and of course, photographers were busy taking pictures of the main attraction. But Stacey barely noticed any of them as Al stopped her at George's side, raising her veil from her fetchingly made-up face to give her one last congratulatory kiss on one moon-rose-blushed cheek. The music stopped as Al took a seat on the front row to the left of her beside Dora Lumas and Rick while all other guests followed his lead in resettling in their own.

Like his father and uncle, Rick had also changed into a designer black suit over a crisp white shirt, around which was placed a bias-striped silk black tie; black shoes on his feet. The wealthy white Alaska-born-Hawaiian had been flirting with her ever since she had fallen into the bridesmaids' line behind Rochelle before Stacey entered on the arm of their father. Rick did that now though Rachel ignored him and averted her gaze to the ceremony about to get underway, causing Rick momentarily to do the same.

Dressed in a black robe—the color of which seemed to dominate the meeting/banquet room-turned-chapel with the exception of the beige-dressed bridesmaids, white-dressed bride and purple-tuxedo-clad groom and groomsmen, Reverend Adomi Claymon started the wedding with the usual 'Dearly Beloveds' to George and Stacey, both holding hands, listening intently. And then the black man who was in his early fifties went into a long spiel about the sanctity of marriage followed by a discussion about the circle of the rings being continuous and therefore having no end and incapable of being broken, the same as should apply to the marriage vows.

A prayer followed that was led by an Alaska Native and old friend of Al Lumas succeeded by another Native who possessed one of the most fabulous soprano voices Rachel had ever heard and who sang *Kisses Sweeter Than Wine* and *Wherever You Walk*. Some Indian woman, a Dena'ina Athabascan, according to the blue cursive-scripted white program Rick showed her from his front-row seat just to the right of her. Rachel recalled Felix telling her all about the tribe as they'd lunched on a slope of the upper Eklutna Valley below East Twin Pass during their visit to Chugach State Park on Wednesday. He had said that Eklutna Historical Park on the other side of Glenn Highway across from Chugach State Park was established by an Alaskan Native Corporation, Eklutna, Inc. around 1990 to preserve the disappearing lifestyles of the Dena'ina Athabascan Indians in South-central Alaska; that in fact, the Dena'ina Athabascan Indians had encountered the white man in the late eighteenth century through the explorations of Vitus Bering and Captain James Cook. Hearing that woman singing served only in reminding her of how sweetly informative Felix had been with her that day when considering how unpalatably bitter he had turned out to be little more than two days later. Rachel didn't need that memory and spent the entire fifteen minutes of the Dena'ina Athabascan Indian's singing listening through numbed ears and staring through numbed eyes at the vamped beige heels covering her feet as numbed as the rest of her.

Everything happened in a blur after that as Rachel stared from a continued state of numbed shock. The Native woman's singing came to an end, as did the beautiful piano accompaniment Rachel had heard through numbed ears and then followed Stacey's vows to George and George's to Stacey. A setting aside of her large flower bouquet to Maid of Honor Diane followed as Stacey slid an expensive gold man's wedding band around George's finger and George slid the equally expensive gold woman's wedding rings carried by ring-bearer Ortis and handed to him by best man Felix onto Stacey's finger. Then Reverend Claymon was pronouncing them as husband and wife and telling George that he could kiss his bride. Stacey lifted her veil from her face; she and George kissed lovingly. Then with the flash of cameras endlessly in evidence behind them, they raced happily down the white-covered aisle while the ending of the Wedding March played beautifully by the pianist signified that the ceremony was over.

The feel of Rick's hand curving over her arm claimed Rachel's attention a split second before he pulled her fully into his arms, program abandoned to his seat.

"Well, congratulations, girl, Rachel, baby, your brother's now married to my sister! What the hell does that make us?" Rick demanded with a laugh over the rush of voices spilling out around them.

"In-laws . . . !" Rochelle interjected with her own laugh as she turned around to take both of them into congratulatory arms.

"And maybe even strange bedfellows!" Dora Lumas grinned as she moved to her feet in front of them, as did Al and the rest of talking and laughing guests beginning to depart the large meeting/banquet room-turned-church.

"Well, Mama, I hope not that strange! Intimate will be quite alright!"

Rachel deliberately ignored the last remark Rick had half whispered in her ear as she saw the knowing look come into the brown eyes Rochelle still had turned on her. Only minutes before the wedding, Dora Lumas had insinuated that Rachel had arrived in Anchorage for her son and both she and Rochelle had ignored it because they had known better. Except that it was no longer because she was interested in Felix as a love object of which Rochelle was still of a wrong assumption. . . . In proof of that, a glance beyond Rochelle showed that Devon had fled past Diane and rushed into Felix's arms, her own and hands all over him while he tolerated her in what he thought Rachel would assume as the game they were playing with her. Except that with all those graphic photos of Felix kissing Devon all over and rolling her all over that hotel bed, Rachel was no longer playing. The game was over. . . .

Rachel hoped Rochelle would assume it to be the same as she turned around in front of her to move toward the aisle along with her and the Lumases, only to find Devon on the opposite side of the aisle hanging all over Felix like a wall decoration. Devon was so aggressive in her attentiveness to him and Felix so eating it up like a lapdog that Rochelle turned an incandescent bronze-shadowed gaze on Rachel that questioned her tolerance of her. Pulling out of the look immediately, Rachel moved out from under the arm Rick had curved around her shoulders to greet her parents as they moved into the aisle in front of her past Felix and Devon.

They were both appropriately dressed for the occasion, Marshall wearing a dark blue suit over a pale blue shirt, a bias-striped silk tie that alternated both hues, shiny black shoes covering dark blue sock-clad feet. Sephora wore a pinstriped suit dress of black alternating with the same lavender color of Dora Lumas' dress that showed off every curve of her still attractive figure, the lavender heels she wore over suntan-stocking-clad feet matching the clutch purse she carried under one arm. Like Rachel's own long hair, Sephora's shoulder-length barely grayed hair had been swept up into a French twist, lavender and black stone earrings pushed through the holes in her ears, the same of which comprised the choker tied around her neck. Lavender ice shadow colored the lids of her black-mascara-lashed luminous brown eyes, mauve blush brushed across her cheeks, lilac lipstick on medium lips, the spring colors contrasting against her dusky skin tone and adding to the fifty-eight-year-old woman's ageless beauty. The lilac lips were curved in a smile at her, as were the well-hewn fuller ones of Marshall, the sixty-one-year-old suntan-skinned salt-and-pepper-haired man as good looking as Harry Belafonte any day. Ignoring the rush of voices coming from the other groomsmen chatting and laughing behind Felix and Devon, Rachel took both parents into her arms as well as the pastel bridesmaid's bouquet she still held in her left hand would allow.

"Hi, Mom, and Dad . . . !" Rachel's shimmering rose lips were curved in a grin as she felt them both reciprocate her embrace, her mother having taken her lavender clutch leather purse from under her arm and into one hand. "Looks like you've lost another one!"

"Well, it's about time!" Marshall rushed out with a laugh that barely wreathed his oval face in age lines. "Especially after all the women George dated before moving over here five years ago!"

"You've got that right!" Rachel's own laugh was one of agreement as he and Sephora dropped their arms from her waist at the same time she dropped hers from their shoulders. It was the second time since arriving in Anchorage on Monday that Rachel recalled all the 'honeys' George had dated during his teens to early-to-mid-twenties before relocating from Georgia to Alaska at twenty six.

However, her laugh dwindled into a frown when Sephora curved her free hand back around her arm suddenly, yanking her halfway down the aisle just as Rick Lumas had stepped forward to shake that of Marshall in friendly welcome into the family.

"And while we're on the subject of time, when are we going to lose you?" asked Sephora with her usual forthrightness, lilac medium lips curved in a grin.

Rachel picked up on her mother's pointed use of the word lose and averted her made-up gaze to Vern Denison as he stood flirting wolfishly with Rochelle farther up the aisle, apparently having approached her from the fifth-row left-aisle seat he had occupied during the wedding. Rachel did not know how to tell her mother just how literally the word 'lose' applied to her. Sephora would not be losing her to Felix as a possible marriage prospect because she had 'lost' him to Devon in a game that was over. . . .

The sight of George and Stacey moving back into the door of the meeting/banquet room-turned-church then brought a relieved smile to Rachel's lips. Quickly moving away from Sephora, Rachel approached the newlyweds in a need to congratulate both as well as evade her mother's last question that she didn't have an answer to.

"Congratulations, my brother!" Rachel's smile brightened into a grin as she curved her arms around his purple-tuxedo-clad shoulders as well as the floral bouquet she still held in her left hand would allow. "How does it feel to be a thirty-one-year-old married man?"

"Wonderful!" George's eyes were as bright as his perfect smile as he slid a deep-purple-sleeved arm round the white-wedding-dress-clad waist of his new wife. Beside him, Stacey stood shining like a new nickel. Or in this case a silver dollar.

"And how are you, Stacey Hardison, my new sister-in-law? Congratulations, best wishes, and welcome to the family—you know, all that stuff!" Despite the fact that Rachel's laugh was genuine, she deliberately veiled the gaze she turned on the woman as she moved past George to curve her arms over her white-clad shoulders, again hugging her as much as both the large wedding bouquet Stacey still carried in front of her and the smaller one Rachel still carried in her own hand would allow.

"Thank you, new sister-in-law, Rachel!" Stacey showed her well-aligned pretty little teeth in a delighted grin as she happily returned her hug while at the same time accustoming herself to the sound of her new name that Rachel had so naturally forced mention of.

They were all there to congratulate the newly married couple after that—Maid of Honor Diane; Rochelle and Vern Denison; Al, Dora and Rick Lumas; A.J., Flip, Ray and Martin; Vic and Brooke Dalene, and Katarine, six, the flower girl, a son, four, and another daughter, two, the latter two of which had been watched before the ceremony by Brooke's mother, Qrona. Sephora and Marshall Hardison to offer son and new daughter-in-law best wishes again. Damon and Mariah Evans, Ortis, two, the ring-bearer, and a five year old, another son. . . . Thacker Muldoon and his wife Sanya (a very unattractive forty). . . . Stu Giddian, the assistant manager and his wife and two sons and two daughters; Stevan Lumas with his three sons and three daughters-in-law, two daughters and two sons-in-law, his two grandsons and two granddaughters, all Stacey and Rick's cousins and second-cousins. And there were Felix and Devon. She was hanging all over the tall attractive sexy deep-purple-tuxedo-clad man like a picture on a wall as he attempted to take his best friend and his new bride into a best wishes hug. Rachel numbed the sensation of fury from her body and gazed purposely away in the distance, again determined to ignore both of them.

Even her inner sigh of relief was a numbed one as a couple of photographers called everyone to gather at the front of the 'church' for pictures then and in fact, they took many. Starting with the newlyweds in their designer wedding finery, George and Stacey, smiling. . . . George and Stacey with his parents, Marshall and Sephora, smiling. George and Stacey with her parents, Al and Dora, smiling. . . . George with his family, smiling. Rachel stayed as far away from Devon in that shot as possible. Stacey with her family, smiling. George and Stacey with both sets of parents, smiling. . . . George and Stacey with both their families, smiling. . . . Again Rachel stayed as far away from Devon in that shot as possible, Rick hanging all over her. George with his seven groomsmen—including best man, Felix, smiling. . . . Stacey with her bridesmaids, smiling. . . . Rachel stood to the left of Rochelle who stood at Stacey's immediate left, again as far as she could get from Devon standing to the right of Diane at Stacey's immediate right. A shot of George and Stacey taken with the entire wedding party minus their parents and Rick, where again, Rachel stood at the far right side of the line as far as she could get from Devon and Felix, she still hanging all over him from his immediate right. A shot of George and Stacey, the entire wedding party and both sets of parents and Rick, smiling. . . . And again, the wealthy white Alaska-born Hawaiian hung all over Rachel from her far right side of the line while at the far left side of the line, Devon continued to hang all over Felix from his immediate right. And throughout the entire picture-taking, Rachel did not look at Felix, did not acknowledge the attractive tenor of his voice; in fact completely ignored him. And Rachel didn't care if she ever set eyes on her bitch of an older sister again! She didn't care how exquisite Devon was. In Brooke Dalene's estimation, anyway!

After the picture-taking was over, they moved out of the 'church' to the second large meeting/banquet room on the opposite end of the corridor, where the reception was about to be held. Rachel filed down the rich blue-carpeted hallway with Rochelle, Vern Denison and Rick, who was still hanging all over her eons behind Diane, Stacey, George and Felix and Devon, still hanging all over him like a wall decoration. Yet Rachel had deliberately chosen to walk ahead of her parents because she had never answered her mother's question as to when were she and her father going to lose her to possible marriage to a man they well-respected and had known for ages, when Devon had blown in from the South and reclaimed his heart just as she had all those years ago. And Rachel didn't want to see the mocking reminder in Sephora's eyes of her awareness of her smooth evasion of a subject that was in no way yet over, just temporarily derailed. For that reason, Rachel shut out her mother's voice sounding behind her along with that of Marshall and Al and Dora Lumas and concentrated on the meeting/banquet room they were approaching in the distance beyond a large coat-check room, which came complete with male attendant in a blue uniform.

The loud blare of music coming from a twelve-piece band from the raised stage in the meeting/banquet room that met her as soon as Rachel stepped through the door behind Rochelle and Vern a moment later only served in aiding in that endeavor. Forget the meeting/banquet part—every padded brown seat had been removed from the large blue, brown, gray and white room by the party planners and it had truly been turned into a ballroom fit for the occasion of a wedding reception. Work tables had been placed up against the entrance wall covered in white tissue paper and were holding a number of cards and fancily-wrapped gifts for the newlyweds. Rachel guessed her three-piece 'Happily Ever After' book and 'Always and Forever' CD and card were among that large assortment somewhere, what with having sent them all down by valet before she'd even left to get dressed in the women's fitting/dressing room hours earlier. The front and center of the brown-carpeted floor had been cleared for dancing, while an endless number of pastel-pink-clothed tables that seated eight were spaced around the adjacent and far walls filling the floor to mid-center—although unfortunately, most of those tables were already occupied by the many guests that had walked over after the concluding of the wedding thirty minutes ago, Rachel guessed. Photographers stood waiting to take pictures—just as they had of the family and wedding party back at the other large meeting/banquet room-turned-church—no doubt having taken several of the gathered guests and surroundings and more of each eventful moment that would follow. And work done by the florists was constantly in evidence, as floral arrangements of the same ivory and peach roses, purple lisianthus, lavender statice, blue delphinium, pink carnations, yellow daisies and fern greenery that made up the bridal bouquets were all over the many tables while an endless number of helium balloons glittered colorfully from the ceiling, shiny multi-colored ribbons streaming down from them. And then there were all the many caterers that George and Stacey had hired to cater the reception, providing everything all the way down from the napkin to the champagne, from the silverware to the wedding cake for the bride and groom.

However, Rachel found it annoying that despite all the careful planning of the wedding coordinators, she, Rochelle and Vern Denison had been prearranged to be seated at a table to the right of the floor's mid-center—which was only half occupied in evidence of that—Rick settling in the last empty chair to the right of her—despite the lack of a place card indicating him to be seated there or not. And while Marshall and Sephora—parents of the groom—were seated at a table toward the room's back and Al and Dora Lumas—parents of the bride—at another one, Rachel supposed she should be grateful that the distance would keep her mother from trying to pry into her personal business. Still as she lowered her bridesmaid's bouquet to the table and settled in the padded chair between Rick and Rochelle with Vern seating himself to the left of Rochelle, Rachel couldn't help but be further ticked at the discovery that while Stacey and George were seated at a prominent front wall table along with Diane, Martin and Flip and an apparent couple of dates for the evening, Devon was seated at one directly in front of them with Ray, an apparent date, another couple wedding guests and Felix who Devon sat next to, as usual hanging all over him! Rachel pushed that sensation down immediately as pictures flashed through her head of Felix kissing Devon and rolling her all over that damned bed, again determined to feel nothing for the man!

"Are you okay?"

Rachel prided herself on the smile she managed in response to the question Rick had asked her over the blare of the background music the band was playing then.

"Yeah!" she forced a laugh to cover the utter rage she'd been feeling at the moment. "I was just thinking about how ridiculous these seating arrangements are! I mean, I'm over here, Mom and Dad are back there, your parents are halfway over there, and Devon's all the way up front at a table in front of that of George and Stacey! And as Stacey's brother, there wasn't even a place set for you. You just sat here next to me because there was no place card for that spot, whether it was planned for you, or not!"

Rick showed his teeth in a laugh at what he thought to be something so simple. "Don't sweat it, Rachel, baby, the point is I'm next to you, which is where I want to be!"

"I see," Rachel replied with a smile, interjecting the two words quickly to cut him off, not wanting to hear another word as to just how closely the white man really wanted to get next to her.

"Don't worry, girlfriend," smiled Rochelle to the left of her, having heard the complaints she had voiced to Rick, "stupid arrangements or no, I don't mind sitting next to you, either. I'm glad to be seated next to you. As a matter of fact, I believe I shared a booth with you at the Downtown Deli & Café for a time yesterday afternoon in proof of that!"

"Yea, I remember that!" Rachel laughed as for the umpteenth time in as many hours she recalled the explicit details of her hot thing with Felix that she had shared with the amber-skinned woman during their near-hour of sharing that booth at said Downtown Deli & Café. That is, before Devon had turned it into a cold thing, Rachel thought with the sudden return of her anger.

"And while we're on the subject," went on Rochelle, leaning over and whispering intimately in her ear, "when is Rick going to get off this wanting to get next to you thing? He's not blind. He has to see that you don't want to get next to him, no matter how much he might want you to. Besides, we both know that the only man you want to get next to is Felix Latham, Mr. Serious Fox! That is, if you can get that artificial sister of yours off of him!"

The mention of that artificial sister heightened all the anger that had returned with Rachel's last thought and that she'd not had time to push down before Rochelle's following number of comments, inspired by the very conversation they had shared at said downtown restaurant the afternoon before brought it back to full-blown fury. Rachel steamed all over again at the ease with which Devon ruined her hot thing with Felix in little more than several hours after telling Rochelle all that, her eyes hot, not even wanting to look at the bitch in the distance. She hoped to God nobody saw her quick flare-up of rage—least of all Rick sitting to the right of her—as she struggled again to numb the sensation from her body. Yet she was hardly surprised when Rochelle, observant as ever, pulled away from something Vern had been about to say to her and curved a glimmering-rose-tipped hand over her arm, causing Rachel's gaze to settle back on her.

"What's going on with you and Miss Artificial?" Rochelle insisted quietly over the blare of the music and for the second time that afternoon and evening.

Having seen the question on her mind several times in between, Rachel fought the urge to scream as the concern in the brown eyes made up identical to hers encouraged her to tell Rochelle the truth. Instead, Rachel pushed that sensation down immediately until her body was again numb, dead from her neck down.

"Nothing," she replied in a voice as numb as the rest of her. After all, what else could it be?

She heaved an inner sigh of relief when a male waiter, a number of the catering firm that had been hired to cater the reception, set a plate of food before her, thereby breaking her out of the curious gaze Rochelle still had turned on her. George had said they'd have everything, and they did. The white china plate was loaded with an assortment of colorful foods: Beef filet mignon topped with fois gras and black truffles—one of three main dishes along with veal steak covered in a mixed vegetable white wine sauce and Alaskan salmon drenched in fried white onion topped with black caviar; green onion mashed potatoes; a thyme roasted Portobello mushroom and sweet onion compote in red wine sauce and with a serving of red caviar on the side; there was squash casserole cooked in a small gold ramekin; skewered shrimp kabobs; and there were the Jalapeño chili wedges, or Spanish cornbread accompanying the meal. A second plate was placed in front of it, containing a colorful frisée, escarole and Belgian endive salad, while a dessert plate holding a slice of Swiss chocolate mousse adorned with the Half-Hersheyed Fruit Berries, or chocolate dipped strawberries, was set to the left of her—one of a number of fancy pies offered with the dinner along with a fluted crystal glass of both a Napa Valley red wine and a champagne from France, a Tattinger Blanc de Blanc in addition to the tall glass of ice water already having been set on the ivory placemat on the table in front of her. Rachel guessed she had not had anything to eat since breakfast eight hours earlier as a quick glance at the silver-toned watch on her left wrist confirmed the time as five o'clock and she was indeed starved because of it. Yet as she raised her fork—one of several silverware pieces placed on a pink napkin either side of her plate—and began to dig into the meal, she hoped to God she wouldn't vomit—so completely was she churning inside out of disgust and frustration.

Thankfully, that twelve-piece mixed-race band that Stacey and George had hired played a number of songs fitted to the occasion that succeeded in relaxing her turbulent mind, enabling Rachel to eat without literally losing her lunch along with it. That, plus she derived amusement from Vern Denison's endless come-ons to an equally amused Rochelle as the two of them sat emptying their own plates to the left of her. At thirty years of age as Rachel had previously guessed, Vern was a veterinarian for the City of Anchorage who dealt mainly in treating animals in the wild—a job which to hear Rochelle put it explained why he had the hands of a wolf! What a laugh, Rachel thought, and she'd needed one. Of course to the right of her, Rick came all on to her amid emptying his own plate, telling her what all he wanted to do for her, what he wanted to do to her, how he wanted to get in her, on her and all over her. Slight variation from A.J. Over—who had completely gotten over her and sat two tables to the left of her trying to get over the short-haired black woman seated to the right of him as they emptied their own plates in tune to the other six wedding guests around them.

She let her gaze wander on around the room as Rick continued to rant about what all he wanted to do for her, what he wanted to do to her. Vic and Brooke Dalene, her mother Qrona, Katarine and their other two children sat eating from a side table, Damon and Mariah Evans and Ortis and their other son occupied one a short distance to the left of them and Stevan Lumas and his three sons, two daughters and their children occupied two even farther to the left toward the back of the large festively decorated meeting/banquet room-turned-ballroom. Swinging her gaze back to the right, Rachel was surprised to find Thacker Muldoon gazing at her from his seat at the side front table he occupied with his too young, too plain wife Sanya and six other wedding attendees. The look the octogenarian had fixed on her amid emptying his own plate translated to Rachel exactly what the old man was thinking. What had happened to her and Felix in just two days of hanging all over each other at his home for her to presently have Stacey's brother hanging all over her while her sister hung all over Felix at an up-front table, a sight that was clearly in evidence to him from his vantage point of being seated at his table on the side farthest from the stage? Rachel dropped her eyes back to her plate, having almost emptied it, meal almost over, dead from her neck down again.

    However, her eyes flashed away from her near-emptied plate and back to the front when the music ended as the band stopped playing suddenly, filling the large room with a disquieting silence. The realization that the break signified the start of the Best Man speech was immediately evidenced by the flash of cameras as the photographers raced forward to photograph the Daytime Emmy Award-winning soap opera actor giving said speech. Rachel had expected it, known it was going to happen; in fact, known who was going to give it, but in her pain she had completely forgotten it, stopped anticipating it. For that reason, she continued to watch from a numbed state as Felix then stepped onto the stage and approached a mike—despite not wanting to look at the man, hear the man, not even wanting to think about the man.

Chapter Nineteen

"I first met George Alver Hardison thirteen years ago, when we were both freshmen attending Georgia State University in Atlanta, Georgia," Felix began with a laugh. "We had the displeasure of meeting up in math class—Professor Dunston's trigonometry class, as a matter of fact," the attractive tenor went on reminiscently. "George occupied the desk to the immediate left of me, and he didn't know a thing about trig. And that was very unfortunate for him, because Professor Dunston was devoted to the subject. In harmony with that, he threw us a pop quiz the first day to test us on what we remembered from high school. George looked at the test in total confusion. I remember him saying, 'What the hell is this! You call this trigonometry? Or is this twigonometry—twigs with numbers on the bottom? Or is this trickonometry—as in Trick or Treat? This isn't Halloween, is it? Because I certainly don't see no treat in this!' Well, I said to myself: listen to this backwoods hick from Villa Rica—wherever the hell that is—don't know a thing about trig! So, I said to George, 'Look, man, whatever day of the year it is, you don't know what that is. You don't belong in this class. You need to go back to whatever high school you came from and take that ninth grade Algebra 101 all over again.' George said to me, 'Shut up, smart ass, and let me copy off of you!' Insulted, I looked at George and said, 'What the hell do I owe you? I don't know you from Adam!' George looked at me and said, 'And while we're on the subject, you know, you look like Eve, pretty boy.' So, I said, 'You're doggone right. As a matter of fact, my looks are going to get me far. I'm going to be a famous actor, someday.' George looked at me and said, 'In case you haven't noticed, I don't exactly look like Freddy Kreuger, myself. I can get any girl I want.' So, I put George to the test. I pointed out the prettiest girl in the class—what was her name—? Tania Dobson, I think it was. Tania was a stuck-up snob who had gone to my high school and who no guy had been able to get next to—not even me, can you believe that?" Felix asked with a laugh. "Anyway, I told George, 'I'll bet you can't get her.' George looked over at Tania and said, 'No problem.' So, I said, 'Fine. I'll set it up. Come over to my house around nine. I'll have her waiting for you.' George said, 'Where do you live?' I said, 'Chamblee,' which is about fifteen miles northeast of Atlanta. George said to me, 'You think I'm going to drive all the way up there to get a girl?' I looked at George and challenged, 'Can't do it?' George looked back and said, 'Just set the date up, man. I'll be there. In the meantime, let me copy off your paper. I need to make a good grade on this test.' So, I let him copy off my test, and I later set up the date. Well, unfortunately, we both flunked the pop quiz. But boy, did George nail Tania!" Felix indulged a laugh that Rachel watched everyone share in to George's complete embarrassment as he recalled the girl he had forgotten ages ago.

"Anyway," Felix went on after a moment as photographers still flashed pictures of him, "as you can see, George and I became best friends, after that. Hey, what can I say—back then, I was young and adventurous. And as a result of that, I got George—small-town boy from Villa Rica—into some of everything. I took him to his first bar, first bowling alley, first nightclub, first strip joint—the man hadn't been anywhere. And of course, with both of us having comparable looks, we met girls all over the place. Of course, most of mine, I threw back, disinterested. George said, 'That's alright, man, I'll take 'em.' And he did! George even found a couple of girls who helped us with our trigonometry class, which I'm happy to say we did pass," Felix smiled. "But George just moved right along with the girls while I sort of hung back on the sidelines. I just wasn't interested in all those girls chasing me because of my looks—you know, too easy come, too easy go, not to mention the fact that I sort of fashioned myself as a gentleman. Of course, eventually, I got hung up on one, it didn't work out. George didn't miss a stroke, though. He was serious road dog with the girls. He never got his heart broke.

"The sad thing about George and me is that eventually, we had to split up," Felix continued after a moment. "As I said before, I was studying to be an actor while George was studying management. As a result of that, after graduating college, I went to New York in further pursuit of acting while George remained in Atlanta, where he got a job as manager of a paint company. But as you can see, it didn't end our friendship, because we spent many a night talking on the phone, reminiscing on the many antics we pulled during our college days, discussing life, our careers, women—how much did we run up in long-distance bills a month—two thousand dollars?" Felix asked George with a laugh. "Plus, we tore up the mail service writing letters to each other. George sent me pictures of all his women. And I sent him pictures of mine. And I mean, obviously, there've been some!"

Rachel knew nobody would doubt that for a minute as she watched Felix indulge a brief reflective pause from her state of total paralysis.

"Then, George called me five years ago with the news that he had gotten an out-of-state job as a general manager at some hotel. I said, 'What state?' He said, 'Alaska.' I had just completed my first year on *As The Star Shines* then, and I remember saying to him, 'What are you going to do all the way over there in Alaska? I hear that it's cold over there.' George gave me the typical response: 'I'm going to cuddle with the ladies, what else, man?' But who knew then that his road dogging days were over, because he would meet the woman here who would steal his heart. Stacey Lumas." Felix turned a smile on the freckle-faced white woman sitting at the table next to her new husband smiling broadly.

"As a matter of fact, I remember when George lost his heart to you," Rachel watched Felix continue to her new sister-in-law. "He called me in New York about a week after arriving here to work for you and told me all about you. George said to me, 'Man, this Stacey Lumas is as cool as the damned weather. You know I'm not used to that. But I can see some heat when I look at her. So, I'm going to work on turning up her thermostat!'" Felix laughed. "The man hasn't looked at another woman since; he's been so busy trying to heat your Bunsen burner up! As a result of that, I was hardly surprised when he called me back in March of this year with the news that he was going to marry you. George said, 'I want you to be my best man. When can you get over here?' I said, 'I don't have a hiatus coming up until June.' George said, 'Perfect. It'll be warmer here then. I'll start making arrangements. I'll see you here then, man.' So, I started clearing my calendar in New York in order to spend most of my hiatus here, and I arrived here—what—? It'll be two weeks tomorrow. And after meeting you, Stacey, I can see how my boy lost his heart to you. You're adorable. You're short, but you're cool, you're soft-spoken, you're composed and incredibly insightful and understanding, not to mention rich as hell!" Felix indulged another brief laugh. "And you've got a good man in George. He's strong, he's good looking—although not as good looking as me—he's compassionate, and even though he's a little quick tempered, most times, he keeps his head. But I'm going to tell you that you have the memories of a lot of women to live up to. So, when you get to the Riviera tonight, I hope you have your salt peter and Mayan's Damiana in your bag in order to keep up with George so that he won't have any of those flashbacks—do you know what I mean?" Felix asked with another totally outrageous laugh to both Stacey and George's complete embarrassment.

"Anyway, George, I know I've embarrassed the hell out of you by bringing up all this, but what I said at the beginning of this speech about it having been a displeasure meeting up with you in Professor Dunston's class, forget that," Felix went on, his dancing gaze turned back on his long-time friend. "It has been a pleasure knowing you all these years. You are the best friend I have ever had. I love you like a brother. And I wish you and Stacey the best now, on your honeymoon, and afterward. As a matter of fact, when you get a chance, you've got to come to New York and let me put you up for a couple of weeks. I'll show you guys around. I'll take you on the set of my soap opera. Introduce you to the three costars that play my boss, her daughter, and her stepdaughter. You know, that I'm sleeping with all at the same time, with none of them knowing of the others!"

Rachel strained to push back the sensation of anger that returned immediately as she raised her near-emptied champagne glass in a toast along with everyone else laughing at the funny note on which Felix ended his speech. Only three days ago while they sat lunching on the slope of the upper Eklutna Valley below East Twin

Pass, Felix had invited her to fly up and visit him on the set of his soap opera, at which point, he would introduce *her* to the women who played his boss, her daughter, and her stepdaughter. Now, the man was sleeping with her sister. A woman he had told her he was over!

She was glad her expression was hidden by her champagne glass when Rochelle leaned over and whispered in her ear again. "God, that man is a serious fox!" the larger woman grinned, her twinkling gaze briefly swinging past her and onto Felix's attractive figure as he leaned over to hug both George and Stacey at their table after having stepped from the stage, photographers again busy taking pictures of the eventful moment. "Not only is he good looking—just like he said—but he can talk, too. I mean, that man is seriously into conversation! Plus, he has a sense of humor! No wonder you've fallen for him! And that was your sister he was referring to when he spoke about the girl he got hung up on, but with whom it didn't work out, wasn't it?"

". . . Yeah." Rachel could only force a dull nod over the lip of her glass in her renewed utter disgust and frustration.

"And now, she's trying with everything she's got to get him back. Look at her over there. All over him . . . !"

As she was, Rachel saw as her gaze lingered in the direction of Rochelle's. Also having known who Felix had been referring to when he'd mentioned the girl who he had fallen for but with whom it had not worked out, Devon had flung to his side at George and Stacey's table and was draped all over him like a Damask curtain.

"Awful!" Rochelle continued in an aside to her as she watched the couple return to their table, Devon hanging all over Felix's arm. "If I were you, I'd go up there and yank her eyes out so bad that she wouldn't be able to see him in a dream."

If only you knew how much I wanted to, Rochelle! Rachel thought as she averted her still angry gaze quickly onto A.J. Over, who sat at his table trying literally to get over another woman—and another black one—seated at his left . . . !

Grateful that Vern said something to Rochelle then, therefore distracting the larger woman's attention away from her, Rachel sliced her eyes onto a woman sitting at a far left table touching up her lipstick, having nothing to say to that.

The beginning strains of *I Swear* being played by the band again taking control of the raised stage signified the First Dance of the newlywed couple. Quietly Rachel watched as George moved to his feet, took Stacey by the hand and escorted her quickly away from their prominent front wall table at the call of the slow tune. The song, an All-4-One ballad, was beautiful indeed—aided by the fact that that eight men/four women band knew it by rote, playing every rift of the bass, every note of the electronic keyboard, the occasional sax, all of its vocal harmony. And the song was made all the more beautiful when one of the lead male vocalists—and a very sensual alto—added his voice to the harmony with the singing of the song's main and romantic lyrics a moment later.

With all the 'honeys'—or as Felix had put it in his speech, women—George had dated while still living in Georgia, it was no surprise to Rachel that George could move. In fact, that was evidenced by the number of pictures Rick had snapped at his bachelor party the night before of him doing the tootsie roll with several hookers—pictures that Rick had left with Rachel that afternoon, in second fact. And George showed his ability to move at the ease with which he pulled Stacey into a rumba once they'd reached the front center of the brown-carpeted floor left cleared of tables and chairs for dancing, photographers again taking pictures of the two of them. But what staggered Rachel was seeing Stacey's easy ability to keep up with her brother, a man taller than his diminutive bride by six inches. She swayed easily around in George's arms, never once getting caught up in the three-foot train of her flower-laced-detailed designer wedding dress. In third fact, not until Rachel had watched the couple twirl gracefully around the floor a couple of times did Rachel realize the true gem they had in each other. In her five days since meeting Stacey, she had found her to be all the things Felix had said in his Best Man speech—soft-spoken, composed, mostly quiet although incredibly insightful and understanding and totally unassuming despite being—also as Felix had put it—rich as hell. Add to that the fact that the stout woman had other skills. What fun she and George must have had when they went out dancing and Stacey came out of her shell and showed those other skills in her easy ability to keep up with him. Small wonder George had fallen for her.

With George and Stacey having gotten the First Dance off to a start, other couples began to join them on the floor at the romantic call of the slow song still being sung by the sensuous alto male lead. Rachel saw Vic and Brooke Dalene step away from their table to move onto the dance floor along with the bride and groom, Damon and Mariah Evans moved away from their table, A.J. Over managed to get one of the two black women he had been schmoozing at his table onto the floor with him, Flip Hart and Martin Rolf got their dates to join them—Rochelle even obliged Vern in accompanying him in a dance—as did several other guests attending the reception. And of course, the flash of cameras was busily in evidence as photographers took pictures of the goings-on. And Rachel was surprised to discover that she wouldn't have minded a dance herself as she watched the many couples begin to twirl around George and Stacey rumbaing to the complete oblivion of all of them from the floor's front center. But there would be no dance for Rachel, because Rick didn't ask her. Despite the fact that his sister appeared to be an Arthur Murray Studio graduate, Rick couldn't dance. Rachel had seen that at Darwin's Theory the night before when Rick had let all that good music go to waste theirs and Rochelle's entire hour or so stay there in preference of sitting contentedly nursing a Coke amidst hanging all over her as he was doing presently. And Rachel tried not to think of all the fun she and Felix had had at Club Oasis only three nights ago, where they had torn up the floor fast dancing and slow dragging. She wondered if he was recalling any of that as she chanced a stealthy glance in his direction. Felix wasn't dancing either, but sat at his up-front table engaged in conversation with Ray Marlboro and his apparent date for the evening. Devon was hanging all over him as usual.

Her eyes were forced off the foursome and back onto Stacey as the band's playing of Luther Vandross' *Dance With My Father* signified the start of the Father/Daughter dance. With the many dancing couples departing the floor—including Rochelle and Vern, who quickly resettled in their seats to the left of Rachel, Al Lumas was quickly at Stacey's side pulling her from George's arms and whirling her around the empty floor in a slow swing to the smooth somewhat up-tempo tune. And again photographers took pictures of the two of them. Al glowed down at Stacey like the proud father he was, Stacey glowed up at him with equal pride, each expressing with their eyes the sentiment behind the lyrics of the song they were dancing to, which told the story about a boy's natural love for his father and his for him. Or as it would be in this case, a girl's natural love for her father and hers for him. Indeed, it was with such emotion that father and daughter Al and Stacey danced that Rachel felt a tug of her own heart despite the fact that it had been numbed of most of its feeling ever since her afternoon discovery of betrayal by a man who only two days ago had told her he thought he was falling in love with her.

"They look really nice together, don't they?"

"Yeah, they do." Rochelle's smiling question uttered over the Luther Vandross song Al and Stacey were dancing to, prompted Rachel's similar response as she continued to watch the pair along with her. "As a matter of fact, I was just remembering how Dad danced with Devon this same way during her reception after her marriages to both Dustin and Richard."

"Lot of good either one of those dances did her," Rochelle responded dryly.

Rachel fell silent at yet another insinuation from her as to her older sister's lack of worth of love from her father much less the two ex-husbands who cheated on her, not needing to know the reasons behind either one of them. After all, as far as Rochelle was concerned, Devon was beautiful but artificial, a name that she had even dubbed her. Well, if only Rochelle knew just how close her assessments were to the truth, Rachel thought with the return of her anger, steam rising to the surface again.

Yet the playing of the band's beginning strains of *A Song For Mama*, signifying the start of the Mother/Son dance, checked its quick rise just before it could blow the lid off the pot. Rachel calmed considerably as Al Lumas and Stacey Lumas Hardison left the floor and George and Sephora replaced them. As they began to dance laughingly to the up-tempo Boyz II Men tune with the photographers again snapping pictures of the two of them, Rachel recalled telling her and her father earlier after the wedding ceremony that it looked like they had lost another one, only for Marshall to laugh back that it was about time! Too bad he and Sephora were never going to lose her, Rachel thought as she recalled the question her mother had privately and smilingly voiced to her not much longer after that, a question she had luckily evaded and a question she had no intention of ever answering.

"Wow, look at George," grinned Rochelle, her musing tone over the blare of the music from Rachel's left again claiming her attention. "Your brother's just married a millionairess! Can you believe it? George is now a millionaire! Your brother's into serious big bucks now, girlfriend!"

"Yes, I'm aware of that!" Rachel shared her grinning look, which she briefly turned back on George dancing proudly to the a-tempo Boyz II Men song with their mother. "As a matter of fact, it was just the other night when George was in the midst of introducing our parents to Stacey that Dad said it was going to be nice having money in the family! Although I don't know where my father got that joke from, when the last thing that man will never need is money!"

"Oh—so that that explains why he's so rich looking, huh?" Rochelle persisted with her shimmering rose full-lipped grin while the twinkle in her bronze-shadowed brown eyes conveyed the exact initial thought Rachel sensed she had had upon meeting her dad the day before as that of him as a sugar daddy. "You remember him, Vern," Rochelle said in a reminding aside to the boyfriend still sitting to the left of her. "You saw him in the other meeting room-turned-church shortly after George and Stacey's wedding ceremony a while ago. His name's Marshall—or did I introduce you? Anyway, he's in his—what—early sixties, and looks like a movie star. George looks just like him." Rochelle was unaware that Stacey had said the same thing upon Rachel's previous mention of George's introduction of her to their father Thursday night. "And you see what his mother looks like," Rochelle continued as Vern listened with interest, at present following the direction of her gaze and letting his resettle on the stylishly dressed seductive dusky-skinned ageless woman dancing with George that he had seen earlier in the other meeting/banquet room-turned-church. "Her name's Sephora, and she's beautiful, isn't she?" Rochelle persisted with her fawning praise. "Plus, she looks forty, despite the fact that she has to be at least sixty. She doesn't look at all as if she's given birth, does she? Together, she and Marshall had George and Rachel—two beautiful children, not to mention that artificial one up there."

"So, you say," said Vern as he recalled her telling him that earlier, his gaze, like hers, slicing from Sephora and George and onto Devon hanging all over Felix at their upfront table.

Rachel didn't hazard a glance in Devon's direction.

After followed the Father-In-Law/Daughter-In-Law and Mother-In Law/Son-In-law dance to the band's lilting playing of Madonna's *Take A Bow*, succeeding in taking Rachel's mind off her sister for the moment. Again Stacey and George took center floor, except that this time, Stacey was on the arms of father-in-law, Marshall while George carried his new mother-in-law, Dora Lumas, around in his arms. The eight men/four women mixed-race band's playing of the percussion, clackers, bells and violins-filled song, which told the story of a woman telling her masquerading lover to take a bow because the show was over seemed inappropriate for a wedding reception, yet was sung as exquisitely as it was played—the woman lead, a sultry second soprano, outdoing Madonna on any given day while the male lead, a second tenor, bested Babyface's background accompaniment with ease. And while Dora

Lumas wasn't a bad dancer next to her daughter, she kept up well enough as a partner for George. But as a dance partner, Dora had nothing on Marshall, who provided seeming Arthur Murray Studios graduate Stacey serious competition as he spun her around to the beautiful song's smooth flowing up-tempo beat.

"Wow, look at your Dad!" crowed Rochelle in Rachel's ear then, her excited tone over the ringing intonations of the music nearly pulling her out of her absorption of the dance taking place between her father and Stacey. "His age has nothing on him, does it! Apparently, Marshall is, and always has been, as good a dancer as George!" Rochelle continued in further praise of the sixty-one-year-old salt-and-pepper-haired black man dancing with Stacey and who she had just said looked like a movie star—and a rich one, at that.

"Hey, who do you think we got it from!" insisted Rachel with a laugh, gazing briefly away from the couple to pin the larger woman with a teasing look that Rochelle translated immediately.

"Hey, my Mom's not too bad a dancer, either!" laughed Rick, having listened in on Rachel and Rochelle's conversation, as had Vern to the left of Rochelle.

"I guess so," Rochelle agreed with a sudden dry boredom that only served only in heightening Rick's amusement.

Together he, Rachel, Rochelle and Vern watched as Marshall and Stacey, George and Dora danced until the song came to its inevitable end, where each did as expressed in the song title and took a bow to his or her partner.

"Oh, that's too sweet!" Rochelle grinned as the foursome then moved off the floor.

"Isn't it . . . !" Rachel grinned in agreement. She couldn't have found a more fitting way to end a dance to a song that carried the gesture in its name.

The cutting of the cake by the bride and groom followed, accompanied by the band's lively playing of Average White Band's *Cut The Cake*. The five-tiered concoction rolled out on a lavish serving cart by a local baker hired by the caterer who specialized in wedding cakes consisted of buttery yellow layers, with rich French Vanilla frostings drizzled in cream and covered in marzipan half-dipped in chocolate. Again the flash of several cameras went off to preserve the moment as George and Stacey cut the first slice and fed it to each other. The serving of the cake by the many waiters employed by the catering firm to all the guests followed and though Rachel found her slice delicious, she simply had nowhere to put it after the large meal she had consumed before the Best Man speech thirty minutes earlier, hazarding a guess. Nor for that matter did Rochelle and Vern, like her leaving the cake barely touched on their plates. Rick, on the other hand, not only ate his slice but went back for two more, as big in appetite as Felix was. Mr. Fox, better known as Mr. Dog. . . . Atomic Dog. . . . Nasty Dog. . . . The Original Dog. . . . And Rachel wasn't thinking about his appetite for food either, but his long-denied appetite for sex, which he thought he could satisfy with both her and Devon at that same time. Well, their lives were not a soap opera and his *star* no longer *shone* with her. If he wanted Devon, he could have her. As he already had obviously, Rachel thought viciously as memories of all those pictures of him rolling Devon all over that damned bed in the process of doing just that again flashed vividly from her mind.

She jumped guiltily when Felix sudden glanced around from his up-front table next to Devon and caught her glaring at him intently from her own right of the floor's mid center. Hotly Rachel yanked her eyes away from his dancing gaze, all the time glad Rick had been too busy with finishing his third slice of cake and Rochelle too busy conversing with Vern to notice. Rachel hoped nobody else noticed her flare of silent rage, which she knew had to have shown on her face as she pushed that sensation down immediately until she again felt nothing and sat numbed from head to toe, dead from her neck down.

She had just managed to gaze at Rick in response to the black-sleeved arm he had curved around her beige-clad shoulders to reclaim her attention when Stacey suddenly appeared at their table behind her and Rochelle.

"Hey, how's everybody doing?" inquired the soft-spoken Alaska Native over the blare of *Recipe For Love*, a Harry Connick Jr. tune being played in the interim by the band, her glittery white-shadowed brown mascara-lashed brown eyes encompassing everyone at the table, including Vern and Rick. "How'd you like the wedding cake?" asked the new bride with a pink-lipped smile, having eaten all the attractive deep red lipstick from her lips, the same of which Rochelle had done to hers and Rachel guessed she had done to hers.

"It was delicious," Rick answered, having just been about to tell Rachel that about the third slice of which he had just finished off his plate. "As a matter of fact, I just finished my third piece."

"You always were a bottomless pit, Brother," Stacey teased Rick with a good-natured smile.

Rick responded to her suggestion that he was a glutton with a show of his own teeth, more even in size than her little bitty ones. "Funny, how my food consumption hasn't shown up on me," he taunted with the meaningful roving of his vivid blue eyes over her stout figure in the expensive long-sleeved flower-laced wedding dress she wore.

Stacey hid her resentment of her tall trimmer brother's deliberate reference to her size behind another show of her small aligned teeth.

"I don't think George is going to have a problem with that," she said over the blare of *Recipe For Love* still being played by the eight-men/four-women band on the stage.

"I surely hope not," Rick agreed indifferently.

Already having guessed herself that George was going to have a feast on the woman when they arrived at their honeymoon destination, Rachel veiled the venom blazing in her eyes and determined to defuse the very same beginning between her and her brother.

"Yes, the cake is good." She got back on the subject with a smile of agreement with Rick's earlier statement amid turning a brief glance on the slice of cake barely touched on her own plate. "But I'm afraid I couldn't enjoy mine," she went on to her new sister-in-law regretfully. "Just had nowhere to put it after all that food I ate a while ago."

"Neither did I!" Vern said of the cake still untouched on his own plate, forcing Stacey to shift her gaze away from Rachel and back onto him sitting to the left of Rochelle.

"Neither did I—!" parroted Rochelle with an engaging show of her own teeth at her old friend, at the same time gesturing the untouched sliced of cake on her own plate. "And as you can see, I have plenty of body with which to put cake!"

"That's for sure!" Vern agreed with a roguish grin, wolfish hands going for their usual places on her body that she had plenty of with which usually to put cake.

Rochelle pulled his hands from her large bust-line with a disinterested snort. "Not now, Vern, we're at a wedding reception!"

"And hopefully, we're going to keep it that way!" Stacey punctuated the tactful suggestion that they maintain proper decorum with a deep red-tipped white hand that she then curved over Rachel's arm, thereby breaking her out the brief spate of amusement she had been deriving from the antics of Rochelle and Vern. "May I talk to you a minute, new sister-in-law?" asked Stacey with a continued show of her small even teeth, causing Rachel's continued show of her own to become one of surprise.

"Sure, Stacey. . . ." Pulling out from the circle of the arm Rick had curved around her shoulders, Rachel moved to her feet to follow Stacey away from the table, all the while wondering what the white woman wanted to say to her.

Ignoring the number of guests still cluttering its center and front since the band's playing of the fast and loose dance tune *Cut The Cake* several minutes earlier, Stacey led her all the way across the brown-carpeted floor before stopping her in front of the white-tissue-paper-covered tables with their large assortment of cards and wedding gifts along the entrance wall. The location put them out of earshot of everyone and way out of sight of George joking with Felix on the far side of the large meeting/banquet room-turned-ballroom. Stacey turned around to face Rachel then, both of them terribly overdressed—although Rachel looked a dud in the short-sleeved scarf-draped boat-neck designer's beige bridesmaid's dress she wore in comparison to the far more expensive equally designer's flower-and-lace-detailed white wedding dress Stacey wore. The matching white flower-and-lace-detailed veil still flowed down Stacey's back, the dress's three-foot train scrunched in her right hand to pull the equally flower-and-lace-detailed white satin material off the floor.

"What's with you this evening, Rachel?" asked the soft-spoken woman quietly then, small aligned teeth again showing in a smile. "You told Thacker when he asked you how were things with you and Felix before the wedding this evening that they weren't bad, and I didn't question the simple response or think it a lie, because I knew you didn't want Devon to get the idea that something was going on with you and Felix. For that reason, when George and I returned to the 'church' after our wedding ceremony, I still didn't question your ignoring of Felix, thinking it part of the game you and he were playing with Devon. But what you said to Thacker was a lie, wasn't it? I've been watching you, new sister-in-law," Stacey said with the meaningful blink of her glittery white-shadowed brown-mascara-lashed brown eyes at her. "Through all our picture-taking back there, I couldn't help noticing that not once did you look at Felix, not even when Devon was looking in the other way—which wasn't often, because she was hanging on him before the pictures started, and she's been hanging all over him ever since. Plus, you made sure you were lined up in those pictures at the end farthest from him. And yet still, not once did you look at Felix. You did not acknowledge the sound of his voice, nor even his name, you completely ignored him, leaving me to believe you were no longer playing a game. And I don't know what happened to the seating arrangements in here, because you and Rochelle were not supposed to have been seated way back there, but up front with George, Diane, myself, Flip, Ray and Felix, while your and George's and my parents were supposed to be seated at the table to the right of us, with my brother being nowhere around you. Yet despite that mix-up, from the table you did manage to find a seat at along with Rochelle and Vern, you've sat with my slug of a brother slung all over you and continued to ignore Felix, and the man has tried repeatedly to catch your eye in all the time we've been here. Except for a while ago when I looked away from something stupid George had said to me, only to find you sitting at your table glaring at Felix with a temperature hotter than that Bunsen burner of mine that he had said in his Best Man speech that George was concentrating on trying to heat up. And then, in yet another attempt to catch your eye, Felix glanced around at the same time and caught it, only for you to yank it and the other one away from his gaze with a heat higher than boiling point, practically sending that Bunsen Burner bubbling out, over, all the way down its fragile sides and into the flames. What's going on, Rachel?" Stacey inquired curiously. "What's happened with you and Felix?"

Rachel blinked her incandescent-bronze-shadowed black-mascara-lashed brown eyes in stunned stupefaction at the freckle-faced white woman shorter than her by four inches despite her lace-detailed designer white satin heels or even her own designer beige leather ones, it being all she could think of to do. Obviously, Stacey wasn't the owner of a multi-million-dollar swanky sophisticated Anchorage, Alaska hotel for nothing, Rachel thought. George had not married a stupid woman. Not only could the stout woman dance, but there were all those other abilities she had that seemed out of character with her normally composed quiet nature in addition to her incredible insight and understanding, such as the inner rage that had flashed from her eyes over the debacle Devon had made of Thursday's dinner, the same inner rage of which Stacey had vociferated all over the cafeteria that morning, and the way she had teased Rachel so unexpectedly in the penthouse yesterday afternoon and then subtly tried to pry into her business after spending most of the week sitting back watching her from the sidelines. In fact, in the last minute, Stacey had said more to her than in the five days since meeting her on Monday. But how could Rachel tell her that the cause of what was 'no longer' going on between her and Felix lay in the very woman Stacey herself had just said had been hanging on him since after said wedding ceremony, the one who had turned Thursday's dinner into a debacle? That in fact, because of that very one, the game was over? Again Rachel determined not to make a scene and blow her and George's perfect day by turning the heat down under that Bunsen Burner until its contents were barely simmering.

"Do you remember what you said to me at breakfast this morning about how you didn't think I'd be waiting for much longer for my rescue?" Rachel asked finally.

Stacey nodded as the question jogged her memory of the object of the very subject to which she had been implying before offering that cryptic statement, the object of which was dominating their present subject.

"It's not going to happen."

Rachel left her to figure out the simple response as she moved away from her to admire a gold-wrapped wedding gift among the large colorful assortment of others and cards on one of the white tissue-covered tables in front of her. And as Stacey turned away from her after a moment of doing exactly that, Rachel rebuked her continued loss of control over the rage she had been experiencing ever since Devon had greeted her in the women's fitting/dressing room about two o'clock that afternoon. To think that she had spent the entire afternoon and evening veiling her eyes from Stacey because she did not know how to tell the woman that the very other woman who had caused Thursday's dinner debacle, the very woman Stacey had warned her not to let see the ridiculous-or-no hot thing she and Felix had going on—the very woman who had bubbled innocently in both their faces during all their preparations for the wedding in the women's fitting/dressing room that afternoon and the very woman Stacey had just said had been hanging all over Felix since after the wedding ceremony—had done what Rachel and Stacey had both feared and roped him back in and Rachel had the pictures—compliments of her brother Rick—to prove it? Rachel was going to have to somehow get control over her inner anger at Devon and not let anyone else see it—least of all Rochelle, who had been suspicious ever since witnessing the greeting between Rachel and Devon in the women's fitting/dressing room earlier that afternoon that something was going on with her and Devon and was presently of the same opinion. For that reason and thankful that Rochelle had moved onto the floor in a dance with Vern to the slow song the band was currently playing, Rachel walked blindly back to their table and resettled in her seat beside Rick, where the slug of a white man was again all over her.

A number of fast tunes followed the slow song as the eight-men/four-women mixed-race band got into the swing of the occasion. They played Pink's *Get The Party Started,* Will Smith's *Party Starter,* Prince's *Musicology* and Madonna's

Music, hitting every key, every drum, every male and female vocal—even Prince's, in addition to the earlier Madonna! They figuratively tore the place up, setting the reception to rocking and sending half the guests in attendance crowding onto the dance floor in response to the thumping music. Of course, Rachel wasn't one of them. She sat at her table with Rick slung all over her, the white man not once asking her to dance, as to hear him laughingly say in her ear, he did his best work off his feet. Rachel deliberately ignored that, as she did all his other come-ons. She couldn't help noticing also that among all the other guests that had remained seated along with her and Rick, Felix remained at his upfront table as well as did Ray Marlboro, Flip Hart, their apparent dates for the evening and a couple other reception attendees. Yet Felix did not glance around and notice her again because he was too busy smiling down at Devon, who remained seated at the table by his side and was hanging all over his arm as usual.

Rachel's eyes flashed away from the couple in surprise when Rochelle suddenly fell into an exhausted heap in her seat to the left of her as the band followed Madonna's *Music* with the playing of Alicia Keys' equally 'music'al *Rock Wit U*, Vern in the seat to the left of her.

"Whew!" Rochelle breathed with a laugh amid struggling to recover from her exertion. "That was some workout, huh?"

"Nothing like the workout I hope you plan for—and have already implied—intending to give me later!" Vern interjected with the charming show of his pretty teeth as he intercepted the question she had intended for Rachel.

Ignoring the innuendo behind the remark borne out of his roguish nature, Rochelle diverted her dismissing gaze past Rachel and onto Devon hanging all over Felix at the upfront table with Flip, Ray and their apparent dates for the evening, immediately noticing as had Rachel that they had remained seated among all the other guests along with Rachel and Rick.

"Is she still hanging all over him? Doesn't she know she looks ridiculous?" The disgusted note went completely out of Rochelle's voice as she leaned over to speak intimately in Rachel's ear. "Doesn't Miss Artificial know Mr. Fox might want to come over here, and ask you to dance with him? You know, so you two can tear up the floor, rock wit each other to Alicia's thumping beat, for example, like you say you did at Club Oasis Wednesday night?"

"I guess not!"

Rachel forced a laugh over the blare of the rocking bass Alicia Keys' tune being played by the band on the stage, not needing to quiet the response to Rochelle's whispered questions that Rick hadn't been able to hear. And she thought it a safe enough answer. While she wouldn't rock wit Felix anywhere-anymore-anyhow, what else could she have said to the woman who didn't yet know that? Rochelle didn't know how deeply inside she disagreed with yet another low assessment from her of her older sister. What would Rochelle do were she to know that however ridiculous she thought Devon was, she had been clever enough to chase Felix until she'd got him back, turning what Stacey'd termed a ridiculous-or-no-hot thing between Rachel and Felix into a cold thing that was totally ridiculous? That in fact, it was Devon who was now 'rocking wit him' and he with her . . . ? A fact Rachel had yet to disclose to Rochelle?

"Ridiculous!" Rochelle snorted.

Rachel fell stiffly silent, again having nothing further to say to that.

Unaware was she that Rochelle was of the same opinion after watching Devon flaunt her charms on Felix throughout the entirety of the band's playing of the Club-Mix-Version of En Vogue's *What Is Love,* a thumping bass fast tune sung by a seductive male lead that she and Vern had also chosen to sit out. Rachel had just managed to extricate herself from a long boring conversation with Rick who still sat drooling all over her, during which she had repeatedly asked the question implied by the song's title—*What Is Love?*—when Rochelle suddenly leaned over and whispered in her ear again.

"Look, girlfriend," she began, incandescent bronze-shadowed gaze still aimed on the couple in the distance, "forget this game you're playing with her, but you need to go up there and get your sister off your man!"

One thing Rachel knew as her own incandescent bronze-shadowed gaze simmered briefly back onto Devon still hanging all over Felix was that she had to stop this game, alright. This party was going to go on all night. George and Stacey had yet to acknowledge all their many gifts and cards, not to mention George's removal of her garter and Stacey's tossing of her wedding bouquet. And Rachel didn't want to be around for that when she knew Devon would be the first single-woman on the floor to catch it in the hopes of snaring Felix for a third husband and he would probably let her. And Rachel had had enough of Rick coming on to her when she had no intention of letting him in. Bending her head at Rochelle in a pardoning nod, Rachel pulled from the circle of Rick's arm and moved to her feet.

She found her parents over at their table farther toward the back of the room in a hurry and promptly announced that she was going home.

Her mother's lavender-ice-shadowed black mascara-lashed brown eyes turned on her in a confused look equally shared by her father as they reacted predictably to the unexpected response.

"Why, Rachel, what do you mean you're going home?" Sephora asked over yet another fast tune currently being played by the band, curving a dusky hand over her same-color arm. "Are you talking about back to Georgia? Why are you leaving now? You're not supposed to check out until tomorrow!"

"Look up there." Without turning to look at them, Rachel watched her parents' gazes follow the direction of the cool angling of her head and settle on Devon and Felix toward the front of the room. "See her hanging all over him?"

"You don't have to tell me, I've been watching her draped all over him ever since the wedding was over this evening," Sephora replied with some embarrassment. "Can't she realize she's making a fool of herself?"

"Not anymore," Rachel said simply.

Sephora's gaze swept back onto her in deepening confusion at the cryptic response, a look equally shared by her father.

"What are you talking about?" Marshall asked in his brusk alto over the fast tune still thumping through the ballroom.

"The game's over." Deliberately Rachel did not offer any further explanation as she watched her parents' gazes linger on her face in a look that clearly transmitted their understanding as to exactly what she had meant. "Anyway, I'm going to go pack my bags and leave here, and let her have him. You guys have a safe trip back cross-country, okay, and I'll see you when you get back to Villa Rica next week. I—I'll call you—or something." Fixing them with one last gaze that met the look of concern deepening in theirs, Rachel pulled her arm gently from Sephora's grasp and turned away from the table in search of George.

She found him just inside the door of the banquet room past a number of guests crowding the dance floor where he stood talking to Stu Giddian, his assistant manager. He turned automatically as the white man moved away from him and back in the direction of the center of the room, his brown gaze twinkling in a welcoming look as he espied her approach on him at the same time.

"Hey, girl," George greeted with a smile as warm as the look in his eyes as she stopped in front of him.

"Hey, Brother!" she forced a medium-lipped grin. "I guess you two really did it, huh?"

"Yea, we did," George agreed, still smiling. "Can you believe it? Stacey and I have been married for a couple of hours now, and will be leaving for our honeymoon in another three!"

"I know you're looking forward to it," Rachel said understandingly, though nowhere near with his excitement.

"You'd better believe it, Kid Sister," George agreed.

Rachel wondered where was the white woman he had married and who had spoken to her privately and at surprising length a while earlier as the brief gaze she swept over the ballroom behind her failed to pick her out of the dancing crowd. Settling it back on George then, Rachel changed the subject.

"That was some speech Felix gave a while ago, huh?" she continued to force a smile.

"Wasn't it . . . !" George feigned a snort of annoyance under his breath as he recalled the moment of more than hour ago. "I have already killed him for bringing up my past women like that, and I am going to kill him some more! He's going to be too dead to walk out of here before this is over! And can you believe what he told Stacey? To bring some salt peter, some Mayan's Damiana, some aphrodisiacs on our honeymoon so that she could keep up with me? Was he crazy, or what . . . !"

"Hey, you said it, the man's crazy." Rachel forced a laugh at his deeply outraged look, at least crediting the actor with that much before her gaze resettled on George in all seriousness. "Anyway, I just wanted to congratulate you again on your marriage to Stacey, and wish you guys a happy honeymoon on the Riviera." Rachel was awed by the poise she managed as she pulled her brother's deep-purple-satin tuxedo-clad body into a smiling hug. "Think of me when you get there. With any luck, I'll be halfway back to Georgia by then."

Fixing the attractive oval face so like her father's with one last parting smile, Rachel dropped her arms from George's shoulders and moved to the door. The sound of 'N Sync's *Bye Bye Bye* blaring from the eight-men/four-women band on the stage behind her Rachel found appropriate and already a distant memory.

However, Rachel was hardly surprised when George curved a hand over her wrist suddenly in equal surprise of her last statement, stopping her before she could step three feet away from his side.

"What do you mean you'll be halfway back to Georgia, by then?" George demanded in his abrupt alto over the blare of the music, brown eyes like hers having resettled on her in all seriousness.

Rachel had to force herself not to pull her wrist from his detaining grip as she let her incandescent-bronze-shadowed gaze resettle on his suntan brown face in a deceptively airy look.

"I'm leaving," Rachel said simply. "I'm going home, tonight."

George's eyes narrowed on her with a curiosity indicating his suspicion that something was going on here for her to want to leave the hotel to fly back to Georgia tonight—hours before her scheduled departure time—and in the middle of his wedding reception—at that.

"Why do you want to leave so soon before checkout time tomorrow at noon?" the abrupt alto persisted insistently.

Rachel found she couldn't answer that as the questioning intensity of his gaze pierced through her outer façade and saw the pain shimmering behind the airy look she had forced at him. Feeling herself beginning to crumble yet not wanting to fall apart before everyone, she curved a glimmering rose-tipped dusky-brown hand over his arm to pull him from the reception.

"Come here, I want to show you something," she said over the band's continued bopping to *Bye Bye Bye* in the background.

George's brown eyes remained narrowed on her in a questioning look as she began to pull him speedily past the coat-check room to the elevator banks down the elegantly sophisticated blue, brown, rust and autumn gold stripe-paper-walled hall.

"What is it, Rachel?" Again George's demand thundered ominously as he hustled to keep up with her fast pace.

"Hold on, I've just got to get my clothes and purse out of the women's fitting room on the third floor, and I'll show you."

Rachel prided herself on the unexpected calm she exuded as she pulled George into the first elevator that opened after she had pushed the 'up' button, imagining it was borne out of necessity. For that reason, she was as unflappable as a breeze as the elevator doors closed and the fast-moving elevator began to ascend to the third floor. Once there with George accompanying her with a look of growing curiosity, Rachel went wordlessly to the large women's sitting/fitting/dressing/powder room across the hall from the equally large one of the men's where she had been made up for the wedding earlier, gathered up the ribbed cream sweater, slacks, socks and white Nikes sneakers—and the beige purse she left in her changing cubicle as well, and then still without a word, she returned to the elevator banks, where she stepped into the first one that opened after she'd prompted it with the punching of the 'up' button, George accompanying her in deepening curiosity. Again Rachel was awed by the outer calm she exuded as the elevator began to ascend from the third floor, clutch leather purse dangling from her left shoulder, her arms curled around her clothes. She stared at the base of the closed elevators doors and therefore did not see the look of bewilderment that had crept into George's still questioning gaze as his deep-purple-satin tuxedo-clad arms curved protectively around her own, wondering what had he missed happening with her all evening that would explain the pain he'd seen behind her earlier façade of deceptive airiness, followed by her unexpected calm and then tense silence, all in the midst of beating a hasty retreat from the hotel hours before her scheduled departure time of checkout time tomorrow at noon?

"What is it, Rachel?" the abrupt alto again persisted insistently.

Yet again Rachel said nothing, not after they'd passed the sixth floor, not after they'd passed the tenth, not even after they had arrived on the eleventh floor and moving in the direction of her suite down the hall from the elevator banks. In fact, it was not until they were safely inside the bedroom of the two-room suite that Rachel dumped her clothes, sneakers and clutch purse onto the bed, lowered her face into her hands and gave in to all the sensations of pain, anger, frustration, utter rage and betrayal she had tried to numb all afternoon and evening, Bunsen Burner bubbling out, over, all down the fragile sides of the glass and into the flames.

Behind her, George stared at her in surprise as she began to cry grievously, a floodgate of tears spilling out of her eyes, all the way down the fragile sides of her face and onto her hands. His arms curved around her in a crushing action as he pulled her back against his chest, his eyes again narrowed on her in a questioning look that demanded to know what was going on here?!

"What is it, Rachel?" George vocalized a repeating of that demand over her loud sobbing.

This time at the insistent question, Rachel managed to force an answer from her throat. "The game's over."

George's brown eyes narrowed on the back of her head in increasing confusion in his failure to have understood the response she had half-sobbed into her hands.

"What'd you say?"

Pushing stiffly out of his arms, Rachel crossed to the dresser and picked up the single packet of photos she had left there that afternoon. Ignoring the running mascara stinging her eyes, she returned to her brother's side, pushed it into his hands and watched him open it from the same state of shock she had experienced upon first having seen them that afternoon.

Apparently, that adage that a picture paints a thousand words appeared to be true. As George pulled the prints from the packet and began quickly to thumb through them, a look of shock slid into his eyes similar to Rachel's own look of stunned stupefaction.

"What the hell is this—?!"

"What does it look like?" Rachel was awed by the return of her calm as she sniffed back the wave of tears and moved coolly away from him around the foot of the frilly blue-print spread-covered king-sized bed. ". . . Pictures of your bachelor party. As you can see, you're all there—you, Flip, Martin, A.J., Damon, Felix, Ray, all of you. And look who else is there! Devon! And look who she's with! Felix! Felix kissing Devon! Devon kissing Felix! Devon crawling all over Felix, and Felix crawling all over her in his damned bed! The man lied to me! He told me it was over between him and Devon! Well, as you can see by those pictures, the only thing over between them is him rolling all over her!"

As Rachel's tears gave way to the return of her frustration, she flounced hotly to the closet while George stared in stunned shock at the graphic pictures of Felix and Devon that had come up in his hands.

"Where did you get these?" George demanded in his abrupt alto.

"Rick brought 'em to me this afternoon, who else?" Moving away from the closet with the large gray Tourister Pullman enclosed in her hands, Rachel threw it onto the bed. "He said he thought I'd like to see how that camera of his performed on the pictures he took at your bachelor party last night. He proceeded to show me the lot of them; letting me see exactly how well that camera performed at last night's party. Rick said as you can see by these pictures, it got quite wild. He said you got crazy. And so did Felix!" Her breath sounded behind the exertion she was making to pile clothes from a six-drawer French Provincial chest of drawers into the Pullman she had unzipped on her bed. "Rick said Felix got busy with Devon! Said he didn't know how she came to be there, but they got seriously busy in the bedroom! It appears that Felix still has a thing for her after all these years, after all! To think that the man stood in here and kissed me three times this afternoon on the way out of here to pick up you-all's tuxes at the formal wear shop—not to mention blew me a fourth kiss from the door, yet he didn't say a word to me about having slept with Devon last night! And to think that for the last couple of days, we've been playing this game of keep-Devon-in-the-dark-as-to-our-involvement-with-each-other—you know what I'm talking about! The man lied to me! Made a fool of me! Almost used me . . . !" Rachel stopped packing and resignedly lowered her face back into her hands as another wave of tears spilled hotly from her eyes at Felix's total betrayal. "So, as you can see, the game's over!" she cried loudly. "If Felix still wants Devon, he can have her! But he can't have both of us at the same time—I don't care how well Mr. Daytime Emmy Award-winning actor is getting paid to sleep with two sisters at the same time on his soap opera, not to mention their mother, his main love interest in the first place. Thus, I have no intention of remaining here to watch him humiliate me with her, any longer! I'm going to call me a cab and have it take me to Ted Stevens Whatever Airport, where I'm going to sit on stand-by until I can catch a plane back to Atlanta! In Felix's own words: I'm getting out of here, quickly! So, you tell me, my Brother—what have I to do to get out of here—!"

Flinging her hands from her tear-streaked dusky-toned face, Rachel slid her bleary-eyed gaze onto the lighter suntan-toned face of George still standing on the other side of the bed, the well-hewn curve of his full lips pulled into a grim line. Though the enraged look in his deep brown gaze again indicated his suspicion that something was going on wrong here, he made no effort to refute Felix's apparent disloyalty to her as evidenced by the incriminating photos of him and Devon he still held in his hands.

"I'll—ahm—I'll call the front desk, and have your full bill charged to my account," George said instead in a worn voice after a moment, at the same time sliding the prints in his hands back into their white packet. "All you'll have to do is turn in your room key and sign out."

"Thank you, George."

Crossing the large bedroom back toward him, Rachel curved her arms around his broad shoulders in a grateful parting hug, which George returned by curving his around her waist. Yet Rachel purposely did not let her wet face come in contact with the smart satin tux he wore, not wanting her makeup, tears and running mascara to smudge, stain and streak the vivid purple material.

Yet with time becoming of the essence and aware that his new wife awaited him at the reception still going on down on the first floor, George pushed regretfully away from her to sweep her bleary-eyed face with a sobering look.

"Look, girl, I want you to call me when you get home tomorrow—no, on second thought, I don't know where I'll be. I'll be on the Riviera, somewhere. I'll call you tomorrow night. See that you got home alright. And let you know how it is out there."

"I would like that," Rachel smiled.

"I'm sorry this happened to you, honey," George apologized after another moment. "And I'm sorry I was so involved in my own happiness not to have noticed all of your pain."

"Hey, it was your wedding day, you were supposed to be happy today," Rachel laughed, a hand flicking an imaginary tear from the lapel of his tux that she hadn't let her face touch. "That's why I hid it all from you—Stacey, included, because I had no intention of ruining you two's special day."

Though George's eyes were kind for her magnanimity in having done all that, he didn't find it a fit recommendation for her to have gone through all that pain all afternoon and evening without once having said anything to him.

"I'll go call the front desk, and have your full bill charged to my account," he repeated finally, his lips curved on her in a last parting smile.

"Thank you, George," Rachel smiled equably. "I love you, George."

"I love you too, Kid Sister."

Lowering his lips to her forehead in a last expression of goodbye, George dropped his arms from her waist and walked purposefully away from her, packet of prints still carried in one hand. Rachel gave them little thought as her brown gaze lingered on George's sturdy five-foot-ten-inch frame in the designer deep purple satin single-breasted tux. He cut a nice swath through the living room on his way to the door, Rachel thought—her brother who looked like the son of a movie star. Again she found it small wonder Stacey had married him.

She stared after George for a long moment after he had stepped from the two-room-suite. Then moving around the foot of the bed, Rachel returned to her packing. She had the five pieces of Tourister luggage fully packed in twenty minutes with everything she had brought there—jeans, sneakers, walking boots, sweaters, pullovers, thermal underwear, socks, slacks, flannel shirts, caps, pumps, black purse, her coat, all her toiletries, her camera. She had even packed her ribbed brown parka—after all, she wouldn't need it—Al Lumas had happily shouted out before the wedding that not only was the sun shining, but it was seventy three degrees outside—not to mention that by the time Rachel arrived at Hartsfield-Jackson International in Atlanta the following evening, it'd probably be a hundred. Rachel wanted no memory of her visit to Alaska to take back with her to Georgia—knowing it would be too painful a one to reflect on and so had dumped all the maps, brochures and guidebooks that she had acquired at the Visitor Center and that Public Lands place that Felix never gave her a chance to read in the first place into the white trash can next to the French Provincial nightstand along with all the other pictures she had taken there as well—barring those she took at Chugach State Park, which were in the possession of her parents. Rachel wanted no memory of the members of the wedding party to take back with her to Georgia, and so would not miss those she took after the wedding rehearsal the day before and had yet to pick up at Stewart's Photo Shop. For the same reason, Rachel wanted no memory of Felix to take back with her either, yet having thought the fetching color photos the teenage boy had snapped of them sharing a smiling and intimate embrace at Delaney Park on Thursday too attractive to dump altogether, she had simply discarded them to the French Provincial dresser. And while Rachel wanted no memory of Rick to take back with her either, she had decided to keep all the pictures he took of her and Rochelle the day before, thinking meeting the woman so like her hometown friend Sydney, the Meg Ryan freak, the only good thing that came out of Anchorage all week other than George and Stacey's wedding. As a result of that, Rachel had slid the glossy color 35mm prints into her strapped gray carry-on, which she had zipped shut before closing the entire bag, pulling its large silver utility zipper around half its circumference and slipping the zipper's clasp into the bag's self-matching lock. Setting the five pieces of luggage to the blue carpeting beside the bed then, Rachel moved to the multi-line phone on the French Provincial nightstand, called the front desk, and had them order her a cab.

Moving into the white-tiled steam bath a moment later, Rachel used the toilet and washed her hands and then her face with a bar of non-comedogenic soap and a white washcloth. Necessity warranted the third action. Not only had her crying succeeded in making all her mascara run, but the shimmering rose pencil that had been drawn at the base of her lashes had disappeared, as had the coral pink blush from her cheeks and as she had guessed earlier, she had eaten all the shimmering rose lipstick from her mouth. Pulling out the beige bag that matched her shoes, Rachel quickly reapplied black mascara to her long lashes, touched up the incandescent brown shadow glittering from her eyelids with a glimmering mocha base that was close to it, replaced the coral pink blush that had been brushed across her curving cheeks with a coral red that came close to it also and applied a raspberry lipstick close to the shimmering rose color she had worn earlier to her luscious medium lips as well. Besides, just because she felt like the Devil didn't mean she had to look like a dog. Removing the pins from her hair, Rachel shook the sophisticated upsweep out of sight and let her hair fall below her shoulders, where she then pulled her white comb from her purse and combed it free of tangles until it flowed long and relaxed and off-black down her back and partially over her beige shoulders.

She decided to let her hair stay loose for a change, putting the no-longer-needed hairpins back into her gray toiletry case. Then she let her chocolate gaze sweep her appearance in one last look. The designer beige knee-length fit-and-flare satin bridesmaid's dress she wore with its short cap sleeves and net scarving all the way down from its boat neck to its cinched waist, flattered every curve of Rachel's figure, her long dusky-colored legs equally curvy in beige stockings that flowed down to well-turned ankles and neat feet pushed into equally designer beige heels while shiny pearly triple-beige drop earrings dangled prettily from diamond studs encased in silver sturdy settings hanging from her lobes. And though the reapplying of makeup to the equally flattering curves of her dusky face was a sheer feminine reflex, Rachel really didn't care if anyone ever thought of her as pretty again. Picking the gray toiletry case and her beige clutch purse up off the white vanity, she carried both back into the bedroom.

Lowering them to the bed she approached then, Rachel picked the multi-line phone up off the nightstand and called for a bellboy to come and take all her luggage down to the first floor. Then she took one last look at the two-room suite. Both rooms were elegantly large—the living and bedroom, outfitted in French Provincial furniture in a sophisticated multi-hued blue theme. Both rooms had Cable-TV, TV/VCR/DVD players, there was a workplace center in the living room, a refrigerator, a mini-bar, a hairdryer came with the suite, there was an additional phone in the tub-and-steam-shower-fitted bath, AM/FM clock radio, security safe, fresh basket of fruit delivered every day. So many amenities that Rachel knew she would never see again in a hotel. Because she would never be able to afford a hotel of this caliber on her teacher's salary! Rachel wasn't too sure she wanted that anyway, for it would invoke too sad memories of Felix and what might have been—if the man hadn't lied to her.

She sighed in relief when the sound of rapping on the white door then indicated that the bellboy had arrived to take her five pieces of luggage down to the first floor. Seeing in the young white man who appeared to be in his upper twenties, Rachel led him to the bedroom and watched him take the pieces up into his arms and hands in a juggling act that reflected years of experience in luggage handling.

"Are you ready, Miss Hardison?"

"I'm right behind you."

Sliding the skinny strap of her beige dressy clutch leather purse onto her equally beige-clad shoulder, Rachel swept her hair away from her face and took one last look around the suite that had been her home for the last five days. George had been truly a sweetheart for covering her tab to stay in a place like this for almost a week; her brother, who would more than likely arrive at Ted Stevens International Airport to leave for his honeymoon on the Riviera with new wife Stacey in a couple of hours only to find her still sitting there on stand-by awaiting a flight out to Atlanta! Rachel took no humor in that thought, wanting only to put as much distance between her and Felix as quickly as possible. With the blue-tagged room key poised in her hand, Rachel turned off the last light and walked out the door.

The cab was already waiting for her when she arrived in the lobby moments later. Rachel took a moment to sweep the circumference of it in one last look of appreciation. It was swanky, truly *muy magnifique*, with armchairs, sofas and love seats grouped in sets of threes around French Provincial tables, where a multiplicity of lamps and chandeliers provided attractive lighting. Rachel's gaze lingered regretfully on the elegant colors of blues, browns, rusts and autumn golds that she would never see again after that day because she was never going to come back here, again. What had started out for her last Monday to be a pleasure trip had morphed into a nightmare that was going to haunt her for the rest of her life. She was never coming to Alaska again after that day. *Goodbye William Seward*, she thought, *goodbye, good ol' Captain James Cook.*

Moving to the service desk behind the bellboy who stood waiting for her to check out, Rachel handed her room key to the brown-haired receptionist, a male, one of three attending the front desk.

"So, you're giving up Suite 1125, Miss Hardison?"

Rachel forced a smile to her raspberry-painted medium lips as the man brought her account number up on his computer. "Yes."

"I trust you enjoyed your stay at the Amber Heights Hotel," the Alaska Native said in his professional tone.

"It wasn't bad," she lied.

"I'm glad to hear that. It appears that Mr. Hardison has absorbed your bill on his own account. All you have to do is fill out this sign-out form."

"Thank you."

Grateful that George had come through for her in this, her largest hour of need, Rachel accepted the white sign-out form and pen the receptionist was handing her and quickly filled it out. Behind her, the bellboy stood, her five pieces of luggage poised under an arm and hanging from his hands and shoulders waiting to see her to the cab likewise parked and waiting for her outside the hotel. Handing the fully filled-out form to the receptionist a second later, Rachel watched the brown-haired man fix her with a smile.

"Very good, Miss Hardison, you have a safe flight back to Georgia. And remember us here at the Amber Heights Hotel for your next stay in Anchorage."

"I'll do that." Like the receptionist, she forced a smile to her raspberry lips, however false—after all, the professional front desk clerk had no way of knowing she was lying. Rachel wished George and Stacey the best, but she was never going to see either of them again after that day. Not if she had to do it over here. Affording the large clock on the wall behind the receptionist's head a quick glance, it surprised her to see that for as long as the afternoon and evening had seemed, it was only ten after seven. Oh, well, who knew what time it would finally be before she could catch a stand-by flight out of Ted Stevens International Airport back to Georgia? Sweeping her luminous brown gaze away from the clock, Rachel half-turned in the brown-carpeted floor; again becoming aware that the bellboy stood with his heavy load waiting to see her out through the double doors attended by a doorman in a red uniform.

Chapter Twenty

A frown creased Rachel's perfectly arched brow when she suddenly became aware of an argument coming from somewhere down the hall behind her.

"Don't touch me! Don't touch me, woman!" came the raised tenor voice, which Rachel was surprised to realize belonged to Felix. "Don't you ever put your lips on me again, do you hear me? Whether or not I'm sober, drugged, drunk, dead, or in the grave! Do you understand me?!"

"There was a time when you used to love for me to put my lips on you." That was Devon's pouting tone.

"You know, you're damned right! When I used to kiss you, I would get a taste off your lips like a Now or Later. Now, I don't want you now or later! These days, I prefer the taste of a Sweet Tart!"

"Who have you been kissing on that tastes like a Sweet Tart! My sister, Rachel . . . ? Don't you know that all she'll ever be is sweet? She doesn't have the experience a woman needs to handle a man like you. Not like I do, anyway. So, admit it. You know you loved kissing on me! And I've got the pictures to prove it!"

"Just get—just—get—get away from me! Don't you ever come near me; again!"

"Where are you going?"

"Where do you think I'm going? I'm going after Rachel! With any luck, I may be able to catch her before she gets out of here!"

Rachel continued to stare in surprise when Felix entered the lobby and espied her standing at the front desk. The man was as gorgeous as ever, the stylish lines of the designer satin deep purple tux, black satin vest and same color bowtie pulled on over and around an equally purple silk shirt up-playing every line of the masculine physique she had barely allowed herself to see all evening. However, the dancing brown eyes in his sexy rectangular face were as furious as the raised voice she'd heard coming from down the hall.

"So, that's it?" Felix snapped from just inside the lobby entrance from the corridor. "You're actually going out of here? You're going to turn this place into the *'heartbreak hotel,'* and leave me *'crying in the chapel'?"*

Rachel ignored his usage of the classic Elvis Presley hit tunes as he began to cross the swanky sophisticated lobby toward her in shiny black dress shoes pushed on over purple-sock-clad feet, wanting to feel nothing for the lying dog. For the same reason she did not look at him as he stopped in front of her, but averted her gaze to a glass-enclosed lamp set on a distant French Provincial side table.

"Put the damned suitcases down!" Felix ordered the bellboy in his attractive tenor, to which the white man complied immediately, dropping the five pieces quickly back onto the carpeted floor at his feet. "And go out there and tell that damned cab she's called that she won't be in need of his services!" His eyes swung back to her in a rage as the bellboy turned to do his further bidding, though Rachel didn't see it for keeping her gaze stiffly averted to the glass-enclosed lamp in the distance. "Why are you going out of here?" the demand came in her ear then.

Rachel forced a look of boredom to hide her total pain, determined that she would call the cab back as soon as she had gotten rid of him.

"Why shouldn't I leave this place?" she demanded, rage simmering in her own attractive medium tone. "It's like Devon said: she has pictures of you all over her, and I've seen them. And you don't look exactly in pain in any of them. But then, why should you be? You mourned the loss of her for years before hooking up with me here last Monday. You even mentioned her in your Best Man speech a while ago when you spoke of the girl you got hung up on, but with whom it didn't work out. So, I understand if you want to go another round with her. My sister's dazzling. For ten years to be exact and apparently, you still do, she's the one you thought was delightful . . . delicious . . . delectable . . . downright damned—divinely—devastating and disturbing."

"The woman is devilish, downright damned despicable, detestable, and disgusting!" Felix snapped between his perfect teeth. "I've never been so happy to be free of the entanglement of a woman in my life as I have this past week! I am completely over her! And with any luck, onto you, which in case you may have forgotten, is where I've been trying to get for the last couple of days! A fact I even expressed earlier to you today, with all that word-play we got involved in about me being the only man I wanted getting over you, not to mention mine being the only man's hands I wanted on you!"

Rachel determined to feel nothing from that last lengthy response as memories of the pictures of him and Devon that had followed that moment continued to flash through her mind, certain the man was still bent on lying to her, even using her. For the same reason, Rachel flinched from the immediate pleasure that slid up to her shoulder from the feel of one of those only man's hands suddenly curving around her arm.

"Don't touch me! Don't touch me, man!" Rachel ordered stiffly. "Don't—Don't you put your hand on me!"

As if sensing her intention of snatching her arm out of his grasp, Felix curved his hand over her arm with even more deliberation, knowing as he did so the effect he had on her.

"Rachel, girl," Felix began in his attractive tenor, anger gone out of his voice as he spoke with sudden gentleness, "I know the pictures you saw of Devon and me were incriminating, but they were meant to be. She set me up. They set me up. They set us both up."

Slowly Rachel allowed her enraged gaze to stray away from the lamp in the distance and back onto his attractive features at his mention of the words *they set us up*. She felt the pull of his raw sex appeal and male virility on her feminine senses despite the strong effort she was making not to.

"What do you mean, they set us up? Who are you talking about?"

"Your sister and your boyfriend, Rick . . . ! Who do you think were responsible for the seating arrangements back there? Devon had Rick order the wedding coordinators to place us as far away from each other as possible in a continued sting to not only split us up, but keep us separate. That way, she could have me, and he could have you."

Her eyes narrowed on the gorgeous golden brown face turned on her in surprised incredulity at the pair's implied complicity, her anger like his, crushed out of existence.

"Wait a minute! What would they do all that for? We knew my sister was after you and wouldn't like it if she learned something was going on between us, but we didn't give her a clue. And it's like I told you this afternoon—I let Rick hang all over me yesterday evening, giving him no clue whatsoever that anything was happening between you and me for him to want to hurt us, either."

"I'm afraid you did, darling, give them both a clue, as did I," Felix contradicted, smiling regretfully. "We messed up one time."

"When?" Rachel wondered, eyes wide in curiosity.

Not wanting to be overheard by the front desk clerks, Felix used the hand still curved over her arm to pull her away from the reception desk and farther into the lobby where they could talk privately. Settling on a deep blue loveseat after settling her in front of him, Felix took her glimmering dark-rose-tipped manicured hand in his after having given her a moment to lower her beige clutch purse to her lap.

"After the wedding rehearsal, yesterday," he said quietly in answer to the question she had put to him. "We played it off well, baby," Felix said. "During the entire thing, I pretended I didn't know you, you pretended you didn't know me. But after the rehearsal, I slipped up behind you down the hall, where you stood talking to a maid. You remember what happened after that, don't you? I took your hand in mine, you went giddy, I told you, 'Calm down, don't float away on me,' you turned around, and we started kissing. And I mean, we were kissing—I mean, you know how I like kissing on you," Felix said, smile broadening into a grin. "However, that's when Devon came out from nowhere and unbeknownst to us, saw us huddled up against the wall."

Rachel hid her face in her free hand in a gesture of embarrassment as she imagined what connotation Devon must have put on witnessing that most heated moment between her and Felix.

"Oh, no!" she gasped into her palm.

"Oh, yeah . . . !" Again Felix contradicted in a low gentle tone. "That kiss confirmed the suspicions you said Devon had that something was going on between us, indeed. The idea that I was screwing her kid sister, left Devon furious, and determined to find some way to get you out of the picture so that she could get me back—the one man who even according to her, she should never have let go of.

"So, what did she do? She went to your boy, Rick, Mr. Alaska-born Hawaiian, who was just as hot for you as she was for me," Felix went on as Rachel sat next to him staring incredulously, listening intently. "Devon told him what was going on between her ex and you, the little innocent. Rick was shocked at hearing this because like I said, he wanted you for himself, so, when Devon saw that, she conceived the idea that would get you for him and me for her by setting us both up. She told Rick that since he was going to be taking pictures at the bachelor party that I would be attending with George and the rest of his friends later to give her the address where the party was going to be because she was intent on crashing it, and having Rick photograph her in bed with me. Devon had to ask for that address because nobody knew at that time where the party was going to be but him, A.J. Over and Flip Hart, remember?"

Rachel nodded blankly as she recalled yet again how she and Rochelle had called Rick a fool for not revealing even to them the day before the address of that very private place that he, A.J. and Flip had arranged for the party to be.

"Anyway, Rick told Devon, who in his own words is a beautiful but vindictive bitch, that there was no way she would be able to get me into bed with her, not after he had seen me reject her twice before his very eyes in a matter of a couple of days," Felix went on informatively in the same quiet low tone. "Not to mention how the hell could she go to her own brother's bachelor party in order to seduce his best friend, anyway, when she would be completely out of place there? Well, let me tell you what your sister did. Devon told Rick—a rich hotel owner who still had connections with the underground circles here, that she would give him $15,000 to find her some kind of drug or drugs that would knock George out while leaving me so dazed that I would barely be aware of what was going on before I, too, passed out. Rick, warm to the idea but not quite sold, repeated to Devon that he was a multi-millionaire who didn't need her measly $15,000! So, Devon offered to screw him if he did as she asked. Well, Rick told Devon that he did not like her, but she was hot, so, he was going to take her up on that."

Rachel stared at the good looking face in deepening disbelief. She didn't know what to react to first: the fact that Devon had actually wanted to hurt her to the point of offering herself to Rick, a man she couldn't stand; the fact that Rick had wanted to hurt her to the point of accepting Devon's offer of sex when he'd even admitted he loathed her; and even worst: when did they have time to have sex?

"But—But baby, I don't understand! When did Rick and Devon have time to sleep together, yesterday? When did they have time to do all this scheming? During the short time-lapse between me returning to the meeting room after our kiss after the wedding rehearsal and the what—ten or fifteen minutes during which Rochelle and I sat talking and I showed her the pictures I took at Chugach State Park on Wednesday after that? When did Rick have time to sleep with Devon? I mean, it's just like George told you this morning and I confirmed to you this afternoon: the man came in and offered to take me to go pick up my pictures at Stewart's Photo Shop when I confided having some I needed to go pick up there, but no way to get there—said in fact, he knew how I must want to get them because he dabbled in photography, himself. Reminded me that in second fact, he had just offered to be the official photographer at George's bachelor party. . . . Anyway, you know the rest, of how I accepted his offer because I couldn't ask you because of the game we were playing with Devon, and because I'd needed to go shopping for the wedding present I hadn't yet gotten for George and Stacey. So, I let Rick take me, and Rochelle accompanied us, saying she needed to go shopping for the same reason and didn't want to do it alone. Rick happily saw her into the car. We talked all the way to Stewart's Jewel and Jade Photo. I asked Rick what kind of camera he used in his practice of photography on the side, since he saw I used a Canon Sure Shot 35mm in mine. He said he favored a couple of Minolta Digitals, but he had left them in his Honolulu, Hawaii hotel. Hence, he was grateful that I'd expressed a need to go pick up my pictures and go shopping, because he had to go out anyway to go visit a friend in the hopes of borrowing a camera with which to take pictures at George's bachelor party last night. Rochelle and I sat in the Downtown Deli and Café waiting for fifty minutes for him to get back after going in search of that friend from whom he planned to borrow that camera—"

Felix's free hand curved purposefully over her arm as her voice trailed off in her throat.

"Ah—oh—"

"I'm afraid so," Felix agreed gently as he watched the realization dawn on her attractively made up beautiful dusky face. "During the short time-lapse between you returning to the meeting room after our kiss after the wedding rehearsal and the ten or fifteen minutes during which you and Rochelle sat talking and you showed her the pictures you took at Chugach State Park on Wednesday, Devon and Rick were out scheming. That's why neither of them was there while you and Rochelle did all that. Rick returned later, knowing he wanted to hurt you, but he didn't know how he was going to do it—that is, until you started talking about your pictures. You must have still been showing them to Rochelle then, so, Rick took an interest in them. And when you told him you had some film you needed to go pick up if you could find a way to get to Stewart's, you fell right into his lap. He played you like a violin after that, darling," Felix said in a tone as sympathetic as that of the hand pumping hers as he watched the deepening realization that showed behind her shocked gaze and gaping mouth. "He took you and Rochelle to Stewart's Photo, where he then left you to go pick up the camera he would use to take the incriminating photos of me and your sister, while at the same time using the opportunity to pick up the drug that he would give to George to knock him out, and one that would leave me so dazed that I would barely be aware of what was going on before I, too, passed out."

"Oh, no . . . !" Rachel pulled her hand and arm free of his to cover her face with both her hands in her increased shock at the ease with which the Alaska-born Hawaiian had manipulated her. "I knew something was wrong! Devon and Rick had been out of the meeting/banquet room when I'd returned after the wedding rehearsal yesterday, although I'd given that little thought at the time, thinking Rick was still out making arrangements with Flip and A.J. for George's bachelor party, and that Devon may have been out flirting with Ray Marlboro, or something. Anyway, it's like you just said: it was about fifteen minutes later after Rochelle and I had sat talking that I showed her the pictures I'd taken at Chugach State Park on Wednesday. She told me they were beautiful, that I'd really captured Eklutna Lake, and asked me excitedly who I'd gotten to take me to the Park. I simply told her George had gotten me a tour guide, not telling her it was you. For the same reason, I kept the pictures I'd taken of you during our lunch on the upper Eklutna Valley slope below East Twin Pass hidden from Rochelle's eyes. And I was glad I did, for Rick suddenly appeared beside my seat, his footsteps having been muffled by the plush carpeting, which otherwise would have alerted me to his return to the room. Anyway, that's when I asked him how it had gone, did he, Flip and A.J. make the arrangements for George's bachelor party. Rick grinned, saying they sure did and just like you said, at a very private place; that in fact, George wasn't going to know what hit him. Well, I didn't like the sound of that, so, I warned him the same way Stacey'd warned George only moments before for Rick and the other guys not to do anything that was going to hurt my brother. Rick grinned, again. He said, 'Don't worry about it, girl, Rachel, baby, it's going to be great!' That's when Rick zoomed immediately in on the pictures that Rochelle still held in her hands. In fact, I couldn't help wondering at the time if it weren't a deliberate ploy to get me off the subject as I sensed a hidden meaning behind the sudden quick lowering of his eyes from mine. He made all that fuss about how beautiful they were, praising me for my photographic prowess and asking me if I were a photographer on the side. I told him the pictures were just a little something I had taken to reflect on after my visit here; that in fact, I had some to pick up at the photo shop if I could but find a way to get there. Rick asked me what shop I needed to go to, I told him Stewart's on West Fourth Avenue, and he jumped on the idea of taking me there. I was reluctant until he told me just like I told you how he knew how much I must want to get them because he dabbled in photography, too, reminding me in fact, as I just said, that he had just offered to be the official photographer at George's bachelor party. Well, it wasn't until Rick said that that I remembered that, so, I accepted his offer for the aforementioned reasons and because I hadn't yet bought a wedding present for George and Stacey. Rochelle said she needed to go shopping for the same reason, but she didn't relish the idea of doing it alone. Rick screamed, 'Well, then, come on, ladies, go grab your coats, and let's hit the road!' You are right, baby, I fell right into his lap. Rick played me like a violin after that. Happily took Rochelle and me to Stewart's Photo Shop without giving me the slightest idea that he had in mind this plan to get revenge on me, nor did he give me the least clue when he returned to the Downtown Deli & Café to pick up Rochelle and me close to an hour later. Instead, he gave us some line about getting back late because he'd arrived at his friend's portrait studio while he was in the middle of trying to photograph a couple and their quintuplets. Rick said the three-year-olds were crawling all over the place—said in fact, that it was fifteen minutes before his friend could get to him after finally settling the babies down long enough to photograph them with their parents. And then, he showed us this camera his friend had loaned him—in fact, like I told you, he blew a whole roll of film taking pictures of Rochelle and me all the way around the block and part-ways up West Fifth Avenue. And then, after that, Rick kept me and Rochelle out for the rest of the evening, just like I told you. The man took us shopping, he took us to dinner; he took us all over the place. Rochelle even made a joke about it, calling us the three R's: Rachel, Rochelle, and Rick. Rick ate it up. Laughingly told her back, 'You got it, baby!' Rick literally played me like a violin, not once letting on his knowledge of my involvement with you, nor his plan with Devon to split us up. Took me and Rochelle all over the place, hung all over me the whole time, he didn't give us the slightest clue, like I said—although at some point, amidst all our running around, Rochelle began to get suspicious of his motives. It was about two—two and a half hours later and we were sitting listening to the music and sipping Cokes at that place I told you about—Darwin's Theory, I think it was. Rick was hanging all over me—you know, like I said, and telling me all about the bar which had inspired the Indigo Girls to write their 1995 hit tune 'Cut It Out,' when Rochelle suddenly yanked me away from him, pulled me to the side, and told me that while we were on the subject, I needed to seriously cut it out with Rick. She said, 'Look, girlfriend, I know that man doesn't mean anything to you, but you need to stop letting Rick hang all over you. That man is not playing with you. He hasn't been hanging all over you all evening for nothing. He wants to get on you to the point where he might even be willing to do something to hurt you to get you.' Well, with Rochelle simply having voiced the thought I was already having that Rick cut it out with me, I looked at him innocently sipping on his drink and brushed off her warning that he wanted me to the point of being willing to do something to hurt me to get me as nonsense. I said, 'Don't worry, I can handle him.' I had no idea he'd long been in the process of doing just that!"

The dancing brown eyes in Felix's golden brown face were again sympathetic on her dusky brown one, the beautiful made-up features of which were frozen in an expression of stoned shock. Again extending a hand, Felix curved it along with his other one back over one of hers as stunned stupefaction and delayed realization continued to show there as well.

"Anyway, come the party last night, just like he said, Rick took the pictures," Felix picked up the story quietly after a moment. "And as you saw by them, and just like I told you, things got kind of wild," he went on gently. "But you have to have noticed now, that Devon was not in any of those pictures. And there's a reason for that—because it's just like Rick had said: she would look out of place at her own brother's bachelor party. And for that reason, nobody saw her there.

"Anyway, like George told Stacey, he didn't drink and was not going to let us get him drunk. For that reason, I think he had maybe one glass of wine, while I had the same. We must have been there for about an hour, maybe, when all of a sudden, I started to get kind of dizzy—you know, like I was in a daze. I remember one of the strippers took George by the hand and led him into the bedroom, while another woman took me by the hand and led me in behind him. All of a sudden, George fell out onto the first bed and passed out. The woman who had led me in behind George took me to the second bed, where I passed out cold beside him. Neither one of us knew at that time that we passed out because we had been drugged."

Rachel stared at the golden brown handsome features in deepening disbelief, not only because Felix had not told her that he and George had actually passed out, but because there had been nothing in the pictures Rick had shown her to support this last revelation.

"Well, come about four o'clock this morning, I was roused to consciousness by George tapping me on the shoulder, having just come out of his own stupor," Felix went on quietly while Rachel's glimmering mocha-lidded brown gaze aimed on him intently. "George said to me, 'What the hell did we drink! We haven't gotten drunk since we were in college! We haven't done anything like this since we were nineteen!' He said, 'I can't tell Stacey I got drunk and passed out!' and so, he didn't tell her. For the same reason, I didn't tell you I got drunk and passed out, either. Anyway, we stepped out of the bedroom, and the place was deserted. All the guys were gone—including Rick, who had probably returned here ages ago. So, George said to me, 'Man, let's get the hell out of here!' Which, we did. But on the way here, I couldn't help remembering that I'd had the sexiest dream about you while I was passed out. I was lying on the bed in the hotel room, George had passed out on the one next to me, and you came to me. Well, I was so glad to see you that I called out your name. I said, Rachel, Rachel, darling, sweetheart, what are you doing here—whatever? That's when I pulled you down on the bed on top of me, and I started to kiss you everywhere. The dream was so intense—I mean I literally felt you. In fact, I even told George that. Although I knew you couldn't possibly have been there for real, knowing you hadn't been at the party physically. I'll tell you more about that in a little bit."

Felix paused to catch his breath, leaving Rachel to stare at him in continued shock. While she could not believe Rick had actually given him and her brother drugs that had knocked them out until four o'clock in the morning, she found it no wonder George had still been sleeping when she and their mother had roused him in the penthouse later on that morning at a quarter till ten, when he'd not long gotten back to the hotel! Same with Felix, whom Rachel had also thought was simply sleeping in from a late night out partying with the boys and whom she'd heard nothing from until he'd shown up at her suite at noon. And Rachel thanked God neither he nor George had manifested any residual effects of the drugs Rick had plied to them, thinking the man a son-of-a-bitch to do something that low to his own brother-in-law-to-be and his own sister's husband-to-be. And all orchestrated at the hands of his brother-in-law-to-be's sister and his sister-in-law-to-be, Devon—the true bitch in the equation—in a vengeful sting to get her—her and George's kid sister—to dump Felix so Rick could have her and Devon could get Felix back, a man who as Rochelle had put it, Devon dumped ten years ago and hadn't thought of since! Curving her free hand over both of Felix's holding her other one in a protective action, Rachel was hardly surprised to find sensations of arousal stirring despite it being a most inappropriate time.

"Anyway, this has been a very busy day," Felix went on then in the same low confiding tone, his hands curving warmly over both of hers. "We got up late and then had to meet the guys at the formal wear shop, pick up the tuxes and shoes, go pick up George and Stacey's tickets to the Riviera, confirm their departure time, a whole lot of running around. And you were sweet—and rather hot—" Felix added with a laugh "to me when I saw you briefly at noon—you know—to kiss you a belated hello and an 'I'll-see-you-later' kiss goodbye, even though a let's-think-about-it-in-the-middle-of-it kiss did kind of add itself into the mix!" Again Felix showed his perfect teeth in a laugh, to which Rachel did the same. "And you look like a damned dream in that dress," Felix said with further impertinence to her own further amusement, his eyes roving over her figure in the satin beige fit-and-flare knee-length bridesmaid's dress she wore with same color stockings and heels in an arrogantly admiring look. "Yet I couldn't help thinking during the entire wedding that something was wrong. You would not catch my eye; you would not look at me, the same way it was during all the picture-taking and reception. Except for that one time I did catch your eye, only for you to snatch your gaze quickly away from me and in the other direction. Well, I said to myself: I guess you're just playing the game we've been playing with Devon. I had sat there for ages watching the way Rick was hanging all over you at your table and I couldn't stand it, but I couldn't do anything about it, because at my table, Devon was hanging all over me. Well, I looked at her and smiled and said to myself, 'That's alright, I'm going to put up with you until this reception is over, George and Stacey are gone out of here, and this game's going to be over.' And I played that game so well that I didn't even notice that you had left. Nor did I notice that George had left, either.

"Anyway, it must have been what—a half hour later, when George came to me all serious and said, 'Come here, man, let me talk to you,'" Felix went on quietly after another moment of pausing to catch his breath. "He pulled me from the table I sat at with Devon still hanging all over me, took me to the side, and said suspiciously,

'Tell me again about this dream you had while you were passed out last night.' So, I told him again about the dream I'd had about you, when George said to me, 'Felix, it wasn't a dream. And it wasn't Rachel.' That's when George showed me all those pictures you had just shown him of the bachelor party that Rick took last night and left with you this afternoon. And like I told you a while ago and also before that this afternoon, the party did get wild, and the pictures reflected that. Except when I got to all those pictures of me kissing some woman in the bedroom. That's when I realized just like George had said: I didn't have a dream, it was real. Except that the woman I was kissing wasn't you, it was Devon! Well, let me tell you something about your brother. I may have painted him as a road dog at the reception back there, but I don't love him for nothing. The man is shrewd. He said as soon as you showed him the photos of me and Devon—incriminating as they are—he smelled a setup. For three reasons: one, he was stretched out on the bed next to me and yet he was not in any of the pictures taken in the bedroom; and two, none of us had seen Devon all evening—none of us, she had not shown. And number three: who took the pictures of Devon and me—the very person who—and who you said showed them to you—Rick, who wanted you to think we were getting back together so that you would dump me and he could have you. Rick, the very man who's been hanging innocently all over you this evening like curtains on a window. . . .

"George said to me, 'Come here, man, I'm fixing to go kill my brand new brother-in-law,'" Felix went on quietly in his attractive tenor. "We went over to Rick's table—you know, where you had been sitting previously and George grabbed him by the throat. Showed Rick the pictures that he had taken of me and Devon and conveniently left with you earlier in the day and demanded to know, 'What the hell have you two done to my kid sister!' That's when the skumbucket spilled all of it. Told us all about the arrangement Devon had made to set me up at the party, how he put a fast-acting drug in George's drink so that he would pass out quickly and not be a witness to what would follow next, how he put a slower-acting drug in mine so that it would daze me, and of how as soon as I fell onto the bed in the bedroom, the stripper who had brought me in there was replaced by Devon, who Rick slipped in unseen by the others and who I in my dazed state, thought was you. Anyway, while I thought I was calling out to you and kissing you, Devon was busy saying, 'Yes, baby; it's Rachel; it's Rachel,' while Rick took all those incriminating pictures of us from every angle. As soon as they were satisfied with enough photos, they left while I passed out and returned here, where despite the fact that they cannot stand each other, just as Devon offered, she screwed him as payment for services rendered. And to seal the sting, she requested the added service of having Rick arrange with the wedding coordinators to seat us as far away from each other at this evening's wedding reception as possible.

"Ten things happened in quick succession after that. One: After seeing the pictures of me and Devon, Rochelle, who had been resting from dancing with her boyfriend and wondering where you'd gone off to, jumped up from the table, and freaked. Rochelle said to me, 'I have not liked Devon from first sight: she's too artificial looking; in fact, I even gave her the name Miss Artificial. Rachel confided everything to me about you and her because I saw the pictures of you and her taken at Delaney Park that she picked up at Stewart's Photo Shop yesterday and put two and two together. I'm hardly surprised that Devon did something like this to get you back after watching her hang all over you yesterday and today; in fact, Rachel even told me yesterday that you and she were playing a game with her, because were she to find out you had a thing going with Rachel, in fact, was already suspicious of her, Devon would not take it well.'

"Two: That's when Rochelle really freaked at the realization that all the time you were telling her all that yesterday, Devon was already in the process of setting you up," Felix continued quietly in his seductive tenor. "Rochelle said to me, 'It was no wonder Rachel was so steamed with her after having seen all those pictures of her and you that Rick deliberately—and at Devon's instigation—left with her this afternoon. When Devon walked into the women's fitting/dressing room and asked Rachel innocently where she was all yesterday afternoon and evening, Rachel looked at her as if she could have spewed molten lava all over her, though she covered her rage with the simple answer that she and I had been out with Rick. I saw that look and even asked Rachel what was going on with her and Miss Artificial, though again, she covered her rage with the simple answer of nothing.' Rochelle said to me, 'I even told my boyfriend, Vern—' and which he then confirmed '—that Devon was artificial. I watched all afternoon as Rachel quietly steamed every time she looked at her, somebody said something about her, even when Rachel introduced someone to her. As badly as it had bothered me, it must have killed Rachel all evening to watch that heifer hang all over you—especially after how explicit she was with me yesterday about you and her and your hot thing. Yet again, when I asked her what was going on with her and Miss Artificial, Rachel covered her pain, rage, and frustration with the simple answer of nothing.'

"Three: That's when Rochelle turned on Rick," Felix went on quietly while Rachel sat similarly, listening intently. "Told Rick, 'You played Rachel right from the beginning—an opportunity that fell right in your lap when Rachel expressed a need to go pick her pictures up at Stewart's Photo, where you then left her to go in pursuit of a friend from whom to borrow the very camera you would use to set Felix up and destroy her, while at the same time using the outing to pick up drugs that you would ply to George and Felix in order to facilitate that wicked scheme.' Rochelle said to Rick the same thing you said to me: 'You left Rachel and I up there at the Downtown Deli for ages yesterday before finally returning, where you then hung all over her for the rest of the evening without giving her the slightest clue of your intentions.' Rochelle said to Rick, 'You may be Stacey's brother, but you are nothing but a skumdog who I knew was out to hurt Rachel—although I never dreamed to this length—and in fact, I even tried to warn Rachel about you yesterday, though she hadn't listened to me. Not that it would have done her any good anyway, when you had set her up from the moment she and I left here with you yesterday. And then, to continue the sting you had set up with Devon to keep her and Felix separate, you hung innocently all over her all evening. Even when Rachel complained about the seating arrangements at the reception here, you brushed it off as nothing, telling her you didn't care where you were seated as long as you were next to her, which was where you wanted to be.' Rochelle said to Rick, 'And to think that the three of us had that most precious scene on West Fifth Avenue yesterday evening, when those two outrageously dressed flamboyant black gays and Indian transsexual, apparently on the way from the Days Inn to attend the drag show held at Mad Myrna's Gay Bar down the street every Friday, approached us in front of the William A. Egan Civic and Convention Center. The two gays hit on all three of us and all three of us rejected them with a laugh, at which point, they walked off with the Indian transsexual totally insulted. Rachel begged you: 'Get the picture! Get the picture, baby! Get the picture!' and you told her, 'Hold on, Rachel, baby, I'm going to get it! I'm going to get it!' You raised your camera to your eye, only to discover you were out of film! The three of us laughed at the lost photo opportunity for five minutes standing out there in front of the William A. Egan Civic and Convention Center on West Fifth Avenue. If you had cared anything about Rachel, you could have dumped that plot to sting her right then. Yet despite that most bonding experience shared between you and her—and I—you persisted with this scheme to alienate her from her presumed lover—and all for the cheap prize of screwing Devon, who you hate—just so you could get Rachel into your bed? Stacey's brother or no, you are a total dog!' Rochelle was incredulous!

"Four," Felix went on in his attractive tenor, "George freaked. After seeing how Rick had used your desire to go pick up your pictures as an opportunity to go pick up the camera he'd needed to set us up as well as buy the drugs he'd needed to knock us out, at the same time realizing that he and I had not passed out from drinking last night but because in fact, Rick had drugged us, George lost his temper—and you know he has one. Anyway, he grabbed Rick by the throat again. George growled down at him, 'You played up to my kid sister yesterday and then dumped her in a restaurant so you could go purchase drugs with which to set us up, while at the same time setting her up as well, just so you could get her into your bed? And then, you actually put those drugs in our drinks, man? And that's why we passed out last night, only to come to around four o'clock this morning and find all the guys—including you—gone? You actually thought possibly overdosing us, maybe even killing us worth all this just to get a little ass, and which you did get from Devon? I swear to God that if you weren't Stacey's brother, I'd break your damned neck right now!'

"Thing five: Diane and Stacey who had both heard George scream Stacey's name over the blare of the music in the distance, rushed over to the table and asked what was going on. When George both told and showed them, Diane freaked. Glared at Rick and said: ' . . . You did that to her? You actually did something that cheap to

Rachel with her own sister so you could have her and Devon could have Felix, a man she's been trying to get back practically from the moment she showed up here at the hotel Thursday evening? Oh, good Lord . . . !' Diane was so shocked all she could do was stare speechlessly off into space after that.

"Thing six: Stacey freaked. She said to me, 'From the moment Devon grabbed you to leave the penthouse to go down with her to my suite to try on her silly bridesmaid's dress and shoes Thursday evening, I was suspicious of her; in fact, as I watched Devon coming so boldly and brazenly onto you at dinner later on trying to get you back, I said to myself: *Oh, yeah, you're going to have trouble with this one.* But that was before George set me straight on everything Thursday night that I realized my oversight. You hadn't mentioned Devon's name since Rachel showed up here on Monday, because you've been too busy getting hung up on her. You even evidenced that over Monday's dinner, when you called Rachel a girl after your own heart because she loves Elvis. That's why I could still kick myself for sitting there staring in confusion when you dumped Devon after Thursday's dinner with the claim that you had a woman waiting for you and that you and she had a date to watch Elvis and not realize the woman was Rachel.' Stacey said to me, 'To think that Rachel lied to appease George's rage over seeing that picture of you and her kissing on the floor of the Dimond Center Ice Chalet in Wednesday morning's paper by telling George she was not interested in you and you were not interested in her; that in fact, you were still hung up on Devon, anyway, and I could have kicked myself twice when George later told me on Thursday night that Rachel was just as hung up on you. I warned Rachel just yesterday not to let Devon see this ridiculous-or-no hot thing you and her had going on because I sensed Devon would not take it well; and in fact, Rachel told me you and her were playing a game with Devon for the same reason—which had not been necessary because George had already made me aware of that.' Stacey said to me, 'Although I never dreamed Devon would go to this length to destroy Rachel by setting her up so that she would dump you, while setting you up at the same time in order to get you back.'

"Thing seven: And then, Stacey turned on Rick," Felix went on quietly without taking a breath. "Glared at him the same way Diane had and screamed, 'I can't believe you actually conspired with Devon to give George—my husband—drugs in order to set up his best friend—Felix—whom you had also drugged—with Devon, Felix's ex-flame—in order to get him back and destroy Rachel, Devon and George's kid sister and Felix's present flame, actually sleeping with Devon as cheap payment for the service! And then, to continue the sting, not only did you leave Rachel all those disgusting pictures of Devon and Felix—and at Devon's instigation—but hung innocently all over Rachel all evening in further alienation of her affection from Felix just so you could get her into your bed?' Stacey screamed at Rick, 'I had just pulled Rachel aside a while earlier, apologized for the seating arrangements that I didn't know had been altered by you and Devon and asked her why she insisted on sitting here with you—my slug of a brother—slung all over her in a game with

Devon that I had already begun to suspect by the way she had completely ignored Felix all evening—and particularly when I saw her flash her eyes away from Felix's gaze at the same time he did—that she was no longer playing.' Stacey said to Rick, 'It was no wonder Rachel could barely say anything to me after that when she had all these graphic pictures of Felix and Devon to reflect on and that had been taken by your duplicitous hand—so that as far as Rachel was concerned, obviously all afternoon, that game was over.' Stacey said to Rick, 'As a last gift to Rachel, I'm going to go put Devon in a cab to another hotel, because she's definitely going to get out of mine. And then, you take your ass back to Hawaii and never come back here!'

"Thing eight: Your parents, who had witnessed the commotion in the distance, also arrived at the table and demanded to know what was going on. When George both told and showed them, they freaked. Now, I've always thought of your father as a lighthearted man, but all of a sudden, I saw from where George gets his temper. Like George, Marshall grabbed Rick by the throat. He said to Rick, 'What the hell do you mean you played up to my daughter Rachel yesterday by offering to take her to pick up her pictures at the photo shop, where you then left her in pursuit of drugs? What the hell do you mean? And what the hell do you mean you then gave my son one of those drugs at his bachelor party last night that knocked him out? What the hell do you mean, you rich slimebag? And what the hell do you mean you then slipped my daughter Devon in, where she then proceeded to seduce Felix—whom you had also drugged—while you took all these degrading pictures of them? What the hell do you mean! And what the hell do you mean you then gave these pictures to Rachel, so that she would think the worst about Felix and dump him so Devon could get him back? You stood right next to Rachel when she introduced us to you a couple nights ago and actually invited me and my wife to come to your hotel, the Kaikilani, in Honolulu, on Oahu, need I remind you? Now, you mean to tell me that you actually conspired this plot with Devon in order to split Rachel and Felix up so Devon could have him and you could have Rachel, who you've been hanging innocently all over all evening, even going as far as screwing up the dinner arrangements in order to keep her next to you and Devon next to Felix in a continued sting to hurt her, just so you could get her into your bed after already having bedded Devon? What the hell do you mean doing this to my baby daughter—?!'

"Your mother, Sephora, said to me, 'Rachel told us just yesterday that you and her were playing a game with Devon because she did not take rejection well! Well, now I know what Rachel meant when she came over to our table a while ago and told us the game was over. But I never dreamed Devon would come up with a scheme like this to get you back! To think how Stacey was in a panic at breakfast this morning thinking you and George's other friends had gotten him drunk last night and that he was up in his suite passed out since neither you nor he showed up for breakfast in all the time Stacey, her parents, her uncle, Marshall, Rachel and I were there. Rachel and I had thought the same thing—and I'm sure Rachel was worried about your absence, also—which was why we went up to the penthouse to see whether George was passed out drunk, sick or dead considering the lateness of the hour. To think how Stacey had wondered where was Rick also, choosing to think as did she Devon—who was also absent at breakfast—that they were sleeping in late because it was a Saturday—same thing all of us had thought, as a matter of fact. Now, to find out Devon was not in the cafeteria for breakfast this morning—in fact, Marshall and I hadn't heard from her all day and I don't think Rachel had, either—not because she was sleeping in late because it was a Saturday, but because of her late night activities screwing this dog last night as payment for services rendered in a sting to set up both you and Rachel so that she would dump you and Devon could get you back? Marshall, go up there; get your daughter and let's get her out of here!"

"George said, 'Naw, Dad, she's mine!' Then, he turned to me and said, 'Man, I'll tell you something—Devon is my sister, my parents' daughter, and we love her, but like Rick said, she's a beautiful but vindictive bitch! I told Rachel that she was suspicious of you two, and that you'd better watch out, because like Rochelle said, I told her—same thing she apparently told Mom and Dad and also that Stacey both knew and warned Rachel about because of what I'd told her—that Devon would not take it well were she to find out the actual truth of your involvement. But it's like Stacey and Mama said: I never dreamed she would go this far to get you back, while destroying Rachel in the process! She's been hanging innocently all over you all evening, man, smiling all in your face and mine without giving us the slightest clue that she set all this in motion to destroy her own sister just to get you back. And to think I'm going to be leaving for my honeymoon in less than three hours! But I'm going to have to do it with a guilty conscience, because for coming up with this scheme to drug us and set up both you and Rachel, I'm going up there and break Devon's damned neck, as well!'

"Thing nine: Well, I somehow managed to circumvent George's rage by saying, 'Never mind that, man, where's Rachel?' You see, you had not yet returned to the table you had been sharing with Rick, Rochelle, and Vern," Felix went on quietly in his attractive tenor. "Sephora said, 'She's gone! Like she told us over at our table, the game's over!' I said, 'What do you mean, the game's over?' George said, 'Exactly that, man, the game's over.' He said you were upstairs in your suite in tears. He said you think I lied to you. He said you think I've made a fool of you, almost used you. He said you think I still have it going with Devon! He said you said if I wanted her, I could have her, because Mr. Daytime Emmy Award-winning actor, me, could not have both of you at the same time, you didn't care how well I was getting paid to sleep with two sisters on my soap opera, not to mention their mother also, my main love interest on the show!" Felix went on with sudden laughter as he parroted the words her brother said she had put to him. "George said you weren't going to be around to see it, though. He said you were not sticking around until checkout time tomorrow to go back home, but that you were packing your bags, calling a cab, and getting ready to check out of here with the intention of sitting at the airport on standby until you could catch a flight back to Georgia tonight. He said to put it in your own words, words that you stole from me and words that George didn't understand, you said, 'I'm getting out of here, quickly!' George said that had happened twenty five minutes ago and that you ought to be gone by now. Well, I knew I had to catch you before you got away. Same thing your Mom and Dad and George and Stacey and Rochelle and Diane and Vern knew. So, that's when I threw the incriminating pictures in Rick's face and turned to race out of there.

"And thing ten," went on the seductive tenor, "as I approached the door of the banquet room, Devon jumped out of a conversation she had been having with a waiter and grabbed me. I loathe her. I can't believe I ever loved her. I told her to go to hell. I told her I knew exactly what she and Rick had done to George, me and you in order to try and get me back. She was neither regretful nor apologetic. Instead, she followed me all the way down the hall and tried to kiss me, still trying to get me back. I told her, woman, don't you ever put your lips on me, again. She told me I knew I loved kissing her and in fact, she had the pictures to prove it. It had never even occurred to me that Rick would have made two sets of the incriminating prints—one for him to give to you to forever turn you off of me, and one for Devon to give to me. In Rick's own words to George, 'Your sister's beautiful, but she's damned twisted!' Well, he wasn't lying. I told Devon to just—just—get—get away from me! And with any luck, she'll never come near me, again!" Felix fell silent as he came to the end of his summary, aware that she had been close enough standing at the front desk when he entered the lobby to have heard the end of his and Devon's argument.

Beside him, Rachel's glimmering mocha-shadowed brown gaze lingered on his golden brown attractive face and sexy features in a look of her usual amazement. She found it incredible that that apparently fabulous brain of his had been able to retain all that; again finding it no wonder he had become an actor. Felix had told her he'd done so/and had always wanted to because of that fact—that he had a good memory. Well, Rachel no longer had cause to doubt that, as he'd just proved his ability to remember forty pages of dialogue a day for the soap he worked on. Another small wonder that the man had won three Daytime Emmys in his six-year stint playing the slick character of Joe Murray. . . . A man presently sleeping with his boss, her daughter and her stepdaughter. . . .

"I hardly know what to say after all that!" Rachel was almost beyond words as she pulled her hands from the warm clasps of both of his to cup her face in a gesture of amusement, gratitude, renewed shock, disgust and self-disgust. "I—I mean, it's both like you and Rick said: my sister is a beautiful, but vindictive bitch! We all knew she wanted you back—like Diane said: she made that known to everybody practically from the moment she showed up at the hotel. Stacey didn't lie, either. She did not go into all that detail with me that she did with you about how you hadn't mentioned Devon's name since I showed up here on Monday because you've been too busy getting hung up on me, nor how you evidenced that over Monday's dinner when you called me a girl after your own heart because I love Elvis. Stacey did not tell me she could still kick herself for sitting there staring in confusion when you dumped Devon after Thursday's dinner with the claim that you had a woman waiting for you and that we had a date to watch Elvis and not realize the woman was me. Neither did Stacey bring up that part about me lying to appease George's rage over seeing that picture of us sprawled out kissing on the floor of the Dimond Center Ice Chalet that came out in Wednesday morning's paper by telling George that I wasn't interested in you, that you weren't interested in me; and that in fact, you were still hung up on Devon, anyway, nor did Stacey tell me she could have kicked herself twice when George later told her I was just as hung up on you. But because of knowing all those things, we were totally transparent to her and George just like you'd said and I'd known. The second I stepped into the penthouse after leaving you yesterday afternoon, George got right on my case, asking me if I'd been where he'd thought I'd been, or did he need to ask, because if his suspicions were correct— And then, as if to catch the ball she had dropped in her oversight after Thursday's dinner, Stacey grabbed it and ran with it by answering her own question as to whether I'd been holed up in your suite with you all morning watching that Elvis Presley movie marathon that had come on the Encore Channel at seven thirty yesterday morning and that we'd paid very little attention to. I like to died, I was so embarrassed!" Rachel laughed and watched Felix do the same; his hands again curving warmly back over both of hers. "Stacey went on to tell me that George had told her it was all this crazy stuff we have in common, more of which we'd learned we had upon returning here on Thursday evening, and that we had this thing going on that was hotter than the sun. I ended up confiding to her the same thing I'd told George: that I knew it was ridiculous for something like this to happen in only three days when considering we hadn't seen each other in ten years. Stacey warned me ridiculous or no, hot as this thing is that you and I had going on, I'd better not let Devon see it. That's when I told Stacey that we'd already come to the conclusion that we were going to have to play the game of keep-Devon-in-the-dark-as-to-our-feelings-for-each-other until the wedding was over this evening. Told Stacey in fact, that what she'd seen at dinner on Thursday night with you completely ignoring me while laughing it up and lapping it up as Devon chewed the scenery in the restaurant and came all onto you like that was part of that game. Which just as Stacey told you—was totally unnecessary, because George had told her all about it.

"And Rochelle certainly didn't lie," Rachel went on in the same quiet tone, it being her turn now to take over the conversation. "She didn't like Devon upon first glance at the wedding rehearsal yesterday. Said she looked too artificial, called her Miss Artificial, just like you said. And it's amazing to hear you say she was hardly surprised Devon did this because just like Mom, George and Stacey, I never dreamed she would go to this length to get you back. To think that she actually conspired with Rick to give George a drug that would knock him out cold, give you one that would daze you—both of which he did, risking just like George said, possibly overdosing you, maybe even killing both of you; had Rick slip her in so she could attempt to seduce you while he took pictures of the two of you and then left, leaving you to pass out, after which she came back here to the hotel and slept with Rick as cheap payment for services rendered? And to think how just like Rochelle said: she walked into the women's sitting/fitting/dressing/powder room this afternoon, asked me as innocently as you please, 'Where were you all yesterday afternoon and evening?' smiled all in my face for the rest of our time there preparing for the wedding chattering endlessly and excitedly about the preparations she went through on the days of her weddings and trying to draw me into it because I was a bridesmaid at both of them—until I had to stop looking at her. And even though I knew Rick wanted me—I mean, he made that known to practically everybody here, too—like Rochelle said: after that most bonding experience the three of us had with those two black gays and that Indian transsexual in front of the William Egan Civic and Convention Center that I told you about earlier today that you said Rochelle said were heading to the drag show at this nearby Mad Myrna's Gay Bar, and also as I said before, I can't believe Rick actually went to all this length to get me, either!"

Felix raised a hand to her cheek that was as tender as the smile that suddenly curved his slender lips. "You know, you're so innocent. You're so sweet. Those are two things I really adore about you. But didn't you suspect that man of duplicity when he left you all those pictures this afternoon? Pictures that nobody else had seen . . . ?"

"How could I? They're so incriminating!" Rachel's cry was a defensive one as he made the two qualities he so adored about her sound like an accusation. "And you should have seen the way Rick played it off! The man had actually slept with my sister, a woman who like you said: he couldn't stand, and there he was smiling and laughing all in my face! First, he showed me the pictures that he took of me and Rochelle yesterday evening, which was hardly suspect because I'd expected him to show me those sometime, anyway. Said he'd wanted to show me the capabilities of that camera, which shot off what—three frames a second. That's when he moved in with his real intention. He said, 'And by the way, before we get completely off the subject of your brother—' who we had not long mentioned was sharing his sister's wedding day," Rachel added informatively, "'let me show you how well that camera performed on the pictures I took at his bachelor party. Oh, yea, it got wild last night. George got crazy! And so did Felix! He got really busy with your sister! I don't know how she came to be there, but she and her ex-flame got seriously busy in the bedroom! It appears that Felix still has a thing for her after all these years, after all!'" Rachel repeated everything she'd told George to him, Felix staring gently, listening intently. "And I mean, that camera with its three frames per second picked up every shot, every motion; every heated movement—in sequence and as a result, like I said, were very incriminating! And all the while Rick was showing me all those graphic pictures of you and Devon, all I could do was smile in agreement with him because I did not want him to know there was something going on between the two of us. Yet after Rick left a moment later—smilingly, of course—with the claim that he was going to go talk to his uncle down on the first floor and would see me at the wedding in what—less than three hours, 'Okay, Rachel, baby?', I knew there was literally going to be nothing going on between us as I went numb all over. The game was over."

"I know." Despite his understanding of her usage of it, Felix smiled at the clever way she applied the game they had been playing with Devon to a game he had presumably been playing with her. "I had no idea you were in that much pain all afternoon and evening. Now, I know why you wouldn't look at me—neither during the wedding, nor throughout the picture-taking, and then only to snatch your eyes hotly away from me the one time I did catch your eye at the reception."

"No." Rachel shook her head, sending her long hair bobbing prettily over her beige-clad shoulders as she again pulled her hands free from the claims of both of his. "Like I said, after Rick left, I went numb. It was my brother's wedding day, the happiest day his life and a day I should have been happy for him, yet I determined to go throughout the whole afternoon feeling nothing. I walked into the women's sitting/dressing room about two o'clock, and Diane came straight for me. Apologized for the blunder she made at yesterday's wedding rehearsal when she tactlessly blurted out the private business about Devon's divorce and unexpected arrival here on Thursday to all and sundry, nearly embarrassing everyone—and herself—in the process. And even worst: mentioning that arrival, which had since put us in the position of having to play a game to keep her in the dark about our feelings for each other, because she was your ex-flame from ten years ago. Something Diane knew, because she was standing right there at the reception desk last Monday when we met for the first time in those ten years and you asked if Devon was coming to the wedding, and I sadly had to tell you the same thing I'd told her—that she was in the process of getting a divorce and so wouldn't be free to fly out until next week. Diane said that Devon even evidenced your affair in the way she asked for your suite number along with mine first thing after arriving here Thursday evening. And now, two days after the aforementioned divorce, she is trying to get you back? Something Diane saw with her own eyes in the aggressive way Devon came all onto you at the wedding rehearsal, yesterday?

"Well, I'd already expected Diane to put two and two together just as she'd said from what she'd heard and seen between us on Monday and Stacey to have filled in the blanks at the wedding rehearsal about the same game Devon's unexpected arrival on Thursday had forced us into playing with her, so, I somehow managed to smile tactfully and tell Diane not to worry, that she didn't blow anything between us, that everything was still alright. Yet as she walked off with a pleased smile on her own lips to get dressed, I went numb all over again at the realization that I was going to have to keep up the lie I'd just told her about everything being still alright between us when everything was far from alright both to Stacey, my sister-in-law-to-be, and Rochelle, my new best friend. And I'd wondered how I was going to be so dishonest with Rochelle considering how honest—or as she'd put it, explicit—I was with her about our hot thing at that restaurant yesterday.

"Anyway, that's when Rochelle came bustling into the sitting room, greeting me all excitedly and pulling me over to introduce me to her boyfriend, addressing me as her new best friend," Rachel went on quietly with loud irony as Felix sat quietly listening with same. "Said I was Stacey's fiancé George's kid sister; also a bridesmaid in the wedding along with her, as she'd told him. I had not needed to force an interest as I had smilingly shaken the hand of the man Rochelle had explained meeting at her dental office a month ago, thinking him charming, about thirty, nicely tall, although big—who just as Rochelle had said, looked like a cougar and had the hands of a wolf, yet the prettiest teeth I had ever seen—with the exception of yours, of course—finding it no wonder Rochelle had been so explicit in her bedroom antics with him after the wedding rehearsal yesterday, and to a woman who was practically a virtual stranger to her. That's right, baby, she blabbed to me first. That's what we spent those fifteen minutes before I showed her the pictures I took at the Park talking about—her hot thing with Vern," Rachel confided with continued quiet and a lack of shame as she watched the obvious realization dawn in Felix's dancing gaze. "Rochelle then told Vern I had a hot thing going on with you, Felix Latham, actor on a soap opera, George's best friend and best man from the days you both lived in Georgia. Told him that our sister Devon was also here and a bridesmaid in the wedding. . . . 'Wait'll you meet her, Vern,' Rochelle had said, 'the woman's totally artificial. No offense, girlfriend,' she'd said to me, totally remorseless. 'None taken,' I'd said back to her, totally understanding. After all, I'd hardly expected her to say anything nice about her after all I'd told her yesterday about Devon's history with you and determination to get you back after having dumped you all those years ago. And I'd thanked God Rochelle had possessed the tact not to go into the details about our hot thing, which she was unaware had become a cold thing due to Devon's determination to/and success in having done just that and gotten you back. That's when the blood receded from my veins as all the numbness returned.

"Rochelle then asked me how things were going with you and me," Rachel continued with the same low irony as she pondered on the events that had followed that moment. "I managed to lie that they were not bad, and then stood listening through dead ears as Vern went on to tell Rochelle that he didn't think he wanted to meet this sister of mine she had just described to him as artificial. That's when Devon walked in and gave him a look on his way out because Vern didn't bother to notice her, the woman Rochelle had just described to him as artificial. Rochelle saw that look, which I imagine must have made her think of Devon as even more artificial, yet nevertheless, as Devon came over, Rochelle introduced herself to her anyway, told Devon her name, and reminded her that she was a bridesmaid in the wedding, too; that in fact, she was in the lineup behind her and Flip Hart with Martin Rolf. Devon brushed off her greeting to her with a tepid handshake and a smile and then came straight to me and asked where I was all yesterday afternoon and evening. Sensation returned immediately; in fact, it was like Rochelle said: I was so hot I could have spewed molten lava all over her! And then she sat there and bubbled innocently all during our preparations for the wedding—smiling all in my face—leaving me so with the desire to spit on her, like I said before, I had to stop looking at her.

"And that's why, for the same betrayal I'd presumed you'd done to me—although I didn't want to spit on you, I refused to look at you during the wedding, as well," Rachel continued in the same low intimate vein as Felix sat quietly understanding, still listening intently. "After all, why would I, when I'd seen you at noon, a time during which you kissed me a belated hello, gave me a let's-think-about-it-in-the-middle-of-it kiss, kissed me a reluctant I'll-see-you-later-goodbye, not to mention blew me a kiss at the door, and all without once letting on that you'd slept with my sister last night? Like I told George, I thought you had lied to me, I thought you'd made a fool of me, almost used me; I thought you still had it going on with Devon. And I especially felt all those things during the wedding reception after watching my bitch of a sister drape all over you while you tolerated her. I kept trying to numb all those sensations of pain, anger, rage, disgust, frustration and jealousy that I was feeling, but they kept coming up every time I as much as looked at you! That's what you saw the one time you turned around from your table and caught my eye, which I snatched hotly away from you, a look Stacey saw at the same time. And then, to suffer the ignominy of her arriving at my table and asking me if she could speak to new sister-in-law me for a minute, which as Stacey told you, she did. I had been trying to hide my pain from her all afternoon because I had not wanted to ruin her perfect day, so, when she told me she'd noticed how I'd ignored you all evening and voiced her suspicions as to the fact that I was no longer playing the game and asked me what was going on and what had happened to us, I didn't know how to tell her that the cause of what was no longer going on, that in fact, what had happened between us, lay in the very woman she had just said to me had been hanging all over you since after the wedding and all over you ever since. I'd not known how to tell her that the woman she had warned me not to let see our ridiculous-or-no hot thing had done what she and I had both feared and roped you back in, and I had the pictures—courtesy of her brother Rick—to prove it? That in fact, the game was over? Stacey was right: I could hardly say anything to her, after that. And after she moved away, I rebuked myself for my continued loss of control over the rage I had been experiencing ever since Devon had greeted me in the women's fitting/dressing/powder room this afternoon, knowing I couldn't let anyone else see it—certainly not Rochelle, who as you already know by what she said to you back there had sensed an undercurrent going on between Devon and me ever since that greeting, had already asked me twice what was going on with me and Miss Artificial, and was still of the same opinion. I went blindly back to my seat where Rick was again all over me—and just like you all said: innocently—and we sat listening to some song the band was playing, the whole of which he spent flirting and coming all onto me, which was too bad for him because I had no intention of letting him in. Rochelle and Vern were taking a break from dancing at the time and unbeknownst to me, Rochelle had sat there watching Devon hang all over you with an aggression that Rochelle had described as ridiculous during the entire song she and Vern had sat out. All of a sudden, she leaned over and said to me in a voice that Rick couldn't hear, 'Look, girlfriend, forget this game you're playing with her, but you need to go up there and get your sister off your man!"

"Well, one thing I knew, it was time to stop that game, alright," Rachel went on in the same low confiding tone as Felix continued to sit listening quietly. "That party was going to go on all night, with George and Stacey yet to go through all their cards and gifts, not to mention his removal of her garter and her tossing of her wedding bouquet. And I certainly didn't want to be around for that, knowing Devon would be the first single woman on the floor to catch it in the hopes of snaring you for a third husband, and you'd probably let her. So, I gave Rochelle a pardoning nod, pulled out of the circle of Rick's arm, went to Mom and Dad's table and announced that I was going home. And when they naturally asked me why I was leaving when I wasn't supposed to check out until tomorrow, I simply told them to look up at your table and observe the way Devon was hanging all over you—which Mom didn't even want to do, because she had watched her do that ever since the wedding was over this evening—as had Rochelle and Stacey—and Devon was a complete source of embarrassment to her. Mama asked me, 'Can't she see she's making a fool of herself?' to which I replied simply, 'Not anymore.' And when Dad asked me what I meant by that, I told them simply that the game was over, and as you've seen, they knew exactly what I was talking about. They figured out what was going on between us and questioned me about it at the wedding rehearsal yesterday," Rachel added unnecessarily, as foreknowledge of the private conversation Felix had previously mentioned her mother speaking about flashed in the brown of his dancing gaze. "And then, I went and found George, congratulated him again on his marriage to Stacey, wished him a happy honeymoon on the Riviera, and announced again that I was going home. However, being the shrewd man you say he is, Big Brother saw the pain in my eyes and asked me same as Mom and Dad why I wanted to leave so soon before checkout time tomorrow afternoon. So, I took him up to the third floor, where I collected my clothes, purse and shoes from the women's dressing/sitting/powder room—a brief stop-off on the way to my suite, where I showed him the incriminating pictures Rick had left me of you and Devon through a floodgate of tears." Rachel gazed swiftly away from him as she relived every bit of the grievous pain that moment had brought her.

Epilogue

Beside her, Felix smiled softly again at the still pained look Rachel was trying to hide from him, already having noticed her change of makeup and known of its reason.

"Silly woman," he laughed, a hand again reaching out to claim one of hers. "Do you actually think I would go back to your sister after all the fun I've had with you this past week—hiking through the woods, running from grizzly bears, partying on the dance floor, not to mention discovering all those other incredible things we have in common, like I told George, same as you said you told George, same as George told Stacey and Stacey then told you yesterday afternoon? I love you, girl. Not think I'm falling, but have slipped, tripped, fallen head-over-heels, and hit the ground. *'I want you, I need you, I love you.'*"

Rachel twisted her lips in a pout as Felix used another Elvis Presley tune to express his feelings for her. "Oh, when did you come to that realization?"

". . . Yesterday morning, when I was kissing you all over my bed."

Rachel managed a laugh out of the corner of her mouth in a dry response to the shameless remark. That must have been when he pulled out of that second one *(kiss)!*

"Do you love me?"

Her mouth pulled to the other side in resignation of the response she was about to give him and his silliness in not having already guessed the cause behind all the hurt feelings she had just expressed having all afternoon and evening.

"Yes."

"Oh, really . . . ?" Felix continued to smile. "When did you come to that realization?"

". . . Thursday evening, when you were kissing me all over your bed." She laughed suddenly at the humor behind her similar response, her gaze again flashing away and onto a distant wall painting in embarrassment.

"Oh, really . . . ?" Felix repeated, laughing along with her despite the fact that his was one of delight.

". . . Uhm-hmm."

Although Felix's laugh sobered, he continued to smile at the way she insisted on playing her equal delight of his confession of his love for her down.

"I'm sorry your sister did this to you," he apologized after a moment, his golden brown hand playing with the darker-toned fingers of hers clasped warmly in his. "And I'm sorry that woman's going to be my sister-in-law."

Rachel's luminous black-mascara-lashed brown gaze narrowed on his gorgeous face in a look of shock at the implication behind his last statement despite the fact that he had averted his own gaze away from her in a momentary look of disgust.

"What did you say?"

"What I'm trying to say," Felix began as his gaze swung smilingly back to her, the hand around hers barely giving her a chance to discard the beige purse in her lap to the blue loveseat cushion to one side of her as it pulled her to her feet as he rose to his, "is will you *'wear my ring around your neck'*? Or in this case, your finger . . . ?"

Rachel returned the grin he had turned on her with a toothy one of her own as he used the Elvis Presley tune to ask her to marry him. Apparently, her parents were going to *'lose'* her, after all!

"Honey, if that's a proposal, I'll wear your ring around my head!" she exclaimed excitedly.

"I don't think it'll fit," Felix answered, toothy grin all over his own face as he let his gaze slide over the circumference of that head from which off-black hair hung long and straight down over her beige shoulders. "But let's see if it'll fit this."

Not quite knowing how to take the remark, Rachel stared at him in surprise when he suddenly lowered himself to one knee on the brown-carpeted floor in front of her. Her surprise quickly turned into shock as he reached into the left pocket of his deep purple tux and pulled a black felt ring box out into his hand.

The realization as to just what the moment indicated left Rachel able only to stare down at him with her mouth open in an expression of stunned shock. Stacey was smarter than Rachel had thought. Apparently, she had been right when she implied cryptically to Rachel that morning that judging by what she'd seen over the last few days with her and Felix; she didn't think Rachel would be waiting for her rescue much longer. To think that Rachel had spent her entire afternoon and evening hating him, despising him, loathing him, refusing to look at him—thinking the absolute worst of him because of what she'd thought he had done to her—when all the time the man had innocently gone out and bought her a ring with the intention of officially proposing to her.

A cry of disbelief sounded in Rachel's throat as Felix then flipped the top up on the black felt box and exposed the engagement ring that set tucked into its satin bed. Of a platinum tone, it was exquisite, with a large glimmering diamond and attractive smaller diamonds all over the circular band.

Her mouth continued to hang open in incredible shock as Felix then removed the ring from its white satin bed before sliding the empty box back into his tux pocket. She could only stare in amazement as he then took her left hand in his and spanned out her glimmering-rose-tipped fingers to slide the expensive band onto her fourth one.

"Felix—Felix, when did you get this . . . !"

". . . This afternoon while out picking up my tux with George and the others. I went into the jewelry store and bought it for you in the hopes of proposing to you after George and Stacey had left for the Riviera and I could get you alone—somewhere far away from Rick and Devon. Well, we're not exactly alone out here in the lobby, but it'll have to do in a pinch." Gazing lovingly up at her as he slid the sturdy diamond-laced platinum band snugly onto her left fourth finger, Felix smiled with the intention of officially popping the question. "I love you, Rachel Hardison, George's kid sister, girl after my own heart. Will you officially consent to be my wife and marry me? Rescue me from my state of—you know, being single. And hating every minute of it?"

She met the playful grin he had directed up at her with a delighted one of her own in her previous revelation from what Stacey'd told her that her own rescue was imminent.

"So long as you promise to rescue me from that same state of—you know, being single. And hating every minute of it . . . !"

"I do!"

"I do, too!"

Rising smoothly back to his full six-foot-one-inch height, Felix encircled his arms around her waist to pin her happily to his torso. "So, tell me again, that you love me, Little Sister."

"I love you, Felix Latham," Rachel smiled, raising her own arms to encircle his neck. "My brother's old friend; and I do mean old!"

"Hey, girl, it's like I told you—I am not old!" Felix laughed back challengingly. "I am just well-seasoned."

"Like the beefcake you are?" she teased playfully.

"That's right, cheesecake," Felix agreed, smilingly using the same response to the question she had put to him the day before. Anyway, cheesecake, now that you've given up your suite, which you did—what—about an hour ago," he half joked, "shall we have the bellboy take your luggage up to mine? Will you stay with me tonight? This slob of a man who loves you . . . ?"

"Most definitely," Rachel agreed, smiling sincerely. "I'll make sure you're even more of a slob to the maid by helping you tear up the bed!"

Felix laughed at the shameless remark he knew she had meant at the same time she did. Then he sobered, returning to seriousness.

"And then, tomorrow when we check out of here, will you fly back to New York City with me?"

"Goodbye, Atlanta," she smiled her agreement. "Besides, you already promised me you were going to take me on the set you mentioned during your Best Man speech. You know; introduce me to the three women who play your boss, her daughter, and her stepdaughter?"

"Oh, that's right—I did say I'd do that, didn't I?" Like her, Felix smiled at the memory of him telling her that while they lunched on the slope of upper Eklutna Valley below East Twin Pass at Chugach State Park three days ago.

"And once there," Felix went on in his attractive tenor, "will you continue to be my fun-mate, my chat-mate, my playmate and my soul mate? Will you be my roommate and my love mate in addition to being my marriage mate? Will you bear my babies out of that gorgeous body of yours, and all that other junk?"

"Uhm-hmm . . . !" Rachel's smile broadened with that most assured affirmation.

"And will you accompany me when I go to Hollywood and become a world famous actor?" the seductive tenor persisted insistently. "Be by my side when I go to accept my Oscar?"

"And your nighttime Emmy and your Academy Award, and your Golden Globe and your People's Choice . . . the list goes on and on!"

The perfect teeth flashed in a grin of pleasure. "I do love you, girl!" Felix said.

"I do love you, too, boy!" she laughed.

"There goes that sound again." Felix's grin broadened into a similar laugh as he picked up on the gurgling noise she had forced from her throat along with her laugh. "And I want to hear it for the rest of my life."

"Most definitely, you will," Rachel promised with a grin.

"And now, that we've gotten all of this out of the way, shall we go tell George that he's going to have a new brother-in-law, Stacey that she's going to have a new brother-in-law-by-marriage, and also tell your parents that they're going to have a new son-in-law? And let that new best friend of yours and her boyfriend, Vern, and Diane see that everything really is alright with us?"

"A good idea on all counts . . . !" Rachel laughed happily at his deliberate wording of letting Diane know everything really was alright with them, not that everything was still alright when everything was far from alright. "And Rochelle is definitely going to love seeing that I got my man, after all! The woman thinks you're a fox. I'm not going to tell you what else she said about you!" Rachel continued to laugh.

"I can imagine!" Felix laughed too, having heard it all before. Then he sobered again and turned the subject back to her. "So, what do you think of me?" he asked after a moment.

"I think you're a fox, too."

"Really . . . ?"

". . . Uhm-hmm." Rachel nodded. "You are a gorgeous, fine specimen of a man, who needs to be loved by a simple plain old ordinary kindergarten teacher."

"And you are a beautiful, fine specimen of a woman, who is going to be loved by a soap actor. I am going to teach you everything there is to know about love. And it will not be a performance. It will not be Joe Murray who'll be making love to you, but Felix Latham, lonely man who's been waiting for you to grow up for ten years!"

"Well, I finally caught up with you, and you've got me forever *'stuck on you.'* And all you have to do is *'love me'* in return."

Felix threw back his head and showed his perfect teeth in a laugh of extreme pleasure at her mention of the Elvis Presley classic tunes he so favored.

"This has got to be the craziest relationship I've ever had. I never thought it possible for a man to fall in love with a woman in three days, much less have her fall in love with me at the same speed."

"Well, baby, I guess this is what you call love on a whirlwind," Rachel offered smilingly.

"I guess so," Felix's agreeing smile rivaled hers. ". . . Because I'm definitely whirling over you!"

"I'm whirling in a wind!"

"Anyway, girl, don't you think it's about time we wrapped this scene?" asked Felix with a laugh between his perfect teeth. ". . . Because as they say in acting circles, this is a take!"

"Well, as they say in teaching circles, class is dismissed!" Rachel forced a laugh between her own perfect teeth.

And mindless to the two concierges, hovering bellboys and three front desk clerks looking smilingly on from the distance, the two differing professions found a common ground as Felix pulled her into a kiss that left them both whirling in a wind.